The Leviathan

The Leviathan

The Greatest Untold Story of the Civil War

PAUL STACK

Certain characters in this work are historical figures, and certain events portrayed did take place. However, this is a work of fiction. All of the other characters, names, and events as well as all places, incidents, organizations, and dialogue in this novel are either the products of the author's imagination or are used fictitiously.

Archway Publishing books may be ordered through booksellers or by contacting:

Archway Publishing
1663 Liberty Drive
Bloomington, IN 47403
www.archwaypublishing.com
1 (888) 242-5904

Scripture taken from the King James Version of the Bible.

Scripture taken from the American Standard Version of the Bible.

ISBN: 978-1-4808-7388-9 (sc)
ISBN: 978-1-4808-7390-2 (hc)
ISBN: 978-1-4808-7389-6 (e)

Library of Congress Control Number: 2019900799

Printed in the United States of America.

Archway Publishing rev. date: 04/05/2019

To librarians, past and present, for without their contribution to knowledge this book could not have been written

Acknowledgments

As will be explained shortly, my interest in the *Great Eastern* began when Nea, my wife, purchased a used book. During the years I researched and wrote this book, she was my constant cheerleader and proofreader. My daughters Nea Elizabeth and Sera always gave me encouragement, and Sera helped me with the book's graphics.

My friend Barbara Purdy helped me understand the use of dialogue to tell a story. She also suggested the creation of a character who filled a void in my narrative. Barbara's son, Bill, is a natural storyteller with insight into human motivation. I used him repeatedly to check the authenticity of my fictional characters' actions.

My friend Gabrielle Kelly helped me get started on this book, the hardest thing for any author. Hannah Cunliffe, my English researcher, skillfully dug out documents from British sources, many of which had been unseen for over a century. Elizabeth Barbour translated copies of correspondence from almost unreadable handwriting into written text. Many of the source documents that I have posted at www.september1861.com are a result of Hannah's and Elizabeth's work.

As the book neared completion, I sought and received comments and criticisms from friends whose opinions I respected. These friends, in alphabetical order, included Tim Fraser, Alexander Kerr, Ira Mirochnick, William O'Connor, Thomas Rickner, and Cheryl Zeigler. Finally, I want to thank Bayo Ojikutu and David Aretha, two experienced Chicago authors, for their reviews and comments.

Leviathan A sea monster mentioned in the book of Job, where it is associated with the forces of chaos and evil.

—*The New Dictionary of Cultural Literacy* (2002)

The Trochus Shell

In 1999, my wife and I attended the opening of a new reading room in our village's library. While I was taking a tour, my wife, a school librarian, rummaged through the library's discarded-book bin. As we were leaving, she handed me a book she had bought for a quarter—*The Great Iron Ship*, first published in 1953.

The book was a quick and enjoyable read. James Dugan, the author, was more a raconteur than a historian, but there were enough of both elements to provide a lively retelling of an amazing ship. On finishing the book, I wanted to learn more about the ship, initially christened *Leviathan* but later known as the *Great Eastern*, so, using the internet, I began to locate other books and collectibles relating to her. Through internet auctions, I acquired old issues of the *Illustrated London News* and *Harper's Weekly*, located two other books and various periodicals, and even purchased an original Currier and Ives print of the ship for my library. In August 2001, however, I ran across an object that gave me pause.

A dealer in Australia was offering for sale a carved trochus shell. The seashell was a cone comprised of ring like layers. The carving on the lowest and largest ring read "The Great Eastern Steam Ship" and contained a detailed profile of the ship along with the words "24500 Tons." The next higher ring had a carving of what appeared to be a gate next to a large tree. The scene was engraved "Tomb of A Lincoln Presidt. of U.S." An examination of photographs and prints of Lincoln's tomb in Springfield, Illinois, led me to the conclusion that the carved tomb was a somewhat inaccurate representation of an early tomb in Springfield, one in which Lincoln was interred from his death in 1865 until 1871.

The shell was puzzling. Why would a person have an image of a ship launched in London carved on one part and then have a likeness of the Midwestern tomb of a US president carved on another? I could think of no connection between these objects. The *Great Eastern* was launched on the River Thames in January 1858, and Lincoln was interred in the spring of 1865. A quick review of different biographies of Lincoln disclosed no reference to the *Great Eastern*, and nothing in the books on the *Great Eastern* I had acquired made any reference to Lincoln. Yet both ship and tomb were on the shell. Curious, I placed a large enough bid on the shell to ensure that, barring the appearance of some fanatical collector, it was mine. I was successful. Shortly after I mailed my check to Australia, the events of September 11, 2001, occurred. The shell and many other things were forgotten in the aftermath of that shocking event. In early October, however, a package arrived at my office. It was the shell.

The shell was more beautiful than I had anticipated. It had been polished so that it had a luster similar to mother-of-pearl. The detailed carvings of the ship and tomb showed considerable artistic skill, as did the accompanying cursive lettering. Looking closely, I saw something not mentioned in the internet listing. Above the carving of the tomb, toward the top of the cone, was a faintly carved symbol—two crossed objects that could have been feathers, quills, or wings. No writing accompanied this symbol. The dealer in Australia, responding to my email, could provide no information about the shell, other than to relate secondhand information that it had been brought to Australia from England many years ago by an unidentified gentleman.

One fall evening, while sitting in my library, I studied the shell closely under a magnifying glass. I could find no further carvings, but a thought occurred to me. Had someone used the shell to record an event? I decided to find out.

I believed that if the shell indeed depicted a true event, the event most likely occurred during the Civil War. Accordingly, I began my initial research by searching a vast collection of documents written during the war. As early as 1866, the federal government began the mammoth task of collecting and typesetting as many Civil War documents as it could locate from both the Union and Confederate sides. The ultimate product, entitled *The Official Records of the War of the Rebellion: A Compilation of the Official Records of the Union and Confederate Armies*, consists of nearly

140,000 pages assembled in 128 volumes. Although the sheer size of the collection was daunting, I learned that it had been digitized and that a website offered by Cornell University allowed the public to freely view and search it. There were only a few entries for "Great Eastern," but one caught my attention. On September 9, 1861, Charles Francis Adams, the American envoy to Great Britain, wrote a letter to William Henry Seward, the US secretary of state. After summarizing communications he had had with the British government, Adams wrote,

> I had hoped to send something by Captain Schultz, who returns in the Great Eastern, and I shall yet do so if it should come before the bag closes.

I now had a name. But who was "Captain Schultz," and what role, if any, did he play in the war then raging?

Introduction

SHORTLY after the attack on Fort Sumter, General Winfield Scott devised a military strategy that became as known as the Anaconda Plan, named for the giant serpent that encircles and crushes its prey. The cornerstone of the plan was a Union blockade of Southern ports in order to cripple the seceding states both financially, by preventing the sale of their cotton to England and France, and militarily, by blocking the importation of weapons, food, and even medicine. Historians have generally concluded that despite horrific battles and terrible losses over a bloody four years, there was no single turning point in the Civil War. Instead, the North, with its superior industrial and financial strength, combined with its much larger population, slowly and inexorably encircled and crushed the agricultural South to the point where the Confederacy could no longer maintain an army.

The story I have come upon, however, which was excavated from thousands of documents collected over more than a decade, leads me to believe that early in the war there may have been a single turning point. Specifically, on September 12, 1861, an incident occurred aboard a ship in the North Atlantic Ocean. While it is interesting to imagine how the change of a single event could impact the course of history, there can be no certainty as to the potential outcome. Nevertheless, I believe that the incident on board the ship disrupted a string of events that were intended to achieve, and might well have achieved, the independence of the Confederate States of America, an event so momentous that had it come to pass its ramifications would still be felt today.

Details about the incident of September 12 and some of the activities leading up to it are sparse. Other than the person who caused the cryptic information to be carved into the trochus shell, no one ever attempted to record these events. While the identities of certain individuals present at the incident are established by historical documents, circumstantial evidence about the nature of the incident and how it was likely carried out has led me to believe that another person whose existence was heretofore unknown was also present. Since it is unlikely history will ever shed any light on this individual's identity, I have named him Kit and described him as I imagine he might have been. The story of his participation in these events, therefore, is fictional. However, I have attempted to construct the story of his background in a manner consistent with stories and documents from the same period.

Other than characters described in the development of Kit's story or characters added to make the story flow, all the major characters in this book are real. Some meetings of these characters are real; others are fictional. Every document quoted in this book is both genuine and accurately quoted in context. Instead of using footnotes, I have elected to set forth the complete text of nearly all source documents used in my research in a searchable chronology that is available for free inspection at www.september1861.com. In addition, the website offers for viewing numerous renderings and period photographs of persons, places, ships, and events mentioned in this book.

Part I

September 1841
to
July 1859

1

Piermont, New York
September 23, 1841

THE *Utica* blazed so brightly in the early-afternoon sun that an admirer would have had to squint just to gaze at her. She had been freshly painted gleaming white with new gold gilding on her trim. Her brass had been buffed and waxed to a mirror finish, and the freshly applied linseed oil on her mahogany cabin doors shimmered. From the stern stanchion, an enormous American flag waved desultorily, and a blue pennant at her bow displayed the letters "ERC" to identify her owner, the Erie Railroad Company. Her side wheels were encased in paddle boxes, the uppermost portions of which were decorated with carved and painted American eagles. More than two hundred feet long and sleekly built, she attracted sightseers to the banks of the Hudson River whenever she majestically passed by. At present, however, she was tied to a broad, heavily built wharf that jutted out nearly a mile into the Hudson.

Captain Alexander Hamilton Schultz stood on the *Utica*'s deck supervising crewmen who were readying the vessel for her return trip to New York City. The ship's passengers had boarded at eight o'clock that morning at Cortlandt Street in the city, and what a boarding it had been! More than two hundred men, led by New York governor William Henry Seward and his staff, had boarded as a uniformed brass band blared out patriotic airs and a crowd of onlookers jostled and cheered. The passengers included Robert Morris, New York City's mayor; Benjamin Onderdonk, the Episcopal bishop of the city; prominent members of the city's common council; and the crème de la crème of the city's business community—the heads and subalterns of its banks, insurance companies, shipping firms, board of trade, law firms, and newspapers. Well-scrubbed and properly attired in dark dress coats with white starched shirts, the men represented the commercial and civic power of their city. They knew each other well from countless deals as well as stabs in the back, but so far today they'd acted like a smiling, hail-fellow-well-met group of aging boys. Outsiders from this cozy group, but welcome nonetheless, were Senator Samuel Phelps of Vermont and T. Butler King, a congressman from Georgia. The voyage today was to show off the completion of the eastern terminus of the New York and Erie Railroad, a task that had involved thousands of skilled laborers and a huge amount of capital. The *Utica*'s passengers toured the two newly constructed roundhouses, each capable of holding fifteen locomotives, and walked through the ninety-acre yard hewed by hand and gunpowder from the rocky cliffs of the Hudson.

Captain Schultz was more impressive than handsome in his freshly brushed dark-blue uniform with gold braid. Stoutly built with thinning blond hair, he'd been born thirty-seven years earlier in Rhinebeck, New York, a small town on the banks of the Hudson. His father, Luke, was a farmer, while his mother, Eleanor Knickerbocker, was a member of an old and respected but not particularly prosperous New York family. His maternal grandfather, John Knickerbocker, had fought the British under the command of George Washington in the battles of Harlem Heights and White Plains. From his mother, Schultz had learned to read and write; from his grandfather, he'd learned stories of the sacrifices and bravery involved in the creation of his country; and from his father, he'd learned how difficult it was to support a large family by farming.

Schultz left his family home in his early teens to seek a livelihood. For a short while he worked as a clerk and for an even shorter while as a green-grocer. When he started working on a small steamer plying the rivers of New York, he entered a profession for which he felt well suited. A few years later, the Erie Canal was completed, and he was hired as captain of a canal boat; for several years thereafter he shuttled passengers and freight between New York City and stops on the canal. Serious and intense when on duty, warm and outgoing among acquaintances, the ambitious young man acquired many friends on his route. One day several years ago Seward, then a young state senator, had boarded Schultz's canal boat. By the time the trip ended, the two men had established what would become a lifelong friendship.

Schultz turned to look at the shore as laughter and loud talk announced the return of the passengers. He watched as the men walked down the long wharf in groups of four and five. Seward and Bishop Onderdonk walked arm in arm at the front of the procession, followed closely by Seward's staff. When everyone had boarded, men on the wharf pushed the *Utica* off with pikes. Her side wheels began slowly turning as she headed into the middle of the broad Hudson.

About twenty minutes into the return voyage, Schultz was surprised to see Seward standing outside the pilothouse. When Schultz opened the door, Seward stepped in and closed the door behind him. Seward was shorter and slighter than Schultz. He had a large nose and a full head of dark hair that stuck out in different directions, an appearance reminding more than a few persons of an exotic bird. Seward spoke first.

"Captain, do you mind if I stay up here for a few minutes?"

Schultz was not happy to have a distraction in the pilothouse but remained polite to his friend.

"Governor, I won't be able to talk very much. I've got to keep my eyes on the river."

"Oh, I'll only be here shortly." After a pause, Seward said in a low voice, "I just wanted to get away from our guests for a few minutes."

"Too loud?"

"No, too angry."

Schultz glanced at Seward with a confused look. He immediately turned back to the river. "I don't understand."

"The whole Virginia thing, Captain. They're angry at me about it. They think it's going to hurt their profits."

With an audible "ah!" Schultz nodded. He knew what the "Virginia thing" was, as did everyone else in New York. It had started out harmlessly enough. Two years earlier a schooner named *Robert Center* carrying a load of live oak beams from Louisiana to New York City had limped into Norfolk badly damaged from a storm. Repairs were going to take a while, so the white crewmen had all gone ashore while the schooner's three black crewmen, aware of the dangers facing them if they wandered around a Virginia port, stayed aboard. The ship's captain contracted with a local shop to make repairs, and shortly thereafter a slave named Isaac, a highly skilled ship's carpenter, boarded the vessel. As Isaac worked on the schooner, the three black sailors included him in their conversations. Over the course of a week, one of the sailors mentioned that a skilled worker like Isaac could make a lot of money in New York City. When the repaired schooner left Norfolk, Isaac was nowhere to be found. Isaac's owner immediately suspected that his slave was aboard the ship and hired two slave chasers to take an express stagecoach to New York City. Incredibly, the stagecoach arrived ahead of the schooner, and Isaac was found in the hold hiding among the oak beams. The hapless slave was seized and taken back to Virginia in irons.

Had things ended there, the *Robert Center* affair would have been unremarkable; after all, fugitive slaves were reclaimed on an almost daily basis. However, Isaac's owner was not satisfied with merely recovering Isaac. He demanded that the Commonwealth of Virginia extradite the three black sailors to face charges of stealing his slave. In July 1839, Virginia's lieutenant governor wrote to Seward asking for the extradition of the sailors. Seward pondered the request, knowing that if the men were delivered to Virginia, they'd likely be hanged or enslaved. Finally, he responded in a letter by noting that the United States Constitution required that a state deliver to another state to face trial a person charged with "treason, felony, or other crime." Alluding to the fact that New York had abolished slavery twelve years earlier, he wrote, "There is no law of this state which recognizes slavery, no statute which admits that one person can be the property of another, or that one man can be stolen from another." Since stealing a slave was not a crime in New York, Seward concluded that he was powerless to return the three freedmen.

Seward's letter was reciprocated with a long-winded argument to the contrary from Virginia's governor. Thereafter the two governors engaged in a literary game of battledore and shuttlecock, lobbing back and forth interminable letters filled with arcane authorities that each contended supported his position. However, in June 1841, Seward strayed from his legal arguments and wrote Virginia's governor a letter containing the following:

> I cannot believe that a being of human substance, form and image … can, by the force of any human constitution or laws, be converted into a chattel or a thing, in which another being like himself can have property.

Until he received this letter, Virginia's governor had kept his correspondence with Seward private. However, this latest opinion expressed by Seward, the second most powerful political leader in the country, was so hostile to the slave states that Virginia's governor gave the correspondence to a local newspaper, and soon it was reprinted in papers throughout the country.

Other than land, slaves were the most valuable asset in the United States, particularly in the slave states. The protection of slavery, therefore, had high priority in Southern legislatures. As retaliation for Seward's effrontery, the Virginia legislature started passing laws imposing punitive fees and duties on ships leaving Virginia for New York City, a cause soon joined by South Carolina and watched closely by other states. New York businessmen began criticizing Seward for causing difficulties in trade between the Southern states and New York. This trade had made many people in the city very wealthy, including most of the passengers on the *Utica*. Some of these passengers owned ships that coasted down to Southern ports to bring cotton to New York, where it could be stored and then sold. Still others owned warehouses that stored the cotton until it could be shipped to Europe. Others owned insurance companies that insured the cotton and the ships carrying it. Some owned banks that financed the cotton trade and lent money to Southern planters for the purchase of land and slaves, and still others acted as brokers for the purchase and sale of the cotton. A few owned deepwater sailing vessels that carried raw cotton across the Atlantic to the power looms of Lancashire and Le Havre and returned with pallets loaded with English machinery and bolts of finished cotton cloth. This vast web of wealth-producing dealings, which was known as the "cotton triangle," all began with millions of slaves toiling in sweltering cotton fields.

"You know, Governor, there's a lot of us that agree with what you're doing," Schultz said, eyes focused straight ahead on the river. "I don't see how buying and selling men and women, much less their children, can be right."

"Thank you, Captain," Seward said. After a pause, he continued, "Someday slavery will end. I just hope it ends peacefully." With an audible sigh, Seward gave Schultz a small pat on the back and said, "Well, I'd better go back down on the deck. The bishop and I are supposed to make speeches. I think I'll limit mine to the new railroad."

2

Clarke County, Alabama
November 1847

Kit shivered as he stood ankle deep in a washtub while his mother scrubbed his naked body with a small piece of lye soap and a rag. Nearby,

Aunt Sissy stood ready with a bucket of water to douse the boy before the soap began to burn. Today was the day that Kit and his mother would be separated, at least for years and possibly forever.

Three months earlier Massa Simmons had been standing on the porch, getting ready to go out into the fields. The next moment he was lying face down on the stairs writhing in pain and clutching his chest. A male house slave named Linzy saw him fall and immediately yelled for help. During the few seconds it took Missus Simmons to come downstairs, Massa had stopped writhing and was lying still, covered in sweat. The slave overseer, alerted by Linzy's yell, had immediately begun running to the house. Linzy and the overseer carried Simmons into the parlor and laid him on a black horsehair settee. The overseer ripped open the unconscious man's shirt and tried unsuccessfully to feel a pulse in his neck. He was familiar enough with dead bodies to know in a few seconds that his employer was dead. However, he continued trying to locate a pulse and even massaged the dead man's face in a show of effort. Finally, however, he opened his knife, polished the blade against his pants leg, and placed the shiny blade under Massa's nose. When it didn't fog up, the two men looked up at Missus Simmons. The tears streaming down Linzy's black face confirmed what everyone else already suspected.

That night, the dread of upheaval swept throughout the plantation. In the great house, Misses Simmons had seen her life upended in mere seconds. As she sat alone in her dark parlor, she reviewed her circumstances. She was fifty-five years old and, after thirty-seven years of an unhappy marriage, had no interest in remarrying. She quickly concluded that the plantation and slaves would have to be sold as soon as possible. She'd move to Grove Hill to be close to her daughter. For a moment, she was embarrassed about thinking of her own situation with her husband's body wrapped in a sheet on the settee only a few feet away. However, she was a practical woman, not given to sentimentalism, and she needed to make plans to protect her interests.

In the log cabins inhabited by the slaves, the evening's dread was fed by helplessness. Older slaves knew what was coming—the auction block. Massa Simmons had been a good enough owner, and the slaves knew many that were worse—sometimes much worse. With Massa Simmons, the slaves had eaten regularly and had not been whipped too frequently. Unlike some masters, he had left the slave women alone and had not delighted in inflicting pain or humiliation. "No," the slaves had murmured to each other in the dark, "things were gonna git wo'se."

Kit yelped as Aunt Sissy poured the cold well water over his back. Today he was part of the first shipment of slaves being sent to the market. His mother had begged Misses to allow Kit to stay with her, but Missus had coldly rebuffed the request. Emmie, the name given to Kit's mother by a previous owner, was a good cook and seamstress and would be valuable to Misses Simmons when she moved to Grove Hill. However, Misses Simmons had no use for a seven-year-old boy. Thus, it was decided that Kit would be sold separately. Emmie was nursing a four-month-old daughter, and the infant would be permitted to stay with her mother. Missus Simmons, a stalwart Baptist, would not think of separating a nursing child from her mother. Also, Missus thought, she could keep the girl as an investment. Emmie was a handsome and intelligent Negress, and her daughter ought to inherit those traits. In fifteen years or so, if money was needed, she could sell the girl for a nice sum.

The slave dealer drew up a large wagon pulled by two horses. Massa Simmons's younger brother, who had taken over the affairs of the plantation, greeted the man. A brief discussion occurred, and the brother took the dealer to see each slave who was to be taken away. By the time the dealer came to the back of the house, Kit had been dressed in an enormous old pair of wool pants, held up with a rope, and a canvas sack with armholes for a shirt. Emmie and Aunt Sissy stood behind him. The dealer looked at Kit.

"How old you, boy?"

"Sev'n, suh."

"You ain't too big."

Kit didn't know how to respond to that, so he just remained silent. The dealer looked at the two women behind him.

"One of ya his mammy?"

"I's, suh," Emmie responded.

The dealer looked at Emmie's drawn face. He saw the resemblance.

"He healthy?"

"Yas, suh."

"No broken bones?"

"No, suh."

The dealer did not particularly like separating small children from their mothers, but it wasn't his decision. He moved closer to Emmie and said quietly, "I try ta fin' 'im a good owna."

Caught by surprise at this act of kindness, Emmie started crying and whispered, "Bless ya, suh."

The dealer knew he would have no real say regarding Kit's next owner. At an auction the high bidder won, pure and simple. One thing he could do, however, was notify some of the more decent slave owners of Kit's availability. Maybe someday, like the dealer's mother had told him when he was young, there would be a final reckoning of one's life. A small act of kindness now and then might help protect him from eternal flames. The dealer didn't necessarily believe in that stuff, but he figured you couldn't be sure.

The eight slaves being sent to market were told to come around to the dealer's wagon. Emmie, holding her infant daughter, kneeled down to give Kit one last hug, a strong, tight one, and whispered her goodbyes in his ear. Kit gave his mother and baby sister a hug and kiss in return and was then lifted into the wagon by the dealer. When all the slaves were seated, the dealer pulled iron chains and manacles from a box underneath the back of the wagon and began chaining each slave by the wrist or ankle to the iron rings attached to the sides of the wagon. Kit's small size was an evident problem, so the dealer waited until last to deal with him. Even the smallest manacle was too large for Kit's ankle. The dealer stared at his remaining chains, trying to come to a solution. Finally, he snapped his fingers. He selected the largest remaining ankle manacle and attached it around Kit's neck. It fit surprisingly well. He attached the other part of the manacle to a ring on the wagon, and he was ready to travel. The slaves in the wagon all sat quietly. A young woman cried silently while her companions, their crying exhausted over the last week, sat grim-faced or with their heads hung down and eyes closed.

With a snap of the leather lead lines, the dealer started off. Kit looked at his mother and Aunt Sissy standing next to each other. Emmie was stone-faced, clutching her baby daughter with both arms, tears running down her cheeks. Aunt Sissy was sobbing loudly. Kit stared at his mother, trying to sear into his memory the details of her face. Finally, the wagon rounded a bend, and he could no longer see her.

3

London, England
August 1855

Ambrose Dudley Mann awoke with a start. He sat up on his elbows and, shaking the fog from his head, looked around his room. Faded and peeling wallpaper with mustard- and rose-colored flowers, an old oak wardrobe, and a washstand with a chipped ewer in the corner reminded him as to where he was—alone in a rundown London hotel. He sighed deeply and slowly swung his legs over the side of the iron bed, sitting there while he gathered his thoughts. He reached over to the nightstand, opened a large silver watch—an extravagance from the past—and saw that it was nearly six o'clock. Through the room's one grimy window, morning light was seeping in.

On a piece of paper next to the watch, Mann had written the words "shipyard" and "Scott" followed by street directions. It was Saturday, and an Englishman named Tim Scott was taking him to see a ship under construction. Mann had no desire to visit a muddy shipyard, but lately loneliness had weighed so heavily upon him that he didn't want to give up a day of companionship with a new acquaintance. After a brief wash in the corner basin, Mann dressed in one of his two suits. *Thank heavens I bought good clothing when I could afford it,* he thought. When he was finished dressing, he examined himself in the mirror hanging above the basin. A balding, weary-looking, fifty-one-year-old face peered back at him. Straightening his cravat, he sighed again.

Less than three months earlier, Mann had been one of the most important, if not *the* most important, Americans in Europe. Appointed by President Franklin Pierce in May 1853 as the United States' first assistant secretary of state, Mann had traveled throughout Europe organizing consular offices and making sure Pierce's foreign policies were being carried out.

Mann was born in 1801 into a nondescript family, a serious disability in the haughty culture of his native Virginia. Nevertheless, his intelligence and industriousness, particularly when applied on behalf of Virginia's Democratic Party, had ultimately resulted in an appointment by President John Tyler as counsel to Bremen, one of Europe's most important trading centers. With a garrulous personality and an innate understanding of commerce, Mann had promoted European trade with his young country so effectively that in three years he was directed to negotiate commercial treaties with all the German states. As trade between the United States and Europe flourished, Mann's stature rose so high that it was widely anticipated he would someday become secretary of state.

In late September 1854, Mann was told of a meeting the following month in Ostend, Belgium, that was to be attended by the United States envoys to England, France, and Spain. The purpose of the meeting was to discuss the potential purchase of Cuba by the United States from Spain. Mann attended the three-day meeting in Ostend and listened approvingly to the reasons put forward by the envoys for purchasing Cuba. The most important in Mann's view was that if the island ultimately acquired statehood, the slaveholding states would gain two more US senators. Also, the purchase would prevent Spain from freeing Cuba's large slave population, an act likely to result in a large Africanized country like Haiti but closer to the United States. Spain was in dire financial condition, and Mann believed that there was a strong likelihood of Spain agreeing to the sale. Nothing Mann heard in Ostend was contrary to his understanding of Pierce's policies, and so when the meeting concluded, Mann returned to England.

The remaining three envoys immediately traveled unaccompanied to Aix-la-Chapelle in Prussia to write their recommendation to President Pierce. However, as the recommendation was being finished, one of the envoys, Pierre Soulé, argued for an additional provision. Soulé was the American envoy to Spain, and he knew from past discussions with Spanish diplomats that the country would never voluntarily sell Cuba. Soulé cajoled his two associates to agree to the statement that if Spain refused to sell Cuba, the United States was justified "in wresting it from Spain" by force. In other words, if Spain did not agree to sell Cuba on the terms offered, a military expedition would seize the island.

The recommendation was supposed to be sent to Pierce confidentially, but Soulé was reckless regarding its disclosure with the result that many of its terms, including the threat to Spain, were published in the *New York Herald*. By early 1855, Pierce was forced to release the entire collection of documents, which had by then been anointed the Ostend

Manifesto. Fury erupted in both the Northern states and Europe upon the manifesto's release. A seizure of Cuba would have resulted in a war not only with Spain but with its allies, Great Britain and France, each with a powerful modern navy. The manifesto recommended, in effect, that men be killed, vast sums expended, and commerce with Europe severely disrupted, all for the goal of adding two more senators from a slaveholding state.

In order to mitigate the damage resulting from the manifesto's publication, Pierce obtained Soulé's resignation and let it be known that the manifesto's demand for war was not authorized. The other two envoys went quietly back to their posts. Even though Mann had not participated in the drafting of the manifesto and had never assented to its threat of war, his presence at the meeting in Ostend, together with his status as Pierce's assistant secretary of state, brought the controversy dangerously close to the president. Thus, it was decided that Mann would have to resign.

Out of work and with a family to support, Mann had approached John Letcher, the governor of Virginia, who had offered Mann a position as Virginia's assistant secretary of state, a position with virtually no duties and little pay. Though bitter at the loss of pay and prestige from his former position, Mann had nevertheless gone to Europe to promote Virginia's tobacco and other agricultural products. London was his first destination.

Mann did not want Tim Scott, or anyone else for that matter, to see the shabby hotel in which he was staying. Accordingly, he arranged to meet Scott several blocks away in a better area of the city. When Mann arrived after a brisk walk, he found his companion, an energetic middle-aged Englishman, waiting for him.

"You haven't been waiting long, I hope?" Mann spoke with a soft drawl that Londoners frequently had trouble understanding. Today, he made an effort to speak more loudly than usual.

"No. In fact, I arrived a moment before you," Scott replied. "The shipyard is near Millwall. Now, the best way to get there is to take the Blackwall Railway Line to Limehouse. From there, we'll take the omnibus to Millwall."

The two men walked through the sooty, manure-splattered streets of London until they arrived at the Fenchurch Street Station, a new and impressive gray-brick building with a cavernous interior.

Once inside, Mann craned his neck to look at the ceiling. "Do you know how they built this huge roof with so few pillars?" he asked.

"I'm told that they used a device called a truss, although I'm not sure how it works," Scott said. "English engineers are most clever." He smiled at Mann. "Our trip today should convince you of that."

Mann had been in London for nearly a month. He had passed through it many times earlier in his career and knew parts of it well. However, this time he was going to an area upon which he'd never set eyes. Through the open window of their railroad car, he saw the London Bridge as they passed over the Thames on a railroad bridge. As they traveled further, he saw a changing panorama of redbrick tenements, wooden stables, filthy-looking streams, large and menacing-looking brick-and-stone buildings—most likely factories, warehouses, or perhaps orphanages—and occasionally a desolate-looking pasture with a handful of grazing cows. The air had an acrid scent.

Scott pointed out sights he thought Mann might find interesting, and they discussed, to their limited ability, the technical aspects of the relatively new railroad train on which they were riding. After nearly an hour of slow but steady progress, the train stopped at a wooden platform with a painted sign announcing "Limehouse." The two men, along with other sightseers, walked a short distance from the platform to an omnibus stop.

While they waited, Scott said, "Dudley, I think you're going to be astounded by what you see today. I went for the first time a month ago. I'm anxious to see what progress has been made since my visit."

Millwall, a distant part of London, was composed largely of marshes and ditches interspersed with ramshackle wooden houses and outhouses and occasionally areas of newer terraced houses made of brick. Despite the unsightly landscape, the mood of the passengers who boarded the omnibus was festive, with lots of nods and smiles among the sightseers and even a few quips. Finally, the coachman yelled out, "'Ere we are—out for the great ship!" The two men joined their fellow passengers in walking down a cobbled road.

The omnibus had stopped on the Isle of Dogs, an oddly named piece of land formed by a great loop of the River Thames. It was an "isle" only by being separated from the rest of Millwall by a basin that served as an entrance to the large West India Docks built half a century earlier.

Someone had once described the isle as "an island peopled by a peculiar amphibious race who dwell in peculiar amphibious houses built upon a curious foundation, neither fluid nor solid." The outstanding feature of the Isle of Dogs was mud, in varieties from dry and rock-hard to slimy liquid. It was one of the ugliest places Mann had ever seen.

The passengers from the omnibus began walking in small groups down a road between large gray-brick warehouses. The road's downward slope made it obvious that they were heading toward the shoreline of the Thames. Suddenly, Scott stopped and took his companion by the elbow. Surprised, Mann looked at the Englishman for an explanation. Scott nodded directly ahead and said, "Look!" Mann turned and looked but saw nothing but the warehouses. When he looked back at Scott in bewilderment, the bemused Englishman shook his head and pointed to an area above the warehouses. Mann looked in the direction of Scott's finger and saw looming above the warehouses a giant dark-red wall. Mann stood there puzzled until Scott leaned over to him and whispered loudly, "It's her hull!"

Mann continued to stare at the object as Scott took his arm and guided him down to where the road opened upon a clay-and-mud area. There, the enormity of the rust-covered object hit Mann with full force. The Englishman, wanting to impress his American friend, smiled at his success as Mann stood there in silence, his mouth open, trying to comprehend the scene before him. The hull of a gigantic ship was taking form, and it stretched out for a length of nearly seven hundred feet, hundreds of feet longer than any ship ever conceived. Even more awesome to Mann was the height of the structure. In those areas of the hull where the workers had nearly finished installing the outside plating, the hull stretched from the ground upward nearly seventy feet. Mann found himself looking up at the construction of a seven-story wall of riveted, rust-streaked iron.

The hull was surrounded by wooden scaffolding that was almost ninety feet tall, and various iron and wooden equipment lay around the shipyard on wooden platforms. Mann was no stranger to large ocean-going steamships; he had traveled across the Atlantic several times on some of the largest ships in the world. However, nothing he had ever traveled on, nothing he had ever seen or even envisioned, prepared him for this colossus.

It was some time before Mann broke away from this sight to acknowledge Scott's presence. Scott smiled as he asked, "Dudley, was it worth the trip?"

Shaking his head, Mann answered, "It's almost beyond belief. I don't know what to make of it."

"Everyone has the same reaction," Scott said. "I've seen it twice before, and it's still as incredible as the first time I saw it."

Mann nodded. The two men slowly walked along the edge of the shipyard, traversing nearly the entire length of the hull, and studied the construction closely. Unlike every other ship built in the memory of man, the great ship was not going to be launched stern first. Scott told Mann that the engineers calculated she was far too long and heavy to do so safely. She was to be launched sideways in two giant cradles made of massive timbers. Because she was parallel to the shore of the Thames, her entire starboard flank was exposed to sightseers. Scott explained that on the other side of the hull, the side facing the river, workmen had steam-driven thousands of tree trunks into the mud banks of the Thames. They then had coated the entire area with concrete to make a ramp leading to the river. On this ramp, railroad tracks had been installed on which the ship's cradles were supposed to slide. When the time came to launch the massive vessel, she would slide down the ramp until she was floating in the Thames. Or so the engineers theorized.

The hull had been substantially completed in a few sections, while other sections remained in their earliest stages of construction. From various vantage points the two men could see enormous iron bulwarks spaced throughout the structure, giant riveted walls locking the hull into a number of watertight compartments. From another view, both the inner and outer hulls of the ship, about three feet apart from each other, could be seen. Dozens of men and small boys were working on the hull, most of them riveting by hand the millions of rivets that held the thousands of giant iron plates together. Most riveting crews consisted of two men and one or two small boys, the function of the boys being to squeeze into the three-foot area between the inner and outer hulls. Wedged in the dark, cramped space between the hulls, the boys caught red-hot rivets in gloved hands and then backstopped them by pushing iron blocks against them while the men outside the hull alternated deafening hammer blows on the rivets' heads.

Large wooden cranes lifted precisely shaped one-inch-thick iron plates, each about six by eight feet, to be directed into place by men pulling guide ropes. Everywhere, human muscle and agility worked in confluence with the cruder power of steam-powered cranes and derricks. To Mann, the workmen appeared as ants on the carcass of some giant blood-colored animal.

Before long it was early afternoon and getting much warmer. The stench from the feculent water of the Thames was beginning to have its effect on Mann. Feeling a bit nauseous, he suggested to Scott that it might be time to leave. The Englishman agreed. Both men were reflective and quiet on the return trip to the city. When they arrived at Fenchurch Street Station, Mann impulsively asked Scott to be his guest for an early dinner. Although money was hard to come by, Mann was reluctant to part without learning more about the giant hull. Scott readily accepted the invitation. A respectable-looking tavern on Lombard Street was located, and the two men sat in a quiet corner to talk.

"You see, Dudley, it all goes back to the discovery of gold in Australia a few years ago. I've never been to Australia, but everyone who has gone there describes the trip as ghastly. Going there, a ship must sail west, across the entire Atlantic Ocean, around Cape Horn, and across nearly the entire southern Pacific. The trip takes months, and more than a few ships disappear without a trace. The storms around the Cape can be devastating; in fact, the Cape is so far south that the weather there is freezing much of the year."

The Englishman stopped for a sip from his tankard and then continued, "Coming home is just as bad. To fill its sails, the ship must sail west again, but this time across the Indian Ocean, around the Cape of Good Hope, and up the west side of Africa. Sometimes these ships get into the doldrums and can sit motionless in the middle of the ocean in blistering heat for weeks."

"Why don't they use steamers and take the shortest route around Africa?" Mann asked.

Scott slapped his hand lightly on the table. "There, Dudley, you have the exact point of the ship!" he exclaimed. "Steamers need coal, lots of it, and there is no coal between London and Australia."

Mann sat and thought while his friend talked.

"No coal in Africa, no coal in India, no coal in Madagascar," Scott said, drawing out the last word in a humorous way. "The Eastern Steam Navigation Company very much wanted the Royal Mail contract for Australia, and to get it they had to work out how to get a steamer to Australia and back. The directors hired the famous Sir Isambard Kingdom Brunel, and he told them the only way it could be done was for a ship to carry all the coal she needed for a round-trip. 'How large a ship would that be, Mr. Brunel?' they asked, and he took out his pencil, made a couple of calculations, and said, 'Seven hundred feet and twenty-five thousand tons.'

"Well, once they picked themselves up off the floor, they realized he was right. They asked, 'Can such a ship be built?' to which Mr. Brunel, ever the great optimist, said, 'Of course.' And so, Dudley, you have now seen the offspring of the marriage of British capitalism and Mr. Brunel's optimism."

Mann laughed at Scott's description and toasted him for his wit.

The dinner continued for some time, with the two men engaged in an animated discussion about the ship. Scott seemed to have read everything he could about it and was more than willing to share his knowledge. As a barmaid cleared their table, Mann asked, "Does she have a name? The coachman just referred to her as the 'great ship.'"

Scott replied, "She hasn't been christened yet, so no name is certain. The newspapers usually call her *Leviathan*. However, sometimes she's referred to as the *Great Eastern*, from the name of the company that's building her. It'll be interesting to see what name she's given when christened."

Finally, with dinner long over and two glasses of a decent Madeira drained, Mann thanked the Englishman profusely for taking him to the Isle of Dogs, and Scott reciprocated for the pleasant dinner. The two parted company, and Mann walked slowly to his hotel, his forehead wrinkled in thought. It was well into evening but still quite warm. He wanted to hang up his clothes, lie down on his bed to cool off, and think.

4

Paris, France
April 16, 1856

THE men in the room off the Hall of the Ambassadors were ill-tempered. For two weeks they had lied and been lied to, threatened and been threatened, intrigued, promised, and cajoled. Several had had secrets winnowed out by noblewomen of easy virtue, and all were bloated with food, drink, and false praise. In short, they had participated in a peace conference.

The primary impetus behind the conference was the fiasco in the Crimean Peninsula, where England and France, longtime enemies, found themselves allies against Russia in the Black Sea. Although the allies were the nominal victors, it was death alone that had triumphed. Yellow fever had killed a quarter million of England's finest young men and an equal number of their French, Russian, and Turkish counterparts. An unnecessary, ineptly managed war had doomed nearly an entire generation of young women to finish their lives as widows or spinsters.

The participants at the conference were from England, France, Austria, Prussia, Russia, Saxony, Turkey, and a host of minor duchies and principalities. All the nations had been bloodied and impoverished to some degree by the endless wars they had fought, the Crimean disaster being only the latest. The nobility of Europe was seeking respite from further bloodletting, fearful that an enraged peasantry, tired of heavy taxes and compulsory service as cannon fodder, would take things into its own hands. Fresh in everyone's mind were the ugly events of 1848 when dangerous slogans such as "democracy," "constitutions," and "the rights of man" were on the lips of countless European rabble.

While peace was ostensibly the purpose of the conference, the real negotiations were over territory, which, at the end of the conference, had been divvied up in such a manner that even the most incompetent prognosticator could have foreseen future wars. Nevertheless, the lines had been drawn and agreed upon, peace was likely for at least a few years, and the debauched negotiators were anxious to return home.

Before adjourning, however, Count Walewski, Napoleon Bonaparte's illegitimate son and the chairman of the conference, wished to make a statement.

"Gentlemen, I suggest that we should follow the example of other great congresses and adopt a declaration that will further international law and the cause of peace."

The delegates looked at Walewski with puzzlement. At the beginning of the conference, the delegates had regarded the count with attitudes ranging from patronizing to contemptuous. Yet, despite his reputation as a pompous dunce, he had somehow held the conference together to its conclusion, messy as that might be. As long as he was brief, there was no harm in hearing him out.

The count continued, "The Congress of Westphalia established liberty of conscience. The Congress of Vienna abolished the Negro slave trade. Now, let us consider this. The wars we have just concluded resulted in great damage to neutral countries. Ships of neutrals were seized, goods belonging to neutrals were plundered, piracy has been encouraged by letters of marque, and paper blockades have created unnecessary wars and dreadful hardships. What I propose, gentlemen, is a uniform maritime law that protects the rights of neutral countries."

The delegates thought about this. Surely wars would occur in the future, especially with the boundaries they had just created, and it seemed a shame that a country intelligent enough to stay out of a war should not be able to profit from it. Maybe the count was not quite the simpleton the delegates thought him to be.

"What do you propose, sir?" a delegate asked. In response, Walewski read four resolutions from a piece of paper.

1. Privateering is and remains abolished.
2. The neutral flag covers enemy goods, with the exception of contraband of war.
3. Neutral goods, except contraband of war, are not liable to capture under an enemy flag.
4. Blockades, to be binding, must be effective—that is, maintained by a force really sufficient to prevent access to the enemy's coast.

The delegates nodded to each other. What a remarkably sensible collection of resolutions! Privateers were a nasty bunch, pirates really, acting nominally as a naval force under letters of marque but not bound by any code of military conduct or discipline. God forbid that a man—or, worse, a man's family—should be on a ship overtaken by murderous criminals such as these.

Neutral ships and neutral goods protected—now that was an excellent idea! Already, the delegates could see a financial benefit to staying out of a war. There was nothing more chilling to a merchant of a neutral country than to hear that his entire cargo, perhaps even his ship, had just been swallowed into the maw of a belligerent. A prosperous man could be ruined in a single day. If such a tragic event could be avoided, it would certainly be a step forward for civilization.

The fourth article was particularly popular. "Paper blockades" had meant that a belligerent's cruisers could swoop down on a neutral merchantman in the middle of the ocean and then seize the ship along with her cargo on the pretext that the vessel might have been heading to an enemy's port. France had declared a paper blockade of the British Isles in its wars with England, and England had retaliated with a paper blockade of the continent. The unarmed ships of neutrals, including the United States, had been continuously seized by French and English cruisers. In 1812, the United States had finally fought back against the English cruisers in order to protect its merchantmen. Paper blockades effected more than the seizure of private wealth; they were capable of dragging a neutral nation into a war.

If the fourth article was adopted, paper blockades would be outlawed.

In the future, in order to seize a neutral ship, a country at war must maintain an authentic blockade maintained by a large naval force, one "really sufficient to prevent access" to an enemy's ports. Seizing a neutral ship in furtherance of a paper blockade would constitute an act of war against the neutral country.

The count distributed a paper with the four articles, together with several short preambles that explained to posterity why the articles were necessary. After the delegates had read the document, Walewski said he would entertain a motion to adopt, and the articles were immediately and unanimously adopted. The four articles of the Declaration of Paris of April 16, 1856, were now the law of nations.

5

Marengo County, Alabama
June 1856

THE last of the slaves had come in from the field in the late-afternoon heat to join the other slaves already milling around a corner of the toolshed. Finally, everyone stood silently in a large semicircle. Bolted onto the corner of the toolshed was an iron ring about six feet from the ground. A slave girl, about thirteen, stood facing the corner. Her hands had been tied, and the rope binding her hands had been fastened through the iron ring, pulling her arms above her head and effectively fastening her to the building. She was sobbing loudly.

A sweaty white man in his early thirties stood behind the girl holding a hickory switch. He looked uneasily around him. Some slaves looked directly at him, their faces void of expression. Others looked at the ground, shifting their weight from one foot to another. A few older women sniffled, and a large, heavy woman looked at him with unmistakable disgust.

I wish ta hell Judge Crane was here, the white man thought. *You don't switch a gal for sassing another gal! I'm going ta have nothing but trouble with the niggers for the next couple weeks.* The man, an overseer named Collins, looked past the circle of slaves to the back porch of the main house. Mrs. Crane and her adolescent daughter were standing on the porch staring at him. The mother, a thin, hard-looking woman, had her arms folded, her face grimly fixed. The daughter appeared agitated, swaying back and forth in place, her head tipping from side to side. The mother, staring at Collins, nodded.

"Aw right! Listen!" Collins spoke loudly, addressing the assembled slaves. "Tizzie was sassing li'l Miz Crane today. She was warned ta stop, but she din't. 'Cordinly, Tizzie is going ta git seven switches. If she does it again, she'll git fifteen. Does everyone un'erstand that there's ta be no sassing of a white person, any white person?" Collins looked around at the sullen crowd. A couple of old women nodded; the rest remained motionless.

Kit had been one of the last slaves to arrive from the field. Now in his midteens, he was short but powerfully built. He stood near the middle of the semicircle, about fifteen feet from where Tizzie was standing. Because Tizzie was a house slave and he was a field hand, Kit didn't know her very well. His main impression of her was that she spoke loudly and sometimes sang tuneless, nonsensical songs to herself. Now, she looked small and terrified tied to the switching ring, tears running down her face.

Collins went to pull Tizzie's dress apart so that he could switch her on her bare back and buttocks. When he untied the cord around her neck, the entire sack dress fell around Tizzie's ankles. Kit stared at the naked girl, thin and dark with a well-shaped back, until he got a sharp jab from Molly's elbow. Surprised, he looked at the old slave woman and saw a scowl of disapproval on her face. Embarrassed, he stared at the ground.

Taking a breath, Collins swung the switch, which landed on Tizzie's right shoulder. She cried out with a scream and began gasping. *Hell!* thought Collins. *I hit her too hard. I'm not good with this damned switch.* Taking an even deeper breath, he turned slightly sideways and hit her again, this time on her left shoulder. Tizzie cried again, her body shaking. Collins swung the switch again, this time landing on the girl's right buttocks, and then smacked her on her left. He stood there for a moment, furious at having been ordered to switch the girl by the old witch on the porch. He looked at Tizzie's back. Welts were starting to appear, and blood was beginning to drip from an angry red line on her right shoulder. He turned to the main house. "Mrs. Collins, she's awfully small. I don't know if I can switch her again without doing some bad damage. If we scar her up too much, she'll lose value if we try ta sell her. I'd like ta stop at four."

Mrs. Crane considered the request. The screaming and crying of the girl was small recompense for the fact that the girl had actually talked back to her daughter. These young darkies had to learn. Nevertheless, her husband would be angry if she caused a slave to lose value. She'd have to be satisfied by Tizzie's cries and sobs. She pursed her thin lips and nodded and then silently turned and took her daughter into the house.

Despite Molly's elbow, Kit had glanced up once during the switching and had seen the switch hit Tizzie's buttocks. He'd seen her body jerk in pain while she cried out. He'd gotten a sick feeling in his stomach as he watched her twist, trying somehow to avoid the next blow

The punishment over, Collins put the switch into the shed and headed toward his cabin. A couple of slave women went to Tizzie. One stood on a box and untied her. She fell on her hands and knees, her body heaving with sobs. As she was helped off the ground and then hustled naked into a slave cabin, the male slaves were quickly dispersed with glowering looks from the women. Eventually, Tizzie's sobbing softened as she was ministered to with a small amount of lard that one of the old slaves kept in a jar for such occasions.

The slaves ate their meager meal silently that evening, and as night approached, their brooding silence continued. After dinner, Kit went to his cabin but was too agitated to sleep. He went outside and sat on the ground, his back to the cabin's rough-hewn wall. It was a still, hot night, and in the distance heat lightning silently flared up low-lying clouds. The night was full with the sound of humming insects.

It warn't right, Kit thought. *She's jus' a gal. She shouldn't ha' sassed da white gal, but gals always sass one 'other. It was wrong to switch her.* The vision of the naked girl on her hands and knees, sobbing in pain and humiliation, troubled him as much as anything he had seen since being sold away from his mother. Kit had seen slaves punished in the past, but usually it was young men punished for stealing or sneaking away from the plantation. Once, a slave had attempted to escape and had pulled a knife on the pursuing slave chasers. Kit had seen him lashed with a leather whip until his back looked like raw meat. The man had writhed silently in agony until he fainted. It had been horrible to watch. Even Kit had been tied to a post once and switched when he failed to turn in a slave who had stolen a piece of smoked ham. But Tizzie's switching bothered him more than all the others because Tizzie had meant no harm. She was just a loud girl, only a few years older than his sister would be now. She wasn't running away. She didn't steal nothing.

The words his mother had whispered before he was shackled into the slave dealer's wagon nearly nine years earlier remained in Kit's mind. "Don't talk back. Do what you're told. Don't cause no trouble. Pray to Jesus." He had followed this advice, except that as he got older he rarely prayed. He didn't know really how to pray anymore, and he wasn't even certain what the purpose of prayer was supposed to be. He had prayed many times to be reunited with his mother, and it had never happened. Tonight, to counter his helplessness, he'd try to pray one more time. "Jesus, make Tizzie feel good again real quick, and help me find my mama." He sat for some time, his head down, listening to the insects humming, breathing slowly to calm the turbulence in his mind. After a long while, he calmed down enough to get up and try to sleep in the sweltering cabin.

6

Dutchess County, New York
July 1856

MARGARET Schultz sat in an open carriage at the Fishkill Landing railroad station. It was early afternoon, and the day, although warm, was also windy, a welcome change from the stagnant humidity of the past week. Gusts of wind tore noisily through the trees on both banks of the Hudson River, animating them with waves of different shades of green. She had been waiting for the train from New York City, which was already twenty minutes late. The Hudson River Railroad was new and rarely on time.

At age forty-six, Margaret had retained enough of her youthful attractiveness to still be described as handsome. Her skin was fair and clear, and her stout figure suggested good health. She was stylishly but appropriately attired in a dress made from swaths of light-colored cotton, and her clothing, taken together with her expensive carriage, announced a person of importance. Leonard DeMund, the Schultz family servant, stood by the carriage talking quietly with her. A small, lean Negro in his late twenties, Leonard was dressed in a plain cotton shirt that had been ironed and dark wool trousers. The two conversed quietly and with what appeared to be an easy familiarity, although an observant onlooker would have noticed that the conversation consisted mostly of Margaret talking and Leonard nodding his head in agreement.

The conversation ended when a steam whistle sounded. Leonard helped his mistress from the carriage, and the two climbed to the station platform. The train approached with a cacophony of sounds—a clanging bell, loud hisses from the steam pistons, and the high-pitched screeches of the locomotive's drive wheels spinning in reverse. The power and noise of a steam locomotive coming to a stop always intimidated Margaret. As the train pulled into the station, she instinctively stepped behind Leonard, seeking whatever protection his slight frame could afford her.

Trainmen descended from the train's two coaches and laid down stepping stools for the passengers. Margaret spotted her daughter Mary exiting the second coach and waved excitedly at her. Following Mary from the coach was Alex, her thirteen-year-old brother. Mary smiled and walked quickly toward her mother while Alex approached Leonard. At eighteen years old, Mary had her mother's coloration. Her slender figure was well hidden under a padded and bustled dress of blue cotton that, unfortunately, was covered with a light coating of gray soot. During the sixty-mile trip from New York City, the passengers had had the unenviable choice of closing their coach windows and suffocating in the heat, or opening the windows and allowing the locomotive's acrid smoke to be sucked into the car. The majority of the passengers, predominantly men, had chosen the latter.

Mindful of the soot on her daughter's clothes, Margaret refrained from hugging her. Instead, she leaned forward and gave her daughter a light kiss on the cheek. Stepping back, she then started dabbing at Mary's face with a linen handkerchief to remove some of the soot. Speaking loudly to overcome the hissing sound from the locomotive, Margaret fairly shouted, "We've missed you so much! We'll get you all cleaned up at home. You'll have to tell me everything about your visits with Kate and the Lowbers."

The Lowbers were Margaret's younger sister, Mary Catherine, and her husband, Daniel Lowber, and Kate was their twenty-one-year-old daughter.

Margaret and Mary Catherine had come from Wales as children with their parents and settled near Utica, New York. Thirty-one years ago, when she was fifteen, Margaret Evans had married dashing twenty-one-year Alexander Hamilton Schultz, a riverboat captain. Several children had resulted from this marriage, the second oldest of which was Mary, the young lady who had just disembarked from the train.

"I'll tell you everything, Mother," Mary said, "but first let me find my trunk."

Mary went to where the baggage car had been unloaded and identified a large steamer trunk. Alex and Leonard hauled it to the edge of the platform, and with the help of a boy hovering around the station looking for tips, they loaded the heavy trunk into the back of the Schultzes' carriage. Leonard gave the boy a tip.

The ride home was pleasant. The carriage traveled slowly, first up a steeply inclined Main Street, then across a small creek, and then up again through a succession of shady, tree-lined roads. Mary sat next to her mother in the rear seat of the carriage, while Alex sat on the driver's seat next to Leonard. Mary's trip from Mobile Bay to Fishkill Landing had been long and exhausting. She had taken a coastal steamer from Mobile to New York City, with an overnight stop in Havana, Cuba. Alex, who had been sent to be her escort and protector, had met her in New York. With the warmth of the sunlight and the rustling sound of the wind-blown leaves making her drowsy, Mary rested her head on her mother's shoulder, now protected by a large cloth. She closed her eyes and listened to the clopping of the horse's hooves.

After a bit, however, Mary perked up and turned toward her mother. "Kate and I had a most wonderful stay," she said. "She and Montgomery are very happy together, and they have a lovely little home in Mobile. Their little Willie is perfectly adorable and very fond of his aunt Mary." Mary pointed at herself with a laugh, and Margaret nodded in approval. Mary continued, "Montgomery is very busy, and he travels a lot, mostly up to New York City but sometimes to England. Kate misses him terribly when he is away. She was very glad for my company." Kate's husband was Montgomery Neill, a British-born cotton trader whom she had married two years earlier.

"I'm sure you two had a great deal to reminisce about."

"Mother, we did! We remembered all sorts of things we did as girls, and we laughed a lot. At night, we read poetry to each other, and one night we even got Montgomery to recite one of Shakespeare's sonnets. He has the perfect English accent for it."

"Gracious! He's such a serious young man. You two must have really teased him into it."

Mary laughed. "We did. He said that he could resist one of us but that since he was outnumbered he would surrender and recite the sonnet. Only one, however."

"How did you find the Lowbers?"

"They seem well. Uncle Daniel's business seems very much better, and they have a nice summer house not too far from New Orleans in a place called Lewisburg. You can travel from New Orleans to Mobile by steamer—it's not too far a distance—so Uncle Daniel and Aunt Mary see Kate and Montgomery quite frequently. I had a nice stay with the Lowbers but was only there for a couple of days."

The two cousins, Mary Schultz and Kate Lowber, had been close since childhood. Considering themselves more sisters than cousins, the two girls always looked forward to Mary's spring trips to the Lowber household in New Orleans. When together, they giggled, read poetry to each other, talked about everything that young girls found interesting, and traveled about under the watchful eye of Mary Catherine Lowber or one of the Lowbers' trusted slaves. When, at age nineteen, Kate had accepted Montgomery Neill's proposal of marriage, it had been on the condition that the marriage take place in New York City, where Mary could be bridesmaid and all the Schultz family could attend. The couple had married in July 1854 at the Methodist Episcopal Church on Sullivan Street. After the marriage, the newlyweds had gone to Mobile to start their family, with little William arriving a little more than a year later.

When the carriage arrived at the Schultz home, Leonard and Alex began the work of hauling in Mary's leaden trunk while Margaret and her daughter retired to a parlor. Margaret covered a chair with a sheet so that Mary could sit down without getting soot on the upholstery. After getting Mary a glass of water, Margaret sat down and asked, "So, how many slaves does Uncle Daniel now own?"

Mary knew this was a sensitive issue. She paused to gather her thoughts before she answered. "Ten, Mama."

"Ten! My goodness! Any children?"

“They have a mother who has two small children. The children are very bright, and Uncle Daniel and Aunt Mary treat them like pets. They’re all very happy.”

Margaret did not respond but made a quiet humming sound with her lips tightly closed.

Mary Schultz was a young woman who alternated between two worlds. Her parents were ardent opponents of slavery. Mary had been taught early on that slavery was wrong and contrary to biblical teachings, although she was never certain as to which ones. Most of her friends in Fishkill Landing regarded slavery as hideous and slave owners as depraved. When Mary stayed in New Orleans, however, she lived in a world that accepted slavery as perfectly normal. Years earlier, while visiting the Lowbers, Mary had mentioned to Kate that she thought slavery might be wrong. Kate had given a gentle laugh and, stroking Mary’s hair, responded with an answer that Kate had heard many times before.

“Dearest heart, the people up North always say that slavery is wrong, but they know nothing about it. We keep slaves out of kindness. You’ve seen our slaves—they’re like children! What kind of parent would drive a child from the protection of his home? Freedom to a slave is frightening; it means that they’re free to starve, or maybe even worse.”

While Mary was considering this, Kate continued, “You know that Negroes can’t read, can’t cipher, and have trouble with the simplest task unless they’re watched over. How could they possibly survive by themselves? Could you imagine a Negro running my father’s store?” Kate laughed gently at the thought.

Mary had to admit that running a store like Uncle Daniel’s was a pretty complicated business, and even Mary would find such work daunting. Trying to run such a business without being able to read or cipher would be nigh impossible.

“Mary, you see them. They’re happy with us. They’re not punished, unless one is really naughty, and then what choice do we have? Why would we be mean to our slaves? We’re Christians too, just like the people in the North. In fact, we’ve saved our slaves’ souls by making them Christians. When the good ones are in heaven, they won’t be slaves anymore. They’ll be free, just like you and me.”

Mary had not considered what might have happened to the souls of the Africans if they hadn’t been made Christians. She had heard that a person who died before becoming a Christian was doomed to eternal damnation. It seemed logical that the rule applied to everyone, even Africans.

"I do wish the people up North would stop judging us," Kate said. "And Mrs. Stowe's book! Why, do you think my father is anything like Simon Legree?" Kate looked at Mary with raised eyebrows, and slowly an impish grin grew across Kate's face. Mary laughed and agreed that Uncle Daniel was nothing like Harriet Beecher Stowe's villain.

Mary had never brought the subject up again with Kate and avoided as much as possible any discussion of slavery with her own family. She had concluded that people in the North and people in the South simply looked at things differently. She had resolved not to think any more about whether slavery was good or evil. That afternoon she also resolved not to tell her parents that Kate and Montgomery had just purchased three slaves for themselves.

7

London, England
August 1856

MANN's yearlong stay in England had been frustrating. While he had had some success in his goal of nurturing sympathies for the slaveholding states among important men, he still had not secured a position that would allow him to adequately support his family. He and his wife back home were still living off the small stipend he received as the assistant secretary of state of the Commonwealth of Virginia.

In the evenings, Mann lay on his bed and assembled his thoughts, making plans and weighing options. One subject that was a constant in these solitary deliberations was the ship being constructed on the Isle of Dogs. Mann had been so moved by his first vision of the giant structure that he'd continued to visit the construction site at least monthly. Twice more he had gone with Tim Scott. Sometimes he brought new acquaintances, but most often he traveled alone, his visits pilgrimages to a massive iron shrine. Mann saw the ship's double hull being constructed; saw her giant paddle wheels, each nearly sixty feet in diameter, erected on her sides; saw the shaft for her giant propeller, which would be an astounding twenty-four feet in diameter when finished, hoisted into place; saw everything huge and powerful and awe-inspiring about her. He carefully followed her metamorphosis from a construction project to an oceangoing vessel. At night, he lay on his bed mulling over the ship's awesome potential.

One afternoon, Mann impulsively stopped at a stationery store and bought an expensive packet of writing paper. Once in his hotel room, he took his writing box from under his bed and removed from it his pen and ink bottle. Sitting on his room's single rickety chair, with the writing box resting on the bed, he began writing:

To the Citizens of the Slaveholding States.

8

New Orleans, Louisiana
September 1856

J. D. B. DeBow bent over a large table reviewing the galley sheets he had just received from his typesetter. The October 1856 issue of *DeBow's Review,* his journal of agricultural, commercial, and industrial progress and resources, was going to press shortly, and this was his last opportunity to correct any errors. As he finished his review, the late-afternoon sun was casting long shadows across the dusty room of the *Review*'s offices on Camp Street. Finally, DeBow sighed and sat down on an old Windsor chair. Bending over galleys for long periods was uncomfortable.

A young proofreader from the downstairs office came up to pick up the galleys. "Are you done, sir?" the boy asked. DeBow nodded, and the proofreader began to organize and roll up the galleys. Tomorrow he would send them by Adams Express to the print shop in New York City. Although he had his back to DeBow, the boy heard the publisher make a grunt of pain as he moved in his chair.

"Are you all right, sir?"

"I'm fine. My back just gets tired from bending over," DeBow said. "Thank you for asking." As the boy started to leave the room, DeBow turned around in his chair and asked, "What did you think of the communication from Mr. Mann?"

The boy, who was perhaps fourteen years old, stopped and looked at the older man for a moment. "I'm not sure I understood it, sir."

DeBow sighed. Mann's main point was easy enough to understand—the North was bleeding the South to death. Explaining how the North was doing it was the difficult part.

"Sir, I think I understood about the need for a steam ferry line, but his discussion about the giant iron ship and railroads was difficult to follow," the boy continued. "Maybe I need to read it more closely. It's hard to think about an article when you're searching it for errors."

DeBow smiled. True enough. "Would you like me to explain to you some of Mr. Mann's proposals?"

The boy looked surprised but answered, "Yes, sir."

DeBow pointed to an old wooden chair, and the young proofreader pulled it to where DeBow was sitting.

DeBow had seen and learned much in his thirty-six years. His skill in assembling statistics had resulted in his appointment as superintendent of the 1850 United States census. Four years after the census, he'd published a widely distributed compilation of important findings he'd extracted from it. From his work on the compilation, DeBow had come to believe that the South was in danger of having its destiny, indeed its very freedom, controlled from outside. From the tables and lists he had put together, it had become obvious to him that the moneyed men of the North, primarily from New York City—men who owned shipping lines, banks, insurance companies, land speculation companies, manufactories, indeed everything that had to do with money—were coiling around the South like serpents, sucking wealth out of it at every opportunity. Unless these men were stopped, DeBow believed, the South would end up as little more than an impotent colony.

DeBow sat quietly composing his thoughts and then started talking. "I want you to imagine a ship leaving England carrying one thousand plows," he said to the young proofreader. "Half of the plows are destined for a merchant in New York City, and half are destined for a merchant in Charleston. The English ship goes to New York City and unloads the five hundred plows. What would you expect to happen next?"

"The ship would sail to Charleston and unload the other five hundred."

DeBow smiled slightly. "What if I told you it was illegal for an

English ship to sail from New York City to Charleston? What if I told you that all one thousand plows had to be unloaded in New York and that the five hundred plows destined for Charleston had to be warehoused in New York City, reloaded on a New York coastal ship owned by some Yankee, and then taken to Charleston, where the plows would be unloaded a second time? What if I told you that with the unloading, warehousing, insuring, reloading, reshipping, and unloading yet again the plows cost the Charleston merchant twice what they cost the New York merchant?"

"That'd be terribly unfair. Who'd make such a law?"

"That is the law!" DeBow exclaimed, banging his fist on his chair arm. "And it was made by the United States Congress, or at least those members of Congress who come from the Northern states."

The boy sat quietly as he considered what he had just heard.

"And that's not the worst of it," DeBow said more softly. "Since English and French ships don't often come directly to Southern ports, we have to ship our cotton to New York on those same New York coasting ships. In New York, the cotton is unloaded, warehoused, reloaded on another New York ship, insured, and sent to Liverpool or France. Some sharp Yankee takes a big slice of money at every stage of that process. The money from Europe comes back through New York banks, which make sure everybody in New York gets paid, and by the time the poor Southern planter gets his money, he's lucky to break even. It's no wonder that the New Yorkers are building mansions while Southern farmers have hardly enough to eat."

"How would Mr. Mann's plan change that?"

"We don't have any shipbuilding yards in the South. The Southern states could never build or man a merchant fleet in time to save themselves from bankruptcy, which is coming soon—I'm certain of that. What Mann proposes is that the South buy this giant iron ship, or a couple like her, and shuttle them directly between Virginia and England. They would carry raw cotton directly to the English textile mills and bring manufactured goods like plows back. That way, the Southern planters and English merchants would keep all the profits, instead of those thieves in New York."

"Would Mr. Mann's plan work?"

DeBow thought a moment. "Hand me the galleys for the article."

The young man unrolled the galleys on the table and located the article entitled "Communication between the Southern States and Europe. Letter of A. Dudley Mann to the Citizens of the Slaveholding States, in Relation to a Weekly Ferry Line of Iron Steamships of Thirty Thousand Tons, between the Chesapeake Bay and Milford Haven." He handed the galley pages to DeBow, who reviewed them once more silently.

Finally, DeBow said, "Yes, I think it would work if there really was a single ship capable of carrying so much cotton. But, frankly, I have trouble believing this ship will be launched, even though Mann seems quite confident of it."

"Why do you think so?"

"I can't imagine a ship this large. Boy, picture the biggest ship you've ever seen in New Orleans. Then double the size of that ship in your mind. Now double it again. Are you done? The ship in your mind is still smaller than Mann's ship. This thing is a true monster. I calculated that by weight she is five times larger than any ship ever built. I also calculated that she could carry the entire cotton crop of the South in four, maybe five voyages!" He shook his head in disbelief but continued to scan the article. "One thing Mann states is absolutely correct. Under a federal law passed by the Yankees, Southern states could not even buy this ship."

The young man looked puzzled.

DeBow said, "The Northern shipbuilders passed a law saying that the only ships the South can buy are ships made by Northern shipyards, not European ones. Mann's proposed company would need an act of Congress just to obtain permission to buy the ship! How could anyone have voted for a law like that, knowing the injury it causes the South? Aren't the common folks up North aware of this? Don't they know that we're all supposed to be part of the same country?"

DeBow sat in his chair, a tired and frustrated man. At every opportunity he railed against the domination of the North over the South, and he'd even started *DeBow's Review* to warn others, but it seemed a losing battle. The genteel plantation aristocracy that controlled the South seemed aware that the South's lack of industry left it vulnerable to the North, but with insufficient capital and experience, they could not do much about it. DeBow was embarrassed that he could not even print his journal in the South because the region lacked the sophisticated printing equipment he needed. Instead, he had to send the journal to New

York City, a fact ridiculed in Northern papers. The North was building factories, railroads, and shipyards while the South was planting cotton and breeding slaves.

DeBow continued talking. "Mann makes another point, one I hadn't previously considered. The United States Navy is pretty much under the control of the Yankees, and if the slave states ever decide to leave the Union, as our friends in South Carolina are urging, the North will keep most of the navy and leave the South defenseless on the ocean. The North could blockade the Southern ports and starve us."

The proofreader looked puzzled. "How would Mr. Mann's plan change that?"

"Here's what Mann says about the great iron ship he saw being built." DeBow peered through his spectacles at the galleys, found the passage he was looking for, and began to read out loud. "There is not a war steamer that floats that could resist such a vessel as the *Great Eastern*. She would proceed onward with her cargo 'in the even tenor of her way,' and so rapid would be her movement, and invincible her strength, as to enable her to run the most formidable of them down as easily as a Mississippi steamboat would a canoe that attempted to interrupt its progress."

A giant iron ship that could run down any war steamer in the world! Imagine if the slave-owning states had such a ship! That image pleased DeBow very much. Any attempt by the North to interfere with Southern ocean commerce or to close Southern ports would be swiftly ended by the mere threat of such a monster.

"I remember reading that," the boy said quietly. He needed no explanation of that paragraph.

The man and boy sat in silence with their thoughts as the room slowly darkened. The sun was starting to set.

"Perhaps I should get home, sir."

DeBow looked up. "Of course. I'm keeping you from your dinner. Thank you for keeping me company."

"Thank you, sir, for explaining Mr. Mann's article. Do you think he'll be successful in setting up such a ferry line?"

"I don't know. But we must give him every opportunity to succeed. The *Review* is read throughout the South, and it's read by very important people. It'll be interesting to see what reaction Mann's communication brings."

After the young employee left, DeBow stood up and made ready to go home. His back still hurt, but his mind was occupied with other thoughts. As he locked his building, he mulled over Mann's article. *She has the ability to run down a Yankee warship like it was a canoe … Perhaps,* he thought, *Mann has found an answer.*

9

Washington, DC
November 1856

OTHER than an occasional rustling of a newspaper, the sound of rain drumming against windowpanes was the only noise inside the fashionable parlor of the brick house at the corner of Twenty-First and G Streets. William Henry Seward, the owner of the house, was sitting in a black upholstered armchair reading the *New York Daily Times* by the light of an oil lamp. The last few months had been tumultuous for him, and for the moment he was savoring the quietude of this chilly afternoon. A coal fire glowed in the firebox near his feet, and a shawl kept his shoulders and back warm.

Less than two weeks earlier Seward had been at his home in Auburn, where he'd voted in the presidential election. He'd found it dreary being home. Although Frances, his wife, suffered from no identifiable illness, she had, as always, been somber and frail looking. He no longer asked her to come with him to Washington, because he knew what her answer would be. To his great relief, Frances's sister had recently moved into the family house to keep her company. Despite a difficult marriage, Seward was genuinely fond of his wife. He faithfully wrote her most evenings, setting forth the comings and goings of the nation as he observed it from the viewpoint of a United States senator.

This afternoon, Seward had several editions of the *New York Daily Times* and other newspapers at his disposal, and he was skimming them for political news but finding little that he did not already know. He picked up the November 10 edition and read an article captioned "The Election—Illinois and Tennessee in the Doubtful List." The vote was trickling in, and the article provided no predictions as to the outcome of the presidential election. John Frémont, the self-promoting explorer and first presidential candidate of the Republican Party, was doing well in New England, where his opposition to the expansion of slavery was well received. James Buchanan, the Pennsylvanian, was certain to carry the South on promises of protecting the property rights of slave owners. The effect of Millard Fillmore's third-party candidacy was probably minimal. Despite the paucity of results, Seward was confident that Buchanan would win both the border states and the presidency. None of the candidates was equal to the demands of the presidency, Seward thought. His dour mood was a perfect match for the weather.

Fred Seward walked into the parlor. "Father, the light's too dim. Mother says that reading under a dim light will hurt your eyes." The twenty-six-year-old smiled as he chastised his father.

Seward nodded in agreement. "All right, turn up the lamp. I'm just trying to conserve oil."

The young man raised the wick, and the room noticeably brightened. While Fred physically resembled his father in that both were short and slender, his personality was largely acquired from his mother. He was studious—"bookish," some would say—and slow to reach conclusions or express opinions. Unlike his mercurial father, Fred was cautious when he spoke and was content to sit quietly and listen during heated political debates.

Frances's unwillingness to come to Washington had been hard for Seward for two reasons. First, he missed his wife's company, even in her current melancholy state. Second, and perhaps more importantly, her absence severely crimped his social life. One could not easily invite politicians and other friends over for dinner and cigars without a lady to preside over the domestic aspects of such affairs. A partial answer to Seward's social drought had arrived when Fred married Anna Wharton, a pretty young woman from the Auburn area. Seward had insisted that the couple live with him in Washington, where Fred could work as his assistant and Anna could take over the role of the lady of the house. The couple had accepted, and although Anna was inexperienced in the management of a household, her beguiling smile made her a favorite among Seward's cronies.

"Dinner is going to be served in about twenty minutes," Anna announced from the entrance to the parlor.

Seward responded loudly, "Whatever it is, it smells wonderful."

Anna smiled and said it was something new that she and the cook had been working on and she hoped it would be a pleasant surprise. Fred sat down on a chair on the other side of the lamp and picked up one of the newspapers on the floor. The elder Seward had just finished the front page of the *Times* and was glancing through the remaining articles to see any items of interest. On one of the inside pages, he saw the following headline: "Enterprise for a Weekly Steamship Ferry Run between Chesapeake Bay and Milford Haven."

"Fred, listen to this," Seward said. He began reading out loud.

> Honorable A. Dudley Mann, the late accomplished and talented Assistant Secretary of State, has addressed a letter to the citizens of the Slaveholding States, in which he announces his purpose, in connection with others, to establish a weekly run steamship ferry line between the Chesapeake Bay and Milford Haven. He described his enterprise and shown its practicality and its great importance in an ably-written pamphlet of thirty pages."

When Seward paused, Fred asked, "What are you reading?"

"The *New York Times.* Fred, do you recognize the name Dudley Mann?"

"Isn't he a diplomat?"

Seward was quiet for a few moments. "Dudley Mann was a man I once admired."

"Is he dead?" Fred asked. "They referred to him as a 'late' something or other."

"No, no." Seward laughed. "I'm certain old Dudley is still alive. They just mean that he used to be the assistant secretary of state but isn't anymore." Leaning toward his son, Seward continued, "Do you remember 1848 when revolutions were breaking out in Europe? The students in Frankfurt were trying to set up their own government, and there was rioting going on in France?"

Fred nodded.

"You remember Kossuth leading a revolution in Hungary against the Austrians?"

"Of course I do. I met Kossuth when he came to the United States and had dinner with us. When I was young, I pretended I was Kossuth, leading his brave revolutionaries. A lot of boys did."

Seward acknowledged this statement with a nod of his head. "Everyone thought at the time that Kossuth was going to be the George Washington of Hungary."

"What does Dudley Mann have to do with this?"

"He was in Europe representing our State Department. When Kossuth was on the verge of seizing control of Hungary from the Austrians, John Clayton, the secretary of state, gave Mann secret orders to go to Budapest and recognize his new government. The orders were inflammatory. They described Kossuth as a 'hero.' Mann stopped at Vienna on his way to Budapest, and while he was changing trains, he learned that things had changed for the worse."

"What happened?"

"The tsar sent troops into Hungary to crush Kossuth's government. Kossuth fled for his life and ended up in Turkey. As you know, he eventually came to the United States."

"What about Mann?"

"He left Vienna in a hurry but remained in Europe. About a year later, when Mann's orders were published, the Austrians were so outraged that they sent a letter to the State Department saying that if Mann had been arrested while carrying those orders, he would have been hanged as a spy."

Fred moved to the ottoman in front of his father and looked at him with interest. Seward went on, "Daniel Webster was secretary of state when that letter was received. Webster wrote back, saying that if Mann had been hanged as a spy, the United States would have declared war on the Austrian Empire."

"I didn't know any of that," Fred said. Thinking the matter over, he asked, "Where would such a war be fought? We couldn't get to the Austrians, and they couldn't get to us."

Seward laughed. "May all future wars be fought between belligerents who can't get to each other."

"You said that you admired Mann?" Fred asked.

Seward nodded. "It took great courage to go into Austria carrying papers recognizing Kossuth. In fact, shortly after the revolution was crushed, I praised Mann on the Senate floor."

"What happened to him?"

"He became part of the Southern attempt to wrest Cuba from Spain. Do you recall the meeting of our Southern diplomats in Ostend, Belgium?"

"Mann was involved in that?"

"Buchanan was involved, which is why he is doing so well in the slaveholding states, and so were Dudley Mann and several others. The Southerners were determined to turn Cuba into a slave state, even if it meant war with Spain. Personally, I don't think Mann ever went along with the threat of war. I think that came entirely from Pierre Soulé. Mann's a diplomat, not a warrior. However, when his presence at Ostend became public, he and President Pierce were savaged by the Northern newspapers. To save himself, Pierce fired Mann from the State Department. Mann loved his job. It must have been very hard on him."

Anna appeared in the doorway. "Gentlemen, dinner is served."

"What does the article say?"

Seward started folding the newspaper. "I haven't finished reading it yet. We've been busy taking about Dudley Mann. After dinner we'll have some cigars and brandy and find out what our old friend Mr. Mann is up to."

10

Marengo County, Alabama
January 1857

No one had ever heard Judge Crane so angry. The slaves pulling tree stumps from the edge of the fields in the early morning stopped when they heard the yelling in the distance, and they strained their eyes to see what was happening. Collins, who was supervising the stump pulling, asked Kit if he could hear what was going on. Kit couldn't.

Near the main house, the judge was yelling at two filthy-looking white men, one tall and fat and the other smaller and younger. The fat one had driven a wagon onto the property, while the smaller man had ridden in on a horse. Both were standing near the wagon, as was the judge. Danny, an older slave, had been working in the toolshed and now stood outside the shed listening to the three men.

The judge was a tall, gaunt man in his early sixties with a remnant of white hair on the sides and back of his otherwise bald head. He had an ample white beard and dressed simply except when leaving for official duties. As the judge was rarely known to yell, the volume he directed to the two men was a subject of wonderment to all on the plantation.

"You're not going to get a cent from me!" the judge roared while glaring at the two men.

"Dere's a reward for this nigga, and we's entitled to da reward!" the fat man yelled back. "You offered hunner dollars for the return of this nigga."

"I offered a hundred dollars for the return of a slave. This," shouted the judge as he pointed at the wagon, "is not a slave. It's a dead body! It's got no value to me at all. In fact, it's going to cost me to bury it."

"How'd we know your nigga was crazy? How'd we know he'd try to fight da dogs? He kilt one'a our best hounds. Who's gonna pay for that?"

The judge seemed surprised at this bit of news and calmed down a bit. "If my slave killed your hound, I'll pay you for the dog. But I'm not paying any reward for a dead slave!"

The volume of the conversation became lower, and finally even Danny could not hear what was being said. After a few more words, the judge went into the main house and returned with a piece of paper, which he handed to the fat slave catcher. The grimy man stared at the paper, folded it, and placed it in his pants pocket. The two men opened the back of the wagon and hauled out by the ankles a body partially covered with a blood-soaked piece of canvas. They dragged the body to the side of the toolshed and dropped its legs on the ground, taking their canvas with them. Their mission accomplished, the men rode off with their wagon.

The judge looked around the field and saw his overseer. Waving his arm, he yelled, "Collins, get a couple of boys up here."

Collins knew that the judge wanted a coffin built as quickly as possible. "Kit," Collins said, "go up there and help Danny with the coffin. Apollo, go get Joe and start digging a grave."

The three slaves put down the levers they were using on the tree trunk and walked briskly to the toolshed.

Danny was a large, amiable slave somewhere in his mid-forties who had been owned by the judge for years. When the judge needed a slave to act as a messenger to go to Mobile or to another plantation, Danny was the usual choice. As Danny was friendly with nearly all the slaves, Collins even used Danny occasionally to persuade a slave to improve his work habits in order to avoid a whipping.

"Well, Kit," Danny said, "we's got to get a coffin put togetta pretty quick. Ol' Ben gonna stink real soon."

Danny and Kit went into the shed to pick out the tools necessary to split pine trunks into boards and build a coffin. The work would take several hours. Danny and Kit worked silently, except for an occasional instruction given by Danny. After working a while on shaping the boards, Kit looked at Danny and ventured a question. "Wha' happened wif da judge? Wha'd you hear?"

"I hear lots," Danny said. "Before de judge come out, de slave catchers was talkin'. Dey chase Ben for most a day, and then de hounds corna him in a barn. Ben, he don't give up. He kilt one hound wit a hoe, and de others 'tacked him. Big old hound got Ben by de neck and tears his throat out. I look at ol' Ben when dey dump him by de shed. You can see part of his neck bone unda his chin." Danny shuddered. "'Nuf to give a man de chills."

Ben, a surly, solitary slave, had run away four days earlier. He hadn't discussed his escape with anyone. Although slaves were usually aware when another slave started making preparations to run away, Ben's escape had caught everyone by surprise.

Kit and Danny continued to work silently until Danny said quietly, "He knew he weren't gonna make it. A slave gotta wo'se chance of 'scaping 'Bama than a hog. At least dey ain't hog chasers all over de place, wif dose bloodhounds."

"Den, why'd he do it?" Kit asked.

The older slave stopped and thought for a moment. Returning to his work, Danny said, "He got tired of bein' a slave, Kit. He was free fo' three days. He wanted to die a free man."

Kit worked silently, considering what Danny had said. Escape from a plantation in Alabama was impossible, and the punishment for attempting an escape could be terrible. If a slave was lucky, he or she would be punished with a severe whipping. If the slave had attempted an earlier escape or if the slave fought back, he or she would most likely be tied to a tree and branded. Sometimes, such unlucky slaves would have their nose or ears cut off; sometimes they might even have an eye put out with a hot iron. Anything that caused terrible pain and disfigurement without harming the slave's ability to work was possible. Ben knew all this.

"Did Ben believe in hev'n?" Kit asked.

Danny shrugged. "Neva axed. I suppose he figga if dey's a heaven, well, dat's good. And if der ain't, well, dying ain't no wo'se than bein' a slave."

"Does you think that, Danny?"

Danny kept working as he said, "Kit, I gits up wit de ol' man sun and goes to bed wit de sun. I gonna do dat till one day I don't get up. I don't think about anything else. When a slave thinks about de nex' day, an de nex' day afta dat, Kit, it's…no…" He trailed off.

The two slaves continued working in silence, but Danny sensed that Kit wanted to talk. "So, Kit, what's you thinkin'?"

"Ben, he die all alone. He din't have no one. Jest us, an' we ain't famly. Dat's hard. I's got a famly. My mama and sista. I jest don' know where's they at."

"You was sold when you was pretty small, warn't you?"

"Sev'n."

Danny shook his head. "Dat's bad, real bad. My ol' mammy is down de road a bit. De judge, he lets me see her a couple of times a yea'. We shu does have a fine time when we gits togetta. Does you wan' me to ax the judge if he can fin' your mammy?"

Kit looked at Danny with amazement on his face. "You can ax Massa to do dat?"

"Shu I can. De judge, he ain't so bad. De wife, she mean as sin, but he ain't. I ax him fo' you."

Kit nodded and smiled at Danny. The men then went back to work in silence.

Finally, in the late afternoon, as the rude planks were being nailed together, Danny chuckled. He looked at Kit and said with a smile, "You knows wha' de say. All de dead, white an' colored alike, is equal when dey's planted in de ground. Da wo'ms, dey don't pick 'n' choose. Tonight, Ben, he be equal to any dead white man." Nodding his head, Danny said, "Ol' Ben, he'd like dat."

The burial was late that evening. It was dark, but as it had been nearly three days since Ben had been mauled to death, the judge wanted the body in the ground before the smell worsened. The judge recited the 23rd Psalm by the light of a torch held by a slave and gave a short homily, asking Jesus to forgive all of Ben's sins, including his running away and killing an expensive hound. As dirt was pushed into the grave in the darkness, the slave women started to clap in a prelude to their farewell song.

11

Isle of Dogs, London
January 1857

As the omnibus moved slowly through the muddy roadway to the Limehouse station, Hamilton Towle sat quietly looking at the grim landscape. It had been a cold, drizzly trip from his hotel, and Towle's black wool cape provided scant protection from the chill. The inside of the omnibus smelled of damp wool. At least the weather would keep down the number of sightseers at the great ship's construction site.

Towle had arrived in Liverpool a few days earlier with his wife, Annie, and their infant daughter, Edith. Towle was the twenty-four-year-old son of a modest New Hampshire family. Almost six feet tall with sandy-brown hair and a runner's physique, Towle often drew admiring glances from women, attentions to which he was oblivious. At age sixteen he'd begun work as a draftsman at the Portsmouth Navy Yard, then at the navy yard in Pensacola, Florida. Unhappy working as a mere draftsman, he and his parents had scraped up money for a private tutor, allowing Towle to enter the Harvard Scientific School. A driven student, he'd graduated in two years with a degree in engineering and immediately begun working on the construction of a new fort at Rouses Point, New York. When his two-year commitment to the fort ended, he'd found himself recommended to the Austrian government. He and his family were now on their way to Pula, by way of Liverpool, to supervise the construction of a shipbuilding yard and dry dock for the Austrian navy.

Like many New Hampshire men, Towle was interested in everything mechanical. Thus, in his spare time he read everything he could get his hands on about the great ship being constructed on the Thames. She would be, after all, the greatest engineering feat in the world, designed by Brunel, the world's greatest engineer. Towle had read the ship's specifications, seen innumerable renderings and schematic diagrams, and absorbed the lofty prose of the journalists who had seen her. When he'd learned he had nearly a week free in England, he'd resolved to bring his little family to the Isle of Dogs. Annie didn't share her husband's enthusiasm for going out in London's blustery weather, and so when the hotel desk clerk had cautioned Towle about bringing his baby to the Thames— "It's an awful stink, sir; the vapors could be very harmful to the little one"—Annie had quickly seen the wisdom of the comments. Towle had elected to go alone, with Annie's encouragement.

Towle had left about noon and had seen London at its worst from his railcar. Rain fell off and on. Few people were out, and the black trails of coal fires rising from drab buildings punctuated the landscape, providing only a slight contrast to a leaden sky. Finally, after arriving at Limehouse and purchasing a ride in the omnibus, Towle was at the construction site.

The first time he saw the hull towering above the large warehouses, the ship had its usual effect. Not prone to emotion, Towle felt overwhelmed, almost dizzy, at her size. He had tried before in his mind to imagine her based upon his readings, but reality proved how far short his imagination fell. Once over the shock of her massiveness, however, he began looking at her critically as only a trained engineer could. The hull was partly built, with the bow mostly completed and the midships and stern only partially constructed. He knew from his reading that she was wide and flat-bottomed like a giant barge. He understood why Brunel had designed her that way—to make her hull as wide as possible to give her more storage space for coal and to give her a shallow draft so she could enter more ports. But Towle mulled about the wisdom of omitting a keel, a feature that had been part of shipbuilding since ancient times. A keel served to steady a sailing ship. Towle understood that if the ship were under constant steam power, it would not need a keel. However, if she lost all power, a storm could easily place the ship at the mercy of the sea. With two separate steam engines, one to power a giant screw located at her stern and the other to power paddle wheels mounted on each side, Towle concluded that Brunel must have reasoned that the likelihood of a total loss of power was so remote that a keel was unnecessary.

The shipyard was chaotic with a crew of perhaps eighty or more scampering around. Towle watched as men slipped and often fell on the slimy mixture of mud and clay under their feet.

Inspecting her hull, Towle saw how enormous strength had been built into the ship. Brunel had established his reputation building soaring bridges for the Great Western Railway, and his method of using partitions to strengthen vast horizontal spans was incorporated into the ship. Great iron walls were placed at various intervals inside her hull, and each was locked into place by thousands of rivets connecting it to the hull and decks. The partitions not only strengthened the hull but also served as watertight compartments in case the hull was breached. Towle knew all about this from his readings, but seeing it in iron instead of on paper convinced him of Brunel's genius.

As he examined the partition closest to him, Towle noticed the ship's double hull. A complete inner hull was separated by about three feet from a complete outer hull. Looking carefully, he thought of the story the hotel clerk had told him that morning about two men who had gone missing at the end of a shift a month or so ago. A search had not been able to find them, and some of the workers had suggested that the men might have been shut up between the inner and outer hulls. However, cracking the hundreds of rivets and breaking open the partition sealing the double hull would have been an immense and time-consuming job. The clerk said that the shipyard manager had immediately dismissed the suggestion, saying the two had probably wandered off earlier. Towle was aware that men sometimes were buried alive in major construction projects, but he'd never heard of a man being sealed inside a ship's hull. On the other hand, he thought, there never had been a ship like this one. Towle was unwilling to accept the story as true without proof but, pulling his cape tightly around him, decided to ask the clerk not to repeat it to Annie, as it might upset her.

"Come on, folks, the bus is making its last trip to Limehouse. Miss that and you'll be 'ere all night!" the driver of the omnibus called, motioning with his arm.

Towle, along with a few other chilly sightseers, carefully walked up the slippery brick path to the carriage. Looking back before boarding, Towle saw workers lighting dozens of gas jets to illuminate the hull. Work was continuing twenty-four hours a day until the hull was done.

As the passengers formed a queue to board the omnibus, Towle noticed an old man with shabby clothes and long, scraggly hair standing in the drizzle staring at the passengers. This odd personage looked at Towle and then surprised him by speaking loudly in his direction. "They's temptin' God, they is!" The other passengers turned to look at the man. "She's called *Leviathan,* and they claims to tame 'er." He shook his head. "Only God can tame Leviathan! That's what the Book says."

"Get on with you, you addlebrained old fool!" the driver yelled. He turned to the passengers. "He ain't quite right. He comes here sometimes to yell this foolishness. He ought to be locked up." The old man said nothing further.

Once everyone was seated, two of the passengers began talking. One noted that he had heard yesterday that a workman had died earlier in the week. "Slipped and fell from 'er deck, he did."

His companion nodded and responded, "I hear there's quite a few that's died there. Poor souls."

On the train ride back to London, Towle looked out the train's window and wondered if he would ever take a voyage on the ship.

12

New Orleans, Louisiana
January 1857

Abram urged the horse to pull the buckboard faster. It rarely got cold in New Orleans, even in January, but during this late afternoon the air had a chill, and Abram pulled his jacket tight with his free hand. The buckboard stopped in front of a small whitewashed building on Camp Street with a painted sign above the door that read:

> D.C. Lowber, General Goods
> Iron, Fertilizer & Farm Equipment

The single room inside the building was furnished with two chairs and a small oak desk covered with papers. An oil lamp sat on a dusty corner of the desk. Behind the building was a large, weed-choked yard enclosed by a high, unpainted wood fence. Scattered throughout the yard were plows, yokes, wagon hardware, barrels containing nails, fertilizers, and a large wagon. In addition, tarpaulins covered a number of unidentifiable items.

"Hea's da stuff from da pos', Massa," Abram told Daniel Lowber, his owner, as he walked into the office. Abram was in his mid-forties and wore a thin cotton shirt and pants, an old cotton jacket, and an ancient pair of shoes with no stockings. Lowber looked up from his paperwork as Abram passed him a small packet of parcels and envelopes. Lowber was now forty-eight years old, a slight, soft-spoken man who spoke with a lisp because of ill-fitting false teeth. Despite or perhaps because of the lisp, he had a pronounced Southern accent, unusual for a man who had grown to adulthood in New York City.

Four years earlier, when Lowber's business had improved, he'd purchased Abram and Betsy, Abram's wife, from a widow in New Orleans. It had been a good purchase. Abram and Betsy were both dependable. If either was given a job, it would eventually get done correctly and without complaint. More importantly, they were both honest. Abram could be trusted to carry money and other documents to and from the bank. Betsy, the family cook, was trusted to work alone in the Lowber home, so

Mary Lowber had the luxury of not worrying about missing silverware or clothing. Mary's few pieces of good jewelry, of course, were always locked up. Trust only went so far.

Going through the mail, Lowber noticed an envelope from Thomas Affleck, a planter in Washington, Mississippi. He smiled as he read the letter inside. "Abram, we have a letter from Mr. Affleck," he said, looking up at his slave. "He wants a quantity of ground bones and phosphated guano sent to his agent in Yazoo City. I'll work out the quantities tonight and tell you in the morning. I'd like to have the shipment ready by Wednesday."

Abram nodded and said that he'd see to it in the morning once Massa told him how much to send.

Something else in the letter pleased Lowber very much. Affleck had written, "Tell me of the engines you have for sale. I shall need one for my Texas place this spring."

At last he was starting to get orders for his engines! He had spent a considerable amount of time and money arranging for the importation from England of iron farm machinery and steam engines. In this effort, he'd been helped immensely by his son-in-law, Montgomery Neill, a cotton broker with extensive contacts in England. Lowber was so excited about Affleck's letter that he had to talk to someone about it. Abram, the only person around, would do. As the two men settled in the buckboard on their way home, Lowber said, "Abram, Mr. Affleck is interested in our engines. If we make a sale to him, I'll bet he can introduce us to many planters. This is good news."

Abram, holding the reins, looked straight ahead and nodded, saying, "Dat do soun' like good news, Massa."

"I think so too, Abram. Some of the engines we'll be bringing in from England may be quite large. We'll have to figure out how to store and move them."

That did not sound like particularly good news to Abram, since he undoubtedly would be the one responsible for moving them. But, in a cheerful voice, he said, "We's got to figga out how to do dat, Massa. I's knows an ol' darky who wo'ks on da wharf fo' long time. He's knows lots 'bout movin' big loads. If you wants, I talk to him."

"That's a good idea. Maybe we can get him a gift for teaching you some tricks of the trade. Something like a jar of honey?"

"Dat's de idea, Massa," Abram said, continuing to look straight ahead and nodding in agreement, although he doubted a jar of honey would do it. "We do sometin' like dat, shu 'nuf."

The two men continued their conversation on the trip back to the house. During the workday, Abram and Lowber talked more to each other than to anyone else. Together they lifted equipment, weighed fertilizer, packed goods, and talked about the business. When Lowber had first moved to the South, he'd thought slavery strange. He'd been raised in New York, where slaves were relatively uncommon. In the South, where slaves were everywhere, he accepted the universally held view that he, as a white man, was superior to any member of the African race. However, he admitted to himself, and even sometimes to his wife, there were times he found it much easier to deal with Abram than with some of the white farmers he had as customers. It seemed to him that Abram was a good deal smarter than quite a few of them. In fact, when Lowber had to go to England to meet suppliers, he let Abram operate the business in his absence. Of course, since Abram was illiterate, Mary had to read all the business correspondence to him, and she also handled the financial matters.

Abram and Betsy considered that their lives were as good as they were likely to get. Mr. and Mrs. Lowber never drank, and they treated Abram and Betsy fairly and, from time to time, even kindly. When Betsy had a fever, Mrs. Lowber cared for her like she was a member of the family. Abram's great fear, like the fear of all slaves owned by tolerable masters, was the day when Lowber died or was forced to sell his slaves. There was no certainty he and Betsy would be sold as a pair. He might find himself a lowly field hand or worse. God only knew what might happen to Betsy. Life was bearable now, Abram thought, but someday it might be awful. His only hope was that Mr. and Mrs. Lowber would live for a long time and that he and Betsy would die before the Lowbers did.

13

London, England
February 1857

THE directors of the Eastern Steam Navigation Company sat quietly in a second-floor room in a commercial area of the city. The room was drab and cold, with the only heat coming from a small coal stove in the corner. The directors sat on a variety of wooden chairs around an oval table covered with a sheet of ink-splattered green felt. Each director had a sheaf of papers before him, and the look on their faces as they read was proof that the information was not good.

"Lord," one director softly mumbled while reading. Another turned to his neighbor and raised his eyebrows with a look of disgust. Shaking heads, nervous coughs, and an occasional loud sigh added to the sense of gathering gloom. The minutes dragged as one by one each of the directors finished reading his sheaf and placed it on the table.

Waiting for the right moment, John McCalmont, one of the directors, looked around at his fellow directors. Finally, he cleared his throat loudly. Everyone looked at him.

"Gentlemen, most of you are familiar with what I am going to relate. However, some of you were not with us from the beginning, and therefore I believe it is appropriate to start from the beginning so all are equally informed."

Chairs scraped against the bare wood floor as the directors swiveled to face the speaker.

McCalmont continued, "I am retiring shortly as a director of the Eastern Steam Navigation Company. Therefore, one of my last duties is to lay before all of you the unvarnished truth. As most of you may recall, when we originally offered the contract for the construction of the great ship in 1853, Mr. Scott Russell bid 332,000 pounds sterling for the construction of its hull, its launch, the paddle engines, screw shaft, and rigging."

This statement was met by a few nodding heads.

"We thought that the bid was quite low, as our engineer, Mr. Brunel, had estimated a cost of 500,000 pounds for the same work. Nevertheless, Mr. Russell was an expert shipbuilder, more experienced in the cost of ship construction than anyone here, and we all accepted his calculations in good faith."

McCalmont's comments were greeted with silence. He paused for a moment, waiting for questions. Hearing none, he continued, "The difficulties we have had in the construction of the *Great Eastern* are well known. Firstly, you all know, or at least most of you know, last year we were shocked to find out that the construction of the *Great Eastern* consumed so much iron that it caused a national shortage of the metal, resulting in a great increase in its price. Thus, Mr. Russell had to pay much more for the iron plates than originally anticipated." He paused and looked around. "Also, gentlemen, all of us, Mr. Russell and Mr. Brunel included, greatly underestimated the cost and complexity of the undertaking. I was personally involved with the acquisition of the crankshaft for the paddle engine. Needless to say, it is the largest crankshaft ever made, so large that our contractor had to build special furnaces before they could even start work. The cost of the construction of those furnaces had to be paid by us before work could begin."

McCalmont waited as this information sank in. He then continued, "As we saw Mr. Russell's costs escalating, we instructed Mr. Brunel to make changes to the design. Many features were eliminated or modified to save money, but the changes were not enough. Mr. Russell came to us in January of last year and told us that he was in dire financial straits. Consequently, we renegotiated our contract with him and agreed to pay 317,200 pounds for just the hull and paddle engines alone. By February of last year we paid out all but 40,000 pounds of this amount and then found to our great distress that Mr. Russell was out of money and could no longer pay for the construction. For want of money, Mr. Russell defaulted on a number of contracts with essential suppliers and discharged all his employees, even though three-quarters of the hull remained unfinished."

"Yes, and then we greatly improved matters by having Mr. Brunel take over the project," said one of the directors with obvious sarcasm.

"We had no other options," McCalmont quickly retorted. "Work stopped on the ship for nearly three months after Mr. Russell discharged his employees, and we were still paying rent on the shipyard. Mr. Russell's creditors were threatening to seize the hull, and our entire investment would have been lost had we done nothing. Unlike Mr. Russell, Mr. Brunel is an engineer, not a shipbuilder. Nearly all the persons working for him on the hull are the same workmen who were fired by Mr. Russell and who were, I might add, quite bitter about not being paid for three months. Mr. Brunel took on a very difficult assignment and has done the best he can. He contacted our suppliers and learned that many were unwilling to continue to deliver materials except on the most exorbitant and indeed often outrageous terms. Despite all these difficulties, construction has continued, and all of you gentlemen can see that Mr. Brunel has made substantial progress toward completing the hull. However, the cost of completion has greatly exceeded our original estimates and, frankly, exceeded the company's ability to pay."

"How much will it take to finish the ship?" a director asked.

"I believe that if we collect an additional sixty thousand pounds from our shareholders, we should be able to finish the project."

There was clear discomfiture with this news. The Eastern Steam Navigation Company was a limited stock company. Historically, large projects in England had been financed by peers and major landowners, men who had inherited so much wealth that they could gamble away hundreds of pounds on a horse race and not trouble their sleep. However, the giant projects of the nineteenth century, and in particular the railways, required so much capital that a new form of organization, the limited stock company, had been created. Instead of one or two enormously wealthy benefactors financing a project, these organizations raised their capital from larger numbers of upper- and middle-class investors. These companies were managed by a small number of directors elected annually by the shareholders.

Railways had both made and lost money for their investors in England. Those investors who were lucky enough to see their railway stock increase in value often regarded their company's directors as honorable men of wisdom and solid judgment. Those investors who saw their investments become worthless usually regarded their directors as either self-dealing cheats, perfect idiots, or some combination thereof. The shareholders of the Eastern Steam Navigation Company had seen the value of their stock plunge to near worthlessness, and their opinions about the company's directors had followed.

John Hope, one of the directors, spoke up. "Gentlemen, once we launch the great ship, these unfortunate financial problems will begin to fade. We are all convinced that she will operate quite profitably, are we not?"

Ignoring this comment, a young, sharp-faced director asked McCalmont, "What assurances will we have that the additional sixty thousand pounds will be sufficient?"

McCalmont said, "Mr. Brunel has binding commitments from his suppliers and feels confident about the cost of labor to complete the ship.

The only unknown is the cost of launching her. Mr. Brunel is confident that the launch will cost twenty thousand pounds or less."

"How would he know?" asked a portly, red-haired man. "There's never been a sideways launch. Every day in the newspaper some engineer or another writes that it can't be done."

"Gentlemen, this is Sir Isambard Kingdom Brunel, the greatest engineer in the world," McCalmont countered forcefully. "If he is confident in his opinion, and he assures me he is, I would certainly take his word over some disgruntled draftsman writing to a newspaper. I believe we should have complete confidence with Mr. Brunel's statements."

A tall, bearded director stood up. After standing silently for a moment, as if collecting his thoughts, he said, "I don't see we have any alternative but to believe Mr. Brunel. If he is right, we may yet see a profit. If he is wrong, our shareholders will rip us apart like ravenous dogs. All we can do is hope he is right."

With the last comment having captured the mood of the meeting, the directors approved by voice vote a call for another sixty thousand pounds from the shareholders and quickly filed out of the room.

14

New Orleans, Louisiana
February 1857

THE *Cahawba*, a 250-foot side-wheeler under the command of Captain J. D. Bulloch, was moving slowly under the morning sun into New Orleans's crowded port. The ship had spent the night anchored offshore waiting for daybreak. Early that morning, a pilot had arrived and directed the ship's final passage. Passengers lined the rails of the ship, some looking for familiar faces and others just taking in the scenery—a forest of masts, spars, and smokestacks sprouting from the multitude of ships berthed in the port. The pilot sounded a loud steam whistle, not so much as a warning but as a notice to the citizens of New Orleans that a prominent ship had arrived.

Captain Schultz and his daughter Mary stood silently on the ship's bridge near the pilothouse, where Captain Bulloch and his pilot controlled the ship's entry. Once the *Cahawba* berthed and the gangplank lowered, the pilot shook hands with Bulloch, climbed down from the bridge, and left. Bulloch surveyed the activity on board the ship for a few minutes and, when satisfied that everything was under control, joined Schultz and his daughter on the bridge.

Schultz spoke first. "Captain Bulloch, my daughter and I enjoyed this voyage very much. I particularly enjoyed watching your ship being brought into port. Thank you for your courtesies."

With a cultured Georgian accent, Bulloch said to Mary, "Miss Schultz, it was an honor having such a pretty young lady as my guest. I want you to know that your father is held in the highest regard by me and the other captains. When a Schultz tugboat attaches a towrope to our ship, we're confident our voyage will end successfully." Turning to Schultz, Bulloch said, "Captain, it's a pleasure to see you somewhere other than on the deck of one of your tugboats. I trust you and your daughter will enjoy your visit in New Orleans. Certainly you'll enjoy the weather much more than in New York."

Indeed, the weather was comfortable. At first Schultz had not been enthused about a late-winter trip to New Orleans. The weather around Cape Hatteras was ugly at that time of year. But Margaret and his daughters had prevailed upon him to let Mary go to New Orleans, and so he'd agreed, on the condition that he accompany his daughter and that they sail on a large, seaworthy ship with an experienced captain. As it turned out, except for a few short rough patches, the trip had been remarkably calm.

After Schultz and Mary had claimed their luggage at the depot on the wharf, they entered a queue waiting for hacks. They didn't have to wait too long before a carriage took them to the St. Charles Hotel.

The St. Charles was a huge five-story structure, almost an entire city block, and far more grandiose than nearly all the hotels in New York. It had particularly beautiful Grecian columns extending over the entrance. As Mary expressed satisfaction that she would be staying at such a stylish hotel, Schultz silently paid the driver and wondered what this excursion was going to cost him. After checking in, Schultz asked the bellman for messages. Daniel Lowber had left a message that he would be by in the morning. Mary and her father agreed that they'd spend the evening unpacking and resting.

The following morning, after breakfast at the hotel, Schultz and his daughter waited in the hotel's ornate lobby. Lowber entered shortly before ten o'clock and was quickly greeted by a hug from his niece.

"Uncle Dan, we're so excited to be here. The news from Kate is so wonderful! She and I are going to have the best time."

Lowber laughed. "Mary, you're an exact image of your mother a few years ago." Looking at Schultz, he said, "Thank goodness she got her looks from Margaret, not from you."

Schultz, not ordinarily prone to mirth, smiled at the comment.

"How's Margaret?" Lowber asked him.

"Margaret's fine. She's busy with the children, of course, and very excited at the prospect of becoming a great-aunt!"

"Well, then, Hamilton, imagine our excitement at becoming grandparents!"

Mary, Schultz, and Lowber all proceeded to Lowber's summer house in a cabriolet. New Orleans was an exciting place, and Mary craned her head to see the variety of current fashions being displayed by the ladies of the city. Even Schultz enjoyed the sunny ride. Operating a tugboat in New York's harbor during November and December was a pretty grim business. Fortunately, he felt his employees were competent enough to manage for a couple of weeks during what was always a slow period.

The cab passed out of New Orleans and traveled to a ferry dock, where it dropped its three passengers off. A small steam ferry eventually appeared, and the travelers boarded it for a trip across Lake Pontchartrain to Lewisburg. On the short walk from the landing pier to Lowber's house, Schultz admired the lushness of the vegetation—particularly the giant, wild-looking live oaks. It all seemed strange, even exotic, to Schultz. Lowber's house in Lewisburg was a small white frame house, sparsely furnished. It sat on about four acres of property bordering the shore of the lake. Mary Lowber greeted them on the small front porch.

"Hamilton, it's a delight to see you. I only wish Margaret could have come as well."

Schultz knew that Margaret would never make the trip. As much as she loved her sister, she would never enter a house in which humans were owned by other humans. Nevertheless, Schultz was diplomatic. "We thought about Margaret coming, Mary, but decided it would be too difficult to leave the children at home without their mother. Of course, you and Dan are always welcome at Fishkill Landing. I know she misses you very much."

Aunt Mary turned to her niece and hugged her tightly. "Here's my namesake! Mary Lowber Schultz, you're prettier every time I see you." Stepping back a bit, she continued, "Kate is so happy you're coming to stay with her. You two are going to have a wonderful time."

Aunt Mary showed Schultz and his daughter to their rooms in the house. After the visitors had rested and cleaned up, but before dinner was ready, they met their hosts on the back porch. Young Mary started the conversation. "I was so pleased when I got Kate's letter. How exciting that she and Montgomery are going to have a baby!"

Aunt Mary nodded. "A first baby is exciting, but it's a little frightening too. With Montgomery out of town so often on his cotton business, we were concerned about Kate being alone so much with just her domestics. She was so pleased when she got your telegraph saying that you were coming right away."

"How could I not? She's like my own sister."

At dinner, Schultz and his daughter learned that the midwife's latest opinion was that the baby would be due at the end of February.

"Kate wrote to you as soon as she learned when the baby was due," Mary Catherine said to her niece.

Lowber joined in, saying to Schultz, "Your daughter's going to be in Mobile for nearly three months. I reckon she'll be a real Southern belle when she returns home—that is, if she returns home. I'm certain there are a number of fine Southern gentlemen that would like to be introduced to her."

Mary blushed. "Uncle Dan, I came down here to be with Kate, to help her with the baby, not to find a husband."

"I know, I know," Lowber said. "But the arrival of such a pretty young lady is bound to be noticed by the bachelors of Mobile."

Schultz and Mary were due to take a steamer from New Orleans to Mobile the following day. Schultz planned to stay two days with Kate and Montgomery at their house in Mobile. Mary would stay with the couple until Kate had the baby and recovered from the birth.

After a dinner of roast chicken and catfish prepared by Betsy and served on the back porch, the two Marys moved to the parlor to talk about family matters. Aunt Mary was starved for information about her sister and other relations in New York, and her niece was delighted to supply as much information as she could offer. While the two women were chatting inside, Schultz and Lowber stayed on the back porch. Looking over the lake, they could see in the distance two men in a punt fishing. Twilight was starting, and it was very peaceful.

Lowber spoke first. "Hamilton, this is our summer house. Our permanent house is in New Orleans. Generally, we only come here when yellow fever is going through New Orleans. However, I thought it might be more comfortable for you to stay here. There's less people." By which, Lowber meant fewer slaves and slave owners.

"Dan, you have a nice little house and grounds. I take it that your business is doing well?"

"I believe it's turned a corner. It was difficult for a while. I made some mistakes early on. Once I was so in debt with inventory that I owed nearly ten thousand dollars."

"Good Lord! I didn't realize it was that bad. How did you deal with that kind of debt?"

"I sold some property, including some slaves I had bought at a good price, and Mary and I watched every penny. Bit by bit I climbed out of the hole. Now, my business is doing well. In fact, I'm looking for new products. Montgomery has introduced me to some fine English machinery manufacturers, and I'm starting to develop that business. Steam pumps, iron pipe, things like that."

"You and I have certainly traveled a long distance since we were a couple of boys on a riverboat." Memories of those days in New York brought smiles to both men. "Those were good days."

Lowber grinned and nodded.

After a period of silence, while staring out over the quiet waters of Lake Pontchartrain, Lowber said, "Hamilton, what's going on in Kansas and Nebraska? We get all sorts of stories in our newspapers. It sounds like a war."

"It is a war," Schultz said. "The Free-Soilers and the slave owners are battling over the territories. Nearly every day we read about some massacre or shoot-up. This is Douglas's 'popular sovereignty.' Let the two sides kill each other for a while and then have the survivors decide whether the territory should be free or slave. It's a ridiculous idea."

"Are the Free-Soilers backed by abolitionists? That's what our papers say."

"Maybe a bit, but that's not the cause of the fighting." Schultz leaned forward on his chair and looked at Lowber. "Dan, you wouldn't recognize New York City today. It's awash with foreigners. Not a day goes by that one of my tugs doesn't pull in a ship crammed full of immigrants—Scots, Irish, Germans, Hungarians, Swedes, you name it. A lot of them are from places I've never heard of. They all want one thing—land of their own. That's something they'll never get in the old country. The best and cheapest land is in the territories. These foreigners have given up everything to get that land, and if necessary, they'll kill for it. They don't need any encouragement from the abolitionists."

Lowber sat silently as he considered these comments.

"Dan, I have a question for you," Schultz said. "Why is the South so insistent upon moving its slaves to these territories? The North is willing to let slavery alone in the South. It just doesn't want additional slave states."

Lowber looked out over the lake as he framed his response. "I can answer that—fear of what's coming down the pike."

"I don't understand."

"It's a long story and one that you don't often hear spoken in the South. You certainly don't see it in our newspapers."

"Fear of what?"

"Hamilton, for years, every square inch of the South has been planted with cotton. Forests have been cut down and plowed; ravines and gullies have been plowed. Every place a cotton plant could grow, the land's been plowed and planted." He paused. "Land that was first plowed ten, fifteen years ago has lost most of its good soil to rain and wind. Each acre yields less than the year before. I hear about it every day from planters asking me about fertilizer, as if guano or bonemeal can restore ruined land. Of course it can't. I've seen many abandoned plantations and many more that are going to be abandoned shortly."

Looking straight out over Lake Pontchartrain, Lowber seemed to be talking to himself as well as to Schultz. "Demand for cotton remains high and so does its price. As cotton goes up, so does the price of slaves. People used to buy only the slaves they needed. Now, people buy slaves willy-nilly for fear their prices will go up." Lowber turned to Schultz. "Look at me, Hamilton. I paid down debt by selling slaves at a profit. I didn't even intend to speculate on slaves, and I made money. A young buck today will bring as much as seven hundred dollars. A breeding wench, if she is large and strong, will bring even more. Slaves are not being born; they're being bred, and the slave population is growing larger and larger. Alabama, Louisiana, the entire South is becoming a sea of black faces." Lowber paused. "A slave is a useless expense without cotton to pick. Unless the South can expand, unless it can move its slaves onto fertile land, someday soon we'll be trapped with barren soil and hordes of slaves. What happens when that day comes, Hamilton? It's coming soon."

"Do you mean slave revolts?"

"Of course I do. We may talk about how much our slaves love us, but let me tell you, we all live in fear of slave revolts. But it's more than just fear of revolts. What happens when hundreds of thousands of slaves are released because their owners can no longer feed them? Many of them will roam the countryside like Mongols, stealing and destroying and God knows what else. Even decent Negroes like my Abram and Betsy will have to resort to scrounging to survive. The North is already making certain that none of the freed slaves can live up there. Illinois and other states have already made it illegal for a Negro to move into those states. Other states will follow."

The two men sat in the darkening afternoon, both staring forward. The fishermen in the punt were rowing slowly to shore. Finally, Schultz said, "There has been a lot of talk about taking the Negroes back to Africa."

"Ah! Liberia! We know all about that. Every time we tell a Northerner that we're terrified of living with marauding bands of Negroes, we're assured that that'll never come about. We're assured that all the freed slaves will be living happily in their native Africa." Lowber made a gentle snorting sound as he shook his head. "Hamilton, the *Cahawba* is one of the larger ships to enter New Orleans. Tell me, how many Negroes could the *Cahawba* transport to Africa in one trip?"

Schultz made some rough calculations in his mind. "About 300, 350 maybe."

"And how long would it take to make the trip there and back?"

"To Africa? About three weeks. But it depends upon the time of year. There are some times when the voyage would be almost impossible because of the trade winds."

"About ten voyages a year?"

"Maybe twelve. Somewhere between ten and twelve."

"So the *Cahawba* could transport four thousand slaves a year to Africa. We have over four million slaves in the South. Their population is increasing by thousands every month. If you had hundreds of *Cahawba*s doing nothing but shipping freed slaves night and day, you'd never catch up. Those people like Clay, those politicians who argue that you can solve slavery by shipping Negroes to Africa, are either simpletons or liars. There aren't enough ships in the world. For better or worse, Negroes—whether free or slave—are not leaving this country. Either they go to the new territories as slaves, or they remain trapped in the Southern states and the gates of hell open up." Lowber turned to look at his brother-in-law. "You have a niece and a sister-in-law in the South, Hamilton. Soon, you're going to have a grandniece or grandnephew. Is this what you want for them?"

For all his hatred of slavery, Schultz looked at Lowber and felt sorry for him. He was not a bad man. In fact, he was a good and kind man, a man who had adopted Kate, his late brother's child, as his own. He was truly afraid for his family and for himself. Schultz struggled unsuccessfully to think of something to say that might relieve that fear. Finally, he said, "Dan, you know I want nothing but the best for you and your family. You know that. Margaret and I love Mary and Kate. You are one of my best friends. I don't have an answer, but there must be a way out of this predicament. The North would never put Southerners at the mercy of their former slaves."

"Hamilton, I pray to God you're right. But I'll tell you, if you honestly believe what you have just said, you have more confidence in your politicians than I have in mine."

The men sat in silence as day darkened and the air turned cool. Finally, Lowber stood. "You'd better get some sleep. Tomorrow will be a long day."

That night, as Schultz lay in his bed, all he could think of was something that he had recently read in a newspaper. It was something Thomas Jefferson had written when he was an old man. Realizing too late the enormous mistake of granting constitutional protection to slavery, Jefferson had written, "We have the wolf by the ears."

15

Fishkill Landing, New York
March 1857

NOT long after his return from New Orleans, Schultz returned home on the Friday evening train from New York City with a packet of newspapers under his arm. He greeted Margaret with a perfunctory kiss and then retired to the front parlor. He was in a quiet mood, and Margaret and the children, clearly sensing that the captain was upset by something, gave him as much privacy as possible. Margaret wondered whether something bad had happened with his newly established tugboat business. That night he went to bed early, without talking to anyone.

The following morning Schultz sat in the parlor, again reading the newspapers. After breakfast Margaret decided to broach the subject of his troubled mood.

"Hamilton, are you feeling well? You've been so quiet."

Schultz furrowed his brow as he read. "No, I feel fine."

"Is something wrong? Did something happen at the wharf?"

Schultz realized that he owed his wife of many years more than curt answers. "Margaret, everything is fine with me and my business. I wish I could say the same for our country."

"Why? What has happened?"

Schultz folded his newspaper and turned to his wife. "The Supreme Court decided *Dred Scott.*"

"*Dred Scott.* That's the case about the slave?"

"That's right, Margaret. Our esteemed Chief Justice Roger Taney and the rest of the slaveholders on the Supreme Court have decided Mr. Scott's fate. Actually, they apparently decided it several days ago but just released their written opinion. That's what I've been reading."

"What did they decide?"

"They decided that Dred Scott is not a human being; he's a piece of property like a table or a cow."

"What? Did they say that?"

"Very nearly. Let me find their language." Schultz looked through the long article he had been reading. "Ah, here's a beautiful passage. The justices found that 'members of the African race were so far inferior that they had no rights which the white man was bound to respect.'" Reading the newspaper further, Schultz said, "Now keep in mind that this next passage applies to Leonard and every other free black. Here it is. Justice Taney says that no member of this unhappy race, as he calls them, can ever be a citizen of the United States. On this point, Taney says that there can be no distinction between a free Negro or a mulatto or a slave, but . . ." Schultz pointed his finger in the air for emphasis. "And, Margaret, this is the court's language I'm quoting: 'this stigma, of the deepest degradation,' is 'fixed upon the whole race.'"

Margaret sat in her chair looking at her husband with concern and puzzlement. "What does this mean for Leonard?"

"Last week, our faithful servant was a citizen. Today, he's no longer a citizen and can never be a citizen. Today, he has no more rights than our horse! He and his heirs can never have any rights. He is fixed, in Taney's words, with a stigma of the deepest degradation."

"That's awful. Why would they say such a terrible thing?"

"Because, Margaret, they are slaveholders who happen to be on the Supreme Court, and nothing matters to them but their damned property. It is the voice of the slave owners speaking through the one branch of government they will always control."

"But what does this mean for the country?"

"Well," Schultz said, "the Supreme Court has tossed out the Missouri Compromise and said that no territory can prevent a slave owner from bringing his human property into it. So how'd you like it if some self-righteous Methodist from Mississippi moved down the road with his slaves and set up shop? Maybe he'd whip them every evening before dinner just to work up an appetite. Maybe go out late at night and ravish the slave girls. Nothing we could do about it. Perfectly legal."

Margaret looked vacantly out the window as she considered what she had just heard. "What can be done about this awful decision, Hamilton? Certainly the people can do something about it."

"We can do nothing about it. To change the decision would take an amendment to the Constitution, and to amend the Constitution we need the consent of at least some of the slaveholding states. That'll never happen. If God is truly merciful, in 1860 he'll give us an honest, freedom-loving president, hopefully Governor Seward, and then strike some of these robed bastards dead so we can get a new Supreme Court. Then the decision could be changed. In the meantime, it stands."

“Hamilton, please. Your language.” Margaret had rarely heard her husband use such vulgar language. Schultz acted as if he hadn’t heard her. His hands were trembling in anger as he put down the newspaper. Margaret was also deeply angered but did not want to show it. She stood up, patted her husband on the shoulder, and said, “Hamilton, I’ll be right back.” As she entered the back parlor, she saw Leonard standing in the doorway to the kitchen, wiping his eyes. He had heard everything. Hot tears of shame started to well up in Margaret’s own eyes, and she walked quickly upstairs to her bedroom.

16

New York Tribune
March 11, 1857

Another most pregnant change is wrought by this decision, in respect of the Northern people. We have been accustomed to regard Slavery as a local matter for which we were in no wise responsible. As we have been used to say, it belonged to the Southern States alone, and they must answer for it before the world. We can say this no more. Now, wherever the stars and stripes wave, they protect Slavery and represent Slavery. The black and cursed stain is thick on our hands also. From Maine to the Pacific, over all future conquests and annexations, wherever in the islands of western seas, or in the South American Continent, or in the Mexican Gulf, the flag of the Union, by just means or unjust, shall be planted, there it plants the curse, and tears, and blood, and unpaid toil of this "institution." The Star of Freedom and the stripes of bondage are henceforth one. American Republicanism and American Slavery are for the future synonymous. This, then, is the final fruit. In this all the labors of our statesmen, the blood of our heroes, the life-long cares and toils of our forefathers, the aspirations of our scholars, the prayers of good men, have finally ended! America the slavebreeder and slaveholder!

17

Washington, DC
June 1857

ANNA surveyed whether anything was left undone for dinner that night. Although it was not yet late afternoon, the cook was already busy at work. Anna examined the parlor, made a few adjustments to a small bouquet of fresh flowers, and was finally satisfied that everything was in its place and ready for the arrival of Fred and his father. Only then did she sit down on her parlor chair and pick up something to read.

With all the vituperation directed at her poor father-in-law in the press, Anna could hardly stand having a newspaper in the house. The journal she selected, *The Living Age*, serialized novels, presented articles on gardening and culture, commented upon the comings and goings of society, and even discussed new scientific theories. Anna liked it because it mostly refrained from politics and, when it did venture into that thicket, tended to be sympathetic to people like her husband and father-in-law who were opposed to slavery.

The main article of the June 1857 issue was a long one, dealing with recent discoveries regarding ocean currents and their relationship to the salinity of the sea, a subject in which Anna had no interest whatsoever. She skimmed the journal looking for other articles. A quick review of the current chapter of *Mr. Gilfil's Love-Story* convinced her that it was no less contrived than its earlier chapters. As she was approaching the end of the journal, she saw an article entitled "The Great Ship."

The article started, "Among the passions which belong to human nature, we may recognize what may be called a passion for size." It continued discussing human fascination with large things, such as giants in fairy tales and gigantic numbers like the speed of light. Addressing an imaginary observer, the article continued, "And now let him get on board a Greenwich steamer and be steamed through the picturesque Pool to Millwall. Just opposite Deptford he will be aware of something pre-Adamitic wallowing in the mud of the Isle of Dogs, a stranded saurian ship, to which even Noah's Ark must yield precedence."

The author described the ship's height and weight, number of rivets and sheets of iron, horsepower, and so forth in great detail, all of which meant little to Anna because she could not place them into perspective. When she measured, Anna used inches and ounces, not yards and tons. She would have stopped reading but for a conversation she'd overheard several months earlier between Fred and his father about a giant ship. Continuing, she ran across some information she could comprehend. The ship was designed to accommodate four thousand passengers or, "on an emergency," ten thousand troops! *Good heavens. The ship is a floating city!* Anna thought. In fact, the article suggested that the ship was so large it would alter the very society of oceangoing passengers. She read with fascination:

> How many immeasurable social chasms will be collected within a few hundred feet? How many Mr. Smiths will there be who will not speak to Mr. Jones during the whole voyage because he is not in the same set? How many Mr. Joneses will pay back Mr. Smith in the same coin? … What flirtations will there not be behind boats, what rivalries and, if many Americans voyage by the Great Eastern, what duellings may we not expect on that ample deck! In short, what an epitome or camera-obscura of the world will the Great Eastern present!

"The *Great Eastern,*" Anna repeated to herself. "That is the ship that Fred and Father were talking about."

The article was long, and Anna went back to the beginning to read it carefully. When she finally finished, she folded the journal and placed it on her lap. *A ship that could carry ten thousand soldiers,* she thought. *How is that possible?* She sat trying to think of a crowd that size and was almost amused by the ridiculousness of the idea that so many people could board a single ship. She would have thought such a ship pure fantasy except that Fred and Father had seemed so interested in it. A noise from the kitchen brought her back to domestic concerns. She glanced at the mantle clock and was surprised at how much time she had spent reading the article. She quickly placed the journal on the table in the foyer and went into the kitchen to see how the cook was doing.

When Fred arrived home late that afternoon, he was greeted by his wife, who, after a proper kiss on his cheek, handed him the journal. He looked at her quizzically, and she opened it to the article about the great ship and pointed him to the piece. Fred stood there quietly reading and then smiled.

"Thank you very much, darling, but I read this exact article almost a week ago. It was published in the *Times*."

"What? Why didn't you tell me?" Anna was peeved that her coup had fallen flat. "I heard you and Father talk about someone's plans to use this ship to take business away from New York and to separate the South from the North. Didn't you think I'd be interested?"

"I'm sorry, darling. I didn't think to tell you about the article."

"This is the ship, isn't it?"

Fred laughed. "I'm sure Dudley Mann would like it to be. However, it appears that this monster, if she's ever launched, is headed for Australia, not for the tidewaters of Virginia. Apparently cotton is not as attractive as gold. It would seem that our concerns were a bit premature. Anyway," Fred said with a sigh, "we have far more pressing problems than some yet-to-be-launched ship stealing business from New York."

"It wasn't a good day?"

"The atmosphere in the Senate is positively poisonous. Thank heavens Sumner is there. The Southerners hate him even more than they hate Father." Fred walked past his wife and sat down in the parlor. "The speeches in the Senate about the *Dred Scott* case are furious. Father has scalded the court for such a horrible decision, and he's being joined by many of the senators from the North. The decision is not having the effect the Southerners thought."

"Why is that?"

"Because the decision could strip states like New York and Massachusetts of their ability to keep slavery out. It also opens all the territories to slavery. Even senators opposed to emancipation are heaping scorn on the court. If Buchanan and Taney thought this decision would douse water on the antislavery forces, they were badly mistaken. It's kerosene, not water."

Fred sat quietly and then looked up at his young wife. "Anna, I'm becoming frightened as to where this is leading. The South is rapidly running out of reasonable men. There's a desperation and anger in their voices that wasn't there even a few months ago. They thought *Dred Scott* would resolve the issue of slavery, and it's had the opposite effect. It was a terrible miscalculation."

Anna did not know what to say. Finally, she touched Fred's hand and said, "Rest before dinner. And please, let's not discuss politics tonight at the dinner table. Father needs something pleasant to talk about."

18

Bristol, Virginia
June 1857

NESTLED in a valley in the Appalachian Mountains, the town of Bristol, Virginia, was shedding its backwoods personality. Roughly equidistant between Roanoke and Knoxville, Tennessee, Bristol was in the process of being connected by railroad lines to those cities as well as to Cincinnati and Norfolk. If all the railroad lines currently planned were built, much of the South's cotton would travel through Bristol on its way to Norfolk, the South's port on the Atlantic Ocean. All that would be needed was a way of transporting the cotton from Norfolk to England.

Bristol's selection as the site for the Railroad and Commercial Convention of Virginia, therefore, was no accident. Indeed, everything about the convention had been well thought out in advance by J. D. B. DeBow. The delegates to the convention were representatives of numerous railroad companies, including the Norfolk & Petersburg; the Virginia & Tennessee; the Virginia & Kentucky; and the Cincinnati, Cumberland Gap & Charleston.

Francis Mallory of Norfolk, a former congressman from Virginia and now the president of the Norfolk & Petersburg Railroad Company, presided over the thirty or so delegates who attended the convention. Besides his duties of calling the convention to order and appointing three gentlemen as its secretaries, Mallory's most important function was to introduce to the delegates William Ballard Preston of Montgomery, Virginia. Preston, an aristocratic-looking gentleman of fifty-one, was the former secretary of the navy under President John Tyler.

After Mallory's introduction, Preston stood before the delegates. Acknowledging polite applause, he said, "Gentlemen, I am honored to be here. I am sure we all wish to thank Mr. DeBow of New Orleans for helping to organize this convention. I understand that he could not attend because of personal reasons, but we all appreciate his many efforts to assist Southern commerce and railroads.

"We have all read Colonel Dudley Mann's letter that was published last year in Mr. DeBow's *Review*. I understand that the officers of many railroad companies throughout the South, and especially those in Virginia, inquired of each other as to whether such a weekly steam ferry, as proposed by Colonel Mann, could carry cotton and manufactured goods back and forth from Chesapeake Bay and England. If such a ferry could operate, it would seem to be a great boon for the Southern states, for at long last we could free ourselves from the shackles of high tariffs and restricted shipping forced on us by the North. Thus, gentlemen, the question before this convention is whether such a steam ferry is feasible.

"Colonel Mann's plan is based upon the use of a giant iron ship called the *Great Eastern*, or at least the use of one or more of the future sisters of this ship. The *Great Eastern* is under construction and is due to be launched in a few months. When his letter was first published, Colonel Mann's description of the *Great Eastern* seemed a flight of the imagination. No one, myself included, accepted as a fact that such an enormous ship could be built and launched. However, we've all read the reports from England that the completion of the ship is at hand and that she's to be launched shortly. Indeed, most of us have seen renderings of this ship in her construction yard, and it appears to a certainty that she will shortly be launched. Therefore, as I've related to some of you privately, I am willing to accept a commission from this convention to go to England to meet the directors of the *Great Eastern*, to see her for myself, and to report back to you my findings. All I ask is your support for such a visit."

Warming to his task, Mallory paused for a moment for dramatic effect. He continued, "If I can convince the directors of the *Great Eastern* that great profits can be made by operating a shuttle between Virginia and England, we may soon see the day when we can enjoy our prosperity and our domestic institutions free of Yankee meddling."

Sounds of "Here, here!" and "That's it!" were exclaimed from the crowd, and the men in the audience started to applaud until the whole room was on its feet clapping. At that point, Mallory took control of the meeting and passed around copies of proposed resolutions. The audience seated itself and began reading the resolutions, including the critical one that appointed Preston as a commissioner and ordered him to travel to Europe and to "place himself in correspondence with the managers and proprietors of the Great Eastern Steamship Company" in order to determine whether Mann's steam ferry line was feasible. When everyone had finished reading the resolutions, Mallory asked if there was a motion to accept them. A motion to approve the resolutions came from the floor, was quickly seconded, and passed without dissent.

The three secretaries of the meeting appointed by Preston were all newspaper editors: A. K. Moore of the *Bristol News*, C. W. Button of the *Lynchburg Virginian*, and R. G. Broughton of the *Norfolk Herald*. Their job was to publish the work of the convention in order to give the widest possible publicity throughout the South to Dudley Mann's plan. It was a job they embraced with enthusiasm.

19

Mobile, Alabama
September 1857

At age sixteen, Rebecca Overdale met nineteen-year-old John Behncke, a strapping son of German immigrants, at a heavily chaperoned barn dance in the small Connecticut town where she and her family lived. A year later, the two were married.

John was a blacksmith, having been apprenticed at age eleven to a middle-aged smith who needed a strong and willing back. During the eight years of his apprenticeship, John had modeled himself after his mentor. He'd become skilled in the art and science of forming, cutting, and bending red-hot iron into hardware and agricultural implements. From his mentor, he'd also learned to avoid gossip and keep his own counsel in all matters but smithing.

Shortly after his marriage to Rebecca, John started a shop in a small town a few miles away from the Overdale home, but paying business was hard to come by. Farmers were usually short of cash and notoriously tight even when they weren't. Although John was always busy, he was underpaid for the quality of his work, and he and Rebecca, his "Becky," struggled to stay self-sufficient. Still, the newlyweds had their happy moments, none more so than when John sat down for dinner. Becky's culinary skills were truly formidable, and with a limited budget she learned to cook meals that were both hearty and tasty. Between the long hours of hard work and Becky's meals, John became a bearded mountain of a man with thick arms and wrists and a rock-hard torso that lacked a discernible waist.

One day, a cousin of John visited the couple. The cousin had just returned from a visit to New Orleans. While describing his trip to John and Becky, he mentioned that he had heard the ship's engineer complaining to another crewman about a broken piece of equipment and about how hard it would be to get it fixed due to the lack of skilled smiths throughout the South. After pondering this information for a few weeks, John and Becky scraped together their savings, borrowed a small amount from Becky's older brother, and booked passage on a coastal steamer, stopping at various ports on the Southern coast. At each stop, the couple conducted a cursory investigation of the town, with John trying to discern the market for his skills and Becky looking at housing and churches.

The cousin's comments were accurate, and John located a small shop for sale very near the port of Mobile. The owner, a smith in bad health, offered to sell it on a purchase mortgage. A deal was struck, and the seller introduced John to harbor masters and others on the wharfs of Mobile. The seller understood that the sooner John became prosperous, the sooner the mortgage would be paid off.

John loved Mobile. There was more work than he could easily handle, and shipowners paid cash on delivery, often with a bonus for a quick turnaround. He usually worked from sunrise to late in the evening by lamplight. Within a year he had paid for the shop, and a few months after that he and Becky bought a little house with a cookhouse in the backyard. The cookhouse was quickly furnished with a beautiful cast-iron stove and shelves for Becky's growing collection of Dutch ovens, frying pans, pots, and crockery. Becky stopped by her husband's shop each midday with a large basket of food, which he'd silently devour in the presence of his adoring wife. When finished, he always complimented her with genuine sincerity.

Becky was less enthused about Mobile than her husband. While she was appreciative of his business and the relative affluence in which they lived, she missed her family and suffered through the South's sultry summers. Then there was the matter of the population. When she'd first arrived in Mobile, Becky had seen more black people than she ever thought existed. They drove carriages, acted as maids and handymen, swept out stores, and tended horses in stables. Most were slaves, but there was a substantial minority who were free. After a while, Becky could pick out slaves from free colored by their clothing, physique, and demeanor. Slaves were usually thinner, particularly slave children, who always seemed hungry. Except for house slaves, slaves also were shabbily dressed and walked slower than the free colored, who walked with confidence. Despite her observations, Becky saw no reason to be particularly critical of slavery until a warm fall day about a year after they had arrived in Mobile, about the time John had finished paying for the shop.

John had just purchased a buggy and wanted to take Becky for a Sunday afternoon ride in the country. A lunch basket was packed, and the couple left Mobile down a rutted dirt road. They traveled through alternating piney woods and cleared land and finally came upon a series of small plantations. The scenery was pleasant as they traveled past cotton fields. In the distance, they could see whitewashed two-story clapboard houses surrounded by smaller unpainted log cabins.

While Becky was taking in the scenery, John was looking down the road, watching for washouts or other obstacles. He saw, perhaps half a mile in front of them, a group of people in a field moving slowly toward the road. He nudged Becky and nodded his head in the direction of the group. Both watched the group intently as their buggy slowly moved toward it. When they grew close to the group, John brought the buggy to a stop. A group of slave women, perhaps as many as twenty, were walking laboriously. A few were carrying heavy and crudely made hoes and shovels, and the others were hauling enormous canvas sacks folded so that they could be carried on a slave's back. The women were of all sizes—some rail thin, a few large and muscular. All were shabbily dressed with dirty and torn cotton dresses, and all wore dingy bandanas around their heads. Several wore crudely made straw hats over the bandanas. A male slave carrying a wooden switch followed the women, and behind him rode a seedy-looking white man on a horse with a coiled whip tied to the saddle. All the slaves kept their eyes fixed on the ground before them as they slowly and silently walked across the road. Becky could see old scars on the legs and arms of several of the women. One had a crescent-shaped branding mark impressed on the back of her neck. Some were shoeless, and the rest wore some sort of shapeless leather covering on their feet.

As the women were crossing the road, the white man on the horse nodded to the couple, tipped his hat, and gave them a gruesome, black-toothed smile. Becky instinctively recoiled at the sight of the man. After the group had passed, John started the buggy once more, and the couple continued in silence for a few minutes. Finally, Becky said, "My God, John, that was awful!"

"What do you mean?"

"John, those are women. They're being herded like cattle. On a Sunday! The switch, the whip, the scars …" Becky had trouble putting her emotions into words. "John, how would you feel if it were me, dressed in rags, barefoot, with scars from whippings and beatings?"

"Becky, they're slaves. That's the way things are down here. Maybe we don't like it, but you can't be surprised."

"John, they're humans. I'm sure some are mothers. You can't think that this is right."

John was silent for the rest of the trip. The couple traveled a short distance, stopped under a grove of trees, and nibbled without much appetite from the basket Becky had packed. They returned to Mobile in silence.

John didn't like slavery, but he had to make a living from people who owned slaves and resolved not to discuss it with anyone. Becky decided on the way back to Mobile that slavery was evil and that she had a moral duty to oppose it or at least to alleviate the suffering it caused, but in such a way so as to not hurt her husband's trade. During the trip, she silently puzzled out how to do that. Before they arrived home, she came up with a plan. She would silently wage her private war to help those suffering from bondage with the weapon with which she had the greatest skill—her cookstove.

20

Isle of Dogs, London
November 3, 1857

THE directors of the Eastern Steam Navigation Company had reached the end of their rope. Threatened by their shareholders, mortified by the taunts of those who had had the good luck not to invest in the giant ship, and possessing funds sufficient only to cover one launch, assuming it occurred quickly, the directors unleashed their anger at Isambard Kingdom Brunel, the man who had assured them that the construction of such a monster was actually and financially possible. In early October, John Yates, the secretary of the Eastern Steam Navigation Company, ordered Brunel with unmistakable panic, "Launch the ship, or we shall be in the hands of the Philistines!"

Although Brunel initially resisted a rushed launch, insisting that proper preparations took time, he succumbed to pressure. He calculated when the tide would be advantageous for the sideways launch and accordingly fixed November 3 as the date.

The morning of the launch date reflected Brunel's mood. It was bitter and gray, with intermittent drizzle. The only advantage offered by the weather was that it somewhat suppressed the putrid smell of the Thames. The ship's completed hull had been painted black, which made it appear even larger and more sinister. Though the ship was painted, rust could be seen streaking down her dark sides from various iron protrusions, looking like dried blood from numerous wounds. It was apparent that no attempt had been made to add beauty or decoration to the ship. She had been designed and built as a seagoing version of a Victorian factory—cold, hard materials; brutally efficient shape; and a vast, dark interior filled with complex and dangerous machinery.

The sideways descent of the great ship was to take place on railroad tracks Brunel had laid years earlier. To control the descent of the ship into the Thames, Brunel had arranged for two giant "checking drums" to be installed. These drums, which resembled gargantuan spools of thread lying on their sides, were encircled by chains, each link of which was the size of a man's torso. When Brunel gave the order to launch the monster, the drums were to be used to slowly lower the ship into the water. Each drum had a great pole sticking out that, when pulled down, tightened a band that braked the drum. A crew of men was assigned to each pole for the purpose of braking or releasing the drum according to Brunel's orders.

Brunel had wanted to ban everyone but necessary workers from the launch site so that his voice commands could be clearly heard. A memorandum he had written days earlier stated, "The success of the operation will depend entirely upon the perfect regularity and absence of all haste or confusion in each stage of the proceeding … and to attain this, nothing is more essential than perfect silence, so that everyone can hear the simple orders quietly and deliberately given by the few who will direct."

Brunel was shocked to learn upon his arrival to the launch site that the directors of the Eastern Steam Navigation Company, desperate to raise money, had ignored his instructions and sold thousands of tickets to this spectacle. News of the launch spread quickly throughout London. Consequently, as the morning went on, a vast crowd gathered around the launching site. Both banks of the Thames were crowded with sightseers and small vessels overloaded with the curious crowd near the launching site.

The crowd, estimated by the newspapers to be in the hundreds of thousands, was a cross section of London. Ladies and gentlemen wearing cold-weather finery had attempted to arrive in carriages but found it impossible to bring their vehicles close to the site. Thus, rich and stylish Londoners found themselves walking manure-laden brick streets next to scarred and gnarled working-class men and women wearing shabby clothes. Middle-class tradesmen and merchants accompanied by their families came as close as possible on omnibuses before making the final walk in the freezing rain to the site, and street urchins crashed the fete in noisy, boisterous fashion. Pickpockets filled gaps in the fluid mass of humanity, briskly practicing their profession. The continued drizzle and cold enveloped all. The rain occasionally came down in sheets.

One newspaper described the scene: "The soil was moist; moist was it overhead; moisture was around; and the coup d'oeil of the Isle of Dogs—especially in the afternoon, when the umbrellas cropped up like Titanic mushrooms after a shower in the tropics—was a patent specific against even a nightmare dream of hydrophobia."

Some members of the crowd, drunken and rowdy, had actually gathered around the checking drums and had to be driven away by the harassed workmen. The more sober members of the crowd were huddled together for warmth while waiting with as much patience as they could muster for what would surely be the greatest spectacle of their lives.

Brunel had developed a complex plan to start the ship on her way into the river. Anchored in the Thames were a number of "lighters," barges that were chained to the opposite bank and that had steam windlasses mounted upon them. Chains were run from various points on the ship to these windlasses. There were also chains at the bow and stern of the ship. These chains ran out to pulleys on other anchored barges and then back to shore, where they were attached to shore-mounted steam windlasses. Finally, steam rams were mounted against the giant wooden cradles in which the ship rested. All totaled, the steam windlasses and rams were capable of exerting about six hundred tons of pressure, an amount Brunel reckoned to be more than sufficient to start the monster on her slide toward freedom. Gravity, he calculated, would do the rest.

All morning, well over a thousand men had scampered around the slips preparing for the launch, all under Brunel's direction. Steam boilers had been fired both on shore and on the lighters in order to power the windlasses and rams. Burly crews of men were assembled at the two checking drums, and chains were tightened all around. Hoarse from screaming over the noise of the crowd, a fuming Brunel had begun to climb a ladder to the top of a tall wooden scaffold next to the ship when he was stopped by a director, who was waving a paper at him.

"Mr. Brunel, a moment please! I must talk to you."

"What is it?"

"We have to select a name for the ship. A number of the directors are not happy with the name *Great Eastern.* The directors and I selected a number of other names and would like your opinion."

Brunel stared at the man incredulously. Could the directors be so idiotic? Now, at the precise moment when the whole world seemed to be watching whether Brunel was to be a hero or a fool, one of them was asking his opinion about names! Brunel looked darkly at the man and spat out his response. "You can name her the *Tom Thumb*, for all I care!" With that, Brunel spun around and climbed to the top of the scaffold.

At 12:30 p.m., Henrietta Hope, the fashionable young daughter of the company's managing director, walked across the scaffold's platform toward the ship. She had started the day beautifully attired with a stylish bonnet, shawl, and bustled and padded gown. She was now soaked and cold and definitely unfashionable but still excited about her role in history. Accompanied by three other maidens attired in similarly soaked clothes, she loosed a bottle of champagne on the ship's hull and, in a voice heard only by those on the platform, announced, "I christen thee *Leviathan.*"

With a wave of a flag, Brunel commanded the launch to begin. The steam winches exerted their tons of steam pressure on the chains attached to the ship's hull, and the chains began to stretch. The rams started their pressure on the cradles, and the *Leviathan* began to inch down toward the river. However, a crew, leaning on one of the poles of a checking drum, was confused by the flag signals and had not heeded an order to hold tight to the brake. Without the brake applied, the rams had jerked the massive chain of the checking drum and in so doing sharply pulled up the braking pole. The sudden action of the pole had injured six men. One of the men lay motionless on the ground, his body twisted.

A cry went up from the crowd. The ship, not even launched, had claimed yet another life! Certainly numerous men and boys had fallen to their death in the construction of the ship's hull, but those sorts of deaths were a common occurrence around shipyards. No, most of the crowd thought of the riveter's boy and the basher who had been accidently sealed in the ship's double hull, their screams drowned out by the cacophony of steam machinery and the hammers of dozens of riveters, their absence not discovered until much later, when any attempt to locate them was deemed hopeless. The thought of their moldering bodies still entombed in their unconsecrated iron coffin sent many a chill down the spines of the onlookers.

The crew members of the other checking drum applied their strength to the braking pole and stopped the movement of the ship. A new crew was hastily assembled, and after an hour of confusion during which the bodies of the dead and injured workmen had been removed, the launch continued. Again, Brunel used a flag to signal the beginning of the launch. Chains snapped rigid, and the sound of the windlasses and rams could be heard above the crowd. The ship moved down the slip about four feet, stopped, and could not be moved further. Her vast weight had overwhelmed all the force that Brunel's machinery could bring to bear.

For the rest of the afternoon, the steam windlasses and rams pushed, tugged, and pulled without effect. Finally, two of four lighters broke their mooring chains and floated freely in the Thames, useless at any effort to assist in the launch. Brunel, finally acknowledging the inevitable, called off the launch. Boilers were shut down, their tenders dispersed. Chains from the lighters were collected and stored on the launch site. The wet and cold crowd, grumbling to itself at this turn of events, slowly disappeared into the gloomy dusk, and as daylight faded, the newly christened *Leviathan* remained a vast and brooding presence on the shores of the Thames.

21

London, England
January 1858

ROBERT Stephenson was one of the greatest engineers in Britain. Brunel had worked with and respected him for many years, and when Brunel heard that the elderly Stephenson had felt slighted for not having been invited to the launch site, he sent him a note asking him to come. Thereafter, Stephenson came to the site several times. What he saw, from the viewpoint of an engineer, could only be described as gruesome.

Twice more in November and twice more again in December, lighters were hired, chains were retrieved and strung out, steam rams and steam winches were fired and manned, and work crews were assembled, all followed by Herculean efforts of man and machine to move the *Leviathan* into the Thames. The newspapers covered each effort. Sometimes she moved six inches, and on one occasion she moved several feet, but by New Year's Day there was widespread concern that she would be forever landlocked. With her great weight, she was sinking deeper and deeper into the wood pilings that had been designed to hold her only momentarily as she slid over them into the river. Unless she was launched within a matter of days, she would be forever trapped in a ditch on the edge of the river.

In the meantime, funds were exhausted. One firm had already reclaimed some of the chains used in the launch attempts, and Brunel had to make do with repaired chains scrounged from other shipyards or hauled up from the bottom of the Thames. It seemed as if everyone involved in the launch was clamoring for payment, and the directors kindly referred the company's angry creditors to a defenseless Brunel.

The newspapers had a field day. One mean-spirited cartoon showed travelers in the year 2000 discovering a giant, vegetation-covered hulk on the shores of the Thames. A writer to the *London Times* chirped in with advice: "Why don't clever men make big ships in big holes and let the water in when the ships are finished, instead of trying to make the ships travel on railroads?" The ridicule literally poured from the press.

Not just London but the whole civilized world seemed to be enjoying a great laugh at Brunel's expense. For a man previously acclaimed as a genius for completing the first tunnel under the Thames; for designing and building many soaring railroad bridges and massive railway stations; for giving birth to the *Great Western*, the first successful transatlantic steamer; and for other accomplishments too numerous to recall, Brunel was humiliated beyond words. Even Prince Albert, Queen Victoria's consort, visited Brunel to give him advice and to remind him that far more than Brunel's reputation rested upon the successful launch of the ship. The reputation of Britannia itself was at stake.

Brunel quietly sent word to Stephenson that he wished to visit him at his townhome in London. Stephenson was not surprised at the request, although when Brunel arrived and removed his hat and overcoat, Stephenson was alarmed to see how exhausted and sickly his friend looked. Brunel had always been a volcano of energy, astounding everyone with his long hours of work and fierce determination. In a nation famous for its energetic eccentrics and creative geniuses, it was hard to imagine a genius more gifted, more energetic, and more eccentric.

Brunel was short, slightly taller than five feet, resulting in newspapers and journals often referring to him as "the Little Giant." Appointed chief engineer of the Great Western Railway at the age of twenty-seven, Brunel's drive and intellect had changed the landscape of England. The plodding horses pulling wagons over dusty roads were now accompanied by loud steam engines pulling dozens, sometimes hundreds, of people at astounding speeds.

To free as many hours as possible for work, Brunel had acquired a britska, a long, black four-wheeled carriage in which he traveled, worked, and lived. Because people predicted that Brunel would work himself to death, the britska had become known as "the Flying Coffin." Stephenson was fifty-three, a year older than Brunel and in poor health himself. Nevertheless, as he looked at the small, crestfallen man before him, Stephenson worried that the coffin prophecy may have been well founded—Brunel was working and worrying himself to death. As Stephenson guided his enfeebled guest to a chair in his study, a small boy, perhaps seven or eight, came into the study to see what was happening.

"Isambard, I want you to meet my grandson. This is Thomas's boy."

Brunel looked at the child with a smile. "I'm pleased to meet you. What is your name?"

The child answered with a snap to attention. "Robert Louis Stephenson, sir." Brunel looked at his friend. "Named after you? You must be very proud."

"Indeed, I am."

Stephenson rubbed his grandson gently on the head. "Today, he's a soldier. Yesterday, a fierce pirate. We'll have to see who visits us tomorrow." Stephenson nodded to a servant, who escorted the boy out of the study and closed the doorway with heavy velvet curtains. The men were alone.

"Robert, thank you for seeing me."

"Isambard, would you join me in having a cup of tea?"

"No. No thank you. I'll come right out and tell you why I'm here."

Stephenson sat silently as the diminutive man seated next to him took a deep breath.

"I'm afraid I may not be able to launch her. Every hour she sinks deeper into the mud. It may already be too late." He paused as he attempted to mentally form the next sentence, but it never came. The small engineer sat silently, his arms bent and his hands turned upward, trembling in frustration.

Stephenson said, more forcefully than he had intended, "Isambard, you must finish it."

Brunel nodded silently. His eyes glistened as he slowly arose. "Robert, I'll take my leave. Good day."

"Wait. I've not finished yet. Please sit."

Brunel hesitated but sat down. When he looked at Stephenson's face, he saw a smile. Stephenson leaned toward his friend and put his hand gently on his guest's knee. "Isambard, in creating this ship you've achieved the greatest engineering achievement of this century. You have to see it through. I've followed the launch attempts very closely after I received your kind invitation."

"I apologize for not inviting you earlier, Robert."

Stephenson waved his hand at the apology. He continued, "I am most disgusted at the rubbish in the newspapers. All I can say is that those jackals cannot construct a proper sentence, much less a ship. Ignoring them, as we must, I can assure you the ship can and will be launched. I have thought very hard about this. What you need is overwhelming power, and it has to be sustained until she is in the river."

"Where can I get that power? I have no money, no resources. Robert, I'm at the end."

"Isambard, I was just writing you a note with the information I'm going to give you now. Do you remember when I was building the Britannia Bridge? I asked for your help, and you came right away and helped me. Anyway, you remember I had to lift and hold in place a tremendously heavy set of girders. To do that, I ordered the construction of two hydraulic rams. They were and certainly still are the most powerful rams in the world. I'm certain you saw them operate." Stephenson shook Brunel's knee gently. "One of the rams blew up under pressure and was completely destroyed. Nevertheless, I've been thinking about your launch for some time, and I telegraphed to find out where the remaining ram is stored. I found it and confirmed yesterday that it can be quickly shipped to the launch site. I'll make the ram available to you, along with a Scotsman who knows how to operate it."

Brunel grew quiet and calm. "Will the ram provide enough power?"

"There's more. I've talked with Richard Tangye, who's an old friend of mine. He's troubled that you've been using his rams and are still unsuccessful. He thinks it's harming his business. I believe if you simply asked, he'd double the number of rams for little or nothing. If we combine these rams with your existing rams and winches, the launch cannot fail. I am absolutely convinced of it."

Brunel was overwhelmed. He had been facing nothing but hopelessness and humiliation when he'd knocked on Stephenson's door. Now, everything had changed. Brunel was silent as he stood up and walked toward the door. After he had put on his coat and hat, he turned to Stephenson and shook his hand solemnly.

"Thank you, Robert."

"Isambard, I'll inform you when the Britannia ram is on its way."

After Brunel left, Stephenson sat down and gazed out the window, watching his visitor depart. *If this doesn't work*, thought Stephenson, *at least I'll share your humiliation.*

Brunel immediately contacted Richard Tangye, who in fact was delighted to increase the number of his rams, together with operators, if Brunel would assist in their publicity. Brunel assured Tangye that he would be unstinting in praise of his rams, and arrangements were quickly made to ship the additional rams to the launch site. To ensure that the entire force of the rams would be applied against the weight of the ship, workmen broke the concrete apron on which the ship rested to build enormous stone abutments against which the rams would exert pressure. Brunel calculated tides and arrived at the final launch date of January 30.

The day arrived, but the wind was howling against the slab side of the ship. Brunel decided to hold off one day. January 31 dawned cold but calm. In the shipyard, rams, winches, and operators were everywhere. Tangye paced from one ram to another to inspect his machines and to talk to his operators. He reminded them that the hydraulic pressure of the rams was to be increased gradually as they pushed against the wooden cradles in order to avoid fracturing the wood. The massive Britannia ram was in place against the stern cradle, a fierce-looking man standing beside her. The lighters were anchored in the river, and chains ran back and forth between them, the ship, and the shore like a spiderweb. Earlier that week, Stephenson had sat with pencil and paper and computed the power available to Brunel. On November 5, the day of the first launch, Brunel had used six hundred tons of power. On this final attempt, Stephenson calculated, when all power was applied, Brunel would have *six thousand* tons of power, nearly half of the weight of the hull. If this failed, Stephenson concluded, there was nothing left to be done but dismantle the ship and sell her as scrap.

Between the second and third launch attempts, a platform had been built on the mud of the shipyard and a tarpaulin pulled over it to provide at least minimal protection from rain and sleet for the persons directing future launches. Despite lingering illness, Stephenson had sat there for two prior launch attempts and was there for this final one. Brunel, far too agitated to sit, paced back and forth on the platform with binoculars around his neck. A small crowd gathered on the roadway behind the launch site.

Brunel's foremen paced the shipyard, inspecting every ram and chain, giving final instructions to the men at the checking drums. Finally, all preparations were over. All boilers were fired and pressure was up, the chains were tightened by the winches, and everyone waited motionlessly for Brunel's signal. Brunel dropped a flag, and the Tangye rams began exerting their tons of hydraulic pressure. The steam winches began, the tightening chains indicating that they also were exerting pressure. Stephenson sat quietly for a moment as the ship remained still. He had consulted with Brunel, and they'd agreed to make certain that the ship was under pressure from all other equipment before the Britannia ram went to work. Finally, she was. After getting a nod from Brunel, Stephenson waved a white cloth to the Scotsman, who nodded back and, with a broad grin spreading across his bearded face, slowly opened the main control valve of the giant ram.

The ship sat motionless for long seconds. Then a voice cried out, "She's moving!" The few onlookers on the roadway started screaming and yelling. Amid the cracking and grinding sounds of the giant wooden cradles being pushed to the river on the railroad tracks and the screams from the band brakes on the checking drums, everyone in the gathering crowd could see that the ship was slowly gathering speed as she descended. It was late afternoon when she finally slid into the murky waters of the Thames.

Cheers and screams punctuated the Isle of Dogs, and grown men wept and hugged at the sight.

The *Leviathan* was afloat.

22

United States Senate
Washington, DC
March 4, 1858

The following excerpts are from a speech by James Henry Hammond, senator from South Carolina:

> What would happen if no cotton was furnished for three years? I will not stop to depict what everyone can imagine, but this is certain: England would topple headlong and carry the whole civilized world with her, save the South. No, you dare not make war on cotton. No power on earth dares to make war upon it. Cotton is king! Until lately the Bank of England was king; but she tried to put her screws as usual, the fall before last, upon the cotton crop, and was utterly vanquished. The last power has been conquered! Who can doubt, that has looked at recent events, that cotton is supreme? . . .
>
> . . . In all social systems there must be a class to do the menial duties, to perform the drudgery of life. That is, a class requiring but a low order of intellect and but little skill. Its requisites are vigor, docility, fidelity. Such a class you must have, or you would not have that other class which leads to progress, civilization, and refinement. It constitutes the very mud-sill of society and of political government; and you might as well attempt to build a house in the air, as to build either the one or the other, except on this mud-sill. Fortunately for the South, she found a race adapted to that purpose to her hand. A race inferior to her own, but eminently qualified in temper, in vigor, in docility, in capacity to stand the climate, to answer all her purposes. We use them for our purpose, and call them slaves.

23

Richmond, Virginia
March 1858

DUDLEY Mann and J. D. B. DeBow made a highly effective team. No minister ever preached redemption with greater fervor than Mann preached his case for a weekly iron steamship ferry line, with the newly launched *Leviathan* as its underpinning. DeBow arranged for one economic conference after another throughout the South, each attended by railroad and banking officials and each recorded by newspaper owners and editors. Newspaper reports of these conferences were often picked up by Northern newspapers. Indeed, Mann and the *Great Eastern*, the name the ship was commonly called in spite of her christening, were becoming a regular item in the *New York Times*. Even the *London Times* carried a report of one such convention held in Old Point, Virginia. Among the attendees at Old Point was John Tyler, former president of the United States, along with numerous delegates from throughout the South. The Old Point convention had collected $8,000 in subscriptions, a fact not lost on the directors of the *Great Eastern*, who were looking for a light at the end of the tunnel, no matter how dim.

William Preston traveled to England and met with the directors of the *Great Eastern* as he had promised the convention in Bristol. What he found was a group of men teetering at the edge of a financial cliff. There had been great miscalculations in the cost of constructing the ship, and her launching had been delayed numerous times. Nevertheless, when Preston inspected the ship, it was apparent to him that she was an astounding piece of naval architecture and would be seaworthy in the not-too-distant future. The ship's directors were receptive to Preston's suggestion that the *Great Eastern* come to Chesapeake Bay, and they promised that they would explore the possibility of the ship serving as a giant shuttle between Virginia and England. However, when they pressed Preston on the possibility of the slaveholding states providing financial help, he demurred, saying that it was unlikely that any funds would be available until she was launched and proved seaworthy. The directors were disappointed but not surprised.

By March 1858, with the giant ship successfully launched and in the process of being fitted out, Mann and DeBow decided it was time to formalize Mann's ideas. On March 15, a bill was laid before the Virginia General Assembly entitled "An Act to Incorporate the Atlantic Steam Ferry Company." Its first provision read as follows:

> Be it enacted by the General Assembly of Virginia, That Ambrose Dudley Mann, his associates, successors and assigns, are hereby created and constituted a body corporate, by title of the ATLANTIC STEAM FERRY COMPANY.

The company was authorized by the bill to raise a maximum of $50 million but could start operations after raising only $1 million. It was to have thirty-six directors, all of whom were required by the act to be resident citizens of slaveholding states. Northerners could invest in this company but could have no say in its operation. The company was empowered to buy ships, build docks, and do anything else necessary to carry out Mann's plan. With little discussion, the bill passed on a voice vote. Governor John Letcher, the man who had earlier appointed Mann to be Virginia's assistant secretary of state, quickly signed it into law.

Mann's plans had come a long way from his first visit to the Isle of Dogs two and a half years earlier. Although he now had a legal mechanism to raise funds, he knew he would not be successful in obtaining investors until the *Great Eastern* was ready for transatlantic travel. That should only be a matter of months.

24

Marengo County, Alabama
August 1858

"KIT, come here. I want to talk to you," Judge Crane called out from the back porch of the main house.

"Yes, suh." Kit left his work in the toolshed and came at a trot. He stopped at the back porch stairs, staring up at his master. The judge stepped down and sat on the bottom stair. "Sit here next to me, Kit."

Kit was surprised at the request. Slaves, or at least field slaves, never sat while talking to their masters. Such familiarity was unbecoming of the relationship between superior and inferior. Nevertheless, Kit had been ordered to sit down, and he did so awkwardly and as far away from the judge as he could sit.

"Kit, I need someone who can operate a forge. Every time a piece of iron breaks, I have to send it to Mobile or New Orleans and then wait weeks before it's repaired. Also, horses are not being shod as frequently as they should be. I've talked to the other plantation owners around here, and they're having the same problems. We need a blacksmith."

Kit nodded his head, wondering where this conversation was headed.

"Since I have the largest spread, I told the other planters that I'd select a good boy to go to Mobile to learn to become a blacksmith. After he learned the trade, he'd come back and do the smithing for plantations around here."

Kit nodded apprehensively. "Yes, suh," he said softly.

"Kit, I've selected you to become our smith. You're obedient, and you work hard. You've always been a good boy, never caused me any real trouble. Danny says that you're good with the woodworking tools. You should be good with forge tools as well. I'm sending you to Mobile to work with a blacksmith named Behncke. You'll work for him about a year, learning the trade. When you're done, I'll order the necessary equipment, and we'll set up a smith shop over beyond the slave cabins."

Kit sat on the stairs, stunned. He didn't know what to say.

"So, Kit, are you ready to become a smith?"

Kit nodded enthusiastically. "Yes, suh, yes, suh." He didn't know what this was all about, but the judge was giving him a chance to live in Mobile for a while and to learn something new. Maybe when he was in Mobile, he could find out where his mother and sister were.

A week later, Danny told Kit that he was going to take him to Mobile and that they were leaving the following day. The day they left, Danny got two slave passes from the judge and hard biscuits and pieces of smoked ham from the cook. The trip to Mobile on the single plodding horse took nearly two days. On the first night, the two slaves slept alongside the road with the horse tied to a tree. Late in the night, they were awakened by three armed white men on horses, accompanied by two large hounds. One of the riders demanded to see their passes. Danny handed the passes up to the night rider, who examined them in the moonlight. None of the riders could read particularly well, but the one who examined the passes recognized Judge Crane's name, which the judge had both printed and signed. The passes were handed back, and the riders moved on.

Kit was scared by the encounter with the night riders and their hounds, but Danny told Kit that their appearance was normal. As long as a slave had proper papers and didn't sass back, the riders didn't cause any trouble. As dawn broke, the two slaves each ate a biscuit and then mounted their horse to continue their journey.

After riding in silence for a while, Danny said, "Kit, you's one lucky boy, goin' to Mobile."

"You think so?"

"You's gonna learn da trade. As you get good, da judge gonna hire you out to folks an' make money from you."

"Why's dat make me lucky?"

"Yous can earn you'self money. De judge, I betcha he gonna let you keep some of dat money you earns, and you can save it. Who knows, maybe somedays you can buy you'self."

Kit hadn't considered all this. He had heard of a slave on another plantation who was skilled in making furniture. His owner would let him go for part of a year to earn his own living. When he returned, he shared part of the money he had earned with his owner and was allowed to keep some for himself. Kit had thought the slave just used the money to buy things. He hadn't thought of him saving the money to buy his freedom.

"Dat's the truf?"

"Could be, Kit."

"How 'bout you, Danny? Can you earn money?"

Danny smiled and shook his head gently. "I's jus' a field han', maybe a little handy with da wood tools. Ain't nobody gonna pay nuthin' for me. I's neva gonna be free." After a moment of silence, Danny said, "Das ok. De judge, he treat me okay. I jes' hope dat de judge, he live longa den de wife. She'd sell my carcass to de hog butcha if she thought she'd make money. Mean!" He looked over his shoulder at Kit. "Real mean!"

Kit felt bad for Danny. To know that one would spend the rest of his life as a slave was hard. Kit had never thought he'd be free, but maybe Danny was right. Maybe this trip to Mobile would somehow, someday allow him to earn his freedom. As they slowly plodded toward Mobile, Kit became aware that he had hope, no matter how slim, and Danny had none.

Mobile was a revelation to Kit. He'd traveled through a few small towns before but never through a city, much less a city that had a port. Mobile had a population of around thirty thousand, making it one of the largest cities in the South. About a third of the population was Negroes, including a few hundred freed slaves. Kit had never seen so many people, so many buildings, horses, wagons, stores, everything that there was, in his life. He and Danny arrived late in the afternoon of the second day. They were both hungry, having finished off the last of the biscuits and ham for lunch. Danny had been to Mobile several times before on errands, and he knew his way around. Before long the two illiterate slaves stood in front of a wooden building with a large sign.

J. Behncke
Black Smith & Iron Work

Danny could not read the sign, but he recognized it and knew what it meant.

The door to the building was open, and Kit and Danny could see inside. Danny recognized the barrel-chested man. Covered with sweat and grime and wearing a leather apron, Behncke was a fearsome apparition. The two slaves stood quietly in the doorway until Behncke noticed that they were there. He squinted a moment at them and then smiled at Danny. He put his tools down and stepped into the sunlight.

"Danny, is this the boy Judge Crane's sending me?"

"Yes, suh."

"His name is Kit?"

"Yes, suh."

"He ain't too big. You sure he's got the muscle to work here?"

"Yes, suh. He ain't too big, but he's plenty strong."

Behncke made a soft humming noise as he walked around Kit. The smith towered over Kit and probably weighed twice as much as the young slave. Danny was right, though. Kit was slender, but his arms and shoulders were muscular. The smith stepped back to appraise the slave from a distance, the way a buyer would appraise a horse. Kit was dark, almost bluish black in color. He had no deformities. Behncke looked at the slave's face, the broad nose and thick lips of the African race, and saw in Kit's eyes what he believed was a good-natured intelligence.

"Kit, if you work hard, you'll learn a trade. If you don't work hard, you'll be sent back and spend your life as a field hand."

Kit winced at those words, knowing the pain they must have caused Danny.

"Massa, I's a good worka. I do my best."

"All right. I can't ask for anything more. Are you boys hungry? I have a whole fried chicken here along with some ham, and the misses brought some fresh bread and baked yams over today."

"Yes, suh, Massa. We're powe'ful hungry," Danny quickly responded.

"Go wash in the barrel over there, and I'll cut you some ham and bread."

Danny and Kit had for them a huge dinner and expressed many thanks to the smith and his legendary wife for their kindness. Finally, it was time for the smith to go home.

"Danny, I'm going to close both of you in the shop. You can sleep over in the corner on those rags and straw. I'll have the misses put together some food for your trip back to the judge's place."

"T'ank you, suh."

"All right. No smoking. I don't want my shop burning down!"

"No, suh. We unnerstan'."

After the shop door was closed, it was too dark inside to make a closer inspection of the dangerous tool-filled shop . The two slaves decided that they'd go to bed early, especially since they were full of ham, chicken, yams, and bread.

"Kit, you's one lucky boy. I ain't neva met de smith's wife, but I's told dat she cooks enuf food to feed haf de colored in Mobile. No slave who goes to de smith's shop leaves witout sometin' ta eat. You's gonna be fat as a hog when you come back," Danny laughed.

Kit didn't respond. He couldn't think of anything to say. He just wished he could share his luck with Danny.

25

Alton, Illinois
October 15, 1858

Abraham Lincoln, candidate for United States Senate, made the following statement during his seventh and final debate with Stephen A. Douglas:

> Now irrespective of the moral aspect of this question as to whether there is a right or wrong in enslaving a negro, I am still in favor of our new Territories being in such a condition that white men may find a home—may find some spot where they can better their condition—where they can settle upon new soil and better their condition in life.
>
> [Great and prolonged cheering]
>
> I am in favor of this not merely, I must say it here as I have elsewhere, for our own people who are born amongst us, but as an outlet for *free white people everywhere*, the world over—in which Hans and Baptiste and Patrick, and all other men from all the world, may find new homes and better their conditions in life.
>
> [Loud and long continued applause]

26

New Orleans, Louisiana
October 1858

"Dan, when are you getting the pumps from Pennsylvania?" Bob Morison asked.

Lowber looked at the papers on his cluttered desk. "I got a letter a few days ago about that shipment. Let's see if I can find it." Lowber picked up and put down clumps of paper. With an exasperated sigh, he said, "It's going to take a while to find it. As I recall, they're due around the end of November. You'll have them in plenty of time for the new year."

Morison, a cheerful farmer with an ample waist and sandy-colored beard, laughed. "Dan, you ought to let Abram do your paperwork. He's a hell of a lot more organized than you are." Abram looked in from the backroom. The slave smiled but shook his head and put his finger to his lips. Morison understood. "Ah, right, I won't drag Abram into this," he said.

Lowber was becoming a little defensive. "I'm usually better with my papers than this. It's just that I've—"

"Dan, I'm just funnin' ya. If I get the pumps by Christmas, it'll be fine." While he was looking at Lowber's desk, Morison saw a copy of the *New York Daily Times.* "You been following that debate Douglas is having in Illinois?"

Lowber nodded. "There's a bunch of debates. I haven't read them all, but I read the one that just came out."

Morison shrugged. "I heard some other guys talking about it. I don't know why it's such a big deal. I don't even know why Douglas is debating that hick. He's just some kind of prairie lawyer."

"I know why," Lowber said soberly. "Lincoln's driving a point that could tear this country apart."

"Slavery?"

"No. It's the territories—keeping slaves out of the territories."

"I thought that was all fixed by Dred Scott. They can't keep slaves out. Ain't that right?"

Lowber, having been raised in New York and being well read, was frequently consulted by businessmen and plantation owners in the New Orleans area regarding national politics. Everyone knew that his brother-in-law, Captain Schultz, was a close friend of the hated "Black Republican" William Seward, and they therefore assumed that Lowber had a special insight into the minds of Yankees. To keep this reputation, which he enjoyed, Lowber read widely from New York newspapers, as well as local papers. He received in the mail the *New-York Daily Tribune* and the *New York Daily Times*, and he read them closely in the evening. However, he avoided strongly abolitionist papers, like the *New York Herald*, for fear that questions would be raised as to his loyalties to the South.

"Bob," Lowber answered, "the territories are being filled with poor whites looking for farmland. They know that if the plantation owners move in, the price of land will jump and they'll be squeezed. Lincoln's not debating Douglas; he's telling these foreigners that they have to keep slavery out of the territories or they'll never get their farms."

Morison nodded slowly as he considered this information. "Someone said Lincoln's an abolitionist. Is that right?"

Lowber laughed. "One day Lincoln says Negroes are equal to white men. Then another day he says they're not equal to white men. One day he says slavery is awful, and another day he says slavery's just fine as long as it stays down South. When it comes to the Africans, Lincoln flops around like a fish in the bottom of a boat. He says whatever his particular audience wants to hear. However, there's one point on which he's firm, and that's the point that's being heard all throughout the country. He doesn't want slave owners coming into the territories and bidding up the property."

"But how can he stop them with the Dred Scott?"

"Bob, how did John Brown stop Kansas from becoming a slave state?"

Morison, like every Southerner, knew the answer to that question. Brown and his henchmen had dragged proslavery men from their homes in the middle of the night and slaughtered them with broadswords. It had been violence and terror that kept Kansas a free state, not the law.

"Is Lincoln talking about violence?"

"Not yet," Lowber said. "But that'll come. If you can't legally stop people from doing something, then you have to stop them illegally. Lincoln's inciting these farmers, and they're a tough bunch, Germans and Swedes mostly, and they'll kill if they need to."

Morison pursed his lips and shook his head slowly. "How's it going to end, Dan?"

Lowber shrugged. "I don't know. But watch Lincoln. He's more than just an ordinary politician. He's smart and he's dangerous, as dangerous as Seward. Maybe even more so, 'cause he's from the West. The small farmers think that he's one of them, and they trust him."

"Well, I guess we hope ol' Douglas will win the election."

"Well, maybe, but even if that happens," Lowber said, "I'm not sure that we'll have seen the last of Lincoln. He knows how to rouse people, and he's hungry for power. A man like that knows how to fish in troubled waters."

27

The Leviathan Steamship, *Scientific American* October 23, 1858

This giant of the seas, which has caused so much speculation, expense, and anxiety, has been in a stand-still condition for some time. It was expected at one period that she would be all ready for sea this autumn, and that the first voyage would be taken to some American port, probably Portland, Me., but at present it is not possible to predict when she will be ready, or what will be her future destination. The cost for her construction having far exceeded the original estimates, and all the funds having been used up, the stockholders did not feel inclined to increase their contributions, hence the delay in completing this great steamer. It is now proposed to form a new company, with a capital sufficient to purchase out the old one, and to finish her at an early date. It is stated that, when completed, she will be able to make eight voyages per annum between London and Portland, and pay a handsome profit.

Rumors have also been circulated that the Emperor of France wishes to purchase the Great Eastern for his navy, and some fears are entertained in England that he may accomplish his object. It has been urged upon the British government to step in and make the purchase for the royal navy. Louis Napoleon is a long-headed genius, and if he can secure the Great Eastern, he might laugh at the power of the whole British navy, because this monster steamer could run down the whole of the largest steamers in any other fleet, one after another, without firing a single shot. We hope that some energetic measures will soon be carried out to complete this noble steamer. The results of such a grand experiment will be looked for with anxiety and interest.

28

London, England
November 1858

In the early night hours following the launch of the *Leviathan*, church bells rang throughout London. Word spread quickly throughout the city that the monster was afloat and Brunel's agonies had come to an end. All of England exulted at the news that what had been a worldwide embarrassment was now going to be a demonstration of the commercial and military power of the British race. It was a time for rejoicing.

The rejoicing of the directors of the Eastern Steam Navigation Company was short-lived, however. Over the previous five years, unpaid debts had piled up. Shareholders had refused to answer calls for more capital, and the company was drowning in red ink. Brunel's herculean but costly efforts to launch the ship, together with the wildly optimistic estimates of her construction costs, had bankrupted the company. That was the bad news. The good news was that the hull, complete with her two massive engines, one for the side wheels and one for the propeller, was floating on the Thames. True, there remained much work to fit her out as a working ship, but the hardest part of her creation was over.

In the fall of 1857, as the Eastern Steam Navigation Company was plunging headfirst into debt and as Brunel struggled to launch his creation, two shareholders had begun to listen to entreaties coming from America. Dudley Mann had met repeatedly with these and other shareholders and had promised vast rewards if the *Great Eastern* shuttled between Chesapeake Bay and England, taking baled cotton on her eastward voyages and returning woven cloth and other manufactured goods to the slaveholding states. His entreaties had been backed up by Preston's earlier fact-finding visit and by statements of John Letcher, Virginia's governor, who had become as enthusiastic as Mann about the great ship.

Virginia was not alone in her enthusiasm for the *Great Eastern*. The citizens of Portland, Maine, had avidly sought to be the port of call for the *Leviathan* and even raised the astounding sum of $125,000 for the construction of a giant pier especially designed for the ship. Indeed, work on the pier was almost complete, and it appeared that Portland, with her naturally deep port, might be the *Leviathan*'s favored port of call.

The commercial class of New York City sniffed at the idea that the owners of the *Great Eastern* might entertain the thought of going to any port other than their own. The *New York Times* dismissed both Virginia and Maine as provincial backwaters and asserted, "The ship must seek a port that can furnish business for her—business sufficient to pay her expenses, and leave a reasonable profit for her owners. Looking at the matter in this light, it must be allowed that New York, as the commercial metropolis of America, is the only proper destination of the Great Eastern."

At the end of October 1858, a new corporation, the Great Ship Company Limited, was formed by these two directors. The new company prepared a prospectus for potential investors that rhapsodized about the profits the ship could earn from the transatlantic trade. Hardly mentioned in the brochure was the gold in Australia, the reason the ship had been built. Instead, potential investors were assured that gold could be more quickly earned by dominating the trade between England and her former colonies across the Atlantic.

The Great Ship Company Limited was authorized to raise a total of £330,000 from the public. For a mere £1 investment, anyone could buy a share and become a part owner of the *Great Eastern.* The stock was snapped up by persons of every description and class, from peers to shopkeepers to butlers. Ultimately, the new company had a total of 2,261 investors, a fantastic number in the days when publicly traded companies were still in their infancy. Hard negotiations took place between the old company and the new, but terms were finally agreed upon. The *Great Eastern* would be purchased for £160,000, leaving the new company £140,000 to complete fitting out the hull and another £30,000 in working capital.

It seemed a bargain enough for a hull with engines which had already cost its previous owners £640,000.

28

Mobile, Alabama
February 1859

"Kit, start pulling."

Kit put down a chisel he had been sharpening and walked over to a knotted rope hanging from the ceiling of the shop. The rope was connected to a large leather bellows used to heat the coals in the forge. Seven months earlier, when Kit had first started working for Behncke, the resistance of the thick leather had prevented him from pulling the rope continuously for more than a quarter hour. Now, he could pull the rope for an hour without stopping. Although Kit hadn't noticed, his appearance had changed during his apprenticeship at the shop. He hadn't grown any taller, but ten hours a day of heavy work, from pulling the bellows rope to swinging fourteen-pound hammers, combined with an abundance of food supplied by Becky, had given the young slave a powerful physique. His arms rippled with muscles, and his chest and shoulders had bulged so much that Becky had needed to make his shirts larger.

A good cook always enjoyed appreciative diners, and Becky, being a very good cook, could not have hoped for a more appreciative audience than her husband and Kit. Each day in the early afternoon, she arrived with a large basket of food. The two men would wash up, sit on opposite benches, and eat. Neither Behncke nor Kit was particularly talkative, and, other than the muffled sounds of appreciation and occasional nods to Becky acknowledging a particularly delicious morsel, their lunches were silent. Years earlier in the woods of Connecticut, Becky had seen in the distance a pack of wolves devouring an elk they had just killed. Watching her husband and Kit eat her carefully prepared lunches always reminded her of that scene.

Behncke continuously tutored Kit in the art of blacksmithing. He taught him what tools to use to hold a red-hot iron bar without getting burned, how to shape iron using different hammers and tongs, how to measure the amount of iron needed for a job, and other skills necessary to be an accomplished smith. One day early in Kit's apprenticeship, Behncke had to replace an iron fitting on a wagon's axle. Kit was amazed to see the smith easily raise the rear of the heavy wagon with a wood-and-iron lever from the shop. Afterward, during a break in their work, Behncke explained to Kit how levers worked, even drawing a diagram of a fulcrum and lever on the dirt floor of the shop. He also gave Kit time to experiment with the shop's lever. Kit had previously used pry bars on the plantation when removing tree stumps but was fascinated when he finally understood how levers and pry bars worked. Once, when the two men had just lifted a particularly large wagon, Behncke mentioned that an ancient Greek had said that with a long enough lever a man could raise the whole world. Behncke was serious when he made the statement, and Kit never forgot it.

Behncke, used to working alone, had learned how to maximize his strength when moving and lifting heavy iron objects. An intelligent man, he had experimented with various ways to strike a hammer on an anvil, ultimately learning how to use his arm in a whiplike fashion. Patiently, he showed Kit the techniques he had developed, techniques which Kit dutifully practiced.

Early one morning, a wagon pulled up to the shop, and two men shoved a heavy iron object, a part of a steamship's walking beam, onto the ground. The beam had been bent in an accident, and the ship's captain needed it fixed as quickly as possible. Behncke and Kit bent over to pick up the piece. Kit struggled to lift his end.

"Kit, put that down and listen to me."

"Yes, suh."

"Tell me, Kit. Which are stronger? Your legs or your arms?"

Before Kit could answer, Behncke put his hands around Kit's bicep and showed Kit the diameter. He then did the same with Kit's thigh, which caused the young slave to start, and showed him the thigh's much larger diameter.

"Which is bigger, Kit?"

"De leg, suh."

"Which is stronger?"

"De leg, suh."

"That's right, Kit. Never use your arms to lift if you can use your legs. Also, get the thing you're picking up as close as possible to your chest." Behncke then squatted down and grasped the beam nearly to his chest, his back bowed inward. With a grunt, he straightened his legs and lifted his end of the beam. It looked easy. Looking at Kit, he then squatted again and put it on the ground.

"Kit, now you lift your end the way I showed you."

Kit felt awkward at first, but finally, after three or four attempts, he lifted the piece—not as easily as Behncke had, but with control.

"Kit," Behncke said, "a blacksmith usually works alone, and he works with heavy things. He must learn to use his whole body as a lever. Your legs, your back, your arms, they're all parts of a lever. You're strong, but if you learn how to use your body properly, you'll be able to do many more things."

Kit loved Mobile. Behncke frequently sent him to the port to pick up and deliver ironwork needed for ships docked there. Initially, he was eyed with suspicion and his pass papers were closely examined, but shortly he became widely known as "the smith's boy." Even some white men would occasionally return his polite nods. Sometimes he took Behncke's wagon to the dock to pick up heavy pieces; other times he walked briskly to deliver an invoice or drop off small pieces of ironwork in a canvas bag. He loved the exotic smell of the port—the fishy, salty aroma of the Gulf mingled with the sulfurous smell of coal-burning steamships. He loved the bustle, the calls of the gulls, and the silent, tough-looking black stevedores with the wide-brimmed hats with whom he exchanged glances.

Becky was a pious woman and, like many Southern women, had concluded that she was duty bound to introduce Christianity to slaves in order to save their souls. Kit was an obvious target for salvation, and so she created a suitable set of clothes—a white cotton shirt and gray cotton pants—for Kit to wear to church on Sunday. Every Monday, Behncke would bring the outfit home to Becky to wash and iron so that it would be ready for the next Sunday. Each Sunday morning, Kit would wash himself in a corner of the closed shop with a bucket of rainwater and put on his Sunday outfit. He would then walk to a small Methodist church where he was escorted by a stern-looking white usher to the balcony with the rest of the slaves. Behncke and his wife attended the same church but, like other white parishioners, did not acknowledge their black acquaintances.

During the service, the minister would read a passage from the Bible. The passages, full of "thees" and "thous" and a lot of other words that Kit could not understand, were always mercifully short. Afterward, the minister would give his sermon based upon the passage. Because some of the white churchgoers were not well educated, the minister kept his sermons simple, avoiding difficult words and hard-to-grasp concepts.

From these sermons, Kit received his first real exposure to Christianity, and from what he could tell, it seemed to be a good religion. There was a lot of discussion about a reward in heaven for those who obeyed the Bible and punishment in hell for those who did not. Kit remembered these concepts from his mother. Jesus being nailed to a wooden cross and left to die sounded to Kit as bad as the punishment he had seen the runaway slave receive from a leather whip. Kit couldn't understand why Jesus had been put to death, but the fact that a white man had suffered so terribly made his words all the more powerful.

One Sunday, the minister began reading a passage from the Bible that seemed familiar to many of the slaves in the balcony. An old slave nudged Kit gently, and when Kit looked at him, the slave rolled his eyes.

The preacher intoned, "Slaves, be subject to your masters with all fear; not only to the good and gentle, but also to the froward. For this is thankworthy, if a man for conscience toward God endure grief, suffering wrongfully. For what glory is it, if, when ye be buffeted for your faults, ye shall take it patiently? But if, when ye do well, and suffer for it, ye take it patiently, this is acceptable with God"

During his sermon, the minister, while looking at the slaves in the loft, stated, "Slaves, Peter says that it is your duty, as commanded by Jesus, to do all your masters tell you to do. Peter also says that you must suffer all punishments given you by your masters with patience and acceptance, even if you think such punishments are wrong or unfair. If you do this, you will be obeying the Word of God. Your masters know what is right for you, and you must never question their orders. If you love and obey your masters and keep all of God's other laws, you may achieve eternal happiness in heaven."

After the service, Kit found himself walking back to the shop alongside the old slave who had nudged him. Kit was troubled by the sermon and wanted to talk about it. Based upon his companion's reaction in the balcony, he seemed a likely candidate for a discussion.

Kit began in a low voice, "I don' unnerstan' why Jesus say dat we's got to be happy when we gits whipped fo' no reason."

The old slave chuckled. "Boy, we gits the same preachin' ever' year, rain or shine. Yous massa always right; you's always wrong. Gits a whippin' for no good reason, and be happy 'bout it. Someday, whens you been whipped enuf an' yous don't grouch, den it's hev'en fo' you!"

Kit looked down, shaking his head. "I don' unnerstan' dis Jesus. He love us, but he okay if'en we gits whipped just outa meanness."

The older slave continued walking alongside Kit. "Boy, you gotta listen closely. Dat wasn't Jesus the preacha was readin'; dat was someone name Peter. Jesus, he don't like it when a slave gets whipped for no good reason. Dey jus' give us dat preachin' to make sure that we do what we's told'."

"So, we ain't goin' again' Jesus if we gets angry 'cause a slave gets whipped for no reason?"

"Not de way I see it."

That afternoon, Kit stayed around the smith's shop. After changing his clothes, he started sharpening tools and tidying up the place. Becky had brought a lot of food for Saturday lunch, so Kit had a wonderful Sunday dinner of fried chicken and biscuits. In the late afternoon, the shop having been placed in good order, Kit rested in his corner and mulled over the church service. He had seen slaves punished many times, some for serious reasons like running away or stealing food, and some for stupid or mean reasons like poor Tizzie. *What's there about us black folk*, Kit thought, *that makes white folks think that whippings and beatings are okay, even if we ain't done nothin' wrong?*

Kit sat quietly in the empty blacksmith shop, looking at his hands and forearms. *They're jus' like a white man's, only dark*, he thought. For several years Kit had reasoned that black folks had done something awful in the past, something for which God was punishing them. But the more he thought that late afternoon, the more he was satisfied with the old slave's comments. That wasn't Jesus who said that slaves should meekly accept unfair punishment; it was someone else, a white man named Peter. Jesus was against people doing mean things to each other. Kit resolved he wasn't going to listen to this Peter. He'd follow his mother's advice and pray to Jesus. Only to Jesus.

29

New York Times
March 11, 1859

A general meeting of the great Ship Company had been held in London. It was confidently predicted that the Great Eastern will be ready by August, and will certainly make her trial trip to Portland.

30

Mobile, Alabama
May 1859

MONTGOMERY Neill locked the door to his office on the second floor of the brick building located at 27 St. Michael's Street and walked a few blocks to his house at the corner of Dauphin and Lafayette Streets. The house was a pretty frame house, painted white, with a picket fence around the front yard. It was small but well maintained with abundant flowers in its small yard. The front door was unlatched, and Neill walked into an empty parlor.

"Hello, Kate. I'm home early," he announced.

Kate called out from a bedroom, "Darling, I'll be right there."

Neill sat down in the parlor, waiting for his wife. A woman entered the room, but when Neill looked up, he shook his head slightly. The woman looked very much like Kate but was younger and, considering Kate's condition, considerably more slender.

"Hello, Montgomery. Kate is bathing Willie."

"Mary! Mary, we weren't expecting you for a few more days. What a surprise!"

"I got tired of waiting to see my nephew," Mary said, "so I came earlier than planned. Willie is, of course, the most amazing baby in the world. I'm very proud to be his auntie."

Neill laughed. He was thirty years old, tall, and elegant looking with large side whiskers. He had an English accent, not surprising in that he'd been nineteen when he immigrated to the United States from Great Britain. Although born and raised in Northern Ireland, Neill was most assuredly not Irish but the son of an English gentleman of good breeding and modest means.

Mary chirped on, "So I'm going to be an aunt all over again. I may be more excited than Kate. Well, not more excited exactly, but just as excited!"

He surveyed his twenty-one-year-old sister-in-law. "Mary, Kate tells me that you're being very choosy regarding suitors. You certainly have a right to be choosy; you must have a legion of them."

"Montgomery, don't start lecturing me about becoming a spinster.

I hear that from my mother all the time. Kate was lucky enough to find the one man for her, and I'm entitled to wait until I find my true love. I'll know him when I meet him."

Laughing, Neill said, "Mary, I can think of nothing more futile than lecturing a member of the Schultz family. On that point, I have personal knowledge."

Mary giggled softly, and as she did, Kate entered the room holding six-month-old Willie. It was still late afternoon, and the kitchen slave had just started working on dinner. To give Neill some privacy, the two women took Willie for a stroll in his new English perambulator while Neill washed up and changed his clothes. When the women returned, it was early evening.

After a pleasant dinner, the three adults settled down in the parlor. Neill, usually reserved to the point of being described as aloof or cold, warmed in the companionship of his young wife and her younger cousin. Normally, he worked long hours and after dinner spent much of the evening reading, his lips pursed, his brow furrowed in concentration. As near as Mary could tell, Neill's reading materials consisted of newspapers, commercial journals, and trade publications. She never saw him read anything for enjoyment or amusement. Tonight, however, there would be talk of family and the goings-on in New York City and the Hudson River valley.

Mary sensed that money was no difficulty in the Neill household, a change from Kate's earlier days when Uncle Dan had so much trouble. Each Monday, Neill gave Kate an envelope of cash, and from this she would pay all household bills, including all of Neill's personal expenses. The Neills operated an efficient household, even more so than the one Mary's parents operated.

Shortly after Mary's arrival, the Neill family reverted to its daily routine. Neill worked late hours, had short family discussions with Kate during dinner, played a bit with Willie, and then settled down in a large, ornate chair with newspapers and journals. He would read until about nine o'clock, when the family would retire. Neill rarely discussed business, but one night, while he was reading one of his journals, Mary heard him exclaim under his breath, "Idiots!" She looked up at him and saw a scowl across his face. Kate was in the bedroom with Willie, and Mary ventured to talk.

"Montgomery, is something wrong?"

Neill looked at Mary, surprised that he had been overheard. "I'm sorry. I didn't mean to be so loud."

"What is it that made you so angry?" Mary asked. Kate entered the room at that moment and sat down facing the two.

"Nothing, really. Nothing that I haven't read before. It's just that people are refusing to face reality, and when that happens, there are dire consequences."

"You're being very mysterious, Montgomery," Kate said. "Who is refusing to face reality?"

"The fire-eaters. I'm sorry to have bothered the two of you. It's really nothing." Neill tried to end the conversation by turning the page of the journal and concentrating on a new article.

"Montgomery, please don't be so secretive. If you're concerned about something, we'd like to know what it is," Kate implored gently. "If it might affect our family, we'd like to know."

Neill was clearly uncomfortable at discussing politics with two women, but he was genuinely disturbed and had no one else immediately available to talk with.

"It was yet another blowhard holding forth about King Cotton. The world will collapse if Southern cotton is cut off, England and France will rush to help the South if the Northern states try to control the flow of cotton, and so forth. It is complete idiocy!"

"I don't understand," Kate responded. "Everyone says that England cannot survive without our cotton, that she'll come to the support of the South if the North continues to threaten us. All the women say as much."

Neill shook his head gently. "Kate, just because a lot of women repeat something doesn't make it so. England will not rush to the aid of the South in order to get cotton. If the fire-eaters in Charleston are convinced that Her Majesty's government will immediately plunge into our disputes, the South is heading for a disaster. England may intervene to save the mill owners in Lancashire, but in her own good time."

"How do you know that?" Kate was actively pursuing this conversation, while Mary sat quietly watching.

"My brother and I are cotton brokers. We buy cotton contracts in the South and sell them in Britain. William stays in England and writes me at least weekly as to the developments in Lancashire and elsewhere. I know more about the sale of our cotton to England than any of our long-winded politicians." Neill sat quietly a while and then asked, "Ladies, do you know what our entire economy, our prosperity, rests upon?"

Mary answered tentatively, "Cotton?"

Neill shook his head. "No, Mary. It rests upon one of the most formidable forces in the world." He paused for effect. "Women's fashion."

Kate responded tartly, "Montgomery, you're playing a joke on us. We're adults!"

"Darling, I'm completely serious. Every year the amount of cotton being shipped to England increases greatly. England and Europe are not growing in population at a rate equal to the increase in the cotton they're using. Why are we shipping so much?"

The two women looked at each other in silence.

Neill continued, "One of my silk shirts was ripped when I was last in London. I couldn't find a tailor but was directed to a seamstress who had a small shop on Oxford Street. She was a very bright woman, and we started talking about clothing. You know what I learned? She said that twenty years ago a woman's dress, including undergarments, took seven yards of cotton."

Kate laughed, no longer put out at her husband. "I have trouble imagining you discussing women's undergarments with me, much less with a complete stranger."

Neill reddened in embarrassment. "She was quite an elderly lady, and I was trying to find out something. This was important for our business."

Kate and Mary were both stifling giggles at Neill's embarrassment.

"You ask me to treat you seriously, and then you laugh when I try to explain something," Neill said with exasperation. "I'm done with my discussion."

Kate smiled. "Go ahead, Montgomery. We'll be perfectly serious."

Kate struck a mock serious face and leaned forward, putting her chin on her fists. Mary did the same, and both sat looking at each other and then staring grimly at the poor man. Finally, he started to laugh at their ridiculous faces. "All right, if you both behave, I'll finish. However, this is a most serious matter and one that you should be aware of."

The two women stopped their comedy and sat quietly waiting for Neill to begin.

"Anyway, this elderly seamstress said that a woman's dress and undergarments now take a hundred yards of cotton. A hundred yards! Everything our economy is built upon—our fields of cotton, our slaves, our railroads, our ports, everything—depends upon women wearing dresses made from these great mountains of cotton."

Mary became a bit defensive. "Montgomery, surely men must use more cotton as well."

"I thought about that," Neill said, "and later asked my own tailor the same question. He said there has been no change. Each of us men may have a couple more shirts than we used to own, but this accounts for only a very small increase."

"But what is your point? Why do you call Southern leaders 'idiots'?"

"Because they think England is itching to go to war to save King Cotton. They blow long and hard that Great Britain cannot survive without our precious cotton and that this desperate need is the ace up the South's sleeve. My God, they talk like the English eat cotton and will starve in a matter of days without it. Ladies, I know the English because I am English. An Englishman will fight and die for many reasons. He'll do so for the queen, for honor, for wealth, for revenge even. However, I've never met an Englishman who was willing to plunge into battle for women's fashion!"

After an awkward period of silence, it appeared that the conversation was over for the evening. Mary stated that she was tired and was retiring early. She kissed Kate good night and patted Neill's hand. Before she undressed for bed, she opened a large mahogany wardrobe and looked at a dress she had carefully hung inside. It was made of layer after layer of cream-colored cotton, with a thick cotton bustle. It was a beautiful and expensive dress, one that she was proud of. Everything she had heard that night was strange and uncomfortable, however, and Mary did not know what to think of her dress. She was still mulling over Montgomery's comments when she fell asleep.

31

Fishkill Landing, New York
June 17, 1859

As usual, Schultz had taken the Friday afternoon train from New York City to Fishkill Landing. If the weather held up, he might go fishing with Alex on the banks of Fish Creek. However, when he arrived at Fishkill Landing, Schultz was greeted by his ashen-faced son. Something was clearly wrong.

"Alex, what's wrong? Is Mama all right?"

"Mama got a telegram from Mary yesterday. She's been crying ever since."

"What is it? Is Mary all right?"

Alex swallowed and then said, "Kate died of a fever."

Schultz was stunned. His beautiful, lively niece was dead. He looked at his son. "Are you sure?" he demanded. Alex looked down silently. Of course he was sure. It was in Mary's telegram. Schultz couldn't say anything but stood there tugging his beard, tears welling up in his eyes. Finally, he asked, "What's Mary going to do?"

"She's going to stay there with Willie and the baby. Aunt Mary is going to Mobile to be with her."

There was nothing further to say. Alex picked up his father's valise and put it in the carriage. Schultz followed slowly, awash in memories of Kate and his late brother. He sat silently on the driver's seat next to Alex as the carriage wended its way to their home.

32

Mobile, Alabama
July 1859

EVERY night Kit was lonely. Somewhere he had a mother and a baby sister, but he didn't know where they were or how to reach them. After Danny asked Judge Crane to help, the judge had written several letters, but each time the response had been the same—no one knew Emmie, or too much time had passed to try to trace her. After all, Kit had been sold well over a decade ago. The judge had learned that Kit had been owned by a widow by the name of Simmons and that the auction house the widow had used was in Clarke County. Beyond that, the judge couldn't find any further information.

When Kit had told Behncke about his mother, the smith had promised that he would ask any slave dealers he came across if they had information. However, Behncke had warned Kit not to keep his hopes up. Slaves moved around a lot as owners died or moved, and a lot of time had passed. Behncke kept his promise, and whenever a slave dealer came by to have a horse shod or wagon repaired, he would ask the man if he knew a slave named Emmie who used to be owned by a woman in Clarke County. The answers were always in the negative—that is, until one afternoon when a wagon driven by an old, tired-looking white man pulled up outside Behncke's shop. When Behncke went outside, he saw that the wagon had rings bolted to its side.

He greeted the driver. "Afternoon. Can I help you?"

The driver was dirty and grim faced. He drew a large cotton bandana from his pants pocket and wiped off his forehead. "My horse threw a shoe yesterday."

Behncke confirmed that only one shoe was missing. "I'm busy, but I'll have my boy do it. Kit, come help this man. His horse needs a shoe."

Kit shortly appeared with the tools needed to shoe a horse. He started filing the hoof while Behncke and the man talked.

"I see your wagon. You a dealer?"

"Yep. I made a delivery to an auction house today and need to get back."

"Where you from?"

"Near Huntsville."

"Long trip."

"Yep. I don't think I'm going to do those long trips no more. Can't afford to have the wagon break down or horse go lame. I might end up havin' to spend the night with a bunch of ornery, hungry niggas in the middle of nowhere. I'm too old for that. I'm glad my horse was able to finish the trip wit'out a shoe."

"You work in Clarke County?"

"Yep. For years."

"I'm trying to locate a slave that might have been there."

This brought an odd look to the driver's face. "'Scribe him."

"Not him, her. Her name is Emmie, and she'd be maybe in her thirties or forties. She used to be owned by a woman named Simmons."

The white man nodded. "I know her. She's daid."

Kit had been listening to this conversation and now stood up, his tools clenched in his hands. He stared at the two white men.

"What happened?" Behncke asked.

"This Emmie hadda girl. The old lady Simmons sol' this girl a couple years ago, and a week or so later this Emmie drowns herself. I talk to one of the slave dealers there. He said she tied rocks in her dress and threw herself in a crick. That was quite a shock to old lady Simmons. Emmie was worth a lot of money. Revenge, I guess."

Behncke stood silently as this news sank in. In a low voice, he asked, "What about the girl?"

"I don't know where she went. She was small, real good looka, I was told. She may've gon' down to the fancy-girl auctions in N'Orleans. She'd fetch a bucket of money there." The driver then cocked his head and squinted at Behncke. "Why are you askin' about this Emmie?"

Behncke pointed to Kit. "Emmie is Kit's mother."

The driver was taken aback by this revelation. He took his hat off and looked directly at Kit. "Boy, I'm sorry. I din't know it was your mama I was talkin' about." Glaring at the blacksmith, the old man growled, "Why din't you tell me?"

Kit continued standing there, his face a mask of shock, his mouth open. He hardly felt Behncke's arm around his shoulders as the big smith took him back into the shop.

"Stay here, Kit, while I take care of the horse. I'll be right back."

Behncke quickly finished shoeing the horse, and the driver paid and rode off. When Behncke came back in the shop, he found Kit was sitting on a wooden bench, tears streaking grime down his face.

"Kit, I'm sorry. I remember when I found out that my mother had died. It was awful."

Kit put his face in his hands and started sobbing deeply. Behncke sat next to him for a long while in silence, trying unsuccessfully to think of something to say. Finally, he got up to get the shop ready for closing. Kit had stopped sobbing and was sitting on the floor in a corner of the shop, his legs pulled close to his chest and his head down, tears running down his face. Just before he left, Behncke patted Kit on the shoulder. The only response was a deep breath.

That evening during dinner, Behncke told his wife about how Kit had learned of his mother's death. Becky sat quietly as her husband tried to recreate the conversation. When he finished, she asked coldly, "What's a fancy-girl auction?"

"I think that's where the whorehouses in New Orleans buy up young girls. Someone told me that once."

Shaking her head and twisting a linen towel between her hands, Becky said, "So! In a single moment, Kit learned that his mother killed herself and his sister has been sold into debauchery."

Behncke shrugged, raising his hands palm upward in a sign of helplessness.

Becky said softly, "John! If God is just, we have much to fear."

With that, Becky went into her kitchen with tears streaming down her face and began to restoke the stove fire. She was going to make a sweet potato pie for Kit. Frustrated and furious, she couldn't figure out anything else to do.

Behncke went to work the following morning and found Kit still sitting in a corner of the shop. It was clear he hadn't slept. "Kit, you take it easy today. We only have a couple of jobs, and I'll get them done. By the way, the misses baked you a sweet potato pie. Even I don't get one of these very often."

Kit acknowledged with a somber nod Behncke's attempt to comfort him, and he looked briefly at the pie laid on the stool before him. He then curled back up in his corner. Thoughts had been racing through Kit's mind during the night. He sat there trying to retrieve from his memory every remembrance, every impression of his mother. He remembered her singing to him, but he couldn't remember the song. He remembered her bathing him and once playing tag with him early one morning. He had so much wanted to see her, to hear her, and now that was all gone. All night despair had come over him in waves, but by morning the pain of his despair had been replaced with anger.

His mother hadn't done anything wrong. He was sure his sister hadn't done anything wrong. Yet his mother had drowned herself, and his sister might be in a whorehouse. In his rage, he recalled a thousand injustices, humiliations, and brutalities he had seen. He remembered the horror of the slave whipped nearly to death for trying to escape, and he recalled poor Tizzie being stripped and switched for just being loud. He had seen slaves with ears cut off and eyes put out as punishment for running away or striking a white man, slave women with brand marks on their backs and breasts. He remembered the countless insults that he and every other slave had received. But mostly he remembered being powerless his entire life, cursed by his skin. During the night he'd remembered what Danny had told him about why Ben had run away even though it meant certain death. "He gots tired of bein' a slave," Danny had said. "He wanted to die a free man."

In addition to the pie, Elizabeth had packed an enormous basket of food for her husband and Kit, but mostly for Kit. She was shaken by what had happened to Kit and reached out to comfort him in the only way she knew how. When Behncke left the shop late that afternoon, the food—fried chicken, ham hocks, corn muffins, and much more—had hardly been touched by either of them.

"Kit, are you all right?" Behncke asked as he was getting ready to go home for the day.

Sitting in his corner, Kit nodded. Unable to think of anything else to do or say, Behncke took the food out of the basket and left it on a stool for Kit to eat later on. He then said good night to the young slave and closed the shop door. Shortly after Behncke left, Kit stood up, his face fixed in grim determination. He found an earthen jug, filled it with fresh water from the rain barrel, and corked it. He took the old canvas bag that he had used to carry iron parts back and forth to the pier and put all the food, including the pie, in it. It would shortly be dusk, and he needed to hurry.

When he got to the pier, he was recognized by a harbor master, who waved him on. Kit walked along the crowded pier, not sure what he was looking for. He saw small sailing schooners, fishing boats, and an occasional bark. Finally, he saw a well-worn coaster, a side-wheeler, tied by hawsers to the pier. A gangplank ran from the pier to the ship's deck. A man was sitting on the ship's stern, the back of his chair leaning against the ship's rail. His chin rested on his chest, and a hat covered part of his face. By his breathing, Kit judged the man to be asleep. He could see no one else on the ship. Kit looked up toward the ship's bridge and saw a large lifeboat behind it covered with a tarpaulin. Kit quickly walked up the gangplank and climbed the stairs to where the lifeboat was lashed to the upper deck. Peering around the smokestack, Kit could see the man on the stern still sleeping in the setting sun. No one else appeared to be on the ship. Kit untied a corner of the tarpaulin, put his water jug and bag full of food into the lifeboat, and climbed in. Once inside, he pulled on a cord to retighten the tarpaulin and tied it from the inside.

It was hot and dark in the lifeboat. Kit curled up in an area between two of the boat's seats. It was uncomfortable lying on the ribs of the boat, but finally Kit got into a position that was tolerable. As he lay in the stifling silence, Kit's mind raced. He had no idea where the ship was going. He couldn't imagine what was going to happen to him. All he knew was that, like Ben, he would not die a slave.

Part II

July 1859
to
December 1860

Canst thou draw out Leviathan with a fishhook? Or press down his tongue with a cord? Canst thou put a rope into his nose? Or pierce his jaw through with a hook? . . .

His strong scales are his pride, Shut up together as with a close seal. One is so near to another, That no air can come between them. They are joined one to another; They stick together, so that they cannot be sundered.

Out of his mouth go burning torches, And sparks of fire leap forth. Out of his nostrils a smoke goeth, As of a boiling pot and burning rushes. His breath kindleth coals, And a flame goeth forth from his mouth.

Job 41:1–2;15–17; 19-21 (ASV)

33

Demopolis, Alabama
July 1859

"JUDGE, I've been expecting you," Wyman Wilcox said as he stood on the wooden porch of his store. Judge Crane walked up the stairs and reluctantly shook the hand that Wilcox had dramatically thrust out. Wilcox was a small, slender man in his late forties with a beard stained with tobacco juice, and clothes that had not been washed recently, if ever. While the judge didn't place Wilcox in the category of vermin, the classification was close.

"I gather you learned about the telegraph message," the judge stated. Wilcox nodded and opened the door beneath the sign that announced Wilcox's name and trade—"Slave Dealer." "Come on in, Judge, and let's figger out a course of action." Wilcox went behind a counter, pulled out some documents, came around to the front of the counter, and laid them out in front of Judge Crane.

"First, Judge, we'll need a number of signed pow'r of attorneys," Wilcox said. "After you sign them, I'll take them to the courthouse and get Myron to put the seal on 'em. The judges up North are gettin' very picky about turnin' over runaways. So we gotta have everythin' done by the book."

The judge nodded as he quietly read the document. "All right," the judge said when he'd finished reading and signing the documents. "Now what?"

"Well, I need a good description, you know—how tall, how dark, scars, brandings, anythin' like that. Then we need a reward."

"All right," the judge said. "His name is Kit. He's about nineteen years old. He's short, maybe five feet, five inches tall, very dark, coal black almost. He was thin but strong, but I understand from letters from Mobile that he's gained weight and become very strong."

"Scars, brandings, whip marks, anythin' like that?"

"No, not really. I only had to have him switched once, and he was never branded. He was always a good boy. That's why I'm so disappointed. I really trusted the boy, and this is how he repays me."

"You din't file his teeth or crop an ear or nothin'?"

The judge looked at Wilcox in disgust. "I'd rather sell a slave than disfigure him."

Wilcox shrugged as he kept writing. "Jest askin'. Have any skills?"

"Yes," said the judge. "He was in Mobile learning how to be a blacksmith. He ought to know the trade tolerably well by now."

Wilcox raised his eyebrows. "A smith? This boy's pretty valuable."

The judge nodded. "I've got great hopes for him. He's smart and a good worker. I could make some good money with him as a blacksmith." Wilcox kept writing as the judge talked.

"Anythin' else, Judge? Was he loud? Could he read?"

"He's very quiet," the judge said. "He didn't talk very much, never shouted. No, he couldn't read."

"Anythin' else?" Wilcox repeated. "Does he have a limp, missing any fingers, anythin' like that?"

The judge shook his head. "No, that's it."

"What else did the telegraph message say?" Wilcox asked.

"Not much. However, I picked up a letter from the smith at the post office on the way here. He gave me more information." The judge laid the letter on the counter and reread it silently. He then said, "Well, according to the smith, Kit learned that his mama had drowned herself, and when the smith came to the shop two days later, Kit was missing." He looked up at Wilcox. "I can understand the boy being upset. He even asked me to help find his mama, but I couldn't get any information. I wrote his previous owner, but she never wrote back."

Wilcox thought quietly for a couple of moments before he spoke. "My guess is he's gonna hang around with the free colored in Mobile, ya know, pass hisself off as free. If that's what he's doing, we should catch him in a month or so. What worries me is that's he's a smith. There's lots of crooked folks in Mobile who'd hire him and claim they thought he was a free nigger."

"Aren't they supposed to examine his papers to make sure that he's free?"

"Well, yeah, Judge, they are. But sometimes folks ain't so fussy."

"So what's next?"

Wilcox arranged the papers before him and then looked up at the judge. "I'll put a notice in the *Register* and get a couple dozen posters printed. Let's give it a month or so and see what happens. I suggest a small reward, maybe one hunner dollars, in case the boy is jest wanderin' 'round Mobile. I'll need fifty dollars now for my costs."

"All right. I'll write out an order for you on my bank," the judge said.

"That's fine, Judge. Your note's always good."

"What happens when someone catches him?"

Wilcox looked puzzled. "Well, ya gotta pay the reward."

"No, I mean, does the boy get punished?"

Wilcox gave a slight smile. "Well, Judge, it's up to you. He's your property. If he was my slave, I'd whip 'im good and hard. He'd 'member the pain for a long, long time. The boy's got to larn he don't run 'way. If you want, I can have Zeb whip him real good, throw some saltwater or vinegar on his back after he's done. I charge three dollars for a good whippin'."

The judge nodded silently. "I see. Well, let's wait until we get hold of the boy."

Wilcox smiled. "I agree, Judge. There'll be time enough for details."

After Judge Crane left, Wilcox went back to his slave pen. It was empty except for a large, fat man cleaning it.

"Zeb, come 'ere," Wilcox called out to the fat man. The man was surprisingly agile as he jogged over.

"Yeah?" he said.

"Zeb, when ya goin' to Mobile next?"

"'Bout four days."

"Okay," Wilcox said. "When you go, I want ya to go to the printers there to get some wanted posters printed and then hang them around the town. Judge Crane's got a runaway."

"Judge Crane! He din't pay me 'n' Tommy the hunner dollars for cotching that runaway Ben."

"Zeb, you now work for me, not Judge Crane. There's a one-hunner-dollar reward on this boy. Catch him and you make thirty dollars."

Zeb looked intently at Wilcox. "You pay the money, not Judge Crane?"

Wilcox nodded. "Yep."

"Then I'll do it. You ain't neva cheated me."

"That's right. I ain't neva cheated ya." With that, Wilcox gave Zeb a gentle poke in the shoulder, and the fat man returned to his work, getting the pens ready for the next shipment of slaves.

34

"The Monster Ship Great Eastern"
Banner of Liberty
Middletown, New York
August 31, 1859

The great event of the week has been the inauguration to the commercial service of the Great Eastern steamship by a grand party, dinner and ball, given on board by the directors and builders of the "great ship." As I was one of the "elect" on the happy occasion, I shall try and give you some idea of my impressions, though language framed by me will utterly fail to give you or your readers a clear conception of this marvelous work. . . .

It is only in connection with vast masses of human beings that the enormous magnitude of this ship can be seen. There were on the day of the festival—day before yesterday—some 2,500 persons on board. When nearly a thousand had gathered together for a dance on the after part of the deck it was not one-third covered, and there was plenty of room to move around and through the immense assembly. Over head was an awning literally covering about half an acre of space, and you may picture to yourself the large band of the Royal Artillery in their glittering uniforms, the gay and expansive dresses of the ladies, with several hundred moving figures in the enlivening dance, and tell me, if you can, if there ever was another such scene since man first became an architect, and emerged from caves, woody tents and mud huts. I have crossed the ocean many times in the largest steamers now running. I have visited all of Paxton's glass houses, stood on the highest minarets of Milan cathedral, crawled up to the tiny ball that overtops the proud cone of St. Peter's at Rome, scaled the lofty spire of Strasburg, and, I believe, seen the grandest monuments of man's architectural skill built in modern times; but no work on human hands that I have looked at comes up to this. I can conceive that money and skill and labor could build up these iron walls; but when I go down to the engine rooms and see the ponderous machinery that obeys the lightest touch, and make the whole mass like a living creature—

Walking the water like a thing of life,

my mind fails to comprehend the achievement. It looks either like a miracle or like the creation of an omnipotent power.

34

In the English Channel off Hastings
September 9, 1859

CAPTAIN Harrison stood by the helm of the *Great Eastern*, his eyes darting constantly across the vast deck. Two days earlier the great ship cast off her moorings on the Thames where she had lingered for nearly nine months and proceeded east toward the open sea. At first, she had been helped by four tugboats but by afternoon she was moving solely under her own power.

By evening of her first full day, she had reached Purfleet where she dropped anchor. The following morning she left Purfleet and arrived in the early afternoon at the Nore lightship, where she dropped anchor for the night.

William Harrison was not merely the *Great Eastern's* captain. He, along with Brunel and Scott Russell, was one of the three individuals who had supervised the design and construction of the giant ship. Nearly three years earlier, before construction of the ship began, Harrison had been selected by the directors of the Eastern Steam Navigation Company to be the ship's captain, winning the position in a competition with more than two hundred rivals. The appointment of a captain of a ship not yet built was unprecedented, but the directors believed that potential investors would find comfort in a man of Harrison's stature monitoring the ship's construction. Humorless and direct, Harrison had won his position with neither charm nor wit but with a well-earned reputation as a competent and disciplined sailor. He had gone to sea promptly upon turning thirteen and had remained a seafarer, finally serving as a captain on the Cunard line. No one was certain as to how many times Harrison had crossed the Atlantic Ocean, but most reckoned it was close to two hundred. As the *Great Eastern' s* captain, he'd worked with Scott Russell on the design of the great ship's masts and spars, advised Brunel on the design of the steering apparatus, participated in all her attempted launches, and, with a small crew, fished chains out of the Thames for use in future launch attempts. He had invested nearly his entire life savings in the great ship and believed fervently that she would be a success.

Harrison firmly insisted that this trip was not the ship's trial run but was being done merely to test her engines and to move her to a site where she could be finished. The trial run would occur later when Harrison had a full crew and the ship was fully fitted out. At present, the deck of the ship was cluttered with wood and iron pieces, and the banging and clanging of carpenters and ironworkers echoed throughout the ship both day and night. When the captain thought of the spotless decks of his former Cunard liners, he gave a shudder.

At the Nore there had been a dinner in the ship's main lounge that Harrison had been required to attend. However, immediately after the toasts he'd left to continue his inspection of the ship. He went below deck to where the stokers and firemen were resting in hammocks alongside the giant boilers. Harrison chatted briefly with them in complimentary terms, which pleased them greatly. Shortly thereafter, Harrison put his young daughter to bed in one of the few finished staterooms. Any questions about the captain's confidence in the safety of the *Great Eastern* were quickly dispelled by the presence of this blonde adolescent.

Later that evening Harrison met Scott Russell while walking the deck under moonlight.

"Captain, everything operating properly?"

"Mr. Russell, seafarers are superstitious, so I'll only say that so far everything seems to be functioning properly. I expect I'll not jinx myself if I go so far as to express my hope that this state of things continues."

Russell gave a slight smile. "I understand. She's a very complicated piece of machinery."

Harrison responded quietly, "Sometimes, I wonder that she may be a bit too complicated."

Brunel had wanted desperately to make this trip, to see his creation move under her own power. The day before the *Great Eastern* was to start this trip, Brunel had come aboard to conduct a final inspection. Harrison had been shocked to see the enfeebled condition of the man he had known for so long. Brunel, with the assistance of a photographer, shuffled to a position in front of one of the ship's five funnels and struck what he hoped was a heroic pose. Harrison was walking back to the helm when an officer ran up to him, yelling, "Captain, Mr. Brunel has fallen. He's lying on the deck!" Harrison ran to where a small crowd had gathered around Brunel. He kneeled to find out from the stricken engineer what had happened. The frightened man could not explain other than to say his leg had collapsed and he could not move it. Harrison had ordered a couple of young sailors to pick up Brunel and carry him back to shore, and soon the Flying Coffin, its owner inside, had headed swiftly to Brunel's home.

Brunel's absence from the trip was fine with Russell, the relationship between the two men having been badly bruised by money disputes. Captain Harrison, on the other hand, wished Brunel were there to see his "Great Babe," as Brunel called her, steaming under her own power. The diminutive engineer had been honest with all his dealings with the captain, and a mutual respect had developed between the two men.

When the *Great Eastern* left the Nore the next morning, the colossal ship, belching thick black smoke and red-hot cinders from her five smokestacks, continued to proceed grandly down the Thames Estuary to shouts and salutes from a flotilla of ships ranging from gigs to fair-sized excursion boats. Massive, roaring crowds gathered on both sides of the river, as church bells announced the coming of the great ship. As Harrison watched the exuberant crowds, he hoped that Brunel could recover well enough to attend the finished ship's maiden voyage and share in the adulation of his countrymen.

By late morning, the filthy black water of the river had become the blue water of the North Sea and then the English Channel. The ship's boilers were now taking in saltwater. It was, all in all, nearly a perfect day. Captain Harrison felt a bit more at ease. Everything had worked, if not perfectly, without serious mishap. A couple of times he had run into Russell on the deck, and they'd exchanged smiles, confirming that all was well. As the ship approached Hastings, Harrison checked his pocket watch to make a rough calculation of her rate of speed. Just as he was closing his watchcase, he felt rather than heard a gigantic explosion behind him. Knocked to his knees, he swiveled his head and saw the first funnel, a massive tube forty feet long, bouncing on the deck. There was a brief silence, followed by confusion and shouting. One man yelled, "We've hit a mine!" Another started scrambling onto one of the boats hanging from the davits.

Harrison almost immediately understood that there had been a steam explosion. What he later learned was that Brunel had designed a water jacket for the first funnel, the function of which was to use the hot exhaust fumes to preheat water going into the boilers. Russell had objected to the idea on the grounds of cost. However, Brunel had been getting his way back then, and the idea had been incorporated into the ship. Something had gone wrong with the jacket. Instead of being filled with water, it had been filled with pressurized steam and finally exploded.

Harrison got to his feet and began to size up the situation. He then remembered that the exploded funnel passed through the main lounge, the place where his daughter had last been seen. *Dear God!* Harrison immediately thought in a panic. *My daughter!*

The frantic man ran down a staircase that led to the main lounge. In the lounge the funnel had been encased on all four sides by mirrored panels. Shrapnel from the shattered mirrors and wood panels had been blasted across the vast open room. Steam was escaping into the lounge, and water was pouring down from the ruined funnel into the boilers below. The lounge appeared empty, but after screaming his daughter's name, Harrison found the terrified child unharmed behind a bulwark. He held her tightly, and together they then heard a horrible sound. It was the sound of men in the boiler room screaming in agony as they were scalded to death.

35

“The Accident”
Frank Leslie’s Illustrated Newspaper
New York City, New York
October 8, 1859

As we steamed grandly on, steamers from Weymouth and Teignmouth, thronged with people in holiday costume, were to be seen making for the great ship. Soon they began to pass under our stern. The crowds on board cheered lustily—nine times nine following three times three. The bands on board the steamers were playing the “National Anthem” and “Rule Britannia.” This is the ovation we expected, and which our ship, her eminent constructors, her admirable captain—who shall deny it?—deserve. But no responsive cheer comes on board the Great Eastern. Not one joyous voice is raised. Passengers and crew are gathered in moody groups about the enormous decks, conversing in low and cheerless tones. Some lean over the bulwarks or stand in the lower rigging, gazing, with sad eyes, at the glittering, shouting crowd below. The music floating upwards grates harshly on ears which within the last sixteen hours have heard very different and very melancholy sounds—the cries of human agony. The gay fluttering banners and pendants have a ghastly garishness in their sheen to us now. We have flags enough on board too. It would be better, perhaps, to hoist a black one half-mast high, to tell the unconscious holiday-makers that we have need of condolence rather than congratulation; that our joy is turned into sorrow; that once more the vanity of vanities in all human aspirations has been displayed; that Death has come down among us, and taken unto himself the “strong man at the furnace side, and those that weld iron from the coals of the brazier;” and that the Almighty, for his own wise and inscrutable purpose, has smitten this magnificent vessel with appalling disaster.

36

Times of London
September 17, 1859

The Death of Mr. Brunel, C.E.—We regret to announce the demise of Mr. Brunel, the eminent civil engineer, who died on Thursday night at his residence, Duke-street, Westminster. The lamented gentleman was brought home from the Great Eastern steamship at midday on the 5th inst, in a very alarming condition, having been seized with paralysis, induced, it was believed, by over mental anxiety. Mr. Brunel, in spite of the most skillful medical treatment, continued to sink, and at half-past 10 on Thursday night he expired at the comparatively early age of 54 years.

37

New York City, New York
October 1859

Six months had passed since Kit had been delivered by the captain of the coastal steamer to one of the eleven harbor masters of the port of New York. In Kit's case, the harbor master happened to be Captain Alexander H. Schultz of Fishkill Landing.

Schultz always considered the day Kit was delivered to him to be a lucky one. Schultz was not only a harbor master but also the owner of a fleet of tugboats ferrying ships and barges in and around New York's harbor. Tugboat duty was demanding and dangerous work, and sober and competent crewmen were scarce. Nevertheless, Schultz had never before thought of using a colored man, much less a fugitive slave, as a crewman. Instead, any fugitive turned over to him, and there had been a few, disappeared into the hands of "conductors" who guided the slave through a route that started near the Schultz house in Fishkill Landing, wound north along the Hudson River, and ended in Auburn, New York, near the home of Senator Seward. From Auburn, new conductors shuttled the slaves through a different route of the Underground Railroad to Canada, the promised land where the despised Fugitive Slave Act, the "Bloodhound Law," had no effect.

The idea to use Kit as a crewman had been planted in Schultz's mind during the conversation he had with the captain who turned Kit over to him.

"Captain Schultz! I've got a stowaway for you."

"Captain Munro, it's good to see you. You've got a stowaway? Where'd he get on?"

"He boarded in Mobile. My first mate put a drunk in charge of securing the ship in port. I'm lucky I didn't end up with half the darkies in Alabama stowing away."

"He's a slave?" Schultz said in a lower voice. "He cause any trouble?"

"Hell no! We had no passengers, just cotton, so I didn't shackle him. Once we got him cleaned up and gave him something to eat, he worked like a fool. I was short a stoker anyway, and the boy did the work of two. If he was free, I'd hire him on the spot."

"Where is he?"

"He's coming down now."

The two captains looked at the gangplank as the unshackled slave, followed by a white crewman, descended from the steamer. Kit presented himself before Schultz.

"What's your name, boy?"

"Kit, suh."

"Captain Munro says you're a runaway?"

"Yes, suh."

Schultz looked at the slave. He was small but powerfully built. The slave looked directly at Schultz but not defiantly.

"Captain Schultz, you ain't heard the half of it," Munro said. "We hit a squall around Hatteras. We were pretty beaten up, and one of the iron brackets that held the stack broke. I was afraid that the stack would come down and we'd have to limp into port on canvas. Well, I'll be damned if this slave ain't a blacksmith! I didn't believe it at first when he told me, but he got the ship's forge going, rigged a new bracket, and got it hot riveted back into place."

Schultz was incredulous. "He's a *blacksmith*?"

"Yep. I wouldn't believe it if I hadn't seen it myself. A good one. As I said, if only he were free."

Schultz stared at Kit. A strong, good worker who was also a blacksmith. How often had he come across one of those? He motioned Munro to approach him more closely so that they could talk in whispers.

"Captain, did you record his capture on your log?"

Munro smiled. "Well, now that you mention it, I just plain forgot to write it down on the log. Awfully busy, you know, running a ship shorthanded."

"Good. You did the honorable thing, Captain."

"That's why I'm turning him over to you, Schultz. Some of the other harbor masters turn these runaways over for reward. I hope they rot in hell."

"I suspect they will."

The conversation ended with Schultz patting Munro on the back and offering whatever services a harbor master could offer. Afterward, Schultz took Kit into a small building near the end of the wharf where he ran his various businesses. He sat behind a cluttered desk while Kit stood before him.

"Kit, you know you're in New York City?"

"Yes, suh."

"You know that even though slavery is illegal in New York, you're still a slave and can be returned to Mobile?"

"I don't know nuttin' about dat, suh."

"Well, that's the law. Did you commit any crimes in Alabama?"

"Oh, no, suh."

"Kit, I can arrange for you to travel to Canada, where you'll be a free man. If you get to Canada, you can't be sent back to Alabama."

"Dat's good! Suh."

"The trip to Canada is dangerous, and if you get caught by a slave catcher before you arrive there, you'll be sent back as a slave."

Kit nodded. He knew what happened to fugitive slaves who were caught. He also knew that he would never go back alive.

"I can offer something else. Kit, I'm the harbor master for this part of the port. No one can do anything in my part of the harbor without my approval. Do you understand?"

"I think so, suh."

"If you work as a crewman on one of my tugboats, you'll be safe from the slave catchers. The catchers know that if they come on my wharf, they're likely to … umm … Well, anyway, Kit, you needn't worry about them. If you become a crewman, I'd let you live on one of my tugboats. You'd have plenty to eat, warm clothes in the winter, and you'd earn five dollars a month. You couldn't come ashore, but as long as you're on one of my tugboats or on my wharf, you're safe. Anytime you wanted to leave to go to Canada, you could."

Kit nodded slowly to indicate that he mostly understood what was being offered.

"Kit, what do you think?"

"If'in I stayed hea', would I still be a slave, suh?"

"Legally, yes. But you wouldn't be my slave. You'd be my crewman, and I'd treat you like any other crewman."

Kit stood before Schultz, thinking. Captain Schultz looked like an important man, a man of authority. Certainly the captain of the coastal steamer had treated Schultz like he was very important.

"What if you' boats go ta 'Bama? Will dey catch me den?"

"Kit, my tugboats don't leave New York Harbor. You will be safe on my tugboats."

The captain of the coastal steamer had told Kit that if he behaved during the voyage and worked hard, he might not be sent back to Mobile. Kit had had trouble believing him, but now he was being offered freedom aboard a boat! He couldn't believe his luck. His mind was made up. "Suh, I stay wit you."

"Wonderful. The first thing is to stop calling me 'sir.' Call me 'Captain.' That's my title."

"Capt'n … Yas'suh."

"It'll take a little practice, Kit, but you'll get it."

"Yas'suh."

"Next, we've got to change your name. They'll be looking for a slave named Kit. Somebody wants you badly, and there'll be a big reward for your return. You're going to have to go by some other name." Kit stood there thinking, as did Schultz.

"Suh, der's lotsa slaves name a' Bill."

Schultz thought for a moment. "Very well, Kit. From now on you're 'Bill.' Don't tell anyone your true name."

"Yas'suh."

"Kit … Bill, that is, I'm Captain, remember? Not 'sir.'"

"Yas'suh, Capt'n."

Schultz chuckled. "We're getting there, Bill."

38

"The Deck of the Great Eastern"
Frank Leslie's Illustrated Newspaper
September 24, 1859

No words alone could give an idea of the sense of vastness which strikes upon the beholder on looking upon the deck of the Great Eastern. Some drawing is needed to show, by comparison with other objects, the immense expanse which greets the eye, and for this reason we have, in this week's issue, engraved a sketch, taken from the port paddle-box, and looking aft on the upper deck.

39

Fishkill Landing, New York
December 2, 1859

MARGARET Schultz was planning dinner when she first heard the church bell. She pulled a heavy wool shawl over her shoulders and went outside onto the front porch. The wooden floor of the porch was covered with ice, and she walked carefully to where the porch joined the outside staircase. She could hear clearly the bell of a nearby church tolling, and then, in the distance, she heard another church bell start to ring. The day, now in its afternoon, was cold and still, and she could hear faintly even more bells tolling from the churches of Newburgh across the Hudson. She stood silently, the shawl wrapped closely around her shoulders, listening. Mary came outside and wrapped a cotton shawl around her. "Mother, listen to the bells! What happened?"

The Schultz house was on a rise above the town of Fishkill Landing. During the winter, when the trees were barren, a person could stand on its front porch and see glimpses of the Hudson River a mile down the rise. Margaret continued staring straight across the river toward Newburgh, where church bells were still ringing. "They've just hanged John Brown," she said quietly. Mary was going to say something, but she stopped and stood silently alongside her mother.

Leonard came around the side of the house from the stables and saw the two women standing on the veranda. When he looked up at them, Margaret said, "Come up here, Leonard." He climbed the steps and stood on the other side of Margaret, overlooking the same snow-covered valley. The bells kept tolling, each bell ringer trying to outdo the other in expressing grief and anger by pulling on a rope.

"It was a foolish raid," Margaret said softly. "I know he meant well. However, I don't believe anything good will come of it."

The two white women and the Negro servant stood silently looking across the river. Finally, Leonard spoke. "Mrs. Schultz, the folks up North keep praying for an end to slavery, keep preaching on how awful slavery is, but the slave owners, they just laugh. They're more powerful than ever. Ol' John Brown, I think he saw something most folks don't want to see. He saw prayers and preaching wouldn't end slavery."

Margaret looked at Leonard with a surprised expression. She had never heard her quiet, dignified servant utter such thoughts. Leonard became aware of her reaction. He had revealed his innermost thoughts to her, a dangerous thing for a Negro servant to do, but he couldn't stop now.

"Mrs. Schultz, you and Captain are the two finest people I know. You've done more for the colored people than anyone else in the area. But I have to tell you, them slave owners keep getting more and more pushy. Ten years ago, I could go into New York City and I wasn't afraid of being kidnapped, dragged down to the South, and made a slave. Today, I can't go into the city without a white man with me to make sure I don't get grabbed. Five years ago, I was a citizen, born a free man. Good gracious, Mrs. Schultz, my great-grandpa and his mule pulled a cannon around for General Wayne against the redcoats. You know that—I told you once. But today, I got no rights a white man is bound to respect. What I hear from the other colored folk in Baxtertown, the ones who just come up from the South, is that there are more whippings and burnings, that the suffering down there is just awful. Maybe, Mrs. Schultz, maybe it's time for the slaves to take things in their own hands. That's what Captain Brown was trying to do. Jest give the slaves guns and knives and let them fight their way to freedom."

"What about the Lowbers, Leonard?" Mary asked sharply. "Should they be killed by their slaves?"

Leonard was caught short by the question. "I don't want nobody killed, Miz Mary. The Lowbers, they're fine people. I don't want no harm to come to them."

The three stood quietly on the porch as the bells continued to toll. Finally, Leonard said softly, "I don't want no one hurt. I don't think John Brown looked to hurt no one. Maybe with the guns and knives, the slaves can say, 'We's leaving, and don't try to stop us.' No one's got to get hurt."

Margaret continued looking straight across the river at Newburgh. "Leonard, two innocent men were killed by John Brown's raiders. Whenever you put guns and knives into the hands of desperate men, people die. I can't think that violence is going to solve anything. I'll keep praying that the Lowbers and the other Southerners realize the sinfulness of slavery."

Realizing he may have said too much, Leonard answered apologetically, "Mrs. Schultz, your prayers are pretty powerful. Maybe they'll do the trick."

Equally unconvinced about the power of her prayers, Margaret said, "None of us knows what to do. I hope, I pray, God will show us the way." With that, Margaret went back into the warmth of the house with Mary following, and Leonard went into the stables to finish his chores.

40

The Portent

Hanging from the beam,
    Slowly swaying (such the law),
Gaunt the shadow on the green,
Shenandoah!
The cut is on the crown
    (Lo, John Brown),
And the stabs shall heal no more.

Hidden in the cap
    Is the anguish none can draw;
So your future veils its face,
Shenandoah!
But the streaming beard is shown
    (Weird John Brown),
The meteor of the war.

—Herman Melville

41

Auburn, New York
January 1860

THE last of the visitors had just left, and Frances was already upstairs in bed. Seward sat smoking a cigar in his parlor, where his son, Fred, sat watching him.

"Fred, you have to admit, I made quite an entrance back to the United States. The crowds, the cannons, the parades. I don't think there's ever been a grander welcome than the one I received. Well, maybe when Lafayette returned to New York. That was also a glorious entrance." Seward puffed his cigar in contentment.

"I wasn't there for either event, Father. But, from the comments of our visitors, it sounds like a very impressive entrance."

Seward turned to look at his son. "You don't sound very impressed. Your father is going to be the next president of the United States."

"That's what everyone around here says," Fred responded.

Seward continued looking at his son. "What is it? Are you upset about something?"

Fred sat quietly. "Father, you've been out of the United States for nine months. Things have been happening here. I'm not sure you understand all that has happened."

Seward nodded his head slowly. "I read the New York newspapers when I was in England and France. True, they're always two weeks late, but I still understand what's been happening." Fred sat silently, so Seward continued, "Fred, what is it that you think I don't understand?"

Fred stood up and approached the coal fire in the iron firebox. "John Brown's raid. I don't think you understand."

Seward laughed. "I'm well aware of what happened. While I was in Paris, I read the *Herald*'s article stating that Louis Napoleon should arrest me and return me to the United States to stand trial as a traitor. I even asked the emperor if he would do such a thing. He and the empress just laughed."

"Listen to me, please! The South is terrified. Brown was trying to start a slave revolt. He had a warehouse full of rifles, dozens of pikes with bowie knives fixed at one end, and many other weapons. He made it perfectly clear that he wanted a revolt much larger and bloodier than anything we're ever seen in the United States, larger than Nat Turner, even than the revolt in Haiti. He didn't want slaves to just escape. He wanted them to kill their owners!"

Seward listened carefully to his son. "Go on," he said quietly.

"The Northern papers have been ridiculing the South. Brown and a handful of untrained men held a federal armory hostage for hours. The papers are calling the Southerners cowards and saying that they're quaking in their boots. One article said that they were so frightened that they ought to be wearing diapers." Fred sat down close to Seward. "It's known throughout the South that church bells rang throughout the North when Brown was hanged. Southern men were frightened and humiliated by the raid, and when they heard about the church bells, that fear and humiliation turned to rage. Much of that rage is directed at you, Father. More than you know."

"I think you're exaggerating, Fred. I was out of the country when Brown raided Harper's Ferry."

"I'm not exaggerating. Are you aware that Jefferson Davis gave a speech about you in the Senate about two weeks ago?"

"Actually, I'm not. I left England before news of that speech would have arrived."

"I have a copy of the speech here." Fred took a pamphlet off the mantel and began reading it by the light of an oil lamp. "Senator Davis quotes a speech you gave in which you said that free labor has driven slavery back in California and Kansas. He then quotes you as saying, 'It will invade you soon in Delaware, Maryland, Virginia, Missouri, and Texas.'"

"I remember that speech," Seward said. "I gave it in Albany. I was talking about the economic battle between free and slave labor."

Fred continued reading. "Here's what Senator Davis said. 'We *have* been invaded, and that invasion, and the facts connected with it, show Mr. Seward to be a traitor, and deserving of the gallows.'" Fred looked up at his father. "He quotes your language about the invasion and then says, 'Has it not already been done? Has it not invaded us with pike, with spear, with rifles yes, with Sharp's rifles? Have not your murderers already come within the limits of our borders, as announced by the traitor, Seward, that it would be done in a short time?'"

Seward looked at his son incredulously. "Jefferson Davis said that?

He's one of my friends! When Varina gave birth during a snowstorm, I had my carriage driver locate her nurse and bring her to their house. Frances and I have been their guests for dinner." Seward said softly, "How could he have said that?"

"You've been out of the country for months! The South is roiling with fear of slave revolts. Newspapers report that in Texas they're torturing slaves to get them to confess to conspiracies, and when they confess, they burn them alive! Every time a barn catches fire in the South, they immediately suspect a slave revolt. John Brown has taken every nightmare of the slave states and made it real." Fred sat down close to his father and continued, "All your rivals immediately condemned Brown and called for his hanging. Chase, Stanton, even Lincoln, all the contenders for the Republican nomination—all demanded his hanging. You were silent because you weren't here, and your silence has been used against you. Ruffin and the other fanatics in Charleston have placed the blame for the raid squarely on you, and you couldn't defend yourself. Now, Senator Davis apparently believes you were part of John Brown's conspiracy."

"Dear God," Seward said quietly. "Fred, you know I had nothing to do with the raid."

"Of course I do, but I'm not the one who needs to be convinced. You must make clear that you deplore the raid, that you think Brown to be a madman, and that you're thankful he was hanged. Otherwise, the Republicans will be afraid to nominate you."

Both men sat quietly in the dimly lit room. "I've been surrounded by nothing but flattery since I arrived. I'm mortified to find that my own son is the only one who can tell me the truth. I'll start preparing a speech tomorrow. I'll make it clear I had nothing to do with the raid." Seward suddenly felt old and weak. Part of the feeling was exhaustion, no doubt—he had just returned from a sea voyage from England and had been feted at New York and a dozen other places on his trip up to Albany. But much of the feeling of age came from his conversation with Fred, from the horrible realization that a person he considered a friend, not to say millions of his fellow citizens, considered him a traitor and wanted him dead.

After a long pause, Seward stood up silently and patted his son on the back. "I'm going to bed now, Fred. Good night."

"Good night, Father." Fred sat alone in the room, staring at the glowing embers.

42

New York City, New York
January 1860

MANY of Schultz's crewmen were Irish, and he knew that there'd be trouble if he put a colored crewman on one of their boats. After some thought, Schultz put Kit on the *Ella,* a small, four-man tugboat. Her captain was an old, eight-fingered Dutchman named VanDer Hooven who had worked for Schultz for many years and had long shared his abolitionist beliefs. The other crewmen were two young German brothers, Felix and Matthias Kiel. The brothers had recently arrived in the United States determined to earn enough money to buy a farm. VanDer Hooven and the two Germans didn't know quite what to make of Kit, or Bill as they knew him, but as long as he did his fair share of work, he would be accepted as the most junior crew member.

Kit showed a remarkable aptitude for tugboat work. He was light, agile, and capable of jumping from a tugboat to a barge and back again, a dangerous but necessary duty. He was strong and could haul rope as well as any man. He lived night and day aboard the tugboat, sleeping in a berth in the bow of the boat most nights but sleeping on the deck when summer temperatures made the berth uncomfortably hot.

Schultz quietly let it be known among his tugboat captains that he had hired a free black named Bill and that they should watch out for any trouble that might arise from slave catchers or malicious tugmen. Early on, Schultz introduced Kit to Boris, the wharf's fierce-looking watchman. Boris was broad-shouldered and of medium height. His black hair and beard were long and matted, and what little skin that could be seen beneath the hair was scarred by smallpox. He always wore a heavily patched red-and-white-checked shirt and equally shabby gray wool pants held up by a wide leather belt. Tucked into the belt was an enormous, unsheathed, single-edged timber ax with a handle that nearly touched the ground. Boris was mute and couldn't read or write. He had come to the wharf a few years earlier, obviously hungry and looking for work. Schultz had needed a night watchman, and the two men, through the use of pantomime, had settled into an employment agreement. Schultz paid the man five dollars a month, the same amount paid to a young seaman, and the bearded man dutifully terrified strangers who approached any of Schultz's wharfs. No one knew the man's true name, but his adroit handling of the ax led Schultz to believe the man was a Russian, and so he was simply called Boris, a name that the man appeared to accept.

"Boris, I want you to meet Bill. He's going to work for me."

Boris stared at Kit through deep-set, watery eyes and then turned back and looked at Schultz. *Hmmm,* Schultz thought. *He is so used to scaring off Africans that he doesn't understand that Kit's going to work for me.* Schultz put his arm around Kit's shoulders and smiled. He then pointed to Kit and made an "okay" sign with his hand. Boris turned back to Kit, stared at him a few more seconds, and then nodded his head at Schultz. He understood.

Kit, who had been mightily impressed by Boris's ax, wasn't as confident of the watchman's comprehension as Schultz. "Capt'n, you sure he unnerstan'?"

Schultz nodded. "He understands. At night you'll be under Boris's protection. I don't think you'll have much to fear from slave chasers or criminals. Boris is very effective."

The *Ella* did a variety of jobs during summers. At high tide, the tug could usually be found towing sailing vessels, mostly coastal schooners and barks, to moorings in Schultz's wharfs. At low tide, when sailing vessels large enough to need towing stayed away from the bar, the little side-wheeler traveled up and down the Hudson pulling barges filled with lumber, stone, and brick to construction yards surrounding the port. One job Kit found fascinating was a trip up the Hudson to a giant icehouse near Catskill to pick up and tow a barge loaded with large blocks of ice. Kit had never seen chunks of ice before, and so Felix chipped off a piece and put it in a pot on the deck to show Kit that ice was just frozen water.

Initially, the language difficulties aboard the *Ella* were considerable. Captain VanDer Hooven spoke English well enough but with a thick Dutch accent. Kit had only a limited vocabulary and spoke with a Southern slave dialect, and the two Germans had an even more limited though rapidly expanding vocabulary enunciated with heavy German accents. The captain taught the three crewmen a series of hand and arm gestures that were sufficient for most of the routine work on the tug. During the warm months, when things were slow and there was no barge work to be had, the crew would have the little tug hover around the bar, hoping for some small coaster to show up in need of a tow. On those slow days, the four men talked, and each began to decipher the others' spoken words.

Barges were always dangerous to tow. They had no rudder and no means of quickly stopping except by ramming into the tugboat pulling them. To allow the tugboat to go around bends, barges were fixed with two towropes connected to stanchions on each side of the tugboat's stern. When the tugboat turned, the crewmen had to quickly shorten or lengthen these ropes, as the case might be, to allow the barge to turn with the tugboat without ramming it or drifting too far away. To do this, the crewmen had to quickly wrap or unwrap the towropes, a strenuous and dangerous job. Sometimes it required a crewman to leap from the tug to the barge in order to shorten the rope on the barge's stanchion. Kit and Matthias each were responsible for a stern stanchion, while Felix, the older brother, worked the boiler and steam engine. The captain controlled the helm and gave commands.

The winter of 1859–60 was brutal, with freezing rain that seemed endless. On a windy January day, during low tide, the *Ella* was traveling down the Hudson to New York towing a large barge loaded with cut brownstone. Shortly after the tugboat entered the harbor, the water became choppy as the wind picked up. The deck was covered with ice, and Matthias and Kit slipped and slid in their heavy leather shoes as they shortened and lengthened their towropes. A large oceangoing tugboat belonging to one of Schultz's competitors passed at full speed, suspiciously close to the *Ella*, and the wake from the ship hit the side of the tugboat full on, causing both it and the barge to rock. Matthias slipped on the deck and fell on his knees against the low wooden railing. As he struggled to stand again, the *Ella* was hit by another wave from the wake, and the young German lost his footing and tumbled over the railing. He clung desperately to one of the wooden stanchions of the railing as he bobbed in the frigid water. He tried to scream, but his terrified voice came out as a feeble croak. Kit had been following the movement of the barge closely and did not see what had happened to his crewmate.

VanDer Hooven saw what was happening. Matthias was being pulled under by the weight of his soaked woolen clothes and the friction of the water as the tug continued to move. He'd be lost in seconds.

The captain knew that the *Ella* couldn't stop without having Matthias crushed between the stern and the barge. Screaming against the wind, VanDer Hooven got Kit's attention. The young slave looked around trying to find his crewmate and then looked toward the pilothouse at the captain, who was frantically pointing to the stricken sailor. All Kit could see was Matthias's hands holding the stanchion. When he got to the railing, Kit leaned over the rail and grabbed the back of Matthias's jacket and pulled as hard as he could. The crewman didn't budge. He had become a petrified man weighted down with soaked clothing.

Kit motioned to the captain to turn the tugboat to the port side, to bring its stern closer to the barge. The captain understood and turned the *Ella* sharply. When the corner of the barge was only two feet or so from the tugboat's stern, Kit stepped over the tug's railing, put one foot on the barge, and straddled the two vessels. Both the boat and barge were rocking in the choppy water, and Kit knew he wouldn't be able to hold his balance long. He bent down to Matthias, who was almost neck high in water, and pried his crewmate's hands from the stanchion. As the captain watched, Kit then quickly squatted down and thrust his arms under Matthias's armpits. *What's he doing?* thought VanDer Hooven.

As VanDer Hooven watched, Kit screamed—a primal, guttural scream. His legs sprang straight, his back snapped into an arch, and Matthias came flying out of the water. For a moment the two young men, joined at the chest by Kit's embrace, were airborne. They crashed onto the deck, Matthias landing on top of Kit and sliding headfirst into the wall of the cabin. Kit landed squarely on the back of his head, which bounced on the deck, the force of the impact increased by the weight of the young German.

VanDer Hooven watched in stunned silence but then quickly recovered. He straightened out the course of the *Ella* to put some distance between her and the barge, looped a rope around one of the spokes of her wheel, and then came down from the pilothouse to yell down at Felix, who had been below deck tending the boiler. Hearing the captain's shout, Felix flew up the stairs to the deck. VanDer Hooven pointed to the stern, and Felix walked there as quickly as the slippery deck would allow. He found his brother and Kit lying on the deck, both motionless. His first thought was that there had been a fight, and he quickly went down on his knees to examine his brother. He was surprised to find that his brother's clothes were soaking wet. Matthias, shaking with cold, had started to slowly move his legs. Felix looked up at the captain in puzzlement. Calling down from the pilothouse, VanDer Hooven yelled, "He fell over der vater! Bill threw him out!"

Felix dragged his semiconscious brother across the deck and down the narrow stairs into the cramped space of the berth. He set him on the floor near the bunks and then went back on deck and did the same with Kit, who was still motionless. Felix moved the oil light into the berth and began working on the two moaning bodies. He stripped his brother, a laborious task with all the layers of wet, frigid clothes, and finally put him in one of the tug's three bunks. He retrieved a heavy wool blanket from the boat's locker and spread it over Matthias, who was shaking uncontrollably. After removing Kit's wet jacket, Felix found a canvas tarpaulin near the ship's locker to cover him. When both men were bunked, Felix loaded the berth's small iron stove with kindling, which he lit with a match. He worked at the fire until the stove started to radiate heat.

VanDer Hooven had no choice but to stay at the wheel and continue the tow or risk being rammed by the heavy barge. After the passage of what seemed to be a very long time, Felix emerged and climbed the stairs to the pilothouse. He told the captain that both men were alive and that he wanted to go back down to take care of them. VanDer Hooven stared at the distant harbor to estimate how much time he'd have before he needed Felix on deck. It would be another three-quarters of an hour before they were close to Schultz's wharf, so he told Felix to tend to the men with the understanding that every few minutes he should come on deck to see how close they were to shore.

In the berth, Matthias was now awake. His teeth chattering, he sat on the edge of his bunk in the tiny and crowded berth, nearly naked except for the wool blanket wrapped around him. Kit was still lying on his back, moaning and now slowly moving his legs but still unconscious. The two brothers talked in German, with Felix telling his brother what he thought had happened. Matthias, sobbing loudly, told his brother that he'd been certain he was going to drown, that he had been terrified, and then he'd seen Bill lean over him. He remembered being jerked hard and then didn't remember anything until Felix was taking his clothes off. After sitting with his brother and Kit in silence for a moment, Felix went up on the deck and saw that the *Ella* was closing in on the wharf.

He went up to the captain and told him that his brother was all right but that Bill was still unconscious.

As they approached the moorings, VanDer Hooven yelled out to the dockhands on the pier to get help, that he had injured men on board. A handful of men came walking gingerly down the frozen wharf and stood ready to haul in rope from the tug. A crewman on the wharf lassoed one of the barge's rear stanchions with a strong hawser fixed to a pier on the lengthy wharf. When the hawser was pulled taut, the tug and barge came to a stop. Quickly and efficiently, the little tug was untied from the barge and secured to its mooring.

When VanDer Hooven ordered a man to get Captain Schultz out to the tug, he was told that Schultz had earlier left for his rooms in the city. Nevertheless, a young wharf hand volunteered to get him, and within half an hour Schultz arrived in a hack. VanDer Hooven told Schultz what had happened, that Matthias had been up to his neck in water and that Bill had picked him up under his arms and thrown him on the deck. As Schultz looked incredulously at VanDer Hooven, the old Dutchman threw up his hands and said, "By Gott, dot's vhat happened!" Puzzled, Schultz went down to the tug's berth to check on the young crewmen.

Kit had started moving, and when Schultz felt the back of his head, the slave winced in pain. Schultz concluded that Kit had just been knocked out, a not particularly rare occurrence on the docks, and would recover in a few hours. He sent Felix to the brothers' lodging to get dry clothes for Matthias and then sat on the edge of Matthias's bunk, looking at Kit in the light of the lamp. When Felix returned with the clothes, Matthias dressed with difficulty in the cramped quarters. He appeared almost fully recovered, although his hair was still wet and his face was a sickly white. Schultz sent the young brothers to their lodgings and told them not to come the next day. Matthias, he said, should stay in bed for a day to recover, and Felix should watch over him. They'd both be paid for the day off. Schultz went on deck and told VanDer Hooven he should go home as well, saying that he'd close up the tug. Nodding solemnly, the old Dutchman left Schultz and Kit alone.

Back in the berth, Schultz noticed that Kit's eyes were open and were looking at him.

"Kit, you're going to be all right. You've a goose egg on the back of your head, but that'll go away in a couple of days. Can you tell me what happened?"

"Matty, he fall over de side, and I reach't in an' grabbed 'im."

"How did you pull him out? With those wet, heavy clothes, he had to weigh two hundred, maybe two hundred fifty pounds!"

Kit lay on his bunk trying to figure out how to explain what had happened. With effort, he swung his legs over the edge of the bunk and sat up. He shook his head to clear out the cobwebs and then said softly, "Capt'n, wif a leva, yous can lif' anyting, even the whole erf."

"What are you saying?"

"I make a leva, Capt'n."

Schultz sat in silence. *A* lever, *that's what Kit's talking about. He made his body a lever!*

"Where'd you learn how to do that?"

"The blacksmif, he done show me, suh."

"The one you used to work for in Mobile?"

"Yes, suh … Capt'n."

That Kit was powerful had been obvious on the day Schultz first saw him. But no one Schultz knew could have thrown a two-hundred-plus-pound man out of chest-deep water and into the air. Somehow, Kit had learned to use his body as some kind of lever or spring. Schultz sat in silence, thinking about this. Kit had closed his eyes.

"Kit, go to sleep. I'll stay a bit and then lock up."

"Yes, suh, Capt'n."

Schultz threw a few more pieces of coal in the small iron stove to keep the berth warm. In the glow of the oil lamp, Schultz sat on Matthias's bunk and looked at Kit, who was now lying still on his side, his back facing Schultz. When Schultz felt that Kit was asleep, he used a poker to put out the flame in the stove but left glowing embers. Just before putting out the lamp, however, Schultz took one more look at the young slave. "Amazing," he said softly and shook his head. He put out the lamp and climbed the narrow stairs to the deck in darkness. He closed the cabin door and carefully walked back in the frigid air to the end of the wharf, where the hack was still waiting, vapor pouring from the horse's nostrils. The sky had cleared, and Schultz could see the nearly full moon. As he left the wharf, he nodded to Boris, who was standing in the shadows, ax in hand. Boris nodded back.

Early the following morning Schultz picked up an iron pail full of hot oatmeal from his landlady, wrapped it in a towel for Kit, and took another hack to the wharf. Although the slave ate well, he spent most of the day in his bunk because he felt dizzy when he stood. By the next day, however, Kit felt well, save tenderness at the back of his head, and he dressed and worked around the tug. The two brothers showed up at their usual hour after their day off. Matthias was carrying a package wrapped in paper and string, and he motioned that Kit, or Bill as he knew him, should go down into the berth. Once there, Kit watched as Matthias opened the package on Kit's bunk. It contained three clay pipes identical to the one smoked by Captain VanDer Hooven and a foil package of tobacco. Matthias handed one of the pipes to Kit, who held it but had no idea as to what was happening. The brothers, seeing Kit's confusion, started to laugh and told him that the pipe was a gift. Kit had never received a gift before.

The old Dutch captain, flattered that his young crewmen wanted to imitate him, showed them how to smoke their pipes, an elaborate procedure that initially involved burnt tongues and singed fingers. However, a few months later, when the *Ella* hovered near Sandy Hook in the late afternoon waiting for some straggling schooner or bark to appear, a passerby would have been amused to see an old sea captain and three young boatmen, one of them black, sitting on the roof of the tug's deckhouse, each smoking a pipe in contemplative silence.

Every night, Kit placed his pipe carefully in a small sea chest in which he kept his clothes. It was, after all, the most valuable thing he had ever owned.

43

On board the *Great Eastern*, near the entrance of the Southampton Docks
January 22, 1860

It was nearly four o'clock. Captain Harrison snapped his watchcase shut and looked toward the docks. It had been a cold and breezy day, with the sky and the sea the color of lead. The ambient light, what little there was, was rapidly disappearing, and Harrison was anxious to leave. Tomorrow was Sunday, and he looked forward to spending the day with his family.

Progress on the fitting out of the *Great Eastern* had gone as well as could be expected, and Harrison was satisfied at the amount of work that had been completed during the week. As he continued to look toward the docks, he saw the ship's gig, a thirty-foot long sailboat, approaching. He smiled at the thought that he'd soon be in the snug little house he had rented for his family.

When the gig was tied to the *Great Eastern*, Harrison, along with the ship's surgeon, its purser, the purser's fourteen-year-old son, and six crewmen, boarded. As the passengers seated themselves in the open gig, they could feel the wind becoming stronger and the temperature dropping. When the gig was pushed off and its sail hoisted, all but one of the skeleton crew aboard the great ship quickly returned to the warmth of their quarters. In a few minutes, the one man who had remained on deck watched with horror as the wind blew the gig over.

44

"Capt. Harrison, of the 'Great Eastern,' Drowned," *York Herald* North Yorkshire, England January 28, 1860

The year which opened so gloomily for all connected with the Great Eastern, has already more than fulfilled the most sinister auguries of continued ill-fortune. Another most tragic incident has been added to the long list of catastrophes which seemed to have dogged the course of this ill-fated vessel from the very first day of her existence. The victims in this case, however, are not poor stokers. The lot of death in this instance has fallen, among others, on no less than Captain Harrison himself—the very type of an English sailor, of all that was frank and manly, of all that was skillful and brave.

45

Washington, DC
February 1860

"Colonel Mann, did you see the article about the *Great Eastern* in yesterday's *Times*?"

Dudley Mann, looking out the window of his office at the *Washington States and Union* newspaper, turned around and saw a young copywriter in his doorway holding a newspaper.

"No, Tom. I wasn't aware there was an article."

"I brought it to you as soon as I saw it," the young man responded.

Mann sighed. "How bad is it?"

"I didn't read it very closely," the copywriter lied. "I just saw the headline and thought you'd want to see it."

"I see. Thank you," Mann said flatly. "Just leave it on my desk."

In the eighteen months following the creation of the Atlantic Steam Ferry Company by the Virginia legislature, Mann had traveled throughout the South, giving stump speeches about his proposal and urging Southerners to invest in the company. However, nearly all his attempts to raise money had been thwarted by the incompetence of the directors of the Great Ship Company. Potential investors always agreed that Mann's idea of a giant ferry between England and the South was sound, but they needed proof that the *Great Eastern* would turn out to be everything that Mann promised she would. Through numerous newspaper articles, the capitalists in the Southern states had learned of the carnage being suffered by successive generations of English investors in the *Great Eastern*, and they were not anxious to walk down the same path. "No, Colonel Mann," they would all say, "when we see that she is real, when we see that she can sail to Chesapeake Bay, then come back to us, and we'll talk. Until then …"

Mann had eventually decided he had to do something to make a living, so in September 1859 he'd assumed the editorship of the *Washington States*, a pro-Democratic newspaper published in Washington, DC. As a close acquaintance of President Buchanan and many of his cabinet officers, Mann was privy to the information that the Buchanan administration wished to circulate. Thus, Mann eked out a living publishing articles lauding the efforts of the Buchanan administration and ripping into the "Black Republicans," the blackest of whom was Senator William H. Seward. Although the editor's position did not pay very well, Mann's ability to shovel printed invective on his enemies was nevertheless the source of considerable pleasure.

Despite his innate optimism, Mann was reaching the conclusion that the investors in England had already reached—that the greed of the directors of the Great Ship Company was exceeded only by their ineptitude. The directors had repeatedly and publicly promised that the *Great Eastern* would make her maiden voyage to America in 1859. They'd promised with such conviction that Portland Maine would be her *entrepôt* that the normally tightfisted New Englanders had built a giant and expensive pier that they'd christened the Great Eastern Pier. Newspaper articles in London, reprinted in America, had promised the ship would arrive in Portland in March 1859. Later, due to "circumstances," the maiden voyage had been rescheduled for September 1859. It was now January 1860, and the Portlandians were looking at the local promoters of the ship with deepening suspicion.

Mann had been promised by the directors that the *Great Eastern*'s maiden voyage would be to Chesapeake Bay in fulfillment of his long-pending dream. In September 1859, just after he had accepted the editorship of the *Washington States*, Mann had written an article for the *Richmond Enquirer* predicting that the *Great Eastern* would soon travel to Norfolk, Virginia, and that the "event would 'stir tide-water Virginia to its very depths.'" What Mann didn't know was that on almost the very day his article appeared, the *Great Eastern*, on a test run up the Thames to the Nore, suffered a massive explosion, scalding six men to death. An investigation disclosed that some nincompoop had failed to open a valve on a preheater for a smoke funnel and the funnel had exploded, spreading shrapnel throughout the lower deck. Six days later, Brunel was dead. It was widely accepted that the fifty-three-year-old engineer had been killed by his own monstrous creation.

The only kernel of good news among the abundant bad was that prior to the explosion the ship had performed well during her trial run. Giant crowds at Greenwich, Blackwall, Woolwich, and other points had lined the banks of the Thames during the ship's brief run to the Nore. At each stop, there had been bands and dignitaries and, had the *Great*

Eastern not been stopped by the devastating explosion, there would be considerably more optimism, even enthusiasm, for her. Of course, the explosion had done more than kill Brunel. It had also mortally wounded the already weak finances of the Great Ship Company.

Even prior to the trial run, work on the finishing of the ship had been halted repeatedly as the Board of Trade, the authority responsible for the safety of passenger steamers, demanded more modifications, more equipment, more boats, more everything, before she would be authorized to take her maiden voyage. To the Board of Trade, it seemed that the directors were more interested in the ship's mahogany paneling or formal china than in the safety of her passengers. The ugly specter of insolvency loomed yet again. All this was well known to Mann as he finally drew up his courage and began reading the newspaper left by the copywriter.

The Great Eastern.

Meeting of the Shareholders—A Stormy Session —Result of the Debate—

Correspondence of the New York Times.
London, Saturday, Jan. 14, 1860.

A most stormy and discreditable meeting of the shareholders of the Great Eastern took place on the 11th inst. at the London Tavern, famous for its noisy demonstrations. It was what you call in America an indignation meeting. The Chairman made his report and offered the resignation of the directors. Then came an amendment that a committee should be appointed to examine into and report upon the alleged misdeeds of the managing directors. This was finally referred to a ballot. The result of this will, I am told will be against the directors, and for their immediate resignation. The chief adverse factions are those of Magnus—a Jew merchant—and Campbell, the Chairman. Then there are sections of enraged shareholders. Among these a florid clergyman, with red hair, was most conspicuous. Ever and anon he

> popped up in the middle of the crowded meeting, like the hammer of a piano when the key is touched, and vociferated in the most amusing style. All kinds of accusations and terms of opprobrium were freely bandied about, but the *odium theologicum*, as usual, was the most bitter and violent. The fact is that Messrs. Campbell and Jackson, M.P., (a quondam trader on the Gold Coast of by no means brilliant antecedents,) had everything their own way, until the bursting of the heater or funnel casement on the occasion of the trial trip ...
>
> Mr. Jackson, who had called Mr. Magnus a liar at a previous meeting, having split with Campbell, owing to a quarrel, it is said, about an anticipated knighthood which was not conferred upon either, now sides with Magnus, and magnanimously wishes to resign to make way for Magnus and Bold, the latter being a nominee of his own. Then one Guedella, of the Stock Exchange, another Jew, calls a meeting of his own, and abuses everything that has been done. Him the valiant Magnus threatens and dares to single combat, and the matter was a day or two since brought before the Lord Mayor by means of a summons obtained by the timorous Guedella, who was big enough to annihilate Magnus had he so dared. Magnus, be it remarked, heard the appellation of "liar" affixed to him by Jackson, with the meekness of a lamb.

The article continued at length, heaping ridicule and scorn upon the directors. Mann, his hands shaking, could read no further. *Good God,* Mann thought as he dropped the newspaper on his desk, *this article is being read by everyone I talked to about investing money in her.*

When the copywriter came back to see how Mann was doing, he saw the back of the short, pudgy man. He was facing a window, his hands on either side of the window's frame, his head hanging down. Unable to think of anything comforting to say to his despondent editor, the copywriter turned and silently moved away from the door.

45

Demopolis, Alabama
March 1860

"Mr. Wilcox! Have you a moment?"

Wilcox turned around and saw Judge Crane standing at the public entrance to his slave pen. "Be right there!" he yelled back. Both men walked into what was Wilcox's office, a small, dusty room with a pigeon-hole table pushed up against a wall and three plain wooden chairs. "Sit down, Judge." Wilcox motioned to one of the chairs.

"Mr. Wilcox, it's been many months, and we've heard nothing about Kit. Do you think he's still in Mobile?"

Wilcox rubbed his chin as he considered the question. "Well, Judge, thar's only a few thousand free niggers in Mobile, and I woulda thought that the reward money woulda smoked him out by now. A lotta those darkies would turn their mammies in for two hunner dollars. He might still be there, but the odds ain't looking so good."

"What now?" the judge asked. "That boy's worth a lot of money."

"Don't rightly know," answered Wilcox. "I'll tell you what. I gotta send Zeb to Mobile the end of next month. I'll have him ask around. He's pretty good at sniffing out runaways. Let's see what he finds out."

The judge was not particularly satisfied at this answer but had no alternative plan. "All right, Mr. Wilcox. Send me a note when your man returns and let me know what he found out."

"Ah promise, Judge. Keep your hopes up. I think we'll get your boy yet."

46

London, England
April 1860

The January debacle at the London Tavern had consequences. The *Great Eastern* was more than a commercial venture; she was a highly visible symbol of British might and ingenuity. During her construction, Queen Victoria's husband, Prince Albert, had come repeatedly and offered advice and consolation to poor Brunel. Even the queen herself had taken a well-publicized visit to the hull after the launching, her nose buried in a massive nosegay to mitigate the putrid stink of the Thames. The human personification of the wealth and power of the British Empire had toured the massive hull and nodded her head in approval. If the world deemed the *Great Eastern* a ridiculous failure, then a large share of the humiliation was sure to be attributed to the arrogance and ineptitude of the British Empire by its many enemies, including those in America.

In England, there existed powerful forces that acted silently and out of public view. After the shareholders' meeting, these powerful forces interceded in the affairs of the ship. Daniel Gooch, a protégé of Brunel, appeared with orders to take charge of the ship. What Gooch lacked in Brunel's engineering brilliance, he more than made up in organizational and leadership skills. He had been operating the Great Western Railway at a considerable profit, and for that he was much beloved by that company's shareholders. While Gooch gave nominal deference to the directors of the Great Ship Company, no one was confused as to where authority lay.

Gooch headed immediately to Southampton to take control of the ship's fitting and completion. His instructions from the powerful forces were to take the ship to New York City in June. Capital previously impossible to obtain was quickly and quietly secured in the form of £100,000 of debentures. The requirements of the Board of Trade that Gooch thought were reasonable and necessary were quickly implemented. Those he thought unnecessary rapidly evaporated.

Gooch remained with the ship, supervising the fitting and completion work, contacting longtime suppliers to his railway to secure better prices, and making sure journeymen were timely and fairly paid. Although the entire atmosphere about the ship had changed for the better, Gooch released little publicity of the fact. In his opinion, the *Great Eastern* had had enough publicity. What she needed was a successful maiden voyage. Nothing would come between him and that goal.

In the midst of this work, Gooch wrote to an old friend in the United States, Colonel Dudley Mann. The ship was going directly to New York City, he informed Mann, because the Great Ship Company needed the anticipated revenue from sightseers. However, when the *Great Eastern* left New York City, she would go directly to Chesapeake Bay. Gooch invited Colonel Mann and his friends to visit her when she dropped anchor in Virginia's tidewaters.

47

Mobile, Alabama
April 1860

ZEB knew his way around Mobile tolerably well, and he located John Behncke's shop without difficulty. He dismounted and looked into the dark shop. "John Bankey, you here?" he yelled out.

A large figure moved from a corner of the shop to the door. "I'm John Behncke. Do you need something?"

The two large men quickly sized each other up and decided they didn't like each other. Zeb said, "You used ta have a boy named Kit?"

Behncke nodded slowly. "Yeah," he answered.

"I'm lookin' for him," Zeb answered.

"I see," Behncke said. "I don't think I can be much help. I haven't seen the boy since he ran away."

"Who'd he run with? Have any friends?"

Behncke didn't like this conversation. "Who you working for?" he asked.

"Judge Crane wants the boy back."

Okay, Behncke thought. *If this tub is working for Judge Crane, I've got to go along.* He answered out loud, "He didn't run with anyone. He had no friends. He lived in my shop, and the only places he went were to church and to the wharf to fetch and deliver ironwork."

Zeb listened carefully. "The wharf?" he asked. "How often he'd go to the wharf?"

Behncke shrugged. "Depends. Maybe a couple of times a week."

"Did he always have papers?"

Behncke shook his head. "Nah, after a couple of months everyone there knew him to be my boy."

"Did you talk to anyone at the wharf after he run 'way?"

"No. What would I talk to them about? I notified the sheriff he was a runaway the day he was missing. If anyone knew where he was, they'd tell me."

"Anythin' else?" Zeb asked.

"I've told you all I know," Behncke said curtly. "I'm sorry it happened, but it wasn't my fault."

Zeb walked away without further comment and mounted his horse. *Well,* he thought as he started back for Demopolis, *that 'splains that. The nigger done stowed away. Where he is, who the hell knows?*

48

Chicago, Illinois
May 17, 1860

"WELL, Schultz, tomorrow's the day!" With that, the middle-aged man who had spoken gave Schultz a gentle punch in the shoulder. "Today, everything went perfectly. Tomorrow morning it'll all be over."

The smoke-filled lobby of the Richmond Hotel was jammed with middle-aged men and a handful of wives. The room was loud, and small groups of men bantered, their voices increasing in volume so that they could be heard over the other groups.

At the end of the first day of the Republican convention, everything did seem to have gone perfectly for Seward. Every battle, from recognizing delegates from Texas, where Seward had some strength, to establishing the right-sized quorum to nominate the presidential candidate, had gone Seward's way. Yet Schultz was troubled. As he looked over the boisterous crowd celebrating Seward's imminent coronation as the candidate of the Republican Party, he recalled the events of five months earlier when, during a two-night stay in Chicago while traveling to New Orleans, he'd had a meeting with "Long John" Wentworth, Chicago's mayor. The meeting had been arranged by Thurlow Weed, Seward's wealthy, politically astute "mentor." Schultz shook his head as he remembered that Weed had warned him not to meet Wentworth around mealtime lest he get stuck with the cost of feeding him.

The meeting with the mayor had been scheduled for 10:00 a.m. Although he arrived early, Schultz had found himself waiting in an anteroom. At around eleven o'clock, a thin man with oiled hair appeared and introduced himself as the mayor's secretary. He apologized for the delay, saying only that some unanticipated business had sprung up and that the mayor would make himself available as soon as possible. Still, no mayor appeared until nearly one o'clock, when Schultz looked up to see a colossal man enter the anteroom. At six feet, six inches tall and well over three hundred pounds, John Wentworth dwarfed Schultz, no small man himself. Grabbing Schultz's hand with his beefy paw, Wentworth announced that he was delighted to meet Captain Schultz and loudly proclaimed, "Any friend of Governor Seward is a friend of mine." He then pulled out a mammoth gold watch from his vest and, looking at it, said, "Good heavens! Look how late it is! Dear sir, I do apologize for the delay in meeting you. I think you must be very hungry, and I know I am." Turning to his well-oiled secretary, he said, "We'll head over to Underhill's. Don't disturb us unless it's an emergency." As the secretary nodded, Schultz thought he saw a slight smirk on the man's face.

When they reached the establishment of Messrs. Underhill and Pew, Wentworth barged through the front door with Schultz scuttling in his wake. The moment he entered, the room became animated with nods, smiles, and waves all in Long John's direction. Although the restaurant was crowded, a prime booth remained empty, and a waiter quickly escorted the two men to it. Standing on a stool, the waiter helped the mayor remove his coat while leaving Schultz to fend for himself. As soon as the two men were seated, a man appeared at their table. "Your Excellency, it is a delight to see you," the man said.

"Ah, Charles," Wentworth responded, "I want you to meet Captain Schultz, the famous sea captain from New York City and a good friend of Governor Seward."

The man, the Underhill part of the establishment's name, responded, "Captain Schultz, we've all heard about you! What an honor to have you in Chicago." At this point, Underhill turned to the other diners and announced, "Gentlemen, we have the famous Captain Schultz from New York with us today!" At this, Underhill stood aside and extended his arm toward Schultz. This was followed by clapping and shouts of "Hear, hear!" and "We're honored, Captain," among other accolades. Schultz forced a smile and waved weakly toward his admirers while wondering what this performance was going to cost him.

Food was not ordered. Instead, as if by some secret instructions, waiters brought out course after course—roasted pigeons, rack of lamb, pork roast, veal medallions, a roast turkey leg. Schultz tried to calculate how quickly his cash was being used up. Finally, after a vast amount of food and two full tumblers of fine whiskey had disappeared into Long John's maw, the mammoth politician dabbed at his lips with his napkin and settled back on his cushions with a lightly suppressed burp. He then looked at Schultz with what could only be described as a sweet smile.

"Well, Captain, how is my good friend Governor Seward?"

It took Schultz a couple of seconds to recover from this performance. "He's fine," Schultz finally answered. "Of course, he's looking forward to the convention this May."

"Ah, aren't we all!" Wentworth said. "It'll be a grand event, one that will be a credit to the whole Republican Party."

"Yes, well, we certainly want to have a grand send-off for Governor Seward," Schultz ventured.

Mayor Wentworth continued to smile at Schultz. "Indeed, at present, Governor Seward seems to be the leading candidate. However, Captain, I'm sure you know that in politics, like on the prairie, winds constantly change."

The conversation went on with Schultz probing into any pitfalls that awaited Seward at the upcoming convention and with Wentworth evading. It was an unfair fight, with the mayor evading with far greater skill than Schultz had at posing questions.

Finally, somewhat frustrated, Schultz brought up a new subject. "I talked to a man at the Briggs House this morning at breakfast. He told me about a 'Cameron and Lincoln Club' formed in Chicago. He said it had thirteen hundred members. I was surprised to hear about it."

Wentworth's face broke out in a big grin. "Ah, Senator Cameron! I've heard about his club. I'll admit that it's odd to see the names of Senator Cameron and Mr. Lincoln together. Cameron spends more on a cigar than Lincoln does on a suit of clothes."

"But why is Lincoln associated with the man? Cameron's utterly corrupt!" Schultz responded.

"Oh, I don't think Lincoln has anything to do with the club," Wentworth said. "My guess is that Cameron doesn't want to strain his back carrying all of his bags of money to the convention in one trip, so he sent a couple of lackeys with a bag or two ahead of time. We have a lot of young men in Chicago in need of a few extra dollars. They'd form a club on behalf of Beelzebub if the loot was there." At this, Wentworth sat and looked at Schultz for a moment. He then continued, "Well, maybe that's a bit harsh. Let's just say that we're letting these young men satisfy their whims for a while. Lincoln's name is included with the club because he has a good following in Illinois. If Governor Seward is afraid of Senator Cameron getting the nomination, tell him his worries are unjustified. When it counts, these club members will come back to the fold *if* they receive sufficient enticements."

There was another moment of silence as another grin spread across Long John's face. "Speaking of enticements, Captain, how much is my friend Thurlow Weed bringing to the convention? Someone told me one hundred thousand dollars, but that seems rich even for good old Thurlow."

Weed, a wealthy New York newspaper publisher, was commonly known to spread his largesse on behalf of Seward at just the right moment. How much Weed was willing to spend to secure the presidency for his protégé was not known to Schultz. The amount quoted by Wentworth seemed high but not improbable, though Schultz could honestly plead ignorance.

"Your Honor, Mr. Weed has not invited me into his confidence on matters of finance."

Wentworth did not expect a different answer. However, he was certain that his knowledge of Weed's reputed munificence at the upcoming convention would be transmitted by Schultz to Seward.

"Is Lincoln willing to be nominated as vice president?" Schultz asked.

Wentworth's face became serious. "I don't know. He'd make a wonderful candidate—that's for certain."

Schultz followed up. "I don't know much about Lincoln," he said. "Just the debates he had with Douglas."

"I didn't know much about him until four years ago," Wentworth said. "It was then that I went to Bloomington to hear a speech he was giving. I went as a reporter for my newspaper. What happened was unforgettable. Lincoln spoke without notes for over an hour. He wasn't talking as a politician; he was talking just as … an ordinary man. His speech was powerful, so much so that the reporters covering it simply put their pencils down and listened. We were all mesmerized! When he stopped talking, everyone jumped to their feet and cheered—and cheered even more. No one to this day is quite certain as to what Lincoln said. He mentioned slavery, I recall that, but beyond that I have trouble remembering, and I have a pretty good memory. I do remember thinking that he showed great courage and eloquence. It was an incredible moment." Wentworth was silent for a few moments and then continued his thought. "He'd make a fine candidate."

"For vice president?" Schultz tendered.

Wentworth's face broke into a grin. "Certainly! A fine candidate!"

At this point, Wentworth looked at Underhill, who nodded and approached the table. "Captain Schultz, it was an honor to meet you," Underhill intoned as he laid the invoice for the meal in front of Schultz.

Wentworth had immediately begun to remove himself from the booth with a "My goodness, where did the time go? I've got to get back. Captain Schultz, it was a delight to meet you, and I look forward to seeing you at the convention." With that, he'd fled the restaurant.

As Schultz was reminiscing over the pain of picking up that invoice five months earlier, his thoughts were suddenly brought back to the hotel's crowded lobby by a poke from one of Schultz's fellow directors of a New York insurance company. When Seward became president, the New Yorkers understood, the patronage and contracts would start to flow. Weed had promised Schultz that Seward would appoint him United States marshal for New York City. Schultz didn't particularly need the money, but he was honest enough to admit, at least to himself, that he wanted the position because of the title and the prestige. Also, he could lower the boom on some of his competitors who were engaged in shady dealings. Schultz wondered what his fellow director had been promised.

In spite of the merrymaking and boisterous optimism, Schultz was uneasy. If the vote had come this afternoon, Seward would have won. But when the vote had been called, the clerk of the convention had announced that the tally paper was mysteriously missing and the vote could not be counted. Accordingly, the vote had been put off until the following morning. While Seward's supporters saw mere incompetence in the failure to have the tally paper at the ready, Schultz saw something more ominous. Dan Lowber was right. Lincoln and his supporters were cunning. Why Seward had agreed to let the convention take place in Chicago was difficult to understand. The city was totally in the control of Wentworth and the Illinoisans. The giant convention hall, "the Wigwam," would be an embarrassment to any proper city, a huge, unpainted wooden barn hastily thrown up by Chicagoans at the corner of Lake and Market Streets. Its entrances were controlled by thuggish-looking men whom Schultz strongly suspected were Lincoln supporters.

"Captain, a drink?" The poking acquaintance tendered an open bottle of whiskey.

"No, thank you," Schultz muttered.

The man stood there a moment. "Well, suit yourself," he said, and he staggered to another person with an offer of a drink.

As Schultz looked around, the whole lobby, with the exception of the ladies and a few disgusted-looking men, was drinking whiskey and other spirits out of bottles and glasses. Loud laughter, shouts, and insults about Lincoln filled the room. One group of men began singing a bawdy song, oblivious to the fact that women were present. Schultz didn't drink. His father, a member of the Dutch Reformed Church, was a teetotaler. His mother, whenever she saw a man taking a drink, usually intoned Shakespeare's line about spirits: "Oh God, that men should put an enemy in their mouths to steal away their brains!" As Schultz surveyed the lobby, he thought gloomily, *There's a lot of brains being stolen here tonight.* Schultz left the hot, smoke-filled lobby and walked alone down South Water Street. He didn't want to walk far for fear of being robbed, but he craved quiet and fresh air.

The group in the Richmond Hotel, Seward's men, were composed mainly of wealthy New Yorkers. Schultz knew many of them. There were bankers and insurance executives, lawyers and real estate magnates. Tomorrow there was going to be a giant parade. Weed had hired a huge band, everyone was going to be given a Seward badge to wear, and the giant procession was going to march into the Wigwam to watch Seward receive the nomination. Horace Greeley, the publisher of the *New York Tribune* and Seward's implacable political foe, had come from New York for the sole purpose of denying Seward the nomination, and even he seemed to accept the inevitability of Seward's nomination. But Schultz knew something that these wealthy and pampered men did not. Although Schultz had made money and enjoyed his spacious, well-built house on the Hudson River, he was no dilettante. For years he had worked on sailing vessels, steamboats, and tugs. For more times than he cared to recall, he had used his bare hands to haul ice-covered rope out of the harbor, had been scalded by steam from malfunctioning boiler valves, and had faced down drunken or rebellious crewmen with nothing but his fists. He was a hard man, with no time for parades and pomp. When he saw Lincoln's supporters, he understood them immediately. They were just like him except they hadn't made their money yet.

They were hard-faced, mostly poorly dressed, and all determined not to die in poverty. Schultz understood that Lincoln's supporters included Germans who had fled penniless from European tyrants, and poor men from Sweden and other Nordic countries who had watched their wives and children die from exposure and hunger on windswept prairies. These men had no scruples about taking the law into their own hands and killing robbers and murderers without trial. They were hard men, and parades, bands, and badges meant nothing to them.

Schultz had learned much at the convention about Lincoln. The story of Lincoln being raised in a log cabin was true. A delegate from Massachusetts had told Schultz that when Lincoln's mother had died during the winter, her body had remained several days in the single-room cabin while young Abraham and his father had whipsawed trees into planks in order to assemble a coffin. She'd finally been buried after other settler women had come to prepare the body. It wasn't an uncommon story for the dirt-poor settlers of Indiana and Illinois. Lincoln didn't have to advertise his poverty and hard life, because his followers already knew the story; they had lived it themselves. Now, these men were determined to get their farmland and would not be driven off by anyone—not by bankers or government agents or slave owners. Lincoln was judged the candidate most likely to give them their land. African bondage, the issue roiling the East and South, was of no concern to them except for its ability to drive up the price of land—land that they intended to acquire cheaply and turn into their homesteads.

No, I don't think tomorrow is going to go well, Schultz thought gloomily as he walked slowly past darkened buildings. *Governor Seward will win the battle of show. But, tonight, Lincoln's supporters are winning the battle for delegates. They'll promise the sun and the moon for a delegate's votes, and if that doesn't' work, they'll simply threaten.* In the end, Schultz feared a number of delegates from the East would be either seduced or intimidated by Lincoln's supporters.

Schultz suddenly became aware of his surroundings. He was alone, and the street was dark. He could no longer hear the loud laughter and shouts from the Richmond Hotel a few blocks away. He didn't want to go back, but he understood he was an easy target for cutthroats. He slowly walked back, hoping his instincts about what was going to happen the next day were wrong.

The Wigwam, Chicago, Illinois

49

New York Times
May 19, 1860

The Republican Ticket for 1860.

Abram Lincoln, of Illinois, Nominated for President.

The Late Senatorial Contest in Illinois
to be Re-Fought on a Wider Field

Hannibal Hamlin, of Maine,
the Candidate for Vice-President.

Disappointment of the Friends of Mr. Seward.

Special Dispatch to the New-York Times.

Chicago, Friday, May 18.

The work of the Convention is ended. The youngster who, with ragged trousers, used barefoot to drive his father's oxen and spend his days in splitting rails, has risen to high eminence, and Abram Lincoln, of Illinois, is declared its candidate for President by the National Republican Party.

The result was effected by the change of votes in the Pennsylvania, New-Jersey, Vermont, and Massachusetts Delegations.

Mr. Seward's friends assert indignantly, and with a great deal of feeling, that they were grossly deceived and betrayed. The recusants endeavored to mollify New-York by offering her the Vice-Presidency, and agreeing to support any man she might name, but they declined the position, though they remain firm in the ranks, having moved to make Mr. Lincoln's nomination unanimous.

50

Southampton, England
June 1860

DANIEL Gooch was furious. After months of using every power of coercion and persuasion at his disposal, the *Great Eastern* was finally fitted out and ready for her maiden voyage. The end was hectic with carpenters, painters, victuallers, and riggers stumbling over each other to finish their respective jobs. The ship was only hours away from leaving Southampton with a meager three hundred paying passengers when the Board of Trade stepped in and required final modifications. Among other things, the lifeboats hanging in front of the giant paddle wheels had to be moved from the davits to the deck so there was no possibility of the boats becoming entangled in the paddle wheels. Gooch could not risk a departure in the face of the board's new demands, and so the trip was rescheduled, the crew was let go, and the would-be passengers were given a refund.

Nearly all of the £100,000 Gooch had raised had been spent in the fitting and completion of the ship. Trying to do a thousand things at once, he left the securing of a replacement crew to the directors of the Great Ship Company. Sailors were naturally superstitious, and many a seaman thought the *Great Eastern* was cursed. The story of the riveter's boy and the basher sealed in the double hull was universally accepted as true by seafarers. Further, the death of Brunel, literally at the hands of his creation, and the drowning of Captain Harrison a short distance from his ship seemed confirmation of the "hoodoo" nature of the ship. Gooch's procurement of Captain John Vine Hall, a respected but vain and imperious officer, helped alleviate some of the concerns about the ship. If the directors had offered fair wages, as Gooch had previously offered, a competent replacement crew could have been obtained.

However, the directors, ever mindful of doing things in the worst possible way, hired "agents" to assemble a crew at the lowest possible cost. Engaging in the ancient art of crimping, cudgel-carrying thugs scoured the alleys, ginhouses, and brothels of Southampton for crewmen. Lucky was the seaman who was found lying in a drunken stupor, for he thereby avoided getting a blow to the head. During the night, bodies were carried, dragged, and, for a fortunate few, assisted onto the great ship. On the morning of Saturday, June 16, the day the *Great Eastern* was scheduled to leave, Captain Hall was horrified to find the greater part of his newly assembled crew lying on the deck of his ship or moaning and stumbling around. Hall announced that the ship's departure would be delayed yet another day to sober up the crew. For several days crowds had gathered near Southampton to see the ship leave and then dispersed in disappointment when it became clear the ship was remaining firmly in place. However, word was passed that the ship was actually going to leave on Sunday.

The morning of Sunday, June 17, 1860, broke to reveal a leaden sky with a half gale coming from the north-northwest. Most of the crewmen were now sober and somewhat functional, and by eight in the morning black smoke billowed from the five funnels as steam pressure was brought up for the ship's two giant engines. Tugboats appeared and pulled her away from her berth. Captain Hall was resplendent in his immaculately tailored uniform, and most of his officers, while of minimal competence, were handsomely turned out as well. At 8:12 a.m., Captain Hall ordered engines started, and with a stupefying blast of her great steam whistle, the *Great Eastern* was on her way.

From a distance, the great ship looked majestic. Gooch had arranged for a two-foot-wide white stripe to be painted around her to break the black bleakness of her gigantic slab sides. The upper portion of her paddle boxes had been painted a cream color, the smokestacks had been painted a yellowish gold, and she looked stately, even dignified. Massive crowds had formed on the piers, on the roofs of buildings, and on the shore. Gawkers even crowded in church steeples. Sightseers had piled on every vessel in the port, and all waited with anticipation for the greatest ship ever built to begin her maiden voyage. As the last tug was untied, a great cheer went up from the crowd, and the paddle wheels began turning slowly. When she was moving entirely under her own power, Captain Hall ordered the propeller engaged, and the water at the stern began to churn furiously. A band on shore began playing "God Save the Queen," and Hall ordered the ship's cannons to fire a salute. It was, by all accounts, the most magnificent start to a voyage that anyone could imagine. Even the crew rose to the occasion and looked presentable, at least at a distance. While Captain Hall was strutting about the deck, basking in the adulation of hundreds of thousands of his countrymen,

Gooch was busy below decks checking out every aspect of the ship's mechanical works. Amazingly, she was working perfectly.

Because of fears and canceled departure dates, the giant ship, designed to accommodate four thousand passengers in luxury, carried a grand total of thirty-five paying passengers, three of whom were women, and nine company deadheads, one of whom was Gooch's wife. The *Great Eastern* carried a crew of 418. The directors were keenly aware that the ratio of these figures did not bode well for any claim of commercial success. Nevertheless, the ship kept steaming out to sea as crowds cheered her passage. At 9:45 a.m. she returned a cannon salute from Hurst Castle, and at 10:03 she passed the Needles, entering at last the open sea. The crowds gathered on every promontory available to them and continued to cheer and wave. A journalist from the *New York Times* wrote:

> One poor little faithful tug, which had come alongside to take the last messages and letters, with half a dozen shivering gentlemen on her paddle-boxes, followed us down to the Isle of Wight, reminding us, the few "foolhardy" who were venturing on an "unfortunate and ill-fated ship"—clinging to the howling rigging under that Wintry sky—of the picture of "the last mourner," familiar to our youth—the drunkard's dog following his body—all alone—to the Potter's Field. One English cheer from the pilot's boat, as we cast it adrift, was the only sound of comfort. Under such auspices did the Great Eastern start for New-York.

51

New York City, New York
June 1860

At one in the morning on June 27, a telegraph message from Sandy Hook, New Jersey, was received at the offices of the *New York Times* and the *New York Tribune*. It read, "A large steamship has stopped outside the bar and from present appearances I am most sure it is the Great Eastern as she shows a great many lights."

Reporters scrambled to the port only to find that the large steamship was not the *Great Eastern.* The citizens of New York were not even certain the *Great Eastern* had left England, there being no direct line of communication across the Atlantic. Nerves were becoming frayed. Had she left? If so, had some catastrophe befallen her? She had been due to leave on the fifteenth. If she'd left on that date, she was overdue. Speculation among the public and in the press was rife.

Later that morning, a giant shape emerged out of the mist near Sandy Hook. Its colossal size left no doubt in anyone's mind that the *Great Eastern* had safely arrived. The great iron ship hovered offshore until the midday tide made it possible for her to cross the bar. She seemed to increase in size as she slowly passed by Sandy Hook and entered New York's harbor. Word flew throughout the city that *the* ship had been seen offshore. Church bells rang, and crowds flocked to any vantage point offered by the harbor.

The *Great Eastern* came up the North River under her own steam. Her sails were furled, and her five funnels, rising like factory chimneys from the flat deck of the ship, belched out thick black smoke. A Union Jack nearly twelve hundred square feet in size fluttered from a stanchion on her stern. When she passed Fort Hamilton, fourteen of the fort's guns fired a salute, which the *Great Eastern* returned with four thunderous blasts from her Dahlgren guns. When she passed close by the wooden steam frigate *Niagara,* the largest ship in the United States Navy, the crowd could see the relative size of the two ships. The *Niagara* was utterly dwarfed. Nevertheless, the frigate gamely dipped her ensign in silent recognition to the passing monster.

The *Great Eastern* was greeted in the harbor by hundreds of vessels of every description—yachts, ferries, tugboats, fishing boats, schooners, trawlers, ships, and boats, each packed with sightseers who were staring at her with amazement. The air was filled with a cacophony of steam whistles, bells, and human screams from these escorts, and every so often the *Great Eastern* would acknowledge their presence with a blast from her steam whistle, a sound so powerful that there was no doubt from which ship it emanated.

Captain VanDer Hooven and his three crewmen stood on the upper deck of the *Ella* smoking their pipes and watching the proceedings from a distance. The old Dutchman had decided to stay clear of the monster because he was afraid of being tangled up with one of the hundreds of other vessels recklessly trying to keep up with her. Even from across the bay, the *Great Eastern* looked like a slowly moving mountain to the four men who stood in silence as she glided in. It was only when the ship sounded its whistle that they became animated. Captain VanDer Hooven pointed his pipe in the direction of the *Great Eastern* and, with a broad smile, said something incomprehensible. Kit and two Germans nodded their heads in full agreement.

As the *Great Eastern* approached her mooring at the quay at Hammond Street, tens of thousands of New Yorkers started running to keep up with her. All attempts by the police to control the crowd were abandoned. Under the command of Commodore Murphy, a pilot who had boarded her at the bar, the *Great Eastern* slowly headed toward her mooring. When she reached the mooring, she sharply turned her rudder, reversed her screw, and turned 180 degrees almost within her own length. The crowd roared its approval at this amazing feat, and when the ship was facing seaward again, Commodore Murphy started inching her toward the wooden wharf. In an unceremonious end to what had been a most beautiful entry, the ship leisurely collided with the wharf, her giant paddle box gouging a sizable chunk out of it. Murphy quickly mastered the situation, and the *Great Eastern* was shortly properly moored. Many in the crowd had been trampled, but none were reported killed.

Those who saw the *Great Eastern*'s maiden entry into the port of New York always recalled it with feelings of awe and grandeur. Even Gooch, phlegmatic by nature, was moved and wrote the following in his diary:

> As we passed up through that beautiful entrance to the Hudson, the banks were lined with thousands of people, and the forts and American men of war saluted as we passed, so that it was one continued firing of guns and shouting of thousands of people all the way up to New York, and when we came close to that town the scene was wonderful. The wharfs, house tops, church towers and every spot where a human being could stand and get a sight of the ship was crowded. We reached the wharf where we were to lay about 5 or 6 oclock, and I

> was very glad when it was time for bed; I will, however, never forget the beauty of the scene.

In the summer of 1860 New York City was the most exciting place in the world. It was estimated that the city's population now exceeded a million. The harbor was filled with ships headed to and arriving from both transatlantic and coastal ports, and financial institutions like banks and insurance companies were cropping up to support the increasing demands of this vast shipping industry. Olmsted and Vaux had just finished laying out their magnificent Central Park. Hotels were being built in record time, and immigrants from Ireland, the German states, Hungary, and a dozen other countries were pouring into the city, bringing both skills and a desire to make money in peaceful pursuits. That summer, in addition to being the terminus of the *Great Eastern*'s maiden voyage, the city was to host the Prince of Wales, the handsome sixteen-year-old heir to the British throne. His visit was almost immediately followed by a visit from Louis Napoleon, the French emperor. A national hero, heavyweight boxer John C. Heenan, known professionally as the "Benicia Boy," was to return shortly from a victorious prize fight in England. The social columns of New York's newspapers could hardly keep up with the comings and goings of the various levels of society as they readied themselves for these momentous occasions. To top it off, the Japanese government had just sent to New York its first delegation to the United States. An editor of the *New York Times* wrote:

> Sensations and excitements are now multiplying so fast in New York that it is sincerely to be hoped that they will result in infusing a little of *nil admirari* spirit in the population. Grown men are just ridiculous when they clap their hands and cut capers for joy. This summer we have already had the Japanese, are now in ecstasies over the *Great Eastern*, have the arrival of the Benicia Boy to look forward to next week, and are promised the Prince of Wales and Prince Napoleon. We must not and cannot get into hysterics over them all.

Amazingly, the trip across the Atlantic went well for the *Great Eastern*. The weather was generally calm, giving the few passengers ample opportunity to explore the ship's cavernous interior. Some passengers went down to the engine room to see the movement of the gargantuan pistons that drove the paddle wheel engine. Other passengers climbed aboard the paddle box and stood fifteen feet outside the hull of the ship, where they could see her entire length. From the stern, passengers could see three wide paths of wake, one from the ship's propeller and one from each of the side paddles. Five of the paying passengers were newspaper reporters, and each related a story replete with breathtaking sunsets, footraces around the quarter-mile perimeter of the deck, phosphorescent seas glowing eerily in the night, and betting on porpoises as they raced to keep pace with the giant hull. The stories had already been written when the *Great Eastern* arrived in New York, and hardworking typesetters had them in print the following day.

While the passengers amused themselves during the voyage, a small number of crewmen were busy at work in the ship's carpentry shop. They were making something never seen in the United States before—a turnstile. The forces that had caused the successful completion of the ship now demanded that she make money. If she could not make a profit on passengers or cargo, she'd make it off sightseers. The dignified Gooch later wrote in his diary:

> I now had to undertake a new kind of life, that was, to become a show man, as we expected to earn a very large sum of money by exhibiting the ship. We therefore had to advertise and organize our plans, and I cannot say, now it is all over, we were very clever at our work … Before leaving England we were told it would not do to charge less than a dollar for admission as the Yankies knew no less coin than the dollar. We soon found out this was a mistake, as the papers abused us for making so high a charge, and we after a few days had to reduce it to half a dollar.

Crowds gathered daily at the wharf where the monster ship was moored. Although she had been awe-inspiring coming in from the mists of the Atlantic, her mystique quickly evaporated as she engaged in the tawdry business of making money. During the day, the wharf was a veritable circus. Merchants, hucksters, and showmen leased space on various sections of the quay and set up refreshment booths, shooting galleries, games of chance, a menagerie complete with bears, and even a freak show advertising "the Great French Giant." Late in the evening, the booths were closed and their contents guarded by toughs who would be paid the following morning only if everything was still intact.

Gooch's description of being "abused" by the papers for charging a dollar a person was an understatement. The *New York Times* had long been hostile to everything English, and the gouging of Americans by the proprietors of an English ship was grist for its mill. Even the *Scientific American* complained about the fee, noting that lowering the admission price would allow more people to experience the scientific wonders of the ship.

When the fee was halved, the paid attendance quickly rose. At times the ship was packed, and many persons felt the admission fee allowed them to return with a souvenir, usually in the form of something not securely bolted to the ship. Chairs, paintings, china, and of course all sorts of nautical hardware left the ship as the distraught directors sought to control the thieves among the surging crowds. The *New York Herald* described a visit to the ship thusly:

> Reader, do you want to see a crowd? To be squeezed, reduced, contracted and epitomized, dovetailed and wedged in; to be scowled at by women and anathematized by men; to have your uninsured corn plantations remorselessly trod upon ... to have parasols stuck in your eyes, and elbows in your ribs; your hat smashed, your bosom mussed ... to take your wife and daughter to see the show and be treated to intermittent glimpses of it between your neighbors' legs or the summits of their heads? ... If so, go on board the Great Eastern.

The presidential campaign was in full swing, and the papers were full of threats of secession from South Carolina and other slave states if Lincoln was elected. Elmer Ellsworth, a young, dashing admirer of Lincoln, took his military drill team, the Chicago Zouaves, to New York. Dressed in flashy uniforms in the style of the French colonial forces in

Algeria, the young men performed drills in Central Park for enthusiastic crowds. Acting upon an invitation from Captain Hall, Ellsworth took his Zouaves to the *Great Eastern*, where they performed their drills on the ship's quarter-acre-sized deck, but only after the lifeboats were moved back to their davits to accommodate the drill team. It was an exhibition that displeased Dudley Mann greatly.

The Great Eastern *in New York, July 1860*

52

Washington, DC
July 11, 1860

DUDLEY Mann had been waiting on the platform of the railway station for over an hour. Finally, the train from New York arrived in all of its hissing, clanging splendor, and Mann looked up and down the wooden platform anxiously. Before long, he saw what he was looking for.

"Daniel! Hello, Daniel, I'm here." Mann waved his arm as people exiting the train walked by him. Daniel Gooch had just stepped down from his railroad car, saw Mann waving, and walked briskly toward him.

"Hello, Dudley. I got your telegram," he said, shaking hands. "It's delightful to see you."

Mann hailed a hack, and when they were settled in and heading for their hotel, they were able to talk without competing with steam engines. "Daniel, you've got to tell me about her! I want every detail of her voyage, everything about her. I can't tell you how wonderful it is that she's finally in America."

"Well, to my amazement, it was an uneventful trip. And thank goodness for that! She behaved beautifully and shows off very well. I must tell you, however, that New York is detestable. It's filthier than London and populated with the lowest class of people I could ever imagine. They're utterly shameless. Every day we catch your fellow citizens trying to sneak off mirrors, china, you name it. And the New York newspapers! Their hostility to everything English is virulent. I know we burned the President's Mansion down fifty years or so ago, but I thought amends had been made."

"Daniel, I share your opinion of the New Yorkers. I assure you that Virginia is populated with true ladies and gentlemen. I know you'll enjoy their company far more than the rabble in New York. Now, speaking of the Executive Mansion, tomorrow morning we have a meeting there with President Buchanan and some of his cabinet members. He's well familiar with the plan to use the *Great Eastern* as a shuttle between Chesapeake Bay and England, and he wants to discuss it further with you."

Gooch nodded his approval at this news. "I'm looking forward to meeting him. I told Lord Russell that you had suggested such a meeting.

He seemed surprised that the president would be so interested in the *Great Eastern*, considering all that is going on in your country."

Mann was quiet as the two men continued walking. He then said, "Yes, we have quite a bit going on in our country. If Abraham Lincoln is elected president this November, it will be the end of the United States as we know it."

"Dudley, certainly that's an overstatement. Your country has survived both good and bad presidents."

"It's no overstatement. His election would endanger every man, woman, and child in the South. Plans are already afoot for the secession of the slaveholding states if Lincoln assumes power." Looking directly at Gooch, Mann continued, "For many years, I was one of the most influential Americans in Europe. I worked very hard to promote the United States. But if a tyrant like Lincoln comes into power, then free men must do what they need to do. I only hope and pray that he doesn't get elected."

Gooch sat silently as he absorbed this information. He then said, more to himself than to Mann, "I see. It's worse than I thought, worse than any of us in England thought."

53

New York City, New York
July 20, 1860

In May 1860, a huge meteor shower passed over Ohio and Pennsylvania, dropping aeroliths as it went. The newspapers reported that the largest stone that dropped out of the sky weighed more than a hundred pounds, and at least thirty other stones were located. Instead of a single explosion, there were "twenty-three distinct sounds first heard like cannon-shots, and then the sounds were blended together like musketry," which lasted two minutes.

Kit was unaware of these reports, but on the hot, torpid night of July 20, while he was lying on his rag-filled mattress on the roof of the *Ella*'s cabin, the harbor became bathed in a blood red light. Looking around for a source of the light, he saw an object in the western sky. Kit had seen many shooting stars before, but this was different. The fireball was huge, the size of a full moon, and it was flaming. It lit up the entire harbor. As it passed slowly and directly over the harbor, Kit sat up and looked around. The glow of the fireball reflected on the ships and structures around him. Pitch-black shadows and dark-red light oozed over the features of the *Great Eastern* as the fireball continued its movement. Kit followed the fireball as it moved to the east. Finally, just before it disappeared over the ocean, there was a loud explosion.

Kit's heart was pumping wildly. In the distance he heard a young man yelling, and then another. A dog started barking on shore. Then the harbor became quiet again. He wondered what he had just seen. There were no other crewmen on the little tug, and Kit looked around in vain to see if anyone else around the harbor had seen the fireball. He was alone.

It's a sign, Kit thought. He knew that the fireball meant something, but he didn't know what. The old slaves would have known; they would have told the young slaves exactly what such an apparition meant. Kit wondered if he could ask someone what it meant and then realized there was no one to ask. He turned to stare at the western sky, wondering whether another such fireball would appear. None did, and Kit finally lay down on the deck and tried to sleep.

54

"The Great Meteor of Friday Night."
New York Times
July 23, 1860

The meteor of Friday night which astonished all our citizens who happened to be unhoused at the time was seen, it would appear, far over the country, and was, in its way, a most astonishing phenomenon. We have had the Japanese and the Zouaves. The *Great Eastern* still abides with us, and the Prince of Wales is coming. The foreign and domestic excitements, however, were, are, and are to be, of this earth, earthy, or of the sea, nautically. A celestial, or at least a supraterranean visitant was needed, and the meteor came. The rule of parallax, evidently not understood by our ordinary street sight-seers, proves, according to the reports from various distances, that the globe of fire with the glowing tail of light must have been from thirty to forty miles above the surface of our planet. It was seen at Philadelphia at about 9 1/2 o'clock, say the papers of that city—rose suddenly from the horizon, about the size of the full moon, traversed an easterly line, dropping fire in its course, like a rocket, till it passed away in the southeast, like a red ball, about twice the size of the planet Mars. It was seen, under similar circumstances, at Danville, Penn., at New-Haven, along the whole line of the Hudson River, at Buffalo, Utica, Albany, and Troy, also at Newport, Rhode Island, and undoubtedly at other places from which we have no report—at each place, appearing to be at no great distance from the spires of the churches ...

The provincial papers in this and adjoining States come to us filled with accounts of the marvel. It is amusing to read of some of the events to come which some of them predict therefrom. The old superstition of "portents dire," it would seem is not yet quite *effete*.

55

Chesapeake Bay, Maryland
August 9, 1860

AFTER five weeks of paying sightseers boarding her deck, the *Great Eastern* weighed anchor and steamed to Chesapeake Bay carrying about one hundred excursionists. She entered the bay on August 2 and anchored at Old Point Comfort, as Daniel Gooch had promised to Dudley Mann. While she was there, she again sought sightseers. Gooch recorded the visit in his diary:

> We reached Old Point Comfort early the next morning and spent that day and night there; thousands of people crowded the little village to see the ship. I went over the large fort here and had also an opportunity of seeing a number of slaves who were brought by their masters to see the ship. The kindest and most friendly feeling seemed to exist amongst them, and I have never seen more happiness expressed in the face and manner of the working classes than appeared in these slaves.

The *Great Eastern* stayed off the Virginia coast until August 5, when it again weighed anchor and proceeded from Chesapeake Bay to Cape May. On the way there, a "Yankee steamer" tried to pass the great ship. Captain Hall ordered "full speed ahead," and the *Great Eastern* pulled away at a speed of eighteen knots. When she stopped at Baltimore, she again received paying customers, although this time she was to receive an additional party. On August 9, a small steam yacht pulled up to the *Great Eastern* and was greeted with a twenty-one-gun salute from the *Great Eastern*'s crew. With great ceremony, President Buchanan and a number of his cabinet members were granted permission to board the great ship. Gooch was waiting to receive the president. "Your Excellency, welcome aboard the *Great Eastern*."

"Mr. Gooch, thank you for your kind invitation. Colonel Mann has described this ship to me so many times during the last four years that I began to fairly wonder if she really existed. Now that I see her, I realize Colonel Mann's claims were too modest. She's a marvel."

The president and his cabinet members were introduced to Captain Hall and to two of the directors. Although the day was blisteringly hot, a tour was provided of the engine rooms, the great parlors, and some of the cabins. Afterward, the group sat under a canopy on the deck of the ship. Buchanan and Gooch sat aside from the group where they could talk in some confidence.

"Mr. Gooch, I gather from our conversation the other day that you have some awareness of the political events going on in our country."

"Your Excellency, Colonel Mann has discussed them with me. I'm aware that the upcoming election may have some serious ramifications."

"That's well put," Buchanan said. "The Southern states are of the firm opinion that Mr. Lincoln's election would pose a deadly threat to their well-being. Throughout the South, there is open talk of secession. So far, it's only talk. I believe the Union must be preserved, but not by force of arms. I believe if we can convince the Southern states that they have the possibility of economic independence, the fear may subside."

"Mr. President, I gather that this is background for Colonel Mann's plans?"

Buchanan nodded. "That's correct. Mann's trying to convince the slave states that this ship and others like her are the means by which the South can achieve economic independence from the North. Frankly, few believed they'd ever see this ship dropping anchor in Chesapeake Bay. Now that she's here, Mann's plans will be seriously considered by the slave states. My question to you, sir, is whether the shipowners will reject these plans out of hand?"

Gooch laughed. "Mr. President, I can assure you that any plan that reasonably proposes a profitable use of this ship will be most seriously and sincerely considered. We have been so distracted by the problems of construction that we have not had ample opportunity to consider what use of the ship is most appropriate. I can further assure you that we'll give Colonel Mann's plan very serious consideration."

Buchanan nodded. "That's all I wanted to hear from you, Mr. Gooch." With that, Buchanan and Gooch rejoined their group.

56

New York Herald
August 9, 1860

The Great Eastern at the South.—The Great Eastern festival, as the Virginia papers call the visit of the big ship to Southern waters, has made a tremendous sensation down there. The newspapers talk of "untold numbers" visiting and to visit her. Ten thousand people were on board during her first day in Hampton Roads, and it appears that Old Virginia is quite waked up by the event. Every available thing in the shape of a boat was brought into requisition for the use of excursionists from all the neighboring points, and on Saturday last one train of cars on the Norfolk and Petersburg road actually carried 850 people—a rare occurrence in Virginia, as the Richmond *Enquirer* says.

The directors of the Great Eastern will make a good thing out of their Southern trip, between the visitors' fees and the fifteen thousand dollars' worth of coal they are to get for making the trip to Annapolis. As for the steamboat proprietors and railroad companies of Virginia, they will make a small fortune out of it. But, at the same time, we are afraid that the visit of the Great Eastern has not done much for direct trade. It is understood, however, that if she can be insured a full cargo of cotton, the directors now with her will lay the matter before the general Board on their return to England, and probably come back for the thirty thousand bales of cotton.

In this way who knows but that the Great Eastern may realize the Southern dream of direct trade with Europe after all?

57

New York Times
September 4, 1860

The Great Eastern.

Mr. A. Dudley Mann in a Reverie.

The following card, addressed to the "citizens of the Slaveholding States," appears in the Richmond *Enquirer*:

Washington, Thursday, Aug. 30, 1860.

In less than two months from this date, the Great Eastern, from assurances which I have just received, and upon which I can implicitly rely, will reenter Hampton Roads, if it is your wish that she shall do so.

In that case she will come prepared to convey to Milford Haven thirty thousand bales of cotton.

* * *

A. Dudley Mann.

58

Mobile, Alabama
October 1860

THE judge didn't take it well when he found out that Kit had likely escaped as a stowaway. He could be anywhere, Wilcox explained. Ships came in and out of Mobile every day bound for Savannah, Liverpool, Cuba, Baltimore, and dozens of other ports, large and small. Wilcox understood a slave owner's despair at losing such a valuable piece of property, but he sensed that Judge Crane's feelings alternated somewhere between affection and betrayal.

Wilcox had seen such feelings before, and they reminded him of the feelings that crazy old ladies had for their cats. "Little Sheba, are you hungry?" they would coo, as if the cat could understand them. Slaves often did a great job of convincing their masters of their fondness and devotion. *Why not?* thought Wilcox. *Get your master to like you, and you might avoid a well-deserved whipping.* In Wilcox's slave yard, however, there was no fondness or affection. The only emotions that the black-skinned property locked in his pen showed was fear and hatred. Any slave given a good chance to run to freedom would do so. They hated slavery, each of them, and the bonds that held them to a plantation were not of affection but of terror. Families were the easiest to terrorize. "Try to run away or act insolent, and we'll sell your little children, and you'll never see them again. Or we'll sell your wife, and she'll become some other buck's woman, whether she wants to or not." Fear of separation was far greater than fear of whippings. That was the problem with Kit, thought Wilcox. As long as he'd had hope that he'd see his mother again, he'd stayed around and been the good boy. Once he'd learned that his mother was dead, he'd taken to his heels.

Wilcox didn't blame Kit for running away. He figured he'd do the same if the tables were turned. But they weren't turned, and Wilcox felt an emotion akin to irritation when he listened to Judge Crane give the old "sharper than a serpent's tooth" lament. *He ain't your child, Judge,* thought Wilcox. *He's your property, nothing more.*

Nevertheless, Kit was a very valuable piece of property—young, strong, and trained as a blacksmith. If there was even a remote possibility of reclaiming him, it should be explored. Accordingly, when Wilcox went to Mobile to examine some slaves who were now part of an estate, he took an afternoon off and went to the wharf to ask around. The harbormaster told Wilcox that he remembered the young slave but had nothing to add. Most everyone else gave a blank look when questioned. "Do you remember a young slave?" Wilcox would ask. "Hah!" was the answer. "There's thousands, and most of them look alike."

As Wilcox was leaving the wharf, a man stumbled up to him. The man was in his forties, more or less, and was dirty and red-eyed. It was obvious that he slept in the open, probably on the wharf. Wilcox figured he was about to be confronted by a beggar, and he said, "Go away," before the man said anything.

"Okay, I'll go away," the man muttered. "But maybe I know somethin' 'bout this here slave you was askin' 'bout."

Wilcox stopped. "What do you know?"

"Oh, nows we wants ta talk," the man muttered. "Maybe I should jest go 'way."

"If you have solid information, I'm willin' to barter," Wilcox said.

"I got info'mashun, fer sure," the man sputtered. "The slave you wants is a little guy, wi' big muscles. Right?"

Wilcox listened. The man could have overheard Wilcox talking to the harbormaster, but he didn't recall seeing anyone close enough to hear.

"Yeah, small and strong."

The drunk nodded his head as he slightly swayed to and fro.

"He's pretty good wit a anvil too, ain't he?"

Wilcox looked carefully at the man. He knew something. "He was trained as a smith," Wilcox answered.

"Come here." The man summoned Wilcox with a finger. "Come closer."

Wilcox examined the man to make certain he wasn't armed and then leaned forward into an odor of cheap whiskey and rotting teeth. The drunk nodded his head. "His name," the drunk whispered, "is …"

"What's his name?" Wilcox spoke forcefully.

The drunk smiled a revolting smile and then yelled into Wilcox's ear, "Kit! That's his name. Kit!"

Wilcox lurched back. His first instinct was to give the drunk a blow to the head. That instinct quickly passed. Regaining his composure, he asked, "How do you know this slave?"

The drunk's smile disappeared. "I was hired on a ship. While the ship was in the wharf, I's supposed to watch it. I got tired and closed my eyes for jest a minute. Sure 'nuf, this here nigger sneaked on board while my eyes was closed. We found him two days out. The captain liked to throw me in chains, but we was short of men, so he din't."

"Where was your ship heading?" Wilcox asked.

The man's smile returned. "Lessee, I ain't sure. My memory ain't so good. Was it Havana? Maybe Pens'cola … or was it China? I jest can't 'member."

"How much to get your memory to work?" Wilcox asked.

"How bad you want this nigger?" the drunk asked in return.

"That's none of your damn business," Wilcox said. "I'll give you two bucks for your ship's name and destination."

"Two bucks!" the drunk muttered. "We ain't talkin' 'bout the same slave. Your slave must be eighty years old 'n' blind."

"Two bucks, or I walk off the wharf." Wilcox would go to forty dollars if necessary, but this drunk needed a drink badly and was in no shape to bargain.

The drunk stood there silent, slowly thinking over his next move. Before he could say anything, Wilcox turned around and began walking away.

"Where's you goin'?" the drunk called out.

"I offered you two dollars," said Wilcox. "Take it or leave it."

"Make it four bucks, an' I'll guarantee it's the truth," the drunk called out.

Wilcox thought that the likelihood of a drunk telling the truth would be greater if Wilcox appeared generous. "I'll tell you what," said Wilcox in his friendliest tone. "You guarantee it's the truth, swear to God, and I'll give you five dollars." Wilcox stood there as the man smiled in appreciation.

"I's 'board the *Cetus*. We was bound for New York. Swear to God."

"Spell *Cetus*," Wilcox snapped.

"C-e-t-u-s," the drunk said. Wilcox spelled it silently to himself to make sure he'd remember it.

"Did he get off in New York?" Wilcox asked.

"Don't know. The captain kicked me off the ship 'fore anyone else. I only got quarter pay. It took long time to git back to Mobile."

Wilcox stood there as he absorbed the information. "New York! Sweet Jesus, the boy's probably in Canada by now." Still, a deal was a deal. He took five dollars in Alabama currency from his wallet and counted it out for the drunk. The drunk bowed in appreciation and then hurried off to buy a jug of corn whiskey.

On his ride back to Demopolis, Wilcox puzzled over what to do with this information.

59

Beechwood, Virginia
November 6, 1860

The following is an excerpt from Edmund Ruffin's diary:

> Nov. 6. This is the day for the election of electors—the momentous election which, if showing the subsequent election of Lincoln to be certain, will serve to show whether these southern states are to remain free, or to be politically enslaved—whether the institution of negro slavery, on which the social & political existence of the south rests, is to be secured by our resistance, or to be abolished in a short time, as the certain result of our present submission to northern domination.—We went to the Court House, where we gave our vote for Breckinridge & Lane, & thence the carriage took me to Petersburg.

60

Charleston Mercury
December 20, 1860

EXTRA:

Passed unanimously at* 1.15 *o'clock,
***P.M. December* 20th, 1860.**

AN ORDINANCE

To dissolve the Union between the State of South Carolina and other States united with her under the compact entitled "The Constitution of the United States of America."

We, the People of the State of South Carolina, in Convention assembled, do declare and ordain, and it is hereby declared and ordained,

That the Ordinance adopted by us in Convention, on the twenty-third day of May, in the year of our Lord one thousand seven hundred and eighty-eight, whereby the Constitution of the United States of America was ratified, and also all Act and parts of Acts of the General Assembly of this State, ratifying amendments of the said Constitution, are hereby repealed; and that the union now subsisting between South Carolina and other States, under the name of "The United States of America," is hereby dissolved.

THE
UNION
is
DISSOLVED

61

New York City, New York
December 1860

In the eleven months since Kit had become a crew member of the *Ella*, the language difficulties aboard the craft had eased considerably. Felix and Matthias now understood most of what Kit was saying, and all three could understand their old Dutch captain well enough. Sitting on the roof of the cabin waiting for a stray schooner or brigantine to cross the bar, the men would talk. The captain, who had gone to sea as a cabin boy at the age of ten, had no shortage of sea stories. He told of pirates in the seas of China, of giant waves and terrible storms, of monstrous sharks, doomed ships, and endless other tales. The young men listened raptly to these stories as the old Dutchman waved his arms and raised and lowered his voice for dramatic effect. VanDer Hooven had told these stories many times on many ships because he knew, like all old sea captains knew, that boredom was an enemy once it boarded a ship.

Sometimes, the captain would retreat to his pilothouse and smoke his pipe contemplatively. When that happened, the three young men would talk. Several months earlier, the two brothers had stopped talking to each other in German, at least on the *Ella*. They'd decided that since they were in the United States to stay, they'd attempt to learn English. They received free lessons from their landlady's pretty daughter and practiced by reading old newspapers that they found. The three men frequently talked about their work and whether all the old captain's stories were really true. They talked about war and the breaking up of the United States, about how a man who had been a poor farmer had been elected president, about how the brothers wanted to go west to buy a farm. The one issue they never directly discussed was slavery. Both brothers suspected that Kit—or Bill, as they knew him—had been a slave, but neither felt it proper to question him on the subject.

On Christmas Day 1860, the *Ella* crew worked a short shift. It was dark early, and any ship that hadn't made it to the bar by 5:00 p.m. would have to spend the night offshore. Since there were no prospective customers in sight, the captain brought the *Ella* around and headed for Schultz's wharf. It wasn't particularly cold, and the three crewmen remained on deck, listening to the gulls and the chugging sounds of the *Ella*'s steam engine. Felix disappeared below deck for a moment and then came out with a wrapped package. "*Frohe Weihnachten*, Bill," he said, handing the package to Kit. Kit looked at Matthias in puzzlement. "Merry Christmas," Matthias said with a German accent.

Kit had celebrated Christmas before. Before he'd gone to Mobile, he had celebrated the holiday several times at Judge Crane's plantation. In early December, Judge Crane would talk to the slaves and get a list of all their parents and children who lived on nearby plantations. He would then write letters to the various owners of these slaves asking if they could come to his plantation for Christmas. These invitations were usually accepted, and on Christmas morning wagons would come by with old men, women, and teenage children looking for their relatives. A slave named Joe always left on a mule with a note from the judge giving him permission to spend the day with his mother.

The judge gave the slaves the day off and usually contributed a huge pig for a roast. There'd be squash soup, cornbread, and an abundance of roasted corn that had been shucked earlier in the week. There'd be singing and footraces and jump rope. Collins had the day off, and the judge would walk around the slave quarters talking with the older male slaves and wishing them a merry Christmas. The judge's wife never appeared but could be seen occasionally glowering from behind a curtain. After the meal, the judge would read from a large black book the story about Jesus's birth. It was amazing to the slaves to hear that Jesus had been born as poor and as powerless as the son of any slave. Why a rich white man like the judge, or any other plantation owner for that matter, would worship such a god was mysterious, but the tale of Mary giving birth in a stable had the ring of truth for many of the slave women. It was a good story, and most of the slaves concluded that Jesus must be a good god.

There was much hugging and crying during those Christmases as children were reunited with parents and sometimes siblings. Kit had usually stayed by himself, sometimes glancing with envy as mothers hugged their sons. Occasionally, after much urging, he'd participate in the wrestling competition, his strength and agility confounding much larger men, but his heart had never really been in it. He'd ached to be hugged, and there had been no one there to hug him.

"Open, Bill!" Matthias gestured with his hands as if he were ripping the paper off the package. Kit did that and found himself holding a good-sized metal cylinder. A new tin of tobacco! Kit unscrewed the lid and opened the waxed paper container inside, and the heady, rich smell of Virginia tobacco wafted up. The brothers smiled at Kit's happy face as he put his nose into the can. Kit held the can out, and each of the brothers inhaled the aroma, each in turn nodding with satisfaction. Kit bounded to the pilothouse and showed the captain, who also smelled the tobacco and nodded his head. Kit didn't want to smoke now. The clay pipe was fragile, and he didn't want to take it out when he was moving around, as he soon would be tying up the *Ella*. He told the brothers, and they understood. They didn't smoke either until they had a chance to sit.

That evening, after the *Ella* was tied up and Kit was alone, he sat on the roof of the cabin with his pipe, his new can of tobacco, and a couple of matches. He packed the pipe slowly and carefully, the way he had learned from the captain, and then lit it. A few deep puffs, and the pipe was emitting the delicious smell of smoldering tobacco. It had become much colder, and Kit wrapped himself in a heavy wool blanket. The night was quiet and cloudless, and Kit could see far across the harbor. As the evening grew later, he could see oil lamps being extinguished. Folks were going to bed. The peacefulness of the night and the wonderful gift he had received eased the loneliness of the young man. Finally, the pipe began to give out, and the air grew colder. Kit went down into the berth. Lying down fully clothed, except for his shoes, he went to sleep under the woolen blanket.

62

Washington, DC
December 31, 1860

RICHARD Bickerton Pemell Lyons, second baron, sat in the evening gloom of his library. Before him was a desk, lit by an oil lamp, a stack of writing paper, and an inkwell. *And so this is how 1860 ends,* thought Lord Lyons. *Not with a gala dance, not with "Auld Lang Syne," not even with a quiet toast with a friend. It ends alone, in this godforsaken city.*

Lyons had come to Washington two years earlier as Her Majesty's "Envoy Extraordinary and Minister Plenipotentiary," Britain's most senior officer in North America. It was an important posting for the forty-one-year-old bachelor, and although he found most Americans annoying, he kept his opinions to himself and worked to present Her Majesty's government as a calm and levelheaded institution by adopting the same characteristics. His reputation as a dour but honest bureaucrat accurately reflected the man.

Lyons found many things troubling about America, but the most troublesome was the propensity of Americans to resolve matters by violence. He was astounded to learn from his predecessor, Lord Napier, that a Southern legislator named Brooks had beaten Senator Sumner of Massachusetts nearly to death in the Senate chamber with his cane and yet had not been charged as a criminal. In fact, Brooks had been lionized throughout much of the South for his cowardly act and frequently received "honorary canes" from grateful citizens. Lyons was equally amazed at the outpouring of grief in the North at the hanging of John Brown, a murderous fanatic who had tried to foment a violent slave revolt. Sometimes the prevalence of violence, real and threatened, was almost comical. He had looked in amazement at a picture in *Harper's Weekly* of an eight-foot-long bowie knife on display a few weeks earlier at the Republican convention in Chicago. It was a gift from Missouri Republicans to an Ohio congressman who, when challenged on the House floor by a Georgia congressman to a duel, had accepted the challenge and chosen bowie knives as the dueling weapons. The Georgian had declined, to the universal derision of the Northern Republicans.

Lyons had arrived just as Kansas and Nebraska had erupted with conflict, and he'd read about the armed thugs from both sides of the conflict killing and maiming each other as well as innocent citizens. During the sultry Washington summers, he'd watched with disgust as slaves in chains marched through the dusty streets of the capital of the United States followed by men carrying whips. He'd once seen a whipping of a slave so vicious that in England it would have brought a rebuke if it had been done to a horse. Unlike members of Parliament, the men in Congress were coarse, often uneducated, and prone to belligerence. It was said that the only men in Congress who did not carry a knife and a gun were those who carried two guns. Duels were so common that even Lincoln, the ugly giant who was now the president-elect, had once agreed to a duel, albeit under somewhat ridiculous circumstances.

Tonight, with violence of massive proportions being threatened from many quarters, Lord Lyons was drafting his final dispatch of the year to Lord Russell, Her Majesty's secretary of state for foreign affairs. Lyons carefully started his dispatch by noting, "The events of the last week have not been encouraging to those who desire to maintain the Union." He took a sheet of paper from his jacket pocket and unfolded it. It was the text of a speech that Louisiana senator Judah Benjamin had given that day in the Senate. Benjamin had been considered one of the more moderate men in the South, but on this day Benjamin had shown that he too was now a man of violence. Lyons quoted a portion of Benjamin's speech in his letter to Lord Russell.

> I desire and hope that it is no stain upon the honour of my State that we part in peace; but if the issue be forced upon us we will endeavor to meet it like men, and, trusting to the God of Battle, strive to merit victory. The fortune of war may be adverse; you may fill our land with bloodshed and ruin; you may desolate us with fire and sword; you may in emulation of those who incited the savages in our Revolution, loose upon us those who are so eager for dissolution, and add to our miseries all the horrors of a servile insurrection; you may do all this, but you can never break the spirit of a Free People—you can never subjugate us; *never, never, never.*

Lyons finished his letter of unremitting bad news, folded it, and put it into a diplomatic pouch. A courier would pick it up the next day, and it should be delivered to Lord Russell in less than two weeks.

Lyons straightened his desk, extinguished the desk lamp, and walked to his cold bedroom using a candle to light his way. As he lay in his bed, he imagined himself in a boat being sucked into a giant whirlpool. He struggled to get the image out of his mind and finally lapsed into a restless sleep.

63

Year of Meteors

Year of meteors! brooding year!
I would bind in words retrospective, some of your deeds and signs;
I would sing your contest for the 19th Presidentiad;
I would sing how an old man, tall, with white hair, mounted the scaffold in Virginia;
(I was at hand—silent I stood, with teeth shut close—I watch'd;
I stood very near you, old man, when cool and indifferent, but trembling with age and your unheal'd wounds, you mounted the scaffold;)

—I would sing in my copious song your census returns of The States,
The tables of population and products—I would sing of your ships and their cargoes,
The proud black ships of Manhattan, arriving, some fill'd with immigrants, some from the isthmus with cargoes of gold;
Songs thereof would I sing—to all that hitherward comes would I welcome give;

And you would I sing, fair stripling! welcome to you from me, sweet boy of England!
Remember you surging Manhattan's crowds, as you pass'd with your cortege of nobles?
There in the crowds stood I, and singled you out with attachment;
I know not why, but I loved you … (and so go forth little song,
Far over sea speed like an arrow, carrying my love all folded,
And find in his palace the youth I love, and drop these lines at his feet;)

—Nor forget I to sing of the wonder, the ship as she swam up my bay,
Well-shaped and stately the Great Eastern swam up my bay, she was 600 feet long,
Her, moving swiftly, surrounded by myriads of small craft, I forget not to sing;

—Nor the comet that came unannounced out of the north, flaring in heaven;
Nor the strange huge meteor procession, dazzling and clear, shooting over our heads,
(A moment, a moment long, it sail'd its balls of unearthly light over our heads,
Then departed, dropt in the night, and was gone;)
—Of such, and fitful as they, I sing—with gleams from them would I gleam and patch these chants;

Your chants, O year all mottled with evil and good! year of forebodings! year of the youth I love!
Year of comets and meteors transient and strange!—lo! even here, one equally transient and strange!
As I flit through you hastily, soon to fall and be gone, what is this book,
What am I myself but one of your meteors?

—Walt Whitman, January 1861

Part III

January 3, 1861
to
April 14, 1861

[Leviathan's] heart is as firm as a stone; yea, firm as the nether millstone.

—Job 41:24 (ASV)

64

New York City, New York
January 3, 1861

"CAPTAIN Schultz?"

Schultz looked up at the middle-aged man standing in the doorway of his shanty.

"I'm Schultz. Can I help you?"

The man looked around to see if anyone else was in the shanty. "May we talk inside, Captain?" Schultz nodded and motioned to a chair. While the stranger was unbuttoning his coat, Schultz closed the door.

"Captain, I'm General Lorenzo Thomas. I'm an adjutant to General Scott. We've received your proposal, and we're prepared to act upon it." Gesturing at his civilian clothes, Thomas continued, "I'm not in uniform, because the matters we are to discuss are highly confidential."

Schultz sat on a chair behind his desk. "The proposal was that a number of my tugboats be used to ferry men and material to a ship in the harbor. Beyond that, I know nothing. If my proposal is accepted, I need to know what this is about."

"Captain, your confidentiality is essential. Your reputation is that of an honest Union man, a man we can completely trust."

"I am a Union man, and I can be completely trusted. Now, sir, what's this about?"

"Captain, you're obviously aware of the rebellion in South Carolina. The rebels lay claim to Fort Sumter. The fort is garrisoned by Union troops but has limited provisions. A siege would result in the fall of the fort to the rebels."

"So you're going to bring additional supplies to the fort?"

"Additional supplies and additional men."

"I see. Go ahead, General."

"Captain, we've chartered the *Star of the West.* We want to use your tugboats to bring men and supplies to the *Star.* The movement must be done under complete secrecy and in the dead of the night."

Schultz looked puzzled. "The *Star of the West*? She's a coaster, not a warship. If she's fired upon, she'll have no way of defending herself. Why not use the *Cumberland* or the *Niagara*?"

"General Scott is under orders not to use any military vessels to resupply the garrison. There's to be no force used."

Schultz leaned forward. "That's idiocy! You've got rebel cannon all over Charleston Harbor, and you're going to bring in an unarmed vessel to resupply a fort. What's Scott thinking?"

General Thomas sat quietly, framing his response. "Captain, General Scott isn't the commander in chief. He's a good officer, and he'll follow the orders he's given, even if he disagrees with them."

Schultz nodded. "Ah, yes. President Buchanan, our commander in chief. A true leader. A man who claims that the Southern states have no right to secede but then says that the North can't use force to stop them. Even for a politician, it is a remarkably craven position."

Thomas let out a sigh of exasperation. "Captain, we have no authority to question the orders we are given. My inquiry is whether you're willing to bring men and supplies to the *Star*."

"General, you've read the reports of the traitors walking their horses over our flag in Charleston, of strumpets dancing on it in the streets?" Thomas nodded, and Schultz added, "And all we can do is send an unarmed civilian supply ship?" Thomas sat motionless. It wasn't a question for which Schultz expected an answer.

The men sat in silence as Schultz thought. Finally, he said, "General, the War Department is full of traitors. If the rebels get an advance warning, they'll be able to sink the *Star*. Is it worth the risk?"

"I'm told it is," Thomas responded. "There's nothing more we can do."

Schultz let out an audible sigh. "If this is all the fool in the President's House will permit, I suppose I've no choice but to go along. Maybe we'll be lucky. Give me the details."

"Captain, tonight you and I need to see Mr. Roberts, the owner of the *Star of the West*, to confirm his arrangements. We'll go through the details with both of you then."

Schultz pulled on a heavy wool coat, and the two men headed toward Thomas's coach waiting at the end of the wharf.

65

New York City, New York
January 4, 1861

Lieut. Gen. Winfield Scott,
Washington, D.C.:

Dear General: I had an interview with Mr. Schultz at 8 o'clock last evening, and found him to be, as you supposed, and together we visited Mr. M. O. Roberts. The latter looks exclusively to the dollars, whilst Mr. S. is acting for the good of his country. Mr. R. Required $1,500 per day for ten days, besides the cost of 300 tons of coal, which I declined; but, after a long conversation, I became satisfied that the movement could be made with his vessel, the *Star of the West*, without exciting suspicion. I finally chartered her at $1,250 per day. She is running on the New Orleans route, and will clear for that port; but no notice will be put in the papers, and persons seeing the ship moving from the dock will suppose she is on her regular trip. Major Eaton, commissary of subsistence, fully enters into my views. He will see Mr. Roberts, hand him a list of the supplies with the places where they may be procured, and the purchases will be made on the ship's account. In this way no public machinery will be used.

To-night I pass over to Governor's Island to do what is necessary, i.e., have 300 stand of arms and ammunition on the wharf, and 200 men ready to march on board Mr. Schultz's steam-tugs about nightfall to-morrow, to go to the steamer, passing very slowly down the bay. I shall cut off all communication between the island and the cities until Tuesday morning, when I expect the steamer will be safely moored at Fort Sumter.

L. Thomas, Assistant Adjutant-General

66

New York City, New York
January 5, 1861

"Tonight at seven o'clock, ve go to Governors Island," Captain VanDer Hooven told his three crewmen as the sky was beginning to darken.

"Vhy?" Matthias asked.

VanDer Hooven shrugged his shoulders and said simply, "Captain Schultz say so."

With several hours to go before their mission, Felix and Matthias went below deck to play cards by lamplight. Kit went down to tend the boiler, and the captain stayed in the frigid pilothouse, warming his hands against his pipe's hot bowl.

When night came, the quarter moon was hidden by black clouds. VanDer Hooven had to go below deck to read his pocket watch by lamplight. On the final reading, there were only eight minutes left. "Okay, boys, ve go now. Get ready." After about forty minutes, the tug, running without lamps, passed the Battery on her starboard. The captain could not see Governors Island, but he knew precisely where it was. After twenty minutes or so, he saw a lantern wagging from the island. He headed directly toward it.

As he approached the island's wharf, VanDer Hooven could see a number of tugs already docked. Men and equipment were being quietly loaded onto them. He waited offshore until one of the tugs had left, and then he promptly eased the *Ella* into the empty space. Kit and Matthias threw out ropes and silently drew the tug in.. Schultz was standing on the wharf and quickly boarded the *Ella.* VanDer Hooven and the three crewmen came on deck to learn what was going on. Schultz talked in a normal voice, although he was hard to hear with the rising wind.

"Captain," Schultz said, "we're going to load your tug with supplies and a number of soldiers. When we're done, you're to go out to the Narrows. The *Star of the West* will be waiting for you. She and my other tugs are running without lamps, so you'll have to be careful. When you get to her, unload the men and supplies as quickly as possible and return to your home wharf slowly and quietly. When you're done, you and your men cannot talk to anyone about this. Do you understand?"

VanDer Hooven looked at his crewmen, who nodded in return. "Yah, Captain. Ve understand."

A gangplank went up, and a handful of soldiers began carrying heavy wooden crates onto the deck. By now, the wind had dispersed the clouds, and the moon gave enough light for the men to work without lamps. Kit and the two German brothers began piling the crates around on the deck. The crates were followed by covered baskets and then large canvas bags. A dozen or so soldiers finally came aboard to help the crewmen pile and secure the supplies onto the tug's deck. A man on shore walked to the tug and said, "That's enough." The soldiers then sat on the tug's deck with their backs against the cabin. Matthias and Kit pushed the tug from the wharf with pikes, and Felix engaged the engine. Captain VanDer Hooven pointed the little boat toward the Narrows.

The *Star of the West* was a large side-wheel coaster, and in the moonlight it was not difficult to find her in the narrow area of the bay between Brooklyn and Staten Island. There were tugs ahead of the *Ella* unloading their men and supplies, so VanDer Hooven ordered the paddle wheels stopped well short of the *Star*. The wind was continuing to blow sharply, and the *Ella* rocked silently in the water. During this pause, Kit had a chance to look closely at the *Ella*'s passengers. They were young men, some perhaps younger than Kit. They sat in their dark greatcoats in crevices between crates and bags trying to shelter themselves from the wind. A couple of the young men looked at Kit with curiosity but said nothing. One seemed visibly nervous. Each man carried a musket and a canvas knapsack.

Captain VanDer Hooven saw a lamp wiggle near the waterline of the *Star*, and he came down from the pilothouse to tell Felix to engage the paddle wheels. Slowly the tug headed toward stairs hanging from the side of the *Star*. An officer waited on the bottom step with the lamp. When they arrived, Kit jumped over the rail of the tug onto the step with a rope, which he and the officer used to secure the tug. The soldiers silently formed a human chain up the *Star*'s staircase, and the *Ella*'s crew, together with two soldiers who remained on board, began passing up the crates and sacks of supplies. Within minutes, the *Ella* was fully unloaded and the two remaining soldiers had boarded the *Star*. Kit untied the *Ella* and jumped from the step to his boat's deck, and the tug began her journey to her home wharf. As she was pulling away, Kit and one of the young soldiers standing on the *Star*'s stairs acknowledged each other with a silent wave of the hand.

On the way back to their home wharf, Matthias and Felix went below deck to tend the engine and warm up. Kit stayed in the pilothouse with the captain. Kit spoke first. "Capt'n, suh, whey you s'pose those soldiers goin'?"

"I don't know, Bill, but I tink I guess. I tink they go to Fort Sum'er."

Kit had heard of Fort Sumter from the German boys. "Why dey go there, Capt'n?"

"Tere's a rebellion, Bill. South Carolina wants to leave the United States, and tey want to take the fort at Charleston."

Kit was confused at this answer. "Why dey want to leave da United States?" he asked.

Captain VanDer Hooven mulled over this question as he scanned the harbor. They were going past Governors Island, which remained in nearly total darkness. Finally, he said, "I tink it's 'cause they scared a their slaves."

Kit was taken aback by this answer. "Why dey scared?"

"The slave owners say that if the slaves are free, tey'll kill the white folks."

"Why dey say dat? Slaves, dey wanna be free, but dey don't want to kill no one." After he said this, Kit paused, thinking that he had let on more about himself than he should have.

Captain VanDer Hooven tamped down the hot ashes of his pipe with his calloused index finger. Taking a puff, he was satisfied the smoke would last a while longer. He looked briefly at Kit and turned to stare out into the darkness. "Bill, if you want people to do sometin', you scare 'em first, den say you'll save 'em from the ting dey scared of. Works all the time, at least for a while."

Kit considered VanDer Hooven's statement. He remembered Collins, Judge Crane's overseer, telling a group of young slaves about the catawampus cat, a terrible beast that attacked runaway slaves at night and tore their throats out. Collins had said that the cat didn't kill white folks because it knew they had guns. If the slaves wanted to be safe from the catawampus cat, they'd better stay on the plantation at night. It had made perfect sense to the young slaves, but one day Kit had asked Danny about it. Danny had looked at him from his workbench with a grin and then started laughing.

“Dat ol’ catawampus. He only eat colored folk! Kit, I seen lotsa things eat chick’ns ’n’ ducks, but I ain’t never seen nuttin’ eat only da dark meat ’n’ leave da white meat ’lone.”

Danny, still laughing, had turned back to his workbench. “Yep, that ol’ catawampus, it sure one *strange* cat.”

Peering into the darkness, Kit pondered what Captain VanDer Hooven had just said—scare them first and then protect them from the thing they’re scared of.

The Star of the West *approaching Fort Sumter*

67

"The First of the War," *Harper's Weekly* January 19, 1861

On Wednesday morning, January 6, 1861, the first shots were fired. At daybreak on that morning the steamship Star of the West, with 250 United States troops on board, attempted to enter the harbor of Charleston for the purpose of communicating with Fort Sumter. The people of Charleston had been warned of her coming and of her errand by telegraph. They determined to prevent her reaching Fort Sumter. Accordingly, as soon as she came within range, batteries on Morris Island and at Fort Moultrie opened on her. The first shot was fired across her bows; whereupon she increased her speed and hoisted the stars and stripes. Other shots were then fired in rapid succession from Morris Island, two or more of which hulled the steamer, and compelled her to put about and go to sea.

68

Demopolis, Alabama
January 1861

ZEB watched from a distance as Wilcox and Judge Crane talked near the entrance to the slave pen. Finally, the judge nodded and walked off without shaking Wilcox's hand. When the judge was out of earshot, Wilcox motioned to Zeb to come to him.

"Zeb, the judge agreed to pay for a trip to New York to get his boy. You and Tommy are going to the big city to find him. If you nab him, the judge has agreed to a reward. You and Tommy can split three hunner dollars of that reward."

Zeb's head shot back when he heard the amount. He and Tommy had been catching slaves for fifteen and twenty dollars for years. Three hundred dollars! That was more than he and Tommy had made in the previous couple of years combined.

"Why so much?" Zeb asked.

"Well, he's young and strong and has been trained as a blacksmith, so on the auction block he's worth maybe two or three thousand dollars," Wilcox answered. However, to Wilcox that hardly explained the thousand-dollar reward the judge had offered him. "Frankly," Wilcox continued, "it's more than that. The judge, he's got a liking for the boy. Thinks the boy went crazy when he larned his mammy kilt herself. He thinks if we nab him and bring him back, a good whippin' will straighten everything out and he and his boy'll live happily ever after. Now, I ain't too sure 'bout that, but that ain't my call. The way I see it, once a nigger becomes a runaway, he stays a runaway. I've seen some niggers get their fingers and toes chopped off, their ears cut off, all sorts of stuff, and they still run away. But …" Wilcox shrugged. "It's the judge's money, not mine."

Wilcox opened an envelope that the judge had given him. "Here's the one hundred fifty dollars for you and Tommy to go to New York and bring Kit back. It's more than you need, so bring some back."

"How we gonna find him?"

"I know the ship he left on. It's called the *Cetus.* I also pretty much know the day it went into New York. I'll write the ship's name and the time of its arrival for you. If you check the Customs House in New York, you may be able to find out where it docked. Then, you ask around. There can't be too many colored blacksmiths who know how to make ironwork for a ship. My guess is that if Kit ain't gone to Canada, he's still near the harbor working as a blacksmith. There's some smart Yankee making money offa him."

"Tommy and me, we ain't never been to New York. I ain't sure we can find our way around so good," Zeb said.

"I know," Wilcox said. "That's why you're going to take Jack wit you. He's been in New York before, and he's a pretty good chaser. Jack will be waitin' for you in Mobile."

"You gonna pay Jack, or I gotta split some of da three hundred?" Zeb asked.

"I got my own arrangements wit Jack," answered Wilcox.

"Okay, boss," Zeb said. "I'll get Tommy, and we'll head to Mobile to pick up Jack. We take a boat to New York?"

"Yeah," Wilcox said. "They got ships leaving all the time. Find one that ain't too dear."

As Zeb was just about to leave, he had a thought. "Boss, let me cut my own deal with Tommy. Don't tell 'im how much da reward is."

Wilcox smiled. Greed in a slave catcher was a wonderful thing. It made them work all that much harder. "Sure 'nuf, Zeb. Mum's da word."

69

British legation, Rush House
Washington, DC
January 1861

"LORD Lyons, the meal was excellent, and the duck was perfect. I thank you heartily for the wonderful dinner." Seward put his knife and fork upon his plate as a gesture that he had finally finished. The dining room of Lord Lyons, the British ambassador to the United States, was dark and gloomy but also warm and comfortable, and the food really was excellent.

"Senator, thank you for your compliment, but I cannot take credit for the meal. The cook was hired by Lord Napier, and I was simply fortunate she was here when I arrived a few years ago. I understand Lord Napier encouraged her to learn how to cook English dishes but without much success."

"Well, thank goodness."

Lord Lyons's eyebrows rose at the comment. Although he had been in the United States for more than two years, he still was amazed at the candor of Americans. In that regard, Seward was a particularly fine example of Yankee bluntness.

"Indeed!" Lord Lyons responded softly.

Seward realized that he had committed an indiscretion, possibly even an insult to his host's country, or its cooking at least.

"What I meant, Your Lordship, is that American cooking is best for American food, whilst English cooking is best for English food."

Lord Lyons decided to remain silent while Seward's ridiculous statement lingered in the room. He then responded flatly, "We have ducks in England."

"Ah, yes, I know you do. But they are ... different. They, uh, are ..."

After an embarrassing silence, Lyons offered, "They're English ducks?"

"Exactly right, Your Lordship. Perfect for English cooking but perhaps not quite right for American cooking."

Behind his bland appearance, Lyons was enjoying Seward's discomfiture immensely. However, there were important matters to discuss, and he needed to probe his dinner companion for information.

"Senator, I very much appreciate your company tonight. When I learned that you had accepted President-Elect Lincoln's offer to become secretary of state, I thought it would be propitious for the two of us to meet in an informal setting."

"An excellent idea, Your Lordship. We have much to discuss."

"As you know, Her Majesty's government seeks no involvement in your country's domestic affairs, but we are still interested in them nonetheless."

Seward responded, "Well, I can well recall when Her Majesty's government had more than a passing interest in our domestic affairs."

Lyons was surprised. "I'm sorry, but I don't understand."

"I was, I believe, about ten years old when His Majesty's troops first came down from Canada and sacked Detroit. Afterward, they encouraged their Indian friends to massacre the settlers at Fort Dearborn in what is now Chicago. Even women and children were butchered. I think I was thirteen when His Majesty's troops burned the Executive Mansion to the ground. As I recall, most Americans considered those activities interference in our domestic affairs."

Lyons was surprised at this rejoinder. "Senator Seward, that was many years ago—indeed, before I was born. Nothing of that sort has happened since that unfortunate period."

Seward, affecting absentmindedness, continued to ramble. "After burning down the Executive Mansion, let's see, the British troops burned the Library of Congress. I remember the stories of soldiers throwing armfuls of books into a great bonfire. It was quite a vicious war, and many an American town was attacked." Then, focusing on Lord Lyons, Seward said softly, "The battles raged throughout the United States, Your Lordship. British troops and their Indian allies sacked cities and towns in nearly every state. Charleston and Savannah were blockaded for months, New Orleans was attacked and forced to defend herself, and Baltimore was shelled by British ships. Even after fifty years, there are many like me throughout the United States, North and South alike, who still remember those events. Indeed, your current prime minister, Lord Palmerston, must remember those events. After all, he was Britain's secretary of war at the time."

It was now Lyons's turn to be discomfited. "That's all history, Senator. What has happened has happened. Nothing we can do can alter those events, unfortunate as they are. I believe it more profitable to deal with the present than look to the past."

"I couldn't agree more, Your Lordship. What now I see at present is troubling. France has decided to install an Austrian prince as the emperor of Mexico with, I might note, British assistance. Even as we speak, French and British troops are establishing military bases just a few miles south of our country's borders. Spain is looking to annex Dominica a few miles from our coast. While I suppose that there may be some harmless motive on the part of the European powers in all these activities, I'm at a loss to see it. What I see, Lord Lyons, is England, France, and Spain circling the United States, attempting to meddle within the American sphere. Someone, my lord, has gotten the impression that the United States has been weakened by all the silly talk of secession, and I can assure you that that is a very dangerous impression."

Lyons looked at Seward in the dim light of the room's oil lamps. He saw bright, intelligent eyes set in an intense, pale face featuring a large, protruding nose. Seward's shock of black hair was rumpled and sticking up in places, and Lyons felt as if he were looking into the face of an old but dangerous bird of prey. The conversation, Lyons thought, was truly extraordinary. The *Star of the West* fiasco had just happened, and slave states were declaring their independence from the Union even as they spoke. It would have appeared to any rational observer that the United States was unraveling. Yet here he was being lectured by the next secretary of state about European interference in Mexico and Dominca! Lyons decided to try again.

"You must know, Senator Seward, that I'm quite sincere when I say that Her Majesty's government has no desire or intention to involve itself in your country's domestic matters. Nevertheless, we are still interested in them. Surely, you must recognize that the claimed secession of certain of the slaveholding states from the United States is an extraordinary event, and Her Majesty's government must try to understand what it means, especially as to the supply of cotton."

Seward nodded. "I understand, Your Lordship, and I believe it most important that Her Majesty's government should not misapprehend what is really occurring." Seward sat quietly for a moment, composing his thoughts.

"When Abraham Lincoln was elected two months ago," Seward began, "a newspaper in Charleston wrote that as a result of that election the value of slaves in the South shrank by some four hundred million dollars. You understand, I believe, that outside of land, the most valuable asset in the United States is slaves. The total value of all the slaves is greater than the total value of all our ships or all our railroads or all of anything else. Our situation is not at all like that of Great Britain, which had relatively few slaves when she emancipated them."

Seward paused to let Lyons absorb this information and then continued, "On the other hand, the total number of slaveholders in the United States is quite small, but it consists mostly of wealthy families, politically strong in their states and frequently connected to one another by marriage. These families are desperate not to lose their wealth, much of which is in slaves. Because these families have somehow talked themselves into believing that the North will forcibly free their slaves, they have used their newspapers and public speakers to raise the specter of slave revolts and ravished white women and all other sort of hobgoblins to drum up support from the poor, gullible whites of the South, of which there are many. If these powerful families were convinced that their assets would be unaffected by Mr. Lincoln's election—that is, that the federal government would not interfere with slavery where it presently exists and that fugitive slaves would be promptly returned to their owners—they'd calm down and rethink the difficulties they face if they secede from what has been a very successful union."

"Is Mr. Lincoln prepared to make such a statement?"

"Indeed he is, my lord. I'm working on his inaugural speech right now. However, so the South does not have to wait in suspense, I'm giving a speech in the Senate this Saturday, the twelfth, in which I lay out the position of Mr. Lincoln's party. Even though Alabama and Louisiana are claiming to have already seceded from the Union, Jefferson Davis and Judah Benjamin will be seated as their senators to hear what I have to say. I'll make certain you get a copy of the speech. I am confident that when our position is fully understood, a great calmness will spread throughout the South, and the talk about rebellion will disappear like dew in the morning. That, sir, is why I'm advising the European countries that it would be most foolish to intrude into our affairs or those of our hemisphere."

"Senator, if the South is allowed to keep her slaves, how long will slavery continue in the United States?"

Seward rested his chin on his hand as he thought through his answer. "We've talked about this. Mr. Lincoln told me that he thinks slavery will wither away in a hundred years or so. I think it will be much shorter. No more than fifty years."

"Fifty years! You believe slavery will continue until 1911! Mr. Lincoln believes slavery will continue until 1961! Can the people of the North possibly tolerate the situation for that long?"

"As long as slavery does not spread from its current location, as long as the new territories acquired by the United States are free-soil, there won't be much agitation to end slavery. There will, of course, be abolitionists, and their voices will not die out. But the majority of the people are unwilling to start a war simply to free African slaves. That's but a plain truth."

Lyons sat stunned by this statement. It seemed incomprehensible that the men referred to in the South as "Black Republicans" were willing to accept slavery for generations to come.

Sensing Lyons's reaction, Seward said, "My lord, I loathe slavery, as does Mr. Lincoln, as do you. I fought against it my entire life. However, if allowing slavery to exist in its current state is the price for maintaining our union, it is a price we must pay. The alternative would be endless war between the North and South." Lyons's face showed that he was still puzzled. Seward went on, "Our Constitution recognizes and protects slavery, and all of us, North and South alike, must adhere to the Constitution."

"How about the territories, Senator? Will Mr. Lincoln support the admission of new slave states?"

"The issue of the territories has been debated so many times that the citizens of every state are tired of hearing it. Mr. Lincoln made his position clear in his debates with Judge Douglas. There is no reason to believe he has reconsidered it. However, I intend in my speech to propose a truce, a moratorium if you will, on the debate. There is no urgency right now regarding the territories. Let them alone until calmer heads prevail in the South."

"Senator Seward, Mr. Lincoln will not be inaugurated for another ninety days. How will it be possible to keep the other slaveholding states from seceding during that time?"

"I'll keep talking to them privately. I know many of the leaders of the current movement, and while they're passionate about the institution of slavery, they don't hate the Union, nor are they irrational."

Lyons did not envy the powder keg upon which Seward was sitting. If his guest was not able to calm the slaveholding states that had not yet seceded, there would only be a rump of a country, and certainly no national capital, for Abraham Lincoln to govern. The proslavery leaders hated Seward, and many wished him dead. Instead of fleeing to New York where he'd be safe, Seward had elected to remain in Washington, a Southern city, trying to keep the county together. If Washington fell, it was entirely possible that Seward, like John Brown, would be hanged. Certainly, that was the public demand of many Southern leaders. *I wonder*, Lyons thought, *if Lincoln understands the risks that this man is taking for him.*

"Well, my lord, your mantel clock tells me I have overstayed your kind hospitality," Seward said. "I must get back, or my son and daughter-in-law will be worried that I've been spirited away by the secessionists. I don't know if you saw, but a newspaper in Charleston offered a reward of fifty thousand dollars for my head. Personally, I don't think my head is worth anywhere near that, but I have grown attached to it over the years."

Lyons gave a slight smile, a rare occurrence for the dour diplomat. He walked Seward to the door and then helped his guest put on his heavy coat. It wasn't particularly cold outside, but Seward lately had been bothered by cold weather.

An extraordinary conversation, Lyons thought as Seward stood in the doorway. Already he was composing in his mind a summary of things he had learned on this night. He rather admired Seward. He was impetuous and overly frank, but he was neither a coward nor a fool. Lyons hated slavery but could readily understand the horrors of a civil war. Seward could not be faulted for seeking to avoid such a catastrophe.

As Seward made ready to walk the short distance to his house, Lyons stopped him to shake his hand. He said quietly, "Senator Seward, I have been a diplomat for many years. A famous emissary once said that diplomacy is 'the art of gaining time.' I trust Mr. Lincoln appreciates your efforts."

Lyons presented the statement as a fact, not as a compliment, and Seward accepted it as such.

"Again, my lord, a wonderful dinner and a most delightful roast duck," said Seward with a smile as he walked out the door.

70

New York City, New York
February 1861

"KIT, de' you is, you raskul!"

Kit turned toward the door of Schultz's blacksmith's shanty and saw a middle-aged black man giving him a gap-toothed smile. Kit was just cleaning up by the light of an oil lantern and getting ready to head back to the *Ella* for the evening. He stared at the man in the door.

"Who you?"

"Kit, you don't 'memba me?" The black man continued smiling at Kit.

Kit searched his memory and came up with nothing. He was uncomfortable with the encounter. How'd this man know his name? Who was he?

"I's Bill. I don't know no Kit."

The man shook his head and continued smiling. "Yous don't 'memba me fro' 'Bama? I's Jack. I met you at da smith's shop."

Kit looked at the man. "You fro' Mobile?"

The black man, still smiling, nodded. He then turned his head. "He's da one. Dat's Kit," he said to someone outside the shanty. Immediately, two shabbily dressed white men appeared in the doorway, one on each side of the black man. Zeb held manacles; Tommy held a coiled rope in one hand and a wooden club in the other. Jack took a club from under his tattered jacket.

"Boy, you's a-comin' back ta 'Bama," said Zeb.

Kit quickly sized up the three men. The white man who had just spoken was tall and fat; the other one, a young man, was average size. The black man was larger than Kit.

Kit understood his plight immediately. "I don't know no Kit—ma name's Bill," Kit repeated.

Zeb smiled and shook his head. "Too late, boy. You axed Jack if he was fro' Mobile. How'd you know 'bout Mobile if you ain't Kit? Ther's ain't many niggas who knows how ta smif. Wey's you larned dat? 'Bama, dat's wey. You's da boy we's lookin' fa'."

The three men began circling Kit. Zeb stood in the doorway with the manacles while the other two men began to circle on either side of the forge, approaching Kit on both sides. Kit picked up a twelve-pound hammer and began moving to a corner.

"Boy, put dat hamma down!" Jack motioned to Kit as if he were putting an invisible hammer on the floor. "You's comin' wit, alive or dead. Jest come wit. We ain't gonna hurt ya." Jack tried to get Kit to face him so that Tommy could come up from behind. He kept talking. "Kit, you jus' gotta come with us. You ain't got no choice."

"I ain't goin' nowhere," Kit said. "Comes close, I crack you' head!" Suddenly, Tommy charged Kit from behind. Kit stumbled forward. Trying to catch his balance, he found Jack holding his right arm with both hands. He tried to raise the hammer but couldn't get his footing with the black man pushing his arm down. A rope circled Kit's chest and shoulders, being pulled taut from behind.

The fat man at the door was elated. "We got 'im, boys! Tommy, tighten dat rope on—"

The voice stopped with a sudden gasp and a loud thudding sound. Kit was fighting to get control of his arm and to free himself from the rope when Jack loosened his grip and then let go entirely. "Oh, Jesus!" Jack uttered.

Kit regained his balance and looked around the room. Jack had backed away from the young slave and was staring at the doorway, his mouth agape. Kit also turned to look at the doorway. The fat man who had a moment before been blocking the door was lying face down on the shanty floor. Boris had his foot on the man's back and was tugging at his ax, trying to free it from between the man's neck and shoulder. Blood was gushing from the wound, and the prostrate body was making gurgling sounds.

While Boris was concentrating on retrieving his ax, Jack rushed by him and out of the doorway. With a great tug, Boris freed his ax. Both Boris and Kit then turned to face Tommy, who was standing in a corner of the shanty. In the glare of the oil lantern, the young slave catcher saw Boris holding his gory ax with both hands and Kit, his face contorted with rage, holding the hammer. Both approached him silently.

Tommy looked around the shanty in a panic. Boris blocked any exit through the shanty doorway. He saw a large open window that opened out to the harbor. He dashed toward it, leaped on a box of nails, and dived through the window headfirst. His legs dangled for a second as he teetered on his waist on the window ledge, and then he disappeared with a splash outside the window. Kit and Boris ran to the window and watched the man struggling in the frigid water.

Now that Kit was no longer in danger, he grabbed a smaller hammer and ran out the doorway, looking for Jack. He ran to where the wharf opened up onto a number of streets. Jack could have taken any one of them. Kit ran down a couple of streets in the chance he might see Jack but soon realized that he was in danger straying so far from the wharf. *He's probably still running,* Kit thought. He jogged back to the wharf and walked more slowly toward the shanty, his heart pounding as he breathed heavily.

Boris was still in the shanty, holding the oil lantern by the window through which Tommy had jumped. He motioned to Kit to look. Kit looked out the window into what at first seemed total darkness, but when his eyes got used to the darkness, he saw something bobbing gently in the water, tangled up in a rope that hung down from the pier. It was the body of the slave catcher lying face down in the water.

Kit stood in the shanty trying to catch his breath while Boris continued looking out the window. Finally, Kit spoke. "Boris, we's gotta git rid of dis," he said, pointing to the body of the fat man lying on the floor. Boris nodded in apparent understanding. Kit and Boris each took one of Zeb's legs, and they dragged his body down the wharf to a small rowboat near to where the *Ella* was docked. Kit held the rowboat close to the wharf with one arm while he and Boris pushed the body into the boat. While Kit untied the oars from the wharf, Boris ran back to the shanty and came back a few moments later with his ax, which he put carefully into the boat.

Kit rowed the boat in darkness with Boris and the body in it for almost twenty minutes. While Kit was rowing, Boris trailed the head of his ax in the water to clean it. When the gore had washed off, he lovingly dried it with his jacket. Finally, Kit found himself near another wharf. He didn't know who owned the wharf, but it wasn't Captain Schultz, and that was good enough for him. Pulling up next to a docked fishing schooner for cover, the two men heaved the body overboard, where it floated for a bit and then disappeared. Kit rowed back as quickly and quietly as he could, while Boris sat in the stern of the rowboat looking around in curiosity as if he were on a night excursion.

When they arrived back at their wharf and had tied up the rowboat, Kit looked around at the blood smeared on the wharf all the way from the smith's shanty to the rowboat. He thought of the slave catcher bobbing in the water by the shanty. Kit thought he should do something to clean up the dock and dispose of the other body, but he felt weak and ill. He grasped Boris on the forearm and nodded at him. Boris grinned and nodded in return; he then tucked his ax into his belt and walked to his post at the entrance of the wharf. Kit went on board the *Ella* and down into his berth. He sat on the edge of his bunk, still breathing heavily from exertion, fear, and rage. He knew that if he had found Jack, he would have beaten him to death with his hammer. He knew that if the young slave catcher had not dived out the window and drowned, he and Boris would have killed him. He had felt rage before, especially the day he'd learned his mother had killed herself, but he had never felt murderous rage, a rage so powerful that he was willing to kill another man. For a man like Kit who had always controlled his emotions, the anger he had just experienced was terrifying. His hands were trembling.

The sight of the young slave catcher floating face down in the filthy water of the harbor disturbed Kit greatly. As his fear and anger subsided, the enormity of what had happened made him queasy. The slave catchers had not meant to kill him, he thought, just to capture and return him. He was, after all, a fugitive slave. Kit wondered if in God's eyes he was the sinner, having caused a death when only his freedom and not his life was in danger. To calm himself, Kit tried to pray, tried to get God's approval for his conduct, but there was no revelation, no affirmation. Finally, Kit collapsed on his bed in exhaustion and fell into a troubled sleep.

A few hours later Kit was awakened by the sounds of a heavy man coming below deck. Kit, who was still fully dressed, sat up immediately and saw Schultz standing at the foot of the stairs.

"Bill, what happened last night? Boris is smiling. He points out a body floating next to the wharf, and then he shows me that the shanty floor is covered in blood! He can't tell me, so you'd better!"

Kit sat on the edge of his berth, rubbing his eyes. "Capt'n, come wif me." Kit got up, went past Schultz, and climbed the ladder. Schultz followed him into the shanty. Kit looked around and then saw what he was looking for—the manacles dropped by the fat white catcher. He held them out to Schultz, who took and looked at them.

"Slave catchers! They were looking for you?"

Kit nodded.

"How many?"

"Three."

"Two dead?"

Kit nodded again.

"How about the third? Where is he?"

"He run away. He's black, Capt'n."

"A black man!" Schultz tugged at his beard. "I knew that they were using free blacks, even slaves, as slave catchers. I should've warned you."

Kit shrugged. Black, white, didn't make any difference to him as to the color of the catcher.

"Well, the slavers were trespassing on my wharf. My guard killed them in self-defense. That's the end of it."

"I's in trouble?"

"No. Even if somebody finds out what happened, the story is simply that my guard killed armed trespassers on my wharf. Open and shut. I'll bring the police in and show them the body of the drowned man. Obviously a criminal, a drunk. As far as the black slave chaser is concerned, he'll be lucky to get out of the city alive. The police fish bodies out of the harbor every day. Frankly, as long as it's not a woman or an important citizen they're fishing out, they don't much care who the corpse was or how he got there."

Schultz looked around the shanty. "Get some water and wash away the blood as best you can. When you're done, get some rest. I'll keep the *Emma* docked today. I'll send the other crewmen on another tug for the day so they don't lose pay. And, Bill, be careful. Trust no one. There must be a large reward for your return and no shortage of desperate men trying to get it." Schultz stood for a moment, thinking. "It may be time to get you out of the city. I'm going tomorrow up to Fishkill. You're coming with me. When we get there, we'll figure out what to do with you."

71

British legation, Rush House
Washington, DC
February 18, 1861

LORD Lyons sat at his desk and studied the paper he had just received. After his dinner with Seward, he had wondered whether his guest's hopes of a peaceful reunion of the states were realistic. However, as Lyons read the extracts from Jefferson Davis's speech upon his arrival in Montgomery, Alabama, he concluded Seward's hopes were no more than wishful thinking. Davis said that "the time for compromise" was "now passed" and that the South was determined to make all who opposed her "smell Southern powder and feel Southern steel." Davis's speech continued, "Our separation from the Old Union is now complete. No compromise, no reconstruction is now to be entertained."

No, thought Lyons as he dutifully wrote down these passages in his dispatch to Lord Russell, *the rebellion does not sound like something that's going to evaporate like dew in the morning.*

Lyons also reported on other events to his superior. He wrote:

> Mr. Lincoln is expected to arrive here this day. He is now making a sort of triumphal progress from his residence at Springfield, Illinois, and much to the regret of his friends, making speeches on every possible opportunity. These speeches are generally short, and are apparently intended to afford little or no insight in the intentions of the speaker.

Lyons finished his dispatch with the remaining news of the day and sealed it with a diplomatic seal. It would go out in the morning. He knew that when it arrived two weeks later in London, the information it contained would already be outdated. Things were happening very quickly, and the drumbeat leading to war was becoming louder with each passing day.

"Southern powder and Southern steel," Lyons repeated out loud as he extinguished his oil lamp and headed toward his bedroom. A man like Jefferson Davis did not utter such words lightly.

72

Railroad station
Fishkill Landing, New York
February 19, 1861

MARGARET Schultz shivered in the cold as she stood on the railroad platform. Her daughter Mary, fashionably dressed in a sealskin-lined cape, stood beside her, as did her son Alexander and servant Leonard. The four were part of a crowd of several hundred that had been patiently waiting for nearly an hour. Fishkill's stationmaster had received a telegram a half hour earlier from Poughkeepsie stating that Mr. Lincoln's train had left and was now on its way to Fishkill Landing. Mr. Lincoln was on his way to Washington, DC, to be sworn in as president of the United States.

Margaret looked around the crowd. She smiled at her neighbors but kept to her own little group.

Leonard said quietly to Margaret, "Mrs. Schultz, the crowd of colored folk over there?"

Margaret looked in the direction in which Leonard had nodded his head and saw a group of Negroes standing by the rail lines, quietly talking among themselves. "Yes, I see them, Leonard."

"They're from Baxtertown," Leonard said. "I know a bunch of them. The one Captain Schultz just brought up, Kit, he's there too." Schultz decided that it was not necessary for Kit to use an alias in Baxtertown.

Mrs. Schultz looked for Kit but couldn't see him. "You won't know him, Mrs. Schultz. He's wearing a hat and got a scarf 'round his face. I know him, though. He nodded at me."

Just then, a train whistle sounded in the distance, and the crowd became animated. In less than a minute, a train appeared, a handsome black-and-gold engine pulling three beautiful coaches. To the sound of applause and cheers, the train, its brass bell ringing loudly, pulled slowly into the station, and the crowd began gathering around its rear coach. As soon as the train stopped, the coach door opened, and a tall, dark-complexioned man stepped out onto the coach's rear platform. Abraham Lincoln was dressed in black and was wearing a tall stovepipe hat. He waited for the applause to end, holding up his hands a couple of times in an effort to quiet the crowd. Finally, he spoke. Although his voice was high-pitched, the words were clearly spoken. "I appear before you not to make a speech. I have no sufficient time, if I had the strength, to repeat speeches at every station where the people kindly gather to welcome me as we go along. If I had the strength, and should take the time, I should not get to Washington until *after* inauguration, which you must be aware would not *fit exactly*."

He ended the sentence with a grin and was greeted with laughter and scattered applause. He quieted the crowd again and said, "That such an untoward event might not transpire, I know you will readily forego any further remarks; and I close by bidding you farewell."

With that, Lincoln tipped his hat and bowed to his audience. The gesture was returned with cheers and applause. He then quickly disappeared into the coach, and a trainman waved to the engineer. Almost immediately, the whistle sounded and the train began moving. In a few moments, it had moved out of the station, its whistle still blasting and bell ringing.

The chilled crowd quickly dispersed. Margaret and her three companions began walking back to their house. The day, although cold, was dry and sunny, and Margaret had decided that walking to and from the station would give her little group some exercise and fresh air. Mary was the first to speak as they walked back. "That wasn't much of a speech," she said.

Leonard said, "That weren't no speech at all. He was just saying 'howja do?'"

Margaret nodded in agreement. "I agree. He was just saying hello. However, we can't be disappointed. He has a very tight schedule, and, as he said, he must get to Washington in time. Fishkill Landing is a pretty small stop on the railroad. We should be thankful he stopped at all." She had wondered whether Governor Seward had asked Mr. Lincoln to stop at her little town out of respect for her husband.

The four were quiet on the remainder of their walk. Margaret had been struck by Lincoln's appearance. The newspapers' description of him as the "rail-splitter," the powerfully built frontiersman, didn't square with what she'd seen. He was tall but thin and stoop-shouldered. He'd been wearing a black shawl over his shoulders, which had made him look even older and more stooped. Although the president-elect was about the same age as her husband, Hamilton looked younger and more vigorous. She assumed some of the fatigue shown on Lincoln's face was from the train trip, but there must have been more to it.

Margaret turned to Mary and said quietly, "The poor man. He knows his election is causing the country to split up. There are so many who hate him and wish him dead. It must be terribly hard to be hated by so many."

"What'd you think of him, Mother?" Alexander asked.

"He has a kind face, but he's carrying a heavy burden. I think we should pray for him."

Confederate Capitol, Montgomery, Alabama

73

Montgomery, Alabama
February 26, 1861

Dudley Mann took his spectacles from his breast pocket and began reading the letter that had just been handed to him:

> Executive Department,
> Montgomery, Ala. February 26, 1861.
> Hon. Howell Cobb, President of the Congress.
>
> Sir: I hereby transmit for the advice of the Congress the following nominations, in accordance with a resolution passed February 13, 1861, to provide for a commission to proceed to Europe under instructions to be given: W. L. Yancey, of Alabama; P. A. Rost, of Louisiana; A. Dudley Mann, of Confederate States.
>
> Jeff'n Davis.

Mann read the letter twice to make certain he understood it. When finished, he looked across the large desk at Jefferson Davis, who in turn was looking intently at him. Davis spoke first. "Dudley, I'm sending this letter to Cobb this afternoon."

"Mr. President, this is a great honor."

"It's much more than an honor, Dudley; it's a duty of the gravest importance. Whether the Confederate States of America continue to survive depends in no small measure upon the success of your mission."

"I have a question, Mr. President," said Mann. "Why do you identify me as from the 'Confederate States'? I'm a Virginian."

"Virginia has not yet seceded from the United States," Davis replied. "I felt it presumptuous to send an emissary identified as a Virginian until she joins us." Davis added with a smile, "Dudley, I believe you're the first person identified solely as a citizen of the Confederate States. That's a singular honor. And, please, I gather I'll be 'Mr. President' to many people, but I'll remain 'Jefferson' to you."

Mann sat in his chair, grimy and disheveled from his hasty trip from Washington to Montgomery. He had not checked in at his hotel, had not washed or shaved for three days, but had come right to Davis's office in response to an urgent-sounding request. He had been fighting fatigue, but the letter that he had just read and the words of Davis energized him greatly.

Davis got up from his chair, walked to the door of his office, and pushed the partially closed door until it shut with a click. Mann's eyes followed him until he sat down again.

"Dudley, what I say must be held in the greatest confidence. Do you agree?"

"Absolutely."

"I will tell you, then, how I came to select the three commissioners. Firstly, you know Pierre Rost?"

"I've met him, but only briefly."

"He's from New Orleans, and he speaks French fluently. He's knowledgeable in things French and rather a pleasant fellow. His job is to go to Paris to establish a relationship with Louis Napoleon and his ministers, to persuade them that recognition of the Confederacy will be in France's best interest. However, we're convinced that the French authorities are not likely to recognize the Confederate States until England does. Thus, while France is an important country, it isn't the critical one."

Mann nodded in agreement. Louis Napoleon had been hinting for a while that his recognition would be forthcoming if the Southern states declared their independence. However, the emperor was not one to be trusted, and Mann agreed that he was unlikely to act without the acquiescence of England.

"Dudley, England is the critical country, and it is to her that I am sending Yancey and you. I must tell you, in the greatest confidence, that Yancey isn't my choice. The government you will be dealing with in London is firmly opposed to slavery. While I believe Lord Palmerston is sympathetic to the South, he also opposed slavery for many years and has strongly condemned the African slave trade. There's no reason to believe he has changed his views. As the representative of a country that accepts slavery, you may be expected to receive, at least initially, considerable hostility."

"But, Jefferson, Yancey's been traveling throughout the North giving speeches advocating the reopening of the African slave trade," Mann said. "That'll certainly hurt our mission."

"Precisely why he wasn't my choice," Davis said. "Yancey, like Ruffin, has too wonderful an opinion of slavery. When Ruffin's followers started arguing that slavery was such a noble institution that white men, as well as colored, should be made slaves, well, it was not well received in the North *or* the South. Yancey's rantings that the African slave trade should be reopened were foolish and only energized the abolitionists."

"Then, why are you sending him?"

"Because we're a very young country and I must make concessions that the president of a more mature country could avoid. Despite the fact that he's a blowhard, Yancey is popular among the fire-eaters—men who have been pushing for secession for years—and if we're to succeed in having the other slave states join our Confederacy, I can't alienate that group. I proposed to make Yancey secretary of state so that he would stay here in Montgomery, where I'd have some control over him. He refused. He thinks his oratorical skills can convince the English into supporting us, and the fire-eaters insisted upon his appointment as a commissioner to England. Thus, I'm appointing him."

"Then how shall I deal with the African slave trade issue?"

"We've nearly finished drafting the Constitution of the Confederate States. When adopted, the constitution will contain an absolute ban on the African slave trade. You may show that as proof that the South remains united against reopening the trade. I'm certain that the Northern elements in London will advertise Yancey's foolish remarks, and you'll have to do your best to assure Her Majesty's government that the remarks were just an indiscretion, wholly rejected by the government of the Confederate States."

"But how do we deal with England's hostility to slavery? Surely we can't claim that the Confederate States are opposed to slavery."

"Dudley, we're going to have help in this regard from the one person whom you would think least likely to help," said Davis with a slight smile.

Mann sat in puzzled silence. "Who?"

"A certain Abraham Lincoln of Illinois."

"I don't understand."

"We are confident, based upon the remarks and speeches of Seward, that Mr. Lincoln's inaugural address will state that the federal government has no intention, or indeed right, to interfere with slavery in the states that presently permit slavery. In other words, the Confederate States did not need to form a new nation to protect slavery; it is already protected! And this, Dudley, is from a source of no less than the chief magistrate of the United States."

Mann sat quietly as he considered this. He finally spoke. "So my job is to convince Her Majesty's government that the reason the Southern states are seceding is because of the economic oppression of the North?"

"Precisely, Dudley! Now you can see why I selected you! You've never been a slave owner, am I correct?"

"Frankly, Jefferson, I couldn't afford a slave in my present circumstances. Prior to that, I was in Europe, where slavery was prohibited. So, in short answer to your question, you're correct; I've never owned a slave."

"And you've written and talked about the North's economic exploitation of the South?"

"More times than I care to recall."

"When you were representing Virginia in England, you made that point?"

"Oh, often, and with considerable effect. There is much sympathy there among the better classes for the South. They consider the

North's tariffs odious and would very much like to deal directly with the Southern states."

"Yes! Yes, exactly! Insofar as England is concerned, slavery has nothing whatsoever to do with the formation of our government. We formed a new government to escape the economic prison that the North has built around us, a prison of punishing tariffs and unfair laws. This is the message that must be given to Her Majesty's government and the upper classes of England."

"What do I say if I'm asked about the extension of slavery into the territories?"

"With the creation of the Confederate States, that issue is now behind us. A territory can become part of our country if its citizens desire. Just remember that, as far as the English are concerned, we must emphasize that the creation of the Confederate States is unrelated to the issue of slavery. The agents of the North will be outraged, of course, but you will have plenty of copies of Mr. Lincoln's inaugural address to spread around; I can assure you of that."

"When do I go?"

"As soon as the Senate confirms you. And honestly, Dudley, that's not going to be easy."

Mann looked at Davis in confusion.

"These men, our new senators, know that you were a hero to many up North when you tried to recognize Kossuth in Hungary. They know you used phrases like 'the rights of man' regarding serfs and peasants, and some find that troubling. As far as some of the fire-eaters are concerned, a Hungarian would make as good a slave as an African. They have no sympathy with all men being created equal, and many of them don't trust you."

"Jefferson, I've been a friend of the South all my life. I was forced from my position in the State Department because I tried to bring Cuba in as a slave state. How can they now think me a traitor to the South?"

"I'll deal with them," Davis said. "I'll let them know that my appointment of Yancey depends upon your appointment being approved. I'll stand firm. Let's assume that you will be confirmed."

"Then, when do I go?"

"The precise arrangements are up to Toombs, who will serve as our secretary of state. However, I think you should leave within a month, so start arranging your affairs now. Time is of the essence, Dudley. We must achieve recognition by Her Majesty's government prior to December. If it takes longer than that, the North will have gathered its wits and will move aggressively against us. It is my hope that we can achieve independence without bloodshed, and to do that we need to move quickly."

Fatigued and now overcome with emotion, Mann slumped in his chair. He said quietly, almost pleading, "Jefferson, I'm overwhelmed."

"It's a profound and difficult duty I'm asking you to perform. Nobody in the South could do it as well as you, Dudley. Oh, there's an additional matter I want to bring up."

"Yes, sir."

"Your *Leviathan*."

"Yes?"

"Are you still bringing her to Norfolk this spring?"

"Good God, I'm certainly trying to bring her! Will you support me, Jefferson?"

"Absolutely. I can think of nothing better for our new country than a shuttle directly between England and Chesapeake Bay by your *Leviathan*. It would help convince Lancashire that our cotton is abundant and available to our friends on the most generous terms. And it would impress upon the North that the South has powerful friends."

"Indeed, it would, Mr. President." Mann sat dazed, overwhelmed. Finally he said, "Forgive me, Jefferson, but your appointment of me, your approval of the *Great Eastern* coming here, this is like a dream."

Davis smiled broadly. "Dudley, we've all been dreaming for a long time of freeing ourselves from the dangers into which the North is plunging us. Our dreaming is now over, and each of us has a role to play. Your role may be the most important of all. Without the prompt recognition of England, our existence as a nation will remain perilous."

Although he was exhausted, Mann's mind raced through all that had just transpired. With some difficulty, he rose from his chair and extended his hand to his friend, the new president of the Confederate States of America.

"I won't fail you, Mr. President. I promise."

74

The London Tavern
London, England
February 28, 1861

"GENTLEMEN," Daniel Gooch called out, "the shareholders' meeting of the Great Ship Company will come to order." There was a murmuring among the crowd of men as they turned their chairs to face the speaker. After a few moments, the room became silent.

"Firstly, gentlemen, it is with sadness that I report that Mr. Hope has resigned as a member of the board."

"It's not the first time we've lost hope!" yelled a member of the audience. The comment was greeted from the back of the room with a loud "Har! Har!" which was followed by more-subdued laughter from a number of the shareholders. Over the years the shareholders had received so much bad news about their beloved ship that they were developing a fine sense of gallows humor. Gooch stood with a somber face, waiting for the crowd to quiet down again. After the near riot at the London Tavern a year earlier, Gooch had come prepared. Two stout, young Welsh brothers with wooden clubs under their jackets sat quietly on each side of the room, ready to stop any shareholder who might try to assault the directors.

"We have some good news," Gooch said when the room became quiet again. "I'm pleased to report that after deducting all expenses, our maiden voyage generated a small loss of only 344-odd pounds. We should be proud of that." The financial condition of the *Great Eastern* had been so poor that even a small loss was something to be celebrated. Gooch continued, "I'm sure you're all aware that the maiden voyage was a great success. The ship worked perfectly and was the subject of many articles in the United States, articles which unanimously described her voyage as safe and smooth. I know you're aware that there was great apprehension about the ship, but those concerns have dissipated in light of her successful voyage. The directors and I believe that if we have one more voyage to the United States, the *Great Eastern* will be considered, without question, the safest and most advanced ship in the ocean. Then, we believe we will have many opportunities to operate the ship profitably."

Heads nodded quietly in agreement. A voice called out, "Mr. Gooch, it couldn't have happened without you." A number of loudly muttered cries of "Hear! Hear!" went around the room.

Gooch gave a small smile. "Thank you very much for the compliment, but honestly I believe that many people, including your directors, did an excellent job." At the mention of the directors, the room fell silent, and the directors became the subject of icy stares from the shareholders. Gooch decided to change the subject.

"We're presently doing work on the ship as directed by the Board of Trade. The iron deck was troublesome during her voyage inasmuch as it became quite slippery and leaked water into the rooms below. We're covering the entire deck with tarred felt and then laying a one-and-three-quarter-inch layer of wood on top of it. When done, we'll have a safe, watertight deck. The other major repair is to the bearing of the screw shaft. We had feared that we would have to remove the entire shaft to replace the bearing, but I just learned that this is not necessary. The bearing is being replaced with gunmetal, and, through the ingenuity of our workers, it is being replaced at a much lower cost than we had anticipated. Thus, I believe we can bring the ship into compliance with all the requirements of the Board of Trade without an additional call for capital."

No additional call for capital! The shareholders were shocked by this bit of good news. Their already high opinion of Gooch went even higher.

"Now, gentlemen, as you know, we had plans to bring the *Great Eastern* into Portland Harbor in Maine last October. As it turned out, the ship was not ready, and frankly we did not have the resources to send her even if she was. Accordingly, the ship has not generated any revenue since her maiden voyage, and considering the repairs I've just described, her capital account is becoming quite low. Naturally, the directors and I have had many discussions regarding her next voyage. We are firmly convinced that she should go to America again, to prove once and for all that she is as safe and reliable as any of the Cunard steamers. The only question is, to what port? We've decided against Portland because, frankly, there is not much that Portland can offer England and not much that England can offer Portland. Portland has a wonderful harbor and a beautiful new pier named after our ship, but our decisions must be driven by financial considerations, and Portland offers us little in that regard.

"The two alternatives open to us are the port of New York and

Chesapeake Bay. We have tentatively concluded that we should accept Colonel Dudley Mann's proposal to bring our ship again into Chesapeake Bay for the purpose of accepting a load of cotton. As you may know, Colonel Mann has substantial support in the Southern states for his plan to use the *Great Eastern* as a transatlantic shuttle between Chesapeake Bay and Milford Haven. Our voyage into Chesapeake Bay would be the first step in fulfillment of that proposal. If Colonel Mann's plan is profitable, we may see our ship become the first of the great iron shuttles between England and the Southern states."

Gooch's comments were received with a thoughtful murmur from the shareholders. A voice from the back called out, "Isn't this Chesapeake Bay part of the breakaway states?"

Gooch shook his head. "No, Chesapeake Bay is part of Virginia, and that state has not seceded. The bay is still part of the United States."

"But isn't Virginia a slave state?" the voice called back.

"She is," Gooch said, "but several slave states have not seceded. Your directors and I will watch events in the United States closely. If there is any unrest in Virginia or if Colonel Mann is unable to secure the cotton that he is today confident of securing, we may decide to steam again to New York City. But, as of today, Chesapeake Bay is our first choice. As you may recall, we took the *Great Eastern* into the bay on her maiden voyage, where we were met by President Buchanan and his cabinet. I must say that our reception in Chesapeake Bay was a much more pleasant affair than our stay in New York." Several directors nodded their heads vigorously in agreement.

"There is only one item of business left, and, regretfully, it is an unpleasant matter. Mr. Russell is pressing his claim against us for work performed on the *Great Eastern*, and we have countered with our own claim against him arising out of work he has not performed adequately. His claim is in the amount of sixty thousand pounds, and our counterclaim is in the amount of one hundred thirty thousand pounds. The matter is in the hands of our barristers, and, I must be frank, the outcome is uncertain. If Mr. Russell prevails, his claim will have a strong negative effect upon our corporation's financial condition. We have nothing further on this at the present time, but we will keep you advised at our next shareholders' meeting, although I dare say that any resolution of the claims will almost certainly be reported in the press."

The meeting having concluded, the two club-toting brothers stood quietly until all the shareholders had left. When the room finally emptied, they walked silently home.

75

Washington, DC
March 4, 1861

During his sleepless night before the inauguration, the events of the previous four months tumbled through Seward's mind. The memories of Chicago, of Horace Greeley's treachery—even worse, of being betrayed by members of the political party that he, more than anyone, had created—were still painful and humiliating. Still, while Lincoln had benefited from this betrayal, the Illinoisan had acted honorably enough after obtaining the nomination. Seward recalled the shock of learning that Lincoln actually wanted him to serve as the secretary of state, the most important position short of president, and how that request had deadened the pain of Chicago. The United States was going over rocky shoals, and Lincoln understood the wisdom of having Seward guiding her.

As he tossed and turned, Seward recalled his endless meetings with rebel "envoys," assuring them that in the future Fort Sumter would not be resupplied without the consent of South Carolina. The North, he assured them, would not try another ham-fisted venture like the *Star of the West*. Seward had no idea as to whether he was telling them the truth. What the Lincoln administration would do about the beleaguered fort was unknowable until there actually was such an administration.

At some point during the night, Seward accepted that he was not going to sleep and turned to sit on the edge of his bed. He struck a match to light a bedside candle. By its light, he read his watch—nearly four o'clock in the morning. In a few hours, Lincoln was going to be sworn in as president.

For months, Seward had fought a lonely battle to keep the country together. By making promises he knew he was not likely to keep, he'd kept Virginia and Maryland from seceding and, by so doing, prevented the nation's capital from falling into the hands of the rebels. He and Fred had created a web of informants in Washington and New York to discover what rebel spies and sympathizers were up to. When he'd learned in February of a rebel plot to thwart Lincoln's election by seizing the Capitol building during the counting of Electoral College votes, Seward had hired dozens of street toughs armed with clubs, knives, and other weapons and stationed them in the visitors' galleries. Under the beady gaze of a gang of potential murderers, the counting had proceeded without incident, and Lincoln had been declared the winner.

What would happen after Lincoln's inauguration was unknowable. But, as of this morning, Seward was satisfied that he had done all he could to hold the country together for the new president. He sighed deeply, blew out the candle, and continued his fruitless attempt to sleep.

The day of the inauguration broke gray and stormy, but the weather eventually cleared. Although cool and gusty, it would be a good day for an inauguration. After breakfast with Fred, Anna, and houseguests, of which there were always several, Seward went out intending to take a brief walk. However, he was confronted at his doorstep with a couple hundred job-seeking New Yorkers demanding a speech. Seward, recognizing a number of longtime supporters, obliged with an impromptu address lamenting the small progress that he had made as a senator but expressing the highest confidence in the president-elect and his anticipation of a speedy reunification of the country.

Seward checked his watch. He had intended to go over to the Willard Hotel to see whether Lincoln had accepted his proposed changes to the inaugural address. However, his impromptu speech to the New Yorkers had taken longer than he thought. He'd find out about the changes when Lincoln gave his address.

When it was nearly noon, President Buchanan left the White House in a simple open barouche, accompanied by the president's mounted guard. The carriage stopped at the Willard Hotel to pick up Lincoln. The gangly president-elect quickly sat down next to President Buchanan, and the carriage continued down Pennsylvania Avenue toward the Capitol building.

Seward left earlier than the president. He was accompanied in his carriage only by Anna. Their carriage became part of a small flotilla of carriages carrying various dignitaries down Pennsylvania Avenue. When Seward got to the Capitol, he and Anna went to the Senate chambers, where Anna climbed the stairs to the visitors' gallery and found a seat among the society ladies of Washington. Seward prowled the Senate floor looking for hands to shake and backs to pat. Senator Bright of Indiana was actually droning on about a bill promoting a gas company (which he had undoubtedly been paid to promote), thus providing considerable amusement to the other senators.

At just before noon, Vice President John C. Breckinridge walked into the Senate with Hannibal Hamlin, the vice president elect, on his arm. The handsome young Breckinridge, the South's presidential candidate in the previous election, impressed the ladies in the gallery with his gracious demeanor and a short but sincere speech honoring the sitting senators. After Hamlin's swearing in, Breckinridge walked over to Seward and warmly shook hands with his ideological foe.

The Senate fell into a restless silence for about an hour. Then dignitaries began shuffling in. The diplomatic corps in full court dress was shortly followed by the Supreme Court justices led by Chief Justice Taney. At last the House of Representatives shuffled in, and at one o'clock the doors swung open, and the president and president-elect were loudly announced. Buchanan and Lincoln entered arm in arm, the former pale and fatigued looking, the latter slightly flushed with pursed lips. The two men sat down in front of the Senate president's desk and waited quietly until they were told to proceed to the platform erected in front of the eastern portico of the Capitol. As they walked out to the platform, an immense cheer arose from the waiting crowd.

When all were seated, the ceremonies began. Lincoln was introduced, and as he stood up to address the crowd, he took off his stovepipe hat. Looking around, he could see no place to put it until he saw Senator Douglas, his old friend and enemy, with his hand extended. Douglas sat with the hat in his lap during the entire inaugural speech.

Lincoln's voice, although high-pitched, was strong. Years of speaking on the stump in windswept prairies had given him the ability to be heard by vast crowds. He began speaking.

> Fellow Citizens of the United States:
>
> In compliance with a custom as old as the Government itself, I appear before you to address you briefly and to take in your presence the oath prescribed by the

> Constitution of the United States to be taken by the President before he enters on the execution of this office.

Looking over the crowd of perhaps thirty thousand, Lincoln took a deep breath and increased the volume of his voice. He spoke slowly and carefully, with frequent pauses for emphasis, so that his every word could be heard and understood.

> Apprehension seems to exist among the people of the Southern States that by the accession of a Republican Administration their property and their peace and personal security are to be endangered. There has never been any reasonable cause for such apprehension. Indeed, the most ample evidence to the contrary has all the while existed and been open to their inspection. It is found in nearly all the published speeches of him who now addresses you. I do but quote from one of those speeches when I declare that—"I have no purpose, directly or indirectly, to interfere with the institution of slavery in the States where it exists. I believe I have no lawful right to do so, and I have no inclination to do so."

Seward surveyed the crowd. It was quiet, straining to hear every word. Lincoln continued:

> There is much controversy about the delivering up of fugitives from service or labor. The clause I now read is as plainly written in the Constitution as any other of its provisions.

With this, Lincoln put on his glasses, turned to a printed copy of the United States Constitution he retrieved from his coat pocket, and began reading loudly from a dog-eared page.

> "No person held to service or labor in one State, under the laws thereof, escaping into another, shall in consequence of any law or regulation therein be discharged

> from such service or labor, but shall be delivered up on claim of the party to whom such service or labor may be due."

Taking his glasses off and putting the document down, Lincoln looked at the crowd. Again, in a loud and careful voice, he spoke.

> It is scarcely questioned that this provision was intended by those who made it for the reclaiming of what we call fugitive slaves; and the intention of the lawgiver is the law. All members of Congress swear their support to the whole Constitution—to this provision as much as to any other.

Seward's stomach churned as Lincoln spoke. The North had been appalled by the Fugitive Slave Act. Negroes had been hunted down like animals, doors had been kicked in, mothers torn away from children, men and women and even children beaten and chained, all in full view of Northerners. Lincoln was right, however. If returning fugitive slaves was part of the price of keeping the border states in the Union, it must be paid, no matter how bitter the payment might be.

Seward gazed over the crowd, trying to read faces. The crowd was now impassive, almost like the inscrutable face of a jury. No cheers greeted Lincoln's acceptance of slavery and acquiescence to the return of fugitive slaves, although Douglas was heard to mutter "good" and "that's so." Lincoln continued. In a lawyerlike fashion, he told the crowd that under the Constitution the Union was perpetual and that no state had the right to secede without the consent of all other states, exactly the position taken by Buchanan. However, Lincoln went further:

> The power confided to me will be used to hold, occupy, and possess the property and places belonging to the Government and to collect the duties and imposts; but beyond what may be necessary for these objects, there will be no invasion, no using of force against or among the people anywhere.

Although conciliatory in tone, Lincoln's statement was clear. He would use his power as president to hold onto forts in the seceding states. It was, however, the only bellicose statement in his address. He even went so far as to endorse an amendment to the Constitution recently passed by Congress that promised that the federal government could never interfere with slavery in the slave states.

Charles Sumner sat on the dais depressed. The speech contained no appeals to honor, to greatness, to sacrifice. No grand plans, no vision, no glorious history. The speech was a long and obsequious concession to slave owners. *Lincoln sounds as spineless as Buchanan*, he thought bitterly. He wondered whether the great electoral victory had been squandered.

Seward had been in somewhat of a daze during the speech, a combination of exhaustion and of having previously read and reread the speech many times, but he perked up as Lincoln came to the end. Lincoln was going to end with the passage first drafted by Seward.

> I am loath to close. We are not enemies, but friends. We must not be enemies. Though passion may have strained, it must not break our bonds of affection. The mystic chords of memory, stretching from every battlefield and patriot grave to every living heart and hearthstone all over this broad land, will yet swell the chorus of the Union, when again touched, as surely they will be, by the better angels of our nature.

Following applause, Justice Taney stood and administered the oath to the sixteenth president of the United States.

That night in Montgomery, Alabama, Jefferson Davis read the speech after it arrived by telegraph. When he was done, he nodded his head. The prairie lawyer had just helped the South's case for European recognition. The president of the Confederacy was certain that Colonel Mann would be very pleased with Mr. Lincoln's speech.

76

New York Times
March 8, 1861

The Great Eastern, according to the Daily News, is to leave England the first week in March, for Norfolk, Va., where she has been guaranteed a cargo, chiefly of cotton, for England, the freight of which will amount to $75,000.

77

State Department
Washington, DC
March 9, 1861

SEWARD was now the secretary of state, and he needed to get busy. The first order of business was to prevent foreign recognition of the Confederacy. He worked on a letter that was to be sent immediately to United States envoys in the major European capitals. The letter, copied by State Department scriveners, was identical except for the name of the country in which each envoy was located. It started out by reminding the envoys, most of them left over from the Buchanan administration, of the letter they had received a week earlier from William L. Marcy, the outgoing secretary of state. This letter had instructed the diplomats that they were to use all "proper and necessary measures" to defeat any attempt to have the South recognized as an independent country.

He included with his letter a copy of President Lincoln's inaugural address and instructed them to "truthfully urge" upon their host governments "the consideration that the present disturbances" had "their origin only in popular passions, excited under novel circumstances of very transient character" and that affection for the Union and its Constitution was still widespread. Seward concluded the letter by issuing a subtle warning:

> Any advantage that any foreign nation might derive from a connection that it might form with any dissatisfied or discontented portion, State, or section even if not altogether illusory, would be ephemeral, and would be overbalanced by the evils it would suffer from a disseverance of the whole Union.

Seward was tempted to be more bellicose about the effects of recognizing the Confederacy but had second thoughts. *We've been threatened by the South so many times that their threats are no longer effective*, he thought. *I'll not fall into the same trap.*

78

"Direct Trade of the South with Europe."
New York Times
March 19, 1861

Mr. T. Butler King left this port for Europe, in a recent steamer, to be immediately followed by William L. Yancey, P. A. Rost, and A. Dudley Mann, Commissioners, for the purpose of presenting the new Confederacy to the favorable consideration of the old world, and of opening the era of "direct trade with Europe," so long sighed for at the South ... Mr. A. Dudley Mann has been laboring, we know not how many years, to realize that philosopher's stone, that perennial fountain of wealth and felicity—"direct trade." How eloquently has he painted the beauty of the Sunny South, its vast productiveness, and its spacious harbor of Norfolk, and how this should be the centre of the commercial system of the United States ...

The North are rich—the South poor. Hence the inference to the Southern mind is irresistible, that in some way or other they are humbugged out of a large portion of the annual profits of their industry. They cannot detect the manner, consequently they are determined to put a stop to the imposition by bringing home to their own ports the proceeds of their crops, and administering upon them themselves. The speech of the Commissioners to the European nations, consequently, will be, "Open friendly relations with us, and we will purchase direct from you $150,000,000 worth of merchandise, which we now buy at the North." . . .

It is important for foreigners to understand that the South consumes only a small amount of European goods—probably not one dollar to five consumed at the North for the same population ... If foreigners would increase our commerce with them, they must leave free the internal trade of the country, upon which our foreign commerce depends, and quietly inform Messrs. Yancey, King & Co. that they had better return and patch up our domestic troubles, instead of seeking to aggravate them through foreign interference.

79

The Athenaeum
Savannah, Georgia
March 21, 1861

MAYOR C. C. Jones sat on the stage of the Athenaeum surveying the audience crowded into the Greek Revival meeting house. Next to him sat Alexander H. Stephens, the vice president of the Confederate States. News that Stephens was going to speak that evening had swept through Savannah, and the crowd that had gathered inside the building soon spilled out onto the lawn and streets around it. A shouting match occurred with some men at the doorway demanding that Stephens go outside to speak. Stephens declined out of courtesy to the ladies who wished to remain inside. At 7:30 p.m., Mayor Jones rose and said a few words of introduction. His words were drowned out by the noise of the crowd, but his standing signaled that Stephens would soon start speaking. The crowd began to quiet. Stephens began to speak but still couldn't be heard. Shouts of "Be quiet!" and hushing sounds filled the room. Finally, Stephens restarted his speech.

> I was remarking that we are passing through one of the greatest revolutions in the annals of the world. Seven States have within the last three months thrown off an old government and formed a new. This revolution has been signally marked, up to this time, by the fact of its having been accomplished without the loss of a single drop of blood.

Stephens then related many of the features of the new constitution of the Confederacy. His presentation was detailed and tedious, and after a few minutes the crowd began murmuring and shifting around in their chairs. Stephens sensed he was losing the crowd, and so he turned to the topic everyone wanted to hear. Why had the Confederacy been formed? Stephens held up his hands and then spoke to the quiet crowd in measured tones and as loudly as his poor health would permit.

> The new constitution has put at rest, forever, all the agitating questions relating to our peculiar institution—African slavery as it exists amongst us—the proper status of the negro in our form of civilization. This was the immediate cause of the late rupture and present revolution. Jefferson in his forecast, had anticipated this, as the rock upon which the old Union would split. He was right! The prevailing ideas entertained by him and most of the leading statesmen at the time of the formation of the old constitution were that the enslavement of the African was in violation of the laws of nature; that it was wrong in principle, socially, morally, and politically. It was an evil they knew not well how to deal with, but the general opinion of the men of that day was that, somehow or other in the order of Providence, the institution would be evanescent and pass away. This idea, though not incorporated in the constitution, was the prevailing idea at that time.

The crowd listened closely to Stephens's words. He continued:

> Our new government is founded upon exactly the opposite idea; its foundations are laid, its cornerstone rests, upon the great truth that the negro is not equal to the white man; that slavery—subordination to the superior race—is his natural and normal condition. This, our new government, is the first in the history of the world based upon this great physical, philosophical, and moral truth. This truth has been slow in the process of its development, like all other truths in the various departments of science. It has been so even amongst us. Many who hear me, perhaps, can recollect well, that this truth was not generally admitted, even within their day. The errors of the past generation still clung to by many as late as twenty years ago!

Confronted with silence throughout the Athenaeum, Alexander became concerned that he was treading dangerously close to the idea that slavery might be extended to some inferior classes of white men. He needed to clarify his position quickly. He continued:

> Many governments have been founded upon the principle of the subordination and serfdom of certain classes of the same race; such were and are in violation of the laws of nature. Our system commits no such violation of nature's laws. With us, all of the white race, however high or low, rich or poor, are equal in the eye of the law! Not so with the negro. Subordination is his place! He, by nature, or by the curse against Canaan, is fitted for that condition which he occupies in our system.

The speech was received with polite applause, and when the applause concluded, the crowd quickly dispersed into the evening. Two old men walked slowly out of the building and down a tree-lined street. Separated from the crowd, they shambled together in the moonlight toward their homes.

"Well, what'd you think of the speech?"

"I'm not certain."

"Really? I thought it a pretty good speech. Did he say something that you didn't like?"

The two men strolled along in silence. They had known each other many years, and each understood that silence meant that thinking was in process. Finally, the second one spoke.

"He said that men like Franklin and Jefferson made a mistake when they signed the Declaration of Independence. Maybe he didn't say so exactly, but that's what he said. There were lots of fine men who signed the Declaration. He just said they were all wrong. My grandpa knew Lyman Hall, said he was the finest man he'd ever met. He was a Georgian, and he signed the Declaration. Lyman Hall didn't think it was a mistake."

"Well, you don't think Africans are equal to white men?"

"Of course not. But there's lots of people inferior to white men. Chinamen, Indians, Arabs. Does that mean that they should all be slaves?"

"But there's so many blacks now. What if they all became free? They'd outnumber us."

"That's the problem! I thought that was why we seceded! We have hordes of blacks, and the damned slavers keep breeding more. If we can't keep them as slaves, what the devil do we do with them? I never thought we seceded because the Declaration of Independence was a mistake. Maybe someday some rich planter will decide that you're inferior and would make a dandy slave. How'd you like that?"

The other man chuckled. "That'll never happen. I'm white. Plus, I'm too old to pick cotton. They'd get tired of feeding me."

"Well, maybe you're right. I just hope this secession thing wasn't a mistake. I remember the War of 1812. The North was all for fighting that one, but when it came, it wasn't very pleasant."

"Nay, there's not going to be any fight. The Northerners aren't going to fight and get themselves killed just to free a bunch of niggers."

"I suppose you're right. Anyway, I sure *hope* you're right."

80

Baxtertown, Dutchess County, New York
March 1861

THE part of Baxtertown in which Kit slept was a collection of tents, shacks, and lean-tos located a mile or so north of Fishkill Landing and about two miles inland from the Hudson River. In a clearing a short distance away from Kit's lean-to a church stood, a building made of white-washed planks with wooden benches inside. A few cabins occupied by freedmen and their families surrounded the church. While Baxtertown was originally built and occupied by freedmen, its population had lately swelled due to an influx of fugitive slaves.

During the morning, the residents of Baxtertown would start cooking fires and go about doing whatever other activities they deemed necessary to stay alive. The word "town" in the place's name was misleading. There was no government, no permanent structures other than the church and its cabins, and few permanent residents, and if anyone knew who Baxter was, they kept it to themselves. The population of this settlement ran from perhaps fifty to more than two hundred, and they were all black.

Often during the night, fugitive slaves would arrive. A few would be brought in wagons driven by Quakers. Most, however, were rowed across the Hudson from Newburgh by a combination of free blacks and white abolitionists. Young men were the majority of the arrivals, but sometimes they were accompanied by women and small children. Most of the fugitives had escaped from Maryland and Virginia and had traveled north through Pennsylvania and Delaware. Sometimes the fugitives were guided by human "conductors" and sometimes by nothing more than the North Star. The fugitives slept in woods, barns, root cellars, and open fields. Sometimes they were fed by sympathetic whites, and sometimes they had to steal food. More than a few died on the trip north from exposure or illness. Some were captured on the way to freedom and sent back to be tortured and then re-enslaved. All started out bound for Canada, the "promised land," a land where slavery was banned and a black skin did not deprive a person of their humanity.

When Schultz had brought Kit with him to Fishkill Landing, he'd decided that it would be safer if Kit lived in Baxtertown until some firm decision could be made as to his future. With slave hunters openly pursuing Kit, his continued usefulness to Schultz on tugboats was over. Indeed, his presence could expose Schultz to massive fines. Even though several slave states were in open rebellion, the Fugitive Slave Law remained in effect, and the Lincoln administration was determined to enforce it.

Each day, a small steam ferry shuttled people and carriages across the Hudson between Fishkill Landing and Newburgh. With his small hoard of saved wages safely hidden at all times on his body, Kit was able to travel to Newburgh every few days to buy meat, green groceries, and other goods. The shopkeepers assumed he was buying for a white household, and since Newburgh had a large number of free blacks working as servants and tradesmen, his visits raised no suspicions. On one of his early visits, while walking around Newburgh, Kit came across a blacksmith shop and looked inside. The smith, an old man, was working hard at his forge, but there was a pile of ironware waiting to be worked on. The smith finally noticed Kit.

"What ya looking at, boy?"

"Jes' lookin', suh. I used ta wo'k fo' a smif."

"That so, boy? Would ya like to work for me? I'll pay fifteen cents a day if you're any good."

Kit stood there, smelling the familiar smells of a blacksmith shop. "Suh, I gots ta git back home, but I think about it."

"Okay, boy. 'Member, fifteen cents a day. Lotsa money!"

Kit acknowledged the truthfulness of the statement and left.

Other than the church and its surrounding cabins, the only structures in Baxtertown with even a claim to permanence were a couple of shacks made from planks salvaged from a wrecked railroad car. The other structures were lean-tos and tents. During the first month that he had stayed in Baxtertown, Kit had examined the existing lean-tos and decided to construct his own. He'd used a hatchet to cut small logs to make its frame and then covered the frame with dirt and sod. The open side of the lean-to facing south was covered with a canvas tarp that Kit had purchased in Newburgh. Although the shelter had a dirt floor, Kit had acquired a horse blanket and a sheepskin in Newburgh, and with these, plus heavy wool blankets, the lean-to was passably warm even in February.

Kit closely examined the fugitives arriving in Baxtertown. Many bore marks of past rebelliousness—clipped ears, branding marks on faces and necks, and scars from whippings too numerous to count. Some were thin and raggedy looking, with deep coughs and watery eyes, and hardly a week went by when there was not a twilight burial of one of the fugitives deep in the woods. Kit's evident health and strength, the result of months of meat and fish brought aboard the *Ella*, was noticeable and resulted in some curiosity in the camp. Feeling guilty and conspicuous, Kit accepted the blacksmith's offer and worked in Newburgh so that he'd have a source of income without the other slaves knowing he was holding so much cash. With this income, he bought beef and pork in Newburgh, and upon his return to Baxtertown he walked around delivering chunks of it to groups of fugitives. His generosity was always acknowledged, frequently by a blessing.

Because Kit had lived in the North for a while, he found himself a source of advice and counsel to the fugitives passing through the makeshift camp. Occasionally trouble would flare up, and usually "Bill"—the alias Kit continued to use in Baxtertown—would mediate, speaking quietly to the antagonists, who rarely failed to appreciate the powerful physique of the peacemaker. "See Bill" and "Ax Bill" became common phrases within the shantytown.

Schultz and Kit avoided direct contact while Kit lived in Baxtertown. However, Leonard walked to Baxtertown frequently, usually with a basket of baked goods from Margaret's kitchen, and would convey messages to and from Kit. After a month or so, Kit was told via Leonard that if he wanted to go to Canada, Captain Schultz would understand. The captain couldn't employ him anymore, and Kit would be allowed to take the money he had earned on the tugboat, almost fifty dollars. Kit mulled over this offer. He was totally alone. The German brothers and the crusty old Dutch captain, the only group resembling a family he had known since leaving Mobile, were as far from him as were Danny and the Behnckes. He knew he'd never see or hear from any of these people again. His mother was dead, and his sister was lost to him forever. After years of living a solitary life, Kit needed to be part of something. It was time to go to Canada, to start a new life. He had some money and his skill as a blacksmith, and, with luck, he could start his own family.

That night, as he received the message from Leonard, a small group of fugitives arrived at Baxtertown led by a hard-looking black woman carrying a percussion musket. Kit was sitting on a log near his lean-to, enjoying an evening smoke on his pipe, when the group arrived. Among the fugitives was a family consisting of a young man and his woman, with a boy about eight or nine years old. When Kit looked at the young woman, thin and exhausted, he saw that she was holding an infant. The protective look on her face caused Kit to recall his mother more vividly than he had in years. After watching for a few moments, Kit stood up and offered the man his lean-to. The man looked surprised but quickly accepted. Kit pulled the canvas tarp aside, and the family went in. "I'll get some food for you," Kit said, and he took a metal plate and located a hot pork stew to which he had contributed the meat. He brought the food back to the lean-to and was again thanked warmly by the man. Kit found some young men trying to sleep under a canvas tarp hung between trees and settled in with them for the night.

Kit had trouble sleeping that night, and it wasn't just the night chill. He could always go to Canada, he reasoned, but the folks coming through Baxtertown were so poor, so desperate, that he didn't feel right leaving them just now. Wasn't the old Quaker driving the wagon with the hidden panels risking his life for the slaves? Hadn't Captain Schultz helped Kit when he could have sent him back for a reward? How about the guides, black and white, bringing these people up from Maryland and Virginia? Most important, how about the slaves? They were risking torture and mutilation just by trying to escape. There was the Golden Rule Kit had heard about in the church in Mobile, the rule that said you should treat folks the way you would want to be treated. Kit couldn't bring his mother back, but he could help other mothers. That night, Kit decided that he'd go to Canada in the fall. In the meantime, he'd stay in Baxtertown and do what he could to help the flow of humanity fleeing the United States.

81

Residence of W. H. Seward
Washington, DC
March 26, 1861

DINNER was over, and Fred and Henry Seward sat in their armchairs in the parlor, smoking cigars and reading newspapers that they picked up from time to time off the floor. Anna had recently purchased a standing oil lamp—an organ lamp it was called—and had placed it behind her father-in-law's chair. She had grown tired of the two men squinting at their newspapers in the dim light of a single lamp. *Much better,* she thought as she glanced in from the dining room.

"Father, listen to this," Fred said.

"What is it?"

"It's in yesterday's *New York Times.* It says, 'Most desperate measures have been making to defeat Alexander H. Schultz for Marshal for the Southern District. At one time, yesterday, his opponents thought they had him down, but to-night the indications are that he will win.' Father, is Captain Schultz going to be the marshal for New York City?"

Seward sighed. "I sent a letter to the president today asking for the appointment, but I'm afraid it's not going to happen."

"Why?"

"Unlike the other office seekers, Captain Schultz doesn't need the job. He's already quite wealthy. While he'd like the job, mostly for the title, I'm the one who wants him there. New York is full of traitors, and I want the marshal's office to be in the hands of someone I can trust, someone like Schultz. However, my old enemies in the Republican Party are prevailing upon the president, and he's determined to give one and all a piece of the pie. I'm afraid that another excellent nomination is going to founder on the shoals of avarice."

Fred folded his paper and looked at his father. "How is it?"

"Fred, I like Abraham Lincoln. He's intelligent and has an ability, an instinct almost, to understand people—what motivates them, what frightens them. I've seen him disarm arrogance with humor, and even his enemies agree he's good company. But he has no plan! He's the president and has no plan on how to deal with this crisis! All day, he entertains visitors, mostly rustics from Illinois and other western states. They laugh and tell yarns, discuss jobs and patronage, and when the day is over, nothing is accomplished other than the appointment of some postmaster in Cincinnati or the harbormaster in Portsmouth. He'd be a wonderful mayor of a small town, even the head of a good-sized county. But good heavens, Fred, he's president of the United States! Each day the rebels plot and plan, and each day there's no plotting or planning on our part. We're wholly unprepared for whatever's coming next."

Seward was silent for a while and then continued, "There's one good thing. President Lincoln knows his limitations. He states repeatedly that he knows nothing about foreign affairs and that if there are any questions in that realm, they should be directed to me. However, I have enemies in his cabinet, and—"

"Father, wait a minute. Listen to this. It's in the same article." He started reading. "Col. Dudley Mann, now in Washington, is about starting for Europe on business connected with the consummation of his *Great Eastern* steamer enterprise."

Seward looked at his son. "Read that again." Fred did. Seward rubbed his chin as he thought out loud, "I heard that Dudley Mann's going to England as a commissioner for the rebels. Why would he say that he's going for the *Great Eastern*?"

"Perhaps he's going to try to kill two birds with one stone," Fred said.

"Good God!" Seward suddenly shouted. "If Mann's going to England, he's likely to board a steamer in New York. Fred, send a telegram to Superintendent Kennedy asking him to find whether Mann is on any of the ships' lists and, if so, to arrest him."

81

Cunard wharf
New York City, New York
March 30, 1861

DUDLEY Mann stood in line at the Cunard wharf, waiting to have his boarding papers checked before he walked on the gangplank.

"Next!" The Cunard officer motioned to Mann. After he examined the papers that the tired but dignified-looking man presented, the officer waved him on board the *Europa*, a wooden side-wheeler. At thirteen years old, she was one of the older Cunard ships. However, like all the ships in the line, she was well maintained and expertly staffed. It was early morning, and the *Europa* was due to depart in two hours. Mann lugged two heavy valises, one with a large lock on it, to his cramped cabin. Mann stored the locked valise under the bunk and put the other valise into a cubbyhole on the side of the bunk. The ship was not crowded, and Mann was looking forward to more privacy than was usual on such voyages.

Returning to the main deck, Mann anxiously looked at the gangplank and checked his watch from time to time. He had been scheduled to leave earlier that morning on the *Arago*, but a note had been shoved under his door the night before telling him that Seward's agents would be waiting for him at the *Arago*'s gangplank. Fortunately, the *Arago* and the *Europa* were both Cunard liners, and a short stop by Mann at the office of Cunard's agent had allowed an exchange of tickets. After Mann had carefully scouted the wharf where the *Europa* was docked, he'd decided to board her.

The two-hour wait aboard the *Europa* seemed interminable, but eventually her steam whistle sounded with a loud blast. Shortly, Mann could feel the movement of the ship as a large tugboat pulled her from the wharf. He walked to the port side of the *Europa* and viewed the city of New York. It was early afternoon, and the city was capped with yellowish, foul-smelling air. Mann wondered why so many people, and so many rich people at that, found it a wonderful place to live. He had lived in many large cities in his life, many of them just as filthy as New York, but none had been as prone to violent criminality.

When the *Europa* was well free of the wharf, the tug loosened the hawsers, and the *Europa*'s crew pulled them on board. The big paddle wheels started turning more quickly, and the ship began moving under her own power. After they had passed the Narrows, Mann went to his cabin. He pulled the valise from beneath his berth and unlocked it with a key on his watch chain. Inside was a collection of papers and letters. He sorted through the documents on his berth and pulled out a long handwritten letter from Robert Toombs, the secretary of state of the new Confederacy. The letter, addressed to Mann and his two fellow commissioners, Yancey and Rost, was dated March 16, 1861, and had been given to him, along with other documents and materials, just as he'd been leaving Montgomery for New York. He would review the letter with Yancey and Rost when they met in London, but, in the meantime, he wanted to commit as much of it as he could to memory.

Although the letter was many pages long, Mann quickly noted that it never used the words *slave* or *slavery*. The letter set forth the grievances against the Northern states the commissioners were to express to Her Majesty's secretary of state as justification for why the Southern states had seceded from the Union. In the dim light of the cabin, Mann read the handwritten letter slowly, making notes on a separate sheet of paper. He put a star next to this paragraph:

> You can point with force to the efforts which have been persistently made by the manufacturing States of the North to compel the agricultural interests of the South, out of the proceeds of their industry, to pay bounties to Northern manufacturers in the shape of high protective duties on foreign imports.

Mann noted on his sheet of paper that the United States Congress had just *doubled* customs duties by passing the Morrill Tariff Act the previous month with Lincoln's enthusiastic support. Mann thought of his conversation with Jefferson Davis about Lincoln's inaugural address. *Mr. Lincoln is certainly trying to make my job easier,* Mann thought. *The English will be outraged at the passage of the tariff, and it won't be hard to convince Her Majesty's government that England and the new Confederacy are equally the victims of the greedy Yankee industrialists.* The letter then hammered home the importance of cotton to England:

> There is no extravagance in the assertion that the gross amount of the annual yield of the manufactories of Great Britain from the cotton of the Confederate States reaches $600,000,000. The British Ministry will comprehend fully the condition to which the British realm would be reduced if the supply of our staple should suddenly fail or even be considerably diminished. A delicate allusion to the probability of such an occurrence might not be unkindly received by the Minister of Foreign Affairs, an occurrence, I will add, that is inevitable if this country shall be involved in protracted hostilities with the North.

Mann wasn't certain how the calculation of $600 million of commerce from Southern cotton was made, but even if it was an exaggeration, England would have no difficulty understanding the economic calamity that would result from a long disruption in the cotton trade.

The letter promised that the Confederate States would honor all existing treaties between Her Majesty's government and the United States, except for the Ashburton Treaty, and would also honor all property and contract rights. The Confederate States could not honor the Ashburton Treaty, which required the navies of Great Britain and the United States to patrol the waters off of Africa looking for slave ships, for the simple reason that the Confederate States had no navy. However, Mann was prepared to make clear that the Confederate States wanted nothing to do with the African slave trade and that such trade was specifically outlawed in the Constitution of the Confederate States.

A point Toombs emphasized in his letter was that there was no hope of reconciliation between the North and South. Toombs warned the commissioners that Northern sympathizers would urge Her Majesty's government to withhold recognition of the Confederacy on the grounds that the two factions would shortly reunite. Mann's orders were to make it absolutely clear that such a reunion would never occur. One side might destroy the other in armed conflict, Toombs wrote, but there would never be an amicable reconciliation.

When Mann turned a page, he was surprised to find the end of the letter. He went through the missive again, to make certain he had not missed a page. He hadn't. Toombs had laid out all the grievances the South had suffered at the hands of the North but never laid out any inducements that the South would be willing to offer England in exchange for recognition. Mann shook his head. *Toombs has no idea what he's doing,* he thought. *England will act only in her self-interest. Unless we can offer her concrete advantages—perhaps an exclusive right to our cotton for years or a waiver of tariffs on English goods for a period, something like that—there is nothing for Her Majesty's government to consider.* Mann was incredulous. *Toombs thinks the English will recognize us out of a sense of justice.*

After sitting for a while puzzling over his mission, Mann put the instructions back into the valise, locked it, and stowed it under his berth. He went back on deck. The air was chilly but invigorating, and Mann strolled to the ship's stern. There, in the cold, he silently watched with a group of his fellow passengers as the shore of the United States began to disappear in the distance. He'd seen this view several times before, but today he didn't know when or even if he'd return to America. If, despite the handicaps under which he was laboring, he was successful in England, he'd hope to return to his new country in glory like Ben Franklin had many years earlier. If he failed, Mann thought, it was unlikely he'd ever see this country again.

82

Residence of W. H. Seward
Washington, DC
March 31, 1861

The dark room reeked of cigar smoke. Fred Seward walked silently into the room and saw his father hunched over a desk, reading a document by the light of an oil lamp. The older man was wearing a shawl, and Fred noticed how small, even frail looking, he appeared. Seward sensed that someone had entered the room and looked over his shoulder. Seeing Fred, he nodded and then turned back to his desk. Fred sat silently in a corner of the room, waiting to see what would happen next.

Seward was holding a pencil that he used from time to time to make a change in the document. Finally, he put the pencil down and arched his back, as if to relieve some pain. At this, Fred struck a match and lit another oil lamp close to his chair.

Seward stood up and said, "Fred, I'm going to need you to copy a document."

"All right," Fred said tentatively. "Can you tell me what it is?"

Seward stood silently for a moment. He said, "Before I tell you, I want you to read this." He picked up a newspaper clipping from his desk and handed it to Fred.

Fred turned up the wick on his lamp to examine it. It was captioned "Important from St. Domingo." With obvious puzzlement on his face, he looked back at his father.

"It's from yesterday's *New York Times*," Seward said.

Fred silently read the first paragraph:

> Our intelligence from St. Domingo this morning is of unusual interest. Our domestic dissensions are producing their natural fruits. The terror of the American name is gone, and the Powers of the Old World are flocking to the feast from which the scream of our eagle has hitherto scared them. We are just beginning to suffer the penalties of being a weak and despised Power.

The article went on to say that Spain had just taken over the island of St. Domingo and intended to take over the neighboring republic of Haiti. After that takeover, the article asserted, Spain intended to bring back slavery to the island. The article quoted a "leading Madrid journal" as saying:

> The troubles now threatening the existence of the American Union are not subjects of grief to the people of Spain. Her political integrity, her interests of race, of religion and policy, require that a stop be put to the progress of this swelling population. If it were proper to be pleased with other people's misfortunes, Spain could, perhaps, have reason to rejoice at what is happening on the other side of the ocean.

When Fred finished the article, he handed it back to his father. Seward picked up the document he had been working on and handed it to his son. It was captioned "A memorandum for the President."

Seward said quietly to his son, "You're assistant secretary of state. You should be aware of what I'm doing. Last Friday, I was informed that President Lincoln has decided to ignore my advice. He's going to try to resupply Fort Sumter. I've warned him that this is exactly what Ruffin and the fire-eaters in Charleston want."

"Does the president understand this?"

"I've no idea. I've tried to make it clear to him that if we can simply keep things peaceful for a while, the Unionists down South will regain their footing. We don't need to go to war."

"Why's the president doing this?"

"He's afraid he's going to look weak. At our cabinet meeting, he quoted Andrew Jackson: 'to temporize is to lose.' He said in his inaugural speech that he'd use his powers to maintain federal property, and he feels he can't back out of this commitment."

"What's his plan, then?"

"Beyond provisioning Fort Sumter, who knows? He has no plan. All day long he's chewed upon by a horde of job seekers, and he can't figure out what to do or how to do it. I'm trying to head off a disaster."

"What's in your memorandum?"

"I'm telling him that we are surrounded by hostile European powers, that Spain and France are moving in on what they believe is a weakened country, and that we should demand explanations from them."

"And if they refuse?"

"We should declare war on them."

"Both of them?!"

"The ones that refuse to provide satisfactory explanations."

"Father, you can't be serious!"

"Fred, I've never been more serious. The president and the other members of his cabinet are very insular. They've not been outside the United States. They've not talked to Europeans about the horrors of a civil war. Trust me—a war against Spain or France would be a mere skirmish compared to a civil war in this country."

"Would a war against Spain prevent a civil war?"

"I think so. The South has a real fear of Cuba becoming Africanized by Spain. Like France did to Haiti, only worse. They think Cuba might become a country of black pirates attacking shipping in the Gulf of Mexico. If we told certain Southern leaders that this was Spain's plan, aided by the French, I believe the rebels would join under our flag."

"Will the president listen to you?"

"I don't know, Fred. I've no other recourse but to try. My handwriting's so bad; you'll need to copy this and then deliver it to President Lincoln first thing tomorrow morning. Do you want me to read to you what I've written?"

"Please."

Fred handed back the document, and Seward began reading. "Some thoughts for the President's consideration—First, we are at the end of a month's administration and yet without a policy either domestic or foreign. Second, this, however, is not culpable, and it has even been unavoidable. The presence of the Senate, with the need to meet applications for patronage have prevented attention to other and more grave matters. Third, but further delay to adopt and prosecute our policies for both domestic and foreign affairs would not only bring scandal on the Administration, but danger upon the country."

Seward paused and looked up at his son. "At present we have no policy as to how to deal with the rebellion. I need to make that point clear."

Fred nodded. "It's pretty clear."

"Let me continue reading," Seward said. "The policy—at home. I am aware that my views are singular and perhaps not sufficiently explained. My system is built on this idea as a ruling one, namely that we must change the question before the public from one upon slavery, or about slavery, for a question upon *union or disunion*. In other words, from what would be regarded as a party question to one of patriotism or union."

He made a note on the paper with a pencil. He then continued reading. "The occupation or evacuation of Fort Sumter, although not in fact a slavery or a party question, is so regarded. Witness, the temper manifested by the Republicans in the Free States, and even by Union men in the South. I would therefore terminate it as a safe means for changing the issue."

Seward looked at his son. "Do you understand, Fred? If we simply evacuate our troops from Fort Sumter, we will have removed from the fire-eaters their immediate cause for war. However, it's not enough to simply remove Sumter as an issue. The fire-eaters will simply find another. We need a common enemy, one that'll cause all sections to join together. This is the heart of my memorandum."

He continued reading. "For foreign nations—I would demand explanation from Spain and France, categorically, at once and if satisfactory explanations are not received from Spain and France, would convene Congress and declare war against them if their answers are unsatisfactory."

Seward stopped reading and looked at his son again. "There you are, Fred. A war against Spain and France to prevent Cuba from being made a threat to the South would reunite our country and give Unionists in the South a chance to recover their footing. It's our only hope to avoid a civil war."

"I understand what you're saying, Father."

"This is the last part of the memorandum. It's pretty strong stuff, but I don't know how else to put the issue before the president." He began reading the document. "But whatever policy we adopt, there must be an energetic prosecution of it. For this purpose, it must be somebody's business to pursue and direct it incessantly. Either the president must do it himself and be all the while active in it, or devolve it on some member of his Cabinet. Once adopted, debates on it must end, and all agree and abide. It is not in my especial province but I neither seek to evade nor assume responsibility."

Seward sat for a long while holding the document. Finally, he put it down. *There's nothing more to add,* he thought. *If the president fails to follow it, a civil war will occur, and Americans will be killing their fellow Americans.*

"The ending language is awfully harsh," Fred said. "The president may ask for your resignation."

"If so," Seward replied, "he'll get it immediately."

Both men sat in the dark room, mulling over their thoughts. "Fred, it's late. Go on to bed now. I'll reread the draft and have it ready for you to copy in the morning. I want you to deliver it to the president along with the newspaper clipping I gave you." Fred nodded and left the room. Seward pored over the document one more time and then sat silently in his chair. Finally, he stood up and headed toward the stairs.

As he walked to his bedroom, Seward stopped by Fred and Anna's closed bedroom door. He stood there for a while thinking of all the young men who would die in a civil war, all the young women who would become widows. *I'd let slavery continue for a thousand years if, by so doing, I could avoid such a war,* he thought. He then plodded on to his bedroom.

83

The Executive Mansion
Washington, DC
April 1, 1861

PRESIDENT Lincoln sat at a small desk in his bedroom. It was late morning, and he had just finished editing his reply to Secretary Seward. The reply was methodical, even lawyerlike. He raised Seward's points one by one and politely but coldly rebutted them. He acknowledged that the news clipping about St. Domingo that Seward had included with his memorandum was a "new item" but did not address its implications. Instead, he wrote that he could not see how the reinforcement of Fort Sumter could be done on "a slavery or a party issue." In addressing Seward's closing paragraph about the creation of a policy, Lincoln simply wrote, "If this must be done, I must do it."

He reread his reply carefully, gently tapping his finger on the desk as he did so. When finished, he sat for a few moments looking out the window at what appeared to be a beautiful spring morning. Turning back to his reply, he sighed and shook his head gently. He folded his letter, put it in an envelope and stuck it in a desk drawer, which he quietly closed.

84

Morning Chronicle
London, England
April 5, 1861

Latest Telegrams.

Liverpool, Thursday.

A Washington telegram of the 22nd says:—

Dudley Mann, one of the Commissioners appointed by President Davis to visit Europe, arrived here today. Affairs at Montgomery, he states, are progressing satisfactorily. No apprehensions are entertained of any hostilities, they feeling perfectly sure and able, however, if attacked, to defend themselves. They have no doubt of a speedy recognition by foreign Powers ... They are cheerful and confident of the future.

The object of Colonel Mann's visit here is to confer with friends respecting affairs between the two Governments. He will remain only a few days, and then depart for Europe.

Colonel Mann has assurances from the directors that the Great Eastern will arrive from 1st to 10th April at Hampton Roads. She will avail herself of the Southern Tariff by landing coastwise at Charleston, and unload into tugs off harbour. She will then proceed to Norfolk, and take in cargo for Liverpool.

It has leaked out, through semi-official channels, that the Administration is, and has been for some days, occupied in arranging or devising some plan whereby a solution of the difficulties impending over the country may be solved without resort to arms. It was for this purpose, it is said, that an armistice of ten days, or two weeks, was asked for and assented to by the Commissioners from the Confederate States.

85

Her Majesty's Foreign Office
London, England
April 6, 1861

"WOULD you care for tea, m'lord?"

Lord John Russell looked up briefly at Johnston, a young clerk, and nodded his head. He then looked back down at the packet of documents lying before him. When Johnston returned to Russell's office after ordering tea, he found Lord Russell with his back to the door, looking out the window of his chambers.

"It's a beautiful day, sir."

Russell started, turned around, and looked at Johnston with surprise. Since his concentration had been disrupted, he decided to banter a bit with the young man, who had been hired on the recommendation of a prominent family. "We have a very long dispatch from Lyons," Russell stated, holding up a sheaf of papers. "I must say, the more of it I read, the less I understand about what is happening in the United States."

Johnston frowned at the comment, and Russell quickly added, "That's no criticism of Lyons. He's being quite factual. It's just that the facts don't make any sense. Sit down." Johnston sat on a mahogany chair opposite Russell's desk. It was, as his father used to say, a time to listen.

"I had thought Mr. Lincoln's election was going to mean the end of slavery," Russell said, "but his inaugural address makes him sound as if he's quite content with it. So it would seem that everything is perfectly resolved in the United States. But then, Lord Lyons has a chat with Mr. Seward, who is in a complete panic lest Peru recognize the so-called Confederate States. Peru! What aid does Mr. Seward think Peru could lend to the Southern states? Then Mr. Seward informs Lyons that the Northern states may cut off our access to Southern ports and Southern cotton."

"Sir, what did Lord Lyons say to that?"

"Hmm. Let me see," Russell said as he shuffled the papers on his desk. "Ah, here it is. This is what he said to Mr. Seward." He started reading out loud.

> It was a matter of the greatest consequence to England to procure cheap cotton. If a considerable rise were to take place in the price of cotton, and British Ships were to be at the same time excluded from the Southern Ports, an immense pressure would be put upon Her Majesty's Government to use all the means in their power to open those ports. If Her Majesty's Government felt it their duty to do so, they would naturally endeavor to effect their object in a manner as consistent as possible, first with their friendly feelings towards both section of this Country, and secondly with the recognized principles of International law.

"Here's the interesting part," Russell said, holding up his index finger. He continued reading.

> As regarded that latter point in particular, it certainly appeared that the most simple, if not the only way, would be to recognize the Southern Confederacy. I said a good deal about my hopes that Mr. Seward would never let things come to this, with which it is not necessary to trouble you.

"Good, Lyons, good!" Russell commented as he finished reading. "Cut us off from our cotton, Mr. Seward, and you may end up with a new and very unpleasant neighbor to your south." He looked up at Johnston. "If Mr. Seward is panicked about Peru's recognition of the Confederate States, he must be apoplectic about a possible recognition by Her Majesty's government."

"Is Mr. Seward talking about a blockade?" Johnston asked.

"That's a good question. Apparently Mr. Seward was asked that question by no less than the Russian envoy to the United States, who quite properly stated that a blockade must be effective to be respected. Here's what Lyons says." Lord Russell continued reading.

> Upon his saying that a blockade to be respected must be effective, Mr. Seward replied that it was not a blockade

> that would be established—that the U.S. Cruisers would be stationed off the Southern Coast to collect duties, and enforce penalties for the infraction of the United States Customs Laws. Mr. Seward then appealed to me. I said that it was really a matter so very serious that I was unwilling to discuss it; that his plan seemed to me to amount in fact to a paper blockade of the enormous extent of coast comprised in the seceding States; that the calling it an enforcement of the Revenue Laws appeared to me to increase the gravity of the measure, for it placed Foreign Powers in the dilemma of recognizing the Southern Confederacy or of submitting to the interruption of their Commerce.

"I've heard of a paper blockade before, sir, but I'm not sure what it is."

Russell sat at his desk, thinking for a moment. Then he said, "Johnston, go find a copy of the Declaration of Paris, the 1856 treaty. Go get it, and I'll explain what a paper blockade is. The librarian should be able to locate one for you quickly."

Johnston rushed from the room, and Russell continued his rereading of Lyons's dispatch. A few minutes later, Johnston came into the room with a large folio in his hand. "I've found it, sir."

"Good. Read what it says, out loud."

Johnston started reading. "Declaration respecting maritime law—"

"No, Johnston. Go to the point. What are the obligations regarding blockades imposed by the declaration?"

Johnston read for a few minutes. "Here we are." He read out loud, "Four. Blockades, in order to be binding, must be effective, that is to say, maintained by a force sufficient really to prevent access to the coast of the enemy."

"There you have it, Johnston. Item number four. A blockade is a paper blockade unless it is maintained by a sufficient force."

"Sir, how can you tell if a force is sufficient?"

Russell frowned. "There's no agreed-upon test, but a blockade does not have to be perfect. Small ships can slip in and out of a blockaded port, and it can still be a legal blockade. However, if a big ship—a transoceanic cargo ship, for example—enters a port, I'd say that's proof the port was not sufficiently blockaded."

"So it's the size of the ship that enters into the port, sir?"

Russell nodded. "That's not the only factor, but I think it's the most important one. If the *Arabia* can steam into a port, I'd say the port is not legally blockaded."

Johnston smiled. "I suppose if the *Great Eastern* steamed into a port, it wouldn't be a legal blockade?"

Russell looked up at his aide with an incredulous look. "If that monster steamed into a port, even the dimmest law lord would hold the blockade illegal."

"The folio contains a number of countries that have adhered to the Declaration of Paris, but I don't see the United States. Sir, is the United States a party to the declaration?"

Russell thought for a moment. "Johnston, the answer is no. I recall there were some negotiations with Marcy, the American secretary of state, but he was insisting on adding some odd language, and we couldn't get him to understand that where a treaty exists amongst a number of countries, one has to agree to the whole thing or not at all. You cannot add additional terms and conditions. For such a powerful country, the United States can be quite dense when it comes to matters of diplomacy."

"So is the declaration binding on the United States?"

"Perhaps not. I hadn't considered that. I'll need to think about it." Russell sat with a frown on his face as he concentrated his thoughts.

"Sir?"

"Yes, Johnston?"

"Could the Confederate States join the declaration? If they did, would that make Mr. Seward's blockade illegal?"

Russell covered the lower part of his face with his hand as he turned and stared into a corner of the room. Johnston could see that Russell was puzzling out an answer to his question. The room was completely silent for what seemed to Johnston a very long time. Finally, Russell spoke.

"Johnston, again you have poised a *most* interesting question. If we were to recognize the Confederate States as a belligerent and if the Confederate States adhered to the Declaration of Paris, then Mr. Seward's blockade might very well be illegal unless there was a sufficient blockading force. Any deliberate attempt by the United States to stop British ships from entering Southern ports would be an act of war against Her Majesty's government."

Russell lapsed into silence again as he considered the implications of his conclusion. Finally, he said, "Anyway, I think this is all hypothetical. Mr. Seward assured Lord Lyons that the rebellion would be over in three months and that there was to be no war. Considering how much death and destruction would result from a civil war, I believe Mr. Seward is correct. The Americans are crude but not stupid. I'm certain they'll find a way to muddle out of this mess without killing each other." Russell stood up. "Anyway, I'm going to take a walk to get some fresh air. Would you like to come with me?"

"Yes, sir!" Johnston responded. "I'll take the folio back to the library and be right back."

What a day this has been! the young clerk thought as he scurried to the library. *Wait till the old man hears about this. "A most interesting question," so says Lord Russell!*

86

New York Times
April 10, 1861

The Impending War.

The Steamship Baltic Sent to Provision Fort Sumpter.
The Authorities at Charleston Notified.

Extensive Preparations for Resistance.

Our Washington Dispatches.
Washington, Tuesday, April 9.

Fort Sumpter to be Supplied.

I have information to-night, entirely satisfying me that the steamer *Baltic* has gone to Fort Sumpter, where she will land supplies in small boats.

You are already aware that she is laden with a large quantity of stores, and is supplied with numerous launches, yawls, &c. The soldiers on board are designed to repel attacking parties coming from the rebel forts; for which purpose the *Baltic* is supplied with boat-howitzers. A number of naval officers have recently expressed entire confidence in this method of reinforcing and supplying Fort Sumpter.

Mr. R. S. Chew, a Consular Clerk of the State Department, has gone to Charleston, to notify the authorities of the purpose of the Government to send in these supplies. It is understood that the Government only proposes to send in provisions; but if the landing of these is resisted, the men who fight their way through, and reach the fort, will remain there.

We may therefore expect exciting news from Charleston, accordingly, within thirty-six hours, if the telegraph is allowed to operate from southward.

87

Charleston Harbor, South Carolina
April 12, 1861

The following excerpt is from the diary of Edmund Ruffin:

> Before 4 A.M. the drum beat for parade, & our company was speedily on the march to the batteries which they were to man. At 4:30, a signal shell was thrown from a mortar battery at Fort Johnson, which had been before ordered to be taken as the command for immediate attack—& the first from all the batteries bearing on Fort Sumter next began in the order arranged—which was that the discharges should be two minutes apart, & the round of all the pieces & batteries to be completed in 32 minutes, & then to begin again.
>
> The night before, when expected to engage, Capt. Cuthbert had notified me that his company requested of me to discharge the first cannon to be fired, which was their 64 lb. Columbiad, loaded with shell. By order of Gen. Beauregard, made known the afternoon of the 11th, the attack was to be commenced by the first shot at the fort being fired by the Palmetto Guard, and from the Iron Battery. In accepting & acting upon this highly appreciated compliment, that company made me its instrument ... Of course I was highly gratified by the compliment, & delighted to perform the service—which I did. The shell struck the fort, at the north-east angle of the parapet. The firing then proceeding, as stated, from 14 different batteries, including Fort Moultrie & the floating battery, which had been placed for this purpose in the cove, back of Sullivan's Island. Most of both shot & shells, at first, missed the fort. But many struck, & the proportion of effective balls & shells increased with the practice.
>
> To all this firing, not a gun was fired in return,

for two hours or more—& I was fearful that Major Anderson, relying on the security of his men in the covered casemates, proof against shells, & in the strength of the walls against breaching by balls—& in the impossibility of successful storming of the strong fortress, surrounded by water, did not intend to fire at all. It would have cheapened our conquest of the fort, if effected, if no hostile defence had been made—& still more increased the disgrace of failure. So it was gratifying to all of us when Major Anderson opened his fire.

88

Demopolis, Alabama
April 1861

"So, Judge, how'd you read the Fort Sumter thing?"

Judge Crane was lying nearly horizontal on a barber's chair with his questioner holding a straight razor on his lathered throat. He held up a single finger, signifying that he would prefer to wait to speak until the risk of getting his throat cut passed. When the shaving was done, he sat up in the chair and said, "Well, Ed, it's pretty clear that some more states will join the Confederacy. Beyond that, it's not so clear."

"Do you think the North is really going to fight? I know that there's some preachers up there who are all agitated about freeing the slaves, but why do the rest care?"

"Well, there's two things we need to consider," said the judge, standing up. He walked over to a small mirror hung on the wall and examined his shave. "First, no man likes to be humiliated. Shelling the fort and forcing the flag to be pulled down is pretty dangerous stuff. There'll be some hot tempers in the North. A lot of folks will be demanding revenge."

"What's the second thing?" asked the barber.

"Well, it's not just preachers talking about freeing the slaves. There's a lot of powerful, wealthy businessmen who'd love a war with the South."

"Why? Why would anyone want a war when we can just peacefully separate?"

"Because there's a lot of money to be made in a war. There's going to be big contracts for ships, uniforms, cannons, horses, food, you name it. Whenever there's a war, these contracts go flying out of the government, and nobody much bothers to see how carefully the money is spent. The men with big money in New York and Boston and Philadelphia, they're the ones who want this war. They'll be as rich as Croesus when it's over."

"I hadn't thought about that," the barber said quietly.

"Greed. Simple greed. The big moneymen own the newspapers in the North. They'll get the rabble worked up real good."

"Is war for certain, then?"

"Our best chance is if England helps the South. The English navy would sweep the Yankee fleet right out of the water. But English recognition must come quickly. The longer the war goes on, the worse it'll become for us."

"Hmmm. I wonder if the fire-eaters thought about all this before they shelled the fort."

The judge gave a low laugh. "I'm sure they didn't. The bunch in Charleston are so full of hate for the North that they never think anything through. We should've waited until we shipped out our cotton crop and purchased a bunch of new weapons from Europe." The judge put on his jacket and walked to the shop's door. Just before he opened the door, he turned to the barber and said, "Ed, we can't unring the bell. We just have to wait and see how this plays out." With that, he left to the sound of a tinkling bell affixed to the top of the door.

•

Part IV

April 15, 1861
to
August 29, 1861

Leviathan maketh the deep to boil like a pot: he maketh the sea like a pot of ointment. He maketh a path to shine after him; one would think the deep to be hoary.

Upon earth there is not his like, who is made without fear.

—Job 41:31–33 (KJV)

89

Washington, DC
April 15, 1861

By the President of the United States
a Proclamation.

Whereas the laws of the United States have been for some time past, and now are opposed, and the execution thereof obstructed, in the States of South Carolina, Georgia, Alabama, Florida, Mississippi, Louisiana and Texas, by combinations too powerful to be suppressed by the ordinary course of judicial proceedings, or by the powers vested in the Marshals by law,

Now therefore, I, Abraham Lincoln, President of the United States, in virtue of the power in me vested by the Constitution, and the laws, have thought fit to call forth, and hereby do call forth, the militia of the several States of the Union, to the aggregate number of seventy-five thousand, in order to suppress said combinations, and to cause the laws to be duly executed. . . .

I deem it proper to say that the first service assigned to the forces hereby called forth will probably be to re-possess the forts, places, and property which have been seized from the Union; and in every event, the utmost care will be observed, consistently with the objects aforesaid, to avoid any devastation, any destruction of, or interference with, property, or any disturbance of peaceful citizens in any part of the country.

And I hereby command the persons composing the combinations aforesaid to disperse, and retire peaceably to their respective abodes within twenty days from this date.

Abraham Lincoln

By the President:
William H. Seward, Secretary of State.

90

United States legation
Portland Place, London, England
April 18, 1861

"FATHER, there's a man here to see you. He doesn't have an appointment." Philip Dallas, the secretary of the American legation in London, stood in the doorway to the office of his father, George M. Dallas, the United States' envoy extraordinary and minister plenipotentiary to Her Majesty's government.

"Who is it, Phil?"

"He says his name is Dudley Mann."

"Dudley Mann?" Dallas gave a surprised snort. "Show him in."

Philip nodded and left, returning with Mann in tow. Dallas, a dignified, silver-haired man of nearly seventy years and a former vice president of the United States, walked to the doorway of his chambers.

"Dudley, how are you?" Dallas asked, extending his hand. "Why didn't you let me know you were coming?"

"Minister, I had to leave the United States more quickly than I planned. I arrived in Liverpool four days ago and had to arrange my accommodations. I should've sent you a note as soon as I arrived. I apologize."

"No matter." Dallas waved Mann toward a leather chair and then sat down himself. "I'm leaving here shortly, you know."

"I didn't think Abraham Lincoln was going to reappoint you," Mann said with a smile. "Who's your replacement?"

"As near as I can tell, it'll be Charles Adams. I can't be certain until he walks in the door, however." Looking intently at Mann, Dallas continued, "I think I know why you're here, judging from what I've read in the newspapers. But tell me firsthand, so there's no mistake."

"I've been sent here as a commissioner."

"A commissioner of what?"

"A commissioner of the Confederate States of America."

Dallas rubbed his chin as he looked at Mann. "What is the purpose of your commission?"

"To seek British recognition of the Confederate States."

Dallas sat quietly, absorbing this information. "So it's true. I had no doubts about Yancey—he's been a secessionist for years—and Rost, I don't know him. But I had doubts about you. I didn't think you would reject the country you had served so long. Have you renounced your citizenship?"

Mann fidgeted in his seat at the bluntness of the question. "I'm not a citizen of any country other than the Confederate States."

Dallas sat quietly, continuing to rub his face gently. "Dudley, you may have heard that last year I helped arrange a shipment of British rifles to Virginia. If that had been publicized, I would have been recalled. But the rifles were to be used only to suppress slave revolts, not to kill Americans." He paused. "I've always been sympathetic to the South. I feel the Yankees have been far too greedy in dealing with the Southern planters. However, this secession, this thing you're involved with, I can't support it. I can't support something intended to destroy the United States."

Mann sat quietly, thinking of an appropriate response. Before he could say anything, Dallas said, "Let me find something." Dallas started searching through a drawer of his desk. "Here it is. This is a directive I've received from Seward. It's not confidential. Let me read a portion to you." Dallas put his spectacles on and started to read.

> Sir: My predecessor instructed you to use all proper and necessary measures to prevent the success of efforts which may be made by persons claiming to represent those States of this Union in whose name a provisional government has been announced to procure a recognition of their independence by Her Majesty's Government. I am now instructed by the President of the United States to inform you that he renews the injunction which I have mentioned.

Dallas removed his spectacles as he looked up at Mann. "There you are, Dudley. I'm no supporter of Seward or Lincoln, but I've taken an oath to the United States. I'm honor bound to use all proper and necessary measures to make certain England does not recognize your Confederacy. My successor will be similarly bound as well. I've already seen Lord Russell and communicated to him the position of the United States."

"It's truly unfortunate. The best solution is for the slave states to go peaceably on their own way. British recognition of the Confederacy would help that."

"Perhaps, Dudley, but we'll never know. Seward claims that this dispute will be quickly resolved, but I don't think so. I think we're heading for a civil war, a long and bloody civil war."

Mann responded, "I agree there'll be no reconciliation, but I don't believe there'll be a war. I know there was a lot of posturing about Fort Sumter when I left New York, but I don't think the North would be foolish enough to start a war over what is really an unimportant fort."

Dallas shook his head slowly. "Dudley, I never knew of a war that started except for something unimportant. Some stupid insult, some insignificant piece of land, some triviality. If a country wants to go to war, any excuse is good enough."

The men sat in silence. Finally, Dallas said, "Well, now that you've renounced your citizenship and are seeking to divide my country, I must ask you to leave and not return. I cannot and will not help you in any way. I may not be here long, but so long as I am, I will work to prevent Her Majesty's government from recognizing your Confederacy." Dallas paused and continued in a less stern voice, "When you were in the State Department, you did many fine and honorable things for the United States, Dudley, and it's to be much regretted that we must part this way." With this, Dallas walked briskly to the door of his office, opened it, and stood silently as Mann stood up and walked out.

91

The Confederate capitol building
Montgomery, Alabama
April 19, 1861

JEFFERSON Davis moved from his desk chair to an armchair by the window of his office in the Confederate capitol building. He had just received a letter from F. W. Pickens, the governor of South Carolina. Pickens's writing was terrible, and Davis had to pick through each sentence, teasing words out of scribbles. As he laboriously read the letter, he learned that Pickens had just had a conversation with Ralph Bunch, the

British consul in Charleston. As Davis continued to decipher the letter, he became concerned that his reading was so slow that he might miss its meaning. He moved to his desk, took a pencil, and began copying, as best he could, each paragraph in the letter. When he could not decipher a word, he left it blank. When finished, he read it slowly out loud.

> Mr. Bunch was authorized to inform me that Lord John Russell had distinctly said, & it was communicated to Mr. Bunch not from Lord Lyons, but directly from the British Ministry, that if the U.S. Govt. attempted a blockade of the southern ports or if Congress at Washington declared the Southern ports were no longer ports of entry & ___ that it would immediately lead to the recognition of the Independence of the South by Great Britain, and that free intercourse with us should be maintained. I communicate this immediately to you as a matter of importance, coming the way it does, and I have no doubt of the truth of it.

Davis reread the paragraph silently and carefully until he was sure he understood it. Pickens said that Bunch, the British consul in Charleston, had told him an attempt by the federal government to blockade the Southern ports would immediately lead to British recognition of the Confederacy. Why was Bunch, the British consul, being directly informed of Lord Russell's decision instead of through Lord Lyons? Davis knew of Bunch, knew that despite the fact that he was the British consul, he was reputed to be sympathetic to the South. Could this information be trusted? Pickens thought so. Davis was still sitting in his armchair, tapping Pickens's letter gently against his knee, when there was a knock on his door. He looked up and saw a young clerk standing there.

"What is it?"

"Mr. President. We just got a telegraph message from Richmond. We thought you should know about it right away."

"Well, go ahead."

"President Lincoln has today declared a blockade of all ports in the states of South Carolina, Georgia, Alabama, Florida, Mississippi, Louisiana, and Texas!"

92

Westminster Palace Hotel
Victoria Street
London, England
April 20, 1861

"Sir William, you're as well prepared as one could hope," Mann said at the conclusion of a nearly three-hour session in Mann's room at the Westminster Palace Hotel. Sir William Gregory acknowledged the praise with a slight smile.

Gregory was a forty-seven-year-old member of Parliament representing County Galway in Ireland. Slightly less than six feet tall and well built, he was an impressive figure in Parliament. In most ways, Gregory and Mann were polar opposites. While Mann had been born into a poor family, Gregory had been born into the wealth his grandfather had brought back from India and plowed into Irish land until the Gregory estate was over sixty thousand acres. Mann was always careful with what little money he possessed, while Gregory was a notorious gambler who had occasionally won but usually lost thousands of pounds at racetracks. Mann was a devoted husband and father, while Gregory was a bachelor and womanizer. However, there were similarities between the two men. Both men had been ushered out of college without a degree—Mann from West Point and Gregory from Oxford. Both were ambitious, and now both had a burning desire to see the Confederate States achieve independence.

Prior to 1859, Gregory had given little thought to North America. In the fall of that year, however, he'd decided to tour the United States and Canada. He'd had several reasons for doing so: to gain credibility on foreign affairs in the House of Commons, to visit his uncle in Canada, and to escape a phalanx of solicitors trying to collect gambling debts. As the son of a wealthy Irish protestant aristocrat, Gregory had long abhorred the concept of universal suffrage. However, even with his preconceptions, he was not prepared for the violent, corrupt, and turbulent brew that he found in the United States.

Attending a fair in the small river town of Quincy, Illinois, Gregory was warned, upon checking into a hotel, that "a murder or two was expected during the night, not premeditated certainly, but owing to difficulties arising among gentlemen from transactions during the fair." At Hannibal, Missouri, he met prospectors from the western states who were "in rags and unkempt" when they boarded the paddle-wheeler on which he was traveling. When Gregory asked the ruffians about gold robbers, the prospectors assured him that they had no problems. As one said, "If a man steals, we jest hang him up right off at once." Shortly thereafter, the captain of the steamer had to pull out his pistol to break up a knife fight. So it went for the British tourist, from one lawless, chaotic town to another. His itinerary included a visit to Harper's Ferry, Virginia, and Gregory coincidentally arrived at the arsenal on October 19, 1859, three days after John Brown's raid. Had he not been accidently delayed in Cincinnati, Gregory would have been aboard the train that had arrived during Brown's assault, the train on which the baggage master had been shot and killed and the passengers fired upon. In memoirs written a number of years later, Gregory wrote about the raid:

> Nothing could exceed the panic of the slave States caused by this attempt. They felt they were resting on explosives, and when men are terrified they are cruel. An English gentleman, Mr. Wynne, was in the train that arrived during the conflict; the dead and dying were lying on the grass. One of the unfortunate wretches, dreadfully wounded and rolling in agony, called for water, and Mr. Wynne asked permission to give him a cupful. "If you do," said a volunteer, who was standing close by, "I'll jest shoot you as I shot him. I guess he shall die an uglier death than a dog or a horse."

Gregory's thoughts on American democracy were finally hardened when he arrived in Baltimore. As he wrote home:

> The mob have got the upper hand, judges are elected by them, many of them notorious scamps, justice is a mockery, all respectable men hold aloof from the jury box.
>
> ... it was stated publicly to me before twenty persons who all agreed that hardly a crime can be committed

> which may not go unpunished if a proper distribution of money be made in the right quarter. All this is the legitimate and immediate effect of universal suffrage.

From Baltimore Gregory went to New York, where the situation was no better. He traveled to Washington, DC, where Lord Lyons introduced him to President Buchanan, "better known as 'Old Buck.'" In the nation's capital, he found a "perfect maelstrom of political excitement. There had been bitter bad blood before between the North and South; now the feeling on the part of the South had been roused to fury by the Brown's raid at Harper's Ferry, and by the tone of the Republican section of the Northern press commenting on it." While in Washington, he was introduced to Virginia's two senators, Robert Hunter and James M. Mason, along with William Porcher Miles, the representative from South Carolina. These men, like Gregory, viewed the world through the eyes of aristocrats, and Gregory felt an immediate attachment to them. For several days they escorted him around the nation's capital and convinced him that if a Republican won the next presidential contest, the slave states would secede from the Union. Despite a personal aversion to slavery, Gregory came to believe that a sudden disruption of the institution would result in a gory racial war. As one of his Southern escorts told him, the insurrection of the slaves in the Southern states would result in atrocities a thousand times worse than Saint Domingue, the site of a slave revolt in Haiti in which more than one hundred thousand people died.

If Gregory had any doubts as to the intensity of the feelings held in the South, they were dispelled when, traveling through Columbia, South Carolina, he ran into a mob that had stripped, whipped, tarred, and feathered a man for expressing abolitionist sentiments. When the poor wretch was proudly displayed to Gregory by his tormentors, the Irishman found the man near death. Gregory left the United States certain that the election of a Republican president would result in a separation of the states. Whether the separation was bloody or peaceful depended on the European states and particularly upon Great Britain. Thus, when approached by Dudley Mann, Gregory agreed to become an advocate for Southern independence. It seemed the only way to avoid the cataclysmic outcome that otherwise seemed inevitable.

“Colonel Mann, I’m optimistic,” Gregory said as he put down a sheaf of papers. “I’ve memorized the materials you’ve given me, and our meeting today gave me a chance to think through our opponents’ arguments.”

“You’re a skilled debater, Sir William. Just remember that your opponents will have to try to explain Lincoln’s new tariff.”

Gregory nodded. “I must say Mr. Lincoln makes a very strong case for Her Majesty’s government granting recognition to the Confederate States. He says in his inaugural speech that slavery is perfectly acceptable, so we can all assume that slavery isn’t the cause for the separation. Then the very first act he takes as president is to *double* an already onerous tax on British goods imported into the United States, and now there’s a suggestion he wants to impose a paper blockade of British ships that will cut off Lancashire’s supply of cotton. Is he truly unaware of how these things will be regarded in England?”

“I’ve never met him, Sir William, but you must understand that he’s just an uneducated country lawyer. I don’t think he’s even seen an ocean, much less crossed one. He’s no more understanding of England than I do of Siam. He’s a skilled orator—I’ll give him his due—but he’s ignorant and crude. Regretfully, it’s these characteristics that endear him to the Northern hordes.”

Gregory started picking up his papers to place them in a folio he’d brought along. “I’m hopeful that Her Majesty’s government will recognize your country within a month,” Gregory said as he stood up to leave. “But, Dudley, you must understand that I’m worried about one thing.”

Mann looked at his guest for the answer.

“War,” Gregory said quietly. “We haven’t yet recovered from the Crimean War, and no one in Britain wants to fight another war for a long time, especially in America. If a war breaks out, your chances of success are greatly diminished. You understand that?”

Mann nodded. “I know there was a lot of puffing and strutting about Fort Sumter when I left, but I don’t believe our leaders would attack the fort, unless they did so purely in defense. Seward keeps assuring our commissioners in Washington that the North will not reinforce the fort. Although Seward isn’t to be trusted, I believe he’s truthful in this for the simple reason that the North isn’t prepared for war. No, Sir William, I don’t think there will be any shooting for a while, particularly if Her Majesty’s government quickly recognizes the Confederate States.

Indeed," Mann said, "that is the best argument for a prompt recognition. It would promote peace and save lives. That's why you've joined us, Sir William."

"Well, yes," Gregory said. After a pause he further said, "Dudley, I've no love for slavery. But I've learned how violent Americans can be. If there's a civil war in America, it will be a long and bloody one. Cities and villages will be burned, and thousands will die, including, I believe, many civilians. If there's something I can do to stop such a war, I feel I must try."

"I understand, Sir. William," Mann said. "Your thoughts are not dissimilar to mine."

With that the two men shook hands, and Mann closed the door silently after Gregory left.

Nearly two weeks pass before I know what's going on in America, Mann thought. *I hope we had the sense not to start shooting.* Mann walked to a small desk in his room and started writing a letter to Jefferson Davis. In his letter, Mann briefly recounted his meeting with Gregory. He concluded:

> If we can take the stand in the family of nations which we deserve to enjoy without unsheathing the sword we shall accomplish the most glorious achievement that the world ever witnessed. This is said on all sides. How much they do dread a war!
>
> Yours Sincerely,
> A. Dudley Mann

93

London Shipping Gazette
April 26, 1861

We have at last the intelligence that hostilities have broken out between the Federal Government and the Southern States. Fort Sumter has fallen, after what is described as a gallant resistance on the part of Major Anderson and his force of forty hours' duration. But, singular enough—and fortunate as it is singular—during this protracted cannonade, in the course of which some 1,700 rounds of shot and shell were fired by both parties, not one single man was killed on either side, and it is doubtful whether any one has been wounded. This bloodless conclusion of the first encounter, taken in connection with the circumstances which preceded and followed it, seems to indicate that there is no very bitter or rancorous feeling on either side, and favors the hope that a good deal of the pent-up irritation of the Southerners has found vent in the first and comparatively harmless passage of arms.

94

Times of London
April 27, 1861

Seven batteries breached and bombarded Fort Sumter for forty hours, burnt down its barracks, blew up several magazines, threw shells into it innumerable, and did a vast show of destruction. The fort replied with like spirit. At length it surrendered, the garrison marched out prisoners of war, and it was then found that not a man was killed or an officer wounded on either side. Many a "difficulty" at a bar has cost more bloodshed. Was this a preconceived feat of conjuring? Were the rival Presidents saluting one another in harmless fireworks to amuse the groundlings? The whole affair is utterly inexplicable. It sounds like the battles when the coat of mail had come to its perfection, and when the only casualty, after a day's hard fighting, was a case of suffocation and a few bruises ... But, perhaps, this is only the interchange of courtesies which in olden times preceded real war. The result is utterly different from all we are accustomed to hear of the Americans. There, "a word and a blow" has been the rule. In this case, the blow, when it does at last come, falls like snow and lights as gently as thistle-down. Surely it cannot be a "cross?" If it be, half the Old Union is in the conspiracy, for all are arming and rushing to war as if they expected serious work.

What next? An attempt to recapture Fort Sumter? A contest for Fort Pickens? A struggle for the Capitol? A diversion in Texas? A renewal of negotiations? No one knows, and what is worse, no one credits President Lincoln for any plan. We can only compare the two sides, and strike a balance. In the North there is an army and a navy, and money, and a more numerous white population, without, too, the incubus of slavery. There is also the tradition of the Union, the Capitol, and the successor of Washington. Modern warfare cannot go on without money, and the Northern States can more easily raise and spend a hundred millions of dollars a year than the South can raise ten millions. All that is outside, and material, is in favor of the North. It has the preponderance of everything that can be counted, measured and weighed; that can be bought and sold; that can be entered in ledgers and put on a balance-sheet. It has the manufactories, the building yards, the dock yards,—the whole apparatus of national wealth and strength. It has the money market, and it borrows more easily than the South, where, however, political zeal sustains a fictitious credit. So in the North we read of numerous gatherings of State forces—of many steamers chartered, stripped of their finery, filled with soldiers, food, and ammunition, and steaming southward. So much for the North. In the South, on the contrary, there is little or nothing but that which often becomes the counterbalance to everything else. There are the men of action, who can combine, conspire, keep the secret, have a plan, and carry it out without wavering or flinching. The politicians at Washington have been vacillating between war and peace, between compromise and resistance. In the South there has been one steady, uninterrupted progress towards secession and war. To the very last, President Lincoln has been behindhand. His ships, sent to relieve Fort Sumter, only arrived in time to be distant spectators of the scene; they came, in fact, but to contribute to the glory of the captors, and to bring shame and distrust on themselves and their cause. If this is to be an omen of the result, the rich and unready North will be no match for the fiery forwardness of the South.

95

Baxtertown, New York
May 1861

Kit walked briskly in the twilight toward Baxtertown from Fishkill Landing's ferry dock. He was carrying a heavy canvas sack draped over his shoulder. He'd just been paid a week's wages for his blacksmithing work, and using that money, along with twenty-five cents of his own money, he'd bought nearly a quarter of a hog and a couple of chickens from Krause, the German butcher. When Kit had first entered Krause's shop several months earlier, the old German had been understandably suspicious of the young black man who had cash to buy more meat than a family would normally eat. With his soot-blackened clothes and powerful physique, Kit clearly was not a domestic for some affluent white family. However, after talking with Kit, Krause had learned that the young man was buying meat with money that he had earned, not stolen. The butcher rightly assumed that Kit was taking the meat to the fugitive slaves in Baxtertown but saw nothing wrong with that. He was no friend of slavery.

The walk from the shore of the Hudson to Baxtertown was nearly an hour. It was daunting during frigid winter days, but on warm and breezy days like today it was enjoyable, and the sack of meat, more than sixty pounds in weight, was carried lightly on Kit's powerful shoulder. As Kit walked into Baxtertown, he was greeted by smiles and offers of help. He dropped the sack at a firepit, where it was quickly surrounded by a handful of women who began collecting wood, assembling utensils, and digging potatoes out of a sack buried in the ground. In less than three hours there would be enough hog stew to give all the residents of Baxtertown a good dinner.

As Kit walked to his lean-to, he glanced at an old slave named Reeba who was sitting on the ground, her dirty skirt spread before her. Reeba was blind in one eye and nearly toothless. Kit had learned from other fugitives in Baxtertown that Reeba's owner in Maryland had concluded that she was no longer worth feeding and had accordingly "freed" her by giving her a small sack of food and a letter of emancipation. She'd then been ordered off the plantation. She'd limped north for several days, sleeping in the fields and begging for food from field hands until a Quaker driving a wagon had found her. She'd promptly been delivered to a station on the Underground Railroad and carried along to Baxtertown. She had been in Baxtertown for nearly two months in an old lean-to that Kit and the other fugitives had fixed up, and she seemed content to stay put, at least for a while.

Reeba enjoyed considerable popularity in Baxtertown because of her ability to tell the future. A fugitive slave wanting to know what lay before him would ask Reeba to read the magic stones she had brought with her. The request was usually accompanied by an offering of food or a piece of clothing, but sometimes there was nothing to offer. Nevertheless, Reeba would open a leather pouch tied to her waist by a cord and retrieve a number of small objects—bones, smooth stones, and a jagged piece of quartz. She would smooth out an area in the dirt in front of her, cry out a series of guttural sounds, and then, with her eyes closed, toss the objects gently onto the dirt. She would open her eyes and with her one good eye stare at the objects for a long time. She would then begin to trace around the objects with her finger, drawing lines in the dirt connecting the objects to one another. When she was done, she'd close her eyes and rock back and forth making a humming sound. She'd then sit motionless in silence. When finished with her silence, she'd take the hand of her visitor to draw him closer so she could tell him his future. The visitor would listen silently, nodding to show understanding. When the fortune-telling was over, the visitor left quietly, bound by Reeba not to tell his future to anyone else.

Kit didn't put much stock in fortune-telling, but the other slaves had a high opinion of Reeba's abilities, and this got Kit to wondering. He had a question that no one had ever answered, and he decided to see if Reeba could answer it. With the offering of one of the freshly killed chickens, Kit sat before her. Reeba started to open her leather pouch, but Kit raised his hand and shook his head. Reeba turned her head to stare at him with her one good eye.

"I seen a fireball. Is dat a sign?"

Reeba nodded her head warily, looking closely at Kit.

"What does it mean?"

Reeba sat silently for a moment and then asked, "What'd you see, boy? What'd you hea'?"

"I's on a boat. De fireball, it came ov'a the harbo'. It lit up the boats in the harbo'."

"Didja hear anythin'?"

"At fi'st, just a dog barkin'. The fireball, I think it sizzled a bit. Den, it sank in the ocean."

"Tell me 'bout the boats."

"Well, dar's this giant ship. When the fireball passed, the ship was lit up red. Dark red. As the fireball moved, wit da shadows it look like blood ooze down da ship. Like to give me shiva's."

With this, Reeba jerked upright. "Boy, dat's blood a' slaves. Dat's a *slave ship*."

Kit shook his head. "Naw, ain't no slave ship. It just a big ocean steama."

"Boy, dat ship's death to slaves!" Reeba was agitated, and her speech, normally a loud whisper, was audible to a few slaves close by. They stared at Kit and Reeba, wondering what was going on.

"Boy," she repeated, "dat ship's death to slaves! Stay 'way from dat ship. *Stay 'way*!"

Activity in Baxtertown ceased as the residents stared at Kit and Reeba. Kit, embarrassed by the commotion, nodded his head to her and stood up. He walked quickly to his lean-to. *Well,* he thought, *that chick'n din't get me much good.* But he reasoned that as a young man he had a duty to bring food to old folks like Reeba, so he didn't regret his gift to her. *However,* he thought, *I'll just give her food in the future and not ask for any more advice.*

96

Pembroke Lodge, Richmond Park
London, England
May 3, 1861

"WELL, gentlemen, I found your presentation most interesting and informative." Lord Russell started straightening the papers on his desk as he talked. "As we close this meeting, I will repeat what I said at its beginning. Whilst Her Majesty's declaration of neutrality recognizes both the Confederate States and the United States as belligerents, with equal rights accorded that status, Her Majesty's government does not recognize your Confederacy as a sovereign state. Consequently, our meeting today was purely unofficial and is not to be interpreted as a step toward such recognition."

"We understand, Your Lordship," William Yancey said. "Again, we appreciate the opportunity to meet with you and look forward to future meetings as matters progress."

Russell did not respond to this comment but stood and walked around his desk. He shook hands with William Gregory, Yancey, Mann, and Pierre Rost. A butler quickly appeared and softly announced, "Gentlemen, I'll show you the way out."

The following day, Edmund Hammond, the permanent undersecretary for foreign affairs, knocked gently on Russell's partially opened door in the Foreign Office. "Come in," Russell said when he saw who had knocked. "Well, Mr. Hammond, would you like some information on our three visitors from America's South?"

"Yes, Your Lordship."

"Well, let's see. I've received a letter from Ralph Bunch, our consul in Charleston, that supplied some information that I combined with information thrust at me from supporters of the Northern states. From all this, I have learned that Mr. Yancey, who made nearly the entire presentation, is an orator of some note, that he has long argued for reopening the African slave trade to America but claims a recent conversion and is now opposed to it, that he once beat his uncle to death with a club because of a slight of some kind, and that he went to prison because of that crime. I'm informed, based upon that record, that Mr. Yancey perceives himself as a gentleman of the most impeccable honor and hopes to ingratiate himself with England's better classes. Mr. Yancey did nearly the entire presentation. Mr. Rost seems to be wholly innocent of any knowledge of diplomacy but having been raised in France can speak the language. Therefore, he is to be the Confederacy's representative in the Tuileries on that qualification alone. Dudley Mann is an experienced diplomat who has spent many years in Europe, including England, although I'm informed that his father was a grocer who became insolvent, and Mann has apparently inherited his father's tardiness in paying bills."

"Mann is an experienced diplomat, Your Lordship. I don't know him, but I certainly know of him. Why didn't he make the presentation?"

"Why, indeed? Lord Palmerston and I consider the closing of the African slave trade as one of the Crown's greatest achievements, yet this so-called Confederacy sends us as a diplomat a man who has argued for reopening the trade? I can only put it down to the naïveté on the part of Jefferson Davis. I don't think it was intended as an insult to Her Majesty's government, although some might interpret it as such. The Southern states would have been much better represented if Mann had come alone. He's not regarded as a fanatic on the issue of slavery, and he understands the importance of free trade. I detected a pained look on Mann's face when Yancey was holding forth on the inalienable rights of man. An amazing speech from a man who buys and sells other men."

Hammond gave a small sniff of amusement at this comment.

"Mr. Hammond, do you think it odd that we met for nearly two hours and my visitors never once mentioned slavery except when questioned in connection with the African slave trade?" Russell asked. When Hammond nodded, Russell continued, "The truth is that but for that loathsome institution, the Southern states present a compelling argument for recognition. The so-called Confederacy is becoming a real government. Mann related, when Yancey finally gave him an opportunity to speak, that in 1848 he was sent by the United States to recognize Kossuth's government in Hungary. Kossuth and his horde had none of the indicia of a de facto government, while the Confederacy will shortly have nearly all of them. It has a legislature, a judicial system, an army, a post office, everything necessary to maintain a modern nation. By what standard can the United States complain if we recognize the Confederacy when they were ready to recognize an unorganized group of rebels?"

"What of the effect on our economy?" Hammond asked.

"Ah, that's the proper question! What does this all mean to us? We don't need cotton as badly as our Southern visitors think we need it, at least for a while, but it is an important staple, and things will get very ugly in Lancashire if Mr. Lincoln's blockade becomes effective. On the other hand, our trade with the North is still substantial, and the Yankees owe London banks very large sums."

Hammond sat quietly, waiting for Russell to continue.

"For the time being," Russell said, "we'll do nothing but watch developments across the Atlantic. It seems unlikely the two halves will ever reunite. Gregory may be right—much blood could be shed before they come to an armistice. What concerns me, however, is the blockade. Our trade with America is one of the most important elements of our economy. Right now the blockade is merely a declaration on a piece of paper, but if it ultimately becomes effective, it could do us great harm. Also, there may be confrontations between the blockaders and British merchantmen, which could easily give rise to armed conflicts. This is exactly how our dispute with America began during the Napoleonic Wars. Every act we take must be measured and cautious and done strictly in accordance with international law. At some point the Southern states will demonstrate their strength of arms, and then it'll be time to recognize them."

Having finished his discourse, Russell sat quietly, deep in his thoughts. Seeing that the conversation was over, Hammond said, "If you do not need me, Your Lordship, I'll tend to my other duties."

"Yes. Thank you for listening to my thoughts."

97

"The Great Eastern: A Chance Not To Be Lost."
New York Times
May 12, 1861

The Administration now has an opportunity of striking a blow at the rebels, which to omit will go very far to destroy all confidence in its sincerity and energy. The Great Eastern is here, and we understand its officers have authority to arrange a charter with Government, looking to its immediate conversion into a transport ship. Let it be hired at once. It will be remembered that the Leviathan will comfortably accommodate an army of 10,000 men, with horses, artillery, and the most liberal stores for a long voyage. So furnished and dispatched to the Gulf of Mexico, the vessel would almost supersede the presence of a squadron, save the few frigates engaged in the blockade of three or four principal ports; for passing with the utmost speed from point to point, it would render the Gulf too hot for privateer; and threatening now one sea-port, and now another, it would furnish ample occupation for a rebel army of fifty thousand men. It is needless to remind the reader of its numerous and ample boats, by which a landing could be effected anywhere,—or a hostile vessel taking shelter in shore, could be pursued and cut out. We trust the obvious economy of the warfare, the Great Eastern thus insures, will have such weight with the authorities as to cause its immediate charter and dispatch to Southern waters.

98

Residence of D. C. Lowber
New Orleans, Louisiana
May 1861

Mary Lowber heard the buckboard stop in front of the house and went to the front door. Her husband climbed down while Abram waited with the reins in his hand. "Daniel, did you have a good day?" she asked.

Lowber gave his wife a kiss on the cheek. "It was slow. Abram and I were doing an inventory of small iron parts—nuts, bolts, things like that. It's tedious."

"Well, dinner should be soon. I'm serving a lovely roast chicken."

Lowber snapped his fingers as he remembered something. "I received a letter today from Montgomery." He reached into his jacket pocket and pulled it out.

"What does he say? Does he have any news on the babies?"

"I haven't read the letter yet. Give me a moment." Lowber pulled out his spectacles from a small wooden box he carried and sat down with the letter. "It's a pretty short letter, Mary. Nothing about the boys."

"Well, what does he say?"

"He's concerned about Lincoln's blockade. He thinks that I should go to England, buy as much iron and machinery as I can, and have it shipped here as quickly as possible. He says the blockade won't become effective for a while, but when it does, it will drive up the price of iron in the South."

"Do you think you should go?"

"Montgomery's right. If there's a war, it'll use up all of the South's iron. There'll be a big demand for farm machinery. The prices should be good. I'll go as soon as I can get organized."

"Can I come with you to see our grandsons?" Mary asked hopefully.

Lowber shook his head. "Mary, you and Abram have to run the business while I'm gone. Abram knows the business pretty well, but he can't read or write. You'll have to do the paperwork."

"I understand," Mary said softly. She went into the kitchen and returned shortly with a dish of sliced pickles for her husband. "Will you stop and see the babies? I miss them so much."

"If it's at all possible, I'll visit William and his wife to see the grandchildren."

"It's just so hard, Daniel. First we lose Katy, and then Montgomery ships the babies off to his brother in England. They're so far away!"

"I know, Mary, but Montgomery did the right thing. The boys are being raised as part of a family. You and I are too old to raise a couple of children, and Montgomery can't raise them by himself."

"I'm not faulting Montgomery, Daniel, but I hope he remarries before too long so that he can bring our grandchildren back home. Margaret wrote and said that Montgomery and Mary have been writing to each other. We're both hopeful something will happen with them."

Lowber looked up at Mary with surprise at this news. "Well, I'm sure Montgomery is fond of Mary, but he's still grieving. Let's just wait and see." He nodded his head in thought. "That would be a pretty good marriage," he said to his wife. He picked up one of the pickle slices and began to eat it.

"How will you leave the United States? Won't the blockade try to stop you?"

"Montgomery suggests that I take a coaster to Halifax and then ferry down to New York City. I'll be just a Canadian iron merchant going to England to do business. Nobody will be interested in me."

"How will your iron enter the United States? Won't it be stopped by the blockade?"

Lowber sighed. "That's a good question, Mary. I guess we won't know for certain until it's ready to ship."

Mary shook her head in disgust. "I don't know why that awful Mr. Lincoln started this blockade. They say that he won't even let medicine come into the South. The Northerners don't want us or even like us. Why don't they just let us go? We don't mean them any harm."

"The North needs our cotton. It's our crops that keep the bankers and shipowners in New York City fat and happy. If we separate, the South will develop its own banks and shipping lines, and we'll ultimately become rich and they'll become poor. Plus, we'd control the mouth of the Mississippi River. The North couldn't even ship its wheat out of the territories without paying us a tariff. It's all about money, Mary."

"Are they really willing to fight to keep us in the Union?"

"If you asked me a month ago, I would have said probably not. But then the Fort Sumter attack came along. The North had to pull down its flag under fire and surrender. All the dashing young men in the South think the Northerners are cowards, that they're incapable of fighting. They're talking about invading Washington and hanging Lincoln and Seward! You and I have lived up North. Do you think the Northerners are cowards?"

"Certainly not! The men in New York are as hard and tough as the men in the South."

"And they've been humiliated, Mary, and they need to draw blood to avenge their honor. This war has not yet started."

"How bad will it be, Daniel?"

Lowber shrugged his shoulders and shook his head.

"Dinner's ready, Ms. Lowber," Betsy called from the kitchen. Lowber finished his pickle and followed Mary into the house.

99

En route to Buckingham Palace
London, England
May 16, 1861

THE black lacquered phaeton traveled slowly through the streets of London on its way to Buckingham Palace during an early-afternoon drizzle. The driver and doorman sat in the open, and two men sat inside on opposite seats.

George Dallas sat quietly, lost in his thoughts. He had been at various stages of his life the vice president, a United States senator, America's envoy to Russia, the mayor of Philadelphia, and Pennsylvania's attorney general. He was now finishing his professional life as America's envoy to Great Britain. The one position he truly wanted, president of the United States, had been denied him by his longtime political rival James Buchanan. In 1856 President Franklin Pierce had appointed Dallas to the Court of St. James, an appointment reconfirmed by Buchanan when he became president in 1857. However, Buchanan had treated Dallas as an exiled functionary rather than a diplomat, and all significant communications with Her Majesty's government had come directly from the Executive Mansion. A frustrated Dallas had been eagerly awaiting his successor so he could return home.

The man sitting across from Dallas was Charles Francis Adams. Fifteen years younger than Dallas, Adams had resigned his position as a United States representative from Massachusetts in order to be appointed by President Lincoln to replace Dallas. Propelled by family history—he was the son of one president and the grandson of another—Adams had run as Martin Van Buren's vice presidential candidate on the Free-Soil ticket in 1848. The loss of that election had turned Adams to the career he loved: writing history and in particular recording the lives of his illustrious forebears. Seward had successfully urged Lincoln to appoint the reserved and intellectual Adams over Charles Sumner, the hotheaded and arrogant senator from Massachusetts, to the London post.

Both men sat silently, each dressed in mourning clothes because of the recent death of the Duchess of Kent. Dallas finally turned to Adams and spoke.

"Charles, the queen is very practiced at this sort of thing. I'll present my letter of withdrawal as the United States envoy to the Court of St. James. I'll introduce you as my successor, and you say you'll be honored to serve as my replacement. The queen will graciously accept my withdrawal and your appointment and will wish a continued harmonious relationship between the two countries. Nothing else will occur."

Adams looked at Dallas with surprise and then realized that Dallas thought his silence was nervousness at meeting the queen. Adams nodded and said dryly, "I promise I won't say, 'Pleased to meet you, Queen.'" Dallas smiled at the retort. With the ice broken, the two men began to talk.

Adams said, "George, three days ago I got off a ship at Liverpool only to find that Her Majesty's government had just issued a declaration of neutrality. My main task was to prevent that from happening, but it was a fait accompli while I was still at sea. You have to admit it's a rough beginning for a new envoy."

Dallas smiled wanly. "I'm certain Seward will be apoplectic when he finds out about it, but honestly it comes as no surprise to me. When Lincoln declared the blockade, it concerned Britain at least as much, and perhaps more, than it concerned the rebellious states. Her Majesty's government was well within its rights in issuing the declaration."

"Do you think England will recognize the Confederacy?" asked Adams.

Dallas shook his head. "Not at present. England has no desire to become involved. The South foolishly thought that the threat of losing the cotton trade would compel England to assist them. Unfortunately for the South, the mills at Lancashire aren't owned by fools. The owners saw troubles brewing in the South years ago and laid up a substantial inventory of raw cotton. It may be several months before any cotton shortage is felt."

"The English think the rebellion is going to lead to war?" Adams asked.

"They do. They had trouble understanding what happened at Fort Sumter. At first, they wondered how two sides could engage in sustained cannon fire for the better part of a week and not end up with so much as a broken arm. Finally, Whitehall concluded that the Americans really were trying to kill each other but were just poor marksmen. After all, it's been years since America has been in a war. Whitehall is now convinced that with some practice the two sides will get better at killing each other."

"Do you also think it's going to be a war?"

Dallas nodded slowly. "The hatred and fear have been building up for years. There's no compromise, no middle road. Lincoln will soon learn that. Either the South will become independent with Europe's help after a short war, or Europe will stay out and the South will be crushed and subjugated after a long and bloody war. I see no third way."

Adams sat silently and gazed out the phaeton's window. The rain was letting up, and he could see patches of blue in the distant sky. Dallas sat silently, so Adams spoke. "I'm told there's a vote coming up in the House of Commons to recognize the South."

Dallas nodded. "That's correct. Gregory will bring his motion up for a vote, most likely in early June. It will be unsuccessful."

"How do you know that?"

"Because Lord Russell opposes it. He said as much. He believes that recognizing the South so soon would mean that England will get drawn into our war, and that's not acceptable. At least, not for now."

"So, at least for a while, we have nothing to worry about?"

"I didn't say that. Dudley Mann is here, and he's working hard to involve England. He won't succeed with Gregory's motion, but he's not going to give up." Dallas leaned forward. "Understand this. Mann has always been underrated. He's devious and wily and is a friend to many prominent Englishmen. He's renounced his citizenship and has no country to return to but his Confederate States. His mission here is to entangle England in our dispute, and he'll play any card he has to achieve that." Dallas leaned back on his seat and was quiet for a moment. He then continued, "Unfortunately, he is being helped by Mr. Lincoln. In signing the tariff act and imposing the blockade, the president has angered the British." Adams sat quietly, so Dallas posed a question. "Charles, when you arrived at Liverpool, what did you see?"

Adams was puzzled by the question and looked at Dallas quizzically.

"Didn't you see a forest of ships' masts?" Dallas asked. "Dozens of oceangoing ships? Charles, England survives by buying cotton in our Southern ports and selling manufactured goods in our Northern ports. The blockade shuts them from the Southern ports, and the tariff makes their manufactured goods so expensive they're difficult to sell in our Northern ports. In a couple of months, Lincoln and the Republicans in Congress have undercut the entire British economy. Into that caldron, you throw Seward, who apparently believes that the way to reunite the United States is to start a war with Europe! Can you imagine how hard it's been to keep the lid on here?"

Adams nodded. "I expect I'll receive a frosty reception from Palmerston."

"I expect you will. Just remember that Mann will exploit every weakness in your position, will try to drive wedges between the North and England at every opportunity, and we've given him no shortage of opportunities. Charles, watch him closely."

Adams absorbed this warning in silence. Shortly, Dallas looked out his window and stated, "There's St. James now. We'll be there in a few minutes."

100

Punch
May 25, 1861

O Jonathan and Jefferson,
Come listen to my song;
I can't decide, my word upon,
Which of you is most wrong.
I do declare I am afraid
To say which worse behaves,
The North, imposing bonds on Trade,
Or South, that Man enslaves.

101

Her Majesty's Foreign Office
London, England
June 1, 1861

"Mr. Hammond, have you collected all the information required for your response to Admiral Milne?" Lord Russell asked as he looked in Edmond Hammond's crowded office.

"Yes, sir. I've finally obtained the opinion of the law lords on his questions. I'm drafting the response today."

"Good. We seem to have left the poor admiral out on a limb. He's in Bermuda wondering what, if anything, he should be doing to protect our shipping, and the Admiralty keeps dawdling on giving him instructions. I must say that his list of questions was right to the point."

"Indeed, sir."

"Please let me see the response before it is sent."

"Of course."

In his letter, Hammond carefully wrote each question asked by the admiral and the response. The first question was, "Are the U.S. of North America and the so styled Confederate States to be considered as in a state of actual War with each other?" The answer: "They are to be considered as in a state of actual War." The other questions, save the last, were technical questions about the rights of British ships under the law of blockade. The admiral's final question was the easiest to answer. Admiral Milne asked whether the validity of a blockade was held to be dependent as to its "efficiency," and Hammond answered "decidedly in the affirmative."

Hammond took the draft to Lord Russell to review. After reading it quickly, Russell looked up at Hammond and said, "Well, there you are, my dear Milne. If the blockade is not 'efficient,' it is not valid. So sayeth the law lords. When is a blockade not efficient? The good admiral didn't ask us *that* question. However, he's an intelligent and experienced officer. We must trust that if anyone can tell whether a blockade is efficient, it is Admiral Milne."

102

Thorngrove House
Worcestershire, England
June 1861

DANIEL Gooch knocked on the door of the Thorngrove House, home to Samuel Baker. A servant appeared and greeted the visitor. "Mr. Gooch, please come in. I'll tell Mr. Baker you're here." Without waiting, Gooch followed the servant into the library, where Baker was sitting.

Surprised, Baker said, "Daniel, I wasn't expecting you, but I'm glad to see you. Sit down." He gestured toward a large armchair. Baker started the conversation. "Well, Daniel, I trust you know that she arrived safe and sound at Milford Haven."

Samuel Baker, now in his sixty-seventh year, had been one of the first investors in the various companies that had built and owned the *Great Eastern*, as well as one of the first directors. While Gooch believed most of the ship's directors were incompetent, he had great respect for Baker, and the two men had learned to confide in each other.

"I found out yesterday, Sam. I was told she worked perfectly."

"Yes," Baker said quietly. "She is an absolute marvel of engineering. Brunel was a genius." Baker's voice dropped off at the end of the sentence, and he sat silently.

"And?" Gooch prompted.

Baker heaved a sigh. "And she's a financial disaster. She carried less than one hundred paying passengers on her second trip to New York. Daniel, a ship designed to carry four thousand paying passengers has carried a total of fewer than two hundred passengers in her first two trips across the Atlantic."

"Well," Gooch said, "it didn't help that our friend Scott Russell slapped a writ of execution on her just before she left."

In spite of his gloom, Baker let out a little chuckle. "Yes, I must say that our Scottish friend has exquisite timing. I'm told that never has a writ of execution been executed with more pomp and ceremony than on the deck of the *Great Eastern*. It's true that the delay in her departure resulting from the writ likely cost us two or three hundred paying passengers. Still, even with an additional three hundred passengers, we're operating at a loss. Plus, we had to empty our coffers to get Russell to release the writ. She sailed with half a crew because that was all we could afford."

The two men sat silently, staring into the cold fireplace. Finally, Baker said, "We're trapped, Daniel. Our giant ship has no purpose. She was built to go to Australia, but at the rate she burns coal, no one's confident she can make it there and back. Even if she could, we don't have the money to prepare her for such a trip, and we've only a limited ability to raise any additional capital. Even though she's been operating flawlessly, everyone believes she's unlucky, that there's always some disaster awaiting her. Her career as a curiosity is over. Nobody in New York was willing to pay money to see her during her second visit. The only thing I can see in the future is a giant empty hull shuttling between Liverpool and New York, losing money every mile of the way."

After a period of silence, Gooch said, "I wouldn't be so pessimistic, Sam."

Baker looked at his guest. "What are you saying?"

Gooch smiled. "The Americans seem to have come to our rescue."

Baker leaned forward in his chair. "Are they going to buy her, Daniel? I thought they weren't even willing to talk to us."

"No, they're not going to buy her. Their help is coming in a different direction."

"Daniel, I don't care for riddles. What's this about?"

Gooch licked his lips and began, "Well, you know Dudley Mann?"

Baker nodded. He had met Mann several times.

"Well, Dudley told me on several occasions that Seward, Lincoln's secretary of state, is quite mad. Lately, Whitehall has learned that Seward has been advocating war between the United States and Europe as a way to avoid a civil war."

"Well, that does sound quite mad. But how does that help us?"

"Be patient, Sam." Gooch leaned forward in his chair. "So it appears that President Lincoln, although he's a bit of a rustic, is not as deranged as Seward, and he refuses to start a war with all of Europe. Now, Sam, this is the interesting part. Whitehall believes that Seward has a different plan to involve England in a war."

Baker nodded his head, albeit in confusion. "Go ahead."

"Well, you know that over the past thirty years or so thousands of Irish have moved into New York and Boston."

"That's the result of the famine."

"That's right. The Irish moved there and, being Irish, had huge families, with the result that there are many, many Irish in America. And, you can be sure, their hatred of England is as strong as ever."

"All right," Baker said slowly, nodding. "And?"

"It's been reported that many of the Irish are joining a group called the Fenians. Their goal is to inflict injury on England in any way they can. Mann said that Seward has always been sympathetic to the cause of the Irish, and so he naturally supports the Fenians but not so publicly."

"All right," Baker said. "Daniel, I must say I'm getting confused."

"Then I'll go right to the point. Whitehall believes that the Fenians intend to form a militia, invade Canada, drive out Her Majesty's government, and make Canada part of the United States."

"Good heavens! Lincoln would permit this?"

"President Lincoln has nothing to say about this. The Fenians are not his troops. They don't obey his orders. But, Dudley Mann has assured me, one can see the hand of Seward in all this."

"Well, Daniel, this is most interesting, but I'm waiting for the part where the *Great Eastern* walks on stage."

"And here, Sam, is where she does. Whitehall is being implored for help by the Canadians, who do not relish being invaded by a bunch of wild Irishmen who will, undoubtedly, drink all their good whiskey and pay for none. Lord Palmerston has decided to make a show of strength, one that will catch the attention of President Lincoln and the Congress. He feels the best way to show Her Majesty's military power is by putting her greatest weapon on display."

Baker was leaning forward, nodding his head in approval at the direction of this conversation.

Gooch continued, "Her Majesty's government is going to charter the *Great Eastern*, refit her as a troop carrier, and rush her to Canada with several thousand troops on board, including horses, cannons, and supplies. Palmerston believes that the sight of England shipping thousands of troops and supplies on two weeks' notice would be very sobering to the United States. If we can land the troops in Quebec in a fortnight, we can surely land them just as quickly in Savannah or other places, which could cause great discomfort in the Northern states. Further, there's nothing in the United States Navy that could slow down, much less stop, the *Great Eastern*."

Baker was so excited he could no longer sit. He paced around the small library. "My God, this is wonderful! This is the destiny for which she was created. Her Majesty's most powerful weapon. But …" He paused. "Why just a charter? Won't they buy her?"

"We talked about that, Sam, but it's too early. Whitehall wants to see how she does. However, if she's successful, I've been promised that they will seriously consider purchasing her or signing a long-term charter. Either way, our shareholders may be able to reduce their losses considerably and perhaps even make a nice profit."

Baker smiled at his friend. "Daniel, I feel like you removed a millstone around my neck. A twenty-five-thousand-ton millstone!"

"She's been due for a little good luck," Gooch responded. "Perhaps her luck will change for good."

103

London Herald
June 1861

The Blockade.
It Must Be Made Effectual to Be Respected.

"It's an ill wind that blows nobody good." The much neglected Great Eastern, after all sorts of misadventures, has at last found its way into Government employ, and we venture to think its capacity as a troop-ship will prove so extraordinary as to recommend its permanent appropriation to the Government service ... The intelligence brought by the last mail from America is of a very grave, if not of a startling character, and has compelled the authorities to take immediate steps for placing the defences of our North American dependencies on a proper footing. Three infantry regiments, we are informed, are under orders for Canada, with a corresponding force of artillery. These troops, with all the requisite material, horses, &c., will easily be stowed away in the Great Eastern; and we may hope very soon to hear that there is no need of further anxiety about the safety of British interests on the North American continent.

There is apparently something very mysterious now going on at Charleston. The ports of South Carolina were declared blockaded. The Niagara was for some time stationed off the harbor of Charleston, and the blockade was effectively maintained. Suddenly we hear of the departure of the Niagara southward. Such a state of things can hardly fail to produce very mischievous results; and it seems to be inevitable that before long the question of a paper blockade will become a subject of serious discussion.

104

The House of Commons
London, England
June 7, 1861

If bystanders who saw Dudley Mann leave the House of Commons that afternoon surmised that his furrowed brow and fixed jaw signified anger, they guessed wrong. What they saw was fear.

True to his word, Lord Gregory had made the final presentation of his motion to recognize the Confederacy. In April, Lord Russell had addressed the motion when Gregory had first brought it up. To resounding cheers, Russell had declared his position on America's war. "We have not been involved in any way in that contest by any act or giving any advice in the matter, and, for God's sake, let us if possible keep out of it!" Russell's position had not changed, except this afternoon he'd made clear that the motion was opposed, at least for the time being, not merely by him but also by Her Majesty's government. In desperation, Gregory had improvised a tortured argument that recognition would restrict slavery and result in its early demise. The argument had been greeted with jeers. Finally, faced with certain defeat, Lord Gregory had withdrawn his motion. He'd looked at the spectator area trying to find Mann, but the Virginian, unwilling to watch the final acts of defeat, had left.

As Mann stood on the street outside of the House of Commons, Yancey approached him. "Well, Mann, it seems we've been sent on a fool's mission." Mann glared at Yancey and nearly blasted out his thoughts, but years of diplomatic training interceded, and he remained quiet. He walked alone back to his hotel. The enormity of the day's events was still sinking in. He had gambled everything on the success of the Confederacy—his life, the welfare of his family, his future. If the Confederacy failed, he would be forever a traitor to the United States, perhaps subject to hanging if he returned. He knew, perhaps more than anyone else in the Confederacy, that Britain's prompt recognition was the only hope for victory. Prior to the shelling of Fort Sumter, the fire-eaters had talked only to themselves, convincing each other of their intellectual and military superiority to the North and the inevitability of their cause. England would dance to the Southern fiddle, they all knew, because of King Cotton. On these points they all agreed, at least with each other. Mann, however, had communicated with people outside of the Confederacy, including many in London, and knew that England could not be threatened into granting recognition; it could only be coaxed into doing so. Recognition by England was the South's only hope, and that hope had just been crippled, if not destroyed, before his eyes.

When he sat down on the bed in his hotel room, Mann saw that his hands were shaking. He was furious at fire-eaters like Ruffin, blowhards who had started the war before he'd had a chance to convince Her Majesty's government to assist in a peaceful division of the United States. He was furious that he had been saddled with Yancey, the most odious person that the South could have sent as a diplomat. He was furious at Louis Napoleon for continuously hinting to the South that France's recognition would be forthcoming. He was furious with Southern leaders for believing Louis Napoleon, a duplicitous Frenchman for God's sake! Most of all, however, he was furious with himself. He had cast his lot, and that of his wife and son, with men ignorant of the task that lay before them.

Mann sat for a while in this mood and then tried to calm down, to collect his thoughts. He was alone, and he understood that the fate of the Confederacy now rested upon him. He had no choice but to come up with a new plan. During the next week he was scheduled to go to Paris to meet with representatives of Louis Napoleon. Nothing would come of it, of course. However, the trip would give him time to think.

105

Residence of D. C. Lowber
New Orleans, Louisiana
June 21, 1861

Mary Lowber called out the back door to her husband, who was hoeing his vegetable garden in the early-evening heat.

"Daniel, Tom Higgins is here to see you."

"Okay," answered a puzzled Lowber. He walked up and placed the hoe next to the doorframe. "Where is he?"

"In the front parlor."

As Lowber entered the parlor, Higgins approached him with an open hand. The men shook hands and exchanged brief pleasantries.

"So, Tom," Lowber finally said, "what brings you here?"

"Dan, can we speak privately?"

"Well, okay, but I don't keep any secrets from Mary."

Higgins shook his head. "I'm not concerned about Mary. I don't want your servants overhearing us."

Lowber signaled for Higgins to follow him, and they walked out of the house back to Lowber's vegetable garden. Both men could see that there was nobody within listening distance. Lowber stood there waiting for Higgins to speak.

"Dan, I heard you're going to England pretty soon. Is that correct?"

Lowber nodded. "I plan to leave four days from now. I'm meeting some iron merchants in England to see if I can pick up some new products."

"Toombs has important dispatches he needs to deliver to the commissioners in England. He sent a messenger to me asking if I could locate a safe courier, someone who was going to England on business. You immediately came to mind."

Lowber puffed his cheeks and slowly exhaled. "I don't know, Tom. If I get caught with the darn things, I'd get arrested, maybe hanged."

"Nah, you wouldn't get hanged. We made it clear to the Yankees that if they hang one of ours, we'll hang one of theirs. There's a very slim chance of being arrested, I'll concede that, but that would only happen if you were careless. You're not a careless person. Now, tell me, how are you getting to England?"

"Well, I'm going to take a coaster up to Halifax and then ferry on down to New York City. I thought I'd pass myself off as a Canadian businessman on a trip to England."

"That sounds like an excellent plan, Dan! If I can get the dispatches before you leave, I assume you'll be willing to take them. Toombs told me to get someone loyal and smart. You're obviously the right fellow."

"Doesn't Toombs have his own couriers?"

"Dan, the Yankees have been arresting our couriers in New York and seizing our communications. Seward has an army of spies at the port, and young men from the South boarding ships to England are searched. These dispatches are important, or at least Jeff Davis thinks so, and they need to get through. An older man coming in from Canada isn't the kind of person Seward's spies are on the lookout for."

Lowber stood quietly for a moment. He didn't like at all the idea of risking his freedom. At the same time, young men from the South were joining the army in droves, willing to die if necessary for their new country. He certainly didn't want to be thought a coward, and he feared that that would be the result of his outright refusal. Finally, he said, "Tom, if it's absolutely necessary, I'll take dispatches with me. But how will I locate these commissioners? I know Rost, but I thought he was in France. I don't know the others."

"You'll be given complete instructions. Toombs wants these dispatches in the hands of Dudley Mann, if possible. If not, to Yancey."

Both men looked at each other for a moment. Then Higgins said, "Well, there we are. I knew you were the right man for the job. I'm not going to identify you to Toombs, since we may have spies in the telegraph offices. I'll simply say I have a man and then wait for the dispatches to arrive. If I get them in time, I'll see you three days from now."

After Higgins walked out the front door, Lowber turned around and found his wife standing in the parlor, staring at him.

106

Residence of D. C. Lowber
New Orleans, Louisiana
June 24, 1861

Daniel Lowber packed his valise while Mary looked on. At the bottom of the valise he placed the envelope of papers he had received from Higgins.

"Are you going to tell Montgomery about the dispatches?" Mary asked.

Lowber shook his head. "I don't think so. Montgomery's a British subject. There's no reason he should know about this."

"Daniel, what happens if you're arrested?"

"Well, I'm pretty certain I'd be jailed. Beyond that, I don't know."

"Is it really worth the risk? What would happen to me if you were jailed?"

"Montgomery would take care of you. He's a smart broker and makes a lot of money. You wouldn't have to worry."

"Except that my husband would be rotting in jail." Mary started crying.

"Mary, I'm not going to get caught. I'm going into New York City on a ferry from Halifax. I'm familiar with New York. Why would anyone suspect that I'm carrying anything of interest to the federal government? I'm just a dealer going to England to purchase more farm machinery."

"I'll be worried to death all the while you're gone," Mary said and then blew her nose. Seeking to compose herself, she asked with a quiver in her voice, "Promise me again you'll see our grandchildren?"

"Darling, if it's at all possible, I'll see them." Mary continued to sniffle. Lowber looked at his wife with affection. "Now, Mary, when I get back, I'll have all sorts of stories about Kate's babies. I promise." He smiled. "Don't worry about me. I'll be fine. Someday this war, if we can call it that, will be over, and everything will be peaceful. However, until that day, each of us has a part to play. Mine is far less heroic than most."

When he finished packing his valise, he went out to the barn to see if Abram was ready to take him to the port.

107

Fishkill Landing, New York
July 2, 1861

"No, don't get down." Schultz put his hand up to keep Leonard from getting off the buckboard. He threw his valise into the back of the wagon and climbed aboard, sitting next to his servant. "Train is always late coming in," Schultz muttered. "Sorry to keep you waiting."

"That's okay, Captain. I sharpened my knife waiting for you."

Schultz smiled. Leonard always found a way to keep busy. "Everything well at the house?" Schultz asked.

"Mista Lowber's here. He got here early this morn."

This news was surprising. "What's he doing here, Leonard?"

"Don't know. When I left, he was on the porch talkin' to Mary."

"About what?"

"Don't know, Captain. You know Mista Lowber's got those fake teeth—they move around, and he kinda mumbles. Mary sat close to him to listen. I couldn't hear nothin'."

"Is Margaret around?" Schultz asked.

"She's home, but she's layin' down. Says her head hurts bad."

Schultz was silent for the remainder of the short trip. When the buckboard pulled up to the front of the house, Lowber was sitting alone on the porch.

"Dan, what are you doing here?" Schultz called out as the buckboard stopped.

"Hamilton, I'm delighted to see you too," Lowber responded with a smile.

Schultz shook his head slightly as he walked up the porch stairs. "I meant, is everything all right with you and Mary?"

"Couldn't be better," Lowber said.

"Well, why are you in New York?"

"I'm going to England tomorrow. I can stay here for another half hour or so. Then Leonard has got to take me back to the station."

"Why didn't you write and let me know that you were coming?"

Lowber laughed. "Hamilton, I live in New Orleans. Any letter that I sent to you would have been read first by your good friend Governor Seward, who would be waiting to offer me free accommodations in Fort Lafayette."

"No, I don't believe so," said Schultz. "You're no threat."

"You may not think so, but your friend may have a different opinion. Anyways, here I am."

Taking a break from their conversation, Schultz went on the porch and sat close to Lowber.

"I used to think weather like this was hot," said Lowber. "Then, I moved to New Orleans. I tell you, Hamilton, you don't know what hot weather is until you've been in New Orleans."

"Why are you going to England?" Schultz asked.

"Montgomery wrote and said that he had met some iron merchants in England and that they would like to talk to me. I figured that with the election of Lincoln, the price of iron is likely to go way up in the South. So I'm trying to build up my inventory and also see if I can pick up some new suppliers of farm equipment."

"That's a good idea. Montgomery's got a nose for money."

"I think he does pretty well," Lowber agreed. "Oh, I'm also going to try to see the grandchildren if I have enough time. They're living with Montgomery's brother. Mary wanted to go, but I didn't think it was a good idea."

The two men then discussed the price of iron and farm equipment, talked about whether Lowber could come back with names of agents who sell brass fittings for ships that Schultz's son might be able to represent, and otherwise made small talk about their prior lives. Finally, Lowber said, "Hamilton, we're sitting here talking, and we've not mentioned Fort Sumter."

"It's nothing to worry about," said Schultz. "Nobody got hurt. I think it was just a bunch of hotheads in Charleston letting off steam."

"You're wrong, Hamilton. It's the start of our battle for independence."

"*Our* battle? Dan, you're not part of this nonsense?"

At this point, Lowber stood up and stretched slightly. He said, "It's no longer nonsense. It stopped being nonsense when we learned that John Brown was given a lot of money by rich Northerners to buy weapons so that our slaves could murder us in the middle of the night. It stopped being nonsense when we heard about the church bells ringing throughout the North when John Brown was hanged. The election of Lincoln was the final insult. Hamilton, the South has suffered in silence every indignity the North has given it, but it's not going to take any more. The South *is* independent, and Mary and I are part of the South."

Schultz tried to move the conversation to business again, but it was hopeless. Neither man really wanted to talk any further. Finally, Lowber pulled out a watch from his vest. "Good God, I've got to get going just in case the train actually leaves on time. Leonard said that he'd take me to the station. Is that all right with you?"

Schultz nodded, and Leonard appeared on the porch as if by magic. He took Lowber's valise and put it in the buckboard.

"Where's Mary?" Lowber asked. "I wanted to say goodbye to my favorite niece."

"Misses Schultz and her went for a walk to see if that would help her head pain," Leonard said.

"I can't wait. Hamilton, give my love to Margaret and Mary and of course your son. Wish me luck in England." The two men shook hands, and Schultz stood silently as the buckboard left.

108

New York Times
July 4, 1861

The Southern Commissioners, Messrs. Dudley Mann, Yancey and Rost, have crossed the Channel, and sought the chances of another battle-field. To us loyalists their retreat seems a rout. They have failed in every single object that they tried for. They wished recognition, and they were never further from it than now. They wished agitation, but the House of Commons swept down on their poor champion, and overwhelmed him remorselessly. They wished to organize a fleet of privateers, and the British Government shut their ports in their faces. They wished to borrow money, and their bonds remain untaken.

Yet, like good Generals, these three gentlemen "bate not a jot of heart or hope." With the pleasing and kindly, though-erring, disposition to see, or pretend to see, all his own projects in the rosiest colors—that disposition which has made the originator of Southern Commercial Conventions and Southern European steamship lines, so harmlessly and humorously famous—Mr. Dudley Mann still trusts that England will reverse her policy.

109

"Departure of the *Great Eastern* with the Canadian Contingent." *Illustrated London News* July 6, 1861

Shortly after noon on Thursday week the Great Eastern sailed out of the Mersey on her voyage to Quebec with troops to reinforce the Canadian garrisons. The day was cloudless, there was brilliant sunshine, and the piers and dock walls for five miles, as well as the landing-stages, were lined with spectators, who, as the great ship passed them, responded most heartily to the cheers raised by the soldiers who thronged the deck and the lower portions of the rigging. As she passed the landing-stages she fired salutes, and another on passing the fort. Both paddles and screw were in motion. In her wake were a score or two of tugs, occasional steamers, and other boats, filled with passengers, whose intention was to accompany the Great Eastern as far as the Bell buoy. The troops seemed in high spirits, and during the passage down the river a band on board the steamer played several favorite airs. There were on board the Great Eastern 2079 men and 46 officers; the former having with them 159 wives and 244 children. The cabin passengers (civilians) who went at the same time numbered about 40.

Departure of the Great Eastern *from the Mersey with the Canadian Contingent*

110

Government House
Quebec City, Quebec
July 8, 1861

THE two officers, attired in their finest dress uniforms as members of Her Majesty's Sixtieth Rifles, stood next to each other and glanced around the ballroom of the Government House. The older of the two, a captain, commented on the scene from time to time to his companion, a lieutenant. Having run out of comments on the paucity of attractive women and the oppressive heat in the room, the older man changed the subject.

"So, Crosley, what'd you think of our voyage?"

"Sir, I've never been on a ship before. I've nothing to compare it to."

"Well, I've been on a voyage or two," the older man said. "I went down to the Crimea and back again. If I had to choose between the Crimea and Quebec, I'd definitely pick Quebec. Although I must say that our trip on the *Great Eastern* was most unusual."

"In what way, sir?"

"Well, to begin with, troop ships usually do not carry women and children. We had nearly five hundred women and children on board. Also, I'm not familiar with troop ships carrying large numbers of stowaways, most of them women."

"I wondered about that."

"Some of them were wives, but more than a few … well, it's fortunate that the *Great Eastern* is so large that the ladies and children on board were not exposed to very immoral behavior."

The young man, having nothing to say on this observation, remained silent, so the captain continued, "Also, births aboard troopships are considered rare, and we had two."

"Yes, I wondered about that too."

"And, finally, troopships are usually not commanded by madmen who are determined to break speed records."

"Sir, is that your opinion of Captain Kennedy?"

"Most definitely! Kennedy was so anxious to set a record that we almost died in the process."

The young man looked at the older man with a puzzled look. The captain nodded and asked, "Did you hear the lookouts crying out about the icebergs?"

The lieutenant nodded.

The captain continued, "I'm told that usually they cry out in a singsong voice, like, 'Icebergs on the port side.'" The older man said the phrase slowly and melodically. "Now, how did the lookouts sound to you?"

"They were screaming, 'Icebergs! Icebergs!' It didn't sound very singsong."

"No, it didn't. It's because they were scared to death. The madman never slowed up once. I was on the deck one night when a giant iceberg loomed up out of the fog. We missed it by no more than a hundred feet. A slight change of course and we'd all have been in Davy Jones's locker."

The lieutenant nodded slowly. "Dead, sir?"

"Dead. Drowned in the briny deep. And it's even worse than that. We just missed the *Arabia* steaming in a fog toward Quebec. If we had rammed her, hundreds of her passengers would have drowned as well. Just plain reckless, if you ask me."

The lieutenant slowly sucked in some air as he looked around the room. He thought, perhaps, it was time to change the subject. "So, sir, what will duty in Canada be like?"

"Crosley, you will experience cold like you've never felt before. You'll go marching in weather so frigid that if you open your mouth for too long, your teeth will crack. However, trust me, it's immeasurably better than the Crimea. It's too cold here for the yellow fever, and there aren't any Russians within miles." He smiled. "Plus, you may develop a taste for moose and whiskey, the two staples of a Canadian diet."

"Sir, why were we sent here?"

"Orders. I don't know much besides that. There are rumors about Irishmen coming up from America to attack Canada, but I can't believe they're true. Your typical Irishman can't cross the road from the pub to his shanty without getting lost or falling down, so how they'd make it from New York to Canada is beyond me."

"How long will we be here, sir?"

The captain clapped the younger man on the shoulder. "Until they tell us to leave and not a day before. Lad, someday when you're a grandfather, you'll have a good story to tell by the fireside, a story about your voyage on the *Leviathan* and your duty in the frozen north!" Seeing a waiter carrying drinks, the captain waved. "I say, over here! We need some drinks."

III

Baxtertown, New York
July 1861

It was dusk as Kit approached Baxtertown. As usual, he had a sack with food purchased in Newburgh, and this time it contained green groceries and a chunk of smoked ham. As he approached the center of the encampment, he saw Reeba sitting near a fire. He stopped when he noted that a man was resting on one knee, talking with her. The stones and bones were not out, and she did not appear to be telling his fortune. The man had his back to Kit, and so Kit circled around to see what this was about. Finally, he was able to see the side of the man's grinning face and heard his voice. Kit dropped his sack, broke into a sprint, and drove his elbow into the side of the man's head, knocking him to the ground.

Jack wondered what had hit him and scrambled to his feet, looking around. When finally standing, he found himself staring at Kit. Jack instantly understood and reached into his pants pocket to draw out a large folding knife. Just as he was in the process of opening it, Kit smashed Jack in the face with his fist, leveling the larger man. Kit then stomped on Jack's hand to force him to release the knife, which Kit then kicked away. All throughout Baxtertown activity stopped as the slaves stood amazed at the violent actions of their previously quiet companion.

As Jack struggled to his feet, Kit turned him around and grabbed the back of his clothes. He picked up the slave chaser as if he were a doll and swung him face-first into a large tree. Jack was still struggling, and Kit swung him again and drove him even harder into the tree. Jack went limp, and Kit dropped him on the ground. The slave chaser lay on his back, dazed, blood oozing from his nose and mouth, while Kit stood over him contemplating his next move.

Finally, an old slave, keeping a respectable distance from Kit, pointed at the prostrate Jack and asked, "Boy, who dat?"

Kit answered between breaths, "Slave chasa." The entire community recoiled at the words and then stared at Jack with rage.

A young boy ran up to Kit. "Hea's his sack!" he said, handing Kit a canvas bag tied with a rope.

Kit opened the sack and proceeded to dump its contents on the ground. Clothing, food wrapped in oiled paper, and rolled-up posters and other papers fell out. Kit grabbed the bottom of the bag and shook it, and iron manacles and a small wooden club fell on the ground. The gathering crowd gasped. Kit bent over and picked up a rolled-up poster. It had an etching of a slave running above printed words. No one at the camp could read, but the two German brothers had taught Kit enough about the alphabet that he could recognize his name. "Dat's me," Kit said quietly as he held up the poster.

"Get a rope," one of the other fugitives said as three male fugitives roughly picked Jack up. The only rope long enough to do the job was tied to a wagon, so everyone stood silently as the rope was untied. Jack had regained consciousness and now understood what was happening.

"I's a slave too," Jack cried out, blood seeping from his mouth. "Dey's got my woman and chilt'n in 'Bama, and dey's forced me to be a chasa." Jack started crying, and his words came out in sobs. "I's got three chilt'n, and dey say dey set dem free if'n I kitch dis Kit. I don't mean no harm to Kit, but …" Jack's sentence died out in sobs.

A young man raced up with the rope retrieved from the wagon. An older slave, acquainted with the art of tying a noose, took the rope from him and started wrapping the knot. Jack continued to sob, restrained now by several more men. Kit, his rage dying, stood silently and watched. Finally, he said, "We can't kill 'im." The other slaves looked in bewilderment at the young fugitive. Kit shook his head and said, "We ain't supposed ta kill."

"Well, den, what's we gonna do wif 'im?" an old man asked. "He's a catcha! We can't let 'im go." That was true. There were other names on posters carried in Jack's sack. Kit thought silently as the residents of the fugitive shanty town stared at him. All wanted to hang Jack right then and there, but no one wanted to cross Kit.

"Tonight, they's a group goin' North," Kit finally said. "Tie 'im to de wagon and take 'im wif. When you get to Canada, let 'im go." Kit looked at Jack. "If'n you come back, den I got no choice—I'll kill you wif my bare hands!"

Jack nodded, tears running down his cheeks.

Jack was tied to a tree while the other slaves went about getting their dinner and getting ready for their trip. Kit went to his lean-to but sat outside it where he could keep an eye on Jack.

After sundown, Jack was tied to a wagon pulled by a pair of mules. A group of fifteen or so fugitives, all but three of whom were men, left to follow the Hudson River north to Auburn. Kit saw them off and then retired to his lean-to. A handful of women slaves had made an excellent stew with the meat Kit had brought, but Kit wasn't hungry and didn't eat much.

After the northbound group had traveled for more than three hours, one of the men signaled for the caravan to stop. A group of men silently untied Jack and dragged him screaming and begging into the woods. They threw him on his back and held him there while one of the men kneeled on his chest and slashed his throat several times. When the gurgling and thrashing stopped, they stripped the dead man of his clothes. The group then continued their trip to Canada, leaving the naked corpse in the woods.

112

Thorngrove House
Worcestershire, England
July 5, 1861

Samuel Baker stepped out of the doorway of his house and allowed Daniel Gooch to enter. Baker said, "I received your telegraph message that you had some information for me. I've been waiting for you."

Gooch followed Baker into the latter's study and sat down. From the expression on Gooch's face, Baker knew the news would not be good. "Well, what is it, Daniel?"

"I've heard from Lord Russell. Lord Palmerston wants to renew the charter, but he's getting strong resistance from Parliament."

Baker slapped his hand on his thigh. "Why? The ship performed perfectly as a troop carrier. My God, it broke all records in crossing the Atlantic. What more do they want?"

"It's not the ship, Sam. It's the mission. It seems that the opposition in the House of Commons is demanding to know why the government rushed to send troops to Canada. Lord Russell is concerned that he may be embarrassed by the entire incident. It seems that most of the cabinet have concluded that Mr. Seward pulled a trick on Lord Russell, that the whole story of the Fenians invading Canada was pure cock and bull."

"But why would Seward make up such a story?"

"They don't even know that he did. It was all rumors. Lord Russell wasn't sure, and he sent the *Great Eastern* as a show of strength. As I said, Palmerston is willing to charter her again, but he's having trouble with his ministers, who are afraid of the issue becoming a laughingstock in Parliament. The end result is that she is to return to Liverpool in early August, we'll be paid the balance of the charter fee, and then …" Gooch fell silent.

Baker let out an audible sigh. "Yes, Daniel, and then. Then what? Without the charter being renewed, the ship has no mission, no purpose! Three perfect trips back and forth to North America, and people still believe she's unlucky. Cunard's ships run like shuttles and are cutting us to the quick with the New York trade. Even if she could make it to Australia without coaling, the Suez Canal will be open very shortly, and all voyages to Australia will be through the canal. And, of course, she's too large for the canal." Baker got so agitated by his own words that he stood up. "She has yet to carry more passengers than crew. She consumes coal like a monster from hell. She costs a fortune to maintain. Our shareholders are bleeding from every pore. Exactly what do we do with her, Daniel?"

"I don't know, Sam. We offered her to the United States, and they wouldn't even respond to our proposal. Then, Lord Russell tells us that even if the United States had accepted our proposal, we'd have to withdraw it because she's served as a troop carrier and her sale would violate the declaration of neutrality. Even Louis Napoleon has told us he's not interested, although if we were willing to give the ship to him, he might be generous enough to accept her as a gift."

"Bastard," Baker muttered as he sat down. For a long time, he sat in silence, motionless, his head bowed down, eyes closed. Gooch looked at his friend with pity. Baker was no longer a young man and was not in good health. Gooch remembered him from years earlier when he was a vigorous, often impetuous marketer of goods and ideas. As a young man, Baker had started a small bank with a partner. This somehow had led to investments in sugar plantations in Jamaica, which had led to him becoming wealthy as one of England's largest sugar merchants. In 1832, while visiting his plantations, he'd gotten caught up in the bloody slave rebellion they now called the Baptist War. He'd told his friends, including Gooch, that he was lucky to have escaped with his life. He'd seen his Jamaican slaves freed two years later when the United Kingdom abolished slavery.

But mostly Gooch recalled Baker's ceaseless promotion of the great iron ship. Ten years earlier, Baker had been one of the directors of the Eastern Steam Navigation Company that had listened to Brunel describe the building of a monstrous ship. He'd been the one who had urged hiring the diminutive engineer to create it. He'd attended all the abortive launchings and suffered all the ridicule the public could throw at him and his fellow directors. He'd been aboard the *Great Eastern* when the terrible explosion had occurred and had heard the screams of men dying deep in her hull. Through two insolvencies, endless lawsuits, and stockholder revolts, through the death of Brunel and the chicanery of Scott Russell, Baker had resolutely maintained his faith in the "*Great Babe*," as Brunel had called her. He had paid a terrible price for this faith. Baker used to be greatly admired in London. Now the old man had to stay out of the city in order to avoid a confrontation by any of the dozens of individuals whom he had persuaded to invest in the ship, almost always to their great financial loss. He was coming to the end of his life being called a fool, a charlatan, and worse.

Gooch sighed and then said quietly, "Sam, I must get back home. There's an evening train I must catch."

113

Aboard the *Kangaroo*
New York Harbor
July 6, 1861

WHILE most passengers on the Inman steamship *Kangaroo* stood on the deck watching the landmarks in New York's harbor go by, Daniel Lowber stayed in his small cabin with his door closed and bolted. His locked valise was safely placed in his cabin's small locker. During the nearly two weeks that he had traveled with the valise, he'd been continuously fearful of the moment when a hand would clasp his shoulder from behind and a stern voice would announce his arrest. The dreaded moment never happened. He was now aboard a British vessel, heading for open sea. He was safe.

He disliked New York City. What relatives he had there, other than the Schultz family, had effectively disowned him. The city was the site of several of his business failures, the memories of which still evoked anger. It was a dirty, dangerous city, and he had never regretted settling in Louisiana, an area that had accepted him as readily as New York had spurned him.

As he sat in his cabin on the *Kangaroo*, Lowber unsuccessfully tried to convince himself that his recent meeting with Hamilton Schultz had ended well. For two men so close for so long, their inability to find common ground on the issue of secession was troubling. If Schultz had known that Lowber was carrying messages from Jefferson Davis to the Confederate commissioners in England, a brawl might have broken out between the two of them. *How does this all end?* Lowber thought.

A loud blast from the *Kangaroo*'s steam whistle stirred Lowber from his bunk to a porthole in the cabin. The ship was sounding a salute as it passed Governors Island. Lowber's uneasiness over his meeting with Schultz was gradually being replaced by the satisfaction of knowing that he was proving his courage and patriotism to his new country. He didn't know what was in the papers he was carrying, but he was certain that they were important. Perhaps when the history of the Confederate States was written, the name of Daniel Cole Lowber would be honorably mentioned.

114

En route to Thorngrove House
Worcestershire, England
July 8, 1861

DUDLEY Mann was apprehensive as the carriage approached the century-old home of Samuel Baker. He had earlier sent Baker a note asking if he could visit him but hadn't given any explanation as to why. Baker had responded with a short note stating he would be at home for a prolonged period and asking the date that Mann intended to arrive. Baker had assured the Virginian that he would have a servant meet him at the new Malvern Link train station.

During the lengthy train ride from London to Malvern, Mann had mulled over the events leading up to this meeting. The French had been polite to the point of unctuousness, the food had been deemed excellent, and the hosts had tendered vague and meaningless assurances of help and sympathy. Rost had conversed in his Louisiana French, which Mann was convinced produced howls of laughter once the hosts were out of earshot. Yancey had enjoyed the food, wine, and flattery, and Mann had spent as much time as possible by himself, pleading indigestion. Mann knew that France would not do anything to help the Confederacy unless England did so first and had concluded that his time would be better spent thinking than being entertained.

Mann had known that British recognition was the key to Southern success before he'd left the United States, and had Fort Sumter not been shelled, Lord Gregory's motion would have had a better-than-even chance of success. However, with the shelling of Fort Sumter, London was inclined to wait until it could determine which side was likely to win. If the war were protracted, Mann had no doubt as to the outcome. He had seen enough European wars to know that numbers counted—the number of soldiers, the number of cannons, the number of ships, and most importantly the amount of money. Kossuth had had the people, the Austrians had had the troops and the treasury, and Kossuth had needed to flee for his life. Mann was convinced that unless England recognized the Confederacy within a few months, the war would be lost and a terrible price would be extracted from the leaders of the Confederacy, including himself.

Prior to his trip to France, Mann had talked with a solicitor in London about the legality of the blockade. The conversation had confirmed Mann's understanding that unless the blockade was capable of stopping large vessels, it would be considered ineffective and could be ignored by neutral countries. However, after talking with English friends and acquaintances, Mann had concluded that the British government would resist declaring the blockade illegal unless there was incontrovertible proof of its ineffectiveness. This would require some dramatic event that left no doubt to even Union sympathizers in Britain that the blockade was a mere paper blockade. Given these facts, Mann had used his time in Paris to form a plan that could be fleshed out on his return to England.

Thereafter, Mann had sought information from a variety of London acquaintances and Confederate supporters, always asking hypothetical questions and never too many from a single source. He'd learned that Chesapeake Bay was guarded by massive Union cannons that could destroy any ship in the world. He'd been given a list of the few deepwater ports in the South. A dinner with a London solicitor had confirmed that Her Majesty's government had not yet recognized the legitimacy of the blockade of Port Royal, South Carolina, one of the deepwater ports on his list.

From a South Carolinian banker, Mann had obtained a recent nautical map of Port Royal prepared by Commander John Maffitt shortly before Maffitt had resigned his post in the United States Navy to join the Confederate Navy. From a Virginian involved in purchasing vessels for blockade running, he'd obtained the names and qualifications of a number of British captains who had expressed an interest in running a blockade.

While assembling details of the plan, Mann had pondered the problem of how to persuade the owners of the *Great Eastern* to agree to it. After repeated maulings by shareholders, the giant ship's board of directors had only four members left. Of these, only Daniel Gooch and Samuel Baker were of consequence. Mann knew Gooch well. He had walked him into the Executive Mansion to meet President Buchanan and had stayed at his house at Clewer Park, and the two men had formed a genuine friendship. However, Gooch had been made a director to ensure the completion and fitting out of the great ship and to supervise her maiden voyage to America. He'd accomplished both tasks. Mann concluded that determining the ship's commercial mission was far beyond the quiet engineer's remit.

Mann's relationship with Samuel Baker was cordial but superficial. He had met Baker several times, and the two men had had several conversations about Mann's plans to use the ship as a shuttle between Milford Haven and Chesapeake Bay. Everyone thought those plans had been dashed when Lord Gregory's motion to recognize the Confederacy was defeated. Everyone now wondered how much time would pass before the *Great Eastern* become insolvent again. Everyone except Dudley Mann.

While in Paris, Mann had reread his instructions from Toombs and been again distressed at their naïveté. Page after page of platitudes about the righteousness of the Southern cause and nothing offered that might be of value to Her Majesty's government. When he'd been working for the United States government, Mann had successfully negotiated many commercial treaties with European states. He knew that one must give something to get something. Now, he was prepared to give Baker something of value, something that Baker desperately wanted—a profitable mission for his giant ship. Although Toombs had not authorized him to do so, Mann was going to offer Baker a monopoly on transatlantic trade with the South. Once the blockade was lifted, the *Great Eastern* and her future sister ships would shuttle between Chesapeake Bay and England carrying all the cotton produced by the South to British ports and returning with heavy industrial and railroad goods needed by the South. The *Great Eastern* would be the most profitable ship the world had ever seen, generating hundreds of thousands of pounds on each voyage. The battered shareholders of the Great Ship Company would receive enormous dividends, and throughout the kingdom Baker's name would be spoken of with respect, even reverence.

In return for this offer, all Baker had to do was agree to a single commercial voyage of his great ship. Because the voyage would be to a port without a blockade recognized by Her Majesty's government and because the ship would carry no contraband of war, the voyage would not violate the queen's declaration of neutrality. Any well-regarded London solicitor would give such an opinion. Although advertised as going to New York City, the *Great Eastern* would head for Port Royal, South Carolina, a deepwater port under the control and cannons of the Confederacy. No shots would be fired, no one injured. There would be only a minor inconvenience for a small number of passengers who thought they were going to New York and found themselves in South Carolina. These passengers would be treated as royalty by the families of South Carolina and would quickly be sent to New York by railroad. The minor inconvenience would be considered an adventure of a lifetime. Once the telegraph confirmed that the *Great Eastern* was lying in Port Royal with a Union Jack flying at her stern, Admiral Milne would have no choice but to declare the blockade ineffective. Thereafter London would be obligated to order the blockade lifted. This would rapidly result in British recognition of the Confederacy, and the Great Ship Company's monopoly would thereafter begin under the protection of the British navy.

There were numerous details to Mann's plan that he was prepared to discuss, but they would have to wait until Baker expressed a serious interest in the offer. One thing was clear, however. For the plan to work, it had to be executed quickly. The North was buying all the vessels it could, putting cannons on them, and sending them out to blockade. In another ten weeks or so, the blockade might actually be effective, and the *Great Eastern* would be unable to enter a Southern port without fear of being seized.

When the carriage stopped at the front door of Thorngrove House, Mann hopped out with the help of the driver and was surprised to see Baker standing at the open door. The old man, hunched over with a shawl covering his shoulders, appeared to be sickly. However, he had a slight smile and said, "Colonel Mann, I'm glad you've come."

115

Residence of W. H. Seward
Washington, DC
July 20, 1861

WILLIAM Seward sat at his writing table. Usually his letters to his wife were filled with the events of daily life. Tonight, however, Seward's mind was racing with troubling thoughts, and he could only write a few lines. He scribbled quickly.

> I snatch a moment to write a few words. We are on the eve of a conflict on the Virginia side of the Potomac, probably some day this week. It will be very important.
>
> So, in Western Virginia, a battle is looked for daily. We are past danger in Europe, if we meet with no disaster.

Before he signed, he reread the note and then underlined the words "if we meet with no disaster."

116

Manassas, Virginia
July 22, 1861

Private John Singleton Mosby, serving with the Virginia Volunteers of the Confederate States of America, wrote the following to his wife:

> *There was a great battle yesterday. The Yankees are overwhelmingly routed. Thousands of them killed. I was in the fight. We at one time stood for two hours under a perfect storm of shot and shell—it was a miracle that none of our company was killed. We took all of their cannon from them; among the batteries captured was Sherman's—battle lasted about 7 hours—about 90,000 Yankees, 45,000 of our men. The cavalry pursued them till dark—followed 6 or 7 miles. General Scott commanded them. I just snatch this moment to write—am out doors in a rain—will write you all particulars when I get a chance. We start just as soon as we can get our breakfast to follow them to Alexandria. We made a forced march to get here to the battle—travelled about 65 miles without stopping. My love to all of you. In haste.*

117

15 Half Moon Street
London, England
July 21, 1861

DUDLEY Mann was sweating heavily. It had been unusually hot in London that week, and he was anxious to go to his room that evening and lie down. As he walked into his small hotel, a substantial step down from his previous one, the desk clerk nodded at him and pointed to a man sitting on a chair in the small lobby. Puzzled, Mann walked over to the man.

"Are you looking for someone, sir?" Mann asked.

"I'm looking for Colonel Mann."

"You've found him. May I help you?"

The man stood and asked quietly, "May we talk privately?" Mann detected a Southern accent.

"Yes, come to my room," Mann responded. The two men proceeded up a narrow staircase to Mann's small room. When they entered, Mann's guest placed a valise on the bed.

"Colonel Mann, my name is Daniel Lowber. I'm a messenger from Secretary Toombs. I have dispatches for you. They're in my valise."

Mann nodded. This was not the first time he had received communications from his government via a Southern traveler. Lowber opened his valise and fished down to its bottom. He pulled up an envelope closed with a red wax seal.

Mann broke open the seal and pulled out a sheaf of documents. He recognized Jefferson Davis's handwriting on the first page. The documents were authentic.

"Mr. Lowber, my thanks for delivering these documents. I gather no one has seen them?"

"That's correct. They've been in my possession since I left Louisiana."

"Ah, Louisiana," Mann said. "Then you must know Pierre Rost, my fellow commissioner?"

"I've met Judge Rost several times," Lowber said. "I'm going tomorrow to visit him in France to see if he'll inquire about a potential supplier. I'm in the business of importing farm machinery, and I'm always looking for new products."

"Excellent. I don't have any dispatches for Judge Rost, or otherwise I'd ask you to take them." The two men stood silently for a moment while Mann studied his visitor. Lowber seemed sober and mature, a man who could be trusted.

"Mr. Lowber, when are you returning to America?"

"I leave Liverpool on the *Edinburgh* on August 7."

"Can you come by my hotel a week from today? Say, on Tuesday, the thirtieth, at about two o'clock? I'll have a packet of dispatches for you to take to President Davis."

Lowber thought he had taken himself out of harm's way when he delivered the documents to Mann. Now, he was being asked to sneak dispatches *into* the United States! His initial reaction was to find a plausible excuse for declining, but he wasn't able to think of one quickly. He finally concluded that he had a patriotic obligation to honor Mann's request. Clearing his throat, he asked, "Colonel Mann, since you're asking me to take a substantial risk, can you give me assurances that the dispatches are truly important?"

Mann laughed. "Mr. Lowber, more important than you could guess. I have something big for the Confederacy, very, very big. Sir, I'm confident that the blockade will be over by Christmas." Then, realizing he had said more than he intended, Mann quickly added, "It has to do with … ah, a financial matter."

"I see," replied Lowber, who despite his answer didn't really see the connection between a financial matter and the lifting of the blockade.

Mann saw in Lowber's face that his misdirection had not been entirely effective, so he continued, "It involves a loan, Mr. Lowber—a loan from some gentlemen in England. With the loan we can buy weapons in Europe."

Lowber accepted the expanded statement at face value. He responded, "I'll get your dispatches to President Davis."

"Good! Then I'll see you on July 30, at two o'clock," Mann said. "Good day, sir." The men shook hands, and Lowber left.

Mann took his coat off, put it on a door hook, and then lay on the bed. It was stuffy in the room, but he rested quietly. The storm of thoughts that had been ravaging his ability to sleep since the fiasco in Parliament slowly calmed, and he finally fell into a deep and sweaty sleep.

Lowber went back to his hotel room, both excited and frightened by his new mission. For years he had envied Schultz, watching his brother-in-law acquire ships and important friends while Lowber had struggled to support his wife and daughter. Schultz had never flaunted his wealth or power, but Lowber had always been intimidated by it. In an unguarded moment several years earlier, Lowber had learned that his wife, Mary, had envied the prosperous life her sister enjoyed as Schultz's wife. Now, Lowber was a moderately prosperous iron merchant, and, more importantly, he had been entrusted with a task—bringing an important document to Jefferson Davis. If successful, he likely would play a role in securing the independence of a new nation. He was finally a man of importance, perhaps more important than his brother-in-law had ever been. He felt powerfully the urge to tell someone, anyone, about his new importance but understood the risk of doing so. Finally, he resolved that he would write his son-in-law.

Montgomery had left Liverpool three or four days earlier and was expected to be in his New York office by the end of the next week. Addressing the letter to Montgomery Neill at the New York address of Neill Brothers, Lowber wrote that he had been asked to carry dispatches. To emphasize the significance of his task, he wrote that he had "succeeded in getting a big thing from some moneyed men in England." He wrote that he was confident that the blockade would be over by the new year. Finally, he related that he looked forward to seeing Montgomery within a fortnight. Lowber didn't sign the letter. He knew Montgomery would know the author.

After he had finished the letter and sealed it in an envelope, he looked at the envelope for a while to convince himself that it was not likely to generate any suspicion. He used as a return address the Irish address of William Neill, Montgomery's brother and partner. Satisfied that the envelope looked like one of hundreds of ordinary business letters that arrived in New York with each steamer from Europe, he walked briskly to the nearby postal office to purchase postage. With luck, it would leave in two days.

118

New York Times
July 25, 1861

Important from Fort Pickens.

The British Admiral's Opinion of the Blockade.
His Report to the British Admiralty.
He Considers the Blockade Totally Inefficient.

From our own correspondent.

Fort Pickens, Sunday, July 7, 1861.

Through a third party I have been endeavoring for some time to obtain something like the substance of a report of our blockade, made to the British Admiralty by Admiral Milne, the Commander-in-Chief of Her Britannic Majesty's naval forces here. I had learned three things from undoubted authority: first, that Lord Paget had instructed the Admiral to detail vessels to look after the cutting off of egress to the Southern ports; second, that the Admiral had obtained one or two copies of Commodore Mervin's official orders; third, that his Admiralship was reported in Havana to have laughed at the idea "of the United States being able to effectively cut off maritime communication with the harbors of revolted States."

119

15 Half Moon Street
London, England
July 30, 1861

LOWBER knocked on the door to Mann's room at 2:00 sharp. A few moments later, the door opened, and Mann literally pulled Lowber into the room.

"Mr. Lowber, your plans must change immediately."

"What's wrong?"

"Come to the window."

Mann took Lowber and placed him at the side of the window facing Half Moon Street.

"See the man standing there?"

Lowber nodded silently.

"I was watching you walk up," Mann said. "That man followed you and is now waiting for you to leave. He's obviously one of Seward's spies."

Lowber moved back from the window. "What do I do?" he asked Mann.

"You can't leave on the *Edinburgh*. If Seward's spies followed you here, they know who you are and are likely to have checked on the New York steamship lines. You'd be arrested the moment you land in New York."

Lowber was distressed. "If I'm not carrying any dispatches, then they'd have no reason to arrest me. Just meeting a fellow Southerner in London is no crime."

"Mr. Lowber—Dan. May I call you Dan? The dispatches I'm going to give to you are critically important. They have to be delivered to President Davis. You're the only hope I have of having them delivered in time."

"Colonel Mann, how do I get into the United States? There are no steamers heading to Southern ports, and if the customs officers are looking for me in New York, I'm going to be thoroughly searched."

"Dan, please call me Dudley."

"All right, Dudley. I don't think I can bring in the dispatches."

Mann sat on his bed and motioned Lowber to the wooden chair in the corner. Lowber pulled the chair up to the bed and sat down.

"Dan, how did you get into New York from Louisiana?"

"I took a coaster to Halifax and then took a ferry down to New York City. I have relatives on the Hudson and stayed with them a day and then went back down into New York City."

"So there was no way of knowing you were from the South?"

"No. I was just a businessman who boarded the train at Fishkill Landing, New York, and took a short ride to the city."

Mann stood up and went to his dresser. He put on his spectacles and unfolded a newspaper lying on the dresser. He turned the pages of the paper, skimming each page, while Lowber sat silently watching him.

"There, Dan. There's the answer," Mann said, poking his finger on a page of the newspaper. "There's a steamer leaving Liverpool August 8 for Quebec. It's the *Bohemian.* Take that steamer and follow the same path you followed before. No one can stop you in Quebec; that's for certain."

Lowber sat silently listening to this. This was becoming thorny. But for his letter to Montgomery Neill, Lowber would have refused to take the dispatches. However, the mailed letter sealed his fate. He couldn't back down. Nodding his head, he said, "It might work. I could take a steamer from Quebec to Halifax and then a ferry into New York City. I could stay a day or so with my relatives north of the city and then take a train to the South. I had no trouble the last time I did that. It could work."

"There you go, Dan! An excellent plan! Leave for Liverpool tonight. Stay away from the *Edinburgh* and board the *Bohemian.*"

Lowber thought through the plan. There was no alternative. "I'll do it, Dudley. I'll take your dispatches with me now. But what do we do about him?" Lowber motioned with his thumb toward the window. Mann stood up and saw that the man was still there, smoking a cigar.

"Well, Dan, I hope you won't be offended if you leave by the servants' entrance?" Mann said with a smile. "We'll let him finish his cigar."

120

Cunard wharf
New York City, New York
August 13, 1861

At the Cunard wharf, passengers climbed slowly up the gangplank of the *Africa* under the watchful eye of a ship's officer marking off names in a journal. Standing close to the officer were two men in dark suits. Their presence was explained only after a tired-looking man approached the gangplank.

"Your name, sir?"

"Robert Mure."

"Spell your last name," the officer requested. After the man did so, the officer nodded his head. At that signal, the two men walked around the officer and approached the would-be passenger.

The larger of the two, a burly man in his mid-thirties with a thick black mustache and a ruddy complexion, asked, "Are you Robert Mure?"

The man looked surprised. "That's me. Who are you?"

"I'm Detective King of the New York Police."

"What do you want with me?"

"Mr. Mure, step aside for a moment." The two men escorted Mure away from the gangplank. King said, "Mr. Mure, are you a citizen of the United States?"

"No, I'm a British subject. I have a passport." King noted a Scottish burr in Mure's accent.

"Show it to me," King said. Mure handed King a folded document, which the detective unfolded and slowly read. When finished, the detective folded the document and placed it in his suit pocket.

"You'll have to come with us, Mr. Mure."

"Am I under arrest?"

"Yes."

Mure was outraged. "For what? I've done nothing wrong!"

"For treason against the United States," King said. Motioning to his companion, King stated, "Go aboard and get his steamer trunk and bring it to the station." King then escorted his charge to a waiting carriage.

121

State Department
Washington, DC
August 14, 1861

Fred Seward ushered the visitor into his father's office. "Detective King, this is my father." The detective nodded a greeting, placed a canvas sack on Seward's desk, and handed him a package of documents. They then shook hands.

"So our information about Mure was accurate?" Seward asked. The detective nodded again. Seward looked at the canvas sack on his desk. "He was carrying this at the time of his arrest?"

"It was in his steamer trunk. Here's a letter from Superintendent Kennedy. He wrote it yesterday afternoon and told me to take the night train to deliver it to you."

Fred looked at his father for clarification. "Kennedy is the superintendent of police in New York. I've known him for years." Seward read the note and then handed it to his son, who read it silently:

> Sir: Your telegram of 13th was received last night, and this morning a short time before the departure of the steamer Africa Mr. Robert Mure, of Charleston, to whom you referred went on board with his baggage, whereupon the officers to whom I had intrusted the business took him in custody and brought him and his baggage to my office. He immediately presented me with his credentials as bearer of dispatches from Mr. Robert Bunch, consul of Her Britannic Majesty at Charleston, S.C., and an open letter of instruction from Mr. Bunch dated Charleston, August 7, 1861, the original of both of which are herewith inclosed. On examining his baggage the canvas bag alluded to in the instructions addressed to "Lord John Russell" was found and apparently sealed with a genuine consular seal. No other papers or documents were found in his possession except a large number of what appears to be private letters from persons

> in the South to others in England, but which I have not yet had an opportunity to examine carefully. A portion of these letters are unsealed and the rest are sealed, by which I believe he renders himself subject to treatment under the postal laws.
>
> The bag addressed to "Lord John Russell" I intrust to the charge of Detective Robert King to deliver with this note to you in Washington, pursuant to the instructions received in your telegram of to-day.

While Fred read the note, Seward closely examined the paper seal on the canvas bag. It looked genuine and was still intact.

"Father, what's this about?" Fred asked.

Seward responded, "I got word from an informer that Mure was going to England with dispatches for the Confederate commissioners. I had no idea he'd be arrested with a consular bag addressed to Lord Russell."

"What'll we do with it?"

"I suspect it's full of treasonable material. However, we can't break a consular seal. Before we do anything, I want to see the other letters Mure was carrying. While we can't open a British consular bag, I'm not fussy about opening mail from the rebels." Motioning for King to sit down, Seward began writing a note to Superintendent Kennedy on his official stationery:

> SIR: The bearer, Mr. Robert King, has delivered to me a letter addressed to Mure and inclosed in an envelope directed to me; also a bag addressed to Lord John Russell and a pamphlet, thus fully executing the trust reposed in him. You will please send me all other papers and documents found in the prisoner's possession, allowing him to retain none, and thus enable me to understand and properly decide upon the case.

Seward showed the note to King, who, after reading it silently, folded it and put it into coat pocket. "I'll leave tonight," King said.

Seward shook his hand. "Please give my regards to the superintendent. And, please, get those letters to me as quickly as you can."

122

15 Half Moon Street
London, England
August 14, 1861

MANN sat alone in his hotel room, reading the instructions from Jefferson Davis that had been delivered to him by Lowber. The instructions contained a long recitation of all the reasons previously urged by Mann and Yancey for England's recognition of the Confederacy. The arguments had been futile then and would be futile now. Of course, President Davis did not yet know of Mann's "big thing" for the Confederacy. Nevertheless, Mann was a commissioner, and his job was to follow the orders of his government. Accordingly, he wrote a long letter to Lord Russell in accordance with the instructions. However, before the final draft was written, Mann made certain the following language was included: "Since the establishment of the blockade, there have been repeated instances of vessels breaking it, at Wilmington, Charleston, Savannah, Mobile, and New Orleans. It will be for the neutral powers whose commerce has been so seriously damaged to determine how long such a blockade shall be permitted to interfere with that commerce."

Well, Mann thought when his letter to Lord Russell was complete, *we shall soon see if Her Majesty's government can continue to ignore breaches of the blockade when it is confronted with the greatest breach of all.*

123

Aboard the *Bohemian*
Quebec, Canada
August 19, 1861

AT the end of an uneventful voyage, Lowber stood at the port rail of the *Bohemian,* a small steamship of about two thousand tons. He had never seen Quebec before and looked around at the church spires, which rose from the banks of the St. Lawrence River. Mann had warned him that Union spies were on nearly every ship leaving England for North America, so Lowber had kept to himself, rarely speaking and then only in a soft mumble so as to hide his Southern accent.

He had boarded the ship using the name of Montgomery Neill. He hated to continue to invoke his son-in-law's name, but he had some of Montgomery's stationery and other papers in his trunk, so if someone had challenged him, he would have been able to prove his identity. As it turned out, the ruse was unnecessary. Nobody asked about him or even noticed him. The two hundred or so passengers on the ship were primarily men of commerce, some with their families, shuttling between England and Canada.

His trip in Great Britain had been rushed. He'd seen Montgomery's brother and his wife and spent an emotional afternoon with his two grandsons. They were both healthy and happy in their temporary family, and Lowber looked forward to giving his wife a glowing description of her "babies." The older boy had scrawled a drawing of a house for his grandmother, a treasure that was sure to end up in a place of honor in the china cabinet.

He was nervous about the next stage of his trip. His plan was to catch a steamer from Quebec to Halifax and then a ferry to New York City. He figured that if the authorities were waiting for him at all, it would be when the *Edinburgh* came into the port of New York. They couldn't be waiting for every ferry arriving in New York, as there were dozens every day.

He had a couple of stories to tell his wife. He was sure he'd entertain her at length talking about their grandsons and how happy they were. Several days into his voyage, he had stepped out of his cabin to see a fellow passenger moving quickly up the stairs to the deck of the *Bohemian*. When he'd asked what was happening, the passenger had told him, "It's the *Great Eastern*!"

Lowber had gone to the deck and found a place on the crowded rail. He'd looked at the colossal ship as she'd steamed in the opposite direction. She'd had no sails out, but thick black smoke had poured out of her five funnels as her gigantic side wheels turned. "She's on her way back from Quebec," a man behind Lowber had said to no one in particular. "Ain't she a sight!" Indeed, she had been a sight, her massive bow calmly breaking the waves, a gigantic Union Jack fluttering in the stiff ocean breeze from her stern. He didn't know if Mary would be impressed by his brush with the *Great Eastern*, but he was sure the men in New Orleans would be.

Throughout his voyage, Lowber couldn't help but wonder about the "big thing" he was bringing back for the Confederacy in the sealed packet Mann had given him. Mann had told him it was a loan, but he was still puzzled as to why it was so secret. Surely the announcement of a loan would boost the morale of the Confederacy. Also, the loan would almost certainly become public when it was drawn upon. Nevertheless, Lowber concluded that Mann must have had his reasons to keep the matter secret. Lowber would do everything he could to ensure that the packet arrived in President Davis's hands with its seal intact.

124

Residence of A. H. Schultz
Matteawan, New York
August 16, 1861

THE station wagon was already gone when Montgomery Neill arrived at the railroad station at Fishkill Landing. Not willing to wait for its return, he walked briskly past the shops of Main Street, crossed the creek separating Fishkill Landing from Matteawan, and climbed a steep hill until he finally reached the Schultzes' house. He stood for a moment at the front door, catching his breath. When he felt composed, he knocked sharply on the door. Margaret answered.

"Good afternoon, Mrs. Schultz."

"Montgomery! What are you doing here? Is everything all right?"

Neill smiled faintly and nodded his head. "Yes, everything's fine. I just had the afternoon free and wanted to visit with Mary."

Margaret didn't believe everything was fine. Montgomery looked pale, and he was still breathing hard. His thick hair glistened with perspiration.

"Sit in the parlor, Montgomery," Margaret said, "and I'll go find Mary."

Neill paced around the parlor, tapping his hat sharply against the side of his leg. He heard voices from upstairs. Finally, Mary came down the stairs with a worried look on her face.

"Montgomery, what a pleasant surprise! I wasn't expecting to see you until this weekend."

"I'm sorry to arrive unannounced, Mary, but as I told your mother, I had the afternoon free and thought it would be nice to spend it with you."

Margaret interceded. "Montgomery, I hope you'll spend the night with us. The night train gets into New York quite late."

"Thank you, Mrs. Schultz, but I have quite a bit of work waiting for me. I don't mind staying up late."

The three people stood silently in the parlor, each one waiting for another to speak. Finally, Neill spoke. "Mary, it's a beautiful afternoon," he said stiffly. "Would you like to go for a walk?"

"It's actually a little hot for me," said Mary. "I'd be more comfortable sitting on the porch in the shade."

Neill nodded and, with a forced smile to Margaret, followed Mary out of the front door.

Margaret turned around and saw Leonard standing in the kitchen, listening to the conversation. She walked closely to him and whispered, "Leonard, Mr. Neill showed up unannounced. He doesn't look well. I'm afraid something's wrong. He and Mary are on the porch now."

Leonard's suspicion as to why he was becoming involved in family matters was shortly confirmed as Margaret continued, "You have ears like a rabbit. Go 'round on the side of the house to see if you can hear what's going on."

"Yes'm."

Leonard quietly left through the back door, and Margaret went into the kitchen, where she fidgeted with a sack of peas, slowly shucking them and wondering what was happening. At last, the front door opened, and Mary came inside. She was red-faced and went directly upstairs. Neill stood at the doorway looking at Margaret in the kitchen. "Mrs. Schultz, I need to leave to catch the afternoon train. I've enjoyed seeing you. Goodbye." With that, Neill left, walking away from the house as quickly as he had walked toward it.

A few moments later, Margaret heard the back door open and saw Leonard standing in the doorway. Leonard signaled that Margaret should join him on the back porch. She quickly obeyed.

"What did you hear, Leonard?"

"Mr. Neill, he got a letter from Mr. Lowber from England. Mr. Lowber, he going to carry some dispatches from the leader of the rebels in England to Jeff Davis hisself. Mr. Lowber, he writes that he got something big for the Confederacy, that he got it from some moneymen, and that the blockade going break by the new year. Mr. Neill, he show Miz Mary the letter."

Margaret was stunned. She knew that her brother-in-law was a slave owner, but she'd never imagined him a traitor.

Leonard continued, "Mr. Neill, he's real angry. Says that Mr. Lowber saw Mr. Neill's brother when he was in England and that Mr. Seward got spies all over England, and now Mr. Neill 'fraid he gonna get arrested as a spy. He said that Mr. Seward throwing everyone in jail. Miz Mary, she starts to cry. She then says to Mr. Neill that Uncle Dan stop by the house on his way to England and tol' her he was carryin' papers *from* Jeff Davis when he goes *to* England, but she was sworn to secret. Mr. Neill's really mad now. He says, 'Don't you unnerstan' that this is a war, that men are getting killed, that this is no game?'"

Margaret's face was white with fright. Leonard, afraid she might faint, held out his arm, and she took it as they walked back into the parlor. She sat down heavily on her husband's armchair.

"I get you some water, Ms. Schultz." Leonard left and returned with a goblet of water. Margaret drank a bit and then gave the glass back. Leonard stood by her until she recovered. He kneeled down beside her and lowered his voice. "It gets worse, Ms. Schultz. Miz Mary say that Mr. Lowber, he used Mr. Neill's name 'stead his own when he go to England. Mr. Neill just 'bout had a fit when he hear that! Says, 'They could hang me!' He then get quiet, and then he walks Mary to the door. I then scoot aroun' to the back door. They don't know I was there."

"Dear God," Margaret said. "Leonard, I'm going to tell the captain as soon as he arrives. Do not say anything about this to anyone else! Not to Mary, not to anyone! Please promise me."

Leonard smiled. "Ms. Schultz, if you can't trust ol' Leonard, well, then who can you trust?"

Margaret patted his arm. "I know that. I can always trust you."

125

State Department
Washington, DC
August 17, 1861

It was nearly six o'clock in the evening when Fred walked into Seward's office with a canvas bag. "These are the documents that Mure was carrying," he said. "I met Superintendent Kennedy's messenger at the train station and signed a receipt." Fred cleared off a side table in a corner of his father's office and dumped out the contents of the bag. The two men each picked up a pile of letters and envelopes and began silently reading. Fred started by reading the open documents, but when he saw his father opening envelopes and taking out the enclosures, he started doing likewise. Most of the letters were mundane, dealing with family and business issues and local news. Quite a few made comments that were insulting to Lincoln or Seward, but nothing provided any intelligence. Then Fred walked over to Seward and handed him a short letter. Seward picked up the letter and after a brief examination started reading it out loud. "Mr. B, on oath of secrecy …"

"Who's Mr. B?" Fred asked.

"From the context," Seward said, "it can only be Robert Bunch, the British consul in Charleston." Seward continued reading. "Mr. B, on oath of secrecy, communicated to me also that the first step to recognition was taken." Seward, looking up at his son, said, "The author has blanked out certain words, apparently to keep the message secret." He continued reading the letter. "He and Mr. Belligny together sent Mr. Trescot to Richmond yesterday, to ask Jeff. Davis, President, to 'blank' the treaty of 'blank' to 'blank' the neutral flag covering neutral goods to be respected."

"What does *that* mean?" Fred asked.

Seward rubbed his face slowly as he considered the message. "It means that with the help of Mr. Bunch, the British consul, the Confederacy has secretly been asked to become a party to the Declaration of Paris. That's the only treaty I know that deals with neutral flags. The writer closes the letter with the following: 'This is the first step of direct treating with our government. So prepare for active business by January 1.'"

"So what does all that mean?" Fred asked.

"Well," Seward said, "this morning I received a dispatch from Charles Adams in which he says that Lord Russell is willing to have the United States become a signatory to the Declaration of Paris. However, there is a condition." Seward picked up Adams's dispatch. "Lord Russell writes, 'I need scarcely add that on the part of Great Britain the engagement will be prospective, and will not invalidate anything already done.'"

"What's Lord Russell talking about?"

"I was suspicious but not certain," Seward answered. "However, if you put the two documents together, it's now clear that Britain and the Southern states have secretly entered into the Declaration of Paris. Lord Russell knows our position that the Confederacy is simply a group of rebels, not a legitimate government with the power to enter into a treaty. What he's saying by his rather crafty language is that the United States' adherence to the Declaration of Paris will not invalidate Britain's secret agreement with the rebels."

Seward sat for a few more minutes, closely examining the two documents. "Something's afoot between Dudley Mann and Lord Russell, but I'm not sure what. Well, anyway, I'm not very good at thinking deep thoughts on an empty stomach. Let's go home, have dinner, and discuss this over cigars."

Both men were silent in the coach on the way home. Seward was deep in thought, and Fred was closely examining passersby looking for possible threats. There were more than a few residents of the District of Columbia who would like to see his father dead. When they entered the foyer of their home, Anna came up to them. "Captain Schultz is here. He's been waiting for you. He says it's very important."

Father and son exchanged puzzled looks. "Dear God, I hope it's not about the marshal's position," Seward whispered to Fred. "Lincoln did me no favors on that one." Seward walked into the parlor, where Schultz was already standing.

"Captain Schultz, it's so good to see you. I hope you will join us for dinner?"

Schultz was slightly flushed from the heat and from the exertion of making a series of train connections. "Governor, I'm sorry to burst in on you like this, but this matter is extremely important." Schultz was visibly agitated.

This isn't about the marshal's position, Seward thought.

"Firstly, Captain, we're going to have dinner shortly. I insist that you join us. My demand is nonnegotiable."

"Thank you, Governor. I'm not very hungry, I'm afraid, but I'll accept your kind invitation."

"Also, Captain, we'd be pleased if you spent the night with us."

"Thank you, Governor, but I've already checked in at the Willard and left my luggage there."

"All right. Well, now, while Anna arranges dinner, let's talk." The three men sat down. Seward and his son were silent, waiting for Schultz to speak.

"Governor, I believe I've mentioned Dan Lowber to you before."

Seward nodded slightly. The name was familiar.

"He's my brother-in-law. He's also one of my dearest friends. He's done something stupid, and I'm terrified that he might hang as a traitor. I've come to beg you for his life."

Seward was taken aback. "Captain, I promise I'll help you to the extent it's within my power. I can't promise any more than that. Tell me what this is about. Don't leave out any details."

Schultz sat quietly for a few moments, his shoulders hunched, his gaze downward as he concentrated his thoughts. On the train trip to Washington, he had carefully thought out how he would tell his story. "I had a younger brother named William," he began. "He passed away about fifteen years ago. When he was young, he married a young woman, and they had a daughter named Kate. William's wife died while Kate was still very small, and he struggled to raise her alone. It was finally decided that Dan Lowber and his wife would raise the little girl in New Orleans. William later remarried, but he left Kate with the Lowbers because they had no children of their own and William planned on having more children with his new wife. As you may know, Dan's wife and my wife are sisters, so the Lowbers really are part of our family. Kate always thought of the Lowbers as her parents." Schultz paused and looked directly at Seward. "Dan became the father of my niece and was a good father to her."

"Go ahead, Captain. We're listening."

Schultz took a deep breath and then audibly sighed. "Dan was born and raised in New York, but he had a hard time making a living there.

When he got married to Margaret's sister, he was working as a master on coastal steamers and was traveling mostly between New York and New Orleans. He spent quite a bit of time in the South and finally decided to move his family there. He went to Mobile and started a business supplying equipment to planters. He later moved his business to New Orleans."

"All right," Seward said quietly. "Go on."

"Dan is now a Southerner through and through. He owns slaves, which troubles Margaret and me greatly. However, he still remains one of my best friends. In fact, Governor, you know my daughter Mary."

Seward nodded. He had met the young woman several times, even corresponded with her a couple of times.

Schultz continued, "Her full name is Mary Lowber Schultz. We named her in honor of both Mary and Dan."

"Captain, there's no crime in being a Southern sympathizer. If it *was* a crime, we wouldn't have enough jails to lock up all the criminals."

"It's worse than that, Governor."

"I'm sorry, Captain. Go ahead; we're listening."

"My daughter Mary was only a couple of years younger than Kate. Mary used to spend several months a year in New Orleans and considered Dan and Mary as her second parents. Kate eventually married a man named Montgomery Neill, an Englishman, and moved to Mobile. Kate and Montgomery had two children, but Kate died shortly after the birth of her second child. My daughter was there when she died."

Seward and Fred glanced at each other. *Where is this all going?* they both thought.

"Gentlemen, dinner is served," Anna called out. Seeing the serious looks on the faces of the three men, Anna decided that she'd have dinner with the cook in the kitchen.

"Captain, we'll continue at the dinner table," Seward said. Schultz nodded.

Schultz continued his story after Seward said grace. "After Kate died, Montgomery sent his two small boys to his brother and sister-in-law in Britain to be raised until he remarried. Not so long ago, Montgomery began seeing my daughter Mary. He would come up from New York on the train to visit her at our house."

"Well, that seems to be good news, Captain, but I haven't heard any treason yet. Are you sure that you are not overly concerned about something unimportant?"

Schultz shook his head. "Dan went to England in mid-July to see his grandsons and to do some business. He stopped at our house and told me he was going to order a quantity of iron and machinery before the blockade went into effect. However, I just learned two days ago that Dan was carrying communications from Jeff Davis to the rebel commissioners in England."

"How do you know this?"

"My wife overhead Mary and Montgomery talking. My daughter said that Dan told her about this but swore her to secrecy. Montgomery was very upset when he heard about this."

"Well, Captain, that's treasonous, but it doesn't sound like a hanging offense. Southerners are crossing the Atlantic every day with all kinds of dispatches and messages, most of which aren't very important. However, you need to keep Lowber away from your family. It was wrong of him to compromise your daughter, although I must tell you that your family is wholly beyond any suspicion of wrongdoing."

"Governor, I'm not done yet. My wife overheard Montgomery telling Mary that Dan Lowber wrote him a letter from England and said that he's bringing back a dispatch from the rebel commissioner to Jeff Davis. Dan wrote that he had a big thing for the Confederacy and that the blockade would be over by the new year."

Seward and Fred looked at each other. Fred asked, "Was there any explanation as to the 'big thing'?"

Schultz shook his head. "No. Just a 'big thing.'"

"How's Lowber returning, Captain?"

"I don't know."

The men finished their dinner in silence, eating little. Seward then arose. "Captain, join Fred and me in our parlor for cigars. Please."

The three arose silently, and Fred retrieved a heavily carved oak cigar box. When the two older men were settled in their chairs, each with a cigar, Fred went into the kitchen and returned with a glowing taper. After the three men went through the ritual of lighting up their cigars, Seward spoke. "Captain, we're trying to understand what the rebels are doing in England."

"Governor, any help I can give is yours."

"We learned today that the South has secretly entered into the Declaration of Paris with Britain."

Schultz asked, "What does that mean?"

"The declaration protects the rights of neutrals during a war," Seward said. "It outlaws privateers and paper blockades, among other things."

"What does it call a paper blockade?"

"The declaration doesn't provide any detail other than to say that a real blockade has to be effective—a port has to be blockaded by a large enough number of warships so that commercial ships cannot enter or leave the port. A mere declaration of blockade isn't enough."

The three men took a puff on their cigars in silence. Seward then asked, "Captain, Lowber wrote that he had met the Southern commissioner in England?"

"That's my understanding. I didn't see the letter but heard about it from my wife."

"Did he say which one? I believe Yancey and Mann are still both in London"

"No," said Schultz. "All I know is that it was the rebel commissioner."

Seward turned to Fred and said, "I think it's likely that he met with Dudley Mann. Mann has many more contacts in London than does Yancey. Mann must have told Lowber that he has a 'big thing' for the Confederacy and that the blockade will end in a few months." His voice trailed off.

Seward put his cigar down on an ash stand. He leaned forward in his chair and, looking at the floor, began running his fingers through his thick, rumpled hair. He appeared to be concentrating his thoughts, and both Schultz and Fred watched him in silence. Finally, he looked up, his face ashen.

"Fred, Mann has been obsessed with something for years, right?"

"Well, yes, direct trade between England and the South."

"No, no, Fred! A *thing*! He's been obsessed with a 'big thing'!"

Fred sat quietly for a moment. "The steamship? The *Great Eastern*?"

"Fred, remember you read that article in the newspaper that said he was going to England to consummate some *Great Eastern* transaction? Remember we wondered why it said that when Mann was really going as a rebel commissioner?"

Fred nodded. "I remember the article. It was in the *Times*."

Seward started rubbing his forehead. "Good God, she's such a financial disaster her owners even tried to sell her to us! Mann must have sounded like a godsend to them."

Schultz interjected, "Why are you talking about the *Great Eastern*?"

Seward responded, "Captain, the rebels now have a treaty under which Britain is obligated to declare the blockade of Southern ports illegal if the blockade's not effective. Now, how can we claim that the blockade's effective if the largest ship in the world steams into a Southern port?"

Schultz was taken aback by the statement. Fred asked, "What happens if Britain declares our blockade to be illegal?"

"I think that any attempt to enforce the blockade against a British ship would be an act of war," Seward said.

"So if the blockade's not effective, we can't stop British ships from going into Southern ports?" Fred asked.

"Not just the British, Fred. The French as well. The trade routes between the Confederacy and Europe would be wide open. The South would be flush with cotton money and could buy all the weapons and mercenaries that Europe has to offer. Our navy is hopelessly outmatched by the British and French navies."

"And the war?" Fred asked.

"I don't know," Seward said. "It could lead to early recognition of the Confederacy by Britain and France."

"Couldn't we protest to Lord Russell?"

"Protest what? Nothing's happened—there's no violation of any treaty. At this point Britain does not recognize the legality of our blockade. It's still trying to determine whether it's effective. We could let Lord Russell know our suspicions, but all we would be doing is confessing that we can't maintain a real blockade. If we had such a blockade, a ship the size of the *Great Eastern* could get nowhere close to a Southern port. The truth is that we only have a couple of dozen ships at most patrolling thousands of miles of shoreline. Most of the time they're coming and going to Northern ports for refueling. We're pretending it's an effective blockade, and for the time being, Britain is not challenging the pretense. We can't say or do anything to prove that it's all an illusion."

"You think that the 'big thing' Dan wrote about is the *Great Eastern*?" Schultz asked.

"I don't know, Captain, but it fits everything that we've learned so far."

"If it is, Governor?"

Seward looked at Schultz for a few moments. "Someone has to go to England immediately to find out if we're right."

The implication was clear. After a deep breath, Schultz said, "Dan's my brother-in-law. If he's involved in treason, it's my duty to find out. I'll go. But what do I do when I'm there?"

"See if you can find anyone who talked to Lowber when he was there. We need to confirm our suspicions."

"What if I can't find anyone who knows anything?"

"Then, you'll have to use your best judgment as to whether we're right."

The three men fell into silence. Fred saw Schultz's face knotted with worry and decided to try a different approach. "Captain Schultz, it seems to me that a highly regarded captain would be unlikely to attempt this. Unless she goes to Canada again, the *Great Eastern* has always been scheduled to go to New York. To divert the ship and her passengers secretly into a Southern port would destroy the reputation of her captain. I think that if she had a prominent captain, she'd not be likely to attempt to break the blockade."

Schultz nodded. "So far she's had Captain Hall and this young Kennedy. I can't believe either of them would ruin his career. So I agree with you, Fred. I need to learn who the captain will be. If he's a man of little or no reputation, it'd be a warning sign."

"Captain," Seward said, "is there anything you can think of that might be a warning sign?"

Schultz gently tugged at his bearded chin in thought. "Well, Governor, the South has lots of ports, but most of them are pretty shallow. The deep port at Norfolk is under our cannons at Fort Monroe, so the *Great Eastern* won't go there. With the other ports, she'd need to go in very lightly loaded and at high tide. If she went in on a high tide and had a shallow draft, I think that she could go into a number of ports—Charleston, Savannah, Port Royal, Beaufort, maybe some others."

"How would we know when it's high tide?"

"An almanac shows when the tide is high. Also, by late August the wind from the east picks up, and that raises the tide. I'd look to see when there's a high tide in late August or early September."

"So if the ship is scheduled to arrive in New York about that time, it's possible that she's really headed for a Southern port?"

"Well," said Schultz, "it's some proof. It's certainly not conclusive. The *Great Eastern* also wants a good tide to come into New York, and all things considered, the higher the tide, the better. She doesn't need a spring tide to go into New York, but she'd need one to break the blockade at any place but the Chesapeake."

"Anything else you can think of, Captain?"

"Not offhand."

"Captain, we know that we have Southern sympathizers in the State Department that report our activities to the rebels. Therefore, we need an excuse for your quick trip to England." Turning to Fred, Seward said, "I'm going to send the captain to England as a courier to carry the diplomatic pouch we seized from Mure. I was going to turn it over to Lord Lyons, but now I can say that the matter is so important I wanted it delivered directly to Lord Russell in England."

"That should work," Fred said. "The fact that the diplomatic pouch was seized from Mure has been in the newspapers. Everyone knows about it. Would the captain give it directly to Lord Russell?"

"No, he'd deliver it to Charles Adams. Adams would deliver it."

Seward leaned in his chair toward Schultz. "When you get to England, Captain, try to confirm whether our suspicions are correct. If you think they are, you've got to act."

"What do you mean?"

"I'm not certain. If there's time, send me a message, and I'll notify the blockading fleet. However, remember it takes two weeks to get a message to me," Seward said.

"What if there's not enough time?" Schultz said. "Should I notify Mr. Adams?"

Seward thought and then said, "No. He could protest to Lord Russell, but Russell wouldn't do anything, because sending a neutral ship into a belligerent's port isn't a violation of anything. All it would do is show our helplessness. I want to keep Adams out of this affair entirely."

The implications of the situation began to sink in for Schultz.

"Governor, I'm not sure what to do if I suspect that she's going into a Southern port and there's not sufficient time to notify you."

"I'm not certain either, Captain." Seward snapped his fingers and turned to his son. "Fred, where is that young engineer—Towle?"

"He's in France right now. He's watching the shipbuilding yards at Havre for any signs of rebel activity, but he has lodgings in Paris."

Schultz looked at Seward for an explanation.

"One of our agents keeping track of the rebels in Europe is a young engineer named Hamilton Towle," Seward explained. "He's quite clever, went to Harvard. I'll give you his address. He can help you figure out a way of stopping the *Great Eastern* from making the voyage if it comes to that."

Both Sewards saw that Schultz was being overwhelmed. Seward leaned over and clasped Schultz's thick forearm. "Captain, the 'big thing' may well be something other than the *Great Eastern.* We may find that we're sitting here like nervous old ladies worrying about something that's not going to occur. All we want to do is be sure that this ship does not enter a Southern port."

Fred said, "Captain, we don't know when she's leaving England, so you'll need to get there as soon as possible. When can you leave?"

"In a couple of days. I have to go back home first. But I don't know what ship is available."

Fred picked up and scanned a recent edition of the *New York Times.* "The *Europa* leaves Boston on the twenty-first for Liverpool."

Schultz nodded. "She's a good Cunard steamer. That's next Wednesday. I can take her."

Fred walked to a desk in the parlor and took a piece of plain stationery from a drawer. He sat at the desk and began writing. As he was doing so, he asked Schultz, "Captain, what time does the train to New York leave tomorrow?"

"Half past two."

Fred nodded and continued writing. When done, he handed the letter to Schultz.

Washington August 17 1861

Hon F. W. Seward
Assistant Sec of State

Sir

I propose leaving this city tomorrow (Sunday) at 2½ O'ck PM to make the necessary arrangements in New York, for leaving Boston in the "Europa" on the 21st inst, in obedience to your orders. Be pleased to prepare my instructions as of today, if entirely convenient.

Very Respectfully
Your Obt Servant

"Is this satisfactory, Captain?" Fred asked. Schultz read the letter and then nodded.

"Take the letter with you and rewrite it in your handwriting," Seward said. "You can give it to Fred tomorrow when he delivers the diplomatic pouch. With this letter, we'll have a perfectly innocent request for instructions." With a smile, Seward explained, "The rebel spies in the State Department will examine this letter and my response and find nothing suspicious about them. Your real mission will remain secret to Fred and me."

"If you have spies, can't you arrest them?"

"Of course. But we know who they are, or at least some of them, and it's helpful to use them to send false information to our friends down South. They'd find out about your trip to England anyway. With these letters, it'll seem innocent enough."

Fred asked, "Will four hundred dollars be enough to cover your expenses, Captain? I'm concerned if it's any more than that, the amount will be suspicious."

"No, that should be plenty. I'll take some of my own money from my bank just before I leave."

After a brief but awkward silence, Seward said, "Captain, early tomorrow morning Fred will come to your room at the Willard. He'll have the diplomatic pouch, an open letter of instructions to you, a sealed letter from me to Adams, and four hundred dollars in cash. You'll give him a copy of the letter he just wrote. When you reach Liverpool, you should see Henry Wilding, our vice consul. He'll arrange your transportation to London and back. However, your mission must remain a secret from everyone but Hamilton Towle, and then only if you think you need his help. I'll not see you again until you return to the United States."

Schultz nodded, and Seward continued, "You know how much now rests on your shoulders. There's no one else I trust more than you. Remember—never discuss this with anyone, ever, even Charles Adams."

"Governor, I'll have to tell Margaret. She needs to know." Seward's face was impassive. Schultz pleaded, "You can trust her. She's kept many secrets and never betrayed a single one."

Seward thought. He knew Margaret to be a sober, mature woman. They'd have to trust her. "Of course, Captain; you can tell Margaret, but only under the strictest confidence. No one else must ever know."

Schultz nodded. "Governor, I'll do my best for you; I promise."

"I know that."

With that, Schultz shook hands with the father and son. Fred left to call for the carriage while Seward and Schultz remained standing at the doorway. After one more brief handshake between the two men, Schultz was on his way to the Willard Hotel. As he traveled in the early evening, his stomach was churning, and his hands seemed cold, even in the hot weather. As his carriage progressed down Pennsylvania Avenue, he glanced at wagons drawn by teams of horses carrying barrels, wooden boxes, and even furniture. He was only vaguely aware when his carriage passed a wagon moving slowly down Pennsylvania Avenue carrying a load of slaves in chains.

Times of London
August 17, 1861

The Great Eastern, which left Quebec on the 6th, arrived last evening, but brought no news.

Captain Kennedy, who commanded the Great Eastern this voyage, will not go in the vessel again, having merely consented, with the permission of the Liverpool, New York, and Philadelphia Steamship Company, to take charge of her for one voyage only. He will immediately rejoin his own vessel, the Etna.

126

Aboard the Baltimore & Ohio Railroad
Somewhere in Maryland
August 18, 1861

During his night at the Willard, Schultz had alternated between looking at the ceiling while lying on the bed and standing and looking blankly out the open window into the dark. It had been a humid night, which would have made it difficult to sleep even in the best of circumstances. With the thoughts of his mission frightening him, sleep had no chance. Finally, when the first light of dawn entered the room, he washed, shaved, and began to dress. He stopped when he heard a knock at the door. He opened it to allow Fred Seward into the room.

"Captain Schultz, here's the diplomatic pouch we seized from Mure." Fred placed the canvas pouch on Schultz's rumpled bed. "I also have a dispatch you're to deliver to Mr. Adams. I have your official instructions and the money for your expenses." Fred handed three envelopes, two open and one sealed, to Schultz. "Your official instructions say you're to deliver dispatches to Mr. Dayton, our minister in Paris. I have put together a dispatch for Mr. Dayton in this envelope with the money for you. It doesn't contain anything important, but it gives you a reason to go to France to find Hamilton Towle if you think you need his help. Mr. Dayton is to know nothing about this."

Schultz silently took the envelopes and placed two of them, his official instructions and the cash, into the breast pocket of his suit jacket, which was hanging on a hook. The third envelope, the sealed dispatch to Charles Francis Adams, Schultz placed in the bottom of a leather valise. Fred waited for a response from Schultz, and when there was none, Fred asked quietly, "Captain, are you all right?"

Schultz gave a slight shrug. "I think so. Here's my letter requesting instructions. I copied it last night."

Sensing further conversation might be unwelcome, Fred offered his hand to Schultz. Schultz took it and shook it firmly.

"Good luck, Captain. Our thoughts will be with you."

Schultz pursed his lips and nodded and then opened the door to his room. "Goodbye, Fred." Schultz finished dressing and packing and took a hack to the railroad station to board a train to New York.

The railroad car was not crowded in the early morning, and Schultz was able to sit by himself. He sat next to the aisle and placed the leather valise between himself and the window on the wicker seat. When he had been on the train for about an hour, he pulled an envelope from his jacket pocket. It was his official instructions.

> Sir: With the dispatches herewith intrusted to you you will proceed to London by the Cunard Steamer which will start from Boston on Wednesday next. On arriving at London you will deliver the dispatches for Mr. Adams to him and as soon as convenient you will proceed to Paris and deliver to Mr. Dayton those addressed to him also. You will remain in Paris for any dispatches which Mr. Dayton may have to send by you and you will return by the way of London for any which Mr. Adams may have. You will exercise all practicable diligence in the discharge of this duty for which you will be allowed a compensation at the rate of $6 a day and your necessary traveling expenses of which you will keep an account, to be supported by vouchers in every instance where they can be obtained. The sum of $400 is now advanced to you on account of your expense.

He put the letter back into his suit pocket.

It was late Sunday when Schultz arrived in New York City. He took a hack and headed directly to his harbor master's office. The following morning he told his clerk that he was going to England on business. From there, it was a short ride to his wharf, where he gave instructions to be followed in his absence. In both cases, he was comforted by the fact that the men he had hired and trained over the years were reliable. He went to his bank, withdrew cash, and then headed for the Hudson River Railroad Station to take a train to Fishkill Landing. With luck, he'd be home in time for a late dinner.

127

Office of the Superintendent of Police
413 Broome Street
New York City, New York
August 18, 1861

"Come in," Superintendent Kennedy responded to a knock on the door to his office. A police sergeant opened the door and walked in. Both men were dressed in their blue uniforms, Kennedy in his ornate single-breasted dress coat and the sergeant wearing a simpler version of the same.

"Superintendent, there's a gentleman here to see you. Says it's urgent."

"Does he look like a crank?" Kennedy asked warily. He had had his fill of deranged individuals conjuring up conspiracies.

"No, sir. He looks like he's got money, though."

"Show him in. Stand behind him in case he pulls a weapon."

The sergeant nodded and returned with a slender man in his thirties, well dressed with a well-groomed mustache. "Superintendent, my name is Benjamin James. I have information about a man working as a spy for the Confederacy." The man spoke as if he were well educated.

"Mr. James, what's your information?" Kennedy asked.

"I'm going to discuss a member of my family, Superintendent Kennedy. You must promise not to disclose that I'm the source of the information."

"Unless you're a party to a crime, Mr. James, I'll keep your information confidential. You can count on that. Now, what's your information?"

"A man named Daniel C. Lowber is coming into the United States with dispatches for Jefferson Davis."

"I see. Where is Lowber now?"

"Somewhere on the Atlantic."

"All right. Can you give me a description of the man?"

"He's in his fifties, average weight, average height. He has whiskers that are mostly gray. He speaks with a Southern accent, but he wears false teeth and has a pronounced lisp because of them. His teeth move about when he eats. He speaks softly."

"Where's he from?"

"New Orleans. He's originally from New York City, and he knows the city well. But he's thoroughly Southern. He fancies himself a great hero of the Confederacy."

"Do you know what ship he's aboard?"

"No."

Kennedy carefully took notes of this conversation. When he caught up, he looked at his visitor.

"Mr. James, how do you come by this information?"

"I was told by my brother, who was told by a family acquaintance in whom we have complete confidence. My brother has offered to sign an affidavit as to these facts."

"I see," said Kennedy. "Mr. James, the police department has received all sorts of claims that Mr. So-and-So is a Confederate spy. Several times we've arrested respectable and loyal men because they were denounced by someone who had a grudge against them. It has sometimes put us in a very hard position. Now, sir, I'm not saying that's the case with you, but I need to satisfy myself that this Lowber really is a spy. In other words, Mr. James, I still need facts."

James stood silently for a moment. "Superintendent, do you know Captain Schultz, the man with the tugboats?"

Kennedy nodded. "I've met him when he was harbor master. I don't know him well, but I know he's a friend of Governor Seward."

"Lowber is his brother-in-law. Their wives are sisters."

Kennedy's thick eyebrows raised noticeably. "Did Captain Schultz tell you that Lowber was a spy?"

"No, I don't think it likely the captain knows anything about this."

"Mr. James, I've told you I'd keep your confidences. Please tell me the entire story."

James pointed to a chair. "May I sit down?"

"Of course, I'm sorry," Kennedy responded. Kennedy waved his hand at the sergeant standing at the door, who came over quickly and removed a stack of papers from the chair.

"My brother, Eddie, and I are Captain Schultz's nephews," James said. "I received this information from my brother, who in turn received it from Montgomery Neill, who's Lowber's son-in-law. He's a well-known cotton trader."

"All right. How does Neill know that Lowber is a spy?"

"Lowber sent Neill a letter from England in which he admits he's acting as a spy for Jefferson Davis."

Kennedy was incredulous. "Why would Lowber do that?"

"I don't know. Lowber's got a bit of a reputation for boasting. He might think Neill is sympathetic to the Confederacy because he's a cotton trader. I don't know."

"Have you seen the letter?"

"No, I just heard about it."

"I see," Kennedy said as he wrote his notes. He looked up when finished. "Go on."

"Lowber may be using the name Montgomery Neill. I think that's why Neill is so upset, why he told my brother about all this. I'm sure Neill expected us to go to the police."

"Well, having your good name purloined by a spy is certainly grounds for anger," Kennedy said. "You say that Captain Schultz and Lowber are brothers-in-law?"

"That's correct. They married sisters. Lowber lives in New Orleans."

"Where does Schultz live?"

"In Matteawan. It's a little town next to Fishkill Landing, across the Hudson from Newburgh."

Kennedy wrote silently, and when he finished, James said, "Superintendent, it's our hope that Lowber can be quietly arrested and his papers seized. The more the public knows about this, the more likely it is to distress Captain Schultz and his family. The captain is a good Union man and, as you said, a friend of Governor Seward. We don't want to embarrass a good family. In all events, you must keep Montgomery Neill's name out of this."

"Mr. James, we'll do everything we can to handle this matter with discretion. Now, anything further?"

"I don't believe so."

"How can I contact you for further information?"

"Send a telegraph message to Thomas Richardson and Company in Philadelphia. I'm one of the managers of that company. I live in Burlington, New Jersey, but I'm at the company nearly every day but Sunday. You can send the message to me or my brother. His full name is Edward."

When he finished writing, Kennedy looked at James approvingly. "You've done the right thing, Mr. James."

"Thank you, Superintendent."

After a brief handshake, Kennedy asked the sergeant to escort James out.

128

Residence of W. H. Seward
Washington, DC
August 19, 1861

The dinner table had been cleared; Seward and Fred were in the parlor smoking cigars and reading newspapers. Anna peered out from the kitchen from time to time, but the silence from the parlor indicated that she'd be wise not to break the concentration of the two men.

"Father, listen to this." Holding the newspaper up to the oil lamp, Fred began to read:

> Lord Palmerston, on the last day of the session of Parliament, which had been prorogued by the Queen in person, had stated his views in reference to the blockade, in which he declared that, should *one* vessel be allowed to enter a blockaded port, that moment the blockade must be considered raised. A belligerent has a right to seal up a port, but if he lets *one* vessel in, his right is gone.

Fred had twice emphasized the word *one* as Seward listened intently. Finally, Seward asked, "Fred, what are you reading?"

"Today's *New York Times*."

"Does the article say anything else?"

"Nothing important. It doesn't give the date of Lord Palmerston's speech, but it must have been around the fifth or sixth of August."

"One vessel gets in, and the blockade is raised," Seward said quietly. "One vessel gets in, and the war is lost?"

"Do you think Lord Palmerston knows of Mann's plan?"

"I don't know," Seward said. "Sending a British merchantman on a blockade running trip is pretty dirty work for a prime minister, even one like Palmerston. I would guess he doesn't know what Mann is up to and is simply repeating a thought someone planted in his mind."

"Someone like a Southern sympathizer?"

"That seems likely."

Fred stood up and stretched his back. "I wonder where Captain Schultz is now."

"He must be somewhere in New York. He leaves the day after tomorrow from Boston on the *Europa*."

"Do you think he'll succeed?"

Seward sat silently. "I don't know. The captain is a resourceful man. If he needs it, he'll have the help of Towle. All we can do is pray that they're equal to the task." The two men continued to scour the newspapers silently until they retired for the night.

129

Residence of A. H. Schultz
Matteawan, New York
August 19, 1861

A breeze quietly moved the muslin curtains hanging in the bedroom window. The night was clear, and the light of a nearly full moon coming through the thin curtains gave the room a dreamlike peacefulness. Margaret was sound asleep, occasionally snoring gently, but Schultz lay staring at the ceiling. He had tried to sleep, but back and leg pain from the long train ride, coupled with an overwhelming feeling of despair, made sleep impossible. He lay utterly exhausted but wide awake.

Schultz thought over and over about the *Great Eastern.* He had toured the ship when she'd arrived in New York on her maiden voyage. Indeed, Captain Hall had given a warm welcome to Schultz after being informed that he was addressing the harbor master. As he lay next to his wife, Schultz recalled everything he could about the great ship—her boilers, controls, communication systems. He was astounded by the size of her engines. While they were no more complex than the ordinary steam engines with which he was familiar, their size made them otherworldly, like seeing for the first time the chair of a giant. Lying in bed, Schultz considered putting sand or grit in the bearings to which the piston rods were connected, but the control rooms for both the paddle and screw engines were always manned, and the bearings were impossible to reach without a ladder or scaffold.

How in the devil can I sabotage her without being seen by the ship's crew? he thought. The steering system was impregnable; the rudder was operated by chains, each link of which was the size of a watermelon. As Schultz mentally recalled each detail of the ship's mechanical operation, the hopelessness of his task increased.

To avoid a dead end to his thought process, he retreated to the very act of first boarding the *Great Eastern* that hot July day a year earlier. He recalled being brought over to Captain Hall and introduced. Hall, a vain man, had been delighted to meet someone of position and authority, as opposed to the crowd of gawkers and ruffians that crowded his ship. As they'd walked around the deck, Hall had pointed out the skylights that illuminated the berths and saloons below deck. The two men had walked forward when …

Schultz sat up in bed. *The lifeboats!* he thought. As he had walked up the deck to the ship's bow, Schultz had noted that certain lifeboats were tied down on the deck, not hanging from their davits. The large wooden boats had blocked the view of the forward deck and been an obstacle to the crowds trying to move around them. When Schultz had asked why the lifeboats were not hanging on the davits, Hall had said that the Board of Trade was sometimes like a "gathering of old ladies," and apparently one of the fussiest of them worried that someone, a drunk perhaps, might cut the ropes hanging the forward lifeboats from the davits. If that happened, Hall had explained, the lifeboat could be sucked into a paddle wheel and end up destroying the wheel.

Schultz got out of bed and sat in a chair by the bedroom window. He closed his eyes, attempting to recall whether the lifeboats had been put back on the davits when the *Great Eastern* returned the second time to New York. He hadn't boarded her that time, but he recalled seeing her enter the harbor. He thought that he would remember if the davits had been empty. He was an experienced sailor, and the sight of empty davits usually meant that something ominous had happened. He was sure he'd have noticed such a sign. By the time he had searched his memory,

Schultz was convinced that the lifeboats had indeed been put back on the davits for the second voyage. All that held them to the davits were ropes wound through block and tackle.

Schultz thought out the consequences of this discovery. If one of the ropes holding up a lifeboat forward of a paddle wheel could be cut loose and the boat lowered into the water, it would indeed be sucked into the moving paddle wheel. The wooden blades of the giant paddle wheel would smash into the wooden lifeboat, and the entire wheel would end up mangled. If that happened, the ship would have to stop her paddle engines and could only use her screw. The ship wouldn't sink, wouldn't even be damaged except for the paddle wheel, but could only travel at a very slow rate of speed. The stopped paddle wheels dragging in the water would act as a brake. She could never make a port at the scheduled high tide and would have to limp to the nearest port for repairs. The repairs could take weeks. Nobody would be hurt; nobody would be in danger. If done properly, it was possible that no one could be certain it was an act of sabotage.

But the rope, Schultz thought. If the rope was cut, it could only mean that there had been sabotage. There would be an investigation in England upon the ship's return. Schultz, as a confidant of Seward, would be immediately under suspicion. But what if a lifeboat were unslung, unhooked from the block and tackle, without cutting the rope? That was easy enough when the lifeboat was weightless in the water, but how could this be done while the boat was hanging from a davit? The boats were large, but if a powerful man was aboard the lifeboat, he might be able to lift it a fraction of an inch or so high enough to unsling it when the ship was rolling from side to side. *Who could do this?* Schultz thought. Schultz knew that at fifty-seven he was years past when he could scramble into a lifeboat hanging on davits. Seward had said that Towle was young, but would he be strong enough? A safety rope could be tied to the man, but the task would still be incredibly dangerous. He could be crushed between the dangling lifeboat and the *Great Eastern*'s hull. *I need an agile, powerful man* ... Schultz thought.

"Dear God!" he said out loud.

Margaret rolled over and cleared her throat. She put her head up to look around and was surprised to see her husband sitting on a chair in the darkness.

"Hamilton, are you all right?"

"Yes, dear. I … I just had a thought. I'm sorry I woke you up."

Margaret pushed herself to a sitting position. "What is it, Hamilton? Is something wrong?"

"No, dear. I'm just a bit worked up about my trip." Schultz had told Margaret about his trip to England to deliver the diplomatic pouch but had not mentioned anything about the *Great Eastern*. He still wasn't sure he was going to tell her.

"Margaret, I need to talk to Leonard."

"About what, Hamilton?"

"Uh, taking me to the train station. I need to talk to him."

"Hamilton, it's the middle of the night. Let him sleep. Come on back to bed and get some rest."

Schultz lay back down, and Margaret put her head on his chest. "I'm going to miss you when you're gone," she said. "Be sure to come back with some good stories about London and the queen and all that." She gave a small chuckle and then lay quietly. As Margaret began to doze off, Schultz stared at the wallpapered ceiling. He thought silently, *I pray to God that he's still in Baxtertown.*

130

Baxtertown, New York
August 20, 1861

"Kit, you in there?" Leonard knelt down by Kit's lean-to in the early-morning light. A black hand reached out from inside the lean-to and flipped over a corner of the canvas cloth that covered its open side.

"I's here." A sleepy Kit looked at Leonard. Usually Leonard was neatly dressed. This morning, he was wearing a nightshirt covered by a blanket. Kit looked at him closely. "You all right?"

"Kit, Capt'n needs you at the house right 'way. You going on a trip with him. Take everything you got."

Kit started laughing. "I's wearin' everythin' I got. What you think, I's got a mule in here?"

"Just hurry. Capt'n and you takin' the train in less than three hours."

"Where to?"

"Don't know. I reckon Capt'n will tell you."

Leonard left, and Kit came out of the lean-to and flipped the entire canvas cloth over the structure. He looked carefully at the interior of his home. He had an extra shirt, the wooden box containing his clay pipe and some tobacco, the folding knife that used to belong to Jack, and a leather pouch with his money. The rest of the lean-to's contents—a couple of wool blankets, a sheepskin, an ax—he would leave to the residents of Baxtertown. Kit figured that if he needed something for the trip, Captain Schultz would get it for him.

The rest of Baxtertown was still asleep, so Kit decided to leave quietly. As he started toward the path to Fishkill Landing, however, Kit saw a thin plume of smoke from a fire. He looked and saw Reeba facing a firepit trying to warm up a piece of potato over the remnants of a fire. She was wearing an old plaid blanket as a shawl. He stopped before her.

"I's leaving," he said softly.

She looked at him and nodded. He felt sorry for the poor woman and wondered if he had embarrassed her when he had walked away from her ramblings.

"You tell ma fortune?" he asked.

Reeba nodded and turned away from the firepit. She smoothed out the ground before her and untied the leather pouch from her waistband. With her finger she pointed to where Kit was to sit. He obeyed.

With the stones and bones in her hand, she began to cry out, and then, with her eyes closed, she tossed the objects gently onto the dirt. She cocked her head so that she could see the objects with her good eye and, after staring for a few moments, began tracing lines and circles around the objects. When she finished, she closed her eyes and rocked back and forth, humming a wandering melody to herself as she did so. She then became silent, her eyes still closed. Finally, she opened her eyes and held her hand out to Kit. Kit reached out and held her hand gently. She pulled him closer to her.

"Boy, you's goin' on long jou'ney."

Kit smiled. *Well,* he thought, *I suppose dat's true for eve'yone in Baxtatown.*

Reeba swallowed deeply and wet her lips with her tongue. "Da ship," she said softly. Puzzled, Kit leaned forward. Reeba continued more loudly, "Da ship! Da ship wif da fi'eball! Da blood ship!"

Kit remembered that he had talked to Reeba about the fireball and the *Great Eastern.* That must have been what Reeba was talking about.

"Da blood ship is death ta slaves!" Reeba said. "Stay 'way, boy!" she said loudly. She then went silent for a period. Then, almost in resignation, she said softly, "Stay 'way."

Kit felt sorry for Reeba. She was obviously teched in the head. Here he was leaving, and she was ranting about something that they had talked about a couple of months earlier. Reeba was becoming agitated, working her mouth but not saying anything, so Kit decided to leave. He reached into his money pouch and found two coins, two dollars each. It was an awful lot of money, but Kit figured that Reeba needed it more than he did. He gave them to Reeba, who nodded her head as she put them in her leather pouch along with her stones and bones. Kit began walking toward the pathway that led to Fishkill Landing.

As he walked out of sight, Reeba sat motionless watching him, tears running silently down the weathered grooves on her cheeks.

131

Matteawan, New York
August 20, 1861

As Leonard was getting the carriage ready to take Schultz and Kit to the Fishkill Landing train station, Schultz took Margaret out to the back porch. He had waited until the last moment to tell his wife the truth so that he didn't have to endure what he knew would be a fierce encounter. Pledging her to a reluctant but absolute secrecy, he told her that while he was going to England in the guise of a courier, he was in fact being sent by Governor Seward to foil a rebel plot to break the blockade, a plot in which Daniel Lowber had entangled himself. Margaret was aghast when she heard that her husband might have to figure out a way to stop the *Great Eastern* from completing her voyage. She began her protest.

"You can't do this, Hamilton. You're risking your life!"

"Margaret, there's no going back. The family's honor's at stake."

"What family honor?" Margaret burst out. "What are you talking about? We've done nothing wrong! This is all Daniel's doing. Why do you have to risk your life? What's to become of me if I'm a widow?

Who would take care of our family? Alex? He's too young! What would we do?"

"Quiet, darling. We don't want the whole house to know what's going on. I'll be all right. I've spent my entire life on ships, and I'm still in one piece. I have an idea of how to do it without any risk to me. I'm also going to have help from a young engineer that Governor Seward has in France. You'll just have to trust me."

Margaret's angry rejoinder was interrupted when Leonard called from the front porch, "Capt'n, we're ready! We don't got much time!"

"When Mary and Alex wake up, tell them I said goodbye. I love you, Margaret." With that, Schultz gave his wife's stiff body a brief hug and a kiss on the cheek, and he quickly went outside. Margaret followed and stood numbly on the front porch watching the carriage with the three men go down the entrance road. When the carriage was out of sight, she went inside, collapsed in a chair, and began weeping. A short while later, Mary came downstairs in a dressing gown and found her mother curled in her chair, her face buried in a towel.

"Mother, are you all right? Are you ill?"

Margaret shook her head. She looked up at Mary, and her daughter saw that she had been weeping. Margaret sniffled loudly and wiped her eyes.

"Where's father?"

After clearing her throat, Margaret answered, "He's left for England."

"Already? Why didn't anyone wake me up? I wanted to say goodbye."

Margaret struggled to compose herself. Sniffing loudly, she said, "They had to move quickly to catch the train. I thought you said goodbye last night."

"Well, I did. I just wanted to say goodbye one more time. Well, anyway, he'll be back before we know. I wouldn't be surprised if he buys something fancy for you in England, maybe some silk."

Margaret didn't respond but blew her nose quite loudly into the towel.

"Oh, Mother. Don't be so worried. He's just going to deliver some silly packages, and I'm sure he'll be back shortly, safe and sound. He'll be a lot safer on the *Europa* than on one of his tugboats. Montgomery goes back and forth across the Atlantic all the time, and nothing ever happens to him. Father will be fine."

Leonard stopped the carriage next to the railroad station's platform. Kit and Leonard carried Schultz's trunk from the carriage to the platform while Schultz carried three large satchels. The trunk was tagged by the stationmaster, and then the three men stood silently on the platform. The morning was cool and quiet, and fog was still lying on the river. Schultz wore a black wool jacket and a clean blue shirt. Margaret had ironed his shirts the evening before. Leonard, normally meticulous about his appearance, looked disheveled, not having had the time to wash or shave or even comb his hair. Kit wore one of the captain's white shirts, with sleeves so long that he had to roll them up to his elbows, along with a pair of Leonard's pants that Margaret had tacked up earlier that morning.

Before too long, the southbound train to New York arrived. As the train was coming in, Schultz leaned close to Leonard and spoke into his ear. "Leonard, watch over the house while I'm gone."

"Yes, Capt'n. I take good care'a things."

Schultz patted his servant on the back.

Leonard turned to Kit. When Kit had first arrived, Leonard had resented the captain's fondness for the young slave. However, whenever Leonard went to Baxtertown, he saw the respect the other fugitives had for Kit. He understood that in similar circumstances lesser men might have become arrogant or demanding, lording over these poor refugees, but Kit never did. Quiet and even-tempered, and occasionally even good-natured, Kit won over a lot of people. Leonard was one of them.

"Good luck, Kit."

At first Kit returned the sentiments with a small smile and a nod, but when Leonard held out his hand, Kit took it. The two men, the freeman and the slave, shook hands for the first time. Schultz then picked up one of the leather valises, and Kit picked up the other two. Leonard and the stationmaster loaded the trunk into the luggage car. When Leonard called out that the trunk was loaded, Kit and Schultz entered the car, Schultz walking toward the front of the car and Kit staying in the back where the colored passengers were required to sit.

Silence shrouded the Schultz house after the captain's departure. Alex went out later that morning to the stable and saddled a horse for a ride. Leonard took a late-morning nap, and Margaret went to the bedroom to lie down. Mary worked with the cook, trying to assemble a good dinner for her dispirited mother. As she took inventory of the pantry, Mary decided to walk down to the greengrocer on Main Street to purchase freshly picked vegetables. She'd also stop to see what looked good at the butcher's shop.

Shortly after the mantel clock chimed one, Mary started off on her shopping trip. It took about forty minutes to walk to Main Street, which left nearly two hours before the shops closed. She'd made this trip many times and really didn't consider it a chore, because she got to amble into the dry goods shops to examine their latest offerings in cloth and millinery before she did her grocery shopping. Around four o'clock, her shopping complete, Mary began walking up Main Street back toward her home. Most of the storekeepers were in the process of closing for the day. As she walked toting her string bag loaded with late-summer vegetables and a freshly killed chicken, Mary heard a horse pulling a wagon slowly up Main Street. She saw it was the station wagon coming from the railway station. Then she stopped and stared at the man sitting next to the driver.

"Uncle Daniel!"

Lowber looked around and then saw Mary waving at him. "Stop the wagon!" he ordered. With considerable effort, Lowber dismounted from the wagon and walked stiffly to his niece.

"Mary, I was just heading to your house. What a delight to see you!" The two shared a brief hug. "Come up on the wagon, and let's ride together."

"Uncle Daniel, what are you doing here? We weren't expecting you, were we?"

Mindful of the driver, who was listening to every word, Lowber said, "I happened to be in New York and wanted to come up and see everyone—especially my favorite niece."

Mary was about to burst forth with all the matters that had occurred in the last couple of days, but when Lowber nodded his head in the direction of the driver, she became quiet, and the two sat silently on the wagon's bench as they rode to the Schultz residence. When they arrived, Lowber and the driver unloaded a steamer trunk and two valises from the back of the wagon. When the station wagon was out of earshot, Lowber asked, "Where are your parents?"

"Father left this morning for England."

Lowber was stunned. His brother-in-law had never before traveled to Europe. "Did he go on business?"

"He went to deliver a package for Governor Seward. He has to pick up and deliver some government dispatches."

This was puzzling. Why would Seward send Schultz as a courier? There had to be dozens of young men who would have jumped at a chance to go to England. What was the package Schultz was to deliver? "Do you know why Seward asked him to go?"

Mary shrugged her shoulders. "I think he just trusts him. Otherwise, I don't know."

"Do you know what the package was?"

"No. Something to do with the government, I guess."

"Where's your mother?"

"She's inside. I think she's resting. She's very upset about father's trip, and I don't think she slept well last night."

"I see. Well, let's not disturb her. Why don't you give the groceries to the cook and then come join me on the porch?"

Mary did so, and when she returned to the porch, Lowber was sitting on an old Windsor chair that her father liked to sit on. Mary pulled up another chair.

"Uncle Daniel, you've just returned from England?"

"That's right. I had some business there. I was also in France. Did Montgomery tell you about my trip?"

At this point, Mary saw no purpose in holding anything back. "Uncle Daniel, Montgomery came up from New York just after he received your letter, the one that said you had a big thing for the Confederacy. He's very worried and angry. He's afraid you're going to involve him and his brother in treason. He said that Governor Seward is arresting people on mere suspicion and that if that letter got into the hands of Governor Seward, he'd likely be arrested and his business ruined."

Lowber was shocked by this news. "How stupid of me," he said softly. He had wanted to impress his son-in-law with his importance and had succeeded only in making him irate and fearful. He wondered if he had irreparably ruptured his relationship with him.

"Uncle Daniel, I think other people know of the letter. I'm certain that the police were told you'd be coming into New York. How'd you escape?"

Lowber became fearful when he heard this. "Do you know who notified the police?"

"No," Mary lied. In fact, after Montgomery's visit to her house, she had sought advice from her uncle George Evans, who lived a short distance away. She'd told Uncle George about Montgomery's visit and the letter Lowber had written to him, and she was sure he had notified the police. She had wanted to do everything she could to protect Montgomery from being arrested, even if it meant her uncle would be arrested instead. From Mary's comments, Lowber concluded that either Montgomery or Mary had notified the police about his impending arrival. He decided not to inquire any further into the matter.

"There were spies following me in England," Lowber said softly. "Instead of coming into New York, I took a steamer to Quebec and then a coaster to Halifax. Do the police know I'm here?"

"I don't think so, Uncle Daniel. I didn't even know you were coming here."

Lowber rubbed his chin as he thought. "Mary, I need to get back to the South as soon as possible, but I'm exhausted. I'd like to sleep here tonight and leave tomorrow morning. Can you ask your mother for me?"

Mary, unaware of her father's confession to her mother about the purpose of his trip, assumed that the request would be accepted. She went upstairs to her mother's bedroom and found her sitting in a disheveled state on the side of bed.

"Mother, Uncle Daniel's just arrived. He'd like to stay the night. Shall I get the guest room ready?"

"What!" Margaret exclaimed. "He's here? What's he doing here?"

Mary was taken aback by the vehemence of her mother's answer. "He just got back from England, and he looks exhausted. Before starting home, he came up to visit us."

"We can't have him here!"

"Mother, what's the matter? There's no place else for him to stay. We can't turn him out."

"I don't want him here!"

Mary tried to figure out what was happening. "Is there something wrong, Mother? Is there something going on that I don't know about?"

Margaret was about to tell Mary the entire story when she remembered the pledge of secrecy she had given her husband. Further, she reasoned that if Lowber knew the real reason her husband was on the way to England, she might be endangering her husband's life. As she thought about her options, the least dangerous was to let her brother-in-law stay.

"No, there's nothing going on, Mary. I'm just exhausted. Go ahead and get the guest room ready. I'll go downstairs as soon as I'm put together."

Mary came down the stairs. "Uncle Daniel, I'll get the guest room ready in a few minutes. I'll have Leonard bring the chest into the library. You won't need it upstairs, will you?"

"No, that'll be just fine. Is your mother all right?"

"Yes. She's just tired, as I mentioned. She'll be down shortly."

True to Mary's word, Margaret came down the staircase. She had fixed her hair, but her eyes were red from crying. Her face was grim and drawn. "Daniel, I'm surprised to see you," she said coldly.

Obviously things were not right. Lowber responded as kindly as possible. "Margaret, I'm sorry I didn't let you know, but my travel plans were interrupted, and I just got into New York this morning. I hope I'm not a great inconvenience."

"No, not at all. We'll be starting dinner soon. You'll have to excuse me while I go into the kitchen."

"Of course, Margaret. I was hoping to see Hamilton. I saw his two grandnephews in England and thought he'd like to hear firsthand as to how they're doing."

Margaret gave a slight smile. "I'm sure he would have been delighted to hear about them. If you tell Mary and me the details, we'll pass them on when Hamilton comes home."

Satisfied that the smile meant the worst was over, Lowber settled in the library while Mary and Margaret worked with the cook in the kitchen.

After dinner was eaten in almost complete silence, Margaret went back up to bed while Mary and Lowber sat in the parlor.

"Your mother hardly spoke a word during dinner," Lowber said. "Is she upset with me?"

"I think she's just tired and worried about Father."

Lowber went to the library by himself and, using a key on a chain attached to his belt, unlocked his trunk's brass padlock. He opened the trunk and removed a leather folio. He removed various envelopes from the folio and put them on a round table next to his chair. As it was becoming darker, he took a match out of a metal canister and lit the oil lamp on the table. In the glare of the light, Mary could see from the wrinkles on his face how much her uncle had appeared to age since she'd seen him just weeks earlier. Lowber started talking in a quiet, tired voice.

"Mary, Montgomery told you that I'm carrying documents from the Confederate commissioner in England. I know your mother has very strong feelings about slavery, so I don't expect her to understand. However, I want you to listen and understand why I'm doing this. Unless the war ends soon, many thousands of young men are going to die on the battlefield. I'm told the information in these envelopes will result in England recognizing the Confederacy. Once that happens, the war will be over. There'll be two countries living in peace with each other. Mary, you more than anyone understand both the North and the South. What you don't fully understand, what most young men and women don't understand, are the horrors of war. In England, there are still thousands of widows and mothers grieving over the young men killed in their last war. I don't want the same thing to happen here. I don't want your brothers risking their lives on the battlefield. I don't want to see any young men dying on the battlefield. But unless the war ends soon, there'll be horrible bloodletting."

Mary sat silently as she absorbed this information. Lowber continued, "Mary, when the war's over and there's a new country, you'll still be welcome in New Orleans. I'll still be your uncle and Mary'll be your aunt, and we'll still love you like always. Montgomery's cotton business will be better than ever. There won't be any difference other than a new flag."

Sensing that her uncle's comments were leading to a request, she asked, "Is there something you want me to do?"

"Well, first, don't tell anyone I'm here. Your father's old friend Mr. Seward is undoubtedly looking for me, and I'm too old to last long in prison. I'm going to leave for the South early tomorrow, so have Leonard get the carriage ready early in the morning. I have some dispatches for the Confederacy that I'd like you to have delivered to Adams Express. I'll write the addresses on them. If Adams refuses to take them, deliver them to John Jackson. He's a young man from New Orleans who's a courier for the Confederacy. Here's his address." Lowber took a pencil out and wrote "Richards & Co., 15 Broadway" on an envelope, which he then handed to Mary. "However, the important dispatch …" At this point Lowber reached into his valise and pulled out a flat envelope with a red wax seal. "This dispatch is from the Confederate commissioner in London, and I'm to deliver it personally to President Davis." He placed the envelope on a table next to him.

"Is that the dispatch about the 'big thing'?" asked Mary.

Lowber nodded. "It is."

"What is the big thing?" she asked.

"I'm not certain, but I've been told it's a loan for the Confederacy," he replied. "It's all very confidential. Mary, once I'm on the morning train to New York, you probably won't hear from me again for quite some time."

"Uncle Daniel," Mary asked, "why did you use the Neill name? That may implicate Montgomery."

"That's the name I was using when I left for England," Lowber said. "Mary, don't worry. Most of the dispatches I'm bringing back are unimportant—gossip and rumors and things like that. If they fall into the wrong hands, I don't think they'd amount to much. The important dispatch, the one I have to deliver personally, will stay with me."

Mary was far from satisfied with her uncle's answer. She thought that even an unimportant dispatch, if intercepted, might implicate Montgomery and his brother. The thought of Montgomery being jailed or exiled made her ill.

Mary and Lowber sat quietly in the lamplight, each thinking of risks they were assuming. Finally, Lowber said, "Mary, I'm very tired. I'm going to bed now. Please, I love your father and mother, but don't tell them anything. Everything I tell you has to be kept secret. Promise me."

Mary nodded. Lowber stood up, kissed his niece on the forehead, and slowly lumbered up the stairs. Mary stayed in the parlor for a bit, sitting quietly and thinking. *How did I get myself into this? What about Montgomery?* After a few minutes of nervous hand-wringing, she calmed down. Finally, she took a piece of writing paper from her father's desk and began writing a letter to Mr. Monell, a friend of her father who lived in Newburgh. When she finished, she folded and sealed the letter and then went outside looking for Alex, her younger brother. She found him in the kitchen reading by lamplight.

“Alex,” she said, “I need this letter delivered to Mr. Monell right away.”

Alex looked puzzled. “He’s in Newburgh. The ferry’s shut down for the night.”

“All right. But you have to be there first thing in the morning.”

“What’s it about?”

“I can’t tell you now. I promise I’ll tell you later. But you have to believe me that it’s very important. Father would want us to do this if he were here.”

Alex nodded as he took the letter from Mary. “First thing in the morning, I promise.”

132

New York Times
August 21, 1861

Capt. Alexander H. Schultz sails from New York to-morrow for Europe. He is intrusted with an important mission to the posts of England and France, and will be absent for two months.

133

Office of the Superintendent of Police
413 Broome Street
New York City, New York
August 21, 1861

"YOU'VE a telegraph message, sir," the sergeant said as he handed a folded paper to Kennedy.

As Kennedy was looking for his glasses on his desk, he asked, "Have we heard back from the officers at the *Edinburgh*?" After his conversation with Schultz's nephew, Kennedy had asked for and received information from the State Department that Lowber would be returning on her.

"No, sir. She was coming in early this morning, so she should be searched shortly."

Kennedy nodded and silently read the telegraph message:

Newburgh, August 21, 1861

> D.C. Lowber, of New Orleans, at 15 Broadway, New York, house of Richards & Co., came out in the last steamer as a bearer of dispatches from England and France in relation to a loan for the Confederates. He came over the country this morning from Halifax. He intends to send his dispatches to Adams & Co.'s Express if he can safely to-day. If not, he may send them by a young man by the name of John Jackson, a Southerner, at the above-mentioned house, 15 Broadway. Inform the chief of police or the U.S. marshal at once. Keep the source of this dispatch to yourself.

"Damn," said Kennedy softly.

"Sir, is there a problem?"

Kennedy nodded. "Lowber gave us the slip. He's not on the *Edinburgh*. He came in from Halifax. He's up somewhere near Newburgh." The sergeant stood silently as Kennedy mulled things over in his mind.

"Sergeant, send two detectives to Richards and Company at 15

Broadway. They're to watch everyone coming and going there. If there's a young man named John Jackson there, arrest him for treason and bring him here. Also, send two officers to Adams Express. No package bound for a Southern state should leave that company before it's been opened and examined. Lowber may try to send his dispatches through Adams."

The sergeant repeated the orders from his notes, and Kennedy confirmed their accuracy. Kennedy continued, "You remember what that James fellow told us? Lowber is Captain Schultz's brother-in-law. Schultz lives in Matteawan, just across the Hudson from Newburgh. I think that explains the source of this telegraph message. Send men on the next train up there. I think James said the train stop is Fishkill Landing. Lowber may still be in the area."

Kennedy sat silently as the sergeant finished writing down his orders. When done, the sergeant looked at Kennedy, who asked simply, "Sergeant, what would you do if you were Lowber?"

"Well, sir, if I suspected I'd been found out, I'd get out of New York fast," the sergeant said. "If I was him, I'd take the train up to Buffalo and then head west to Pennsylvania. I wouldn't go into New York City. Too many people looking for me. Once I was in Pennsylvania, I'd take a train down to Cincinnati or Indianapolis, and then I'd have a clear shot to the South."

Kennedy nodded in agreement. "That makes sense. If we go the same direction, we might get lucky. There's not that many railroad junctions in Pennsylvania. Go find Detective King. I want him to take the next train to Pennsylvania. He should get off at a main stop that has connections to the South and wait for Lowber. Be sure and give him Lowber's description, false teeth and all. It's a long shot, but we've got to do our best."

The sergeant finished writing and looked up. "Repeat your orders," Kennedy said, which the sergeant did correctly. Kennedy waved his hand. "Go ahead, Sergeant, and get those men out immediately. Lowber's on the move. I don't know what's in those dispatches, but it could be something important. Tell the officer on duty that when the detectives return from the *Edinburgh* they should come right to me for further orders."

"Yes, sir."

"One thing, Sergeant. You were here when that James fellow came in. You remember our talk about keeping Captain Schultz's name out of this if possible?"

"Yes, sir."

Hearing nothing further, the sergeant turned and left. Kennedy looked back at the telegram. It had been sent by a Mr. J. J. Monell.

134

Residence of A. H. Schultz
Matteawan, New York
August 21, 1861

MARGARET and Mary stood on the front porch. The morning sun was lighting up the clouds with its pink and gold rays but had not yet appeared. Both women were dressed in cotton housecoats, and neither looked like she had had a good night's sleep. Leonard and Lowber had just left in the station wagon to the relief of both women. When the wagon was out of sight, Mary followed her mother into the kitchen, where both sat down. The two women had always been open with each other. As the early-morning light seeped into the kitchen, however, both women were silent, each holding secrets from the other. Finally, Margaret spoke.

"Well, darling, I'm going back to bed. I don't think I'm going to get any sleep, but I'm not feeling well, and maybe what I need is rest."

"Is there something I can do for you?" Mary asked. "Would you like breakfast?"

Margaret shook her head. "No, I'm not hungry. I just feel a little light-headed and would be more comfortable back in bed. Maybe I'm getting a summer cold." With that, Margaret arose from her chair with some effort, stroked Mary's head, and went upstairs to her bedroom.

Mary felt clammy. She wasn't hungry, and she certainly didn't want to lie down and toss and turn the way she had most of the previous night. She rubbed her damp palms against the housecoat where it covered her knees. She was scared. Uncle Daniel was a traitor, or at least that was what her father would have called him. Worse, he was close to implicating Montgomery in his treachery. She looked at the mantel clock. In another hour or so, her uncle would be on a train approaching New York City. By tonight, he and the dispatch for Jeff Davis would be hundreds of miles away. She still loved him but was deeply troubled by the danger in which he had placed her and her family, particularly Montgomery.

The day dragged on, and by lunchtime Margaret had dressed and come downstairs. She and Mary had a quiet lunch, and then Margaret announced that she was going to visit a neighbor. Leonard had taken the rest of the day off to go fishing. Alex had left to visit a friend. Mary was alone in the house. She went upstairs to wash and dress and then returned to the parlor to stare at the mantel clock, trying to estimate where her uncle would be.

At around three o'clock, Mary heard a horse and wagon pulling up to the house. She went to the porch just as the station wagon was pulling up. To her shock and dismay, Lowber was sitting next to the colored driver!

"Uncle Daniel, what's wrong?" she cried out as she came down the porch stairs.

"Just stay here a bit," Lowber said to the driver. With some effort, he came down off the wagon. "Mary, let's go inside," he said to her.

When in the entry room, Lowber looked around. "Is your mother here?" Mary shook her head. "She's visiting a neighbor."

Lowber was sweating, and he licked his lips. "Is anyone else home?"

"No, Uncle Daniel, everyone's gone. I'm home alone."

With that, Lowber quickly walked past Mary into the library. The envelope with the red seal was still on the library table. "Mary, did anyone look at this?"

"Dear God." Mary shook her head. "I didn't know it was still there. I thought you had packed it."

Lowber exhaled. "I was so tired and agitated this morning that it wasn't until I was on the train for New York that I realized I had forgotten to pack it. How stupid of me! I exited at some stop and got on the next train back to Fishkill." Lowber collapsed into a chair in the library and started mopping the sweat from his face with a large handkerchief.

Mary sat down on a chair opposite her uncle. Her stomach was churning. Everything was going wrong, and she had no one to turn to for advice. When Lowber's breathing slowed down, he said, "Mary, I've got to get back to the South. The dispatch is critical." He opened up his valise, pulled all the papers and clothing out, put the sealed envelope at the bottom, and repacked it. "If I can get back into New York City by tonight, I'll be lost in the crowd and can figure out some way of getting home. The next train leaves Fishkill Landing a little after five o'clock."

He sat motionless, breathing deeply. Finally, he said, "Mary, I can't get arrested with these papers. Go with the station wagon back to the station and check my trunk through to Indianapolis under the name of Henry Neill. See if there's any problem. If not, come back right away and get me."

"What kind of problem, Uncle Daniel?"

"I don't know. Hopefully none. If anyone asks you about me, tell them I left this morning and you haven't seen me since. Tell them I asked you to forward my trunk. Don't worry about me using the Neill name. They can search the trunk all they want. There's nothing in it of concern. It's all in here." He patted the valise.

Mary became frantic. She was engaging in treason. She saw no other course other than to turn her uncle over to the authorities, in which case he would be imprisoned, maybe hanged, as a traitor. While Mary stood frozen in the parlor, Lowber dragged his trunk out to the porch. The driver climbed down from the wagon, and the two men heaved it into the back of the wagon. "Mary, please get on the wagon," Lowber said. "We're running out of time."

Mary snapped out of her stupor and climbed aboard the wagon while Lowber went back into the house. "Driver, take me to the station, please," she said. The driver looked at Mary oddly but nevertheless snapped the leads, and the wagon began its slow trip. Mary saw a couple of ladies she knew as the wagon plodded down Main Street toward the station, and she gave a slight wave in response to their curious faces. When she arrived at the station, the driver hauled the trunk onto a handcart and pulled it over to the luggage room. Mary went inside to see the stationmaster, a middle-aged man whom she had seen before but whose name she did not know.

"Hello, miss. Can I help you?"

"Please, I want to check a trunk."

"All right." The stationmaster took out a destination tag. "Now, what's the name?"

"Henry Neill." She spelled out the last name.

"Okay, miss. Where's it going?"

"Indianapolis."

The stationmaster looked up at her with curiosity. "We don't get many folks going there."

Mary shrugged her shoulders in a feigned nonchalance. "He's an iron dealer. He goes all over the country."

The stationmaster went outside to the hand wagon, tied the tag to the trunk, and gave Mary the receipt. "Are you going to pay for it now, or will Mr. Neill pay me when he buys his ticket?"

As she considered her answer, she suddenly realized that if Mr. Monell had sent a telegram as she'd requested, the police would be coming quickly to Fishkill Landing. *If I bring Uncle Daniel here,* she thought, *he'll be arrested for certain.* Mary looked around the station to see if anyone resembling a policeman was present, but the station was empty except for an old couple waiting for a train. *I can't let him be arrested,* she thought. *I've got to send the police on a wild-goose chase.*

Taking a breath first to bring herself under control, Mary said to the stationmaster, "I'm not certain Mr. Neill will be coming to this station. He may take a wagon up to Poughkeepsie tonight. I'll pay for the trunk now. Can you hold it until tomorrow evening to see if he shows up? If he doesn't, then please ship it. Can you do that?"

"Well, sure," the stationmaster said. "If he don't show up by tomorrow night, I'll send it on to Indianapolis." Mary nodded her approval.

The stationmaster headed back to his counter while Mary pulled the fee out of her beaded purse. The transaction completed, Mary boarded the wagon and gave instructions to return home. She was startled when the stationmaster yelled out, "Hey, wait a minute, young lady!" Her heart was racing as she turned to look at him.

"We got a telegraph message last night for a Mr. Neill. That must be your fella. Do you want to take it?"

Mary nodded numbly, and he walked to the wagon and handed her a Western Union envelope with "Neill" written on the outside. The stationmaster was looking at her oddly, she thought, as she forced a smile and said, "Thank you."

On her short trip back home, Mary desperately thought over her dilemma. She knew it was likely that the police would arrive shortly at Fishkill Landing. If her uncle wasn't arrested at the station, he'd be arrested when he arrived in New York. If she told him that, however, he'd know that she was the person who had informed the police. By the time she arrived at her house, she had arrived at a plan.

"Mary," Lowber said as he came down the front stairs, "did you check the luggage?"

"Come inside, Uncle Daniel." To the driver she said, "Please wait." When the two were alone in the parlor, Mary said, "When I told the stationmaster the trunk belonged to Henry Neill, he refused to put a tag on it. He just locked it in his storage room. Before he did that, however, he gave me this." She handed him the telegraph message.

Lowber visibly blanched at the news. He then ripped open the envelope Mary had given him.

"What is it, Uncle Daniel?"

"It's in cipher. Just a minute." Lowber pulled a folded sheet of paper from the valise and started writing in pencil on the telegram. He finished in a couple of minutes. "It's from John Jackson. He says that the police are looking for him. They're also asking about me." Lowber looked up at Mary. "I need to get out of here."

"Uncle Daniel, when the stationmaster asked when you were coming to the station, I lied and told him you might ride up to Poughkeepsie. If the police come here, I think they'll either wait at the station or go north to Poughkeepsie." Lowber stood quietly for a moment in the entry hall. Then he turned to Mary. "There's nothing in the trunk relating to the Confederacy. I've got the important dispatch with me." He became quiet again as he drummed his fingers on a table. "But what do I do?"

Mary had already thought out the next step. "You can catch the Harlem train at Dover Plains. That goes to a different station in New York than the Hudson line. The police won't be waiting for you there. From there, you can take a train to Philadelphia, and you should be able to make your way down South." Mary had taken the Harlem railroad several times and was familiar with it.

"How far is it to Dover Plains?" asked Lowber.

"It's quite a distance. If you leave now, you probably won't be there until morning."

"You were right to throw the police off our track," he said. "Mary, this is embarrassing, but if you have any extra money, get it. I can't get to a bank in New York, and I'm running low on funds. The police are after me. If I'm arrested, the dispatch will be seized. You'll have to hide the dispatch here and come with me to Dover Plains. When we're there,

I'll send a telegram to John Jackson. He'll come up in a couple of days and get the dispatch from you."

"Uncle Daniel," Mary started to protest. She stopped as tears welled up in her eyes. All her plans had fallen apart. If the police learned that a dispatch for Jefferson Davis had been hidden in the Schultz house, she and her family would be ruined. On the other hand, if she helped the police arrest her uncle, he might die in prison. She'd never let that happen. Lowber dug the dispatch from his valise and handed it to Mary, who ran up to her bedroom and slid it under the carpet underneath her bed. On her knees, she pushed it as far as she could under the bed. She then went into her parents' bedroom and retrieved a leather envelope containing cash her father saved for emergencies. She stuffed the bills into her purse and went downstairs. It was nearly four thirty. Her mother would be home shortly.

"Hurry!" Lowber said as Mary came down the stairs. He opened the door to the porch, and both climbed aboard the station wagon. "We're going to Dover Plains," Lowber said to the driver. The driver lurched with surprise and then turned around and looked at the couple with bewilderment.

"We need to catch the Harlem train," Mary explained.

"Dat's a fur trip," the driver responded. "It near fo'ty miles to Dova. It'd be late night 'fore we gits dere."

"When's the last train from Dover Plains to New York?" Lowber asked.

"It pretty late," the driver responded. "I don't think we can ketch it, but anyhows I's got to stay the night in Dova. Horse gotta rest."

Mary leaned forward to the driver. "We'll pay your fare both ways and your lodging."

Ordinarily the driver would not have been so trusting, but the Schultz house was one of the most prominent in Matteawan, and he had never had any trouble with the people who lived or visited there. So when Lowber and Mary were seated on the second seat, he snapped the leather leads, and the horse began plodding on its journey. As the wagon pulled out of the Schultz entryway and started its journey, Mary started sobbing.

"Darling, what's wrong?" Lowber asked.

Mary blew her nose into a handkerchief. She leaned close to Lowber so she could speak in a whisper without the driver hearing. "Uncle Daniel, I'd do anything for you. You know that. I'll do what I can to help you get back home. But those dispatches in my bedroom, if anyone finds them, I'll be called a traitor. Father and Mother will be called traitors. They'll be ruined. Montgomery might be arrested. I'm terrified someone will find them."

"Driver, wait," Lowber said. The wagon came to a halt. He said to the driver, "Quick, go back to the house; I forgot something." The driver made an exaggerated nod with his body and then pulled the leads to turn the wagon around. Within a few minutes, they were home. Both Mary and Lowber got off the wagon and walked into the house.

"Go get the dispatches and bring them to me," Lowber said, after looking around to see that the house was empty. Mary rushed upstairs and with some difficulty pulled the dispatches from underneath her carpet. She came downstairs and handed them to her uncle. He put his spectacles on and sat in a library chair. Looking up at Mary, he told her, "Tell the driver to wait." He opened the sealed envelope and began to read.

Inside, there were perhaps a couple dozen handwritten sheets. Some of the papers told of contacts that the commissioners had made and of opinions that highly placed government officials had expressed about England not wanting to involve itself in the war. Midway through the documents, Lowber read a separate dispatch from Dudley Mann addressed to Jefferson Davis. Mann told of his meetings with the owners of the *Great Eastern*, of the success he'd had with them. He said that President Davis must make sure that Port Royal was prepared to receive the ship on the date she was next scheduled to arrive in New York. Shortly after her arrival, the letter went on, the law lords would almost certainly declare the blockade illegal, and English and French warships would open Charleston and other Southern ports to trade with Europe. The dispatch concluded with an admonition that the plan could succeed only if it was executed in complete secrecy.

Lowber sat in stunned silence. *My God!* he thought. *This is Mann's big thing! All that talk about a loan was a ruse.*

When Lowber looked up, Mary was standing in the parlor, staring at him. "Mary," he said, "stay with the wagon. I'll be out in just a moment." When Mary left, Lowber slowly reread Mann's letter, trying to remember each item of information. When he finished, he gathered all the papers, including Mann's letter, walked to the fireplace in the library, and lit the papers with a match. In less than a minute, the entire dispatch was ash. He walked outside and climbed aboard the wagon. "All right, driver," he said. "Let's go to Dover Plains."

After a few minutes, Lowber leaned toward Mary and whispered, "I've burned the dispatches. I've memorized them as best I could. Now, there's nothing to implicate you other than you're on a carriage ride with your uncle." With that, he patted her hand. Mary sat in silence, both relieved and frightened. Lowber leaned over toward his niece. "When the war ends, Mary, I'll make certain people realize you helped save thousands of young men's lives. You'll be a heroine to both the South and the North."

The wagon lumbered easterly as twilight began to overtake it. After an hour and a half or so, the wagon reached a fork in the road, and the driver stopped. He turned toward his passengers and said, "I heard you folks talking about the Harlem Train?" Mary nodded. The driver continued, "If you're going into the city, why go all the way to Dover Plains? We can go to Pawling. It's due east, and we can get there much sooner than going to Dover."

"The night train stops at Pawling?" Mary asked.

The driver shook his head at the silliness of the question. "Missy, the night train stops everywhere. Pawling ain't much a station. Matter of fact, it's just a platform. No place there to sit and wait. But the train do stop there."

"Is there enough time to get the night train?" Lowber asked.

"I'm pretty sure there is," the driver said, "but we gotta hurry. You want to go there?" When both Lowber and Mary nodded, the driver turned and snapped the reins of his horse.

135

Hudson River Railroad Station
Fishkill Landing, New York
August 21, 1861

It was just past six in the evening when the northbound train pulled into the station at Fishkill Landing. A detective got out and met three stubble-faced men, one in a dark suit and the two others in police uniforms. The man in the suit went into the station, climbed a staircase to the second floor where the stationmaster lived, and started pounding on the door. The stationmaster quickly appeared at the door, wiping his mouth with a napkin. "Who are you?" he asked the man at the door.

"We're police officers from New York." The man pointed to the uniformed men on the platform. "We're looking for Daniel Lowber."

"I don't know that name," the man said.

"Come on downstairs. We need your help," the officer said. The stationmaster complied. The men gathered around the stationmaster as the officer continued his inquiry. "How about Montgomery Neill? Do you know that name?"

"Yep. I got a trunk for a Neill. Montgomery don't sound familiar, but the name Neill is on the tag. It's checked for Indianapolis. I'm holding it till he shows up. If he don't show up, I'm supposed to ship it without him."

"Where is it?"

"It's in the luggage room. Hold on; I'll get the key." The stationmaster went back upstairs and returned with a ring of keys. He walked to a padlocked door, opened the padlock, and walked inside.

"Here it is," he said, pointing to a trunk. "Like I said, it's tagged for Indianapolis."

"Who brought it here?"

"Well, that's what's kinda odd. A young lady that lives in town. I think she's Captain Schultz's daughter."

"Was she by herself?"

"Yep. Well, she came on the station wagon. The driver—his name's Jeff—he jest sat in the wagon. He din't hear nothing."

"Did she say anything?"

"No, not much. Just wanted to check the trunk. She was really nervous, though. Just about jumped outa her skin when I told her to wait, that I had a telegraph for Mr. Neill."

The officers looked at each other at this bit of news. "Are you the one who took down the telegram?"

"Yep."

"Do you have a copy?"

"Nope. Ain't supposed to copy other folks' messages."

"Do you remember what it said?"

"It was in code. We get lots of messages in cipher. People don't want other folks to know their business." The stationmaster continued, "The young lady, she said that Neill was going to Poughkeepsie. I don't know if that's true or not, but that's what she said."

"How far is Poughkeepsie?"

"'Bout sixteen miles. On the train, it's about thirty minutes due north."

The plainclothes officer whispered to his companion, "Why would they go to Poughkeepsie?"

The stationmaster thought the comment had been directed to him. "Why do folks do all sorts of things? He may have been coming down from Poughkeepsie later in the day. Maybe he just wanted to ship the trunk and wasn't going nowhere. Remember—I didn't see this Neill fellow."

"I need to send a telegraph message to the superintendent of police in New York City right away. Can you send the message?"

"Sure. I'm the telegraph operator. You write down the message on a piece of paper, and I'll send it."

"When you're done sending the message, I want you to retag that luggage and send it to the attention of the superintendent. Send it out on the first train."

"You're the boss. If this Neill fellow shows up and asks about his trunk, I'm gonna tell him I was ordered by you."

"You can tell him anything you want. Just send that trunk down on the next train." He turned to the two uniformed officers. "One of you stay here in case he stops and picks up his trunk. If he comes through, you nab him. The other should take the next northbound train to Poughkeepsie. He may be holed up there." He turned to the stationmaster. "Tell me where this Captain Schultz lives."

136

New Jersey Central train station
Jersey City, New Jersey
August 21, 1861

DETECTIVE Robert King stood at the ticket window of the New Jersey Central terminal for nearly a minute. The young ticket agent was arranging his cash drawer, and King was becoming impatient waiting for him to look up. Finally, King rapped his heavy nickel-plated brass badge on the counter and said, "I'm Detective King of the New York City police." The agent, startled, looked at the mustachioed, powerfully built man before him.

"Yes, sir. Can I help you?"

"I need some information," King replied. "I'm in pursuit of a man who is heading west, probably to Indianapolis. I don't know what railroad he's riding on. Where's a good stop to wait for him?"

"You think he's already left the city?"

"I think so. I suspect he may have gone through Buffalo."

The agent thought for a moment and then went rummaging in a drawer. He returned with several railroad maps, which he studied.

"Mister, there's a bunch of new lines just opened. Give me a minute." King murmured his assent, and the agent closely examined a couple of the maps. While still studying a map, he said, "I'm pretty certain he'd have to go through Pittsburgh. From there, he could take the Fort Wayne Railroad, get off at—let's see—maybe Alliance … hmm, maybe Crestline. That's Ohio. He could connect at either one of those stops to a southbound train. He might go beyond Crestline to Fort Wayne, but that would take him out of his way. I think he'd connect to a train heading to Indianapolis at either Alliance or Crestline. At Crestline he could take the Indianapolis, Pittsburgh, and Cleveland direct to Indianapolis."

"How do I get to Pittsburgh?"

"Take the New Jersey Central to Pittsburgh. In Pittsburgh it connects to the Pittsburgh, Fort Wayne, and Chicago Railroad. That stops at both Alliance and Crestwood. The train to Pittsburgh will be boarding pretty soon."

"Can I see your map?" King asked. The young agent turned the Fort

Wayne Railroad map around so the detective could read it. The agent put his finger on the eastern side of Ohio. "Here's Alliance." He then moved his finger west to Crestline. He tapped his finger on the word *Crestline* a couple of times. "See what I mean, mister? The railroads all meet at Crestline."

"So you think I've got to go all the way to Ohio?" King asked.

"Unless you catch him in Harrisburg or Pittsburgh," the agent answered.

"I need this map," King said.

The agent was about to protest the loss of his only map of the Fort Wayne Railroad, but King didn't look like a person who would much care about the concerns of the agent. "Fine," said the agent. "Now, the next train leaves in less than twenty minutes, so you'd better get your ticket and get on board."

King looked up from his map. "My badge is my ticket. Where do I board?" The agent pointed in the direction of the platform. "Thanks," said King as he moved quickly to the train.

137

Railway station
Alliance, Ohio
August 23, 1861

Lowber shuffled slowly to an empty spot on a long, wooden dining table in a hall near the Alliance railway station. He was exhausted from a lack of sleep and not particularly hungry. However, he had a lot of ground to cover before he arrived in Indianapolis, and he thought it prudent to eat something. He placed his bowl of food down and edged in between two men who were eating with a sullen silence. A glance at his bowl showed the reason for the gloomy nature of his companions—two greasy chunks of meat that might or might not be boiled beef, together with a boiled potato, in a broth that shimmered an oily blue color in the sun. This, with a metal cup filled with a dark liquid claimed to be coffee, was the fare available to the poor wretches who rode the Pittsburgh, Fort Wayne & Chicago Railroad.

As Lowber looked around, he saw that Alliance hardly existed as a town. It had a large railroad platform and station and a few wooden buildings nearby. It existed primarily as a railroad interchange, where passengers from the East could head in nearly all directions.

As he summoned his courage to start eating, Lowber thought back on the previous forty-eight hours. His arrival in New York, his railroad trip to Fishkill Landing, his long trip on the wagon with Mary to Dover Plains … it all seemed to be months in the past. Every muscle in his body ached from riding on bouncing and uncomfortable seats and from trying to sleep in strange positions.

He thought about Mary. During the long ride to Dover Plains, he'd had a chance to talk to her about old memories. They hadn't needed to whisper, because there had been nothing incriminating about their long talk. Mary had talked about Katy, and Lowber had recalled vividly what a beautiful and vivacious daughter he had adopted. He'd told Mary how much like Katy she was, and it was true. She wasn't quite as spunky as Katy, but she looked and talked remarkably similar to Katy. It was no wonder that Montgomery had become so quickly attached to Mary after Katy's death. Lowber and Mary had talked about the parties in New Orleans and all the odd and sometimes hilarious characters that showed up. New Orleans and Fishkill Landing were certainly worlds apart, she'd said, and he'd heartily agreed.

When the train had arrived in New York, a man working at the station had said there was a respectable boardinghouse for single women in Staten Island, and Mary had decided to take the ferry over and return home in the morning. When Mary and Lowber had hugged goodbye, Mary had started to cry. As Lowber had ridden on the train out of New York to Philadelphia early that morning, he'd worried that he might have implicated Mary in his work for the Confederacy. If anyone made that claim, he vowed he'd return to New York to testify on her behalf and to face the consequences of treason. He'd hang before he let any harm come to her.

He looked down at the bowl and summoned up his courage. *Good God,* he thought, *how in the devil am I going to get this meat down?* He poked at it with his fork. It was tough, horse maybe. With his false teeth, it was going to be impossible to eat it unless he ripped it into small pieces. With his knife and fork, he set to sawing the meat into shreds and then ripping the shreds into smaller pieces. A couple of times he bumped his elbow into his scowling neighbor, only to be greeted with a grunt of annoyance, considerably louder the second time. While sawing away, he ate part of the potato. He could chew that, but it caused his teeth to move around in his mouth.

From a distance, a powerfully built man in a black coat watched Lowber intently. Finally, the man walked back to the station and asked for the Western Union telegraph operator. He was directed to a small room where a young man sat reading a newspaper.

"I want to send a telegraph message to Crestline," the man said.

"Yes, sir," the operator said, pointing to a pad of paper and a pencil. "Write it out here." The man wrote out a short message and handed it to the operator.

"Hmm … 'United States marshal at Crestline,'" the operator read out loud. He counted the remaining words and said, "Mister, that'll be eighteen cents."

Detective King pulled out his badge. "Son, this is official business. You're authorized to send this without a charge."

The young operator nodded slowly. "Okay," he said as he started tapping the key to alert the operator in Crestline that a message was coming. When he received an acknowledgement that the operator in Crestline was ready to receive, he quickly tapped out the message.

"Good work, son," King said. "I'll let the folks in Crestline know the service you did for your country." He then went outside. The man with the false teeth was still struggling with his meal. King lightly patted the Colt revolver tucked in his waistband. He had used it more than once, and it had never failed to knock a man off his feet. However, there was no sense in taking risks. He had no jurisdiction in Ohio other than that of an ordinary citizen, but the presence of a US marshal would remedy that defect. If the marshal was competent with a gun, all the better.

138

Railway station
Crestline, Ohio
August 23, 1861

AFTER watching his telegraph key sit silent while he counted to twenty, the young Western Union operator tapped out "di-dah-dit" on his key, code for "message received." With that, the operator took a clean sheet of Western Union paper from a stationery box and, using a steel-nibbed pen, carefully wrote in longhand the message he had just received. When he was done, he looked at the pendulum clock on the wall and recorded the time. He blotted the letter, carefully folded it, put it in a yellow envelope, and wrote "Marshal Archer" on the outside. He then stepped outside of his office to look for the delivery boy, whom he found sitting in a shady corner of the train station

"Davy, you gotta get this to the marshal right now," the operator said. The boy stood up.

"Who's the marshal?" the boy asked.

"It's old man Archer," the operator responded. "His office is at the post office."

"Archer?" the boy said. "He works for the railroad, don't he?"

"Used to, but Mr. Lincoln made him a deputy marshal a couple of weeks ago. Now get this message to him fast. Real fast!"

"Yes, sir," the boy said and started running to the post office with the yellow envelope. Within a couple of minutes, the boy was at the unpainted wooden structure that passed for a post office. He looked at the side of the building and saw a "U.S. Marshal" sign above a door. He banged his fist on the door.

"Come in!" said a man's voice. Davy entered and saw M. C. Archer sitting at a desk reading a newspaper. The marshal was a tall, thin man, about forty years old, with a thick mustache. He was wearing a gray shirt with a dark-brown vest.

"Marshal, I got a telegram for you," the boy announced.

"Well, come here and give it to me," Archer said. The boy handed the envelope to the lawman and waited while he read it in case there was a reply.

Archer placed the message flat on his desk and carefully read it. When he finished, he ran his hand through his tangled hair and muttered, "Holy smoke!" The messenger boy was getting the idea that something exciting was going to happen.

"Is there a reply, Marshal?" the boy asked.

Archer looked up at him. "No. No reply." He looked around his new office. "Boy, I need your help. There's a rebel spy on the next train."

Wow! Davy thought. *This is getting good.* It was sure lots better than the usual messages telling folks that someone had missed a train or gotten sick or died. "Yes, sir," he said. "Whatcha want me to do?"

"I'm pretty sure I got some leg irons here in this storage closet. Dig them out and bring them to the telegraph office as soon as you can. Make sure they've got the turnkey so I can clamp them on somebody. I don't know how soon the next train's coming from Alliance, but I have to be ready."

While Davy went rummaging through the storage closet, Archer reviewed his choice of weapons. The marshal's office had a .41-caliber Volcanic carbine that Archer had tested out in the field shortly after he'd gotten notice of his appointment. It was a repeater, and it had worked when he'd tried it. He opened a box of ammunition and carefully filled the rifle's magazine with eight rounds. It held something more than that, but he wasn't sure of the number. He figured if he couldn't kill the traitor with eight rounds at close distance, maybe he shouldn't be wearing a badge. He turned to see young Davy staring at him in admiration.

"Boy, did you find the leg irons?"

"Yes, sir. You got two cuffs and a chain, and one cuff with a ball." Davy hauled the two sets of chains out and laid them on the floor.

Archer looked carefully at the choice. "Take two trips. Bring the double cuffs first and then the ball and chain. Once we arrest the traitor, we'll figure out which set is best. I'm going over to the station now. Now, boy, stay out of the way. Just go to the telegraph office and leave the chains there. Don't come outside on the platform. This guy could be desperate, and there could be lead flying. I hope not, but you don't know."

"Yes, sir."

As Archer walked the short distance to the station, Davy walked just behind carrying the double cuffs. The few folks they met on their walk stopped and stared at the duo. Archer walked in the telegraph office.

The young operator looked up and saw Archer carrying the carbine with Davy and the chains lurking behind.

"Looks like you got the message."

"Yep," Archer said. "I don't know how I'll recognize this Detective King, but he won't have any trouble recognizing me." Archer tapped his badge, a nickel-plated steel star with the words "U.S. Marshal." He had bought it from his predecessor for twenty cents.

"How soon does she arrive?" Archer asked.

"Well, the schedule's pretty much useless, but I'll guess from the time I got the telegraph message. Alliance is a hundred miles away, more or less. She'll stop at Massillon and Mansfield for sure, maybe a couple of other stops. We're talking about four hours. Maybe a little more, maybe a little less. She sometimes hits fifty miles an hour on the straightaway."

Archer wasn't pleased to hear that he had to sit tight for four hours. Looking at the extra chair in the telegraph office, he asked if he could sit down. "Sure," the operator said. "If I get any messages for you, it won't take long to deliver 'em," he said with a smile. In a few minutes, Davy returned lugging the ball and chain, and then he sat down on the floor. The two men and the boy sat silently, the only sound being the loud ticking of the clock.

As the time dragged by, the men shifted in their chairs. Davy went home to get something to eat. Archer stood up and stretched. The telegraph key began to click. When it had finished, Archer asked if it was for him. "Nah, just the time," the operator said as he opened the glass face of the clock and adjusted its minute hand. Davy had returned by this time, and the three settled down for more waiting.

As the day passed, the room became warmer. The telegraph operator stood up and opened a window, letting in a warm breeze. A large black fly promptly entered the room and provided some auditory competition with the pendulum clock. Davy watched it intently, and when it landed on the counter, a fast motion by the boy squashed it. "Got it!" the boy said with a smile. The two men nodded with approval at the boy's feat. The waiting continued. Suddenly, the telegraph key began to click. The operator responded, and the key returned his message. Turning to Archer, the operator said, "She's leaving Mansfield." That meant the train would be in Crestwood in fifteen, twenty minutes. Archer stood up and started stretching but remained silent.

Finally, the sound of a steam whistle was heard through the open window. Archer stood up and looked at Davy. "Boy, you stay here on the floor until I call you!" Davy nodded. Archer picked up the carbine and, holding it with both hands, walked out onto the platform. He stood in a shadowy corner of the station.

The train came into the station, drive wheels screaming in reverse, the brass bell clanging loudly. When it stopped, the only sound was the hissing steam of the engine. There were five cars, two passenger and three freight, including a mail car. The stationmaster opened the freight cars, and the doors to the passenger cars were opened by a conductor. About a dozen people got out. Archer looked carefully at all of them. He stepped into the sunlight so that King could see his badge and rifle. As soon as he did, a man in a black overcoat looked at him, reached into his jacket, and pulled out a nickel-plated badge. He then pointed to a man walking away from the platform. The indicated man was in his fifties, had thick gray whiskers, and was carrying a heavy valise. He walked slowly. Both lawmen converged on the man from behind as he climbed down from the platform and started walking across the dusty street to a hotel.

"Lowber, you're under arrest," said King softly. Lowber stopped but didn't turn around. Archer quickly moved in front of Lowber.

Holding the carbine at the ready, Archer said in an equally soft voice, "I'm Deputy Marshal Archer. You're under arrest. Don't move."

King came in front of Lowber from the other side. "Drop the valise," he ordered. Lowber complied. King walked up to Lowber and searched him for weapons. None were found other than an ordinary pocketknife, which King put into his jacket pocket.

"You're Daniel Lowber," King said directly to his prisoner.

Seeing no purpose in lying, Lowber nodded. He was exhausted, frightened, defeated. He barely had enough energy to walk.

"Marshal, how far's your office?" King asked.

Archer pointed to the post office about eighty yards down the road.

"You got a jail?" King asked.

Archer nodded. He had two cells behind his office.

"All right," King said. "Let's lock him up, and you watch him while I make arrangements to take him back to New York."

"Okay," Archer agreed, and the three men began walking to Archer's office.

From the station platform, Davy yelled, "Marshal, do you want the chains?"

"Yeah, boy, bring them back to my office." Archer turned to look at the boy. Smiling in relief at the peaceful way Lowber had been arrested, he called out, "Boy, you done a good job. I'm proud of you." With that, Davy fairly skipped back to the telegraph office to retrieve the chains.

139

"The Blockade and Neutral Rights," *New York Times* August 24, 1861

The blockade of the Southern ports was formally proclaimed on the 29th of April, fifteen days of grace being allowed for vessels to clear out after the date of the proclamation. We need not repeat what we have so often stated, upon the authority of the most eminent jurists, and especially those of the United States, that no blockade can be maintained without the continued presence of a competent armed force. The ports at which, since the publication of the blockade, this requirement of the law of nations has been complied with are, Hampton Roads, Savannah, Charleston, Pensacola, Mobile, New-Orleans, and since the 7th of July, the port of Galveston. These are the ports at which blockading ships have been stationed, and, consequently, the only ports under such a blockade as can be recognized by a neutral State. At the ports of Wilmington (in North Carolina,) St. Mark's and Apalachicola, (in Florida,) Beaufort and other places, no such steps have been taken to render the blockade effectual. No men-of-war have been stationed, or have even arrived, so far as we can ascertain, with that object. It is by no means improbable, moreover, that the blockade even of those ports where it has been regularly established has been irregularly and inefficiently maintained. We can hardly conceive how it could be otherwise, considering the vast extent of coast line the National Government has undertaken to close against commerce, and the limited resources at their disposal, to effect so extensive a blockade.

The National Government may say that they are at liberty to take their own time in the matter of blockading the Southern coast, seeing that in doing so they are only closing their own ports. This is not an explanation which would for a moment be listened to by any European Government. The National Government must blockade as belligerents, or they cannot blockade at all; and what we have from the first contended for on behalf of neutral commerce is, that the blockade shall be established and maintained according to the strict usages of maritime warfare—that it shall be effectual in form and impartial in its operation. This, we have no doubt, the British Government will insist upon, and they will be supported in their demand by all the maritime States of Europe; and if it shall appear that the National Government is unequal to blockade the whole of the Southern seaboard, then it will be the duty of the neutral fleets in those waters to see that neutral vessels entering or leaving unblockaded ports are not subjected to interference or molestation on the part of the National cruisers.

140

Residence of A. H. Schultz
Matteawan, New York
August 24, 1861

LEONARD heard a horse clumping up the approach to the house and went out to greet the visitor. It was John Monell.

"Hello, Leonard," Monell said to the servant.

"Well, it's good to see you, Mr. Monell, but the captain ain't here. He left for England."

Monell dismounted and handed the bridle to Leonard. "I heard that. Actually, I'm here to see Mary."

This came as a shock to Leonard. Leonard couldn't imagine why Mr. Monell wanted to see the young woman. Monell wasn't no young man—he must've been close to fifty. And Leonard had always been under the impression he was married.

"I'll see if she's in," Leonard said cautiously. In the hallway, he yelled up the stairs, "Miz Mary, you got a visitor!"

"I'll be down in a moment" was the faint response.

Leonard went outside and conveyed the message to Mr. Monell, and the two men stood there making small talk about the weather. Finally, Mary came down and was equally startled to see Monell. As Mary greeted Monell, Leonard started walking with Monell's horse over to the trough at the side of the house.

When the servant was out of hearing, Monell said, "Mary, I got a telegram this morning from New York. Your uncle was arrested in Ohio last night."

Mary put her hands up to her mouth. "My God!" she muttered.

"I know how hard this must be for you," Monell said, "but I want you to know that you did the right thing in sending me that note."

"What will they do with him, Mr. Monell?"

"I'm not certain. I would think it likely that they'll bring him back to New York and question him."

Mary felt panicked. And ill. She had helped her uncle escape, and she knew she was certain to be implicated. The stationmaster had seen her check her uncle's luggage at Fishkill Landing, and the driver of the station wagon would obviously remember the ride to Pawling.

"Are you all right, Mary? You look ill."

Mary shook her head. "No. No, I'm just upset Uncle Daniel's been arrested. I need to sit down."

"Well, I understand that it must be quite hard for you," Monell said. "Now, Mary, until your father gets home, please feel free to call on me for any help you might need. The same goes for your mother."

Mary nodded and gave a small smile. She then went into the house, collapsed on a chair in the library, and started sobbing.

141

"Arrest of a Bearer of Dispatches to Jefferson Davis"
New York Times
August 25, 1861

Cleveland, Ohio, Saturday, Aug. 24.

Detective King, of New-York, assisted by United States Marshal Archer, of Ohio, arrested Daniel C. Lowber, of New-Orleans, at Crestline, Ohio, last night. Mr. Lowber acknowledges himself as bearer of dispatches from England to Jefferson Davis, but professes entire ignorance of their contents. The dispatches are in his trunks, which were seized in New-York some days since. The officers, with their prisoner, leave immediately for Washington, *viá* New-York.

142

Residence of W. H. Seward
Washington, DC
August 27, 1861

FRED heard the front door open and went to greet who he hoped was his father. The elder Seward appeared in the doorway, looking tired. "Hello, Fred," he said quietly.

"Father, come in; sit down. Anna's been keeping the dinner warm. It should be ready in a few minutes."

Seward walked to the parlor and sat in his favorite chair. "I suppose we should wait until after dinner for cigars," he said to Fred. "However, I want you to look at this." Seward handed his son a telegraph message. It was a long message from Superintendent Kennedy detailing the chase and arrest of Lowber, from the first reports that he was to arrive on the *Edinburgh* to his arrest in Ohio. As Fred was reading, Seward said, "It's the last two paragraphs that concern me." Fred continued reading until he came to the end.

> I sent a man by the New Jersey Central, being the first train west, to head him off if possible, supposing he had gone by way of Buffalo; but it so happened that by the time they reached Pittsburg both Officer King and the fugitive were on the same train, and the sagacity of the officer led to his detection and identification at a station on the Fort Wayne railroad (Alliance), where the train stopped to dine, but he prudently telegraphed for help to meet him at the depot at Crestline, where the arrest was made, but nothing found on him to implicate him.
>
> The great pains he took to avoid arrest is the strongest feature against him as it stands unless some of the letters which I this day forward to you by Adams Express may contain matter of treasonable character. He denies having had anything of the kind intrusted to him, either in going out or returning; that his visit was on business and in pursuit of health solely. He is a New

> Yorker by birth, thoroughly southernized by more than twenty years' residence at the South. I am thus particular that you may see the whole case.

"They'd earlier seized his trunk at Fishkill Landing, and it didn't contain any dispatches either," said Seward. "I'm beginning to wonder if the man was just a blowhard and had nothing to do with Jefferson Davis."

"Father, Fred, dinner is served," Anna called out.

"Anna, can you keep it warm just a few more minutes?" Fred asked. "I have to show something to Father."

Silently, Anna and the cook returned the dishes to the kitchen to try to keep them warm.

"Father, a messenger from Reverend Beecher delivered a letter here today," Fred said.

"Beecher!" Seward responded. "What's he doing in this?"

"Well, let me read you the postscript to the letter," said Fred. He read out loud, "For the purpose of keeping this secret from my family I have written from Mrs. Beecher's at Peekskill. Should there be any reply or questions to be asked if you address to Peekskill in cover to H. W. Beecher they will at once forward it to me."

Seward's forehead was furrowed in concentration. "Who wrote the letter, Fred?" he asked quietly.

"Mary Lowber Schultz."

"The captain's daughter?" Seward exclaimed. "What secret is she keeping from her family?"

"That she helped Lowber escape. It's a long, rambling letter, obviously written while she was very agitated. It's full of midnight rides to train stations, checking luggage under false names, and so forth, but at the end of the day she's confessing to helping Lowber try to escape. She doesn't say so, but I think she probably wrote the letter as soon as she heard that Lowber had been arrested."

"Well, we have Lowber now," said Seward. "The letter doesn't sound particularly useful."

"There's one paragraph you might find interesting," Fred said.

"What is it?"

"She writes the following about the papers Lowber was carrying." Fred read aloud from her letter:

> The only means I could contrive to get the papers was to create a panic. I drove to the station in advance with his trunk and returned with news that the station agent had refused to check the trunk; that the detectives were doubtless on his track and gave him a telegram received from John Jackson in confirmation. He handed me the dispatches to conceal, jumped into the carriage which was waiting and we started for Dover Plains where he could take the Harlem train to New York. But a second thought for the safety of our family urged him to return and before we knew what he was about he had burned the dispatch, trusting to his memory to carry the contents safely to Richmond, so I was again checked.

"He burned the dispatches," Seward said. "He memorized them and burned them." Picking up the telegram from Kennedy, Seward said, "He denies having had anything of the kind entrusted to him."

"The man's a liar," said Fred. "Also, Mary saw the same letter that the captain told us about—the letter about the 'big thing' for the Confederacy."

"Gentlemen, we're removing the dinner and offering the two of you some delicious hardtack instead," Anna called out.

"All right, Anna, we're coming!" Fred said irritably.

The two men sat at the table. Before eating, Seward said, "Fred, I'm going to say grace." Fred put his fork down and folded his hands. Seward continued, "Dear God, thank you for this food. And we humbly ask that you help us understand and do your will. Amen."

The two men then ate in silence.

Part V

August 31, 1861
to
September 10, 1861

Let them curse it that curse the day, Who are ready to rouse up Leviathan.

—Job 3:8 (ASV)

The Tower Buildings, Liverpool

143

Consulate of the United States
69 Tower Buildings South
Water Street W.
Liverpool, England
August 31, 1861

"COMING, coming!" Henry Wilding called in response to knocking at the door. When he opened it, Wilding was surprised to see a burly man with a sandy-colored beard and a smaller colored man standing next to him. A steamer trunk and three valises sat on the doorway.

"Can I help you?" Wilding asked.

The bearded man responded, "I'm looking for Henry Wilding."

The man who answered the door was small and slender, in his late fifties, balding with a neatly trimmed gray mustache. "I'm Henry Wilding," he said softly.

"I'm Captain Alexander Schultz. I was told to contact you by Secretary Seward. I'm on a diplomatic mission for him."

"I see," said Wilding. "Well, come in."

"I need to bring my luggage in as well," Schultz said.

"Of course, bring everything in."

As Schultz and Kit brought in the luggage, Wilding stepped outside to look up and down the street to see if anyone was watching. There didn't appear to be.

"Please sit down, Captain," Wilding said as he picked up a pile of papers from an old leather chair. When he noticed Schultz looking around the suite, Wilding assured him, "No one else is here."

Schultz sat down and opened the straps on his valise. He pulled out an envelope and handed it to Wilding. "Mr. Wilding, these are Governor Seward's instructions to me."

Wilding retrieved his spectacles from a bookcase, sat down opposite Schultz, and began reading the letter addressed to Charles Francis Adams. It all seemed straightforward to Wilding; Schultz was just one of many couriers Seward had been using to deliver dispatches. The only thing unusual was the item that was the subject of the dispatch—a British consular bag addressed to Lord Russell. When he finished reading, Wilding handed the letter back. "Captain Schultz, I will assist you in any way I can." Wilding, although a British subject, had served in Liverpool as vice consul for the United States for many years. Over the years, he had proved to be more loyal to the United States than many of her own citizens.

"Thank you, sir," Schultz said. "The consular bag referred to in Governor Seward's letter is in one of the valises held by Kit." Schultz motioned toward the young man, who was still standing near the doorway. "By the way, Kit is my servant. He's here to carry things for me. I find that I'm not as young as I used to be." Wilding acknowledged the statement but silently wondered why Schultz had brought a colored servant instead of a less-noticeable white one.

"Mr. Wilding, tomorrow I have to go to London to deliver the consular bag to Mr. Adams. I want to return to Liverpool tomorrow evening. I need to see some business associates and family members in this area. Governor Seward said you'd help me with trains and such."

"Of course," said Wilding. "There's an early-morning train to London, and after you deliver the bag, there's a late mail train back to Liverpool, so you should be able to make the trip in one day. I'll write out directions on how to get to the legation's offices from the train station."

"Thank you very much, sir. I hope it would not be an inconvenience to leave some of my luggage here for the evening."

Wilding smiled. "Oh no, Captain. Not at all."

"Mr. Wilding, I need to make accommodations for Kit," he said, again motioning to the servant. "Can you help me?"

Wilding's brow furrowed as he considered the request. No reputable hotel or rooming house would take a colored guest. There were some seamen's lodgings where black sailors could stay, but they had a reputation for licentiousness and seemed unsuitable for a servant. Schultz saw the consternation on Wilding's face and volunteered that Kit was an accomplished blacksmith. At this news, Wilding's face brightened.

"Ah! We have an excellent blacksmith who always has more work than he can handle," Wilding said. "I think your young man could stay in his shop in exchange for labor. How long will you be here?"

"About a week, perhaps a bit longer," Schultz answered.

"That may work," Wilding said. "Well, let's get on to the blacksmith. His name is Rodgers. I don't know his first name. He's rather grumpy, but he's honest. As long as Kit does as he says, they should get along well enough." Wilding added in a conspiratorial tone, "However … you both should understand that Liverpool is very much in favor of the secessionists. It is wise to say nothing about who you are, where you are from, or why you are here. No one in Liverpool is to be trusted."

Schultz nodded and turned to Kit, who nodded as well.

With that, Wilding placed the valise containing the consular bag under a table and placed a stack of documents in front of it. Satisfied that it could not easily be seen, Wilding ushered his guests outside and double-locked the door to the offices. Wilding and Schultz walked briskly and silently toward the blacksmith's office, with Kit walking a few steps behind them.

Rodgers was grumpy all right, but if anyone inquired about his mood, which no one ever did, the inquirer would have learned that the old blacksmith was in continuous pain. Forty-seven years of pulling on bellows and lifting, bending, and cutting iron had damaged his back, shoulders, knees—indeed, nearly every part of his body. When Rodgers saw Wilding and his two guests in the doorway, he put down his tongs and limped with a grimace toward them to find out what they wanted. When Wilding told him that the young Negro would help him if Rodgers would feed him and let him sleep in the shop, the blacksmith was curious. Surveying the heavily muscled young man, Rodgers listened as Schultz explained that Kit had worked several years as a blacksmith and that he needed a place to stay for a week or two. Rodgers asked to see Kit at work before he made a decision.

Kit took one of the valises, went to a dark corner of the shop, and changed from his good clothes into old clothes from his tugboat days that Mrs. Schultz had packed for him. He then began pulling the rope on the leather bellows, his powerful strokes quickly bringing the coals in the forge to a near white-hot state. Without speaking, Rodgers seized the opportunity, picked up his tongs, and placed an iron rod into the forge. It was soon glowing red. Schultz and Wilding watched the two smiths work together silently over the forge, Kit pulling the bellows while Rodgers alternated between heating the rod and hammering it into the shape of a bracket. This activity continued for nearly a quarter hour. Finally, Rodgers looked at Wilding and nodded his head. Wilding and Schultz left without further conversation.

It was perhaps an hour later when Rodgers took a short pause to stretch. He held up his palm, signaling Kit to pause, and he gave his young helper a gap-toothed smile. With Kit's help, Rodgers had finished what would have been several hours' worth of work. For his part, Kit was amused by the old blacksmith's mannerisms, which ranged from frequently spitting into the forge to grumbling to himself, but he also respected the high quality of Rodgers's work. All around the shop were iron pieces from various ships and carriages. Kit was impressed at the complexity and workmanship of many of the pieces.

At midday, Rodgers put his tools down and motioned Kit to stop as well. The old smith went over to a barrel and washed his hands and face, and then Kit followed. Rodgers removed a sack from a hook on a rafter, and the two men sat on stools facing each other. Rodgers handed Kit a salted fish and a piece of bread and had the same meal himself. Even though Kit was on the other side of the ocean, working in a blacksmith's shop was familiar to him. His work with Rodgers was no different than his work with Behncke in New Orleans and with the blacksmith in Newburgh. The smell and heat of the red-hot coals, the clang of iron hammers on anvils, the tools, the forge, the water barrels, the iron stock—everything was nearly the same. A blacksmith's shop was one of the few places Kit truly understood. Other than the *Ella*, it was the only place in which he felt at home.

After eating, work recommenced and continued until early evening. Finally, Rodgers held up his hand for the last time that day. He left the shop without saying anything but returned shortly with rolls and a salted fish for Kit's dinner. He showed Kit a straw-filled canvas mat in a corner of the shop, and the two men shook out the mat and kicked the surrounding straw to get rid of any rats that might have been nesting there. "Good night, boy," Rodgers said—the only complete sentence Rodgers had spoken that day to his new assistant. Rodgers shut and locked the door to his shop and left the young man alone in the dim light. Kit rearranged the cot to eliminate a few lumps, took his clothes off, and settled down to rest. He wasn't tired and wouldn't fall asleep for some time, but it felt good to lie down and stretch. From time to time, he sat up and nibbled on his dinner.

As the shop became totally dark, Kit could hear the scratching of what was probably a rat in a corner. It was a sound he was so familiar with that it was actually relaxing. When he finished his meal, he threw the remaining scraps, together with the newspaper in which the meal had been wrapped, into the still-hot forge. The flaring of the paper temporarily illuminated the shop, throwing weird-shaped shadows throughout. Kit moved back to his bedding before the shop became totally dark again.

As he lay in the dark, Kit wondered why Schultz had brought him across the ocean. The captain had said that it was to help carry the valises, but they didn't seem that heavy. He had seen the captain carry lots-heavier things before, and certainly Leonard could have helped the captain. The captain had told Rodgers they'd be there a week or two. Why? They had brought the luggage to England. What else was there to do? However, Kit was used to doing what he was told to do, so he didn't dwell on these questions long. As he lay there, he thought more intensely about a different matter.

During their voyage on the *Europa*, Kit had asked the captain if he'd be considered a runaway slave in England—could they catch him and return him to 'Bama? The captain had said that Kit was no longer a slave once they left the United States. In the middle of the ocean, the captain had said, Kit was a free man. *A free man*, thought Kit. Not a slave, not a fugitive, but free like the captain, like the German brothers on the *Ella*, like Leonard. The captain had said that Kit would not be a slave when they arrived in Liverpool since England had freed its slaves years earlier. "What about when I go back to New York?" Kit had asked.

The captain had been silent for a bit. "You'd become a fugitive slave once again, Kit." Seeing the stricken look on Kit's face, Schultz had continued, "You'll go to Canada when we get back home. I'll see to it. There's nothing in the United States for you."

The thought that he was free—that there were no slave chasers, no whippings, no auction houses—was difficult for a young man born into slavery to comprehend. What he did understand, however, was that when he entered New York Harbor, he'd be a slave once again. The thought angered him, but eventually his fatigue overcame his emotions, and he feel into a fitful sleep.

144

Diary of Benjamin Moran, assistant secretary
United States legation
London, England
Monday, September 2, 1861

Captain Alexander H. Schultz, once master of a North River steamboat, arrived here this morning as special bearer of despatches from Washington, bringing with him a Despatch Bag from Bunch the British Consul at Charleston, addressed to Lord Russell, and found in possession of Robert Mure, a naturalized Scotchman and rebel Colonel, who was arrested while on his way to Europe, with treasonable documents on his person. The bag is supposed to contain communications for the Rebel Representatives in London. There were 60 odd letters found on Mure, nearly all of which were treasonable, and he passed our lines through Bunch's connivance with a Courier's passport in violation of the rule without the proper countersign. One of the letters intercepted reveals the fact that the British and French Consuls at Charleston have been in official correspondence with the Rebel authorities on two of the articles of the Paris Declaration, and Mr. Adams is instructed to ask Bunch's recall for this proceeding and for having violated the rule about passports above described of which he had received official notice. If these Consuls acted by authority on these Declarations, as I suspect, then this and the French Govt. have been acting with bad faith towards us, & neither Consul will be removed.

145

En route to the London and Northwest Railway
London, England
September 2, 1861

SCHULTZ boarded the afternoon train to Liverpool with a quarter hour to spare. As the train filled up, Schultz moved tight against the window to make room if another passenger wished to sit next to him. Fortunately, there were enough empty seats, and no one found it necessary to sit next to the burly man. When the train started moving, Schultz moved away from the window a bit to make himself more comfortable and laid, on the empty bench next to him, all the newspapers he had bought at the train station.

Before he started reading, he glanced out the window as the train pulled out of the station. The station was large, larger than any he had seen in New York. The English trains were superior, Schultz thought. They were on time and clean, features he attributed to their having been in operation over a longer period than their counterparts in America.

The meeting with Adams had gone reasonably well. Moran, the assistant secretary, had been pleasant and had flattered Schultz with his questions about the captain's background. Adams had been cooler but still polite. He had carefully read Governor Seward's letter in Schultz's presence and carefully inspected the consular bag to confirm that the paper seal was intact. Adams had asked Schultz when he planned to return to the United States. Schultz had related that he had to deliver dispatches to the American legation in Paris and that when he returned to England he wanted to visit family members near Holyhead. All in all, Schultz had said, he might stay as long as two weeks. Adams had asked Schultz to come by the legation's offices just before he left to pick up any late dispatches that needed to be sent to the State Department. Given his secret mission, Schultz had been reluctant to make such a commitment, but when pressed by Adams, he'd agreed to do so. To have flatly refused, thought Schultz, would have raised suspicions.

Schultz started picking through the newspapers he had just bought. The *Times* he was familiar with, the others not, so he started reading the *Times*. He almost immediately read the following:

London, Monday, September 2, 1861

> The Army and Navy Gazette has announced that three more regiments of infantry are about to be placed under immediate orders for Canada, and that they will probably embark in the Great Eastern before the middle of the present month.

It took a couple of seconds for the importance of this sentence to sink in. He stopped and read it again, slowly. He then read the entire article about the troops going to Canada.

My God, he thought. *She's going to Canada! Mann didn't get her after all!* He felt as if a great weight was being removed. His whole mission was about a plot that did not exist! He sat back in his chair and breathed slowly to calm himself. As he reread the paragraph, he noticed the word "probably" but gave it little weight. He thought, *Moving three regiments to Canada requires a great deal of planning. The army wouldn't permit her to go to the United States if they were considering sending her to Canada.* He knew that there was no other ship in the world large enough to carry three regiments.

Freed from his dangerous mission, Schultz began to plan the rest of his trip. He'd first try to find the whereabouts of Montgomery's brother Henry and make arrangements to visit his family at Holyhead. He would then travel to Paris to visit the American legation to pick up any dispatches Mr. Dayton wanted to send to Governor Seward, stop by the legation's offices in London for the same purposes, pick up Kit in Liverpool, and then take a steamer to New York. He would be little more than a tourist. It was too bad he hadn't brought Margaret on this trip. She would have enjoyed seeing Montgomery's sons.

As he gazed out the window of the train, Schultz realized how beautiful the weather had become, how the wind had blown away the city's soot and smoke to reveal a mostly blue sky, and how interesting the brick buildings looked even in their grimy condition. For the first time in more than two weeks, he relaxed. Tonight, before he returned to his boardinghouse in New Brighton, he'd buy himself a fine dinner and a good cigar. It had turned out to be a wonderful day.

146

The Serpentine
London, England
September 2, 1861

DUDLEY Mann sat on a bench overlooking the park. Passersby who glanced at him were greeted with a kindly smile and a tip of his hat. He was holding a folded copy of a newspaper in one hand. It was becoming late afternoon, and he needed to head back to his flat. Before he left, however, he wanted to read the article one more time. The *Times* article said that the *Great Eastern* was probably leaving for Canada with three regiments. *My friend has come through!* thought Mann with great satisfaction. His friend, who had close connections to Lord Palmerston, had planted the rumor about the *Great Eastern* with the *Army and Navy Gazette* and had made sure that the *Times* repeated it. With the *Times* picking up the rumor, the story would be an established fact throughout Britain almost to the day the *Great Eastern* left.

Yes, Mr. Seward, thought Mann. *Your spies can crawl through Liverpool looking for blockade runners—puny ships that may make it through the blockade but without much result.* Mann stood up to walk off some of his excitement. *Your spies,* Mann thought, *your paid informers, are all useless. When the* Leviathan *arrives, Mr. Seward, you and your friend Mr. Lincoln will be gnashing your teeth.*

147

Mrs. Kendall's boardinghouse
New Brighton, England
September 3, 1861

Schultz slept late that morning. When he awoke, he shaved, dressed, and went downstairs to the boardinghouse's dining room. He had missed breakfast, but that was no problem. He had eaten so well and so late the previous evening that he wasn't hungry. Mrs. Kendall, the widow who kept the boardinghouse, offered him a cup of the still-warm breakfast tea, and he sat down at the dining table to drink it.

"Captain, would you like to read the newspaper?" she asked. "I think the other tenant has finished with it."

"Please," said Schultz, and she handed him the *Liverpool Mercury*. As Schultz scanned the paper, he came across the following:

> The Government has decided upon augmenting the military force in Canada to the strength at which it stood prior to the outbreak of the Crimean war, and an additional brigade, consisting of three regiments, and numbering 2500 men, will be placed under orders to embark in the Great Eastern before the middle of next month. This decision, though calculated to produce, at the first sight, considerable uneasiness, is simply a matter of precaution, for taking which the Government deserve great credit.

He laid the paper flat on the table and reread it. Unlike the article in the *Times*, this article did not talk in probabilities. There it was in black and white. The *Great Eastern* was going to Canada.

His mind now wonderfully at ease, he thought about how he'd spend his day. He knew that Neill Brothers had a small office in Liverpool and wondered if Montgomery Neill's brother Henry was in town. If he was, Schultz thought, they could have supper together and make plans to travel to Holyhead to see Montgomery's two sons. After all, they might end up being his grandsons if Mary and Montgomery were really interested in each other.

He also wanted to ask Henry whether he had seen Dan Lowber when Dan was in England, although, in light of the information in the newspapers, that issue was no longer particularly pressing.

148

Bremford Hotel
Liverpool, England
September 4, 1861

"Lydia, may I ask your opinion?"

The question was directed to Lydia Smithson by her husband, Captain Midford Smithson of Her Majesty's navy. Lydia, in her late thirties but still pretty, looked up in surprise at her husband. Captain Smithson, more than ten years older than Lydia and generally regarded as an honest but dull functionary, stood before her uncomfortably. In more than twenty years of marriage, she could count on one hand the number of times her husband had requested her opinion on any matter.

"Why, yes, Middie. What is it?" she said as she laid her sewing in her lap.

Smithson quietly asked, "Is Olivia here?"

Lydia was even more surprised. Olivia Burrows was Lydia's seventeen-year-old colored companion whom they had brought with them from Bermuda. "No, I sent her to purchase some baked goods for tomorrow's breakfast." Looking closely at her husband, she asked, "Has she done something wrong?"

"No, no, not at all," Smithson said. "It's just that I wanted your opinion about something. I may need Olivia's help."

Lydia was getting more confused by the second. "Sit down beside me, Middie, and tell me what this is about." She patted the cushion next to her on the love seat. Smithson obeyed.

"Well, darling," Smithson began, "my horse threw a shoe yesterday, and I was directed to a blacksmith's shop on Victoria Street. The old smith who owned the shop was busy, and he handed me off to a young man, a colored one. The young man went right to work and put a new shoe on for me."

"All right," said Lydia quietly. "And?"

"Well, I watched him for a while—the young blacksmith, that is. After he finished with my horse, he went back to shaping an iron gear. It was a very complicated piece and involved hammering an iron rod into a ring and then cutting teeth into it. I talked to the old smith while the young man was working and asked about him. The smith took me outside and said it was a strange story. He said the colored boy's name is Kit and that a Yankee captain and the American consul in Liverpool brought him to the shop. He said that Kit is simply staying with him and will be leaving in a week or so. He said he has no idea why Kit was brought to Liverpool. He said that the boy works hard and is a good blacksmith but says very little."

"I see," said Lydia, who really didn't. "And?"

"Well, you know how hard I work at Dockyards trying to keep our ships serviceable. Frankly, I'm desperate for a blacksmith who's skilled enough to repair a ship's ironwork. There are a few in Bermuda that do a good job, but they're always putting private work ahead of the navy's. They tell me that the private work pays better. I only have a limited amount of money to pay for blacksmithing, and the Admiralty requires that I account for every farthing. It's been very difficult."

Lydia was not quite sure where this conversation was going, so she decided to have some fun. "So you think Olivia could become a blacksmith like this colored boy?"

Smithson gave his wife a stunned look, only to smile when he saw his wife's grin. "Well, that's quite a picture," he said. "I don't think our little Olivia is quite strong enough to work as a blacksmith. No, I'm thinking of the young man at the blacksmith's shop, the boy Kit."

"And this Kit is the sort of blacksmith you need in Bermuda?" Lydia asked.

"Exactly! He's just what I need. I could give him a salary and put him in the forge at Dockyards. It would be a wonderful arrangement for both him and me. I could save money, and he'd have a job."

"Middie, you asked for my opinion. My opinion is that you should ask this young man to come to Bermuda with us."

Smithson took a deep breath and then said, "Darling, I wanted your opinion about how to approach this young man. I want to know if you would approve of having Olivia talk to him on my behalf."

"Why don't you talk to him directly?"

"Firstly, darling, he seems to be very shy. He hardly talks to the other smith. I think he was quite intimidated by me. Secondly, I gather from what the blacksmith told me that he's an American. He may have been a slave, or, at least, he certainly knows someone who's been a slave. Such a person is not likely to talk to white men who are strangers. You've read *Uncle Tom's Cabin.* You know what things are like in America for a young colored man."

"What would you like Olivia to do?"

"Well, we give her Sunday off. I'm sure the smith is also closed on Sunday. What if we arranged for Olivia to spend the day with this Kit?"

Lydia was shocked. "I hardly think so. She's a very proper young woman from a respectable family. We can't ask her to spend a day with a young man who's a total stranger. You know nothing about him."

"Darling, I'm not suggesting anything inappropriate. On Sundays, all sorts of young men and women promenade in public. It's perfectly respectable. All I'm asking is for Olivia to spend part of her day off walking around in a public venue with a young man and telling him how wonderful life is in Bermuda. That's all."

Lydia pondered this. She knew her husband wouldn't have brought the subject up unless he felt strongly about acquiring this young man. "How do you propose arranging such a promenade?" she asked her husband.

"Well," he said, "this is where I need your help. I thought I could visit the smith and suggest that if this Kit has Sunday off, my wife has a colored companion, a young woman of good breeding, who would be willing to be taken on a walk. Olivia knows Liverpool and Merseyside well enough. She'd know the best place to promenade. I thought I'd give the smith a little money to hand to Kit so that if they wanted to cross on the ferry, they could go to Merseyside or New Brighton."

"Middie, this is hardly fair. You know that Olivia idolizes you. She'd do anything you ask. I'm the one who has to speak up for her interests."

"I understand that, darling, which is why I'm asking you. If you say no, the issue is closed. I'll not bring it up again."

The couple sat in silence on the love seat, their eyes not meeting. Finally, Lydia asked, "So what does this young smith look like?"

"Well, he's quite dark," Smithson said. His wife started to frown. Olivia was neither dark nor yellow but what Bermudians sometimes called "coffee colored." Seeing his wife's face, Smithson continued, "But, Lydia, he's got a physique like a miniature Zeus. You've seen pictures of those Greek and Roman statutes of their gods with bulging muscles. Well, that's what he looks like. Not an ounce of fat. Powerful arms and shoulders. He wasn't wearing a shirt when I saw him, just pants and a leather apron. He's short but taller than Olivia. He's clean-shaven. His face gives the appearance of intelligence and soberness. I think Olivia would be favorably impressed."

Lydia listened to her husband's description. *A miniature Zeus,* she thought. She imagined that Olivia might be interested in that description. "Are you sure he's not a brute?"

"I've not seen anything to suggest that, but I can talk with the smith confidentially. He'll not lie to me."

"You'd have to take her to the shop to introduce her to the young man."

"Of course," he said.

"In fact, I'll go with you. If I don't like his looks, we'll return immediately."

"Agreed."

Lydia sat silently as she mulled the matter. "You know that Olivia doesn't have a proper promenade dress," she said.

Smithson knew where this conversation was going and tried to head it off. "Darling," he said, "Sunday is only four days away. We don't have time to have such a dress made. Olivia will have to do with her daily clothes."

"Well, actually," said Lydia, "I have a solution to that problem. The landlady was showing me clothes that her daughter has outgrown and wondering whether I might buy any. She had a lovely dress, turquoise with coral-colored trim. With a nip and tuck it would fit our Olivia beautifully. It's not quite a promenade dress but close. It seems to me that if you wish to impress the young man with the beauty of Bermuda, the best way is to show him a beautiful Bermudian." She gave her husband a big smile at the end of her sentence. Lydia's skills as a coquette had not diminished over the years.

"How much? We haven't much money."

"I've saved a little bit. Darling, if you really want to pursue this Kit, you must consider my relationship with Olivia. I couldn't think of imposing on her without providing her with a proper dress." This statement was greeted by silence. Lydia continued, "After all, you wouldn't send a frigate out of Dockyards unless she was properly equipped, would you?"

Having been speared by an excellent metaphor, Smithson surrendered. "No, dear." The bargain struck, Smithson informed his wife that he'd be going for a walk. He didn't wish to be present when his wife and Olivia discussed the matter.

149

Liverpool, England
September 4, 1861

It had been a wasted day for Schultz. He had wandered around Liverpool until he'd found the offices of Neill Bros. A young clerk was there making entries in a journal, and from him Schultz learned that Henry Neill was in London and not due to come back until Monday. The clerk volunteered that he sent a packet daily by train to London and that he could inform Mr. Neill of his visitor from the United States. Schultz agreed and wrote out a message that he would like to meet Henry in Liverpool on Monday.

After that, Schultz walked down to the riverfront and saw the *Great Eastern* at her moorings. He compared her against the first time he'd seen her more than a year earlier, when she'd arrived in triumph in New York Harbor. He remembered the excitement of that day, the fleet of vessels that had accompanied her, the cannon salutes, the bands, the tens of thousands of sightseers. Now she sat silently at her moorings. A tugboat was passing leisurely by her, its crew taking no particular notice of her.

The white line that ran around her hull and the white paint on the top of her paddle boxes were gone. She was entirely black except for her smokestacks, which had been repainted a dark-red color. She'd never been a beautiful ship, but now she was merely an immense black object, without interest except for her size. As Schultz stared at the ship, he noticed that the lifeboats were hanging from their davits. He *had* remembered correctly! Schultz nodded his head in satisfaction at his powers of observation. He thought of his plot to have Kit climb aboard one of the boats and unsling it so that it would be drawn into the paddle wheel. *It would have worked,* Schultz thought. But he thanked God that he and Kit didn't have to go through with the plan. The thought of the risk they would have been running gave him a queasy feeling.

After staring at the *Great Eastern* for a while longer, Schultz meandered back to the ferry and returned to his boardinghouse in New Brighton. He was in time for dinner, and he dined with a collection of cotton brokers and ships' officers. There was a lively discussion about the Civil War in America, with none of the diners saying anything positive about the North. Although perturbed by the conversation, Schultz remained silent. He saw no point in arguing with men who made money from human slavery, even indirectly.

After dinner, some of the men decided to have a drink while a couple remained in the parlor. Schultz decided to stay in the parlor. Mrs. Kendall lit a whale oil lamp and turned up the wick so that the men could read. Schultz looked around and found a folded copy of the current *Liverpool Mercury* sitting on a table. He read through the articles—nothing about the *Great Eastern.* He then thought that he ought to start making plans to return to the United States. He turned to the advertisements to see what ships would be available next week. He saw the following announcements:

United States.

Goods for Shipment per Great Eastern are received North-east Corner Waterloo Dock.

GREAT EASTERN FOR NEW YORK.

The Steamship

GREAT EASTERN,

JAMES WALKER, Commander;

Will be despatched from LIVERPOOL for NEW YORK, as under:—

TUESDAY.............................September 10.
TUESDAY.............................October 29.

Fares—Cabin Passage, £20 to £28, according to accommodation; Steerage, Seven Guineas and upwards.

Freight, on moderate terms, payable here, or at New York at $4 80c. per pound sterling.

Apply to the Great Ship Company (Limited), 90, Cannon-street, London, E.C.; or to

3s07 C. E. DIXON, 9, Rumford-place.

THE GREAT EASTERN FOR NEW YORK.

PASSAGE TO NEW YORK £7 7s.

The GREAT EASTERN,

13 343 tons register, Captain Kennedy, will sail FROM LIVERPOOL TO NEW YORK on the following dates:—

TUESDAY, SEPTEMBER 10.
TUESDAY, OCTOBER 29.

Steerage Fare Seven Guineas and upwards to Ten Guineas, according to accommodation. The fare includes an unlimited supply of provisions of the best quality. Early application should be made for berths to SABEL & SEARLE,

mwf 19 Water-street.

Southern States.

STEAM COMMUNICATION BETWEEN LIVERPOOL AND CHARLESTON.

On the reopening of the port of Charleston, the undermentioned first-class Screw Steamships will be despatched for that port, taking freight and passengers for all the Southern and Western Cities:—

BERMUDA.............................New Ship.
ADELAIDE.............................2060 tons.
VICTORIA.............................1877 tons.

First-class passage to Charleston, £25.

For further particulars apply to

FRASER, TRENHOLM, & CO.,
10, Rumford-place; or to
M. G. KLINGENDER & CO.,
d 22 Water-street.

Schultz read the three announcements carefully, methodically. They made no sense. The first two announcements stated that the *Great Eastern* was to leave for New York on September 10. That was next Tuesday, five days away! The first announcement said that a Captain Kennedy was going to command her, and the second said that a Captain Walker was in command. Kennedy was likely the same Captain Kennedy who had taken her to Quebec loaded with British soldiers. Who Walker was Schultz had no idea. Each announcement had a different booking agent. Both announcements said that her next departure to New York after the September 10 departure would be on October 29. That date was impossible if the *Great Eastern* was going to Canada early in October, as the newspapers had earlier reported. There wouldn't be enough time between the voyages.

The third announcement was also alarming. There was a small fleet of steamships ready to leave "on the reopening of the port of Charleston."

"Captain, are you unwell?" Mrs. Kendall asked as she entered the room carrying a tray that included a small decanter of sherry and small glasses. Schultz looked at her dumbly. "Captain, you're as white as a ghost." She put the decanter down and placed the back of her hand against Schultz's forehead. "You're clammy," she said. "I hope you don't come down with something."

Schultz wasn't coming down with anything. He was frightened.

150

Liverpool, England
September 5, 1861

"Can I help you?" The young clerk at the offices of Sabel and Searle looked up at Schultz, who had just entered the offices.

"I'm returning to the United States and want some information about passage on the *Great Eastern*," Schultz said.

The young clerk stood up from his desk and walked to a counter. "Are you referring to the departure next week or the one in October?"

"The one next week."

The clerk opened a book on the counter and located the proper page. "Well, sir, we have plenty of open cabins. You'd be traveling first class?"

Schultz laid the previous day's *Liverpool Mercury* on the counter. "I have a question," he told the clerk. "There are two announcements. Is she definitely leaving on the tenth, and if so, who will be her captain?"

"Sir, as far as I know, she's leaving on the tenth under the command of Captain Kennedy."

"Is that the same Kennedy that took her to Quebec?"

"Yes, sir. The same."

"Who is this Captain Walker in the other announcement?"

The clerk shrugged his shoulders. "No one I've heard of. I know the names of all the first-line captains out of Liverpool. He's not among them."

"Do you have any explanation for the two different announcements?" Schultz asked.

The clerk shook his head. "We saw the other announcement for the first time this morning. Mr. Searle was very surprised and, I must tell you, very angry when he saw the announcement. He found the whole matter very questionable since we were appointed booking agents for the Great Ship Company. Mr. Searle's not in right now, but he'll be back later in the day. Perhaps by that time he'll know something. That's all I can tell you." After a pause, the clerk asked, "Do you wish to book passage, sir?"

"No," said Schultz. "Not at this time. Thank you for your help."

Within twenty minutes Schultz arrived at the offices of G. E. Dixon, a small shop at 9 Rumford Place. When he entered, he encountered a middle-aged man. "May I help you?" asked the man.

"I'm interested in returning to the United States next week, and I'm interested in booking a cabin on the *Great Eastern.*"

"I see," the man said. "Well, we have many excellent cabins available. Would you be traveling first class?"

"Before I book a cabin," Schultz said, "I'm trying to understand these two announcements. One says that Captain Kennedy is in charge, and the other, the one placed by your firm, says Captain Walker is in charge. Which is right?"

"Ours is correct, sir. Captain Walker will take the *Great Eastern* to New York."

"What happened to Captain Kennedy?"

"I don't know. All I know is that Captain Walker will command the ship."

"Who is Captain Walker?"

The man was becoming a little irritated by Schultz's questions. Nevertheless, he maintained a formal civility. "Captain Walker is late of the Galway Line. I'm told he's an excellent captain. His last ship was the *Adriatic*."

"The Galway Line," Schultz repeated softly to himself. He had heard of it. It was a small line of disreputable steamers that ran between Galway, Ireland, and New York City. He had heard that it recently went out of business.

"Is that the Galway Line that went out of business?" Schultz asked.

The man was becoming increasingly annoyed by his visitor. "I believe it no longer is in business; that's correct," he said coldly.

Schultz stood in silence as he recalled his last conversation with Fred Seward. "If the captain is a person of little or no reputation …" Fred had said. Kennedy would not have tried to run the blockade. But an out-of-work captain from a small, defunct line of steamers, a man desperate for money?

"Do you wish to book a cabin?" the man asked Schultz.

"Perhaps," Schultz said. "I need to confer with another individual who may be traveling with me. I'll be back."

"Very well," said the man, glad to be rid of the inquisitive visitor.

As Schultz walked to the ferry to return to his boardinghouse, he pondered this new information—the sudden and unexpected decision to send the *Great Eastern* to America, the captain with solid standing apparently being replaced by one with little reputation from an insignificant and now-defunct steamship line … all the warnings were present. He needed to get to Paris quickly to find Hamilton Towle.

151

Hull Packet and East Riding Times
Hull, England
September 6, 1861

An authoritative contradiction is given to the report that the Great Eastern has been chartered for the transport of the three regiments ordered to proceed to Canada. The Great Eastern, it is announced, will leave the Mersey for New York on Tuesday next, under a new commander—Captain Walker, late of the Galway line.

152

Paris, France
September 7, 1861

SCHULTZ left Liverpool Thursday night on the mail train to London. Over the years he had learned to snatch sleep on rolling ships, so he'd been able to doze off and on during his several hours on the train. He arrived in London on late Friday morning, stiff and sweaty, and immediately went to catch a train to Dover. It was shortly after noon when he left Dover on a steam ferry to the port of Calais. In Calais he took a train to Paris and arrived late that evening. He followed his fellow passengers into the hotel district and found a hotel that looked decent enough. A bored matron waited on him, and then Schultz lumbered upstairs to his room, a small but clean space on the third floor. Exhausted, he took off his clothes and hung them in the wardrobe, turned down the gas light, and collapsed into bed. He hadn't eaten since Thursday night, but his hunger was overtaken by his fatigue, and he fell into a fitful sleep.

Early in the morning Schultz fell into a much deeper sleep, before being awoken by light coming into his room. Once he slowly recalled where he was and why he was there, he quickly scrambled from his bed. He washed and dressed in a hurry and made his way downstairs. From the clock in the hotel's parlor, he saw it was a little after nine o'clock. He showed the address Wilding had written down for him to the desk clerk, who proceeded to give directions in French. Schultz couldn't understand a word and tried to ask in English. The desk clerk started responding in mangled English, of no use to Schultz. However, an Englishman in the parlor came to Schultz's rescue and gave him very precise directions to the American legation.

Saturday was a busy day at the American legation's office, and Schultz found himself in the midst of a collection of tourists and travelers waiting to have their visas approved. Schultz approached a harried-looking clerk.

"Sir," said Schultz, "I'm here to see Mr. Dayton. I have dispatches from Governor Seward."

The clerk looked briefly at the letter Schultz handed him, the same letter that Schultz had shown to Charles Francis Adams. The clerk recognized Fred Seward's handwriting and, without reading beyond the salutation, escorted Schultz through the crowd into William Dayton's office. Dayton, a middle-aged man with the quiet demeanor of a judge, which he'd once been, looked up at the two men.

"Mr. Dayton," the young clerk said, "this gentleman has a letter from Secretary Seward. He said he has dispatches for you."

Dayton stood up and extended his hand.

"I'm Captain Alexander Schultz from New York."

Still shaking his hand, Dayton said, "Captain, welcome to Paris. I hope you enjoy your stay here."

"Actually, I'm only here for a day. I need to get back to England."

"I see. Well, let's see what you've brought."

Schultz handed Dayton his letter of instructions. Dayton reviewed the lengthy letter. "How'd you find Mr. Adams?" he asked.

"He seemed well. He was very busy, so we really didn't have much of a conversation."

"Well, yes, we're a little busy keeping Lord Palmerston and Louis Napoleon from sticking their pointy noses into our unfortunate rebellion. The rebels are here in force, poking around the shipyards in Calais looking for ships that can be made into raiders. We're watching them closely."

"I think Mr. Wilding is doing the same thing in Liverpool," Schultz said.

"Exactly. And I hear he's doing a very good job. Liverpool is a festering den of secessionists. Mr. Wilding must be a lonely man indeed."

At this break in the conversation, Schultz dug out from his valise a thin packet of dispatches that he had received from Fred Seward and handed them to Dayton. The latter briefly examined the contents of the packet and then said simply, "Thank you."

"Mr. Dayton," Schultz said after a pause, "can you give me directions? I'm trying to find the home of Mr. Hamilton Towle."

Dayton sat back in his chair and looked closely at Schultz. "Are you a friend of Mr. Towle?" he asked.

"No, sir," said Schultz, surprised at the question. Thinking for a moment, he answered, "We have a mutual friend, and the friend asked me to look him up."

"I see," said Dayton, rubbing his chin as he silently considered Schultz's request. Finally, he said, "I understand that Mr. Towle spends most of his time in Calais, but he has an address in Paris. I'll have my secretary give you his address and directions. It's not far from here." Dayton lowered his voice. "Be careful, Captain. The Union has many enemies in this country."

Schultz nodded, and Dayton arose and called his secretary into the office. The secretary wrote out the address and sketched a map on a piece of paper. With this, Schultz walked briskly through the streets of Paris and within a half hour arrived at the address. Towle's flat was on the second floor, so Schultz entered through a narrow doorway on the street and walked up a flight of stairs. He came to what looked to be a freshly painted black door. Schultz knocked. He could hear an individual closing an interior door, and then the front door opened a crack. "*Oui*?" A young, sandy-haired man stood in the doorway. He was taller than average, slim, and dressed in a shirt and pants that looked freshly ironed.

"I'm an American," Schultz said softly.

"What can I do for you?" Towle asked.

"I've been sent here by Governor Seward," Schultz said, continuing his whisper.

Towle nodded and opened the door to admit Schultz. Before he closed it, he looked down the staircase to ensure that no one else was around. Once the door was closed, Schultz began to speak.

"Mr. Towle, my name is Alexander Schultz. I'm a sea captain who works a line of tugboats in New York Harbor. I'm acting as a courier for Governor Seward. He gave me your name. I got your address from Mr. Dayton's secretary." The flat was small but neat. Towle led Schultz into a small parlor and pointed to an upholstered armchair. When Schultz sat, Towle pulled up a wooden desk chair.

"Captain Schultz, how can I help you?"

"It's a long story," Schultz said, "and we don't have a great deal of time. Governor Seward said you were keeping an eye on the rebels in France, that you were watching to see if they were trying to buy raiders or blockade runners."

Towle was a little flustered at how completely his secret business was known by this stranger. "Captain Schultz, I need some proof that you are who you say you are. Don't be offended, sir. I'm sure you understand the need to be careful."

Schultz dug Fred Seward's letter from his valise, the same letter he had shown to Adams and Dayton. "Mr. Towle, can you recognize Fred Seward's writing?" Towle nodded. Schultz continued, "This is the letter under which I made this journey." He handed it to Towle. Towle moved his chair closer to a window and slowly read the letter. When finished, he handed it back to Schultz.

"The letter says you're acting as a courier," Towle said. "What is my involvement in your mission?"

"Mr. Towle, my real mission is to find out if the rebels have acquired a blockade runner in England. My role as a courier is simply to throw the rebels off the track if they learn I'm here."

"All right," said Towle. "What do you need from me?"

"Well, as I said, I was sent to determine if the rebels have obtained a ship in Liverpool. I'm not entirely positive, but it looks highly likely that they have. Governor Seward thinks that if this ship goes into a Southern port, England and France will recognize the Confederacy and have their warships lift the blockade."

"What ship?" asked Towle.

"The *Great Eastern*."

Towle sat silently as he stared at Schultz. Finally he said, "You can't be serious."

"I am, Mr. Towle. If the largest ship in the world enters a Southern port, the British will declare the blockade illegal."

"Where would she enter?"

"I don't know, but I've thought about it. If she's lightly loaded, there are a few ports she could enter. I think the one most likely would be Port Royal, but there may be others."

Towle nodded. "South Carolina. That would make sense. But why would the owners of the ship run this risk?"

"She's losing money and has no prospect of making any. I'm sure you're aware of that. Now, sir, if a ship can't make money, she has no value except as scrap. However, if she breaks a blockade, the owners will almost certainly be rewarded, richly rewarded, by the government that's being blockaded."

"That's all true, Captain, but what leads you to believe the rebels have her?"

"A number of facts, Mr. Towle. The fact of the matter is that both

Governor Seward and I believe she's going to attempt to break the blockade, and I'm determined to stop her from doing so. I need help."

"What *are* those facts, sir?"

"They're several, and I'll go through them with you on the way to Liverpool. However, we have to leave almost immediately."

Towle asked, "When is the *Great Eastern* due to leave?"

"Tuesday."

"Tuesday! Three days from now!"

"Yes."

"Captain, we have to travel across the channel, travel from London to Liverpool, and come up with a plan to disable her in three days?"

"Yes," Schultz said quietly. "If we leave for Liverpool immediately, we should arrive Monday morning. I have to pick up some dispatches from Mr. Dayton in Paris. You can wait outside while I get them. It shouldn't take but a moment. I then have to stop to pick up dispatches from Mr. Adams in London. That may take a little longer, but you can go directly to Liverpool. In Liverpool, we can both stay at my rooming house Monday night."

Towle sat slowly shaking his head in amazement. "The *Great Eastern*," he said quietly. "Captain… do you have a plan to stop her?"

Schultz nodded. "I do, Mr. Towle. But it needs work. I need your help."

Towle took a deep breath while looking at the floor. "All right, Captain. You've clearly been sent by Secretary Seward. That's good enough for me. I'm going to pack, and we should be on our way in minutes."

153

"England and the Southern States," *The Spectator* London, England September 7, 1861

We fear there is no little reason to apprehend that the leading members of the English Government have already under their consideration the propriety of recognizing, early in the autumn, the independence of the Southern States; and that unless some decisive victory and rapid success of the North intervenes, or English opinion declares very strongly against it, this step may be soon taken. The second reinforcement of Canada, which has taken place since Parliament separated, and the language and sympathies of the Government journals, are some indications of this danger. At all events, there is no doubt that it is a question much canvassed in influential quarters, and that the strong desire of the Government to secure Lancashire against a cotton crisis, together with an impression which is widely prevalent in political circles that it would be a great advantage to England to see the power of the United States broken up into fragments, tends to persuade them to adopt it.

154

Liverpool, England
September 8, 1861

Kit stood outside the closed blacksmith's shop looking up and down the deserted street. On Sunday mornings, respectable Liverpudlians were in church; the remainder were sleeping it away. After washing in the rain barrel, Kit put on the clothes he'd worn when he'd arrived in Liverpool, the best clothes he had. He was thankful that when he had first arrived in the blacksmith's shop, he had folded them and placed them in a canvas bag to keep them clean. Although the clothes had originally been made for a taller man, either Leonard or the captain, Mrs. Schultz had taken them up, and they fit Kit's shorter frame tolerably well.

As Kit waited, he pondered his strange situation. The captain had brought him to London for some task, to carry something or other, but he hadn't seen the captain since the day they'd arrived. He had worked more than a week at the blacksmith's shop with a crotchety old man whose longest sentence seemed to be "Let's eat." A day earlier, the blacksmith had told him that he'd have Sunday off. Then, Kit had listened in amazement as Rodgers had actually tried to hold a conversation with him.

"So, Kit, ya've come inta a bit'a good luck, ya have. Ya see, there's this here navy captain, or some sech title, who's taken a fancy to you—I don't know how else ta put it—and he comes by and says his wife's got a girl, a 'componion' he says, a colored girl from Ba'muda. And he says, 'Why don't that Kit take this girl for a walk on Sunday?' Then knock me over, he give me some money to give ta ya, sos that you can ride da ferry or something. Now, the captain, he says this girl's a lady, real smart and fancy, so he wants ya to act like a proper gentleman, or otherwise you gotta answer to him *and* to me. So, der ya are. The captain, he brings da girl by Sunday morning. So, see, dat's a bit'a good luck. Some coins to jingle in ya pocket and a good-looking girl to boot." At this, Rodgers had given Kit his finest attempt at a smile and a gentle punch to the shoulder.

Kit was unable to understand why the navy captain was making this offer. Thus, his first thought was to decline the offer and stay in the blacksmith's shop in case Captain Schultz came by. On second thought, however, he'd decided that the captain had handed him over to the blacksmith, and if Rodgers thought taking Sunday off was acceptable, Kit assumed Captain Schultz would approve. He was lonely and hadn't talked to a colored person since he'd said goodbye to Leonard on the railroad platform. Thus, on Sunday morning Kit found himself outside the shop, nervously looking up and down the street.

After what seemed to Kit to be a long while, he heard hooves clomping on a cobblestoned street. As he looked in the direction of the sound, he saw a cab pull out of a side street and turn toward him. The driver was perched high above the cab's rear. As it neared, Kit saw three people in the cab, two women and a man. The cab pulled up, and the man, whom Kit now recognized from an earlier visit to the blacksmith's shop, stepped out.

"Hello, Kit," the man said. "Do you remember me?"

Kit nodded. "Yes, suh."

"I'm Captain Smithson. You replaced my horse's shoe a few days ago."

"Yes, suh."

Kit looked closely at the man. He was not wearing a uniform but a black suit and tie. He looked to be an important person.

"I gather Mr. Rodgers told you about today."

"Yes, suh."

"Well, good then. Kit, I want you to meet my wife, Mrs. Smithson, and my wife's companion, Miss Olivia Burrows."

Kit looked into the cab. The white woman smiled broadly at Kit. *That's gotta be the wife*, he thought. He then stared at the other woman. She was small and thin, a colored girl. Kit, however, had never before seen a colored girl dressed like this. She was wearing a dress of a strange blue color, with orange trim on it. She wore a flat straw hat with a feather sticking out of the hatband. The girl gave Kit a small smile and then looked away, staring down the street as if she were looking at something in the distance.

Kit had no idea what to say or how to act. He smiled at Mrs. Smithson and then turned to smile at the man. He bowed to both. He was becoming very uncomfortable with his situation.

"Well, Kit," the captain said, "today is a beautiful day for a perambulation." Kit looked at him in complete confusion. Seeing this, the captain quickly added, "A walk, Kit. A beautiful day just to walk, you know, to stroll."

Kit didn't know whether he should respond, so he just stood there smiling. He looked up at the colored girl, but she was still staring down the street. Kit looked down the street himself. *What's she staring at?* he thought. The street was still deserted.

"Anyway, Kit," the captain continued, "we, my wife and I, thought we would drop you and Miss Burrows off by the ferry. You can cross the river, and then there are lovely places to stroll on the other side of the Mersey. Did Mr. Rodgers give you the money I gave him?"

Kit nodded. "Yes, suh."

"Well, then, you'll have enough for both of you to take the ferry and buy a little something to eat. Does that sound like fun?"

Kit looked at the colored girl staring icily down the street. It didn't sound like fun. Without waiting for an answer, the captain said, "Kit, get on the back of the cab with the driver. We haven't any room in the front. When we get to the ferry, you and Miss Burrows can get off."

Kit obeyed, and the driver slid over to make room for the young man. The cab began its journey, and within twenty minutes they had arrived at the ferry landing. The ferry was in the middle of the river, slowly heading toward them. The party got out of the cab and stood on the ferry landing to watch the vessel approach.

The captain spoke first. "Well, then, Mrs. Smithson and I are going to go on for a bit, and we'll leave you here. Olivia, you know what time you should be back?"

"Yes, Captain."

Kit had never heard a colored girl talk that way. Her words were crisp, just like the white English folks spoke.

"You two have a lovely day," Mrs. Smithson said. "It's a wonderful thing to be young."

Olivia had a pained look on her face, and Kit just smiled vacantly and nodded. With that, the Smithsons reentered the cab and left the two young people alone.

Kit and Olivia stood side by side, keeping a respectable distance from each other. Kit rotated his head, appearing to look around but really trying to avoid looking at his companion. Olivia was the first to speak. "You may call me Olivia. What is your name?"

"Kit."

"What's your last name?"

What should I answer? Kit thought. He didn't have the skill to lie convincingly, so he told her the truth. "It's just Kit. There ain't nothin' else."

"But everyone in Bermuda has a last name. What was your mother's last name?"

Olivia noted discomfort on Kit's face when she said that. *Oh dear,* she thought. *What did I do?*

"My mama din't have no name but Emmie. She's dead now."

Recovering quickly, Olivia went on, "Well, Kit is a perfectly good name. It's short and easy to remember." She gave a small smile, but Kit was staring at the ground. *I made a terrible mistake,* she thought. *I need to change the subject.*

"So, Kit, I'm from an island called Bermuda. Have you ever heard of it?"

Kit nodded.

"You have! Have you ever been there?"

Kit shook his head.

"How did you hear about it?"

"I used ta work on a tug in New York. Sometimes ships would come in from Ba'muda. We'd pull dem inta da wharf."

"New York. You're from America?"

"Yeah."

Olivia was beginning to puzzle some things out. A young man with no last name from the United States.

"Kit, are you from New York?"

Kit shrugged. "I's dar fo' a while," he answered. He wasn't going to say anything further. He didn't know this young woman or her captain. He didn't know how safe he'd be if she discovered he was a fugitive slave. He remembered Jack.

When the ferry arrived, the young couple boarded it and stood by a railing. As the ferry was crossing over the broad river, a gusty breeze was blowing, and Olivia had to hold on to her hat with both hands. She started to laugh. "This wind's so strong my hat and I may blow away, just like a giant kite." Seeing the young woman smile, Kit smiled as well. She really had a pretty smile, he thought. Plus she had all her teeth, at least the ones he could see.

"Kit, have you ever flown a kite?"

He shook his head. In Newburgh, he had stopped to watch a couple of boys flying a kite in a park, but he'd never flown one.

"I like to fly kites," Olivia said. "My father's a deacon, and each year on Easter Sunday he and I used to fly a kite that we made on Good Friday. We painted them, and they were beautiful. My father said that sending a kite into the air is like watching Jesus go up to heaven. I'd write little prayers on paper, and then we'd put them on the kite string, and they'd go right to the kite."

They stood quietly for a few moments. Then Olivia said, "If you came to Bermuda, you'd get to make and fly a kite."

Kit smiled and nodded. "Dat sound nice," he said. Actually, it did.

Because of the wind and the sounds of the steam ferry, Olivia had to often get close to Kit to yell into his ear. The first time she approached him, he looked at her face. There were no scars, no scratches. Her skin was smooth and brown. He had never seen a colored girl with skin like that. The ones he knew in Alabama, the slave girls, were pretty beaten up, their faces scarred from accidents, whippings, and fights.

When they reached the opposite shore, they began walking on the bank of the broad river, heading east toward where the mouth of the Mersey opened into the ocean. A wide road ran along the upper level of the bank, and several couples were walking up and down the road, talking to each other. Every so often, Kit saw a couple walking arm in arm.

The wind was still gusty, but the noise from the ferry was gone, so the couple could talk more easily. In response to a series of questions from Olivia, Kit gave mostly vague answers, except in response to a surprisingly blunt question about whether he had a wife or a sweetheart, the latter of which he understood to mean a woman. Kit answered that he did not. Although she kept a straight face, Olivia was inwardly pleased with this answer. She allowed that she, also, was unattached. The rest of their conversation was carried on by Olivia and dealt with Bermuda. Everyone in Bermuda was free, the island having abolished slavery long before Olivia was born. Colored people could own businesses and houses, could go to whatever church they wanted, and could marry if they wanted to. They didn't have to ask anybody's permission to do things. They couldn't vote, but someday they'd be able to, Olivia said. Kit had only the vaguest idea of what a vote was.

Olivia talked about all the houses in Bermuda being painted white, even their roofs, and said that flowers were everywhere and the weather was always nice, with no ice or snow. On Sundays, everyone dressed up and went to church and then took walks after supper. On Saturdays, just about everyone went fishing. Judging from Olivia's description, Bermuda was the best place in the world, especially for colored people.

Both young people were forming impressions of the other. To Kit, Olivia was otherworldly. She liked to talk—indeed, once she started, she hardly stopped—and she spoke with a beautiful accent. She occasionally flashed him a bright smile, especially when she was telling a funny story about the folks in Bermuda. She was smart, almost scarily so, but she was no show-off. She had been raised in a world Kit could hardly comprehend.

Olivia considered that Mrs. Smithson's description of Kit was accurate. He was very dark, almost black, and when he smiled, the contrast between his teeth and skin was striking. According to Mrs. Smithson, the captain had said that Kit had the physique of a miniature Zeus, and Olivia remembered the pictures of statues of ancient gods she had seen in the captain's books. Kit *was* powerfully built with broad shoulders and a thin waist. Peeking out from his rolled-up sleeves were powerful wrists and forearms, marked with numerous scars from burns and cuts. In spite of his obvious strength, he walked lightly, almost gracefully, and seemed surprisingly gentle. Although he said little, he listened carefully to every word Olivia uttered, which she thought was an admirable trait and one that far too few men possessed.

As they ambled along the walkway, Olivia became quiet. She had simply run out of things to talk about. Also, she didn't want Kit to think her a chatterbox. Silence was an uncomfortable state for Olivia, however, and she cast around for something to start a conversation. She looked around and saw a giant ship moored in the river, its five smokestacks looming over the tiny vessels traveling past her. She looked carefully at its side wheels, enormous even at the distance at which she rested.

"Kit, is that the *Leviathan*?" She stopped and pointed at the ship.

Kit looked. "Yeah. Dat's the *Great Eastern*."

"She's gigantic," Olivia said. "Have you seen her before?"

Kit nodded. "I saw her in New York. I was workin' on a tug, 'n' she came in."

"She's ugly," said Olivia. "Just a giant black ship."

Kit turned to his companion and asked, "Does you believe in signs?"

This was the first nonresponsive sentence Kit had made during the day, and it surprised Olivia. "Do you mean like an omen?" she asked. Kit nodded. Olivia thought carefully, because the question was certainly odd. "I guess I do, Kit. In the Bible, God gives prophets signs, and so, yes, I do believe in signs. But why do you ask?"

"I's tryin' ta sleep one night in New York Harbor, on da deck of da tug. All of a sudden dere's a fi'eball—giant red fi'eball. It goes ova da harbor, jest where I'm tryin' ta sleep. Passes real slow, like. I looks at da *Great Eastern.* Wit da light 'n' shadows from da fi'eball, it look like blood runnin' down her sides. Den, the fi'eball explodes."

"You think that was a sign?"

Kit shrugged. "I dunno. I ask an old lady once. She was tellin' fortunes, and she gets all excited. She said da ship was a slave ship, and she said it was covered with da blood of slaves. I said, 'No, it ain't no slave ship; it just a big steama.' She wouldn't listen to me. She jest went on and on."

"I don't think there are slave ships anymore. Anyway, there are certainly no slave ships that come to Bermuda. If a slave ship came into Bermuda, the captain would be hanged. That's the punishment."

Kit stood looking at the *Great Eastern.* Olivia worked up her courage to ask Kit a question, the answer to which she was quite certain of.

"Kit, you were a slave, weren't you?"

He turned to face her, and at first she thought he was angry. But instead of saying anything, he just nodded and then turned to look back at the ship.

"Where were you a slave?" Olivia asked. "It wasn't in New York, was it?"

"Nah, in 'Bama."

"'Bama?" Olivia thought for a second. "Oh, Alabama. You were a slave in Alabama?"

Kit nodded, still looking over the river toward the ship.

"How did you get to New York?"

This question was greeted by silence. After it became obvious Kit wasn't going to answer, Olivia said, "Kit, you're a runaway, aren't you?"

He turned to face her. He looked at her but said nothing. He then turned back to look at the river.

Olivia was silent for a moment and then asked, "Kit, why are you in England? How did you come here?"

"I come wit da man who help me, Capt'n Schultz. He ask me to come to help him."

"Help him do what?"

"I ain't sure. He ain't really tol' me yet."

"Are you going back to America?"

"Yeah, I think pretty soon."

"Kit, you know you're free here in England. You know that, don't you?"

Kit nodded.

"Why would you go back to slavery? You're free here; you'd be free in Bermuda. In America you'd be a runaway slave. If you got caught, you'd be chained, tortured, maybe killed! Kit, don't go back."

Kit had no response to this, so Olivia continued, "Captain Smithson will pay for you to go to Bermuda. He'll give you a job at Dockyards as a blacksmith. He told me that. He wants you to come to Bermuda. You'll be free and safe and can make your own living. You can start a whole new life."

Olivia decided to be quiet while Kit absorbed all this. Again he faced her, as if to say something, but he turned back, looking over the river. Finally, Olivia said, "I think it's time we should start heading back." It wasn't actually—it was still a little early. However, Olivia didn't know what else to say or do. Captain Smithson's offer was squarely before Kit, in the most forceful way Olivia could make it.

The couple started walking back toward the ferry landing. As they walked, Olivia said, "Stop for a moment, Kit. Give me your arm."

Kit had no idea what Olivia was talking about. Olivia put her hand on Kit's forearm and tried to raise it up. The muscles in his arm stiffened.

"Silly," she laughed. "I'm not going to bite you. We're going to walk like a proper lady and gentleman. Now, give me your arm." She took her two hands and raised his forearm. She was surprised at how thick his forearm was. Once his arm was at the right height, she rested her hand gently upon it.

"There," she said. "Now we look like a proper couple."

With Olivia's hand resting gently on his arm, Kit experienced feelings that were new to him. This beautiful young woman was favoring him with her hand, he thought. For the first time in his life, he felt truly free. And happy.

155

Mrs. Kendall's boardinghouse
New Brighton, England
September 8, 1861

The knocking sound slowly became incorporated into Mrs. Kendall's dream. She rolled over on her back and opened her eyes. A new burst of knocking brought her to full wakefulness. She sat up in bed and lit a candle. Another burst of knocking occurred. "I'll be right there," she called from her first-floor bedroom. After putting on a heavy dressing gown, the widow unlatched her bedroom door and walked into the inner and then outer parlors. The rooms were in total darkness except for the pinpoint of her candle flame. Reaching the front door, she called out, "Who's there?"

A male voice called out, "It's Captain Schultz, madam."

Mrs. Kendall unbolted the front door and thrust the candle into the opening. Schultz's tired face, made eerie by the shadows cast by the candle, returned her look. "It's just me, Mrs. Kendall. The train from London was very late."

Mrs. Kendall moved aside, and Schultz entered. He was accompanied by a younger man. After shutting and bolting the door, Schultz said, "Mrs. Kendall, this is Mr. Towle, a friend of mine. He needs to stay in Liverpool a couple of days, and since we're coming in so late, I said he could stay in my room if that is acceptable to you. Of course, we'll pay the extra charge."

"You don't need to share your room, Captain. I have an extra room available for Mr. Towle." Nodding at Towle, she said, "Please, sir, follow me." As she was leaving with the candle, the only light in the house, she turned to Schultz and said, "Captain, can you wait here until I return? There's something I need to tell you." Schultz agreed, and Mrs. Kendall disappeared into a dark hallway with Towle in tow.

When she returned after a few minutes, Mrs. Kendall had transformed herself from a tired old woman into the efficient and resourceful manageress of her boardinghouse. She placed her candle on the fireplace mantel. "Captain, while you were gone, a messenger delivered a packet for you. I was to turn it over to you as soon as I saw you." With this said, she handed a sealed envelope to Schultz. The envelope bore Schultz's name and nothing else. "If you wish to read it now, I'd be glad to light the oil lamp and then leave you alone."

"Mrs. Kendall, please light the lamp."

Mrs. Kendall took the glass chimney off the whale oil lamp and lit the wick with her candle. When she replaced the chimney, the room lit up. Schultz sat down heavily on a stuffed chair by the lamp. Mrs. Kendall said, "Captain Schultz, please extinguish the lamp when you're done. Good night." She then left with her candle.

After opening the envelope with a pen knife, Schultz found inside only a smaller sealed envelope addressed to Schultz care of the consulate. It had no return address. He opened the second envelope and pulled out a single sheet of stationery. As he unfolded the stationery, a small piece of paper fluttered out. He picked it up from his lap. It was a newspaper clipping.

The letter was short:

Phila August 23, 1861

> I have brief time to write that I hope this will find you safely arrived in the old world and in good health—Uncle Daniel was home Saturday afternoon. He only escaped arrest from me because I found him in my counting room at my desk. Had I seen him in the street I should have had him placed in custody but coming to me, I had to rise to the dignity of a savage & hold him an unwilling guest. It is enough to have one's mere acquaintances engaged in an assault that may not only rob him of his little all but destroy his own, and the lives of those closer still but when the folly and the crime are in his own household the act is past toleration or forgiveness.
>
> Affectionately yours,
> E. G. James

The letter's author was Eddie James, the orphaned son of another sister of Margaret. The letter was hastily scribbled and didn't make a great deal of sense. Schultz then picked up the newspaper clipping. Written by hand on the margin was "Aug. 27" and the words "Daily Tribune." Holding the lengthy article closer to the oil lamp, his hands trembling, Schultz read the first two paragraphs:

The Case of Mr. Lowber

> Mr. Daniel C. Lowber, who is suspected of taking out and bringing home dispatches for Jeff. Davis, was yesterday escorted by Mr. Police Superintendent Kennedy to Fort Lafayette. The capture of this man reflects great credit upon the detective service of the city. His departure for Europe became known to Mr. Kennedy, and his probable return was pretty accurately ascertained. Instead, however, of coming home in the Edinburgh, as he had apprised his friends, and as the police expected, he changed his course, took passage by the Bohemian, and landed at Quebec a week ago yesterday. Thence he came by Rouse's Point and Albany to Fishkill and Mattawean, reaching the residence of his brother-in-law, Alex. H. Schultz, esq., on the afternoon of Tuesday; but a few hours after Mr. Schultz had left for Boston, to take passage for Europe by the steamer, as bearer of Lord Lyon's dispatches, taken from Mr. Muir, which, under the circumstances, international etiquette required we should forward by special messenger.
>
> On Wednesday morning Mr. Lowber came to the city, where he remained for three hours, and returned to Fishkill. In the afternoon, as a friend was checking his trunk at the depot for Indianapolis, a dispatch was sent apprising that friend that there was danger ahead, and that Mr. Lowber, who intended to take the 7 o'clock up-train that night would do well to start earlier. The friend, leaving the trunk, dashed back to Mattawean, and speedily warning Lowber of his danger,

> got him into the wagon and drove off, ostensibly for Poughkeepsie, really for Dover Plains on the Harlem Road, but missing the road, brought him up at Pawling, where he took the late train for New-York.

Schultz was stunned. Lowber had implicated the whole Schultz family in a treasonous plot! As Schultz read the whole article, he found Lowber's "friend" mentioned again and again. He wondered who the "friend" in Fishkill might be, the person who had helped Lowber escape arrest. It then hit him—it was *Mary*, his own daughter! He knew Mary was fond of her uncle, but he'd never imagined that she would help him commit treason.

The *Daily Tribune* was the largest paper in the United States. Every business and political acquaintance that Schultz had must have read the article. As he sat in numbed silence, he considered the implications for his present mission. If the *Great Eastern* got through, Lowber, a braggart, would surely claim credit for it. If the United States were dismembered as a result of the lifting of the blockade, it would always be assumed that the Schultz family had been complicit in its downfall. Where could he and his family live? They'd be hated up North as traitors and despised down South as abolitionists.

His thoughts turned to Lowber. The last time they'd seen each other, Lowber had made no secret of his support for the rebellion. However, Schultz had put his comments down as mere argument, as Lowber was wont to make, and not a commitment to treason. He knew that his daughter Mary loved her uncle. He grew furious at the thought that a friend, an old friend, would involve the Schultz family in treason. If the article was true, Mary had helped a rebel spy try to escape.

Silence could only further the damage, Schultz thought. He needed to immediately declare his innocence to someone of importance. But to whom could he make his protest? Everyone important was in New York. It would be two weeks before his letter arrived. He then recalled that Fred Seward had mentioned that John Bigelow had been appointed United States consul in Paris. Bigelow, the retired publisher of a New York newspaper, was a longtime acquaintance of Schultz and a close friend of Governor Seward. Bigelow may have stayed in London a few days before traveling on to Paris, Schultz reasoned. It was worth a try.

Schultz moved the oil lamp to a small writing desk in the parlor and found a pen, ink, and some stationery that Mrs. Kendall provided for her boarders. Schultz began by stating that a letter from his adopted son had convinced him that Lowber had been arrested and that Lowber was not only a real secessionist but "in the interest of the Rebels." He continued, "Of course I could have not believed it—for I could not think he would compromise me in any way. He talked secession to me following the one half hour I saw him on his way to England but I ridiculed the idea and told him to stop his nonsense, as I wanted to talk about business."

Schultz went on to explain that he and Lowber were married to sisters, but in writing he needed to express the terrible sense of betrayal he was feeling. He had always been kind to Lowber, had enjoyed his company, had let his daughter spend summers with him and his wife. Schultz wrote, "It is strange. I admit how infatuated I have always been with him …" He added, "If I am to lose position and character it will indeed be ruinous." He sat quietly for a few moments reading his letter carefully. He couldn't think of anything else to say in his defense, so he sealed the letter and addressed it to Bigelow care of the American legation in London. The next day, he would deliver it to Wilding, who sent letters daily by train to London.

Schultz had been exhausted when he'd arrived at the boardinghouse. The letter from his adopted son and the enclosed article had brought him to an agitated state of wakefulness. However, there was nothing more that could be done. He turned down the wick on the lamp and stumbled to his room in total darkness.

156

United States legation
Portland Place
London, England
September 9, 1861

Schultz and Towle had arrived in London and roomed together in a small hotel near Portland Place in London. Deciding that sharing the bed would be uncomfortable in the heat, Towle had elected to sleep on the floor on some piled-up bedding and let the older man have the bed. Neither had slept well.

Early in the morning, Towle took the train to Liverpool. He had been fully informed by Schultz as to their situation during the ferry trip from Calais to Dover. Towle's job was to go directly to Liverpool to try to inspect the lifeboats of the *Great Eastern* before she was moved from her moorings. Schultz would briefly visit Adams in London as he'd promised and then take the train to Liverpool. The men agreed to meet later that afternoon at the American consulate in Liverpool.

After a quick breakfast, the two men parted. Schultz walked briskly to the offices of the American legation and found Benjamin Moran, the assistant secretary, dealing with a scruffy collection of men and women. When Schultz told Moran that he had to leave very shortly, the assistant secretary went into Adams's office and returned, asking Schultz to wait a few minutes.

After a few minutes turned into half an hour, Schultz said, "Mr. Moran, I have to leave very shortly. I have to catch a ship tomorrow from Liverpool, and I'm still not prepared for the voyage. Please tell Mr. Adams it's urgent he see me." Moran agreed and shortly returned, motioning Schultz to enter Adams's office.

"Mr. Adams, I have to leave very quickly. As you requested earlier, if you have any dispatches ready to go, I'll take them."

"Captain Schultz, I'm expecting momentarily some communication from Lord Russell regarding that diplomatic bag you brought here. Hopefully it will show up shortly, but if not, I would prefer you stay the night and then leave London tomorrow or perhaps a day later."

Schultz was momentarily flummoxed but recovered quickly. "Mr. Adams, I have some very important dispatches from Mr. Dayton, and he said that I have to get them to the United States as quickly as possible. I'm afraid I can't wait."

"Did Mr. Dayton give you copies of the dispatches for me?"

"No, sir, he did not."

Adams looked at Schultz with an imperious stare. "Surely, if the dispatches were so critically important, I would have been given a copy."

Schultz responded with as much politeness as he could muster, "Sir, I know nothing about that. All I know is that I'm leaving tomorrow on the *Great Eastern*. If I miss her, I'll not be able to leave for several days. I have given my personal assurances to Mr. Dayton to have these dispatches delivered to Governor Seward as quickly as possible."

"All right," Adams responded curtly. "I will draft a short note to

Secretary Seward and will give it to you in a few minutes." At this point, Adams waved his hand dismissively toward the door to his office, and Schultz stalked out. He sat in the anteroom to wait for the letter.

In his office, Adams was peeved. He was anxious to receive and send along the dispatches he expected to receive shortly from Lord Russell. If the dispatches from Dayton were so critical, Adams thought, he would have received copies of them or at least a summary. Schultz just wanted to return home early, Adams thought. These couriers always wanted the government to pay for their travel, but they never wanted to inconvenience themselves to assist the government. Nevertheless, Adams wrote a short letter to Seward. Toward the end of the letter he wrote:

> I had hoped to send something by Captain Schultz, who returns in the Great Eastern, and I shall yet do so if it should come before the bag closes. I have consented to the departure of Captain Schultz mainly because Mr. Dayton has expressed a great desire that he should take charge of his dispatches as soon as possible.

Adams gave the letter to Moran to copy so that Adams could retain the original. When Moran was done making his copy, Adams closed and sealed the copy and waited, hoping for the dispatches to arrive. Shortly, however, Moran came into the office.

"Mr. Adams, Captain Schultz said he's got to leave, with or without your letter. He's quite insistent he has no time left."

"Fine," snapped Adams. He handed the letter to Moran. "Give it to him and tell him to be on his way."

157

Tower Buildings
Liverpool, England
September 9, 1861

HAMILTON Towle sat in the anteroom of the American consulate, drawing sketches on a piece of paper. That morning he'd gone to the wharf from which passengers would board the *Great Eastern*. He'd joined a small group waiting to tour the giant ship and had been taken out to her by a skiff. On deck, Towle watched crew members and suppliers bringing food aboard. Live cattle and fowl were already on deck in a pen. Overall, Towle noted, the ship was messy and ill-prepared for a transatlantic trip. Schultz was right, Towle acknowledged. This trip had been put together at the last minute.

Continuing his tour of the ship, Towle meandered over the vast deck looking at random fixtures and devices so as to appear to be a mere sightseer. When he stood by the lifeboat hanging immediately in front of one of the paddle wheels, he looked around to see if anyone was interested in him. No one was. He looked carefully at the boat's davits, as well the ropes holding the boat. He looked at how the ropes had been tied to a cleat on the deck. There was nothing remarkable about the arrangement. It was just a larger version of the configuration commonly used on Cunard liners. Towle examined the two large threefold blocks that hung from each davit. The blocks would be used to lower the boat in the case of an accident at sea. He assumed that the ropes were attached to the lifeboat by iron shackles, but the lifeboat was hanging too high for Towle to see the shackles. Towle climbed a staircase to the top of the paddle box, where several other visitors stood, and from this vantage point he could look down into the lifeboat. He saw that the ropes terminated in a horseshoe-shaped shackle, the open part of which was closed with an iron pin. When a lifeboat was resting on water, the pin could be easily removed, releasing the boat from the shackle.

As he returned to the deck, Towle imagined various ways to unsling a hanging lifeboat without leaving evidence of sabotage. The most obvious way, he reasoned, was to remove or break the iron pin while the boat was still hanging. After the damage to the paddle wheel from the dangling boat was done, it would be assumed from an inspection of the remaining ropes hanging from the davit that the missing pin had accidently broken. Defective iron parts were not unheard of. There could be no proof that the unslinging of the boat was anything but an accident. As far as it went, Schultz's plan seemed feasible.

The problem, Towle understood, was removing or breaking the pin while the boat was still suspended. The boat was heavy, certainly over a ton, and the pin was locked into place by the boat's weight. Unless the boat was momentarily rendered weightless, the way it would be if it were afloat, it wouldn't be possible to remove the pin. To do this while the boat was still suspended, someone had to get into the boat while the *Great Eastern* was rolling from side to side and push the pin out of the shackle at the exact moment of weightlessness, the moment when the upward roll of the *Great Eastern* ended and its downward roll was just beginning. The pin was large. While the lifeboat was floating, a man could push it out. However, Towle didn't believe a man could push the pin out with his bare hands in the short time that a rolling ship rendered the lifeboat weightless. The easiest way would be to use an iron pry bar to break the pin. The difficulty was that the bar would have to be large, perhaps five feet long. How could such a tool be brought on board without notice?

The captain of the skiff called out, and the sightseers, including Towle, returned to the small boat. The skiff landed back at the pier, and the passengers disbursed.

Towle walked briskly to the Tower Buildings, to sketch out his plans and to wait for Schultz. Wilding was talking to a young woman when Towle arrived, and when the woman left, Wilding turned to Towle.

"Mr. Towle," Wilding said, "I'm going to make tea. Would you care for some?"

"No, no thank you," the engineer answered. "Do you know the time?"

Wilding stepped into his office and looked at the tall case clock. "It's nearly three o'clock."

The Great Eastern *leaves in less than twenty hours,* Towle thought. *Where in the devil is Schultz?* Towle concentrated on the task at hand as he started sketching the shackle from various angles, trying to figure out what sort of tool would work. Within moments, a red-faced Schultz burst into the anteroom.

"Captain, are you all right?" asked Wilding.

Schultz nodded. "We're just running a little late, and I had to hurry. If I sit down for a minute, I'll be fine."

After unsuccessfully offering Schultz a cup of tea, Wilding retreated to his office, leaving his two guests in the anteroom. Towle moved a chair close to where Schultz was sitting to show him his sketches. Just as he was doing so, Wilding reentered the room, surprising both Towle and Schultz. Sensing that something might be afoot, Wilding said merely, "Gentlemen, I have an errand to run. Would you be good enough to watch the consulate for half an hour or so?"

"Of course," said Towle. With a nod, Wilding put on his hat and left the two men alone.

158

Rodgers's blacksmith shop
Liverpool, England
September 9, 1861

It was nearly four thirty when Schultz arrived at Rodgers's shop. Towle had gone on to purchase two first-class tickets on the *Great Eastern* and a large steamer trunk. The two men had arranged to meet later at Schultz's boardinghouse.

"Mr. Rodgers, I'm back," Schultz called out. The smith looked up from an anvil where he had been hammering an iron rod.

"Aye," Rodgers said. He placed the rod into a bucket of water and walked over to Schultz. "I wondered when you'd be back."

"Well, sir, we're leaving tomorrow, and so I'll need to take Kit with me."

"Aye. I'm gonna miss the boy. Hard worker, he is. Ain't much for talkin', which I 'appens ta like."

Kit had been standing by the forge, watching the two men. He approached Schultz. "Hello, Capt'n," he said.

"Hello, Kit. You heard that we're leaving tomorrow?"

"Yeah, Capt'n."

"Mr. Rodgers, I'd like to talk to Kit for a few minutes about the trip tomorrow. Is he in the middle of something?"

"Nay, we're done for the day. I jest gotta clean up."

Schultz led Kit into daylight by the shop door. "Kit, I want your advice on something. We have a shackle that needs to be opened. It's … ah … jammed, and we want to open it without damaging it." At this point, Schultz pulled out Towle's drawings. In the first drawing, the shackle looked like an upside-down horseshoe with a bar closing the open section of the shoe. The second drawing was a profile, showing the bar to be a round pin. Kit studied the drawings.

"We're thinking about something that could break the pin without damaging the shackle," Schultz said.

"How's da pin held in?" Kit asked. "Did they use a shim?"

Schultz shook his head. "No, it's held in by the weight of the object it's holding. There's no lock or shim."

"How big's da pin?"

Schultz held his hands about ten inches apart. *Dat's a big shackle*, Kit thought.

"How big 'round?"

Schultz made a circle with his thumb and forefinger. The pin was about three inches thick.

"Capt'n, da ain't no way ta cut dat witout an anvil." Kit shook his head as he looked at the drawing. "Is da pin rusted? Is dat da problem?"

"No, I don't believe it's rusted. It's just held in by weight."

As Kit studied the drawings, he made a low whistling sound. He then walked away and talked briefly to Rodgers. Schultz couldn't hear the conversation. Kit then walked over to a large wooden toolbox and returned to Schultz, holding a large iron hammer and a steel punch.

"Capt'n, I done dis before wit a hammer and punch. Just put the punch on da side of da pin, give a couple of ha'd whacks, and pretty soon we got it free. It don't harm da shackle."

Schultz considered Kit's recommendation. It made sense, and the hammer and punch would be easy to conceal. There didn't seem to be any alternative.

"Can we buy these from Rodgers?" Schultz asked. Kit shrugged and moved so that Schultz could approach Rodgers directly. The two men talked, Schultz handed the blacksmith the agreed-upon amount, and the deal was done. Kit gathered up his meager belongings and then walked over to Rodgers. The blacksmith held out his hand, and the two men shook hands. With that, Kit and Schultz headed for the ferry landing.

The two men walked in silence, side by side, through the streets of Liverpool. Someone would occasionally glance at Kit, but mostly they were ignored. They crossed the Mersey on the steam ferry, and when they arrived on the other side, they began walking to New Brighton. Daylight was just turning into twilight when Schultz stopped walking. He looked around to see if anyone was near. The walkway was deserted.

"Kit, it's time to tell you why I brought you here," Schultz said as the young man stopped and turned to face him. "You know that there's a war at home, a war between the Northern and Southern states?"

Kit nodded. The fighting had been a frequent topic of conversation at Baxtertown. There was no agreement as to what the war meant to the fugitive slaves, but there was plenty of discussion about the topic.

Schultz continued, "The Southern states attacked because they want to spread slavery across the country, and the Northern states fought back because they want to get rid of slavery altogether." Schultz knew the statement was an exaggeration, but it was one that he felt necessary under the circumstances. "The South is not as big or powerful as the North, and the longer the war goes on, the more likely the North will win. The Northern states have declared a blockade of the Southern ports, to stop ships carrying cotton from leaving and to stop the Southern states from getting cannon and guns shipped in from England. You've heard of the blockade?"

Kit nodded. He had heard of the blockade while working at the blacksmith's shop in Newburgh.

"The only hope the Southern states have is to break the blockade, and the only power that can do that is England. The English government is waiting for an opportunity to send in its navy to open up the Southern ports. If that happens, Kit, the war is over. The South will have won, and slavery will continue forever in the Southern states."

Kit nodded to show that he understood what Schultz was saying. He asked, "Why would dey do dat? Da's no slaves in England. Why dey help da South?"

"Money, Kit. Money, pure and simple. England wants the South's cotton, and the South won't or can't sell cotton to England as long as the blockade's in effect. Most people in England hate slavery, but the rich men, the ones that control the government, love money more than they hate slavery."

That was believable. Kit knew that people could do terrible things for money.

Satisfied that Kit understood, Schultz said, "Kit, we've learned that the South is going to have a big ship from England break the blockade. If this ship gets into a Southern port, England's navy will lift the blockade, and the war will be over. I've been sent by Governor Seward to stop this ship, and I need your help. That's why I brought you to England."

"Wha' you wan' me ta do?"

"We're going to get you on the ship, and when she's underway, I'll help you into a lifeboat. You'll knock the pin out of the lifeboat's shackle, the boat will drop down into the paddle wheel, and that'll stop the ship. The ship will have to go back to England for repairs, and then I can go back to the United States and warn our blockaders." Schultz paused for a moment and looked at Kit. "We'll have a rope tied around you and will haul you back on deck."

Kit stood silently as he considered this. It sounded incredibly dangerous, rope or not. Finally, he said, "Capt'n Schultz, I's got an offa from an English navy capt'n ta go ta Ba'muda. I's gonna work dere as a blacksmith. I won't be slave dere, just a blacksmith. Maybe have a family."

Schultz started to panic. He'd never anticipated Kit having an option.

Kit continued, "Capt'n, I ain't a slave he'. I ain't a slave in Ba'muda. But I gits to America, I's a slave again, just a runaway slave."

"Kit, the ship will never reach America. When we disable it, it'll have to come back to England. When we reach England, I'll give you the money to go to Bermuda, if that's what you want. But I need your help now. If we don't stop the ship, the North will lose. All the slaves you know, the ones you lived with, they'll remain slaves their entire lives. Their children will be slaves as well."

"What happens if I stop da ship?" Kit asked. "Will da slaves be free?"

Schultz nodded. "Yes, Kit, they'll be free. Not immediately, but in months, as the South collapses."

Kit took a step away from Schultz and turned away to look out over the river. He wanted to consider everything he had just heard. Schultz stood quietly, looking at the young man. Kit finally turned back to the older man.

"What ship is dis?"

"The one moored in the river." Schultz nodded in the direction of the ship's mooring. "The *Great Eastern*."

Kit looked at the ship and then turned to Schultz to make certain he understood correctly. He did. Staring at the ship, Kit took several steps toward her, stepping off the roadway and jumping across some large rocks. He stopped on the highest rock and stared at the ship. Although evening was coming, Kit could see every detail of her perfectly. The wind had died down, and the only noise was the screeching of gulls. She was tugging silently at her moorings as the tide went out.

Kit now understood everything—the fireball, the blood running down the side of the ship, Reeba's warnings, everything. The *Great Eastern was* a slave ship, and the blood was the blood of slaves! It was the blood of his mother and sister, of Danny and Ben, of dozens of slaves Kit had known who were doomed to die in slavery. He now knew it was no accident that he had been delivered to Captain Schultz or that he had been lying on the deck of the *Ella* when the fireball went over. Olivia had called the ship "ugly," and she was ugly—not ugly for her massive blackness, but ugly for representing all the death and whippings and brandings, all the broken lives, all the children ripped from the arms of their mothers. Looking at her lying placidly on the river, he was overcome with rage as faces and events raced through his mind. Finally, he remembered the David-and-Goliath story he had heard in church in Mobile, how David had killed the giant. The *Great Eastern* was his Goliath.

Schultz watched the young man from the roadway. From an angle he could see Kit's lips moving silently. Kit was saying something, Schultz thought, but what? Kit's hands were clenched into fists, and when he finally turned around, Schultz was startled by his face. It was filled with hatred and rage, and Schultz at first thought the emotions were directed at him. Then Kit said quietly and calmly, "Tell me how ta do it."

Schultz swallowed. The thought of being attacked by this powerful young man had frightened him. Now, Kit was on his side.

"Come with me, Kit. I'm going to introduce you to another man who's going to help us. Together, we'll make our plans."

The two men walked silently, side by side, into New Brighton, toward Schultz's boardinghouse.

159

London, England
September 9, 1861

ALL day, Dudley Mann assiduously avoided contact with anyone involved with the war in America. He was so excited and apprehensive about the *Great Eastern*'s departure the next day that he was concerned he might say something revelatory. Everything had proceeded so far because of absolute secrecy, and he was not ready to change. He thought of going to

Liverpool to see the ship off but decided that since he had no ostensible reason to do so, questions might be raised about his presence. Instead, he wandered about London, peering into shop windows and eating a light supper at a public house. It was evening when he walked back to his hotel.

When he entered his hotel's lobby, he saw a neatly folded newspaper sitting on an empty chair. A response from the desk clerk confirmed that both the chair and newspaper were free for the taking, and Mann sat down and began reading the *Times of London*. He was pleased to find that it was that day's newspaper.

He quickly turned to the news of America. The *Persia* had arrived in Liverpool the previous day, with news dated August 28 from New York. The *Times* quoted an article from the *New York Tribune* that stated, "Mr. Adams, Minister at St. James's, writes that in the British mind the independence of the rebels is fully admitted as a military and political necessity; that the acknowledgement by England is but a question of time and prudent courtesy."

Mann nodded his head approvingly. All that was needed, Mann knew, was the lifting of the blockade. That would happen shortly, certainly within weeks of the blockade being broken. His years of efforts were close to finally paying off. He continued reading down the column of news from the United States and read the following: "Mr. D.C. Lowber, of New Orleans, a bearer of dispatches from President Davis, had been arrested on his way to embark for England."

After regaining his breath, Mann searched through the rest of the newspaper to see if there was any additional information on Lowber's arrest. Had the dispatches that Lowber had been carrying been seized? Why did it say Lowber was heading to England when he'd been returning from England? Had he lied? After frantically scouring the paper, Mann was convinced that there was no additional information.

What should I do? Mann thought. He could feel sweat on the back of his collar. If Lowber had destroyed the dispatches, the mission was safe. If the dispatches had been seized, however ... *Dear Lord,* Mann thought. *The entire blockading fleet would be waiting for her outside Port Royal.* Mann's mind raced over the possibilities. Captain Walker's instructions were not to run the blockade if it meant taking fire from the blockading squadron, but Mann knew the man was desperate for money. He may well try to ram any blockading ship that attempted to bar his way. If Walker was determined to get in, it would be nearly impossible to stop her.

Mann finally decided that he had to try to stop the *Great Eastern* or at least make Walker take her to New York. He couldn't take the risk of British civilians getting caught in America's war. He knew that if civilians died in furtherance of a Southern plot, it would destroy any chance of England recognizing the Confederacy. But how to tell Walker? He couldn't send a telegram that made any sense without the telegraph operators becoming aware of the plot. He'd have to go to Liverpool himself, to see if he could get a message to Walker. He looked at his watch. He had missed the evening mail train to Liverpool. The following morning, he'd take the earliest train. With a little luck, he'd be able to make it in time.

Shivering with anxiety, Mann went up to his room to wait for the morning. There was nothing else to do.

160

Bremford Hotel
Liverpool, England
September 9, 1861

"THERE! I've finished the letter, and now I'm sealing it," Captain Smithson announced to his wife as he glued a paper wafer onto an envelope.

"What letter?" his wife, Lydia, asked.

"It's a letter to Mr. Wolfe, a solicitor in Liverpool. It gives him instructions about sending Kit to Bermuda. I'm going to have Olivia deliver it to Kit tomorrow. When Kit's ready to leave, he can take the letter to Mr. Wolfe, who will arrange passage for my new blacksmith. I haven't talked to Olivia, but I'm sure you've praised her for her excellent work."

"Indeed, she and I had quite a chat. She's quite taken with this Kit, says he's a perfect gentleman and that he's quiet and listens carefully. My little companion did a wonderful job of convincing your Kit to come to Bermuda. See! I was correct. Her dress was worth every penny."

"Well, yes, I just have to figure out how to get the Admiralty to reimburse me for it. But the important thing is that Olivia was successful. I was confident she would be. By the way, where is she?"

"She's asleep. I saw her yawning and asked her if she was tired. She said she slept badly last night. I think it's the excitement over Kit. For a colored boy, he's quite handsome."

"Yes, well, you two can work on your female designs on him once he's safely in Bermuda. Whether my new blacksmith is a bachelor or a bigamist is no concern of mine, so long as he can repair ironwork."

"So you say, Middie," said Lydia. "I think you're a bit of a matchmaker yourself. You're very fond of Olivia, and this Kit is showing a lot of promise."

Smithson sighed audibly. "Yes, dear, whatever *you* say. However, tomorrow morning I'll send Olivia over to the blacksmith's shop to give this letter to Kit and explain it to him. We should have an early breakfast."

"Duly noted, Captain Smithson," Lydia said, giving her husband a salute. "In the meantime, since there's so much romance in the air, perhaps we should retire." She smiled. "We have so little time alone."

Smithson was going to say something and then stopped. He extended his hand to his wife, and she led him into the bedroom.

161

New Brighton, England
September 9, 1861

SCHULTZ was standing at a corner near his boardinghouse when Towle walked up. There was a cold breeze coming up the Mersey from the ocean, and the last pink tints from what had been a beautiful sunset were fading. With the breeze, the two men had to stand close to each other to talk. There was no chance of their being overheard.

"Is Kit down?" asked Towle.

"I don't know whether he's sleeping," Schultz said. "He's in the stable loft. He should be comfortable enough to sleep tonight."

"That's more than I can say for myself," Towle said.

After standing in silence for a few moments, Towle again spoke. "Nothing's changed? We're committed to this?"

Schultz shook his head. "Nothing's changed. You have every bit of information that I have."

"What happens if we're not successful?" Towle asked.

"We'll be successful," Schultz said. "If we're not, the war is over—our country, as we know it, will no longer exist." Towle stood silently, listening. "Hamilton," Schultz continued, "our soldiers, many of them mere boys, are walking into cannon and musket fire in Virginia. If wounded, they're bayoneted to death. If they can take those kind of risks, we can take the risks we need to as well. Let's go over our plans."

Towle nodded. "I bought the trunk and cut small air holes near the seams for Kit. The trunk will be marked with your name. Kit will carry the hammer in the trunk. I've got the punch in my valise. The trunk will be locked. We need to stuff some clothing in it so Kit doesn't bang from side to side when it's being handled by the stevedores."

"All right," Schultz said. "We'll board separately. If Kit is detected, I'll be implicated by the trunk, but you won't. You'll still have the opportunity to cut the lifeboat loose, although it'll be an obvious act of sabotage. We must try to avoid that at all possible."

"Is Kit committed?" asked Towle. "Does he understand what he's being asked to do?"

"He's with us," Schultz said. "He knows what he's going to do."

"Captain, you know he has little chance of surviving. When the pin is knocked out, the end of the lifeboat will plunge, and it will start slamming against the side of the ship. Even if we pull him up right away, there's a good chance he'll be crushed to death. That thing weighs well over a ton."

Schultz exhaled quietly. "I know that. If he's killed, we drop his body into the ocean. We'll have to hope we can haul him on board before the boat starts swinging."

"How long have you known him?"

"He was delivered to me as a stowaway over two years ago."

"Why's he willing to go along with us?" Towle asked.

"He's an extraordinary young man," Schultz said. "He was sold from his mother when he was a small child, and he never saw her again. She killed herself when her owner sold her youngest child, his sister. He hates slavery, and for plenty of reason."

"And he thinks stopping the *Great Eastern* will end slavery?" Towle asked.

"I *told* him stopping her would help end slavery," Schultz responded sharply. "It will. Unless England recognizes the South and raises the blockade, the South will lose. She'll be choked to death by the North, and the price she'll pay for rebellion will be the freeing of her slaves." Schultz looked at Towle in the dim light thrown from a whale oil light in a house window. "Don't doubt that," he said.

"I hope you're right, Captain," Towle said. "You don't hate slavery any more than I do."

Schultz acknowledged Towle's statement with a nod. "Let's go back," Schultz said. "We need to get some rest."

"Agreed," Towle said as the two men headed slowly to their boardinghouse.

162

Rodgers's blacksmith shop
Liverpool, England
September 10, 1861

All morning Olivia had bumbled around the Smithsons' flat. The envelope that Captain Smithson had sealed the previous night rested on a small table in the parlor, and Mrs. Smithson had told Olivia that morning that she was to deliver it to Kit after breakfast. Olivia quickly went about her chores, laying out her mistress's dress and undergarments. As Olivia was brushing Lydia's long, chestnut-colored hair, the two women talked.

"Are you looking forward to seeing Kit again?" Lydia asked.

"I think so, ma'am."

"I thought him very good-looking. Don't you think so?" Lydia asked, deciding to have a little good-natured fun with her companion.

"Oh, I don't know. He seemed all right."

"You know, when the captain first saw him in the blacksmith shop, he didn't have a shirt on but just a leather apron. Remember how I told you that the captain said he had muscles like a miniature Zeus. Do you think so?"

Olivia audibly gulped. "Well," she said hoarsely, "he had his shirt on, but his arm was very strong."

"Oh, how did you know that?"

"Well, ma'am," Olivia said, "when we were walking, I made him put his arm up, like a gentleman, so that I could rest my hand on it.

Remember, ma'am, the captain wanted me to talk him into coming to Bermuda, and, well, I thought he'd think Bermuda was more wonderful if all the women were ladies and all the men gentlemen, even blacksmiths."

Lydia nodded. "That's good thinking. It seems to have worked."

Olivia continued, "When I put my hand on his arm, it was like putting it on, oh, I don't know, a thick piece of wood, like a log. He must be very powerful."

"Well, blacksmiths are very strong. Usually they have these great bellies, however. Kit is the first one I've seen with a trim waist."

Olivia was getting excited and nervous just talking about Kit. Lydia could see in the dresser mirror the agitation in her companion's face. She decided to stop teasing.

"Olivia, take things slowly. Men who look promising are often great disappointments. Trust me, I know, but I won't say how. Kit may be wonderful, or he may be a complete rascal. It's far too early to say. But I'm pleased you've persuaded him to come to Bermuda. When he's there, your mother and I can examine him more closely to see what he's about."

"Yes, ma'am," Olivia said solemnly as she finished the brushing.

The captain was reading in a chair in the parlor when the two women came into the room. They exchanged their good-morning greetings. The captain walked over to the small table and picked up the envelope.

"Olivia," he said, "you remember the directions to the blacksmith's shop?"

"Yes, sir."

"Good. This envelope is for Kit. Now, I'm not certain he can read, but the outside of the envelope has the name and address of my solicitor. Kit's to take the envelope to the solicitor, and the solicitor will arrange for Kit's passage to Bermuda on the earliest ship. Do you have any questions?"

"No, sir."

"Excellent. Then, you get one more glance in the mirror, and off you go!" he said with a smile.

Olivia picked up her straw hat and faced the parlor mirror. She carefully pinned it into her hair. When the hat was just right, she arranged her collar with the small cameo in the center.

"Just a minute," said Lydia. She walked into her room and returned with a small jar. Olivia knew the jar. It was a lotion containing finely crushed pearl, and Mrs. Smithson used it only on the most important occasions.

"Face me, darling," said Mrs. Smithson. She carefully rubbed a little pearl dust onto each of her companion's cheeks. The effect was striking, making Olivia's cheeks seem to glow. "There, young lady, you are truly beautiful. Poor Kit won't know what happened to him."

"My God, you women," muttered the captain. "Why don't we just buy an animal trap, capture him, and be done with it?"

"Hush, you," said his wife. "You want him in Bermuda? Well, then let us do what needs to be done. Olivia, you look perfect. Now, here's the envelope. We'll wait your return."

The young woman walked briskly from the hotel down streets full of a variety of characters, more than a few disreputable looking. With her starched white blouse and dark-blue skirt highlighting her trim figure, she caught the envious eyes of several women. Normally, she would have been bothered by these looks, but today she was unaware of them.

In about a quarter hour, she arrived at the blacksmith's shop. Her heart was pounding. She could hear a hammer banging on an anvil inside. As she looked in, she saw Rodgers bashing an iron rod. She looked around the shop but couldn't see Kit.

"Mr. Rodgers," she called out during a moment of silence.

The blacksmith looked up and peered at his guest. As he walked toward her, he wondered who she might be.

"Mr. Rodgers, is Kit here?"

Now he knew. "You the componion of the capt'n's wife? The one that went wit Kit on Sunday?"

"Yes, sir. I'm Olivia Burrows. Is Kit here?"

The blacksmith immediately realized things were not going to go well. "Well, missy, ya see, he ain't here."

"I can wait. When will he be back?"

The blacksmith hung his head and shook it slightly. "Missy, he ain't coming back."

Puzzled, Olivia asked, "Well, sir, where is he?"

"I ain't cert'n, missy, but I think he's going back to America."

Olivia stood thunderstruck. *This can't be true*, she thought.

"What makes you think he's going back to America?" she implored.

"The man he come wit, the captain, he come back and took Kit wit him. They ain't coming back here, not so far as I know. The captain, he thanked me, and I said goodbye to the boy. He was a good 'un."

"Are they leaving today? Do you know, Mr. Rodgers?"

"I don't know."

Olivia stood in the doorway with tears starting to run down her pearl-dusted cheeks. Finally, she asked, "Are there any ships heading to America today?"

"Well, I know the *Great Eastern* leaves today, 'cause there's some folks gonna watch her leave. Other than that, I don't know."

Olivia's mind was racing. The *Great Eastern*! That was the ship that Kit had made the odd comment about, the comment about believing in signs. What had he been trying to tell her?

"Do you know where's she leaving from?"

"I don't know. She's got to be by one of the wharfs close to her mooring, I'd venture. But, missy, I don't know for certain."

Olivia looked up and down the street as she calculated which way to run. Finally she took off in the direction that would lead her to the ship's mooring. The blacksmith saw the devastation on the young woman's face and felt terrible about giving her the news. He stepped out in the street and called, "Missy!"

Olivia stopped and looked back. The smith was embarrassed that he had called for her. He simply yelled out, "Good luck." She nodded and returned to her run.

As Olivia ran toward the river, she heard a loud steam whistle followed by two shorter ones. She continued running in the direction of the whistle until she came to an area where she could come close to the riverbank. On her right, where the Mersey started opening to the Atlantic Ocean, she saw the giant ship. It was billowing black smoke from all five stacks, and its paddle wheels were turning slowly. As she watched, the river at the stern of the ship exploded into foam as the screw started. At this, cheering rose from the crowds of people standing on the banks watching the *Great Eastern* leaving.

Olivia stood breathing heavily. There was no purpose in running any farther. If Kit was aboard the ship, he was lost to her. She started to sob, and as she went to wipe her eyes, she remembered she still had the letter for Kit in her hand. As the young woman stood sobbing in the street, she drew stares from passersby and a few sympathetic glances.

Further down the bank, a middle-aged man stood with a stricken look on his face. While waiting at daybreak for the train to Liverpool, Dudley Mann had known that he had but a slim chance to reach Captain Walker with news of Lowber's arrest. The late arrival of his train in Liverpool had eliminated that chance. Now, for good for evil, the great ship was on its way. Mann pulled back and stood against a building, silently praying. He ended his prayer by saying softly to himself, "Her voyage is now in God's hands."

Part VI

September 10, 1861
to
September 12, 1861

Upon earth there is not his like, who is made without fear. He beholdeth all high things:

He is a king over all the children of pride.

—Job 41:33–34 (KJV)

163

Liverpool, England
September 10, 1861

THE loading of the *Great Eastern* was chaotic. The ship had been scheduled to leave at noontime, but the small number of stevedores, combined with confusion over arrangements having been made by two different brokers, forced a delay. Towle and Schultz had earlier agreed to board the ship separately. Towle boarded a tender first, taking only hand luggage. As Towle watched from the deck of his tender, Schultz waited on a wharf for another tender to arrive to take him and his luggage to the *Great Eastern*. Standing next to Schultz was a stevedore holding a handcart on which a large steamer trunk was strapped. Boarding on a separate tender were a cattle and pigs and a number of fowl, including a large swan. The animals would be slaughtered during the voyage to provide fresh meat for the ship's complement.

As his tender approached the *Great Eastern*, Towle saw hull markings showing her depth. She was drawing only twenty-three feet. She would be even lighter when she arrived in a Confederate port because she would have burned off many tons of coal during the voyage. When she arrived, she would be drawing such a shallow draft that she could enter Port Royal and perhaps one other Southern port. Towle agreed with Schultz. It made no sense for her to travel to New York with such a light load.

The *Great Eastern* started her voyage after one o'clock under the guidance of a pilot. The weather was excellent—brisk and clear with a slight breeze. The day before word had passed quickly through Liverpool that the *Leviathan* was leaving, and crowds had gathered on either side of the Mersey to watch her departure. To the sound of cheering, she sounded her steam whistle and began to travel down the river by means of her paddle wheels. Once the pilot was satisfied that she was safely within the channel, he ordered that the screw be engaged as well. The passengers aboard the ship stood on her deck, some at her railings, some on top of the paddle boxes, and waved to the crowd.

At four o'clock in the afternoon the ship stopped at Bell Buoy. The pilot, accompanied by Liverpool's mayor, a few of the ship's directors, various emigration officers, and other dignitaries, left her to board a tender to return to Liverpool. With the Irish Sea in front of him, Captain James Walker now assumed control of the ship and began the voyage. Speed was increased, and she proceeded westerly toward Holyhead. She shortly came upon and passed the incoming *Persia*, the large Cunard liner that she had almost rammed in the fog outside Quebec's harbor a few months earlier. When passing, the *Great Eastern* dipped her flag and fired two guns, a salute that was returned by the *Persia*.

164

Leeds Mercury
September 12, 1861

The Great Eastern left the Mersey on Tuesday for New York. The prospects of profit seem to be poor, for the number of passengers was under 300, and the cargo small.

165

On board the *Great Eastern*
September 11, 1861

The *Great Eastern* made good time, and by noon of her second day, she was close to Kinsale, a town located at the southern coast of Ireland. She had traveled over three hundred miles at a steady fifteen knots per hour. As she was rounding Ireland, her passengers caught sight of the steamship *Underwriter*, a 170-foot packet from New York, and noted that the smaller ship was pitching heavily, while the rolling motion aboard the *Great Eastern* was hardly perceptible. One passenger noted:

> Our deck was like a sea-side esplanade on a holiday; ladies and gentlemen promenading, sitting chatting, reading, and laughing; children playing hide and seek around the deck, and even playing ball in one of the holds! On board any other ship afloat, nine-tenths of these women and children and two-thirds of the men would have been in the agony of sea-sickness.

While the passengers praised the seaworthiness of the ship, they unanimously and loudly condemned its accommodations. Food was badly prepared, attendants were both scarce and churlish, the ship was cluttered and dirty, and there was an obvious lack of both preparation and organization. For most of these passengers, the decision to travel aboard the *Great Eastern* had been made mere hours before her departure in order to capture a once-in-a-lifetime opportunity to cross the Atlantic on the greatest ship ever made.

The next morning broke cloudy, and within two hours a cold drizzle started falling. Around noontime, long swells generated by a distant storm began to appear. A half hour or so later, a second set of swells from yet another distant storm appeared, intercepting the first at an oblique angle, creating a "cross sea." Under these conditions, the great ship began to roll slowly from side to side. Captain Walker ordered relieving tackles attached to the ship's giant rudder as a protective measure. At about one o'clock in the afternoon, a gale came up with wind and heavy rain. Thick, squally clouds darkened the sky. Passengers fled the deck, and the few crewmen required to be on deck took what shelter they could find.

Inside his cabin, Schultz could feel the rolling motion. He looked at Kit, who sat silently on the floor in a corner of the cabin, his head hanging down between his knees. It had been an uncomfortable two days for the two men. Schultz had made trips to the dining hall and on each trip brought food back on a plate and offered it to Kit. The young man had eaten well enough at first but had eaten little or nothing of his latest meals. At night Schultz tossed and turned on his berth, and Kit lay on the floor resting on Schultz's coat. Neither man slept well.

As the rolling became more pronounced, Schultz got down on one knee to get close to Kit's face so he could speak quietly.

"Kit, the ship's rolling. I think it's time."

Kit raised his head and silently nodded.

Schultz continued, "I'm going to talk to Towle. I should be back shortly. I'm going to lock the cabin door, so don't do anything if someone knocks on the door or asks you to open the door. Instead, crawl under my berth with your tools and don't make a sound." Kit again nodded, and Schultz left, locking the door behind him.

When Schultz opened the cabin door and looked into the dim hallway, he saw no one. Most of the cabins were empty. Those cabins that were occupied were likely inhabited by seasick tenants doubled over on their berths. When he came to Towle's cabin, Schultz knocked and announced himself in a loud whisper. Towle answered the door, ghostly white with a napkin at his mouth.

"Seasickness?" Schultz asked.

Towle nodded and sat down on his berth.

"It's time, Hamilton," Schultz said. "The weather's bad, and I'm quite certain no one's on deck except at the helm. I'm going to need your help." After a nod from Towle, Schultz continued, "I need to get you on deck so that Kit and I can come up without being seen. You can do that?"

Towle nodded, pushing his hand across his forehead to wipe off beads of sweat.

"I'll be back with Kit in a few moments."

Before Schultz left, Towle asked, "Captain, is the boy committed to this?"

Schultz nodded.

"Did he talk about it?"

"No," said Schultz. "We didn't talk at all except for a few questions Kit had about Bermuda."

"Bermuda!" Towle responded in a loud whisper. "What did he want to know about Bermuda?"

"He wanted to know how big it was, how hard it would be to find someone there." When Towle looked puzzled, Schultz continued, "He said when this is over, he's going to Bermuda, as I promised him he could, and he's going to look for someone, a young girl I'm pretty certain."

Towle's face became pained. He appeared as if he was going to speak but then said nothing. He covered his mouth with the napkin and shook his head slowly.

Schultz was silent for a moment also and then said, "I'll have a rope tied around his chest and legs. With his help I can get him up quickly. Hamilton, we can't do anything more than that." Not waiting for a response, Schultz left the cabin.

Ten minutes later, there was a knock at Towle's cabin door. When Towle asked who was there, Schultz answered softly. Towle opened the door and saw Kit dressed in Schultz's jacket with the collar turned up and wearing Schultz's cap. The two men stepped into Towle's cabin, and Kit pulled a length of rope from underneath his coat. The rope was tied around Kit's legs just below his groin and then went up and encircled his chest. Schultz grabbed the rope to show how securely it was tied. "It's a bowline on a bight," he said. "We use it when a man goes overboard to inspect a hull. Now, Hamilton, go on deck and tell me what you see. I'll finish getting Kit ready."

Towle, steeling himself against the seasickness inflicting him, climbed the stairs at the end of the hallway to the deck. The wind was howling, hurling the heavy rain into the face of anyone who might approach from the stern. As far as Towle could see, the deck was deserted. The stanchion where the starboard lifeboat was hanging was next to a large wooden pen holding a number of squealing pigs. Towle could feel the *Great Eastern* rolling more strongly than before. Trying to control his nausea, Towle slowly and carefully climbed down the wet stairs and returned to his cabin.

"There's nobody out," Towle said to Schultz when he got back to his cabin.

Schultz nodded and said, "Hamilton, you go up first in case someone is passing by. We'll follow."

Schultz and Kit followed Towle partially up the staircase but stopped about halfway up. After reaching the deck and looking around again, Towle took a couple of steps down the stairs and nodded to the two men. "It's clear," he said. Schultz and Kit climbed the stairs and crouched behind the pigpen. Schultz untied the gripe line which checked the swaying of the lifeboat. He then watched the swinging lifeboat for a few moments to get a sense of the timing of its swings. At a point during the *Great Eastern*'s roll to the starboard, the boat came within a couple of feet of the steamship's railing. Schultz brought Kit next to him and held him, waiting for another roll. Finally, with Schultz's help, Kit climbed on the railing, and when the lifeboat swung close, Kit leaped into the open boat.

Schultz then pulled out the hammer and punch he had purchased from the blacksmith in Liverpool. When the lifeboat swung near the railing, he tossed the hammer into it. He did the same with the punch on the next swing of the boat. Kit picked up both tools and then hunkered at the bottom of the boat. Schultz had previously loosely tied the rope attached to Kit to his own waist. Now that Kit was in the boat with the tools, Schultz untied the rope and tied it near the base of one of the railing's stanchions. He made certain that the knot was tied in such a way it could be used as a slipknot.

Kit remained in the bottom of the boat, feeling the short-lived weightlessness resulting when the boat first started its downward roll. A number of rolls went by before Kit felt he could predict the time when the boat became weightless. Finally, he moved to a seat underneath the buckle holding the bow of the boat. He looked at Schultz for confirmation, and Schultz nodded. On the next roll, just before he felt the weightlessness, he placed the punch on the pin closing the bottom of the buckle. When weightlessness hit, he hammered the punch. The pin moved perhaps an inch but still remained in the buckle. At the next roll, he hit the pin again, and it moved another half inch or so. During the next roll, as Schultz looked on apprehensively, Kit stood and hit the pin with all his strength. The pin popped out of one side of the buckle but dangled out of the remaining side. Kit was looking at the buckle trying to figure out what next to do when suddenly the part of the buckle still holding the remainder of the pin broke under the strain of the increased weight, and the bow of the lifeboat plunged downward. Kit was thrown from the boat, and now both he and the lifeboat were dangling from their respective ropes.

Schultz lay down on the wet deck, hoping that Kit could climb the rope to where he could grab his arm and help pull him aboard. The storm had increased and so had the size of the waves hitting the steamship from two different directions. The *Great Eastern* had a great roll, and both Kit and lifeboat swung far away from the ship. When the roll was reversed, both Kit and the lifeboat slammed into the iron hull. On the next outward roll, Schultz saw Kit swinging away from the ship. He appeared to be inanimate, his head hanging down. Panicked, Schultz tried pulling on the wet rope, but the young man's weight was too great. Towle moved away from the staircase and crouched alongside the pigpen. He got behind Schultz and said in a loud whisper, "They heard the boat crash. Someone's coming to look. I can hear them!"

Schultz now heard men shouting, trying to figure out from which side of the rolling ship the crashing sound of the lifeboat was coming. As the voices grew near, Schultz looked out and saw Kit swinging out again. His body was still motionless. As the voices approached, Schultz dried his hand on his shirt. He pulled the slipknot, and the rope snaked off the deck. Between the roar of the sea and the howl of the wind, no one heard Kit's body plunge into the frigid waters of the North Atlantic, where it was submerged by a blade of the giant paddle wheel.

Part VII

September 12, 1861
to
April 25, 1861

In that day Jehovah with his hard and great and strong sword will punish leviathan the swift serpent, and leviathan the crooked serpent; and he will slay the monster that is in the sea.

—Isaiah 27:1 (ASV)

166

On board the *Great Eastern*
September 12, 1861

At around two o'clock on September 12, a crew member heard a crashing sound coming from toward the bow of the ship. He moved cautiously forward across the wet and rolling deck and finally came to the davits ahead of the starboard paddle wheel. Leaning over the edge, he saw a lifeboat dangling by a single rope slamming against the side of the ship on each roll. He understood immediately that if the wooden lifeboat broke free, it would get sucked into and destroy the starboard paddle. The crewman shouted an alarm, which was carried by other crewmen and finally heard by Captain Walker at the stern of the ship.

Captain Walker gave orders to have the paddle engines stopped and then told the helmsmen to turn the ship into the gale to create a calmer area in which the dangling lifeboat could be cut away. Despite the order, the paddle wheels continued their slow and powerful turning, and the lifeboat continued to slam against the hull, straining the one shackle still holding it up. Walker, fearing the loss of his paddle wheels, ordered the ship's giant screw to reverse in order to drive the ship astern until the paddle engines stopped. However, he failed to warn the helmsmen to hold the rudder straight on so as to avoid it being sucked to one side by the reverse thrust of the screw. The four brawny men at the ship's wheel were flung like ragdolls by the spinning wheel as the twenty-four-foot diameter screw sucked the ship's enormous rudder to one side until it crashed into the stern of the ship. One young helmsman was hit in the head by one of the handles of the spinning wheel and was rendered unconscious. When the remaining helmsmen staggered to their feet and returned to their wheel, they found to their horror that the wheel was spinning freely. The rudder was no longer under their control.

Word was immediately delivered to Captain Walker. After moving quickly to the helm to confirm the bad news, he told the helmsmen to remain at the wheel and to pretend to continue to steer the vessel so a panic would not set in among the passengers. He then went below deck to find out what had happened. By the light of oil lanterns, the ship's engineer carefully examined the steering mechanism and found the problem.

When the rudder had slammed into the stern of the ship, the rudderhead, a nine-inch-thick iron bar, had cracked. The gigantic wooden rudder now swung freely from side to side with each roll of the ship, crashing into the rotating screw, which took large gouges out of the rudder with each collision. The captain ordered the screw engines stopped in order to preserve what was left of the rudder. The *Great Eastern* floated in the ocean powerless and rudderless.

The storm continued to worsen. Walker's decision to turn the ship's flank into the storm was now playing havoc. Brunel had designed the *Great Eastern* as a flat-bottomed ship so that her draft would be shallow enough to enter Calcutta's Hooghly River. The lack of a keel meant that if she ever lost her rudder in a rough sea, she would roll deeply and helplessly from side to side. In nautical terms, she would roll like a log in the trough of the sea. As the gale worsened, that was precisely what happened.

Captain Walker posted fourteen men to try to control the rudder using the relieving gear, ropes attached between the outside of the ship's stern and the rudder, and he ordered the fore staysail and trysail set in the hope of getting the ship out of the trough by positioning her so that the wind was at her back. However, as soon as the enormous sails were pulled into place by steam-powered donkey engines, they were torn to shreds by the howling wind. With the rolling, the giant paddle wheels alternated from being nearly submerged to being totally out of the water, and by six thirty in the evening the port paddle wheel broke under the strain, and large portions of it were carried away. During the night, the storm increased in intensity, and the rolling became so severe that many on board feared the ship would capsize.

Below decks was bedlam. Passengers, furniture, crockery, luggage, and cargo slid and somersaulted from side to side with each roll of the ship. A cast-iron stove broke free and shattered the giant mirrors in the center of the grand saloon. A cowshed on deck containing two cows broke loose and crashed through the skylight of the ladies' cabin, killing both cows. A swan fell down a staircase and killed itself attempting to fly out of the grand saloon. Two large tanks of fish oil broke loose and landed on a hatchway, leading to their foul-smelling contents spreading throughout the lower deck. Great crashing noises echoed throughout the ship as inadequately fastened sheets of lead slid from side to side, smashing into the hull. Some passengers crawled on their hands and knees to their cabins, where they tied themselves to their beds using torn-up bedding. There, violently ill from seasickness and the smell of fish oil, they prayed for both forgiveness and deliverance.

As the passengers were being thrown about in utter terror, Captain Walker decided to try a sea anchor, a large, heavy object thrown from the stern of the vessel. If the anchor worked, the wind might push the ship out of the trough. A large spar, marked as weighing four tons, was located and heavily laden with additional iron. An immense hawser was tied to the spar, and a collection of crew and passengers heaved it overboard. The spar was almost immediately torn away, and the rolling continued.

At times over the next few days the storm abated, and passengers gathered to choke down cold food in the foul-smelling dining hall. During these occasions, the passengers all came to the same conclusion: the *Great Eastern* was utterly unprepared for an ocean voyage. Nothing had been tied or battened down. The injuries the passengers had sustained—including numerous broken bones, gashes, and missing teeth—were largely the result of flying objects, including tables, chairs, and a large rosewood piano. The fear the passengers had felt was now mingled with fury over the ineptitude of the ship's management.

For the next three and a half days, the hellish conditions on board the *Great Eastern* continued. Sometimes the gale would pick up and rock the giant ship; sometimes the storm would abate, and the shaken and wounded passengers would meet to console each other. Captain Walker had his men attempt to gain control of the rampant rudder by dangling young crewmen in bosun's chairs over the edge of the stern in an effort to hook a chain into the newly created gouges on the rudder. The battered crewmen were finally hauled back up when the effort was deemed futile. Finally, Hamilton Towle identified himself as an engineer to Captain Walker and offered his assistance in restoring control over the rudder. Insulted, the ship's engineer repeatedly refused the offer.

A delegation of infuriated passengers then confronted Captain Walker with a demand that he immediately accept Towle's offer to assist in gaining control over the rudder. This time Walker, faced with violence from his passengers, overruled his engineer, and Towle was brought below deck to the location of the steering mechanism. Towle had previously examined the whole apparatus by lantern light and had devised a method of wrapping a chain around the broken rudderhead and using that chain to regain control. Following Towle's orders, a long chain made up of links weighing close to eighty pounds each was located and hauled into place by crewmen. Under Towle's directions, the chain was wrapped around the rudderhead and then around large iron stanchions, where it was then tightened by blocks and tackles. When the apparatus was tested, it appeared to work. For the first time in nearly a week, the *Great Eastern*'s rudder was found to be responsive to her helm. Captain Walker turned the ship toward Ireland, and the *Great Eastern*, powered solely by her screw, began limping back to port. Although Towle's solution was the best possible, no one, not even Towle, was confident it would hold all the way to landfall.

On September 16, the passengers saw a sail in the distance, and the *Great Eastern* fired distress rockets. The sail came closer, and finally the *Persia* came into sight. The *Great Eastern*'s crew and passengers had previously found a large board and painted on it, "HAVE LOST RUDDER COME AROUND LEE SIDE." Although they held the sign up, Captain Judkins of the *Persia* could not read it. However, he could see that the *Great Eastern*'s paddle wheel had been destroyed. He cruised around the ship and saw that the other paddle wheel had likewise been sheared off. The giant ship was now facing Ireland, not America, and she seemed to be proceeding under her own power. Judkins concluded that there was nothing the *Persia* could do for the *Great Eastern*, and so he ordered his ship to continue her journey to New York City.

167

Thorngrove House
Worcestershire, England
September 17, 1861

WHEN Daniel Gooch learned of the hastily arranged voyage of the *Great Eastern*, he was puzzled. He sent a telegram to Samuel Baker and learned by return telegram that the ship had booked many passengers and a great deal of cargo and that the voyage would certainly be profitable. Still perplexed, Gooch traveled to Liverpool and arrived in time to witness the *Great Eastern* steaming down the River Mersey toward the ocean. After staying in Liverpool for two days while working on other matters, Gooch took a train to Worcestershire to visit Baker.

At Thorngrove House Baker's staff prepared an excellent dinner for the two men. During dinner Baker related that he had arranged a quick voyage to boost the morale of the company's shareholders and was surprised by how profitable the voyage would be. Gooch trusted Baker and was relieved at this news, although he was surprised by how optimistic, almost giddy, Baker was about the ship's future. After dinner, when the two men had settled in by the fireplace to talk further about the ship's future, a servant arrived with the news that a telegram had been delivered, and he handed the piece of paper to Baker. The telegram stated that a large ship had been spotted off the coast of Ireland and it was believed to be the *Great Eastern.* Since she had departed for New York only a few days earlier, the men were distressed but wondered whether the ship had been misidentified. Having no further information, both men retired for the evening. The next evening Gooch wrote the following in his diary:

> I had not been very long asleep when a knock at my door awoke me and poor old Baker walked into my room with a fresh telegram in his hand. I will never forget the appearance of the old gentleman as he stood at the foot of my bed to read the telegram, wrapped up in a white flannel dressing gown and one of those old fashioned night caps on his head, a lamp in one hand and the telegram in the other.

The telegram in Baker's hand confirmed that the *Great Eastern* was indeed off the coast of Ireland.

168

Queenstown, Ireland
September 18, 1861

On the morning of September 18, word spread among the residents of Queenstown that the *Great Eastern* was anchored several miles outside of the city's harbor. Since she was still not able to control her rudder with precision, she was ordered to remain outside the harbor until the winds and waves had died down. Finally, on September 20, a combination of steam tenders and tugboats brought the battered ship safely into Queenstown's harbor. Sightseers watched with a mixture of amazement and pity as the passengers limped off tenders onto a wharf. Dirty, covered with dried vomit and blood, unshaven, many with bandaged arms and legs and torn blankets wrapped around their heads, the sullen passengers shuffled off in the direction of hotels. A few had to be carried by their fellow passengers. They had no expectation whatsoever of the ship's owners offering them any assistance, and, indeed, none was offered.

The only reported death was that of the young helmsman who had suffered a head injury from the ship's helm. For several days the surgeons and dentists of Queenstown were busy repairing broken limbs, pulling out broken teeth, and stitching cuts from shards of mirrored glass.

The interest in the crippled ship was great, and one journalist reported on his visit to her on an excursion boat:

> The excursion steamers having twice gone round the Great Eastern, and stopped, in order to take a view of the vessel—as there was no admission on board—an opportunity was thus afforded of getting a near view externally of the ship. And we must confess to a feeling of disappointment, on a close inspection, as naval beauty seems entirely omitted in her construction. Her stem is straight, which gives her bow a heavy appearance, and her round stern is divested of any ornament whatever. "The Great Eastern, London," in plain letters being just inscribed, while the tiers of little windows on her sides have rather an unsightly appearance, gives her a dark, gloomy look. She is, however, a wonder of naval architecture, and her hull, for size and strength, strikes the spectator with amazement. Imagine three first class men-of-war (such as the Duke of Wellington) fastened together, and that will give an idea of the size of the Great Eastern, but we must add that she stands higher out of the water, her bulwarks being loftier than the funnels of the steamers sailing round her.

169

Cape Race, Newfoundland
September 23, 1861

On September 23, the *Persia* arrived at Cape Race, on her way to New York. She stopped her engines about a half mile offshore and waited until the Associated Press yacht came alongside. When the two vessels were side by side, a young man from the yacht climbed a staircase lowered from the side of the *Persia.* Once on deck, the man was handed a large canvas bag and quickly went back down the staircase and boarded the yacht. With a wave, the yacht headed to shore, and the *Persia* recommenced her journey toward New York City. It would be two more days before she arrived.

When the yacht reached a wharf, the young man hurriedly carried the bag into a small wooden building and put it on a table. He opened it and with a smile pulled out a fresh loaf of bread from the *Persia*'s ovens and several choice cuts of beef, both wrapped in butcher paper. They were gifts from Captain Judkins. The young man would share it with his mates as soon as they finished securing the yacht. He then dumped the remainder of the bag's contents on the table and began sorting them. Mostly they were newspapers acquired just before the *Persia* left Liverpool. However, he saw a single piece of the *Persia*'s stationery with handwriting on it. He picked it up and read the short message. Putting the newspapers aside, he immediately began tapping out a telegraph message to the Associated Press operator in New York, inquiring if New York was ready to receive a message. Within a few seconds, he received an acknowledgment that the operator was indeed ready. The young man began tapping out a staccato message on the telegraph key.

The following day, newspapers throughout the United States, from New York City to Bangor, Maine, to Terre Haute, Indiana, carried the following message:

> The Persia makes the following report relative to the Great Eastern:
>
> "On the 16th inst., passed the steamship Great Eastern, which was putting back to Liverpool in a damaged state."

That night, without comment, Fred Seward handed his father a handwritten copy of the telegraph. Before retiring, the elder Seward wrote a letter to his wife, Francis. The letter began, "My fears of foreign intervention are subsiding." He did not explain why.

170

Great Britain
November 1861

THE *Great Eastern* remained moored at Queenstown until she was towed to Milford Haven, where in early November her supply of coal was removed to other ships and she was prepared to be placed on the gridiron at nearby Neyland. When inspected, it was discovered that her hull was solid and that overall structural damage was not as bad as feared. However, it would take several months to repair the side wheels and rudder. A meeting of the ship's shareholders on November 8, 1861, at the London Tavern was predictably grim. Samuel Baker bravely chaired the meeting and assured his beaten-down shareholders that the calamity that had befallen their ship was not the fault of the directors. The shareholders were also informed that it would take £25,000 to repair the ship and that the directors hoped to procure a loan in that amount. When the meeting ended, it was obvious to all that the *Great Eastern* would not sail for many months.

171

Port Royal, South Carolina
November 7, 1861

ON November 7, 1861, a hastily assembled flotilla of seventy-seven Union vessels, consisting of warships, coal tenders, and support ships, descended on Port Royal, South Carolina. Under a lengthy barrage from the warships, the two Confederate forts guarding Port Royal were abandoned, and by the following day Union soldiers occupied the abandoned forts. From that day to the end of the Civil War, the Union army and navy occupied Port Royal and used it as a refueling station for its ships.

172

Fishkill Landing, New York
April 25, 1865

DURING the night and well into the early morning, a cold drizzle fell, creating clouds of fog on the hills on either side of the Hudson River. However, by midday, the fog had lifted, and the sky became a sheet of gray clouds. After lunch, Leonard DeMund walked from his small house toward the railroad depot accompanied by James, his ten-year-old son. DeMund had wanted his wife and four other children to come with him, but she'd demurred, saying that the small children might catch a fever and that they couldn't really understand what was happening anyway. DeMund agreed.

DeMund and his son reached a point on the road leading to the railroad tracks where they could see the Fishkill Landing depot. Already, there was a large crowd of people milling about. DeMund assumed that many of the people were from nearby towns, including Newburgh, and the presence of numerous coaches suggested people had traveled from other inland towns and hamlets. Nearly all the women were dressed in black, and most of the men wore their dark Sunday clothes. The depot was covered with black bunting, and a large display made from pine cuttings had been placed on the far side of the track. When DeMund asked James what the display said, his son read it to him: "IN GOD WE TRUST." DeMund nodded in agreement with that sentiment.

It was obvious that he and his son could not get close to the tracks anywhere near the depot, so DeMund decided that the two of them should walk north on a path that ran parallel to the tracks. As they walked, the crowd thinned out, and finally they came to a hill with relatively few people around. From the top of the hill they had a good view of the tracks below. DeMund sat down on the grass, and his son sat next to him.

After a period of silence, DeMund said to his son, "This is the second time Mr. Lincoln come this way. I was there the first time." He thought back on that visit four years ago. He'd been working for Captain Schultz and his family, and he remembered Mrs. Schultz and Mary walking with him on that cold day. So much had happened since then, he thought.

DeMund had enjoyed working for Captain and Mrs. Schultz, and they had treated him well. Mary, he thought, was a bit spoiled, but she hadn't been around much and had been no trouble. He'd stayed with the family until word had come around that Mr. Lincoln was taking colored men into the army and paying them pretty well. Thus, in December 1863, DeMund had enrolled in the army and become a private in Company D, Twentieth US Colored Infantry.

DeMund recalled a great ceremony in New York City when the Twentieth Colored Infantry received its colors from its sponsor, the Union League. He loved his uniform and the prestige that went with it. He'd been with Company D when it was sent to New Orleans to protect the city from being retaken by the Confederates. Although he'd liked the beauty and exoticness of New Orleans, he'd been astonished at the intensity of hate that he saw in the faces of whites, particularly white women. However, he'd fitted in comfortably with members of Company D and had taken his assignment seriously. In September 1864, he'd reinjured an old injury in his knee, and after an examination he'd been given a disability discharge. He'd returned home to his family in Fishkill Landing and now worked as a laborer and farmhand.

As DeMund reminisced, he thought of Kit's presence at the train station four years ago. It had been cold, and Kit had worn a scarf around his face so he could not be identified by slave chasers. DeMund had never learned what happened to Kit. Shortly after Captain Schultz had returned from his trip to England, DeMund had overheard Schultz and his wife talking quietly in their parlor. He'd thought he heard Captain Schultz mention Kit's name, but he hadn't been able to make out what was said. Once the captain had left the parlor, DeMund had entered and had seen Mrs. Schultz sitting in her chair wiping her eyes with a handkerchief. When she'd looked up at DeMund, she'd shaken her head silently and looked back down. Kit's name had never again been mentioned in the Schultz house.

It was late afternoon when the clanging of a locomotive bell was heard. At this, everyone on the hill stood and looked as far as they could see to their left. A locomotive then appeared. It was black with polished brass fixtures, and it was traveling at a moderate speed. As it came closer, the sightseers saw that it was pulling only a coal tender. There was considerable confusion at that, until someone yelled that the funeral train was behind it. An identical locomotive, named Union, followed the first locomotive. The second locomotive was pulling seven cars, including a long car painted dark maroon and covered with black bunting. No one doubted that this car carried the body of the murdered president.

DeMund pulled a cap from underneath his jacket. It was his blue forage cap, the one issued by the army that he'd worn so proudly in New Orleans. Standing at attention, he saluted his dead commander as the funeral train passed by them. His son watched him with fascination. Once the train was out of sight and sound, DeMund and his son began their long walk home. During the walk, DeMund placed his cap on his son's head, an act that was greeted with a smile from the boy. James wanted to know more about his father's service in the army, but since both father and son were walking in twilight's peaceful silence, James decided he would wait until another day to ask questions.

Epilogue

After his arrest in Crestline, Daniel Lowber was taken by Detective King to New York City, where he was incarcerated in Fort Lafayette, a gloomy prison on an island in New York Harbor. Confined to dungeon-like quarters with both real and suspected traitors, Lowber began writing letters. One of the first such letters, which no longer exists, was to William H. Seward. Seward responded to this letter on September 30, 1861, by sending the following letter to Lieutenant Colonel Martin Burke, the commandant of Fort Lafayette:

> SIR: I have received a letter from Mr. D. C. Lowber, a prisoner confined at Fort Lafayette, asking permission for his niece, Miss Mary L. Schultz, to visit him which under existing circumstances I cannot with propriety grant. You will please communicate to Mr. Lowber the decision of the Department.

A month later, a sentry came upon Lowber outside the prison walls. Lowber was equipped with a life preserver, a valise containing a number of gold coins, and a washtub in which he apparently intended to paddle out to a waiting ship. Lowber tried without success to bribe the sentry but ended up being dragged back into the prison, where he was handcuffed and double chained. How Lowber acquired these implements of escape, particularly the washtub, was the subject of speculation in the New York papers, and there were rumors that they had been smuggled into the prison by a young lady. *Vanity Fair* approached the subject with humor, noting:

> One of the prisoners confined in Fort Lafayette, Lowber by name, attempted to escape lately by embarking in a

> wash-tub. What means of propulsion he meant to employ we are not informed; but, considering the description of the craft selected by him for his conveyance, it is reasonable to suppose that he calculated upon being washed ashore.

On October 30, 1861, Lowber wrote a letter to Thurlow Weed, the prominent New York Republican who had been Seward's most important political advisor for years:

> Dear Sir: Personally we are strangers but I have known you by reputation since my boyhood and you may have heard my name mentioned by my brother-in-law, Capt. A. H. Schultz. I am sadly in need of a friend in my extremity, and stranger as I am to you I thus boldly force myself on your notice and ask your assistance.
>
> Over nine weeks ago I was arrested under very suspicious circumstances at Crestline. I was supposed to be a bearer of dispatches to the Confederate Government. My baggage was taken possession of by the superintendent of police in New York and after a thorough overhauling nothing was found to incriminate me, but it was said that I had ample time to dispose of my dispatches before my arrest.
>
> Permit me to state to you "the truth, the whole truth and nothing but the truth." On the 6th of July I left my home in New Orleans to make a flying trip to Europe partly for the benefit of my health and partly to have a personal interview with my business correspondents in Liverpool and Glasgow. My whole stay in England and France was but eight days, and here let me assert that I neither carried over nor brought back any writing or any verbal message to or from any person directly or indirectly connected with the Confederate Government except a private letter from the Hon. P. A. Rost to Pierre Soulé which Judge Rost, who is an old friend of mine,

told me contained some instructions in relation to a legal suit Mr. Soulé had in charge for him …

Had I been conscious of being in the act of committing any offense against the Federal Government I would not have unhesitatingly paid the friendly visit I did to my relatives at Fishkill Landing knowing how widely we differed in our political views. Had that visit not have been made I would not probably have been arrested.

As I have said before it is now over nine weeks that I have been incarcerated here, shut out from intercourse with all those who make life dear to me. Driven to desperation by the seeming neglect of those who I thought would unasked by me endeavor to effect my release I recently attempted to escape and was caught in the act. The penalty—double irons and a four by six foot cell—I was perfectly aware of before making the attempt. I was faithfully but not harshly imposed and of that I have not one word of complaint to make. But I conceive there was nothing particularly atrocious in my endeavor to free myself surreptitiously. At least twenty officers and men confined as prisoners of war at Richmond have evaded the vigilance of their keepers and on their arrival at Washington have been patted on the back as good and enterprising fellows. It may be said that I can be released if I establish all the foregoing acts on taking the oath of allegiance, but the question arises is it right to require me to take that oath when it is well known it will work the immediate confiscation of my property for the benefit of the Confederate Government and that you are not now in a position to protect that property for me? In regard to giving my parole not to visit or to correspond with a seceded State that I will do and will honorably keep the promise until released from it. May I beg of you the favor to call the attention of him who has the power to open the gates of my prison to this my case? If there are any other explanations I can make they will

> be promptly given as the days here seem like weeks and I confess to a great anxiety to get out.

Although Weed never responded, he forwarded the letter to Seward. Seward received it at about the same time he received a letter from Mary Lowber Schultz. In her letter, Mary described a far different version of her uncle than the one described in the earlier letter she had written to Seward. She related that of her own knowledge Lowber had made himself "to some degree obnoxious in New Orleans by his strong defense of the Union and his condemnation of the precipitate action of the South against an untried Administration." She went on:

> From my own experience I can say that his house was the only one in New Orleans in which I ever heard abolitionism fairly allowed an utterance. In a conversation with Miss Frémont, then visiting at his house in New Orleans in May, 1860, I remember his distinctly avowed disgust at the demagogues who wished by secession to plunge the country into civil war, for which he believed they had not one unfriendly act of Government to show as excuse.

Mary now asserted that she "most sincerely" believed that Lowber had left New Orleans "with the simple and sole purpose of visiting his grandchildren and establishing business relations in Glasgow." Of course, Mary had previously informed Seward that Lowber had burned Mann's dispatches after committing them to memory, so she could say, with some modicum of truthfulness, "I think it can be proved that whatever letters or papers he carried on his return not one found its way South." The finale of Mary's letter to Seward, asking for Lowber's parole to Europe, was an appeal for mercy:

> I have been induced to write thus from the belief forced upon me that Mr. Lowber's health is being seriously affected and his constitution undermined by the inactivity of prison life and by the conviction that if released on parole no harm could result to the cause nearest

> and dearest to me. The disease from which he suffers is peculiarly fostered by confinement and from my knowledge of the family tendency I have been seriously alarmed lately lest it terminate in some form of insanity. Except my parents he is my dearest relative and I could not entertain this belief without longing to save him from such a fate. But for this conviction my perfect trust in the Administration would have forbid my uttering one word on the subject.

When this letter went unanswered, Mary and Lowber redoubled their efforts. In early November 1861, Seward received a lengthy letter from Montgomery Neill's brother William, who was then in New York and was a self-professed personal friend of numerous ardent abolitionists, including Wendell Phillips, W. Lloyd Garrison, Fred. L. Olmsted, and H. Ward Beecher. William stated that he had met Lowber in England. William's letter read as follows:

> As soon as I heard of his arrest which I did in Liverpool from Captain Schultz I informed the latter that from what I had seen of him and the entire tone of his conversation I was satisfied he had no official or other connection with the Confederate Government, for if he had I felt certain he would have been proud of it and told me or my brother of it.

On the same day William Neill wrote the above letter to Seward, Lowber wrote a moving letter to his brother-in-law, Alexander Hamilton Schultz:

> Dear Hamilton: As the break of day is now apparent to all except those who are fattening and battening on this unholy war I stoop to ask a favor of a political enemy, personal friend though he be. I have now been imprisoned so long that it is absolutely necessary on account of my business affairs that I should go to England before I return home and I want you to see President Lincoln

and ask for permission and passport to embark on the steamer that leaves Boston on the 8th. If it is obtained you must also pay my passage on sea as I am entirely out of money. In Liverpool I can obtain what further funds I need. I would prefer that this application should not be mentioned, even in the family, as some of the family are in such intimate companionship with J. A. Kennedy that the first thing we will know will be an account of it in the Tribune, and for a humble private individual my name has been in the papers as often as I care to have it. It is well that you and I have not corresponded since your return from England. The bitter thoughts that this war has created in my heart would have found utterance in bitter words, and the corner stone of something more than an apparent estrangement might have been laid. As it is, the same old love that has filled my heart for you and yours for the last thirty-two years still wells up in it with undiminished force.

Understand me, in asking for my release and passport I do not wish to leave Fort Warren until the day before the steamer sails, so that I can go immediately on board.

Give my love to the old enemy and her inimical scions and believe me, very truly yours,

D. C. Lowber.

Much as I wish to get to England I can take no oath of allegiance to the United States Government, but I will give my parole not to return to the country during the continuance of the war and not to aid, comfort or correspond with the Southern States until peace is made. If you think it worth while you can hand this letter to President Lincoln.

Lowber's timing was unfortunate. While Seward was receiving letters on behalf of Lowber from Mary and her friends, he was occupied with a much larger issue. On November 6, 1861, the warship USS *San*

Jacinto stopped the *Trent*, an unarmed British mail packet, in international waters after firing warning shots across her bow. Officers from the *San Jacinto* boarded the *Trent* and forcibly removed two men, James Mason and John Slidell, who were being sent to England by Jefferson Davis to replace Dudley Mann and William Yancey as Confederate commissioners. While the hotheaded captain of the *San Jacinto*, Charles Wilkes, was feted as a hero in the North for his audacity, the British people and government were infuriated by this gross insult to their flag. At a turbulent meeting of his cabinet, Lord Palmerston roared, "You may stand for this but damned if I will!"

What followed were weeks of tense diplomacy that consumed the Lincoln administration. Initially the American public clamored for war on England. However, the forcible boarding of a neutral merchantman reminded many older Americans of the British conduct that had led to the War of 1812. Also, knowledgeable Union officials compared the strength of the British and Union navies and concluded that any clash was not certain, or even likely, to be favorable to the Union. Ultimately, Lincoln told his cabinet, "One war at a time," and Seward was ordered to implement that policy. By the end of December, Mason and Slidell were released to recommence their trip to England. At the same time Seward issued a somewhat apologetic letter to Lord Russell in which the federal government disavowed Wilkes's actions. By the end of 1861, talk of an impending war had been tamped down on both sides of the Atlantic.

About the time of the *Trent* incident, Lowber was transferred from Fort Lafayette to Fort Warren in Boston's harbor. Since letters to Seward and Seward's friends had had no result, Lowber wrote the following letter on December 31, 1861, to "His Excellency Abraham Lincoln, President of the United States":

> SIR: I was arrested on the 23d of August, and by order of the Secretary of State was committed to Fort Lafayette and thence transferred to this place. Over four months have now elapsed and I have heard of no charges against me, but I presume I am detained as a citizen of Louisiana. As it is not probable I shall ever be brought to trial and the further imprisonment of a humble private individual like myself can be of no benefit to the United

> States Government I respectfully ask permission and a passport to embark for England under a pledge that I will not return to America until the present disturbances are over, nor aid, comfort or hold correspondence with any person in the seceded States.

How this letter was sent to the White House or what events occurred upon its receipt are unknown. What is known is that one week after it was dated, Seward wrote to the commandant of Fort Warren ordering Lowber's release on the condition that Lowber sign a parole under oath confirming that he would leave the United States fifteen days after release and not return during the duration of hostilities. The parole was signed, and Lowber left for England on a trip apparently paid for by Schultz.

Considering the efforts made to release Lowber and the assurances of various gentleman that Lowber would keep his word and not return, Seward must have been amused when he received the following telegram from Superintendent Kennedy on June 10, 1862:

> Daniel Lowber whom you paroled from Ft Warren on condition of his going to and remaining in Great Britain was captured on one of the vessels running the blockade and brought to this port by the store-ship relief—He has been passed over to my custody. Will lay the case before the War Department and obtain my instruction what disposition I should make of him.

The following day Seward sent a telegram to Edwin M. Stanton, secretary of war, who now had jurisdiction over Lowber:

> I send you a copy of Lowber's parole. He is not worth imprisoning. I would discharge him and publish his parole, showing the value of a rebel's oath, as the severest punishment that could be inflicted upon him.

Stanton did not agree with Seward's suggestion and instead sent Lowber to New Orleans to be placed "under surveillance." Admiral David

Farragut and his West Gulf Blockading Squadron had conquered New Orleans a couple of months earlier, and Benjamin Butler, a politician turned Union general, was placed in charge of the city. Known in the South alternatively as "the Beast" for his brutishness and "Spoons" for his purported habit of stealing silverware from Southern houses he occupied, Butler had just issued his infamous General Order No. 28. In an age when chivalry still meant something, Butler's order provocatively stated that any woman who insulted or showed contempt toward a Union soldier would be treated as "a woman plying her trade"—that is, a prostitute.

When Lowber arrived, however, even the Beast was flummoxed. On July 13, 1862, Butler wrote Stanton the following letter:

> Will you have the kindness to send me a certified copy of the parole given by Daniel C. Lowber, of New Orleans, who was released from Warren, with instructions how to dispose of him. He now seems to think that he has been sent down here for the purpose of visiting his wife and is quite indignant that I do not send him home to his family.

Apparently Butler received the copy, because Lowber was soon incarcerated in Fort Pickens in Pensacola, Florida. He remained there until December 1862, when he was again paroled, this time by Butler, upon Lowber's promise "not to commit any act of hostility to the United States or render any aid or comfort to the enemies of the United States during the existing war." This time Lowber lived up to his word.

Life took a different trajectory for Schultz. After the crippling of the *Great Eastern* and the ensuing days of the great ship "rolling like a log in the trough of the sea," New York newspapers were filled with articles discussing the disaster in detail. The individuals aboard the *Great Eastern*, like the survivors aboard the *Titanic* decades later, acquired a celebrity status. Nearly every banker, businessman, and reverend aboard was identified, some immediately and others later when they arrived in New York on other vessels, and their names were usually proceeded by such adjectives as "prominent" and "well-known." However, Alexander

H. Schultz, a former alderman of the City of New York, a former harbor master of the port of New York, a close friend of William H. Seward, and a man important enough to generate an article in the *New York Times* when he'd departed for England a few weeks earlier—indeed, the most well-known individual aboard the ship during the disaster—was never mentioned as being aboard the ship.

John Hay, Lincoln's secretary and biographer, told about Lincoln's use of humor to defuse a difficult situation when he noted that at a gathering at Seward's house, apparently shortly after the 1860 Chicago Republican convention, "a Captain Schultz" showed very bad taste by alluding to Seward's defeat in the Chicago convention. Instead of confronting Schultz, Lincoln responded by telling "a good yarn," one that apparently put the events at the convention in a humorous light. By March 1862, Schultz's opinion of Lincoln had improved, as evidenced by a letter he sent to Fred Seward concerning the CSS *Sumter*, a Confederate raider that was attacking and destroying American merchantmen. The letter, to be delivered to Lincoln, read as follows:

> Mr. President
>
> I respectfully propose to rid the ocean of the rebel pirate steamer Sumter, and in order to avoid any possible conflict of jurisdiction with either the English or Spanish Government, I will do it in this wise.
>
> I will go to England and arrange with the extensive shipping house, Messrs. Richardson Spence & Co, who have at all times upwards of twenty-five ships at sea, for the purchase of the Sumter, and when that shall be effected, she shall be manned by a crew of my selection, to the officers of whom I will give instructions to allow her to be captured at a designated point upon the ocean, on our coast.
>
> The price of the Sumter is understood to be Two hundred and fifty thousand dollars. I shall only require a letter of credit for twenty five hundred or three thousand dollars for the necessary travelling and incidental expenses and this sum will be the only hazard which the Government will incur, to obtain what, in my judgment,

is so great a desideration for the protection of the commerce of the United States.

I have the honor to be
Your obdt servant
Alex Hamilton Schultz

Six weeks after his letter to Lincoln, Schultz was again in England. His ostensible mission was to carry a ratified treaty with Great Britain for the further suppression of the slave trade. Whether his real mission was to execute his plan to purchase and then seize the *Sumter* is unknown, since in April of 1862 the *Sumter* was laid up for repairs in Gibraltar and was never again a threat to Union shipping.

In December 1862, the federal government purchased Schultz's flagship, the 117-foot *A. H. Schultz*, and renamed her the USS *Columbine.* She promptly went to work as a blockader. As the blockade became stronger and the South more desperate for European goods, Schultz created a lucrative business purchasing "prizes," ships captured by the US Navy either running the blockade or carrying contraband, and rebuilding them for resale. The better ones were sold at substantial prices to the US Navy for use in the blockading fleet. The government's demand for his rebuilt shallow-draft boats was so great that Schultz got into the business of building new ones. Thus, while Lowber was struggling to keep his business alive in New Orleans, Schultz was "fattening and battening" on the war in New York.

On July 29, 1863, Mary Lowber Schultz married Montgomery Neill in Christ Church, New York City. She was twenty-four; he was thirty-two. The married couple went to Europe and were reunited with Montgomery's two sons in Ireland, now aged four and three. With this marriage, both Schultz and Lowber became the adopted grandfathers of these boys. Of course, the blockade played havoc with the Neill brothers' business of brokering cotton, so they concentrated efforts on their newsletter, the *Neill Brothers & Co. Circular.* Printed in Manchester, England, and widely distributed in both England and the United States, the circular provided factual information dealing with the projected size of the

Southern cotton crop, the amount of cotton in inventory in England, and all other matters dealing with the cotton trade. The circular was widely cited by both British and American newspapers, and the Neill brothers became the authoritative voice on all things cotton.

In March 1864 Schultz wrote Fred Seward the following letter:

> I have been so busily engaged in purchasing and rebuilding prize steam ships, in the Port, and in building new steam boats that I have not had time to visit Washington for nearly a year—but will be there with my new & beautiful steam boat "Wm H. Seward" in the course of next week. . . .
>
> My Daughter Mary (now Mrs Henry M Neill) will return from Italy to London on or about the 20th of April—there to be confined—some of our family ought to be there, and it has occurred to me that I may be of sufficient service to our Government to justify the State Department in sending me out from the 10th to 15th April—will you please assist me in consummating this for I really must go—and want no one to know it except the department & my immediate family.

The following month the federal government purchased the *William H. Seward*, a 137-foot, steam-powered schooner, as a revenue cutter for the sum of $34,500. Schultz did not say what sort of assistance he was seeking from the State Department, but apparently he was hoping to be a paid courier. That he was successful in his request is shown by a note dated May 5, 1864, in the journal of Benjamin Moran, the acerbic assistant secretary of the United States legation in London, recording a visit to the legation by Schultz.

The Civil War ended in April 1865. In July of that year Mary gave birth to a son, Hamilton, while still living with Montgomery in London. Shortly thereafter, Mary, accompanied by her children, returned to Fishkill Landing just in time to witness her mother's death from "congestive fever" on October 1, 1865. Tragically, Mary's infant son died two weeks later and was waked at the Schultz home. That December, Schultz wrote a poignant letter to Seward:

> In order to bridge over a space of time, and to while away a couple of months—or more if necessary, I want to go to England, France, Belgium, Holland, Germany & Switzerland, or almost anywhere else where I may be sufficiently useful to justify the department in paying my expenses and a remuneration commensurate with the service I may render, and that will not exceed the extra expenses of an American gentleman travelling in Europe—I wanted to go to India, but the remnant of my family will only consent to an European voyage under your protection = the unexpected death of my wife on Sunday Oct 1st, my grandson on Sunday Oct 15th and my youngest brother (our adopted son) at Baltimore Sunday on the 29th of that ill fated month seems to coerce me to seek the ease a sea voyage only can give. I will await as early an answer as you can send me by letter here, or telegraph to "Girard House Philadelphia until 19th inst as I shall return from there that day.
>
> I can leave for Europe at any time in January—
>
> With many thanks—for your life long friendship, I am truly your obedient servant

How long Schultz remained abroad is unknown, but his travel appears to have been intermittent. There are references in the local Fishkill newspaper in 1866 to Captain Schultz suffering from illness. The following obituary appeared in the May 2, 1867, edition of the *New York Times*:

> Capt. Alexander H. Schultz, a native of Rhinebeck, Dutchess County, N.Y., died on Tuesday [April 30, 1867] last in Philadelphia after a protracted illness. Capt. Schultz was the architect of his own fortune. Early in life he left his home and went to reside in Utica, and thence move to Rochester and subsequently to Buffalo. He was first engaged in the steam passenger business and then became interested in canal packet boats. For fifteen years he was captain of a steamboat plying between New Brunswick, Amboy and this City.

> Subsequently, he ran for Alderman of the Fifth Ward, was successful and held the office for several years. Gov. Seward, of whom he was a warm personal friend, conferred on him the office of Harbor Master, for the duties of which he was peculiarly well adapted.
>
> Of a warm and impulsive nature the death of his wife greatly affected his health and spirits, and no doubt hastened his own end. He leaves several children and a large number of friends to deplore his loss.
>
> For the last four years of his life Capt. Schultz acted as confidential agent for the Government and residing during great part of that time abroad.

Schultz was buried next to his wife in the family vault in Rhinebeck's Methodist cemetery.

When the fighting stopped, Lowber and his wife emerged into a blasted world. While the land was still there, there were no slaves to work it and, equally important, no money to plant and fertilize it. Lowber's business was destroyed, so he and his wife traveled to New York, where he joined a company engaged in the manufacture and sale of baling wire. Before long, Lowber was traveling to England and reestablishing contacts with the merchants with whom he had done business in the past. The business grew, and Lowber achieved a respectable level of success in the heady days of Northern commerce after the war. Eventually, he and his wife moved to Liverpool to be closer to his suppliers, although Lowber traveled frequently between Liverpool and New York. In February 1873, during one of his absences from Liverpool, his wife, Mary, died of pneumonia. She was sixty-two. As late as 1876 Lowber was still living in Liverpool, as evidenced by the address on a US patent he received on the configuration of a wire loop. Not long after this, Lowber returned to New York and died there in October 1879, aged sixty-nine years.

Henry Montgomery Neill and his wife Mary Lowber Schultz Neill moved to New Orleans shortly after the end of the war. Montgomery, usually referred to in the press as "Henry Neill," and his brother continued to publish their circular, knowledgeably reporting on cotton-growing conditions in the South and accurately predicting crop yields. Following the law of supply and demand, the circular became the basis for pricing cotton for both English mill owners and Southern planters. By supplying detailed information to both sides of the Atlantic, the Neill brothers were breaking new ground in helping to set prices for America's largest export. As the circular became increasingly prominent, it became very expensive, and the Neill family became wealthy on both sides of the Atlantic.

On August 15, 1899, the *New York Times* published an article under the headline "Largest Cotton Crop Known." It read as follows:

> New Orleans, La., Aug. 14.—Henry M. Neill, the cotton-crop expert of this city, who predicated the enormous crops of 1894–5, 1897–8, and 1898–9, is out with a forecast indicating that the crop now maturing will exceed any of these, and may reach the unprecedented total of 12,000,000 bales.

The aftermath of this information, widely disseminated through the United States and Europe, caused the price of cotton to plunge. European "spinners," mainly English textile mill operators, purchased vast quantities of Southern cotton at a mere five cents a bale.

Whether unintentionally or deliberately, Neill had guessed wrongly. The crop was mediocre, and Southern planters were badly harmed by the low prices. Opinions differed in the South as to whether Neill had simply erred or whether he had participated in a massive fraud. In a series of front-page articles, the *Atlanta Constitution* excoriated the man it called the "Prophet of Evil." An article of November 7, 1899, set the tone of what was to follow:

> The fall of a prophet, under any circumstances, is a matter of note, but when the prophet is an agent of evil, his fall becomes not only an occasion of comment, but of rejoicing.

> Such a prophet was Henry M. Neill, of New Orleans, whose oracles have brought disaster into so many homes, and whose scope of malicious survey covered an empire of territory. With the yield of cotton production on one continent, and of its extensive manufacture upon another, where actual buyer and seller could never meet to compare notes, what an opportunity was presented to the middleman! On the one side there were the owners of from $300,000,000 to $500,000,000 of raw material; on the other the mill owners with a custom calling for $1,500,000,000 to $2,000,000,000 worth of manufactured goods; between them the adroit man, without capital, whose only stock in trade was gall and cheek, who made his profit by playing first to the one and then to the other, and ending up by playing both.

The total amount of damage suffered by the South was never accurately measured. The *Atlanta Constitution* stated:

> The story of how one irresponsible man could so surround himself with mystery and importance as to become able to wreck crops of $300,000,000 in value, while those whom he wrecks are weak in their confusion, is one which points to its counter lesson—that we must attend to our own business ourselves.

Though the Southern planters' total loss was not readily calculable, the *Weekly Age-Herald* of Birmingham, Alabama, in an article entitled "Mr. Henry Neill's Downfall," estimated the loss at $50 million, a staggering sum in 1899. The *Weekly Age-Herald* reached the same conclusion as the *Atlanta Constitution*—that Neill was finished as a predictor of cotton crops:

> Such a result unseats Mr. Henry Neill. Confidence in his infallibility is destroyed even in England, although English buyers have been able to stock up with cheap cotton. But just the same he has been mistook in his

judgment, and that destroys belief in his future predictions. The cotton pope has been shoved off his throne.

It appears, however, that the reports of Montgomery Neill's professional demise were premature. There was a need for information about cotton yields on both sides of the Atlantic, and the circular had been accurate in the past. Eventually, the circular regained its credibility, and so did William and Montgomery Neill. However, the strain of perpetrating what at first appeared to be a multimillion-dollar fraud on one's friends and neighbors must have placed a tremendous burden on the Neills. Thus, it is not surprising that in April 1901, less than two years after the *Constitution*'s broadsides, Mary died from a heart attack at age sixty-six. An obituary in the *Times-Picayune* of New Orleans noted:

> Mrs. Neill was greatly loved in this city, where a large portion of her life has been spent and where she was prominent in the social world and active and devoted in behalf of charities.

Montgomery and his brother William were made of sterner stuff. They continued to publish the circular. In 1906, at the age of seventy-eight, Montgomery went to New York to visit his son Henry, now an editor of a newspaper. While there, Montgomery was lionized by the New York Cotton Exchange, an organization he'd helped to form and make rich. He returned to New Orleans a conquering hero to both planters and brokers alike. Shortly after his arrival, however, he was struck and killed by one of New Orleans's new electric streetcars.

Although over a century has passed since Mary's and Montgomery's deaths, the Neill name is remembered at least once a year in New Orleans. After Mary's death, her friends established and endowed an annual prize to be awarded by Newcomb College (now part of Tulane University) to a student for excellence in watercolor painting. The award, which is still given out annually by Tulane, is known as the Mary L. S. Neill Prize.

Four days after Daniel Lowber was arrested in Crestline, Jefferson Davis wrote a letter to Howell Cobb, president of the Confederate Congress, nominating James Mason to be the Confederate commissioner to England and John Slidell to be the commissioner to France. Following this, Robert Hunter, the Confederate secretary of state, sent a letter to Dudley Mann dated September 23, 1861 (the day that the news of the *Great Eastern*'s disablement was telegraphed throughout North America), to inform Mann that he had now been reassigned as commissioner to Belgium.

Mann's assignment was delayed by the seizure of Mason and Slidell aboard the *Trent*, but when they finally arrived, Mann was off to Belgium. This small country had but few ports and no navy. However, it had King Leopold, whom Mann wooed with considerable success on behalf of the Confederacy. Leopold, a longtime ruler now in his seventies, had several important connections. First, he was the uncle of Queen Victoria. Second, he was, as Mann put it, the *le doyen des souverains de L'Europe* (the dean of the sovereigns of Europe), who had influence in every royal house on the continent. While Mann was in Belgium, an odd event occurred. He wrote about the event to Lord Gregory on November 28, 1862. His letter stated in pertinent part:

> On the 12th Lord Palmerston favored me with an interview. It was of about 65 minutes duration. From the commencement to the end there was no cessation in the conversation. We set directly opposite each other, almost toe to toe—looking at one another steadily in the eye. I never addressed a more attentive listener. I never answered a more earnest enquirer... I could scarcely realize the fact that I was in the presence of a personage who was Minister of War when I was but barely four years old.
>
> His Lordship made no allusion whatever to the subject of slavery in the Confederate States except a mention of the wicked Proclamation of Lincoln ...
>
> The first question that Lord Palmerston addressed to me was, in substance, what immediate benefit do you believe the Confederate States would receive from

> Recognition? This of all others was the one which I wished him to ask, and I responded to it at considerable length—observing, at the outset, that in my candid opinion no European measure could be so effective as occurring an early termination of hostilities.
>
> Earl Russell had fully consented when he was here on the 5th of September to favor Recognition and he returned to London on the 20th of that month prepared to act with as good as an undivided Cabinet upon the subject—the only dissidents being the Duke of Argyll and Sir Cornwall Lewis. A circumstance occurred, however, which I cannot relate, during the final days of October to postpone this decision. . . .
>
> It is not in my nature to conceal any thing of importance from so good a friend as yourself and one who enjoys my unbounded confidence. How I should enjoy a long conversation with you at this time.

What "circumstance" intervened to interrupt the British government from recognizing the Confederacy is not known. Mann had been deeply involved in two different attempts to secure British recognition of the Confederacy—the first being thwarted by the disablement of the *Great Eastern* in September 1861 and the second defeated by an unknown circumstance in October 1862. If either effort had succeeded, the Confederate States of America may very well have achieved independence, and Mann would have entered the pantheon of its heroes. Instead, he failed, and subsequent historians, particularly Frank Owsley in his 1931 book *King Cotton Diplomacy*, ridiculed him for his efforts, not knowing the secrets that Mann took to his grave.

As the war progressed, Mann left no stone unturned in Europe. He went to the Vatican and met with Pope Pius IX, with Mann's son acting as translator, but was only able to secure a letter from the pontiff expressing a hope for a speedy end to the bloodshed. As Mann ran around Europe cultivating royal and wealthy supporters, the Confederacy deteriorated under the North's relentless strangulation. When the Confederacy collapsed, Mann became an "irreconcilable," a Southerner who refused life under Union domination. While Jefferson Davis accepted a pardon and became a United States citizen after the war, Mann refused any such concession to the North. He lived the rest of his life in genteel poverty in Europe, mostly in and near Paris. Nevertheless, Davis and Mann remained close friends, and in the 1870s Davis and his wife Varina came to visit and stay briefly with Mann in France

On December 6, 1886, the following article appeared in the *Philadelphia Ledger*:

> There died the other day in Paris, in his ninetieth year, and with mental faculties unimpaired, an American of the name of Ambrose Dudley Mann. The great mass of his country men will, no doubt, recall with difficulty the man or the name, while those of the present generation will probably recall neither, however indistinctly. Yet Col. A. Dudley Mann was once a very prominent figure in American politics. He was a warm, close friend not only of Andrew Jackson, but of Henry Clay. During President Pierce's Administration he was Assistant Secretary of State, and is credited with having organized the present Consular Service. Between 1829 and 1859, it is stated, "he was variously engaged in the foreign service negotiating many important treaties and commending himself to the Department of State as a man to be trusted with large and difficult transactions." Col Mann was a Virginian, and was among the first of those summoned to Montgomery to assist Jefferson Davis with his counsel. He was appointed by the Confederate President chief of that commission of which Rost of Louisiana and Yancey of Alabama were originally members, and of which Mason and Slidell subsequently became members. Its mission was to represent the Confederacy abroad, and, if possible, to induce the foreign powers to recognize it. Col. Mann was appointed Commissioner in the first year of the war, and then taking up his residence in Europe, he never returned to his native country, preferring to live in voluntary exile after the failure of the South to maintain the Confederacy. Col. Mann's original

> prominence was due to his great abilities, and, had he not made the mistake of going "out of the Union," his subsequent career might probably have been even more brilliant and useful than was that of his earlier years, as the opportunities for usefulness were largely increased by conditions growing out of the war.

Mann's gravesite was unknown for many years. However, Hubert Leroy, a Belgium researcher, believes he has located the grave at the cemetery of Montparnasse in Paris.

The reasons behind James Walker's decision to leave his position as a master on the prestigious Cunard Line and accept a position with the small Galway Line are long since lost. All that is known is that shortly after the Galway Line became insolvent, the unemployed thirty-six-year-old master was hired to command the *Great Eastern* a few days before she was scheduled to leave Liverpool, ostensibly for New York City. The calamitous voyage of the *Great Eastern* is well documented, being one of the major news stories of 1861. For months afterward, Walker was second-guessed, summoned to inquiries, and made the subject of numerous articles. By 1862, however, the incident had been long overshadowed by stories dealing with the American Civil War and turmoil in Europe.

In early 1862, Walker, apparently seeking to reinstate his reputation as a master, gave a speech. The results were reported in the *Shipping and Mercantile Gazette*:

> Captain Walker, late Commander of the Great Eastern, recently gave an account, before a Liverpool audience, of the disasters of the big ship, which might as well have been undelivered. But Captain Walker has a professional reputation, and some public explanation was demanded from him. He gave a description of the gale, and its results on the ship and equipment. Having received charge of the vessel only the day before sailing, he could not have been expected to possess a perfect acquaintance

> with everything on board. His description of the series of accidents adds a little to our previous knowledge of events, and from it we learn that, notwithstanding experience gathered from previous gales, the furniture and gear of the ship were not secured against mischief from the rolling of the vessel. He explains how the boat forward of the paddle-wheels was blown out of the slings, and cut adrift to free the floats. Next, that some heavy pieces of iron were suffered to frolic about, smash through a compartment, and fall into the machinery. . . .
>
> Captain Walker claims the credit for himself and Engineers of planning and fixing the temporary rudder gear, and speaks very disparagingly of the efforts and ingenuity of Mr. Towle, C.E. The passengers, in their letter as published, awarded the merit of invention to Mr. Towle, and this agrees with information furnished to us by disinterested persons.

While Captain Walker was unlikely to command a major passenger ship in the future, there were persons who recognized his daring. Thus, on May 10, 1862, the American consul at Liverpool sent a short message to the State Department, which forwarded it to the United States Navy:

> The steamer Adela has arrived at this port. She is commanded by Captain Walker, late of the Great Eastern, has been purchased for the South, and is one of the expedition of thirty steamers referred to in previous dispatches. She is only 175 tons burden, and very swift. On her voyage from Belfast to this port she made 17 knots per hour, and they say she was not put down to her full speed; that when she is she will run 19 knots. She is to be got ready and dispatched as soon as possible.

The navy acted on this information, and on July 7, 1862, the USS *Quaker City* and the USS *Huntsville* seized the *Adela* near the Bahamas. Captain Walker was in command of the seized ship. The *Adela* was loaded with valuable cargo, and both she and the cargo were condemned as prizes. Her owners appealed her seizure all the way to the United States Supreme Court, claiming she was merely bound for the Bahamas and was not intending to break the blockade. In *The Adela*, 73 U.S. 266 (1867), the Supreme Court rendered a decision. Noting that the chief officer of the *Adela* had testified that she was intending to run the blockade, the court found Captain Walker's contrary testimony impaired by its "evasive character." Captain Walker, the court noted,

> professed himself entirely ignorant of the nature of ownership of the cargo; declared that he had no bill of lading, or any other document relating to the merchandise on board, and knew nothing of the ownership of the vessel except what he derived from the ship's register. He was appointed master by one Burns, of Liverpool, who shipped the goods, whether for himself or as agent for other parties, and on whose real account, risk, and profit, he did not know. . . .
>
> The character of her cargo, of which much the largest part consisted of Enfield rifles and other goods clearly contraband of war, and the destination of the letters found on board, many of which were directed to Charleston, Savannah, and neighboring places, strongly confirm the testimony of the chief officer.

The seizure of the *Adela* was upheld. What became of Captain Walker after the seizure of this blockade runner is unknown.

While Schultz's presence aboard the *Great Eastern* was shrouded in silence, Hamilton E. Towle's presence was widely publicized. This is because Towle was not merely a passenger but, to quote numerous newspaper articles, the man "who saved the *Great Eastern*."

Towle avoided all publicity during his spring 1861 assignment to England and France. Thus, he must have been surprised when his response to an invitation to attend a gala Fourth of July breakfast in

London was published in a London pro-Union newspaper, establishing him as an unabashed Unionist:

> Gentlemen, Please accept my thanks for your kind invitation to join you at breakfast on the glorious Fourth. I am very sorry I cannot have this pleasure, as I must be in Paris to-morrow and for several days following.
>
> Your appropriate mottoed envelope cast a thrill of delight as my eye first met it. Though occasional clouds and shadows may pass over and tint the page of our nation's history, with our banner inscribed "The Union for ever—one and inseparable," our shining Republic will never cease to be the wonder and admiration of the world.—I am gentlemen, your obedient servant,
>
> Hamilton E. Towle

Two months after writing this letter, Towle found himself aboard a rudderless ship, confronting its engineer over the best method to regain control of her. After three days of relentless pounding by the ocean, a desperate Captain James Walker overruled his ship's engineer and permitted Towle to use the ship's crew to install an apparatus that the young American had hastily sketched out. The task was daunting. First, a giant nut holding the freely swinging rudder in place had to be tightened. The author of the *American Annual Cyclopædia and Register of Important Events* of the year 1861 describes the procedure directed by Towle:

> There was a wrench on board fitted to the nut, having projections entering holes drilled in the periphery of the nut. In conformity with all the proportions of the great ship, so massive was this wrench that, in order to handle it, it had to be slung by ropes from a timber overhead. Mr. Towle had the wrench swung in a proper position, with its outer end firmly lashed in place, and then as the rudder was turning the proper way the wrench was pushed into its hold on the nut ... As the rudder started to turn back in the opposite direction the wrench was removed. By three hours' labor in this matter the nut was screwed

> back to its place, the last turn carrying away the lashing, and sending the wrench rattling along the iron deck.

When finished with the nut, Towle went below decks with his crew. There, following Towle's instructions, Captain Walker ordered a length of chain to be lowered to Towle through a freshly cut hole in the ship's main deck. Working mostly by oil light, Towle's crew found the strength to wrap this chain, each link of which weighed about eighty pounds, around the rudderpost. When the chain had been wrapped several times around the post, Towle ordered that the chain be tightened, which was done. Amazingly, the improvised apparatus worked well enough that Captain Walker was able to turn the *Great Eastern* around and limp back to Ireland, using the ship's giant propeller as his source of power.

When the *Great Eastern* was finally berthed at Queenstown, there was a general meeting of the passengers at which certain resolutions were passed. The resolutions heaped scorn on the directors of the Great Ship Company and called upon the Board of Trade to conduct an inquiry into the ship's obvious lack of preparation for the voyage. The passengers found no fault in the conduct of Captain Walker, and as to Towle, the resolutions stated as follows:

> That we would also acknowledge with deep thankfulness the sense we entertain of the valuable scientific suggestions of one of the cabin passengers, E. Towle, of Boston, U.S., civil engineer, made in order to repair the injuries sustained by the steering apparatus of the vessel; and of the patient attention with which, at much personal inconvenience, he assisted Captain Walker until the ship was again enabled to proceed.
>
> That some suitable testimonial of our appreciation of the skill and services of Mr. Towle be provided and presented to him by the passengers.

The directors of the ship, deeply uncomfortable at the suggestion that their great ship had been saved from destruction by a twenty-seven-year-old American, downplayed Towle's contributions. In this regard, they were assisted by Captain Walker, the ship's engineer, and a few of the

English passengers aboard. Americans were outraged by this attitude. Benjamin Moran, the assistant secretary of the American legation in London, must have dipped his pen in acid when he wrote the following entry in his journal:

> That boasted marvel of naval architecture the Great Eastern, has come to grief again. She has returned to Queenstown completely disabled after having encountered an ordinary blow that any common vessel would have rode out harmless. It seems she rolled about like a barrel, smashed everything moveable on board, and for 3 days was a mere log in the sea. A young American Engineer by the name of Hamilton E. Towle happened to be on board, who rigged up a temporary steering apparatus, her rudder gear having early broken down, which brought her into port, and when clear water was gained and the danger over, the English passengers tried to deprive Towle of the honor of his invention. This is characteristic. Had his gearing broken down they would have jeered it as Yankee and ridiculed Towle as a fool.

The American press picked up the fight. The October 19, 1861, edition of the *Scientific American* featured an article entitled "The Great Eastern Saved by the Skill of an American Engineer." The following week a longer article appeared in the *Scientific American* detailing the on-board friction between the ship's engineer and Towle. The article, accompanied by diagrams of Towle's apparatus, noted:

> As the passengers saw themselves rescued from the awful peril in which they had been so long involved, they crowded around Mr. Towle, pouring out their grateful congratulations. Mr. Towle is a young man, and he was so completely overcome that he was obliged to go away in private to escape the demonstrations.

In November, the *New York Times* reported that Towle was making

Boston his "headquarters" and suggested that men like him should be in the employ of the government. The article closed, "We are informed by a gentleman who was a passenger on the big ship that, so far, the proprietors have in no way recognized the services of Mr. Towle."

Between Captain Walker and the directors disparaging Towle's efforts and the American press goading the young engineer to vindicate his honor, Towle took action. He sued in the United States district court in New York for the salvage value of the *Great Eastern*. Settlement did not seem to be an option for either side, and in November 1864 the court rendered its decision—Towle did indeed save the *Great Eastern*. Given the peculiar case of a passenger aboard a ship being found a salvor of the same ship, the court did not award the full salvage value but awarded Towle $15,000, a considerable sum for the time and one that the directors could ill afford to pay. As the *New York Times* editorialized, "If any one thinks that Mr. TOWLE is pretty well paid for his day and a half of labor, let him think of the responsibility which he would have had to bear, in case of failure."

Towle was a restless man, traveling around the world looking for engineering projects suitable for his talents. At the time he boarded the *Great Eastern*, he had already worked for the Austrian government as supervising engineer of a large dry dock and railroad project in what is now Pula, Croatia. In 1865, he was in Venango County, Pennsylvania, working as a boring and mining engineer helping to develop the county's oil fields. Later, he patented a loom for heavy fabrics and founded a company to manufacture it. He then supervised engineering on several railroads in New York and thereafter went to England, where in 1872 he made an associate of that country's Institution of Civil Engineers. In 1874 he and his wife were off to the country of Colombia to work on an engineering report on the Magdalena River, but in 1877 his health worsened, and he returned to the United States. He went to Europe to regain his health, returned to New York in 1878, and went back to England, where he remained until he died in September 1881 at the home of his daughter and son-in-law in Upper Norwood, near London. He was forty-seven years old.

On the registration records of Harvard University, Towle is identified as a member of the class of 1855. Next to his name is a handwritten note: "saved the Great Eastern."

❧

On April 4, 1865, Abraham Lincoln and his son Tad walked through Richmond, Virginia, which the Confederate army had evacuated three days earlier. After inquiries, Lincoln found Jefferson Davis's house and entered it. An eyewitness described the event:

> At the Davis house, [Lincoln] was shown into the reception-room, with the remark that the housekeeper had said that the room was President Davis's office. As he seated himself he remarked, "This must have been President Davis's chair," and, crossing his legs, he looked far off with a serious, dreamy expression.

On the following day, William H. Seward was in Washington, DC, taking a carriage ride with Fred, his daughter Fanny, and a young friend of Fanny's, Mary Titus. The carriage had a balky door, and the coachman stopped the carriage to see if he could repair it. For some reason, the horses bolted while the coachman was working on the door, and Seward tried to grasp the loose reins. In so doing he fell from the coach. The panicked horses continued on to Lafayette Park, where they finally stopped, leaving the other passengers unharmed.

Seward had been knocked unconscious, and he was brought back to his house. His injuries were serious. His right arm was broken and his face badly smashed up. Doctors quickly determined that his jaw was fractured on both sides, and when he finally gained consciousness that night, he was found to have a dislocated shoulder. In terrible pain, he suffered through having his jaw and shoulder reset. Seward's wife, Frances, was telegraphed and came to Washington the following day.

News of Seward's accident traveled quickly. That evening, Schultz, staying at the Girard House, a hotel in Philadelphia, sent a short telegram to Fred Seward: "What can I do. Command me by Telegraph."

Three days later, Robert E. Lee surrendered to Ulysses S. Grant at Appomattox. Since Seward was in and out of a delirium, it is uncertain whether he comprehended the news of the surrender for several days. On April 10, Fred sent a telegram to thank Schultz on behalf of his father for the box of "choice cigars," which Schultz had sent up by Adams Express. Fred assured Schultz, "The critical period is now believed to have passed." Schultz continued to send delicacies from Philadelphia. A stream of cigars, figs, grapes, guava fruit, bananas, and other edibles arrived at the Seward house via the express company. Whether a man with a broken jaw could enjoy any of them is doubtful, but they were clearly a treat for visitors to the house, including President Lincoln. Fred Seward described the meeting with Lincoln:

> "You are back from Richmond?" whispered Seward, who was hardly able to articulate.
>
> "Yes," said Lincoln, "and I think we are near the end, at last."
>
> Then leaning his tall form across the bed, and resting on his elbow, so as to bring his face near that of the wounded man, he gave him an account of his experiences "at the front"... They were left together for half an hour or more. Then the door opened softly, and Mr. Lincoln came out gently, intimating by a silent look and gesture that Seward had fallen into a feverish slumber ... It was their last meeting.

To help Frances Seward cope with the care of her husband, Secretary of War Edwin Stanton supplied a convalescent soldier, George Robinson, to act as a nurse. On April 14, 1865, nine days after Seward's accident, a war-weary Abraham Lincoln and his wife went to see a light comedy at Ford's Theatre. That evening Seward lay in painful misery in a darkened bedroom, with Robinson sitting in the shadows watching his patient. At about the same time that John Wilkes Booth shot Lincoln in the head, the doorbell rang at the Seward house. A young servant, William Bell, answered the door and met a tall, powerfully built young man in a light-colored overcoat. The man said that he had medicine from Dr. Verdi, Seward's physician, and that he was required to deliver it personally to Seward. Although Bell said no one was to be allowed upstairs, the young man insisted, and Bell led the man to the third floor, where Seward's sickroom was located.

Fred Seward met the man on the third-floor landing, and the

messenger told Fred that he had to deliver the medicine personally to Seward. Caught off guard, Fred went to the sickroom and came back, saying that his father was asleep and that he would take the medicine into the room. At this point, the man in the overcoat pulled out a navy pistol and fired it point-blank at Fred. It misfired. The man then began to pistol-whip Fred, hitting him in the head several times with the heavy revolver. Fred collapsed, and the man ran into Seward's sickroom, where he drew a large Bowie knife from the inside of his overcoat. Seward's daughter Fanny had been reading to him, and the man in the overcoat pushed her aside and began slashing at Seward. The room was dark, and Seward was lying on his bed next to the wall. The assailant slashed toward Seward's face and neck but was not able to tell where he was hitting his victim. Robinson, the nurse, jumped on the man, and a fight ensued. Robinson was stabbed, as were other men running to the commotion. Finally, the man in the overcoat ran down the stairs and into the street, leaving a trail of blood and wounded men.

The assailant was Lewis Thornton Powell, also known by his alias Lewis Paine. The son of a Baptist clergyman in Florida, Powell had fought as a Confederate soldier in some of the most brutal battles in the Civil War, including Antietam, Chancellorsville, and Gettysburg, at the latter of which he'd been wounded and captured. He had recently met John Wilkes Booth, and the men had found that they shared a profound hatred of blacks coupled with a desire to avenge the South. A conspiracy was formed between Booth and Powell, joined by a few others, and the assassination of political leaders was discussed. In 1862, when Seward was told of an alleged plot against Lincoln and his cabinet members, he dismissed it, saying, "Assassination is not an American practice or habit." As the sun rose on April 15, 1865, that was no longer the case.

Seward slowly recovered from his cumulative injuries and wounds, although he would be scarred the rest of his life by the knife wounds to his face. Fred's skull had been fractured, and a portion of his brain was visible at two fractures. He remained in a coma for a lengthy period, with his wife and mother watching over him closely. While Fred ultimately recovered, his mother, always frail and now burdened with worry, started to fail, and she died nine weeks after the assassination attempt. Shortly after her death, Paine was tried by a military commission and promptly hanged.

William H. Seward's life is so vast and significant that it is the subject of many books published over many years. To summarize this life in a mere epilogue would do a disservice to a man who, perhaps more than anyone else, save Lincoln, shaped the destiny of America in the nineteenth century. William Seward died a widower in October 1872 at the age of seventy-one.

After an unsuccessful attempt to be elected as New York's secretary of state, Fred Seward, together with his wife, Anna, moved to Montrose, New York, where he quietly practiced law and lectured. Fred edited and published his father's autobiography and thereafter wrote a book about State Department activities during the Civil War. Fred died in April 1915, and Anna died four years later.

Until December 2017, when the new aircraft carrier *Queen Elizabeth* was commissioned, the largest ship in the British navy was the *Ark Royal (R07)*, an aircraft carrier 689 feet long. The *Great Eastern*, launched nearly 150 years before the *Ark Royal*, was six feet longer. In fact, in almost every dimension, the *Great Eastern* exceeded the *Ark Royal.*

Every fact about the *Great Eastern* bespeaks her immense size. Her propeller, approximately two stories tall, is still among the largest propellers ever made. Her paddle wheels were nearly six stories tall. She had the capacity for fifteen thousand tons of coal, nearly three times that of the RMS *Titanic*. Designed to hold ten thousand troops plus their equipment, she was for over one hundred years the largest troop carrier ever made. She was finally topped by two mammoth ocean liners, the *Queen Elizabeth* and *Queen Mary*, both of which were converted to troop carriers during World War II. Each of these ships could carry up to fifteen thousand troops.

Unlike the *Titanic*, the *Great Eastern* was virtually unsinkable. Brunel divided the ship into multiple compartments, with bulkheads riveted firmly to the deck. Further, the *Great Eastern* had an entire inner hull. The double hull, consisting of thousands of iron plates interlocked into a single unit by millions of rivets, was one of the strongest ever made. The *Great Eastern* would have survived the iceberg that sank the pride of the White Star Line.

While it is interesting to compare the *Great Eastern* with ships far younger, it must be remembered that the *Great Eastern* was construed without electricity, welding, or pneumatic tools. The only power available to Brunel came from steam boilers and human muscle.

After the disastrous voyage of September 1861, the *Great Eastern* was out of commission until 1862. While her hull was found to be undamaged, it took time to raise the needed money and then repair her paddle wheels and rudderhead and restore the interior from the damage it had sustained both from water, which had poured in through the skylights, and from the crashing about of loose articles and furniture. The year 1862 did nothing to dispel the ship's reputation as unlucky. In August of that year, she sailed to New York and promptly hit a theretofore unknown underwater rock near Montauk Point, New York. The rock, later identified on nautical maps as the "Great Eastern Rock," cut an eighty-foot-long gash in the bottom of the ship. At some places the gash was four feet wide. Such a cut would have sunk any contemporary ship and, indeed, most modern ships. The *Great Eastern*, with her double hull, only suffered a slight list. A diver was sent down to explore the underwater damage and came back up in a terrified state, having heard a banging from the inside of the hull. It appears that the diver was well aware, as was nearly everyone, of the macabre tale of the entombed riveter's boy. The beleaguered captain of the ship, Walter Paton, had to have his crew explore the ship to find the source of the sound, which was announced to be a swinging shackle hitting the hull. Whether the diver was convinced of this explanation is unknown. What is known is that Paton decided to repair the ship before its return trip to England. What was initially proposed as a simple repair took six months and £70,000. An event that should have showcased the incredible strength and safety of the ship's hull instead convinced everyone that her luck remained bad.

Just as the Civil War ended, a man named Cyrus Field stepped forward with a plan involving the *Great Eastern*. Field, a forty-two-year-old Yankee from Massachusetts, had been obsessed with laying a transatlantic cable for years. In 1858, he led an American-British venture that laid such a cable. It carried telegraph messages for three weeks, including a message from Queen Victoria to President Buchanan, before it went dead and could not be revived. Field's new plan was to manufacture a heavier, more durable cable, and he needed a mammoth ship to lay it. The *Great Eastern*, with her vast bunkers, was perfect.

Daniel Gooch forced this plan on the ship's directors, and the ship was refitted for the job. The *Great Eastern*'s storage capacities were so immense that she carried in a single voyage enough cable to connect Valentia Island, off the southwest coast of Ireland, with Heart's Content, a small fishing village in Newfoundland. The laying of the cable is a story so filled with drama, determination, and ingenuity that it would be unfair to even summarize it. It is sufficient to state that by the summer of 1866 North America and Europe were permanently connected with a telegraph line. The technological leap was enormous. Before the cable, it took weeks for developments in Europe to be learned in the United States. With the cable, a major event occurring in Prussia or France could be read about the next day in the newspapers of Kalamazoo or Terre Haute. The cable had a particularly profound effect upon the commercial interests on both sides of the Atlantic, as the pricing of stock, interest rates, and commodities became known almost instantaneously.

In her mission as a cable layer, the *Great Eastern* performed flawlessly. She laid a cat's cradle of cable across the Atlantic Ocean, connecting and reconnecting both England and France to North America, and then laid a cable across the Indian Ocean connecting Bombay (Mumbai) to Suez. She was laid up for two years at a mooring on the Mersey but, like an old warrior, returned to lay her fourth transatlantic cable. Finally, in 1874, she laid her last cable.

When it became obvious that her sailing days were over, the *Great Eastern* was bought by Louis Cohen, the managing director of a clothing emporium called Lewis's. On the port side of the ship, in large white letters, was written, "LADIES SHOULD VISIT LEWIS'S BON MARCHÉ CHURCH STREET," and on the starboard side, "LEWIS'S ARE THE FRIENDS OF THE PEOPLE." So attired, the *Great Eastern* became a garish nineteenth-century shopping mall, complete with amusements.

The ship's humiliation came to an end in 1889, when she was purchased for breaking up, a process that took years. The vast amount of iron and brass in the ship was melted down and reused in countless bridges, buildings, and railroad tracks. Were the remains of the two workmen found during the ship's demolition? James Dugan, the author of *The Great Iron Ship*, wrote to Captain David Duff, a longtime tugboat captain in Liverpool who more than once worked on a tugboat pulling the *Great Eastern*. Duff wrote back in a letter quoted by Dugan:

> They found a skeleton inside the ship's shell and the tank tops. It was the skeleton of the basher who was missing. Also the frame of the bash boy was found with him. So there you are, sir, that is all I can tell you of the Great Eastern.

There are reminders today of the great ship's existence. In Portland, Maine, there was for years a Great Eastern Wharf, designed to handle the ship which never came. Many of the ship's fittings—bells, chains, china, even furniture—are in the hands of collectors and are scattered throughout the United Kingdom and North America. Her original launching site on the Isle of Dogs has been partly excavated and is open to the public. Most interesting, however, is a statue in Cobh, Ireland, that the passengers of many ocean liners, including the RMS *Titanic*, would have passed on the way to their ships, some of them blessing themselves as they walked by. The statue, called *Our Lady, Star of the Sea*, faces Cobh's harbor. It was paid for by passengers of the *Great Eastern* as a way of giving thanks for having survived the unforgettable voyage of September 1861.

The Trochus Shell

We know something about what happened to most of the real persons in this book save one—the unidentified person aboard the *Great Eastern* whom I have named Kit. For this individual there was no obituary, no article noting his passing, no public grieving by his loved ones. Yet I believe there is a confirmation as to what happened to this person, and it is the trochus shell. As the reader may recall, there were three renderings on the shell. At the bottom was a rendering of the *Great Eastern*, above it a rendering of what was described as Lincoln's tomb, and above both a symbol consisting of crossed wings.

I have not been able to find a symbol identical to the crossed wings. However, the use of wings on tombstones during Victorian times was not uncommon. These symbols signified souls ascending to heaven. Thus, I believe that the shell was used by someone, perhaps Schultz, perhaps Towle, perhaps someone who learned the story under a promise of confidence, to memorialize both the story and the final resting places of two men—one who died fighting to preserve the Union and the other who died fighting to end slavery.